The Decision

The Decision

headline
review

First published in 2011
by HEADLINE REVIEW
An imprint of HEADLINE PUBLISHING GROUP

1

Cataloguing in Publication Data is available from the British Library

ISBN 978 0 7553 2090 5 (Hardback)
ISBN 978 0 7553 2091 2 (Trade paperback)

Typeset in New Caledonia by Avon DataSet Ltd,
Bidford-on-Avon, Warwickshire

Printed and bound in Great Britain by
Clays Ltd, St Ives plc

Headline's policy is to use papers that are natural, renewable and
recyclable products and made from wood grown in sustainable forests.
The logging and manufacturing processes are expected to conform
to the environmental regulations of the country of origin.

HEADLINE PUBLISHING GROUP
An Hachette UK Company
338 Euston Road
London NW1 3BH

www.headline.co.uk
www.hachette.co.uk

For Paul, who was always there. And for Polly, Sophie, Emily and Claudia, for getting me through.

Acknowledgements

As always, the list of couldn't-have-done-without-the-help-of is long, possibly longer even than usual, and huge thanks to so many people.

Michael Drake, legal superbrain, took me painstakingly, patiently and above all inventively through all the complexities of divorce and custody in the 1960s and '70s, escorted me round and indeed into the Royal Courts of Justice and Lincolns Inn Fields, responded to my interminable and often crass emails always within hours and usually minutes, suggested sub-plots, improved upon scenarios and never for an instant even implied that his hugely valuable time might be better sent. A complete star, you are, Michael, and thank you.

James Marshall not only arranged access to some of the great names in advertising in sixties London, he was just the best fun and the most informative guide on a whistle-stop tour of Milan, which took in an evening at La Scala, a trawl of the very best restaurants and shops and an introduction to some truly wonderful characters. Including the lovely Phyllis Achilli, who created for me a whole world in which to set that part of my story, Tai and Rosita Missoni, who hosted us in their box at La Scala and Peter and Mariella Van Shalwick, who cast a further bright light on the lifestyle of the city then.

I would also like to thank Jackie Hollows for so tirelessly and generously sifting through her past as a very glamorous air hostess in the sixties for wonderful funny, intriguing and colourful stories and detail; the book would have been the poorer without her.

The fashion element in the book is crucial; I spent my own early professional life in fashion but I still drew heavily on the recollections and stories of many of the leading stars in journalism. Felicity Green, Fleet Street legend herself, and my mentor indeed, opened up her wonderful memory store for me, especially relating to the Paris collections; Shirley

Lowe, starry journlist, who inspired a whole strand of the story by reliving her own fashion editor past; John Bates, one of the leading fashion designers of the day (I was lucky enough to own not just one, but two, of his dresses) and John Siggins, his director and partner; and Liz Smith iconic fashion editor and also, like my heroine Eliza, fashion consultant to a famous advertising agency.

David Smith, husband to Liz, a dear friend, and a star of both journalism and advertising, provided wonderful anecdotes about both those worlds, but also some brilliantly funny recollections of his own National Service days. Very sadly he died just as this book went to press; his stylish, slightly old-fashioned sense of humour and turn of phrase were truly life enhancing for everyone lucky enough to know him.

Edward Harris provided further legal background, and some particularly brilliant ingenuity over the creation and workings of the Summercourt Trust and I would like to thank Ros Harris too, who provided a most valuable overview, steeped as she is in such matters. Sue Stapely was a fount of knowledge on all manner of things and as always provided me with pathways to all kinds of helpful people; the wedding in the book would not have been the same without the sparkly musical input of John Young of Country Church Wedding Music; Steve Gunnis provided a marvelously expert overview of the cars of the decade, and Lisa Lindsay Gale was a wonderful and witty consultant on gymkhanas and pony etiquette generally. And I am truly indebted to Nicholas Coleridge for generously giving me the run of the Tatler archives. Two dizzy afternoons indeed!

At Headline, I have been particularly well cared for by Jane Morpeth and Leah Woodburn, my editors, who between them have worked an incredible magic with an even-later-than-usual manuscript, remaining calm, patient and appreciative against every odd. It meant so much to me. Susan Opie is the most wonderfully thoughtful and perceptive copyeditor; and as always immense thanks to Kati Nicholl who works some kind of magic on a manuscript and cuts it so brilliantly that even I can't spot what has gone! Jo Liddiard has not only put together the usual gorgeous marketing campaign, she was kind enough to sit with me through a long morning in my study and guide me through the technological intricacies (as I saw them!) of returning to my neglected blog. Louise Page has returned to handling my publicity with all the imaginative determination I remember so fondly; and the sales team, under Aslan Byrne, has been quite simply magnificent. And a special thank to Justinia Baird-Murray for designing the most gorgeous cover I have seen for a very long time.

Finally I would like to once again thank my family; the sons-in-law as well as the daughters, have been completely wonderful. And to welcome two new members, Grace and Niamh to the ever-growing clan.

In retrospect, as always, it looks like just the best fun.

Penny Vincenzi
August 2011

Character List

Eliza Fullerton-Clark, a debutante and subsequently a fashion editor
Sarah Fullerton-Clark, her mother
Adrian Fullerton-Clark, her father
Charles Fullerton-Clark, her brother, a stockbroker

Anna Marchant, her godmother
Piers Marchant, Anna's husband
Sir Charles and Lady Cunninghame, Eliza's grandparents

Matt Shaw, a property developer
Sandra Shaw, his mother
Pete Shaw, his father
Scarlett Shaw, his sister, an airhostess

Diana Forbes, Scarlett's air hostess friend

Mr Barlow and Mr Stein, Matt's first employers

Emmeline, Eliza and Matt's daughter
Margaret Grant, her nanny

Jeremy Northcott, Eliza's millionaire boyfriend and advertising supremo
Emma Northcott, his sister

Louise Mullan, secretary to Matt and subsequently a property tycoon in her own right
Jenny Cox, receptionist and secretary at Simmonds and Shaw
Jimbo Simmonds, Matt's partner
Valerie Hill, a hugely successful businesswoman

Georgina Barker, Matt's girlfriend

Barry Floyd, a successful builder
Roderick Brownlow, a property developer

Juliet Judd, Charles's girlfriend
Geoffrey Judd, her father
Carol Judd, her mother

Lily Berenson, a rich widow from Charleston
David Berenson, her son
Gaby Berenson, her daughter-in-law

Lindy Freeman, Eliza's boss at Woolfe's department store

Maddy Brown, a knitwear designer and friend of Eliza's
Esmond, her boyfriend and a hatter

Jerome Blake, a photographer
Rex Ingham, another photographer
Rob Brigstocke, Creative Director of KPD, advertising agency
Hugh Wallace, account director at KPD

Jack Beckham, editor of *Charisma* and later of the *Daily News*
Fiona Marks, the fashion editor
Annunciata Woburn, the features editor

Johnny Barrett, Louise's journalist friend on the *Daily News*

Giovanni Crespi, wealthy businessman
Mariella Crespi, his wife and socialite
Anna-Maria, a maid
Bruno, Giovanni's valet
Sebastiano, the Crespi's butler

Timothy Fordyce, a friend of Mariella's in Milan
Janey, his wife

Mark Frost, a distinguished travel writer
Persephone Frost, his mother

Heather Connell, a young mother and friend to Eliza
Coral, her daughter
Alan Connell, her husband

Mrs Munroe, Eliza's gynaecologist
Mary Miller, her psychotherapist

Philip Gordon, Eliza's solicitor
Toby Gilmour, Eliza's barrister

Ivor Lewis, Matt's solicitor
Sir Bruce Hayward QC, Matt's barrister

Sir Tristram Selbourne, another QC

Mr Justice Rogers, a judge

Demetrios and Larissa, taverna owners on the Greek island of Trisos

Prologue

1971

It was nearly over then. By this time tomorrow it would be settled. By this time tomorrow she would know. Whether she would still be a mother, a proper mother, the sort that did the ordinary things, got her child up every morning and tucked her up in bed every night, took her to school and picked her up again, knew when she'd had a tummy ache or a bad dream, got cross with her, argued with her, decided when to get her hair cut, or that she needed new shoes, told her off for skimping on her homework or her ballet practice, insisted she made her bed and tidied her room and wrote thank-you letters and cleaned out the hamster's cage . . . Or the other sort, the once-a-week sort, the provider of a perfect room and whatever-you-fancy food, who waited impatiently outside school, aware of the mild curiosity of the other mothers, the purveyor of treats and outings, and ultra-generosity to friends, surprised by a new dress, a fringe, a fad, always with time to give, over-indulgent, never cross, never critical, desperate to know about a school concert, a friend's party, plans for a holiday, watchful for new loyalties, jealous of new traditions . . .

Which would she be?

The mother with custody? Or the mother without?

Part One

The Engagement

Chapter 1

Eliza was in the middle of curtseying to the Queen when she decided it was time she lost her virginity.

She was rather shocked at herself; not for the nature of the decision, but for managing to make it at such a moment. She had had a lot of trouble getting her curtsey absolutely right (one foot lined up perfectly behind the other, both knees bent, head erect, arms at side), it was hardly comfortable and she was inclined to wobble. Concentration was essential. And it was a terribly important moment in her life; both her mother and her godmother (who was actually presenting her) had instilled into her endlessly how lucky she was, that had she been one year younger it would not have been possible, because this was positively the last year of court presentation, it had been declared an anachronism, not in keeping with the new Elizabethan age. And here she was, in her blue silk Belinda Belville cocktail dress, in the presence of the Queen – so much younger and prettier in the flesh than her photographs, and the Duke – so amazingly handsome, and she was thinking not about being part of a deeply important tradition that had lasted for generations, but about who of all the young men she was dancing and flirting with that wonderful summer she might achieve this new ambition with. It really was rather bad of her.

Concentrate, Eliza! What would her mother and godmother say if they knew that after all their organising and lunching and juggling with dates and guest lists and budgets for her Season, that her mind was fixed not on what to them was the almost sacred part of the whole thing, but on something very unsuitable indeed.

She straightened slowly (without a hint of wobble), and moved towards the side of the throne room, making way for the next wave of girls.

Eliza was attracting a lot of attention that summer. Indeed she had become a bit of a favourite with the popular press, had so far appeared in the *Express* three times and the *Mirror* four. Her mother had felt it rather lowered the tone of Eliza's Season, but Eliza thought it was wonderful and a lot of the other girls had been really jealous. She wasn't pretty; she could see it for herself: her features were too large, and her colouring too strong, with slightly olive skin, very dark hair combined with very dark blue eyes, and she had more than once heard her mother saying worriedly to her grandmother that she did hope no one would think there was foreign blood in the family. But she also knew that she was extremely attractive.

Boys had made passes at her from when she had been only fifteen, and she had always had an endless queue of would-be partners at pony-club dances. Indeed, she had first made the pages of *Tatler* the year before her Season, watching her brother Charles play cricket for the Old Etonians on Founders' Day.

But this year was truly hers, and she was proving a star; she had already been granted the Big One, a full-page solo spot at the front of *Tatler*, taken by Tom Hustler, himself once a Debs' Delight and now a society photographer.

'Miss Eliza Fullerton-Clark,' the caption said, 'daughter of Mr and Mrs Adrian Fullerton-Clark. Eliza, a charming girl whose interests include skiing and the History of Art' (I didn't know that, thought Eliza, studying the photograph critically, grateful for Tom's lighting which disguised her slightly too-long nose, and made her eyes look simply enormous) 'will have her dance at the exquisite Fullerton-Clark home, Summercourt, Wellesley, later in the Season.'

The photograph had been granted its prominence by *Tatler*'s social editor, Betty Kenward, the redoubtable Jennifer of 'Jennifer's Diary', the all-powerful goddess of High Society, whose word alone could promote a girl from being just, well, a girl, to a success, someone to be marked down as having a future. Which meant not a future in her own right, but as the wife of someone rich and powerful, at best heir to one of the great estates of rural England.

And Eliza's future had been most carefully planned. Sarah Fullerton-Clark, together with her best friend (and Eliza's godmother) Anna Marchant, or rather the Hon. Mrs Piers Marchant, had visited Mrs Kenward in her eyrie at the top of a small flight of stairs from the *Tatler* editorial floor. Mrs Kenward had given them the regulation small tomato juice and shared with them the almost mystical tools of her trade: her diary of the Season, with every girl's dance and date so far, and a list of eligible young men, rich and well-connected, christened (by the tabloids) the 'Debs' Delights'. The Delights had a longer lifespan than the debs, and were summoned for several summers, at no cost to themselves, to attend dances and parties, Ascot and Henley, and whole weekends at fine country houses, where the only requirement upon them was to wear the right clothes, not to drink too much, to be polite to their hostess and to smile at and charm the prettier debs. (The plainer ones tended to go unsmiled at, and undanced with; Eliza knew more than one girl who regularly arrived on Friday evenings and went right through to Sunday midday totally ignored by everyone, and certainly not asked to dance.)

Charles was on the list of course; he was extremely good-looking, which meant if it was a toss-up between inviting Eliza to a cocktail party or dance or another girl without a brother, Eliza usually won. He was very tall and dark, and charmingly diffident, a favourite with the mothers; Sarah and Anna had left Mrs Kenward's office with a recommendation for the date for Eliza's dance and some starred names of young men on the list, denoting particularly impressive titles or fortunes.

Eliza was staying with the Marchants in London during the week that summer, since she was doing – as well as the Season – a course at one of London's smarter secretarial colleges. Her mother had been anxious that the course would be too much for her and she'd look tired at all the important dances, but the principal assured her that girls doing their Season were permitted to come in at midday after an important party, so they could get their beauty sleep. And as Eliza had assured Sarah, typing along to the strains of Victor Silvester and his Ballroom Orchestra (this was to ensure the steady rhythm essential to a good typist) was hardly arduous.

Eliza was determined to work, and not in some feeble little job either; her allowance from her father was very small and anyway, she wanted a career. She knew what everyone including her mother said, that a job was just something to do until you got married and to earn you a bit of pocket money, but Eliza wanted more; she wanted a job that was interesting and absorbing, something she cared about 'that will make me a person, in my own right,' she said to Charles, 'you know, not just as someone's wife or whatever.'

7

Fashion fascinated her particularly: not just clothes, but the way they worked, how you could tell so much about a person from what they wore, how important they were to the picture you presented to the world. Her college had a tie-up with *Vogue*, and many of their girls got secretarial jobs there; maybe that would be something she might do. It would be a start anyway. A start to her career.

In spite of her decision, taken in such sumptuous circumstances, Eliza was still a virgin as the date for her dance approached. Lots of her friends claimed to have Done It, or rather implied they had – but she suspected most of them were lying. Everyone was petrified of getting pregnant, and it had been dinned into them by their mothers that girls with bad reputations were usually finished in the marriage market. Some boys were very badly behaved, of course, and there were lots of stories of girls being found in compromising situations in bedrooms and libraries and even wine cellars in country houses, but somehow, it just hadn't happened to her; and she really didn't want the occasion rushed through. She wanted it to take place in style.

Besides, she'd been terribly busy, had had a wonderfully successful time. She'd been to literally dozens of dances and cocktail parties; she'd had a starring role in the Berkeley Dress Show, that great annual opportunity for debs to be models for a day, and managed to catch the eye of the photographer from the *Evening Standard* and hit the front page, wearing a white evening dress by Hartnell. And at Queen Charlotte's Ball – the Harlots' Ball as the Debs' Delights called it – she had been quite near the front in the line of girls pulling the giant cake into the ballroom: yet another photograph in the tabloids.

And then there was her own dance, so much discussed and planned – what should she wear, how many of the girls she 'owed to' had to be invited, even whether she should share with someone, which was the classic means of halving the cost – but she categorically refused. It was to be her night, and hers alone. It had passed far too quickly, a magical fairy-tale evening, when she'd felt like a story-book heroine, just drifted by without any clear memories of anything, except fragments: the perfect June night, the garden filled with roses, the white marquee so gorgeously dressed up, the crowds and crowds of friends, the band playing exactly what she wanted, the endless champagne, her father flushed with pride, her mother kissing her and telling her how proud of her they were. She'd danced and danced, literally till dawn, with an endless flow of charming young men and then fallen into bed, amazed that she wasn't drunker, considering how much champagne she had consumed.

It was the crown on a wonderful summer; and she wished it need never end.

Her mother was pale but happy next morning, relieved at the success of the dance, relieved it was finally over. It had occupied her thoughts and fed her anxieties for almost a year; but it seemed to have been worth it.

Worth the bank loan Adrian had had to take out, the sleepless nights, the endless work. The expense hadn't stopped at Eliza's dance, of course, it was all the attendant expenditure: Eliza's six dance dresses, two of them long for the grander dances, one white for Queen Charlotte's Ball, her clothes for Ascot and Henley, Sarah's own dresses, all the hats and shoes and gloves, the mums' luncheons, the pre-dance dinners – but it was all an investment in Eliza's future, and not even to be questioned.

Having her dance at home in the country, rather than in London, had saved a lot, and was so much nicer, everyone had (apparently genuinely) said and certainly numbers had not been in the least affected.

Eliza's dress had been from Belville Sassoon again – but Sarah had had her own dress run up by her dressmaker and Adrian's tailcoat being a little worn and slightly out of date was desirable rather than the reverse. Nothing more common than spanking-new evening clothes on the older generation; people might even think, heaven forbid, they'd been hired. Adrian had bought his coat soon after they had first met; she had invited him to a dance in the country and, seeing where Sarah Cunninghame's infatuation with him could be leading, Adrian had considered it a sound investment for two weeks' salary and twenty-five years later, it still looked superb – a tribute to his own unchanging shape as much as Messrs Hawes & Curtis's skill.

And Charles of course, darling Charles, had looked brilliantly handsome as always; he had danced with her not once but twice, telling her how lovely she looked, how proud of her he was. Not many sons would do that.

All the young people had behaved pretty well; there had been the usual horsing around by some of the male element and a couple of the girls had been really rather drunk, especially the one doing strip-tease by the ladies' loos, but it had all stayed good-natured and Eliza had clearly had a lovely time. And as a final coating of icing on the cake, both *Tatler* and *Queen* had sent photographers.

Sarah was a little anxious that so far into her Season, Eliza had clearly still not found anyone she considered special, but she was only seventeen, a bit too young perhaps to be thinking about marriage.

'Hello, Mummy. Pleased with your night's work?'

'Oh, Charles, hello. Darling, you look tired. Sit down and I'll get you some breakfast.'

'No, I'm fine. Had some earlier. Well, it all went well, didn't it? And Eliza looked jolly nice.'

'Didn't she? And seemed to enjoy herself.'

Sarah smiled at him: her firstborn and the great love of her life. After Adrian, of course. She could hardly believe he was twenty-one, and out in the world. Well, not quite; he'd have to do his National Service first before finally settling down to his career. He was hoping to go overseas: 'Hong Kong, or maybe Gib. See a bit of the world before I have to buckle down in the City.'

'Darling,' she said, patting his shoulder affectionately, 'I shall miss you.'

'Oh, nonsense. Time'll fly by. I'm looking forward to it actually. Some of the chaps are taking a short service commission, doing three years. I did wonder about that, get a bit more out of it.'

Sarah looked at him, slightly alarmed; she and Adrian had been looking forward to stopping Charles's allowance, or at least cutting it drastically. Another year in the army would mean another year of expense.

'But in the end I decided against it,' he said. 'I want to get on with the job, make a bit of dosh, that sort of thing.'

'And you'll be called up soon now you've left Oxford?'

'Yes. Six weeks' basic training in some Nissen hut and then Mons, hopefully, and the regiment. It should be fun.'

'I believe it's awfully tough.'

'Can't be worse than the first half-term at prep school.'

'Charles! Were you really so unhappy?'

'Well, a bit. I was homesick. And quite hungry, the food was awful. But it didn't do me any harm, did it? God, I'll certainly send my kids. The old place looked nice last night, didn't it?' he added.

'Didn't it? Your grandfather would have been so happy.'

The old place was an exquisite small Palladian villa, built at the top of a gentle rise, smiling graciously down on the village of Wellesley, a little to the south of Marlborough and looking just slightly – although beautifully – out of place there, like a fashionable woman wearing her couture clothes to walk down the village street. Built in 1755, it had a charming legend. A young but very well-born architect called Jonathan Becket was looking for work and was at a soirée one evening in Bath. He had actually studied with John Wood the Younger, who, with his father, was responsible for many of Bath's architectural wonders. There he met and fell in love with the beautiful Lady Anne Cunninghame, and she with him; married to Sir Ralph Cunninghame, she was the young and dreadfully spoiled daughter of the eccentric Earl of Grasmere, used to having her own way in all things and not in the least in love with her middle-aged husband apart from his wealth.

Sir Ralph for his part was so afraid of losing her that he could refuse her nothing; and when she spoke longingly of a 'fine house, created precisely for me' young Becket got his commission and created a breath-taking place, not large, set against the grand houses of its day (a mere ten bedrooms, and only three receiving rooms), but very beautiful with its glorious south front 'greeting the morning sun' as Lady Anne described it in her journal, with its classical pillars, its gently curving steps, its wide terrace, its exquisite orangery, set some five hundred yards from the house; 'It is just for me,' she went on, 'created to suit my beauty as my darling says.'

Her darling (presumably Jonathan Becket, rather than Sir Ralph) went on to serve her with a wonderful park behind the house and a small sloping grass sward to the front of it; most of the park had now been sold, leaving only ten acres for the present-day incumbents and as protection against the ever-present threat of building development in its immediate vicinity.

The house was christened Summer Court; it was to be largely a summer residence, for Sir Ralph liked the bustle of Bath for much of the time, and she saw herself holding her own small court there; the name was contracted to a single word by one of her more modest descendants.

It was hugely uncomfortable; always at least five decades behind with its modernisation, impossible to heat satisfactorily. When Eliza arrived for her first term as a boarder at Heathfield, she was astonished at the other girls' complaints about the cold dormitories, the draughty study bedrooms, the 'dribbly' showers. It seemed the height of luxury to her, accustomed as she was to waking to ice on the inside of her windows and a four-inch bath deemed disgracefully wasteful. But she adored the house. It had stayed with the Cunninghames through ten generations; Sarah's mother, the last Lady Cunninghame, had been the first in the line to fail to produce an heir. She had produced only one child, and that was Sarah.

Mercifully – as Sarah saw it – there were no other claimants to the house: no cousins, no male uncles even. And thus it was that Sarah's father, the ninth baronet, had been forced, his signature dragging with dreadful reluctance across the paper, to entail it to her. Or rather, to her and her husband. It was better than selling it, which was the only other option. And Sarah did love it.

'Never let it go' had been his last words to her; and she promised. It was owned by a trust, and they were merely its tenants for life; it was slowly bankrupting them. But keeping it was what mattered and the children loved it as much as she did; Summercourt was their treasure and their home, it was where everything important happened.

Charles, brought up from his earliest years to regard it as his legacy, would roam its woods and fields as a child, pretending to be the son of Lady Anne; as he grew older, he took it very seriously, acquainting himself with such country pursuits as hunting and shooting, as befitted the heir to such a gem. The fact that the estate was far too small to support anything more than rabbit shooting and a few pheasants didn't apparently trouble him; but Eliza once overheard two of the fellow undergraduates he'd invited down for a few days discussing 'Charles's Brideshead fantasies' and that they'd expected something ten times its size, 'Drives and lodges, that sort of thing.'

There was no proper drive even, only a rather pretty tree-lined avenue up from the village, and certainly no lodges. The house had no privacy from the front, which the family rather liked; it had been designed to stand as part of the village. But the charming stone cottages, pretty Norman church, medieval duck pond and seventeenth-century inn that had set the house off so prettily in 1755 and lain at its feet (another of Lady Anne's fanciful phrases) had become extended by a sprawling growth of mock-Tudor bungalows to one side and to the left another of council houses – albeit for the most part with lovely gardens – a garage, a school (late Victorian, not beautiful), a bus shelter, a children's playground and a shop.

But it was a proper village; it had a heart. The school was thriving, the church more than half-full most Sundays, and the inn (now the White

Hart pub) busy; most people knew most people. And the Fullerton-Clark family were popular – the children had all gone to the village school for the first few years of their education, Sarah ran all sorts of local enterprises, opened the grounds several times a year – most famously for the Easter Egg Hunt, in which the whole village took part – and Adrian did his bit as he put it by drinking in the White Hart whenever he could. He also played for the village cricket team, where he was something of a liability and always sent in to bat last, but much appreciated for his good nature and his generosity in the bar afterwards.

The village had even been made to feel part of Eliza's dance; the local band had played a set and the fireworks had been let off on the village green rather than at the back of the house.

Yes, Sarah thought, her father would have been very happy last night, happy with what she had managed to do.

And even forgiven her for marrying Adrian. Perhaps.

Chapter 2

Someone was crying in the darkness. More than one, actually. Muffled, quite heavy sobs. God, it was like being back at prep school, Charles thought. And he hadn't cried even then. It did bring it back, though, being eight years old, staring dry-eyed into the darkness, small fists clenched, fighting the homesickness and the fear . . .

But it was absurd, blubbing like that.

And this hadn't been that bad a day. The next would probably be much worse.

They'd come in lorries, a wildly assorted mass of very young men, mostly eighteen years old, to a depot called Blackdown, near Aldershot, to do the compulsory duty to their Queen and country, two years of military training and experience known as National Service. Charles had sat smoking, offering his pack round to his neighbours, not talking much, all on the advice of a friend who had just survived this ordeal.

'For the first and probably the last time in your life your accent'll be a disadvantage,' he had said, 'so keep mum as much as you can until you get a bit stuck in.'

They'd arrived mid-morning and been hustled out of the back of the lorry against a background of interminable shouting; shouting and a lot of hustling went on all day. Some of the younger-looking lads wore expressions of absolute panic. They'd been shown to their hut, allotted a bed and then hustled off to another hut for kitting out, walking down a long line of tables bearing clothes and equipment, and piling up kit in their arms as they went, the final and most important bit of kit being the huge Lee Enfield rifle. It all had to be stored in the iron wardrobes that stood next to every iron bed.

And then the haircut: pretty brutal, the clippers run straight from the nape of the neck to the forehead and then a swift finish off round the sides, bit of a shock, but it was only hair for God's sake, it would grow again. Charles had been appalled to see a couple of Teddy boys, all swagger in the lorry, near to tears as their DAs, short for Drake's Arse, drifted to the floor.

They had eaten that night in the canteen – pretty disgusting muck on tin plates, using their regulation 'eating irons' in army speak, sausages, some burnt, some almost raw, a heap of oily onions, another heap of watery mash, followed by bread and jam. Charles, used to the horrors of public-school food, found it not too unbearable, but several of the boys silently scraped their still-full plates into the dustbins. Probably, they were the ones crying now.

God, he wanted to pee. He'd have to go and find the latrines. He eased himself out of bed and walked quietly down the hut, carefully avoiding looking at any beds in case he embarrassed one of the blubbers. Actually, why bother with the latrines – which had looked pretty disgusting – when outside would do? He slipped out of the hut, peed with huge relief into the darkness and was just going back when he heard an amused cockney voice.

'That better?'

'Eh? Oh, yes, thanks.'

'I s'pose this is all a bit like your school, isn't it?'

'Well, yes, it is a bit.'

'Yeah, I've heard you public school lot take to it all like ducks to water. Drakes, rather. Ciggy?'

'Oh – yes, thanks.'

Charles took a cigarette from the pack of Woodbines being offered. He could see quite well now, his eyes adjusted to the darkness. Not that it was very dark, there were tall arc lights on every corner of the camp.

'Talking of drakes, did you see that bloke crying as his hair came off?'

'I did, yes.'

'Quite a few crying in there now. Poor little mummy's boys.' He held out his hand. 'Matt Shaw.'

'Charles. Charles Clark.'

'Where you from, then, Charles?'

'Oh – Wiltshire.'

'Yeah? Don't know that area at all. I'm from London. As no doubt you can hear.'

'Sort of,' said Charles carefully.

15

'Pretty recognisable, really. Like your accent, no mistaking that either. What d'you reckon we'll do tomorrow, then?'

'I rather fear it's all the medical stuff. You know, injections and so on. It's Friday.'

'What's that got to do with it?'

'I've heard they make you feel a bit rough. You get the weekend to recover a bit. And after that I expect an introduction to drill.'

'Blimey, those crybabies won't like the needles will they? More tears I reckon. What you been doing up till now then, Charles?'

'I've been at university.'

'Yeah? Thought you was a bit older than the rest of us. Oxford I s'pose? Or Cambridge?'

'Oxford,' said Charles.

'Thought so.' He grinned at Charles. 'As you can see I know all about the upper classes.'

Charles grinned back at him. He liked him. As far as he could make out in the half-light, Matt Shaw was rather good-looking. Dark hair – what was left of it – rather broad face, dark eyes, wide grin, and surprisingly good white teeth. Quite tall – a good six foot. Obviously pretty young.

There was the sound of boots on the concrete; most likely some kind of patrol. Charles jerked his head towards the hut and they shot in.

Charles had been right about the medical stuff. And Matt had been right about the tears. They were woken at five thirty by NCOs banging their pace sticks on their bed ends and fire buckets and shouting at them.

'Come on, you 'orrible lot. Hands off cocks and on socks. Up, up, up.'

They were sent into the latrines – plugless basins, freezing cold, not a door to be seen – and then to breakfast. More bread and jam. And then out onto the parade ground. Their sergeant, a bullet-headed sadist, roared insults at them for what seemed like hours while they discovered the apparent impossibility of keeping in step. Charles had no trouble with that, he'd been in the Combined Cadet Corps at Eton, but he did discover his boots were too big. Better than too small, the other option – there were no half sizes – but he knew what the result would be. Blisters. Not fun.

They were also introduced to bulling: the army's word for cleaning. Kit had to be polished and polished and polished again. Dimples had to be teased out of boots with heated spoons and treated literally with spit and polish; white belts were blancoed, brass shone – 'I want those buttons shining like a shilling up a sheep's arse,' a sergeant shouted. They shouted non-stop; it added to the confusion.

And then at the end of the day, the syringes. Injections against yellow fever, typhoid, tetanus. The needles were alarmingly large: the MO kept a couple hanging casually from his white coat and didn't sterilise them between each use. A couple of the lads fainted. Even Matt Shaw was quite pale afterwards and very quiet.

'Fucking hurt,' he said, managing a grin.

That night there was more muffled weeping.

Three days later, three days of drill and bull and being shouted at and insulted constantly, vile food and too little sleep, even Charles was low. Matt was very low. He missed supper on the Monday night, unlike him since he normally ate everything without complaint – 'My mum don't allow fussy feeders' – and when Charles went to find him he was lying on his bed, clearly unwell.

'Got an 'eadache,' he said. 'Bloody everything aches.'

Charles put a hand on his forehead; it was very hot.

'You've got a temperature,' he said. 'Must be the jabs. Come on, I'll come to the infirmary with you.'

'What, and get ribbed for skiving? Not bloody likely. I'll be all right.'

Next day he passed out on the parade ground and was sent to the infirmary anyway.

'You're reacting to the yellow fever shot,' said the MO. 'Temperature of one hundred and four. Should have told us earlier. We don't want heroics here. Bloody stupid.'

Matt was too wretched to argue.

Charles went to visit him two days later; he found him sitting up, looking much more cheerful.

'Back to the 'oliday camp day after tomorrow. Can't wait.'

'Wish I was lying down,' said Charles, 'I've got some hideous blisters.'

'Yeah?'

'They'll harden up in no time. I'm treating them with meths, that toughens up the skin. We used to use it on our backsides at prep school when we'd been beaten.'

'How old was you then?' said Matt with interest.

'Oh, about ten.'

'And you paid for that, did you?'

'Well, my parents did,' said Charles with a grin.

17

'Blimey. No wonder you've settled down here.'

'Yeah, it's much the same. Anyway, poor little Walton's blisters are really bad. And he was put on jankers today, poor sod. That didn't help.'

Being put on jankers meant having to run round the parade ground in full battle dress, complete with tin hat and bayonet, urged on none too gently by an NCO in running gear.

'Poor bugger.'

Walton had become a friend of theirs, had sat in the NAAFI with them the second night and talked of his life as a Barnardo's Boy. Like Charles, he was finding the army experience bearable, used as he was to institutional life; and he appeared unmoved by the constant criticism hurled at him. He was almost incapable of keeping in step; he had been called out on the third morning, so he could 'show the rest of this shower 'ow it's not done', and quick-marched the width of the parade ground on his own. The drill sergeant watched in silence; then his lip curled.

'Look at 'im,' he roared, 'just like a pregnant bloody fairy!'

'I didn't really care,' Walton had said to Charles and Matt later, 'except half the hut will think he meant it, think I am a fairy. Which I'm not. If I 'ad been I wouldn't be no more. You got beaten for it at the Home – if they caught you that is. Soon cured it, I can tell you.'

The weeks wore painfully on. With the first thirty-six-hour leave in sight, everyone was terrified of doing something that would jeopardise it. Punishment could descend from apparently nowhere, often on unjustly large numbers. But they were lucky, and their inspection more than passed muster, resulting in a cheery 'jolly good, Sergeant, well done' from the inspecting officer.

'As if the bleedin' sergeant done anything,' said Matt bitterly.

Much of the first leave, the thirty-six hours so desperately looked forward to, was spent by the men in their beds. They came home literally exhausted, not only by the physcial trauma of their new lives, but the pressure, from being harried from first light to last, from struggling to cope with the ceaseless criticism and confusion, from the loss of any kind of privacy, from the fear of failure and the threat of punishment.

There was a lot of bravado, of boasting of imminent and immense sexual conquests and drinking, but Charles, looking round the hut as they waited to leave, almost everyone pale and hollow-eyed, thought there would be precious little energy for either activity. All he wanted, after a decent dinner, was to lie down on his own comfortable bed in his own quiet room at Summercourt and stay there until it was time to return.

Matt Shaw had no intention of spending any time in his bed. Since it would be in a room shared with two younger brothers and usually the family dog as well, a constantly yapping terrier called Scruff, there would be little point.

He got off the train at Clapham Junction and walked along the Northcote Road, savouring the freedom to move slowly, to smile and chat with various stallholders in the market who recognised him, ribbed him on his haircut, asked if he was a Field Marshal yet.

The Shaws lived in a small terraced house in a street just south of the Northcote Road; as Matt opened the gate, his two young brothers shot into his arms. He was touched.

'You miss me, then?'

'Not 'arf. No one to talk to,' said twelve-year-old Derek.

'An' I 'ad to walk Scruff on me own,' said nine-year-old Alan.

'Shockin'. Oh, now here's Mum. How's my best girl then, eh?'

His mother smiled at him, gave him a hug.

'Hello, Matt. You all right? You look a bit thin, love. And my word, what they done to your hair? It looks shocking.'

'Mum, it'll grow. Worse things happen than that, I can tell you. You look good, Mum. Like your hair.'

'You noticed! More than your dad did. It was Scarlett's idea, getting it cut.'

'Very nice. Where is she?'

'Away, love. Should be back tonight though, with luck. She's in Rome.'

Sandra's pride in Scarlett and her new career as an air hostess was almost unbearable. For a family to whom the Isle of Wight was abroad, to have a daughter who flew regularly to legendary places like Rome – and Paris and Venice and Madrid – was truly extraordinary.

'She enjoying it still?'

'Loving it. And the people she meets, really Matt, you've no idea—'

Matt, who had every idea of the people Scarlett met, having been regaled with the list of them as well as the destinations, said he was pleased to hear it, and he and Scarlett could catch up later.

'Imagine if you get sent abroad, Matt, that'd be half the family over there. What a thought. Come and sit down, love. Want something to eat? How about a bacon sandwich?'

'Oh, Mum, now you're talking. Army food's disgusting.'

He watched her as she fried the bacon, sipping a cup of her extra-strong, extra-sweet tea. She was great, his mum. She wasn't like the other mothers round their way, she didn't look halfway to old age already. At forty, Sandra Shaw was still pretty – very pretty. She was dark, very slim, with large brown eyes. She'd had a hard life; she'd had to do cleaning work to close the gap between what Peter Shaw brought home from his building job and what their large family needed, but had always claimed cheerfully that as it got her out of the house and away from her own cleaning, she didn't really mind. Sandra was nothing if not upbeat.

Since Scarlett and Matt had been out in the world, she'd been able to retire as she put it, but in a way she missed getting out of the house and having at least a few shillings of her own. Although she'd never had any money for clothes she managed to look as if she did. She was clever at sewing and made herself blouses and dresses from fabric she got at the market, and studied the fashion pages of *Woman* and *Woman's Own* carefully every week.

Today she was wearing a pair of narrow black trousers and a black sweater, as made famous and fashionable by Audrey Hepburn. She did her eye make-up like Audrey's as well, with thick black eyeliner and heavy eyebrows and had now had her hair cut urchin-style like Leslie Caron in *Gigi*. She was very much influenced by the cinema: Scarlett had been named after Scarlett O'Hara. Sandra had read *Gone With the Wind* while she was pregnant and been deeply affected by it, and only some very firm words from Peter Shaw had prevented her from calling their firstborn son Rhett.

'But he looks just like him,' she had said, gazing down at the squinting eyes and black hair of the baby. 'He's going to be really dark and handsome.'

Peter had told her that no son of his would have a sissy name like Rhett and Matt, when he was told, was extremely grateful to his father.

Scarlett arrived home just after six, rushing in looking crisply businesslike in her navy uniform, engulfing Matt in hugs and kisses.

'Oh, it's so lovely to see you. Mum's been so worried about you, thought you wouldn't survive.'

'I'm fine,' said Matt, 'course I am. And it's great to see you too, Scarlett.'

They were very close. There were only seventeen months between them – 'then Pete found out what was causing it,' Sandra would explain with one of her earthy giggles – and they had grown up practically as twins. Scarlett had the same thick, dark hair as Matt, the same large dark eyes, set off by absurdly long eyelashes, the same straight nose, the same neat, sharply carved jaw. She exuded vitality as Matt did; she was quite small and very slim and irrepressibly energetic. She had inherited her mother's eye for clothes and she would devour the fashion magazines noting trends and what they called fashion tips. She had always attracted attention wherever she went, and still more so now, with the sophistication of her new career; indeed the week before she had been photographed at the local dance hall, jiving with a girl friend, a dizzy whirl of flying pony-tail and circular skirt, complete with layers of frilled nylon petticoats – all bought in the market and starched with sugar water – and glorious white-teethed grin. It had appeared in the local paper and Sandra had framed it and hung it in the front room.

Matt was younger than Scarlett, but he had always protected her in the school playground when they were little and guarded her against predatory boys when they grew older, and she acted as dating agent for him, as his good looks turned him into a magnet for her friends.

He was inordinately proud of her and her career, it was a big leap for a girl from Clapham, from a secondary modern. Being an air hostess was about as good a career as a girl could hope for. As good as being a private secretary, only with more prestige. The uniform, the foreign travel, the dashing pilots.

But she had thrown herself into her application, done a Linguaphone course in French, having heard that a second language was a big advantage, and she had a talent for sweeping people along with her enthusiasm, making them believe in whatever she was saying, which had stood her in good stead at her initial interview.

Matt had said he thought you had to be posh to be an air hostess, but Scarlett laughed.

'Matt! I can be posh. If I try. You know I can.'

This was perfectly true; she had a sharp eye and a distinct talent for the social climb. Her accent could move from Clapham Junction to nice suburban at will, and she knew precisely when and how to tone down her rather exuberant manner.

'So – what we going to do tonight?' she said now. 'I thought we might go to the Lyceum, if you feel up to it.'

'Course I do.'

21

They had a good time at the Lyceum; Scarlett invited her friend Josie along, as well as Malcolm, her on–off boyfriend, hauled in when she needed him, dropped again when she didn't.

Josie liked Matt, in fact she fancied him rotten, and she was fun. Matt had a couple of beers with his dad at the pub before they left and a couple more when they arrived at the dance hall. Exhaustion and the excitement of freedom doubled their potency; he danced the evening away through a haze, not only with Josie, but with several other girls as well.

At one stage he felt sick and dizzy, and had to go outside; Josie followed him, sat down on the steps with him and put her arm round him.

'Poor old soldier,' she said. 'I know what it's like there, that basic training, me brother did it last year. You must be all in.'

'Nah,' said Matt firmly, 'I'm fine. Thanks.'

'That's OK.'

She turned to him, pulled his face to hers and pushed her tongue into his mouth; it was a bit of a surprise, but very pleasant. Especially given the hazy feeling. They staggered up the street a bit, found an alley where he kissed her back very thoroughly and pushed his hand up her sweater onto her breast. Josie seemed to like that. God, he'd forgotten what they felt like, breasts. Hadn't had the energy to think about them even, the last few weeks. After a while, he moved to her bottom, which was firm and extremely responsive; he felt her grinding her hips into his and he pushed his hand gingerly up her skirt, feeling his way towards her panties. But this was forbidden territory. She pushed his hand down again.

'No, Matt,' she said, suddenly sober.

He didn't care and returned to her breasts. He knew the rules. He'd done pretty well, he thought, really. Later, going home on the tube, she sat with her head on his shoulder.

'It's been really nice,' she said sleepily. 'I like a soldier boy.'

Matt grinned at her.

'Same again next leave?'

'Yeah. What do you think?'

When they got back to the camp, they felt like old timers. There was a new intake of raw, terrified recruits; Matt went out of his way to speak to a few in the NAAFI, and tell them it wasn't too bad.

'It suddenly all begins to make sense, you'll be OK.'

'You heard about poor old Happy?' said Charles when he saw him.

22

'He's being sent off to Fattening Camp.'

Happy was their nickname for the undersized Walton, partly as reference to his size ('You could play one of them dwarfs,' Nobby Tucker, a Geordie they had befriended, had said one morning), partly his sunny nature.

'What!'

'Yeah. They say he needs building up. Might get deferred. Poor sod.'

Being deferred was the ultimate nightmare; it meant getting returned to a new unit. Which meant losing your mates and a dreadful sense of going back to square one.

Fattening Camp was on Salisbury Plain, near Aldershot; men who were particularly thin and unfit were sent literally to be fattened up.

'But 'e's as strong as a bloody ox,' said Matt.

'I know. Try telling them that, though.'

'Poor old bugger.'

Men were being hauled out now to do their USB (Unit Selection Board). It was the first screening for POM (Potential Officer Material); mostly predictable, anyone who had been to public school and a few wild cards who showed the necessary leadership qualities got picked, and those who passed would be sent off to do the War Office Selection board, known affectionately as Wosby, at Andover.

Charles was summoned together with the one other public schoolboy in the hut; so to his delight were Matt and a couple of others. Matt went off to, as he put it, 'blind them with my fucking potential'. He was pretty confident; if anyone had the gift of the gab he reckoned he did.

The USB procedure was an interview with the CO, no more than that. Matt failed. The only non-public-school boy who passed was a grammar-school boy, who spoke what was known as BBC English. Matt was very upset and angry; Charles tried to comfort him.

'They probably didn't like your ugly face. Doesn't mean a thing, really.'

'Yes, it does,' said Matt bitterly. 'Why else would that wanker Johnson get through?'

'Well,' Charles hesitated. 'Well, I s'pose it was just . . . just luck.'

'No, it fucking wasn't. It was because he'd been to fucking grammar school. Knew how to talk and that.'

'Oh. Matt, I'm sure—'

'No, it's me that's sure. And you know something? I could have gone to grammar school. I passed the scholarship. Only my parents couldn't afford the uniform. Mum was really upset. But Dad just couldn't do it. I even 'eard them talking about borrowing the money from somewhere. I wasn't having that. So I told them I didn't want to go, wanted to go to the secondary modern with me mates. Complete lie, I wanted to go. Course I did. And if I 'ad I'd be going off to do my Wosby with you. Not fucking fair, I tell you.'

'No, it isn't,' said Charles and was surprised to find how indignant he felt on Matt's behalf. 'Come on, Matt, I'll buy you a few beers.'

But Matt was filled with a black rage that lasted for days.

Two weeks later, Charles was sent off to do his Wosby. Having not only the right background, but demonstrably the right qualities – namely an instinct for leadership, a sense of comradeship, a practical intelligence and a clear lack of intellectual pretentiousness – he enjoyed it hugely and passed outright. Attending with him was Nigel Manners, who had been at Eton with him; on the last night they got mildly drunk together in the mess.

Manners said he seemed to remember Charles had a 'jolly pretty sister' and Charles said indeed he had. 'Baby of the family. I'm very fond of her. She had a rather successful Season.'

'Really? Good for her. Quite a good lark this, isn't it?'

'It is. Find your basic training OK?'

'Oh – you know. Not bad. Better than school.'

They both laughed.

'Good chaps in your unit?' asked Manners.

'Some of them, yes. One really bright bloke. He should be here really.'

'Yes? Why isn't he?'

'Because he didn't go to the right school,' said Charles. 'And he'd be a bloody fine officer. Sometimes I think it's not fair, all this stuff.'

Manners stared at him.

'Good lord! You're not a pinko, are you?'

'Not really,' said Charles slowly, 'but knowing Shaw has changed my mind about certain things. He's a good bloke through and through.'

'Well, he's obviously an exceptional fellow,' said Manners, 'but – it's jolly difficult, isn't it? I mean, would you introduce him to your sister, for instance?'

'What – socially?' said Charles. 'Oh, no, I don't think I'd go that far.'

Chapter 3

'Matt, this is my sister, Eliza. Eliza, Matt Shaw, comrade-at-arms.'

'Goodness. How very military. How do you do, Mr Shaw?'

'Fine, thanks,' said Matt, taking her outstretched hand. He stood there, staring at her; he felt an odd sense of disorientation, without being at all sure why. Tall she was, Charles's sister, with dark hair tied back in a ponytail and big blue eyes; she was wearing narrow black trousers and a black-and-white check jacket, which swung open to reveal a black sweater, clinging quite closely to some extremely nice rounded breasts. The hand he held for that moment was warm and smooth, and the smile she gave him had a slightly mocking edge to it.

'I hope you're not off to some battlefield now,' she said, taking back her hand and he was aware that he had held onto it for just too long and felt foolish. 'No, not just yet,' said Charles. 'Rather the reverse. Three days of serious relaxation for both of us; but Matt and I came up together from Warley, and I thought you might be able to drop him off at his place. I told him you were meeting me.'

'Well, of course I will. Where—'

'Really, it's not necessary,' Matt said, pulling himself together, suddenly desperate to be away from them, to escape from a situation he felt illogically uncomfortable in. 'I can get the bus, easy—'

'Of course we'll take you,' said Eliza, taking Charles's arm, reaching up, giving him a kiss. 'I'm taking Charles to see my new flat, so it's fine. Where do you live, Mr Shaw?'

'Matt, please. Well, Clapham, not too near your flat, Kensington I think Chas said it was—'

'Chas! Is that what you call him? I like it!' said Eliza, and Matt felt slightly patronised. 'No, honestly, I'd love to drive to Clapham, I'd take you up to Scotland if you wanted. I've got this heavenly new car, it's a Fiat 500, I can hardly bear to get out of it even.'

'How on earth did you afford that?' said Charles. 'If Pa bought it for you I'll feel very badly done by.'

'Of course he didn't,' said Eliza, 'it was a present from Gommie. You know how she loves to spoil me—'

'Wish my godmother loved to spoil me,' said Charles. 'What colour is it? Come on, Matt, don't look so nervous, she's not that bad a driver . . .'

As if that was what he was nervous about, Matt thought.

The Fiat was parked just below Waterloo station, in The Cut; it was navy blue. 'There she is,' said Eliza, 'love of my life. What do you think, Charles?'

'I think you're a lucky so and so,' said Charles. 'Can I drive it?'

'No you can't, you can get in the back. Matt, you sit next to me.'

'No, really, look – there's my bus. Goes right past my door. Thanks anyway, cheers Chas, see you, bye Eliza, nice to meet you.'

And he ran towards the bus as it was pulling away, seized the rail, jumped onto the platform and then went upstairs, so that he could watch the Fiat as it wove its way rather uncertainly in the opposite direction. He felt much better already.

He had still not got completely over his rage at not getting a commission; and he was depressed at the thought of Charles's departure from Warley barracks. He had become, Matt realised, a genuine friend; of course it wouldn't last, once this extraordinary experience was over, but for now he had come to rely on his company and he was going to miss him. The three days' leave marked their final separation. Charles was off to Mons, and the four of them, tough little Walton and Nobby Clark, the Geordie, had got very drunk the night before and sworn they'd stay in touch. Bloody likely, thought Matt, the three of them working-class lads and Chas the Posho. Basic training might pretend to make you all equal; but it was only skin-deep.

The other public school wallies, as he thought of them, were wallies indeed: 'thick as the proverbial,' he remarked to Nobby one night as they polished their boots. 'I mean Chas, he's got a brain in 'is 'ead, but those two 'aven't. I reckon we could get the better of 'em, you and I, Nobs, if we only got half a chance.'

'Yeah, well maybe,' said Nobby, 'but who's going to give it to us, eh? I don't see either of us being welcomed into the Stock Exchange where old Chas is going.'

'Maybe not,' said Matt. 'Trick is to find a place where we'd be welcome, where we could box clever, you know? I'm not going to be a builder like me dad, I want a cushy job, in an office, with a desk.'

'Yeah, and pigs flying past the window,' said Nobby.

Matt did actually have an idea about what he wanted to do, although he wasn't sure how he could accomplish it. Before he went into the army, he had worked as an office boy for six months in a big insurance company. His sharp eyes had led him to where he was sure a lot of money lay: the world of property.

Big buildings were going up all over London: the Shell building near Waterloo station, Castrol House in the Marylebone Road, Thorn House in Upper St Martin's Lane. The company he was working for insured some of the smaller ones; Matt always read very carefully the memos he carried about from office to office, realising how much he would learn from them, and one of the girls who worked in the typing pool and who fancied him would supply – in all innocence – information on the figures she typed up all day during an evening at the pictures or in a coffee bar. She didn't realise she was doing this; just found Matt's interest in her work rather touching.

It was small-beer stuff, a few thousand here and there, but Matt would work out for himself how the thousands would multiply to the power of millions for the big boys behind the big buildings. And it wasn't just the money; he felt a sense of genuine excitement as he travelled to work each morning on the bus – watching the buildings grow, watching London turn modern, as he put it, staring at the bomb sites that still scarred it, and wondering what might be growing shortly in their place. He had read in his *Daily Mirror* that something like a hundred and forty million more bricks had been cast that year than the one before, and that the money spent on new buildings had almost doubled in the past ten years. It seemed very clear to Matt that this was the industry to go into. Moreover, he sensed that it was a new, go-ahead world, and he would have a better chance to make progress in it.

When he left the army, he'd decided to get a job in one of the commercial estate agents that were multiplying almost daily; he could earn at least eight pounds a week just for starters. The sky towards which the great towers soared could be literally the limit. And Matt would have a part of it.

That was his dream, at any rate.

❁　❁　❁

'So – any news?' Charles said as they drove towards Kensington. 'Got a job yet?'

'Not really,' said Eliza. 'I mean I've got one, but it's not what I want, I'm just a secretary.'

'So, what do you want exactly?'

'Well, I'd like to get into the fashion business, work on a magazine maybe, but I haven't quite got there yet.'

'Jolly good. Well, keep me informed. I can't say I quite understand, but—'

'It's very simple. I want a career, I don't just want to get married. Well, I do one day, but I certainly don't see getting a rich husband as the be-all and end-all, like nearly all my friends do. Even if it is what Mummy and Daddy hope for.'

'They're struggling a bit, aren't they?'

'I really think they are. And the house is a huge expense and worry, lovely as it is. Oh, look, there's another little Fiat, look, a sister for mine.'

'You are absolutely ridiculous,' said Charles, laughing.

'I know, I can't help it. Incidentally I thought he was rather sweet, your Mr Shaw. Awfully good looking.'

'Is he? I suppose he is. Eliza, do look out, you nearly knocked that chap off his bike. Now tell me about your flatmates. Anyone I know? And where are we going tonight? I'm ready for a bit of fun, I can tell you.'

Sarah took a deep breath; she had to broach this subject, she couldn't leave it any longer.

'Adrian?'

He was deep in an article in the *Telegraph*. They were having breakfast outside, on the terrace at the back of the house.

'Interesting. They could start work on this Channel Tunnel in two years. I can't believe it. Wonder if it'd be a good investment.'

'Adrian, please don't talk about investment. We can't afford to buy as much as a premium bond at the moment. And anyway, if—'

'If what, my love?'

She stopped somehow. She'd been about to say one of the unforgivable things, about how Adrian's investments had invariably left them worse off; or that if he'd done a proper job throughout their marriage instead of fooling around with ridiculous schemes, they might not be in quite such a difficult situation now, or, worst of all, that her father had been right.

'If we did have any money, we'd need to spend it on Summercourt.'

'On what exactly? Seems fine to me.'

'It isn't fine, Adrian. It needs painting, the whole house, outside, every door and window, and that would cost at least five hundred pounds.'

'Sounds a bit excessive. And not really necessary, looks all right to me.'

'I know it looks all right at the moment,' Sarah said, 'the sun's shining, the roses are all over the front door, but when it rains, when it gets wet, you can see the cracks in the paintwork. Damp is getting in, it's really serious.'

'Really? I'll have a look next time.'

'We could look at it all now, darling, actually. Like those window frames. The wood's actually crumbling away in one of them.'

He stood up, took his glasses off, walked across to the window, peered at it for a moment, then returned to the table.

'Honestly, darling, I don't think it's too bad. Lick of paint on the worst ones, that'd fix it. No need to do them all.'

'Adrian, there is a need. Really. And there's damp in the cornices of some of the top bedrooms, I think there's quite a lot of water getting in. Really and truly we need a new roof, you know. Mr Travers warned us about that last time he replaced the slates, said he couldn't patch it all up indefinitely.'

'Now darling, think of the money he'd make, if he re-roofed the whole of Summercourt. Of course he's going to say that.'

Sarah took a deep breath.

'I don't agree, Adrian. He's a careful builder, a proper craftsman, and I would put a lot of faith in anything he had to say. And looking at those ceilings, I think the time has come.'

'But sweetheart, we can't afford it.'

'Well, we could if—'

'If what?'

'If we sold a bit more land.'

There. She had said it. It hadn't sounded quite as bad as when it had ground round and round in her head, in the small hours of the morning.

'But I wouldn't even consider it,' he said, 'it would be a dreadful thing to do. We've always agreed that we've kept the absolute minimum necessary to ensure the place is safe, so there's no risk of it being spoilt.'

'We need the money, Adrian, we really do. It only need be a few acres.'

And then it did all sound dreadfully bad, and she was horrified to find herself near to tears. He went over to her, put his arm round her shoulders. 'Hey,' he said, 'don't cry. You know I can't bear you to be upset. It'll be all right, darling. You should have talked to me before, not worked yourself up into this state. Look, leave it with me, I'll find someone to help us.'

'But, Adrian—'

'Now, Sarah. I mean it. It'll be all right. Promise. I'll talk to Bert Chapman, see what he says. He's a bit more realistic about these things than Travers.'

Bert Chapman was what her father would have called a spiv. Adrian liked him because whenever he came in with an estimate it was lower than anyone else's and he got jobs done more quickly, but to her the reason was plain, he botched everything, cut corners and employed people who had no real idea what they were doing.

She opened her mouth to say so, but Adrian was already moving into the next hideously predictable phase of the discussion.

'Oh, Sarah,' he said, his face suddenly infinitely sad. 'I'm sorry, sweetheart. Sorry I don't have more in the way of funds myself. I've been pretty useless to you, haven't I, in lots of ways. Never brought any money in.'

'Don't be silly.'

Of course, she'd known when she fell in love with him that he had no money and only a modest job in the City. Which he'd given up on his fiftieth birthday, because he was finding it so exhausting doing the journey up there every day as he got older, and a friend of his had offered him a partnership in his company, selling guns and fishing rods by mail order. But that had gone bust, taking Adrian's investment with it. Of course he had a small pension. But he was terribly extravagant, spent a lot of money on shooting, on wine, clothes . . .

'I'm not being silly,' he said now. 'I feel bad about it. And I hate to see you so worried.'

'Well, I'm afraid I can't help that.'

'Sometimes,' he said suddenly, 'I think your father was right. You should never have married me. How much better you'd have been with Johnny Robertson, how many millions is he worth now?'

'I have no idea.'

'I think you do,' he said and his eyes were very sad. 'I found that magazine you were reading the other day, and that list of the richest men in Britain. Let me remind you. It was twenty. Twenty million pounds.

That would have sorted out any amount of painting, wouldn't it? And Lord Harry whatever, he was on that list too, he had even more. Oh, Sarah, I'm not surprised you're disappointed.'

'I'm not disappointed,' she said quickly.

He ignored this. 'But there Charles was. So you didn't have much choice, did you?'

'I didn't want a choice.' And she hadn't, in spite of her mother's grief, her father's rage at her announcement she was pregnant. She had wanted to marry Adrian. Had insisted on marrying Adrian.

She reached up and kissed him.

'I've been very happy,' she said, 'as you know, we both have. It's all been lovely.'

'I hope so. Certainly it has for me.' He picked up the paper again, clearly feeling the matter settled. 'Anyway, darling, I'll get Mr Chapman in early next week. Don't worry any more.'

She would of course, but silently. These discussions just made matters worse.

As she went into the house, the phone rang.

'Mummy?'

'Hello, darling. How are you?'

'Very, very well. I've got the most wonderful news.'

Engaged? thought Sarah, her heart leaping. To that nice Barrett boy, perhaps. That would solve an awful lot of problems, he was so rich and so . . . so suitable in every way. 'What's that, then?'

'I've got the most amazing and brilliant job. I'm so excited. It's everything I hoped for, in fashion, not just secretarial – oh, Mummy, I'm so happy . . .'

'That's absolutely marvellous, darling,' said Sarah, forcing her voice into enthusiasm. 'I'm so glad. Tell me all about it.'

Her heart lifted in spite of herself as she listened. It did sound wonderful. And Eliza was only eighteen, was still a little too young to think about getting married . . .

Chapter 4

'Look! Isn't it lovely?'

They all looked obediently at the square-cut sapphire surrounded by small diamonds, glittering in its appointed place, the fourth finger of the left hand, specially manicured for the occasion.

'Oh, it's gorgeous.'

'It's beautiful.'

'How terribly exciting. Congratulations!'

'Marvellous!'

'Thank you. I'm so happy! I don't know how I'm going to get through the day. Thank goodness it's Friday, we're going down to the country tonight, to talk plans with Mummy and Daddy.'

'Well—' Eliza hated to break the charmed circle of beaming rosy faces all peering down at Susannah Godley's ring, in the kitchen of the shared flat, but . . . 'I'm already late. Sorry. Susannah, congratulations again. Let me give you a kiss.'

'Thank you, Eliza. Thank you so much. Work hard! As if she wouldn't,' she added to the other girls, as the door closed on Eliza's back. 'That job is just too important to her. Well, when she does get married, she'll have to give it up, I mean no man's going to agree to his wife working the sort of hours she does.'

The others murmured in agreement and turned their attention back to the ring.

Eliza ran out into the street, feeling the now-familiar mixture of irritation and mild depression that followed any announcement of an engagement among her friends. Irritation because she couldn't understand how they could all get so excited about it, seeing it as the be-all and end-all of their lives – it would be the end as far as she was concerned – and depression because however much she told herself that, and that she was right and they were wrong, she was beginning to feel just a bit of an outsider. Everyone, absolutely everyone was getting married, even Princess Margaret – to a photographer called Antony Armstrong-Jones. Everyone except her, that was. Not that she wanted it, or certainly not at the moment, she hadn't met anyone she would have remotely wished to have a serious relationship with, let alone marry: she was far more interested in her career, it seemed to offer much more than any Mr Right, however wonderful. She supposed when and if he did actually appear, she might change her mind, but he'd have to be pretty impressive in every possible way, and certainly much more so than anyone she had met so far. And that was quite a lot of men . . .

But it was beginning to feel a bit lonely, out there, more so with every friend's engagement. Of course, she still had a terrific social life – although she could see that might dwindle as everyone got married, and started giving married dinner parties, so boring, she had been to a few, where the new dinner service and cut crystal were shown off in the new dining room in the new flat. It was a bit like being shown round some club you weren't a member of. And actually didn't want to join either.

Anyway, at least she wasn't a virgin any more; she'd seen to that, rather unsatisfactorily but with great relief, a few months earlier, at a country-house party. She hadn't exactly planned it, but she did want to get it over and done with, it was such a stupidly old-fashioned condition; he had been the brother of an old friend, who had actually been at her dance, they had both been rather drunk, and she had – well, seen a golden opportunity really.

Her relief was tempered with disappointment that it hadn't been more pleasurable; how could that, which had been uncomfortable rather than anything else, possibly have anything in common, she wondered, with the surge of rapture that Lady Chatterley had clearly experienced with Mellors (the book had just become available on the open market and was being passed from Nice Girl to Nice Girl all over England). She told herself that everything required practice, presumed it must get better and that when she found the right person, it would.

She did, of course, feel considerable guilt that she couldn't yet give her mother the pleasure – and the satisfaction and relief – of seeing her safely engaged to someone rich and appropriate. She was well aware of the investment in her Season and how difficult it was for her parents to find the money; the whole point of the ritual – and it was a ritual – was to pave her way to the altar, as it was for all the girls. Eliza could see she was, in that particular at least, a serious disappointment. But she felt unable to do anything about it.

And she had something far more important, in her opinion, the sort of job she had dreamed of, that had fulfilled all her criteria, in the publicity department of Woolfe's, a medium-size, high-fashion Knightsbridge store on the Kensington side of Harrods. Eliza had gone to Woolfe's as a secretary, but she had recently, and to her great pride, been promoted to Publicity Assistant. She absolutely loved her work, which consisted mostly of driving round London in taxis, delivering clothes that fashion journalists had requested for photographic sessions; she was also sometimes allowed to show the more junior journalists clothes – or more usually accessories – herself, and even suggest that such and such a hat or bag would go beautifully with the dress their magazine was featuring. Of course she wasn't allowed near the real queens of their professions, Audrey Withers of *Vogue*, Ernestine Carter of the *Sunday Times*, Beatrix Miller of *Queen*, but she sometimes would get the chance to sit quietly in a corner and listen to her boss, Lindy Freeman, as she talked to them, studying her apparently gentle persuasion, her skilful suggestions that Woolfe's could not only provide the one garment that had been requested for a feature, but another that was either very similar or dramatically different. She had brilliant ideas, did Lindy; the use of live mannequins in Woolfe's windows to launch the previous autumn's collection being her greatest yet. She was a tough boss and often had Eliza working until nine or even ten at night, and her wrath over mistakes was terrifying, but she was immensely generous, both with her praise and in giving credit where it was due. Eliza had never got over the sheer heady thrill of hearing Lindy tell Clare Rendlesham – the petrifying Lady Rendlesham of *Vogue*'s 'Young Idea' – that the idea of sending a cloud of multi-coloured silk scarves together with a simple black shift dress had come from 'my assistant Eliza'.

'You all right, darling?' asked Lindy when she got to the office. 'You look a bit wan.'

'Yes, of course,' said Eliza, 'absolutely fine, thank you.'

'Good. I want these coats taken over to Audrey Slaughter. I don't know if they're young enough for her, but it's worth a try. And on the way back, you might pop into Ruban's and buy a few yards of ribbon: white, pale blue and lemon. I've got an idea for an advertising shot; kind of weaving them into a model's hair. Nice for our wedding promotion.'

'It sounds lovely,' said Eliza. She loved going into Ruban de Paris, just off Hanover Square, with its rows and racks of ribbons and buttons.

Audrey Slaughter, an inspired young editor, had just launched *Honey*, the first-ever magazine for that new social curiosity, the teenager, and moreover was persuading the big stores to open up Honey Boutiques within their fashion departments, stocking the kind of trendy, young clothes that teenagers would want to buy, rather than near-replicas of what their mothers wore. She liked the coats but said she really couldn't use them, that they were a bit too grown up and certainly too expensive, that no teenager would ever buy them.

'Pity though, they have a really nice line. I haven't seen anything quite so sharp anywhere.'

Eliza reported this to Lindy, who sighed.

'It's a problem for us. Of course *Vogue* and *Queen* sometimes do young fashion, but for the most part our young clothes are ruled out of court as being too expensive. It's such a shame.'

'The customers buy them though,' said Eliza. 'Surely that's what matters?'

'We-ell, not as often as I'd like. We just don't have many young customers, really. And the perception of Woolfe's is still very much for the mothers rather than the daughters. And I can't get as much publicity as I need to change that view.'

'Couldn't you get some younger clothes made up, that were just a bit cheaper?' said Eliza. And then, 'Sorry, sacrilege I know, Woolfe's isn't about cheap, of course.'

'Well – maybe not complete sacrilege,' said Lindy after a long silence. 'Not even sacrilege at all, actually. In fact you might've given me an idea, Eliza. I need to think it through a bit, but meanwhile let's have those ribbons. And I can try this idea out on your hair.'

'Please do,' said Eliza and sat feeling almost unbearably excited as Lindy wove yellow ribbons into her hair. She had given Lindy an idea! If only the rest of your life could be as good as work.

'Oh, God. Here we go. Turbulence ahead. Now they'll all be sick. Oh, the glamorous life of the air stewardess. Scarlett, it's your turn to collect.'

Scarlett didn't mind. She loved her job so much that even collecting and emptying sick bags was bearable. She still adored it, even now she'd been doing it for two years.

Her training, the six weeks in digs near the airport, seemed like a dream from another age. She'd been so nervous, felt so inadequate; now she was self-confident and easy in any situation the job threw at her.

She had made one particularly good friend on the course, a girl called Diana Forbes, who had gone to a private school, had a brother at Cambridge, and spoke with an impeccable accent; she had teased Scarlett out of the social anxieties she had confided to her late one night over one too many gin and tonics.

'Scarlett, honestly! All that class stuff is completely out of date. I'm surprised at you.'

Scarlett didn't say that it might be out of date if you were like Diana and right there at the top to start with, but it was a bit different if you were dead common and trying to claw your way up. Some of the girls had been quite off with her in the beginning, not unfriendly, but not friendly either.

Most of them had been to private schools, or at the very least to grammar schools, their fathers worked in banks and in insurance companies; none of them were builders. And their mothers stayed at home and looked after them and gave dinner parties, and had what they called charladies. It had taken Scarlett quite a long time to admit her mother had been a charlady. She knew it was dreadful of her; and when, buoyed up by her own popularity and success, she did announce it one night, nobody turned a hair and said things like 'good for her'. But she also knew that there was an element of hypocrisy in it, that some of them at least were struggling to show how broad-minded they were, and that if the interviewing board had known it would have been a black mark against her, not an acknowledged one of course, but there, just the same. She hadn't tried to explain all this to Diana; it would have been pointless.

Diana, it turned out, was engaged. 'The trick is to work for a year, and then you get the honeymoon flights free.'

An old hand now, Scarlett had learnt first aid, among other things how to inject people with morphine (practising on the skin of an orange), and to deal with the inevitable air sickness; she knew about crash survival, about catering, how to work the bar, which was sealed before and after take-off. No one could leave the plane until customs – known as the rummage squad – had visited it and checked the contents of the drinks

36

cupboard which was closed with a lead seal before take-off and after landing.

And she had swiftly learnt the real lessons in bar work: how to put white wine through the soda-stream in lieu of champagne, how to knock the top off a Rémy Martin bottle, strain the contents through a tea towel into a jug and report it 'broken in flight' and then how to smuggle the booty out. Flat whisky bottles were the easiest and could easily be contained inside a pantie-girdle – 'make sure it's at least three times too big,' one of the old hands had told them – along with four packets of cigarettes.

Scarlett and Diana both flew Comets. The rotas were mostly European, to Rome, Madrid, Paris and occasionally down to Majorca, in the middle of the night with the fast-developing package tourists, the grockles as they called them, who begged them to tell them where they stayed or to join them for drinks. The other airline, BOAC, did the long-haul flights; the Boack girls, as they were known, were irritatingly superior about their job, their passengers – mostly VIPs – and their destinations: America, Canada, India.

Scarlett loved it; the fun, the glamour, the status of it all. She loved the dizzy excitement of the walk through the terminal, wearing her uniform, the blue-and-white dogtooth suit, the white shirt, the jaunty cap, smiling confidently, being pointed out and stared at admiringly – anyone would think they flew the bloody planes – greeting passengers at the top of the steps, directing them to their places, settling them, flirting very mildly with the men, charming the women, walking up and down slowly, smiling reassuringly, checking they were all safely strapped in. 'It's a bit like being a mannequin,' they'd been told when they were training. 'Everyone will look at you, you're the face of the airline, you have to be calm, confident, perfectly groomed every minute of every trip.'

And they had such fun. The pilots were fantastic, glamorous, dashing figures, made so much more handsome by their uniforms – Scarlett never got over seeing a pilot for the first time without his uniform – without anything actually, but it would have made no difference, he looked smaller, paler, even his teeth seemed less white. The most dashing were the ex-fighter pilots, older, practised charmers; the girls weren't supposed to fraternise with the air crew, they were always booked into separate hotels, 'as if that would make any difference for God's sake,' Scarlett said scornfully.

37

Nor of course were you encouraged to have anything to do with the passengers once off the plane. There was occasional trouble with the men of course, they'd pinch your bottom, or try to stroke your legs, and some of the businessmen travelling alone would ask you to have dinner with them, but a sweet smile and an 'excuse me' or 'sorry, sir' usually did the trick, although now and again, lured by the promise of dinner at the Hilton, say, in Rome, they would succumb. There was a degree of *droit de seigneur* about the whole thing; Scarlett's opinion of her passengers was permanently lowered when an American tipped her out of the taxi one night in the middle of Athens when she refused to go back to his hotel with him. The pilots were more fun and generally nicer.

God, this turbulence was bad. There were bells going all over the place, unpleasant noises coming from various points in the plane, someone trying to get up to go to the loo, they all begged to be allowed, but they weren't, they had to stay in their seats, however humiliating the consequences. That was another thing you became as a stewardess: a nanny. Scarlett didn't even mind that.

They were on the way to Rome. She was looking forward to it, she liked Rome and she specially liked Roman men. Normally it was straight back the same day, but she had a couple of days' leave and she had decided to stay. She was having a little fling with a pilot, who'd adjusted his rota to be with her. Well it was more than a little fling; it was an affair. He was married, but he was getting a divorce, so she didn't feel too bad.

Sometimes Scarlett wondered what on earth her parents would think of her if they knew what she had become. A tart, they would call her. A slut. Which would be unfair, because she never slept with anyone unless she was very fond of him; she had only one relationship at a time and she never slept with anyone who was happily married or who had children. Of course they all lied, and said their wives didn't understand them, but she always did her homework and checked their stories out. And she hadn't actually had that many affairs. Three. Well, four, if you counted the first one.

She often looked back at the Scarlett who had been a strictly-brought-up virgin, who knew that once you'd slept with a boy you lost his respect for ever and you'd never see him again. The other girls had put her straight on all that; the conversations in the hotel rooms late at night were barrack-room lewd. They'd told her what a lot of fun she was missing and where and how to get herself sorted out so she wouldn't get pregnant; she was still worried about the loss of respect, but Diana said that was an old wives' tale – or rather an old mothers'.

'Maybe when you're really young and you don't know the chap very well, but in a relationship, goodness, it's fine.'

Scarlett, thinking herself properly in love for the first time, with an Englishman she had met in Paris, consulted the gynaecologist who was kind and practical, instructed Scarlett in the mysteries of the Dutch cap and sent her back to her boyfriend's bed with her blessing. He was, as it turned out, as so many of them had turned out to be, married; but Scarlett enjoyed several weeks of happiness with him before making the discovery and, as a by-product, learnt to enjoy sex immensely. She just couldn't believe anything could be so wonderful, so all-consuming, so triumphantly intense – and so conducive to self-esteem.

Diana's fiancé was a regular soldier, a First Lieutenant in the Royal Scots Greys, serving out in Hong Kong, and as soon as he got promoted to Captain, they were getting married.

'Can't wait, it's such a wonderful life in the army, and he's an absolute dreamboat, Scarlett, you should see him in his mess kit.'

'What's mess kit?' asked Scarlett curiously. She was learning a whole new vocabulary from Diana, every bit as foreign as the French, Italian and German of her passengers.

'Oh, it's what they wear in the Officers' mess, not khaki, but bright red tunics and frightfully narrow navy trousers, so flattering.'

In spite of everything, Scarlett always felt rather honoured Diana had befriended her.

The plane had settled down again; Scarlett took a deep breath and went to collect the honk bags.

'So, darling, how is the job? Still enjoying it?'

'Oh, Gommie. I just adore it. And I've got the most marvellous news, I've been promoted.'

'Really, darling, how awfully clever. I've never been promoted to anything in my life. Unless you can count getting married. And I don't think Piers has turned out to be a promotion. Not nearly as rich as I'd thought. Good thing I didn't have any brothers and all Pa's money came to me or I'd be in a frightful bind. More champagne, darling?'

'Oh, yes please.'

Eliza beamed happily at her godmother; they were having their monthly dinner at Claridges. Anna liked to keep up with Eliza's life; she said it was much more interesting than her own.

'So what is the new job?'

'Well, Woolfe's are going to do a new young department, called Younger Generation, or something like that. And, they think it deserves a young PR. To talk to the younger journalists. And, oh Gommie, you're looking at her!'

'My darling girl, that is just thrilling. You are clever. Well done. How exciting.'

'Isn't it? And it means I can go into meetings with the buyers, stuff like that. I just can't believe it. Lindy – that's my boss – is so generous too. She says it was something I said that gave her the idea, and she's told Mr Woolfe that. And she's so young-thinking even though she's quite old, I mean at least thirty-five, I'd say—'

'Thirty-five! My God, Eliza, and she can still get herself about?'

'Oh, yes,' said Eliza, missing this irony entirely, 'and she's really with-it, too.'

'With-it? What does that mean, darling?'

'Oh, gosh, well, sort of – sort of young and trendy. You can apply it to anything, cars, clothes, music . . .'

'I shall remember that,' said Anna, smiling at her, raising her glass. 'It's one of the reasons I like seeing you, darling, keep myself up to date. Well, congratulations. Now what about your love life, anything interesting happening there?'

'Absolutely nothing,' said Eliza firmly. 'I'm a career girl, Gommie, and a very ambitious one. Love, getting married, doesn't fit into my plans at all at the moment.'

'Better not let your mother hear you saying that,' said Anna Marchant.

Chapter 5

'What you doing this weekend then, Matt?'

'Oh, not sure.'

Matt grinned at Paul Dickens, one of his fellow negotiators – well, OK, fellow trainee negotiators – at Barlow and Stein, Commercial Estate Agents.

'Group of us going down the coast Sunday. Should be good. Going to be hot, they say. Want to come?'

'Well . . .' Matt did want to go – a lot. But he'd promised Mr Barlow to work on Saturday and if he didn't finish he was quite prepared to work Sunday as well. He wanted to get promoted and fast, and he needed Mr Barlow to be pleased with him for that.

It wasn't exactly a difficult job; the only requirement was legwork. There was a stack of letters to go out to a great many small businesses in the area, asking them if they were looking to expand their offices and letting them know that Barlow and Stein had every type of premises to show them if they were; it would save a lot of money if they could be delivered personally.

Barlow and Stein was a small agency, based just off Great Portland Street and specialising in commercial property. Their clients were the fast-expanding businesses cashing in on the boom in every area of commercial life. London was the place to trade and its commercial heart, the City itself, was the centre of world finance.

'It's got fewer restrictions than any other capital city, that's the thing,' Matt told Scarlett over a drink one evening. 'It's like a bloody magnet, the money just comes pouring in, banks, insurance and that. And they need office space, all these people, loads of it.'

'An awful lot of my passengers are businessmen,' said Scarlett, 'specially in First Class, coming in from God knows where, Paris, Rome, Berlin. It isn't half strange thinking of Germans as customers rather than the enemy, but I've got used to it now. And then Boack fly them in from the States, they all say London is the place to be, you're right.'

Matt knew that he was on the brink of doing well. He woke every morning feeling upbeat and confident, positively looking forward to going to work. All the way in on the bus – where he sat in his new suit from the Fifty Shilling Tailors, a piece of brown paper set carefully down on the seat to keep it clean – and the bowler hat Mr Stein insisted he wore – 'it looks so much more professional, Matthew, puts you up there with the accountants and the bankers, and looks as if you really know what you're doing' – he studied his work place, the great bustling burgeoning city, and felt proud to be a part of it in however small a way.

He knew he had the army to thank for much of his progress. He'd chosen to go into the Royal Engineers, and learnt stuff which he could see he could find very useful in his future life as a property tycoon. They'd done things like constructing Bailey bridges and studying mechanics and road building, and he'd learnt to drive which he could never have afforded otherwise and managed to get himself put on a vehicle maintenance course. And then he'd played every sport available to him, fraternised with the locals – he tried not to think what his father would have to say if he knew he was snogging (and worse) with Germans – and some of the ATS girls were very . . . well, friendly. Sex was one of the things he missed most out in civvy street. There was precious little opportunity of getting a girl into bed when you shared a room with your brothers. It was one of the many reasons he, like Scarlett, yearned for a place of his own.

He'd left the army as Corporal Shaw, RE, with two stripes on his arm, a tough young man rather than the stroppy boy who'd gone in; and he went to the Labour Exchange on the very day of his demob, got a temporary job as an office boy and spotted an advertisement for the job with Barlow and Stein a few weeks later.

'We want someone with energy,' Mr Stein had said at the interview. 'Energy and common sense. And nice manners of course.'

Matt said he had plenty of energy and a fair bit of common sense, and that he hoped they could see he had the other commodity.

'My mum used to box my ears if I was cheeky.'

'Good for your mum,' said Mr Barlow.

Matt got the job and felt immediately as if he had come home. This was a world he was completely comfortable in; he seemed to understand how it worked in the most fundamental way. Wherever you looked there were new buildings going up, or old ones being refurbished.

There were the big boys of course: Jack Cotton, Charles Clore, Joe Levy, and Matt's personal hero and role model Harry Hyams, who'd made twenty-seven million by the time he was thirty-nine. That's what Matt was going to do, possibly rounding it up to thirty million. It wasn't a dream or even a hope, it was what he planned with a hard-edged certainty, he was going to build and own properties and fill them with the thousands of new companies that were also being spawned by the booming economy.

'It's a bit like a blind date,' said Mr Stein when he was explaining the business to Matt. 'There they both are, girl and boy, building and tenant, both perfect for each other, not knowing the other exists, needing an introduction. That's where we come in. You don't have to be a genius, Matthew, just a bit sharp. You'll soon learn.'

Matt didn't have to learn sharpness; it was in his bones. Within weeks Mr Stein was leaving him to show clients round premises on his own.

He didn't realise until much later how fortunate he had been in Mr Stein; how excellent was his grounding, how profound was his advice.

'Two things count in this business, son,' he said over a pint of warm beer one evening. 'One is that you have to be a gentleman. Your word is your bond. You can't let someone think they've got an office and then a week later tell them they haven't, just because someone's come in with a higher offer. This is a small world, Matthew, and people have to trust you. And you've got to be able to get along with people, mix with all sorts. All gossip this business, especially at the higher level.'

There was one thing which Mr Stein didn't mention and which Matt had no need to learn either, and that was the importance of hard work. And not just office work; if there was anything to be done, Matt did it, however disagreeable. The army had taught him that too. Indeed one day when the Barlow and Stein toilets were blocked and no plumber was to be found, Matt went out and bought caustic soda, a rubber plunger and some heavy-duty gloves and cleared the offending pipes – temporarily at least – himself. When some simpering typist said she really didn't know how he could do such a thing, he told her about Charles Fullerton-Clark who had once been ordered to scour the army lavatories with a razor blade, and had sung rugby songs while he did it.

He decided regretfully that he couldn't go down to the coast with Paul Dickens.

He set out for the City as soon as the offices closed that Friday evening, reckoning it'd be better to get that side over so that he could be in the West End on Saturday, good fun even if he was working; he'd delivered about fifty letters when he heard someone calling him.

'Matt! Over here, Matt, it's me, Charles Clark.'

And there he was on the other side of Lombard Street, waving at him. He'd never have recognised him, Matt thought, he looked exactly like all the other toffs round here, rolled umbrella, bowler hat, pinstripe suit. But he seemed genuinely pleased to see Matt, grinning and waving him over.

'It's jolly good to see you, old chap,' said Charles, slapping him round the shoulders. 'What are you doing here? Got time for a pint?'

Matt said he thought so and followed him into the King's Head on Lombard Street.

'Remember Matt Shaw?' said Charles to Eliza next day. 'He was in the army doing basic training with me. You met him with me at Waterloo one day.'

They were having a drink in the Markham in the King's Road: the newly dressed King's Road, filled with pretty young people, glamorous cars, and the clothes boutiques that were replacing the old food shops, all following their leader, Mary Quant, who had opened Bazaar, the very first of them, as early as 1955. No one would believe it had been there that long, Lindy had told Eliza. 'It seems so absolutely brand new, but it's just one more proof of Mary's genius.'

'Yes, course I remember Matt Shaw,' Eliza said. 'He was quite tasty as I recall.'

'I ran into him in the City. He had quite a sharp suit on, filled out a bit, his hair's longer. It was really good to see him. He's working for an estate agent. Commercial variety. He's doing well.'

'Oh, really? Well, good for him.'

'Yes, it's the business to be in at the moment, that's for sure. The potential for development in London is incredible, I know that. Typical Matt, he was delivering letters by hand, seemed embarrassed about it. I told him not to be so bloody silly. He's got a bit of a chip on his shoulder but I do like him a lot. We thought we'd try and track down a couple of the others, have a real reunion.'

'Yes, why don't you?' Eliza sounded distracted suddenly. 'Charles, there's something I want to talk to you about.'

'What's that? You're not getting engaged finally, are you?'

'Oh, for God's sake. Why does everybody think I have to get engaged? No, Summercourt.'

'What about it?'

'I was talking to Mummy last weekend. She's desperately worried. It needs a lot of money spent on it, not just painting it and general refurbishment, but they might need a new roof as well. They had it patched up a couple of years ago, but now it's getting really bad. And they haven't got a bean, she's even talking about selling a bit more land.'

'They can't do that! Anyway, the trustees won't let them. What does Pa say?'

'Not a lot, as far as I can make out. You know how loyal she is, but reading between the lines his head's firmly the sand. Just denies there's a real problem. I can't think what we can do to help, but at least we must show her some support. When are you going down next?'

'Well, I could pop down tomorrow. I really can't have her selling the land. It'd wreck the place. Could you come too?'

'I could actually. OK, let's do that. It would cheer her up if nothing else. She's really worried, can't sleep.'

'Poor Mummy. Yes, let's go and see her. I'm sure we can come up with something. Now, how's the job? I want to hear all about it.'

Eliza was even less inclined towards marriage than usual that summer; gearing up for the autumn opening of Woolfe's Young Generation was consuming all her energy. It had taken longer than even Lindy had expected, had been postponed twice and she had been in despair over the delay; Bernard Woolfe, initially enthusiastic, became slower and more cautious as he and the rest of the board debated endlessly the range of the merchandise, the look and feel of the department, its location within the store and what it would cost. Lindy and Eliza were both insistent that Woolfe's did an own-label range of clothes to stock alongside the other designs, to link the youth and fun of the department more closely with the store and its gilt-edged fashion reputation; Bernard Woolfe said this would be a mistake, that should the new department fail, it would reflect badly on Woolfe's as a whole, a question mark on their judgement.

'Bernard, that's just ridiculous,' said Lindy, trying to keep her voice calm. 'Either we believe in this thing or we don't. If we don't do our own line, it will look as if we're hedging our bets.'

'Perhaps that's exactly what I am doing,' said Woolfe, his dark eyes gleaming with good-natured malice. 'Not such a bad thing, you know, when the going's a bit rough . . .'

If Lindy had had her way, they would have opened within three months, 'to beat the competition that I know there's going to be', but Bernard argued that unless everything was right the competition would win.

Jan Jacobson, the brilliant young buyer hired to work exclusively for Young Generation, had brought in some beautiful clothes; comparatively established designers like John Bates (of Jean Varon) and Sally Tuffin and Marion Foale would hang on rails alongside entirely new talent. He had discovered Mark Derrick, who designed apparently shapeless little shift dresses that still flattered girls' bodies: the bodies that had seemed almost overnight to have been transformed from the shapely curves of the late Fifties to something almost boyish with neat, small breasts and flat, hipless torsos. And then there was Pattie Newton, whose clinched trench coats cut in the finest light gaberdine could be worn to work, to the theatre, even to parties over nothing more substantial than a silk slip; and Eliza herself had discovered Maddy Brown who had reinvented the sweater so that it continued downwards from the waist, to somewhere above the knee, and who also made ribbon-edged, gilt-buttoned mohair jackets in multi-coloured wool, which owed more than a nod in the direction of Chanel in shape, but were nonetheless totally original.

Eliza liked Maddy, she was fun, with a sweet and deceptively gentle manner; beneath it was an ambition as steely as Eliza's own. She was the child of working-class parents, had won a scholarship to a grammar school and then to art school; she was small with long fair hair and huge green eyes, and she still lived at home and used her tiny bedroom as a studio workshop. Selling her range into Younger Generation was her greatest success yet. Eliza had spotted one of her jackets in a journalists' office one day and had brought her into the Woolfe fold.

'It was truly lovely,' she had told Jan Jacobson, 'and the girl at the magazine was so sorry they couldn't use it, but she doesn't have any stockists you see. I think you should see them.'

This was a familiar story; new designers, young and forward-thinking, making clothes for the new young market, had very little in the way of resources; stores liked the clothes, but didn't want to risk unreliability of supply.

Slightly unwillingly, Jan agreed to see Maddy Brown, fell in love with the clothes and persuaded Bernard Woolfe she was worth the risk. Maddy and her one knitter, also working from home, found a couple more girls who met her exacting standards; all four of them were now installed in the unfortunate Mr and Mrs Brown's front room.

The department was due to open at the very beginning of September. It was late to launch autumn and winter merchandise, but they had to make a huge splash with the press and by September everyone would be back from holiday and thinking winter, as Lindy put it. It was all incredibly exciting and Eliza could hardly believe she was going to be part of it.

One night that summer, she and Charles went with a party of friends to Brads, the newest of the new nightspots. It was wonderfully unstuffy, the dress code dizzily informal, the food fun – hamburgers and hot bacon sandwiches – and the music loud, it was as far removed from the polite formality of the traditional nightclub as jeans and open-neck shirts were from dinner jackets. It was soon after midnight when Eliza, lying back temporarily exhausted after an energetic bossa nova, heard someone shouting above the din.

'Charles, old chap! Lovely to see you,' and into view, smiling and waving just slightly drunkenly in their direction, came the most glorious-looking man.

'Jeremy!' said Charles. 'Come and join us. Eliza, I don't think you've met Jeremy. Jeremy Northcott. We were out in Hong Kong together. Jeremy, this is my sister, Eliza.'

'Hello,' said Eliza, smiling just a little coolly while digesting this Adonis: tall, blond, absurdly good-looking, the patrician nose and chiselled jaw saved from cliché by a slightly lopsided grin, showing, of course, perfect teeth.

'Hello to you,' said Jeremy and sat down abruptly next to her, clinging to his glass of red wine with some difficulty. 'I think we met a couple of times at Eton, Fourth of June and so on.'

'Really?'

She was sure she would have remembered him, he was so extra-ordinarily good looking, but then you did get a bit dazzled there, the standard was pretty high.

'Yes, think so. And I was at the Harlot's Ball the year you came out, but I didn't manage to dance with you, too much competition.'

47

Eliza giggled.

'Well, maybe we could put it right some other time,' she said.

'That'd be marvellous.'

He smiled at her again; he really was knee-shakingly attractive.

'Well, what have you been doing with yourself, you old bugger?' asked Charles. 'Where are you living now?'

'In a flat I kind of inherited in Sloane Street,' said Jeremy.

'Lucky you,' said Charles. 'That's the sort of inheritance I'd like.'

'Yes, it's quite jolly there. What are you doing then, Charles? Working in the City, I heard?'

'That's right, with a firm of stockbrokers. Not a bad life. Hours are fairly agreeable, lot of decent chaps there. Pretty good really. How about you?'

'I'm working in advertising,' said Jeremy. 'Terrific fun. Firm called K Parker Dutton, KPD for short. Don't know if you've heard of it?'

'I certainly have,' said Eliza, smiling at him. 'It sounds like complete heaven to me. Is it true you all have your own offices complete with sofas and fridges?'

'Absolutely true.'

'You on your own, Jeremy?' said Charles. 'You're very welcome to join us.'

'No, sorry, whole crowd of us, including a rather tedious cousin who I'm bidden to look after. I must get back in a tick.' He looked at Eliza. 'Lovely to meet you again. Think I can't take you up on your invitation to dance just now. Another time perhaps?'

'Yes, of course.'

'We must arrange an evening,' said Charles. 'Been to the Saddle Room yet?'

'Yes, I'm a member. Great idea. So what are you up to, Eliza? Working girl?'

'Is she ever,' said Charles. 'You're looking at a bona fide career woman, Jeremy. Eliza works in fashion.'

'Really? How amazing.'

'Well, yes, it is a little bit amazing,' said Eliza. 'I love it anyway.'

'So, what exactly is it? Are you a model?'

'No,' said Eliza, not sure whether to be flattered because he should think that possible, or irritated that he should think modelling a career. 'No, I work for Woolfe's, department store in Knightsbridge. I do the publicity.'

48

'Oh, I know Woolfe's. Great store. Publicity, eh? I know what that means, taking all the fashion editors out to lunch?'

'Well, that's only a very small part of the job,' said Eliza, 'but yes, that is one of the perks. And telling them about everything in the store, hoping they'll write about it. And then making sure—'

'Steady on, Eliza,' said Charles, 'Jeremy's supposed to be enjoying himself, he doesn't want a lecture on the PR industry.'

'No, no,' said Jeremy, 'it's my line of country, you know. Look, I must get back to the cousin, I can see her looking a bit wan. Let's have lunch soon, Charles, here's my card, give me a ring. And I'll fix that evening at the Saddle Room. Lovely to meet you, Eliza. Bye for now.'

And he unwound his considerable height from the sofa and made his way back across the room.

'He seems very nice,' said Eliza.

'I knew you'd like him,' said Charles rather complacently, 'and he's fearsomely rich. His family owns a bank. Now if you married him that would solve all our problems. Summercourt included.'

'Charles!' exclaimed Eliza, hurling a packet of cigarettes at him. 'I said he was very nice, not that I wanted to marry him. Please stop going on about it. I am just not interested in getting married at the moment; I'm only interested in my career, OK?'

'OK,' said Charles.

Chapter 6

'Scarlett, could I possibly go up the front on the way back?'

'OK. As long as Brian agrees.'

Brian was one of the stewards on their flight; it was the stewards who decided which girls did Economy (Down the Back as it was known) and which First (Up the Front). The posher a girl, the more likely she was to be sent down the back; it was the totties who got given First Class, acknowledged a cushier number, because they were more likely to reward the stewards – those who weren't homosexual at least – by sleeping with them. No really classy girl would dream of sleeping with the stewards. Scarlett was seldom up the front, in spite of her slightly shaky social credentials, because she wouldn't have dreamed of sleeping with them either; she'd actually hoped to be there this trip, for a treat, it was from Vienna, almost four hours, but Diana was looking dreadful.

'Why, what's wrong?' she said.

'Oh, I've got the curse, feel awful. Now at least I'll be able to sit down occasionally.'

'Course. I'm sorry.' Scarlett looked at her sympathetically. Diana had terrible period pains and was quite often actually sick. 'You go and lie down for half an hour. They're boarding late; I'll make you a nice cup of tea. Got any codeine?'

'I think there's some in first aid. Thanks, Scarlett.'

But when it was time to board, Diana was vomiting and dizzy; the captain sent her back to the sick bay.

'You can't fly like that. No use to anyone. Don't worry, we'll manage.'

The flight was only half full. 'This'll be a piece of cake,' said Scarlett cheerfully to Brian.

'Don't be too sure. Lot of turbulence forecast.'

The turbulence was a while coming; Scarlett began to hope the forecast was wrong. She had enough to cope with without it; there was a difficult meal to serve, beef on the bone, carved in the aisle, and almost every passenger on the plane wanted theirs rare, and a French businessman demanded his blue; an extremely tiresome child insisted on walking up and down the aisle behind her, 'helping her' as she put it, and an American woman called Mrs Berenson was intensely nervous and clutched at Scarlett every time she went past, asking how they were doing, whether there was any turbulence ahead, when they might land, was there a doctor on board.

'I have dreadfully high blood pressure, you see, I could need sedation if there were any difficulties.'

Scarlett assured her there were no difficulties as far as she knew, and that there was first-aid equipment on board.

'My dear girl, that's no use to me, I need a proper doctor.'

Scarlett smiled again and offered her an aspirin. It often soothed the most terrible nerves: placebo effect, she supposed.

'Yes, that might be nice, thank you. Oh, dear God, what was that?'

The plane had dropped slightly; it shook a little and then steadied.

The captain's voice came over the intercom.

'Ladies and gentlemen, we may be about to experience a little turbulence. Please return to your seats and fasten your seat belts.'

'Oh, my God,' moaned Mrs Berenson, 'oh God, what shall I do?'

'Nothing,' said Scarlett gently, 'just do up your seat belt and sit tight. You're perfectly safe.'

She stayed with her for a moment, trying to calm her, and then worked her way round the cabin, reassuring, smiling, plumping pillows, fastening belts. She could feel the plane beginning to shudder.

The child was still running behind her, giggling. 'I'm sorry,' said Scarlett as politely as she could to her mother, 'but I really must ask you to get your girl strapped into her seat.'

'But she's enjoying herself so much,' said the woman.

'She won't enjoy herself getting thrown round the cabin,' Scarlett said coolly. 'Please do what I ask, it's important.'

A wail went up from Mrs Berenson; Scarlett hurried to her.

'There's nothing to worry about, Mrs Berenson. Really. You'll be fine. Please try to stay calm, you're upsetting the other passengers. Here, have a sip of water. Did you take your aspirin?'

'Yes. Maybe I should have a second one.'

The tail seemed to swing round slightly and Mrs Berenson wailed

51

again. Various buzzers were being pressed; Scarlett patted her hand and hurried off.

When she passed the Frenchman's seat he put his hand out, barring her way.

'This wine is terrible. Open a new bottle, if you please.'

'I'm afraid I can't – not just at the moment.'

'Miss, this is not what I have paid my first-class fare for. Please do what I ask.'

Scarlett walked to the service area, and started to open a fresh bottle of claret.

'Scarlett! You can't do that. Not while this is going on.' Brian was frowning at her, sitting in his own seat, doing up his straps. 'Sit down and belt yourself in.'

'It's either giving that frog his bloody wine, or pushing him out the window. Now just stop fussing, and think about something else, like that lovely boy you met last night.'

'Bitch!' said Brian and blew a kiss towards the window. She smiled at him tolerantly. He was a raging queen like most of the others.

Mrs Berenson was screaming now. Such panic was infectious; other passengers were turning to stare at her nervously, and the little girl started to cry.

'I'll go and sit with her,' Scarlett said to Brian who was behind her, proffering a second napkin to the Frenchman, 'otherwise they'll all start screaming.'

'All right, darling. Rather you than me. She's the colour of a billiard table.'

Scarlett started to make her way towards Mrs Berenson, smiled at her and settled herself in the window seat.

'Here,' she said, 'hold my hand. You're going to be fine.'

'I don't think so,' said Mrs Berenson. Her voice was lower now, her teeth chattering. She had a very pretty, Southern-belle-type accent; she was very pretty altogether, Scarlett noticed, honey-blond, with fine, fair, slightly freckled skin and wonderful green eyes. She was far from young, probably about sixty, but slim and beautifully dressed, in a cream silk shirt and camel skirt. 'We're going to crash, aren't we?'

'No, we're not. The captain says it's fine, just a bit of bad weather. Honestly, in about ten minutes it'll be over. Deep breaths, that's right. Now why don't you tell me where you're from, why you're coming to

England, I do love to know more about passengers, and we never usually get the chance. Do you have family here?'

Clinging to Scarlett's hand, Mrs Berenson began to talk, and became calmer, telling her where she lived (Charleston, South Carolina), where she was going (London to visit an elderly aunt), why she'd been in Vienna (to stay with a friend and visit the Opera House for 'the most wonderful "Magic Flute"'), about her three sons, all of whom were extremely good-looking, she said (and what mother didn't claim that for her sons, Scarlett wondered, smiling at her, they were probably as plain as pikestaffs. Although if they were anything like their mother . . .)

The turbulence ended as suddenly as it had begun and the plane became completely steady. Scarlett unbuckled her belt.

'I've love to hear more, Mrs Berenson. But I have lots to do now. Excuse me, won't you?'

'Of course, my dear. How kind you've been. Thank you.'

'It was truly a pleasure.'

They reached London two hours later; the plane landed smoothly, everyone stood up, chattering, the trauma quite forgotten. Scarlett stood at the top of the steps, smiling sweetly at everyone, accepted Mrs Berenson's thanks and a promise to look out for her in future, and a kiss from the tiresome child.

'Told you,' she said to Brian. 'Piece of cake.'

Young Generation had been open for nearly a year now, and was acknowledged by everyone who mattered as a huge success. Bernard Woolfe said so, albeit cautiously, while noting its extremely healthy turnover; the press said so, rather less cautiously, giving it rave reviews from day one (the *Evening Standard* had described the opening party as 'an explosion of colour and music and style') and continuing to feature it and its merchandise on a most satisfyingly regular basis, and the customers said so by flocking to it, day after day. Young, stylish, moneyed, they fell on this treasure trove of clothes that suited them and their lifestyle so perfectly – and carried it away from Woolfe's in the shiny, brilliantly coloured carrier bags that were its trademark. The carrier bags had actually been Eliza's idea and she was very proud of them.

The party had been attended by everyone who mattered in fashion: Anne Trehearn of *Queen*, Ernestine Carter of the *Sunday Times*, Felicity Green of the *Mirror*, and Shirley Conran, creator of the new 'Femail' section in the *Daily Mail*; the fashion photographers and rising star David Bailey, with his friends Terence Donovan and Norman Eales, as well as the more establishment crowd, John French, and Henry Clarke; and the models, Jean Shrimpton, Pagan Grigg, Grace Coddington, and every man's dream of a girl, blue-eyed blonde Celia Hammond.

And then there had been the designers – who would have thought Mary Quant would attend, never mind John Bates, Jean Muir, and the new names such as Maddy Brown who (to quote the *Standard* again) 'has done the impossible and made knitting sexy'.

Eliza had thought it would be hard, settling down after the excitement of the launch, but in fact she simply found herself caught up in an ever-increasing whirlwind timetable of shows, photographic shoots, press releases, and the more mundane but possibly most important task of all, seeing to the nitty-gritty: getting clothes over to the offices of the fashion editors, making sure that *Queen* and *Vogue* – for instance – weren't featuring the same dress, checking prices, suggesting and then rounding up accessories to accompany the clothes that the journalists called in.

Her favourite days were when a fashion editor rang up and said something like, 'We're doing a story on fringed hems – have you got anything?' And if there was nothing fringed to be found in the stockroom, she'd call up one of her favourite designers and ask, 'Got anything with a fringed hem?' Whereupon the more desperate would actually knock up a sample in twenty-four hours for her, on condition Woolfe's would agree to be listed as stockist. It was quite common for none of the garments in question to be sold; but it didn't really matter much, it suited everybody, the journalist who found a page of her feature filled, the designer who got the priceless publicity for his or her name, and Woolfe's who increased their reputation for cutting-edge fashion.

It was hectic, exhausting, and absolutely wonderful. What romantic liaison could possibly compete with that?

'You all right, young Matthew?' said Mr Barlow.

'Yes, fine, thanks.'

It wasn't true; he had terrible toothache. It had been growing quietly but insistently for three days now. He kept hoping it would go away, settle down again.

'Good. You don't look it. Anyway, come in, I've got some news for you.'

Matt followed him into his office.

'You've done well, lad. Very well. We've all done well, of course, got a load of new clients, in fact we'll have to move soon. You'll have to find us an office. Go and see some agents.' He chuckled. He prided himself on being a joker.

'But credit where it's due. A lot of it's down to you. So, I'm promoting you, Matt. Making you up to negotiator.'

'Crikey,' said Matt.

'I hope you don't use words like that to the clients,' said Mr Barlow disapprovingly.

'Course not.'

'Good. And there'll be a rise too. How would twelve pounds a week sound to you?'

'Pretty good,' said Matt, 'but not as good as thirteen.'

'Maybe not. I didn't say thirteen though.'

'I know that, Mr Barlow. But I reckon it's what I'm worth. From what I've heard.'

Mr Barlow looked at him almost severely. 'You've got a cheek. But you could be right. How about twelve pounds, ten shillings?'

'Done. Thank you very much, Mr Barlow.'

Matt went into the golden September evening feeling very happy. He was getting there. Next move would be getting his own agency. In a year or two. He had the energy, and he'd have some clients. He'd have no compunction about taking them away from Barlow and Stein. They'd have had fantastic value out of him; it would be time to get some out of them. Matt felt very bullish suddenly. Taking on the world.

And it was a good evening for his promotion to have happened. Charles had arranged some kind of reunion with Happy and Nobby Clark as well. He could tell them all about it, really hold up his head as a successful man of the world.

Matt had suggested they met at the Salisbury in St Martin's Lane at seven.

'Great,' said Charles, 'and then we might go out for a Chinese after that if we're hungry.'

The Chinese was a new phenomenon in London, everyone was tucking into spring rolls and sweet and sour pork.

The Salisbury was filling up fast; Matt was the last to arrive, the others were sitting at a table in the corner. Charles waved him over.

'Got a beer for you.'

'Thanks, Chas.' He sat down, raised his glass. 'Cheers!'

'Cheers,' said Happy, 'bit of a funny place this, isn't it, dead fancy, all this brass and mirrors and stuff. It's a great meeting place for queers, someone told me.'

'Really?' said Charles. 'Well – we can move if it's not OK.'

Matt looked around him with interest. He supposed there were a lot of men on their own in there. They looked pretty normal to him.

'Here's to us then,' he said, picking up his beer, 'good memories and all that. Thanks for organising it, Chas.'

'Yes, thanks Chas,' said Happy.

He looked just as Matt remembered him, with his seemingly permanent smile, but Nobby was quiet, staring gloomily round the bar and then saying 'sorry' when he saw any of them looking at him.

'What's up then, mate?' said Matt, wincing as a potato crisp touched his tender tooth.

'He's a condemned man,' said Happy, 'got to get married and all. Couple of weeks, isn't it, Nobby?'

Nobby nodded and sighed heavily.

'Go on. You never are. What on earth for?' asked Matt.

'He got a girl in the club, didn't he?' said Happy. 'Silly bastard.'

'Crikey,' said Matt, 'you poor bugger.' He contemplated the dreadfulness of this: married and a father at twenty-two. Life ended before it had properly begun. 'God, bad luck, mate.'

'Yeah, well.' Nobby tried to smile. 'Happens sometimes, don't it?'

'Where you going to live, then?'

'With me mother-in-law,' said Nobby.

'Jesus,' said Charles, 'that does sound bad. Or maybe she's nice?'

'She's a filthy old cow,' said Nobby, 'and when Janice is with her mum, she turns just like her. Gets all mean and bad-tempered. And the fuss! You wouldn't believe it. Oh, I feel sick. Oh, Mum, make me another cup of tea. Oh, Terence, rub my back—'

'Who's Terence?' asked Matt.

'Me, you stupid bugger. Only got called Nobby in the army. Honestly, wish I'd bought it out in Cyprus now. Be better'n this.'

'Well, look on the bright side,' said Charles slightly desperately, 'it'll be jolly nice to have a kid, won't it? To play football with and – and that sort of thing.'

56

'Yeah, s'pose so. Might be a girl though. Then what'd I do?'

There was a silence; Charles suggested another round.

Nobby looked at his watch.

'I'd best go,' he said, 'Janice said I had to be home by nine, she said she didn't know what she was doing letting me out at all when she was feeling so rough. Nice to see you all. Thanks for organising it, Chas.'

He shambled out across the bar; the others looked at one another.

'Poor bugger,' said Charles, 'what rotten luck.' There was a silence; Charles said he'd get another round.

An hour later the party broke up. Nobby's ill-fortune had depressed them all. Matt hadn't liked to talk about his promotion; it seemed tactless. Happy walked away from them both towards Trafalgar Square; Charles asked Matt if he'd like a bite to eat.

'Not sure,' said Matt. 'Got a bit of toothache.'

'Oh, come on. Take an aspirin. I've got some – here you are. Chinese'd be nice and mushy, won't do it any harm.'

They wandered towards Gerrard Street and went into one of the less flashy-looking places.

'I got some good news today anyway,' Matt said, unable to keep it to himself any longer. 'Got promoted. Can't quite believe it myself. '

'That's fantastic, Matt. Well done. I knew you'd do well in life, knew right from the beginning. This calls for another beer. Congratulations.'

'Thanks,' said Matt.

They chatted easily for a while; Matt was surprised how easily. Chas was pretty all right, he reckoned. He'd never been able to talk to any of the other toffs he met, in the course of his work. They were so bloody patronising. But Chas was different: he could even listen to him talking about his work on the Stock Exchange without wanting to throw up. Although now he was talking about his parents' house in the country, which was clearly vast, but which was what he called 'going to rack and ruin'.

'They just can't afford to keep it going, not really. They're really hard up, worried to death, poor old things.'

Really hard up, Matt thought, living in a house with ten bedrooms.

'So Eliza and I are trying to help a bit. They can't sell it, thank God, losing it would be too awful, it's owned by a family trust. It's been in the family for generations. I say, Matt, you OK?'

'Not too good,' said Matt, wincing, 'bit on me bad tooth. Bloody agony it is.'

'When are you seeing your dentist?'

'Dunno. Haven't got one, not really.'

'You haven't got—' Charles's voice tailed off. 'Look, you must make an appointment right away. Your face is quite swollen, you could have an abscess. We go to a chap in Kensington, he's awfully good. I'll give you his number. Mummy and Pa pay I believe, but Eliza and I see him on the National Health. Say you're in pain and you'll get in tomorrow. Damn, now I can't find his number. Stay there and I'll go and ring Eliza, she'll know. There's a phone box right outside. Don't drink my beer, there's a good chap.'

It was Charles who was the good chap, Matt thought – even if he did call his mother Mummy. At twenty-five; it was pretty weird really.

Charles came back smiling.

'Here's the number. Frobisher 7592. Mr Cole. Now, you must go, Matt, no chickening out. Promise.'

'I promise,' said Matt. 'Er – how is your sister, by the way?'

He had never forgotten Eliza that day on Waterloo station; he could still see her there, in her black trousers, and black-and-white coat, her dark blue eyes smiling at him, had never forgotten how the ground had seemed to heave slightly underneath his feet as he looked at her.

'She's absolutely fine, thanks. She's got a fantastic job actually. In the Public Relations department for Woolfe's, you know—'

'Oh yeah,' said Matt again. He wondered what on earth Woolfe's might be. Insurance office? Bank? Law firm?

'Yes, she's doing brilliantly. Always hobnobbing with journalists, buying them lunches. Seems to be a lot of fun.'

'She's not married then?' said Matt. It seemed important to know.

'Good lord, no. Not yet. She's always going out with someone or other, spends her evenings in various discotheques and so on, you know, but no one at all serious. Mummy's getting quite anxious, keeps saying she really ought to be settled, but she's in love with her job. And she just says no man could possibly compete with that.'

'Really?' said Matt. Eliza must have met some very dull men, if that was her view.

'Yes. Anyway, you can see her for yourself. She's at her flat, and she said we could go round, she's at a loose end, only girl not out with a beau.'

'Oh,' said Matt. His toothache suddenly seemed inconsequential. 'But she won't want to see me, surely.'

'She remembered you. Said she'd love it, that we'd be doing her a favour. And that she could pretend you were her boyfriend if any of the others got back.'

'Yeah, right. I bet I'm exactly like one of her boyfriends.'

'Don't be so touchy, Matt. I've told you before. All that stuff is over. Eliza was telling me the other day lots of the people in the fashion world are really – really . . .'

His voice tailed off. Matt looked at him.

'Really working-class? Is that what you mean?' He grinned at Charles. 'It's OK, I know my place.'

'Matt, for God's sake, you don't have a place.'

'OK,' said Matt easily, 'if that's what you think.'

'I do. Anyway, I'm only telling you what Eliza says. There's this fantastic new photographer called David Bailey, and another called Terry something, beginning with D . . . Dudley? No, Donovan, yes that's the one. Both from the East End, left school at fifteen or whatever. Everyone thinks they're wonderful. Come on, Matt, knock that chip off your shoulder and come and see Eliza with me.'

Eliza opened the door to them wearing a pair of calf-length jeans and a very large white man's shirt. Her feet were bare, her dark hair tumbled on her shoulders. And as she leaned forward to kiss Charles and then, slightly tentatively, Matt, laughing as she did so, there was a wave of some infinitely delicious warm scent. She looked perfectly beautiful and Matt, finding himself suddenly invaded by a violence of feeling that came somewhere between pleasure and distinct physical weakness, wondered rather feebly if this was like falling in love.

They were still talking at midnight as the other girls and their braying boyfriends came and went; Eliza chatting and laughing and telling funny stories of a world of which Matt had absolutely no knowledge but which sounded like some enchanted kingdom, peopled with fashion designers and photographers and models and journalists and beautiful clothes and star-studded parties; Charles begging for introductions to 'just one of the models', smiling as he teased her about her ambitions and her career.

Matt listened, hardly speaking, but committing everything that he could to memory: Eliza's voice, her smile, her lovely hands which she waved about as she talked, the way she sat with one long leg curled under her, the way she turned her head to listen intently to people, the way she laughed, teased Charles, managed to appear interested in what few things Matt was able to say. His toothache was forgotten, his last bus missed, none of it of any importance whatsoever. He just stayed and stayed and would have been still there in the morning, had not Charles told him they really should leave, that Eliza needed her beauty sleep and so did he for that matter; and then finally and with infinite reluctance Matt said goodbye to her and was kissed again and told how lovely it had been for Eliza to see him after all this time, and then walked all the way home from Kensington to Clapham, the tube being closed: almost two hours it took and he was happy to do so, for he could live and relive the evening without interruption, replaying every moment.

And thinking that if Eliza really felt no man could compete with her job she must be seeing the wrong sort of men. He could set up in competition with her job, no problem, he was sure of that. If he ever got the chance, which was pretty bloody unlikely.

In fact, much more likely, he would never see her again.

Chapter 7

'Charles? It's me. Look – friend of mine makes the most fabulous jumpers and things; she's looking for a studio/workshop. Would that be the sort of thing your nice friend Matt might be able to help with, do you think?'

'Possibly. Probably. I'll give you his number. Oh, and Juliet wondered if we could go out for a meal together next week. She says she wants to get to know you better.'

'Oh – course. Sounds wonderful. Only thing is, I'm quite busy next week.'

'Well, the one after then. Why don't I get her to ring you?'

'Lovely idea. Yes. I'll look forward to it. Now – Matt's number?'

As she waited, she contemplated Juliet and an evening with her and Charles.

Juliet Judd – her name alone made Eliza want to giggle, it was like a girl in a cartoon – was his new girlfriend, and he appeared oddly besotted by her.

She worked as a secretary for the lawyers who worked for Charles's stockbroking firm and she was a hugely irritating, simpering creature, so much the sort of girl Eliza disapproved of that she found it hard even to be polite to her. She was acutely and self-consciously feminine, a blue-eyed blonde, but her hair was over-styled and, at a time when most girls were wearing simple, ever-shorter shift dresses, or Mary Quant's pinafores over black sweaters or even the latest craze of jeans tucked into knee-high boots, she favoured girly blouses and flared skirts, or neat little suits, and always had matching bags and shoes and gloves. She had left Roedean with two O-levels and gone to finishing school in Paris where she had learnt to cook and sew and do flowers and was always saying things like 'I don't think men like girls to be too clever'.

Eliza was sure it wouldn't last; it was the novelty, she kept telling herself.

'Matt! This one's for you. Nice little building out Paddington way, near the station. Five hundred square feet, three floors, see what you can do with it. Landlord's in a hurry, burnt his fingers a bit with his financing, OK?'

'Fine,' said Matt. He still hadn't got over the excitement of having his own clients, of sorting out a deal. He enjoyed all of it, talking to the landlord, getting out the files, checking potential tenants, fixing appointments, showing them round; it was all dizzy stuff. The day both sides were due to sign, he would wake up feeling as if it was his birthday. He once asked Paul Dickens if he felt the same; Paul was very amused.

'Course not, you silly bugger. It's a job, innit? I'd be just as happy working in the motor trade to be honest with you. Bigger commission too.'

Matt was shocked. How anyone could compare the dizzy matchmaking of landlord and tenant with selling a car was beyond him. Money just wasn't the point. The point was involvement, was feeling part of this mighty fusion of money and bricks and mortar and commercial expertise at a time when the entire city was being reborn.

He phoned the landlord: a sharp young man, no older than Matt himself, called Colin White. They met at the building, which had been a warehouse and had had only the most minimal work done – new windows, whitewash on the walls, reconcreted floors – and White professed great nonchalance over the deal.

'I want the right tenant, and I don't want no hassle, people moving out again in a year. I want it settled, so I don't have to think about it any more, OK?'

Matt said OK but he thought the rent was too high.

'It's a good space but it's the location, I just don't see it as offices, more manufacturing, storage, that sort of thing.'

'Well I don't,' said White coolly. 'I spent a lot of money on this place, Shaw, I want a proper return, I was told you was a good salesman, I think I might be disappointed. I'll give you a couple of weeks, then I might have to take it somewhere else.'

'You won't have to do that,' said Matt firmly. 'I'll find you someone for it well inside a fortnight.'

'Good,' said White, 'and don't bother me till you're sure. I'm a busy man, I don't want a lot of poxy phone calls about this, that and the other.'

Matt went back to the office and trawled through his files. It wasn't going to be easy. The building was in a noisy dirty street, very near the route of the new Westway, the M40 extension leading into Central London. It might make a light factory but it certainly didn't seem suitable for the offices Colin White was so determined on.

Two days later he was three quarters of the way through his list of prospects, feeling increasingly panicky; nobody wanted it. Then Janice, the telephonist, put a call through.

'Potential client, Matt. Sounds really sweet.'

Janice would have described the Kray twins as sweet had they telephoned Barlow and Stein; Matt picked up the phone warily. A female voice said she had heard he might be able to help her.

'My name's Maddy Brown. I'm looking for some premises for my business.'

'What type of business would that be?'

'Well, fashion. I design clothes.'

'Oh yes. And where are you working at the moment?'

'In my parents' house.'

'I see.'

That wasn't going to pay Colin White's rent. He'd heard about these girls, straight out of art school, looking to cash in on what the papers called the youth boom. Probably hadn't got a single customer. As politely as he could, he suggested she took a flat with a spare room, 'Or carry on working at your parents' place. Just till you get going a bit.'

'Well,' she said, 'that's a very interesting idea. Thank you for absolutely nothing.' She put the phone down.

Spoilt brat, Matt thought. He returned to his Rolodex. The phone rang again.

'Matt? It's another young lady. What you been up to?'

'Nothing. Unfortunately. Put her through.'

'Is that Matt Shaw?' said a voice. A voice he recognised at once; a voice that tipped his world on end, stopped it in its tracks, a voice he could have listened to for ever.

'It's Eliza Fullerton-Clark here. I'm ringing about Maddy Brown. Who I work with, incidentally.'

Shit, Matt thought. SHIT! He felt rather sick.

'I had thought, you know, that I could do two good turns here. Silly idea, it seems. Maddy said you were worse than useless, absolutely no help at all and offensive into the bargain.'

'I was not offensive,' said Matt, stung. He'd been perfectly polite he knew, had actually made a suggestion that would save the wretched woman money.

'Well, I'm afraid you were. By making the assumption that she was some silly girl, with not an idea or a business contact in her head. Just because she was a woman.'

This was so true Matt couldn't even begin to deny it.

'Suppose Miss Brown had been Mr Brown? You'd have assumed backing, clients, customers, wouldn't you? You'd have taken all kinds of details from him, what kind of premises he wanted, where, how many thousand feet was he looking for, what kind of rent was he prepared to pay—'

'Well—'

'I don't somehow think you'd have told Mr Brown to use a room in his flat for a while, until he got going.' Matt felt extremely sick. So much for impressing Eliza. He'd really blown it.

'I – that is—'

'Well, just so you know, let me tell you about the client you could have had. Miss – not Mr – Brown has just got a very big contract from a chain of boutiques. Do you know what a boutique is? A shop, selling fashion to young people. They are absolutely the latest thing at the moment, big, big business. And the people who own them are desperate for young designers to supply them with what they need. And Miss Brown, who I might say left the Royal College of Art with a graduation show that made a lot of the papers, has just got a contract from Girlz – that's the name of the chain of boutiques, Girlz spelt with a Z, remember that, you'll hear a lot about them – and backing to the tune of over fifty thousand pounds. More money than you'd ever make in your entire life, I'd say. Pity, you really blew it. Bye then. We've got other agents to call, fortunately.'

Matt put the phone down and felt so angry with himself that he punched his desk so hard the knuckles hurt for days.

He couldn't bear to be in the office, staring at the wall and his own stupidity. He told Mr Stein he was going to meet a prospective client and went for a walk: across Oxford Street, down Regent Street, and along Piccadilly, towards St James's Park. It was a glorious day, and the city looked young; girls in brilliantly coloured shift dresses strode along, their long, loose hair swinging, men in sharp suits and sharper haircuts bumped into one another, grinning as they turned to stare at the girls. Everyone seemed happy.

But even the long legs and the swinging hair failed to distract him. He dimly heard a newsboy shouting 'Profumo case latest' and bought an *Evening Standard* and sank down onto the grass staring at it; photographs of the Minister for War, John Profumo, and Christine Keeler, the call girl he had been sleeping with (and sharing, it appeared, with a Russian naval attaché), covered the front page, along with speculation on a government possibly brought down, a fine political career undoubtedly ruined. The scandal had intrigued Matt hugely; he completely failed to understand how people could risk losing all they had achieved in life for a bit of sexual pleasure. Sex was great; but it wasn't power, it didn't show you'd made it. He was unable to imagine any woman, however beautiful or sexually gifted, could be as important as worldly success.

He sat, smoking rather feverishly, wondering if there was anything, anything at all that he could do that would redeem him in the eyes of Eliza Fullerton-Clark; and he decided next morning he would have to apologise. Really crawl. She might not accept it, of course, but it was worth a try. And then he had another idea.

He went into the office early, dialled Woolfe's number, and asked for the PR department.

'Hello. Eliza Clark speaking.'

So didn't use the Fullerton bit at work; Matt wondered why. He took a very deep breath.

'Miss Clark, good morning. This is Matt Shaw.'

She'd probably put the phone down now.

'Yes?' she said coldly. Very coldly.

'I wanted to apologise. To you and Miss Brown. For yesterday. It was stupid and insensitive of me, and I feel really embarrassed about it. And – and – the thing is I think I might have the perfect space for Miss Brown. As a matter of fact.'

Silence.

'It's in Paddington. It used to be a warehouse. The owner's done a bit of work on it and it's three floors, about three thousand feet, perfect for storing clothes and – and that sort of thing. And room for an office space and – and a studio if that was required. It's not too expensive and I'd really like to show it to Miss Brown if you think she'd agree. And if she hasn't got anywhere else yet.'

Another long silence; then, 'Well I can certainly ask her,' said Eliza finally, her voice just slightly less cool, 'and I don't think she has got anywhere else, no. I'll see if I can get her to call you.'

'Right. And – and if you'd like to come along yourself,' he said, 'see what you think about it, that would be fine.'

She wouldn't. Of course she wouldn't.

But, 'Yes,' she said, 'I think I might. If I have time. I'm extremely busy.'

'Yes, of course.'

'And Matt, thank you for phoning and for apologising.' Her voice was more itself now, warmer, smiley even. 'It was nice of you. We'll be in touch.'

Perfect happiness doesn't come often in life. It came to Matt then.

He arrived at the building an hour before the appointed time, walking round and round it, checking every door and window, even every electrical fitting, anything in fact that might prompt a query. He was determined not to be caught out in any particular.

He watched from an upstairs window as they arrived in Eliza's Fiat. Eliza was wearing a short red shift, long black boots and sunglasses; she looked amazing. Maddy was very pretty too, but looked terribly young: tiny, with long blond hair falling down her back; it was hard to believe she'd got this important contract Eliza had been shouting at him about.

Maddy loved the building, said it was absolutely fab; Eliza had been more practical and indeed critical, had stalked about, peering into corners, out of windows, up into the roof space. She said it needed a lot of money to convert it and that Maddy didn't actually need three floors; what about subletting.

Matt said he didn't think that was possible.

'Could you maybe convert one floor into a flat?' said Maddy.

Matt said it wasn't designated for residential use. 'It would make it far more expensive, you see, entail a completely different rate and rent structure.'

'Well, I think it really is too big,' said Eliza, 'and too expensive. You'd be crazy, Maddy, far too much of an overhead for the business.'

'But—'

'Excuse us,' said Eliza, indicating to Maddy to follow her to the other side of the room; Matt put his hands in his pockets and studied first the ceiling, and then the fit of the windows, even the floorboards, hoping he didn't look as desperate as he felt. They came back.

'Suppose we found you a tenant for the third floor?' said Eliza. 'A photographer we know, Jerome Blake, is looking for a studio. That would solve all our problems.'

'That would be fine,' said Matt, 'as long as he negotiated through us, of course. I'm sure the landlord would be very grateful for an introduction.'

'I should think he would,' said Eliza, 'I would expect a reduction of your fee, as a matter of fact.'

'Well I – that is—'

She grinned at him suddenly.

'I wasn't serious. Maddy'll ring you when she's made a decision. And as you can tell, she does quite like the place.'

'With good reason. It is a remarkable opportunity.'

'For whom exactly?' said Eliza. Then she grinned at him again.

'Well, I'll look forward to hearing from you,' said Matt, hanging onto his professional dignity with an effort.

Jerome Blake (real name Jim Biggs), the photographer, had been very keen to take the top floor as a studio; Matt liked him and he seemed reassuringly red-blooded, not a woofter as Matt had feared. Colin White agreed to a slight reduction in Maddy's rent, and a deal was struck. Mr Stein was particularly pleased with what he called Matt's performance.

'Well done, Matt,' he said, 'that's what I call good business practice. Spotting an opportunity, using your contacts, that's what it's all about.'

Matt had no intention of telling him the contacts were actually both Eliza's.

The whole incident had rather changed his opinion of Eliza. She was gorgeous and she was sexy, but she was very bossy. Not used to being crossed, obviously, or even argued with. It would probably do her good: just as long as it wasn't him that had to do it.

Chapter 8

'My dear, I was just wondering if you would be able to take tea with me one day either this week or next? I am staying at the Connaught hotel with my son, David. He is here on business, while I am taking in some fun!

Leave a message at the hotel and let me know. Any day will do, except next Thursday.

Yrs affectionately,

Lily Berenson.'

Scarlett had never believed in love at first sight; she had frequently declared it, indeed, to be a load of old toot.

'You can fancy someone, obviously,' she would say, 'think they're good-looking and sexy and so on. But that can't be love, it really can't. You'd have to know someone to love them. Otherwise it isn't love.'

And she was thus totally unprepared for it, when it came to her, when love walked towards her in the lounge of the Connaught hotel and stood before her, holding out its hand and smiling: love in the form of a tall, brown-haired man with his mother's green eyes. Beautifully dressed, love was, in a dark grey suit and a light blue shirt, with a deep, slightly drawling voice, and its handshake was firm and warm; and as it spoke her name and told her how delighted it was to be meeting her and that its mother had told it so much about her, she felt the ground shift a little beneath her, felt her knees, only a few moments ago perfectly strong, turn slightly weak, felt a strange, lurching sensation in her stomach and a slow, wondering disturbance in her heart.

She could not have told you what had been said or done over the next hour or so; clearly she had drunk her tea and picked at the smoked salmon and cucumber sandwiches and smiled politely at Mrs Berenson and listened to what she had to say and even responded, but all she was aware of was the presence facing her, sitting side by side with his mother, smiling at her, passing her sugar and plates and pastries, jumping up once when a bellboy came into the room with a sign reading 'Phone Call for Mr David Berenson' and disappearing to take the call.

During his absence, Mrs Berenson said that wasn't it lovely she could meet David – 'he is my firstborn, you know. Always so special to a mother' – and Scarlett was able to ascertain that David was married, to Gabrielle, 'a darling girl, a huge presence on the charity circuit', and that their youngest child was now ten, that David was in charge of the business, and that in so many ways she didn't know what she would do without him.

'He seems – very – very charming,' said Scarlett carefully.

'Oh, my dear, isn't he? Of course all the boys are, but I really think David would win the prize. Duncan is maybe a little better looking and I sometimes think Digby is the cleverest – but David – ah, there you are, darling. Who was that?'

'Oh, the guy I'm having dinner with tonight. Was going to have dinner with tonight.'

'Did he cancel, dear?'

'Postponed. Until tomorrow. So – looks like you and I have a date tonight, Mother. I'm relieved actually, I am a little disoriented. Jet-lagged, I believe you call it, Miss Shaw. It must be quite a problem for you.'

'Oh – no. I don't do the long-haul flights. I work for BEA. It's the BOAC girls who fly to your country and even Australia.'

'Would you prefer the long haul?'

'Well – yes and no. Of course it's much more glamorous, and the BOAC girls do see themselves as rather special – but I love my European flights, certainly for the moment. I go to so many different places, and especially in the summer, it's wonderful, all that sunshine.'

'And have you always been a stewardess?'

'Well, yes. Since I was eighteen. Before that I was a—' Suddenly hairdresser didn't sound quite glamorous enough. '– a beautician.'

'Oh really? How fascinating.' He made it sound as if she had said she was a professor or a sculptor. 'What made you change?'

'Oh, I thought it would – suit me better.'

'And she is a wonderful stewardess,' said Mrs Berenson.

'Yes, Mother told me, Miss Shaw, how you comforted her and made her feel so much more confident. In fact she hasn't stopped talking about you since. And now I can see why.'

69

He smiled at her, the green eyes probing hers. Scarlett felt dizzy again; and something else, a squirm of sexual excitement, reaching into her. Scarlett Shaw for God's sake, pull yourself together.

'You know I just had the nicest idea,' said Mrs Berenson. 'Would you be free to join us for dinner, my dear? It would be so nice to have your company, and you could tell us what shows we should see, and so on. Don't you think so, David?'

'I think it would be wonderful,' said David Berenson, 'but I'm sure Miss Shaw will have better things to do than have dinner with two old people like us.'

'Oh – no! I'd love it. I—' She stopped herself. Stay cool, Scarlett, don't look too keen. 'I'll have to make a phone call, that's all, I had a vague date with a girl friend.'

'Oh, you mustn't change anything on our account.'

'No, no, it was very vague. Really. Perhaps you could excuse me for a moment.'

'Yes, of course. There's a phone booth in the lobby.'

She returned from a visit to the ladies, smiling.

'That's fine. She hadn't even remembered. So I'd really like to have dinner with you both. Thank you. But I should go now, if you'll excuse me, I have a few things to do.'

Like – get her hair done, beg Andre Bernard in Dover Street, the salon she used for special occasions, to fit her in, press her black shift dress, maybe buy one of those long strings of pearls in Fenwicks, and some new black stockings while she was about it, ring Diana about what she thought was good at the theatre – so much to do.

'You sound very excited,' said Diana, her voice amused, 'what's going on, who are you having dinner with? And where?'

'Oh – just that nice American lady I met last autumn, remember I told you about her? She was very nervous and I sat with her through some turbulence. She sent me a Christmas card, care of the airline, and now she's in town and she invited me to tea—'

'Sounds lovely. Well, tell her *Luther* is amazing. Bit heavy, maybe, but Albert Finney is incredible. Oh, and on the lighter side, *Oliver*. Think they've got that over there now, actually. '

'I will. Thanks, Diana.'

'And where are you dining?'

'The Connaught.'

'Goodness. Well, enjoy it. The food's wonderful.'

Scarlett supposed the food was wonderful; she wouldn't have noticed if they had served up porridge with chips. She carefully didn't drink very much, although David Berenson, who had ordered three different wines for the three different courses, urged her constantly to 'drink up'. She devoted herself for the most part, they both did, to listening to Mrs Berenson talk and reminisce, answering any questions that were put directly to her, suggesting they saw *Luther* and also *Oliver* while carefully making it clear that she hadn't actually seen either herself – no point pretending – and through it all, every time she dared to meet David Berenson's eyes, feeling the same slightly whirling dizziness, the same sweet light-headed warmth.

And then, 'I might leave you young people,' said Mrs Berenson, as coffee was ordered, 'I'm a little tired.'

'Oh – and I must go,' said Scarlett, 'I have to be on the coach at seven in the morning.'

'The coach?'

'Yes, to go to the airport. I'm flying out to Milan first thing.'

'Don't go.' David Berenson's voice was suddenly rather intense. 'Stay for a coffee. It's only just after ten.'

'Oh – well, yes, that might be nice But then—'

'Of course. I won't detain you. It'd just be nice to – well, to chat a bit more. I'm feeling rather wide awake now. It's only – what – six or so in Charleston. Goodnight, Mother.' He stood up as she did, went round to her chair, helped her into her fur stole. 'I'll see you to the elevator. Don't turn into a pumpkin will you, Miss Shaw?'

'I won't. And please call me Scarlett.'

He was back in a few minutes, summoned the waiter. 'A brandy and soda. What about you, Scarlett?'

'Oh – no, thank you.'

'Very well. Now – why don't we take our coffee in the lounge?'

'Fine. Yes. Why not?'

Why did he make her feel so flustered? She just wasn't a flustered sort of person. Usually.

The lounge was half empty; he led her to a large sofa by the fireplace, with its back to the room, sat down beside her. Rather close, she couldn't help noticing.

'So,' he said, 'let's talk about you, now. Are you a very independent single girl? Or is there someone in your life? Do you have a boyfriend? I'm sure you do.'

'Well – several, you know, but no one special.'

'Ah. And your family – do you have brothers and sisters?'

She began to talk, decided to be completely honest, describing her childhood, told him about Matt, how proud of him she was, how well he was doing.

'It seems to me you're doing pretty well, too. Your parents must be very proud of you both.'

'Well – I think they are, quite.'

'It must be great,' he said suddenly, 'to have made your own way.'

'What do you mean?'

'Well – you know. It's all very well heading up some big concern, but it's been rather horribly easy for me. I just did what my father told me when he was alive, and now I just go on doing what he told me, more or less, even though he's dead.'

'I'm sure it's not that easy. And it's obviously a very large and successful company, real estate, isn't it?'

'Yes, that's right. How clever of you to know.'

Brian had checked this out for her, intrigued by her friendship with Mrs Berenson. 'Mr Berenson was a millionaire, darling, died of liver disease rather young, that means an alcoholic to you and me.'

'Well, it may be a large company, but I inherited the success along with everything else. I doubt if I would have made it on my own.'

'I'm sure you would,' said Scarlett.

'Now why do you say that? You don't know anything about me?'

'Well – no, but I can see you're very clever—'

'How can you see that?'

He had her there, it had been a ridiculous remark.

'All you can see is someone rather spoilt, someone clearly with a bit of money, running a company that frankly would run itself for quite a long time, given a following wind.'

'Well – it's obviously silly to argue with you,' said Scarlett.

'Very silly. Are you sure about that brandy?'

'OK – maybe just a small one.'

It was all so predictable after that, really, predictable and corny, the fact that he felt if not a failure in his business career very far from a success; and only a partial success as a person; and certainly a failure in his marriage.

'It is not a terribly happy one I'm afraid; we rub along OK, and we love the children and put on a good show for them, but Gaby very much leads her own life, and I think she cares more about her charities than she does for me. We're just biding our time for a while, until the kids are grown, and then we'll go our separate ways. It's very sad, but I guess that's the way of the world these days.'

And why did she believe that, Scarlett wondered, half-amused half-shocked at herself, and how many times had she heard it before? Because she wanted to believe it, she supposed; and because looking into those extraordinary green eyes, and the sadness in them, alternating with what she could see was an attraction, a drawing towards her, together with the leaping excitement in herself, was just too much to resist.

They sat there on the deep sofa, close, so dangerously close, talking for quite a while; he was a wonderful listener too, she discovered, was charmingly amused by her stories of her life as a stewardess, of her passengers, the nice ones like his mother, the tiresome ones, the awkward ones, the spoilt brats.

Time disappeared, into some odd, confusing place; one moment it was half past ten, the next almost midnight. Occasionally he would move, not exactly nearer, for that would scarcely have been possible, but so that the closeness would become somehow rearranged, deliciously different; at one stage he put his arm along the top of the sofa, and then it drifted down to rest on her shoulders. 'Is that OK?' he said and the acknow-ledgement of it, that there was a need to ask, her laughing affirmation that of course, yes, it was perfectly OK, took them further into an intimacy that was yet perfectly respectable, and not the crustiest, most disagreeable Connaught guest could have complained. And all the time, his eyes were on her, attentive, appreciative, sometimes smiling, sometimes thoughtful, and now and again so intense, so probing it was like a physical touch, an embrace indeed, and she had to look away lest she did something unseemly.

And then, 'David, I must go,' she said, 'it's long after midnight, and I'm flying tomorrow,' and he said, 'How sad, how very sad for me, but yes, of course you must go.'

And he picked up her hand and studied it, as if it contained some important message for him, and then raised it and very briefly brushed it with his lips.

'I will see you safely on your way,' he said. 'Come along, my lovely

Cinderella, let us seek out your pumpkin,' and stood up and pulled her to her feet, and then kept her hand in his and walked her to the front lobby.

'Coat?' he said, and 'Yes,' she said. 'Yes, I did have a coat, thank goodness you reminded me, I'd have forgotten it otherwise,' and he fetched her coat from the cloakroom and helped her into it, and very gently, almost imperceptibly, stroked her shoulders and the tops of her arms as he did so and then ushered her towards the swing doors and told the doorman to get a cab.

'It's been lovely,' he said, 'so lovely. You are an enchanting companion and you have given me an enchanted evening, and I am very, very grateful to you. And I would like to do it again, next time I come to London. Which is fairly frequently. Do you think you might be available for dinner?'

And Scarlett, so dizzy with excitement, so confused with desire, so lost in this new, strange, overwhelming emotion, said that yes, she might well be available for another dinner and gave him the telephone number of her flat and got into the cab, having been kissed on the cheek most properly, and sank back in her seat and closed her eyes and wondered how she could be so stupidly, so absurdly, so dangerously happy.

Eliza was eating a sandwich at her desk when Lindy called her into her office; she was leaving Woolfe's at the end of the year, she said, in order to marry a Swiss banker and move to Geneva. Eliza felt rather as if she had announced the earth was flat.

'But you can't! What about your career, what about—'

'I know, I know, Eliza,' said Lindy, reaching for a cigarette, 'but last time someone asked me to marry them, it was ten years ago and I turned him down because I cared so much about my career, it would have meant moving to Edinburgh, and – well, maybe I wasn't in love with him. Anyway, I can't risk another ten years. Jean-Louis wants a proper wife, he says, and I want to be a proper wife. Don't look at me like that, Eliza, I'm thirty-seven, getting a bit old to be having babies even, if I'm not careful. I don't want to end up like some of the women in our profession, lonely and bitter, with only a set of tatty press releases for company.'

Eliza was so shocked she was unable to do more than stammer out a few words of congratulation and then retreat to her own office, where she burst into tears. She wasn't quite sure why: except that Lindy had been her pattern in life, she had had it all, everything Eliza wanted, success, recognition, money, independence, and now she was giving it all up for a man. A man! And for being a stay-at-home wife. She sounded like Juliet.

Later, she went in and apologised and said she was really happy for Lindy and after all, she'd obviously achieved everything she possibly could, so it was time to move on; and Lindy had said she hadn't actually achieved everything, but she supposed it had been quite a lot.

'Now you're not to worry, Eliza, I'm sure whoever takes over will be delighted to have you working for them.'

Eliza hadn't worried until that moment; but then she began to.

She went back to her desk, worrying; worrying about her own future, worrying about what she could do. And grieving that she had lost her role model.

She'd always sworn she'd never put a man before her career. But if Lindy could . . .

Chapter 9

'Eliza? Jeremy Northcott.'

'Oh – hello, Jeremy. Yes. How are you?'

'I'm absolutely fine, thanks. Look – I wonder if you're doing anything on Friday?'

She ought to say she was; Friday was only three days away, and as well as that, it was Friday. When any self-respecting girl was booked up. Saying you weren't made you look like a bit of a disaster. So—

'No,' she said, 'no, I don't think so.'

'Excellent. Well, I know we never made that night of it at the Saddle Room but I thought we might make a visit to the Establishment instead. I've spoken to Charles and he says he and his girlfriend – Juliet, is she called?'

'Yes.' God. Not Juliet. Not at the Establishment. She'd be such an embarrassment, she'd—

'Right. Well, they're free. So – how about it?'

'It sounds wonderful,' said Eliza. 'Thank you very much, Jeremy, I'll really look forward to it.'

She put the phone down and realised her hand was shaking slightly. God. Jeremy Northcott. Rich, handsome, charming Jeremy Northcott. He'd asked her out. He'd actually – actually asked her out.

She was gazing out of the window, when Lindy came into her office.

'What did *The Times* say about those coats?'

'What coats?'

'Eliza! The grey flannel coats. I really need to know.'

'Oh – sorry, Lindy. Yes. I was just going to ring them. I'll – I'll do it now.'

'OK.' Lindy looked mildly irritated and went out, shutting the door a bit too sharply.

This won't do Eliza. This will not do. Pull yourself together. He's only a man.

Now what on earth could she wear on Friday?

76

'I've got some news,' said Matt.

'Oh, yes,' Scarlett smiled at him. They'd met – at his request – in one of the new Italian restaurants he liked so much. 'What's that, then?'

'I'm setting up in business on my own.'

'Really? Matt, that is exciting . . .'

'I know. I can't quite believe it myself. But me and a mate, Jim Simmonds he's called, known as Jimbo, he's a negotiator same as me, we just decided we could make a go of it. He's my age, well, year older maybe, been in the game the same length of time, he did his National Service in the navy, been with a firm a bit bigger than Barlows. You'd like him, you really would.'

'How'd you meet him?'

'Oh, we meet all the time, us negotiators, we go to the same pubs and restaurants, we all know what the others are up to, who our clients are, it's the name of the game. We've pooled resources, Jimbo and I, a lot. Anyway we was having a drink the other night and Jimbo said he reckoned we were doing too well for the old men, got to start doing well for ourselves. I wasn't sure at first, to be honest, but we worked out if we got just one client, then that plus what we might be able to persuade the bank to lend us could keep us going for a bit.'

'Sounds good so far.'

'Yeah. And then right out the blue one day, client of mine, Mike Robertson, took me out for a drink and told me I was wasting my talents working for Barlow and Stein, and if I ever thought of going it alone, he could put a bit of business my way.' Matt was very impressed by Mike Robertson. He had bought a dizzying number of broken-down shops and buildings as close to bomb sites as he could manage and then sat on them, pleased if they were let, but not bothered if they weren't. There was a roaring trade going on in bomb sites. National Car Parks bought them up to convert them – and could be forced to pay a great deal more for adjacent buildings than they were actually worth.

Robertson also put up a fair few buildings of his own, and it was for those that Matt was briefed to find him tenants.

'So that's about the size of it, Scarlett. He's backing us and simply because we can say he's a client we've managed to get an overdraft. Not much, mind, only a thousand, but it's enough to pay ourselves and a girl for a year, we reckon, and he's also letting us use a room in one of his developments dirt cheap. He says he likes to see young people given a chance, that he got lucky and so should we. So – all pretty good really.'

'It sounds incredible,' said Scarlett, 'really, really exciting.'

'Well, I'm glad you think so. Mum and Dad kept going on about risking everything and giving up a good job, all that rubbish.'

'It's just that they don't understand, Matt. Their generation, and their parents and their grandparents, they were stuck with whatever job they'd got and grateful for it. You've got to remember Grandpa Shaw was out of work for years in the Thirties, on the dole, it was hideous, a job was something you fought for, didn't just take for granted. Mum's always telling people how Mr Barlow's promoted you or given you a rise or whatever. It frightens them, seeing you throw that away. Anyway, I think it sounds fantastic. And I'm very, very proud of you. When are you open for business?'

'Well, almost straight away,' said Matt. 'Mr Barlow said he didn't want us pinching any more of his clients, and Jim's boss said the same.'

'But they were quite happy really?'

'Yeah. It's that sort of business, Scarlett, every man for himself and that's understood.'

'I see. And Jimbo, what's he like?'

'You'd like him. He's Jewish, an awful lot of people in the business are of course, very positive, bit pushy, I suppose you could say—'

'I like pushy people,' said Scarlett, 'they get things done.'

'Yeah, well, Jim certainly does. The thing you'd really notice about him is he's really, really tall, six foot four, makes me look like a real little runt, and very skinny. He's still living at home, like I am, fed up with not making any real money—'

'Girlfriend?'

'Not really. There's some girl his family want him to marry but he's just not interested. He's like me, married to the job at the moment . . . nice bracelet, Scarlett,' he said, suddenly reaching for her hand, pulling it towards him. 'Really pretty. All those charms. Where d'you get that then?'

'Oh – second-hand jeweller,' said Scarlett vaguely, 'you know how good I am at finding stuff like this.'

She was acquiring quite a bit of beautiful jewellery. David was very good at presents. The bracelet was her favourite – it had also been the first, and every time she saw him he gave her a new charm for it. The most recent had been a spinning disc that spelt out 'I love you'.

'Because I do,' he said.

'David!' she had said warningly, as he took the bracelet from her wrist with a promise to return it next day, having had the charm fitted. 'David, you mustn't say things like that.'

'But my darling, I do. We may only have met a few times, but I feel I have always known you. I did from the very beginning, the very first time.'

'Well, that's nonsense,' she said, hearing the rather feeble note in her own voice; for had she not experienced precisely the same sensation herself, the feeling that she had found whatever and whoever she was looking for, had tumbled most happily and shockingly into love.

And it was shocking: that she, Scarlett Shaw, most down-to-earth and hard-headed of creatures, should be so easily and swiftly stripped of her common sense, should find her feet removed from the ground and, perhaps most shocking of all, her sense of right and wrong knocked inside out and back to front. In what way was it possible that she could disregard the presence in his life of a wife of more than a dozen years and two much-loved children? And even as she had lain in his bed, tenderly and sweetly seduced, feeling the first tentative shoots of desire move inevitably into the disruption of brilliant, spreading, explosive orgasm, even as he entered her again and yet again, through a long, savagely inexhaustible night, as they fell finally asleep and then awoke to find one another stirring, smiling, reaching yet again, disturbed by a new unsatisfied need: right through that first long night, she was achingly aware of those three people, and indeed of a fourth, sleeping not so far along the corridor of the hotel, the matriarch of his family, who had brought them so innocently and so dangerously together, and she swore to herself that this was a brief, deranged yielding to temptation that would not be repeated, however strongly it might assert itself.

And how little she knew of herself, the strong-willed, self-controlled Scarlett who did what she and not others wanted; for the next time he came to London, only three weeks later, and this time without his mother, and sought her out with presents – a Tiffany necklace, a Dior scarf, as well as the bracelet from Garrard's, things she would never in a hundred years have dreamed of possessing – presents and honeyed words and his own desperate need of her, she resisted for very little more than a moment, and then gave in to him laughingly, joyously, helplessly.

They talked for many hours, that second visit – coinciding most happily with three days of leave – as much as they made love, indeed: of his need for her, his lack of happiness, his sense that at last he had found what he wanted in life.

He pleased her in many more ways than one. He was witty, which took the edge off his sentimentality; he was intuitive, and was able to disabuse her of any doubts and suspicions, almost before she was aware of them herself; he was generous, not just with gifts, which was easy for him, for he was, she discovered, extremely wealthy, but with himself, encouraging her to talk about herself, to lead her into new discoveries and interests, willing to do things she wanted even if he patently didn't. Thus, even that second weekend, he found himself walking in the rain, 'No, we will not go back to the car, this is what life in England is all about,' sitting in smoky country pubs, skating round and round Richmond Ice Rink, 'this was my biggest treat when I was a little girl, always on my birthday we came here,' laughing bravely and dutifully when he fell over.

He could not get enough of her past, of talk of her family, of the war years in London, even of her career as a hairdresser, and loved her stories of difficult passengers, of turbulent flights, of her sister stewardesses, 'I've never really known a working girl before.'

In short, being with him was complete and absolute pleasure; she felt cared for, amused, interested, satisfied in every way. She told him so.

'Every way?'

'Every way,' she said laughing.

'That is so lovely for me,' he said, his green eyes very serious suddenly, 'you have no idea, after years of being tolerated in bed, not even tolerated for the most part, rebuffed, I find myself considered desirable again – and an old man, like me, I cannot believe it.'

'Hardly old,' she said firmly, but of course it was true, he was forty-four, twenty years older than she was, and she could only disregard the fact because he was in superb shape, slim and muscly, with a sports-man's body, honed through three decades of tennis, golf and squash. And he dressed so well: that was something else. He wore beautiful linen and light wool suits, glorious shirts from Brooks Brothers in finest lawn and twill and Madras cotton, cashmere sweaters, handmade shoes or tasselled loafers – he just always looked wonderful.

She was intrigued by the fact that his family were clearly posh: he spoke of nannies, gardeners, of being away at school, of summer houses on the East Coast.

'I thought the whole point of being American was that everyone was the same, it was classless,' she said almost plaintively one day when he had tried to explain the concept of 'preppy' to her, and he had laughed.

'My darling Scarlett, the American is every bit as snobby as the Englishman, possibly more, always stressing how far back his family goes, denying anything remotely nouveau, fighting to get into the right schools and colleges, launching debutantes into society – it's all just the same. You have to be Old Money, with capital letters, or you might as well not have any at all.'

'Did you say debutantes!' exclaimed Scarlett. 'Surely not!'

'Oh yes. There are balls where it is de rigueur to be seen, where girls in white dresses are led in by their parents to find rich and suitable young men—'

'Your wife then,' said Scarlett, 'is she very – very old money?'

'I suppose so, yes,' said David, with a sigh. 'But please can we not talk about her?'

'All right. But you know I'm not, don't you? I've made my own way and I'm proud of it. And I know underneath I'm not really up there at all.'

'To me you are, my darling. Very, very high up there. Beautiful, amusing, chic, and sexy. What more could anyone possibly ask? Now how about we go upstairs and you take some of those – no, all of those – chic clothes off. And I show you how important you are to me.'

He was irresistible: absolutely irresistible. Even while she could see, and with hideous clarity, how stupid she was being, that was what she found him. And – what harm were they doing, after all? Making each other happy. Nothing worse than that.

The evening at the Establishment hadn't begun too well; Eliza, Charles and Juliet had arrived together to find a message from Jeremy.

'Mr Northcott says to tell you, he's very sorry,' said the girl on the reception desk, 'but he's been held up in a meeting. He's ordered a bottle of champagne for you, and there's a table reserved. He'll be about half an hour.'

'Wonderful,' said Charles, taking Juliet's hand, 'come along darling. Eliza?'

'Yes, coming.'

Forty minutes later, there was still no sign of Jeremy.

'I think it's rather extraordinary, I must say,' said Juliet. She often used this phrase, as if it conferred some kind of originality on what she was saying. 'Quite rude, really. I mean, why make an arrangement if you're not going to keep it. And it's very late for a work meeting, surely? Half past nine.'

'Not at all,' said Eliza briskly. 'I know exactly what those sort of advertising meetings are like. Complete nightmare. They end when the client wants them to.'

'Well, all I can say is, I'm glad I'm not in that business,' said Juliet.

As if she would be, Eliza thought. She looked at Charles, who was clearly mildly embarrassed, anxious himself at the turn the evening was taking. He couldn't stand upsets of any sort.

Various people Charles and Eliza knew came over to say hello; Juliet sat silent, sipping at her juice.

'Eliza, 'ow're you doin'?!'

'Rex! Hello, how lovely to see you.'

'You too, darlin'.'

Rex was a photographer she'd worked with once or twice. She had no idea what his surname was, he never used it. He was tall and skinny and always wore tight jeans, Chelsea boots, and some kind of variation of a dinner jacket over white shirts. He had a strong South London accent and told her he'd gone to a secondary modern and hadn't even passed his eleven plus which surprised her, since he was clearly very bright. When she asked him where he'd grown up he said 'sort of Surrey way'. And discouraged any further discussion on the subject. She supposed he was embarrassed about it – although she couldn't think why he should be, it was so old-fashioned, all that stuff, and he was very successful, he'd done work for *Queen* and *Vogue* and lots of advertising campaigns, and had a studio just off World's End. She'd thought he might be queer, until she'd turned up early for a session one afternoon and found him having sex with the model on a couch at the back of his studio, behind the great rolls of background paper. Eliza had been embarrassed; neither Rex nor the model had cared in the least.

'You on your own?' she said now. She was so relieved to have met someone she knew and someone so eminently suitable for the occasion, a brilliant example of the new classless, talented London she worked in, she could have kissed him. She did kiss him.

'Yeah, just for the minute. Waiting for some mates.'

'Come and have a drink.'

'Yeah, well, thanks.' He sat down, smiled rather coolly at Juliet; she was rather gratifyingly thrown by him, Eliza noticed, pleased. Anything that upset Juliet was all right by her.

'Haven't seen you for a bit,' she said to Rex. 'How's it all going?'

'Good, yeah. Done a session for *Vogue* last week.'

'Rex, that's great. I'm so pleased.'

'Me too. Ciggy?'

'Oh, yes, thank you.'

He pulled a pack of Gauloise out of his pocket, offered them round. Charles took one, Juliet shook her head rather over-emphatically. Silly cow, thought Eliza.

'I hear Lindy's leavin'. Shame. You gettin' the job, then?'

She laughed. 'God no, not me. Not nearly important enough.'

'You should. You got talent, girl.'

'Well – thank you, Rex.'

'Bin here before, have you?'

'No, never.'

'It's pretty good. Yeah. Very funny cabaret. You'll like it. Bit near the knuckle mind, but—'

'Eliza! Hello. So sorry I'm late. Charles, old chap, great to see you and you must be Juliet, I've heard such a lot about you.'

Juliet had revived suddenly from her silent disapproval of Rex and started blushing and fluttering her eyelashes.

'It's wonderful to meet you,' she said, 'and I've heard a lot about you too!'

'Not all bad I hope?'

'Oh, goodness no. All about what fun you had at school and in the army and what friends you and Charles are—'

'All quite true,' said Jeremy, smiling at her – God he really was charm on legs, Eliza thought. 'Now, let's get some more champagne shall we, and – God, Reggie,' he said to Rex, 'I didn't see you for a minute, how are you? And your brother – how's he? Charles, you must remember the Hon. Don, as we used to call him, he was Reggie's big brother.'

'I do remember Don, yes,' said Charles, 'but not Reggie here.'

'Well, he was just a little squirt and he looked pretty different of course, his hair was much lighter, and quite curly, but – well, it's really great to see you Reggie. How are you doing? He was my fag at Eton,' he added to Eliza.

'I'm fine,' said Rex, looking at Eliza slightly awkwardly, 'yeah. Good, really good. I'm doing photography.'

'Fantastic! You must come and see us at the agency.'

'Love to. Which one's that, then?'

'KPD.'

'That'd be great.'

His accent was changing already, admitting its true origins. Eliza looked at him.

'Secondary modern!' she said. 'Honestly, Rex.'

'Well, Eton is a secondary school,' said Rex.

'And we did sometimes call it Slough Secondary, it's true,' said Jeremy. 'It's great to see you, Reggie. Shall we get some more champagne? Ah, and here's Emma. Hi, Emma darling.'

Emma, thought Eliza, who for heaven's sake was Emma?

'Everybody, this is my sister Emma.'

Eliza felt dizzy with relief.

Emma, who was meeting some friends later, it turned out, was an editor at a publishing house, very tall and rather beautiful; and great fun. Just like her brother, Eliza thought. She sat down at their table.

'They used the spotlight yet?' she asked, taking a slurp out of Jeremy's champagne.

'The what?' said Juliet.

'Oh, they have a wonderful thing here, idea of Peter Cook's, he owns the place, you know, a spotlight they can turn on any table, usually during the cabaret, if they think anyone specially interesting's here.'

'How scary!' said Juliet. 'Not on me, I hope.'

'Pretty unlikely, I'd say,' said Rex.

'Rex!' said Eliza warningly. He winked at her.

'Sorry.'

He didn't seem too impressed by Juliet; it was another point in his favour.

They did have fun; even Juliet, bowled over by Jeremy's charm, giggled and fluttered her way through the next hour. Charles sat beaming at her, laughing at her feeble jokes, topping up her drink, occasionally leaning forward to kiss her on the cheek; he did seem to be a man in love, Eliza thought, fighting off her resistance to the notion.

The crowd was very what would once have been called Bohemian, very non-establishment, actually, Eliza thought, which was the whole point of the place of course, lots of arty-looking men, and rather serious-looking girls with heavy black eye make-up.

'There are the Ormsby-Gores,' said Emma. 'Look Jeremy, you know them, don't you?'

Two girls sat together at a table; they were both dressed in long lace dresses, and wore a mass of necklaces and rings and large, elaborate hats over their wild dark curly hair.

'Amazing clothes, aren't they?' said Emma. 'They always dress like that, genuine vintage. They're huge fun, ever met them, Eliza?'

Eliza shook her head.

'No, but I've heard about them, of course. They own "Granny Takes a Trip", don't they? You know, that shop at World's End.'

'It seems a bit of a funny idea to me,' said Juliet, 'wearing someone else's old clothes. Is it to save money or something?'

Emma gave her a cool, rather gracious smile.

'I wouldn't imagine so. They are both hugely rich.'

'Even odder,' said Juliet, 'don't you think so, Charles?'

Eliza watched Charles struggling between loyalty and embarrassment; loyalty won.

'Possibly,' he said finally.

The music was wonderful, Eliza thought, provided by the Dudley Moore trio; he was her favourite from the *Beyond the Fringe* quartet. 'He's so so sexy, and so sweet,' she said to Emma; Emma smiled.

'Totally,' she said, 'complete nympho, though. Or so they say. Wish I could speak from more experience but one lives in hope.'

Eliza smiled at her; she really liked her. She seemed very sophisticated. And not married, or even engaged; that was a big plus.

And then the cabaret began, dark and sharp and at times very crude; the Establishment being a club, there was no censorship of any of the material. That was what you came for, of course. Nothing was sacred, no word unspoken; even to Eliza, determined to be totally sophisticated and broad-minded, there was a shock element; even Jeremy, she noticed, occasionally didn't laugh.

After a while, she became aware that Charles was looking anxiously at Juliet. and that she was certainly not laughing, but frowning down into her lap. Silly girl. Well, it served her right. Eliza wasn't sure why it served her right, but she was enjoying her discomfort.

She didn't enjoy it for long, for Juliet suddenly stood up and made her way rather ostentatiously away from the table, towards the cloakrooms. Charles kept craning his neck looking for her, but she didn't return.

'Eliza! Would you mind just checking on Juliet, see if she's all right.'

'I would, yes,' she hissed back. 'I'm enjoying this, he's brilliant.'

'Please, I'm so worried.'

Reluctantly, she went, and found Juliet, flushed, standing alone in front of the mirror.

'Oh, Eliza, there you are. Isn't it awful, so disgusting, I'm simply hating it. I can't stay in there, but I don't want to seem rude.'

'No, of course not.'

'Maybe – maybe you could just tell Charles I'm feeling a bit dizzy or something. I – well, I could wait for him outside. I really would quite like to leave. It just makes me feel so uncomfortable. I'm just a bit old-fashioned, I suppose. Silly, I'm sure. Would you mind, Eliza?'

And so it was that by the time the cabaret had ended, Charles and Juliet had gone, Rex had joined his model, Emma's friends had arrived and she was chatting to them, and Jeremy had suggested a foray to the Saddle Room.

'If you don't mind it being just the two of us.'

Eliza said she didn't mind at all.

Chapter 10

'Engaged! But that's – well, it's – it's – wonderful. Of course. Yes. Goodness. Congratulations. When – how – that is?'

'Oh – only just happened. Last night. Just couldn't wait to tell you. You are pleased, aren't you?'

'Yes. Yes, of course I am. It's – like I said, wonderful.'

How could she be doing this? How could she be saying she was pleased, that it was wonderful, when she just wanted to burst into tears and scream and kick the furniture and then go out and get terribly terribly drunk, and then go round to see him, and beg him not to do it; or just quite simply ask him why, why her, when there had been so many other lovely girls he had seemed to like and who were so much more suitable, why mealy-mouthed, cliché-talking, old-fashioned, just not-up-to-his-standard, totally unsuitable Juliet . . .

'I'm so glad. I want you to be happy for me. And, well, I do know she's not quite your sort of girl, but I know she's right for me, and I know we'll have a terrific life together, she says she can't wait to give up work and just look after me . . .'

Nice dig at me there, thought Eliza. There'd be plenty more where that came from.

'And that's what I need. Getting on a bit now, after all, twenty-six next birthday, time I settled down.'

'Of course. Of course. It's – no, it's lovely, Charles. It really is. Um – have you told Mummy and Daddy?'

'Not yet. We thought we'd go down on Friday, tell them then. Could you come too?'

'Of course.' She quailed at the thought, at having to smile and look pleased and watch her parents being pleased, seeing Juliet being kissed and congratulated by them, fluttering her eyelashes at her father . . . but, 'Yes, of course I will.'

She could hear her own voice, dull and flat; he must realise, he must.

'Well that's fantastic. I think – well, I know Mummy will be pleased. She likes Juliet a lot, I know, she told me so. Now – one more thing.'

'Yes, Charles?'

'I told Juliet I was going to tell you, but no one else yet. Could you give her a ring, do you think? She's so fond of you, and so impressed by you, and she'll be longing to have a chat.'

'I will if I can, Charles. But I'm out of the office most of the day, nowhere near a phone . . .'

'Well, just ring her now quickly. She'll think it a bit odd if you don't.'

No she wouldn't, Eliza thought, she'd think it was exactly what she'd have expected of her. She couldn't resist arguing with Juliet, challenging her ridiculous statements, and she knew Juliet didn't like her either.

'Yes, all right, I will of course,' she said. 'I'd better go now though, Charles, I'm running late already, got so much to do before I leave the flat even.'

'You worry too much about that job of yours,' he said, 'there's more to life than work, Eliza, you know.'

That wasn't him speaking, she knew, it was Juliet; and this she wasn't going to stand for. She'd pretend she was pleased, she'd pretend to understand why he was doing this extraordinarily stupid thing, she'd even pretend she liked Juliet, if she had to and when the occasion required it. But she wasn't going to stand for being told a whole lot of rubbish about her life.

'Please don't talk to me like that, Charles,' she said, and her voice was even colder than she had intended, 'it's insulting. I know what my life is about, and it's my business, not yours, all right?'

'Sorry,' he said and he sounded so hurt she felt quite remorseful, to have spoilt his happiness on this of all mornings; she made herself a very strong cup of coffee and smoked one cigarette, lit another and then phoned Juliet to congratulate her.

Juliet simpered down the phone, said how sweet of her to ring, told her how terribly happy she was, how thrilled about everything, 'and of course I hope you'll be my bridesmaid.'

'Your bridesmaid!' said Eliza, struggling to make horror sound like surprised delight.

'Well, one of them,' said Juliet, her voice cooing down the phone. Was that a put-down or was she really totally insensitive? 'I'll have to have at least eight, seriously, I've got so many girl friends. Now I must go, Eliza, I've got to ring Mummy. Lovely of you to phone, thank you.'

It was a nightmare.

'Maybe she's in the club,' said Maddy Brown. She had come into Eliza's office with the clothes from her spring collection; later they were to present what they felt were the most suitable to Lindy for her consideration.

Eliza had come to regard Maddy as her best friend these days, feeling she had far more in common with her than the girls she had grown up with. Maddy cared about the same things as she did, shared all her attitudes; she too saw men as an obstacle rather than a help in her quest for fulfilment. They found the same things funny (and sad), liked (and disliked) the same people, regarded fashion as something of huge import-ance, rather than a frivolous game, and were both fiercely ambitious. Maddy had met Juliet and been horrified by her, 'she's like a sort of send up of herself', and had also rather liked Charles. In fact at one point, Eliza had harboured a little fantasy where Charles and Maddy might get together, and arranged a couple of evenings, but it hadn't worked. 'I mean, I do love being with him and everything, but there's no – no spark, you know? Can't really explain it.'

'She can't possibly be in the club,' said Eliza now, 'she doesn't believe in sex before marriage. She told me so.'

'Even so. She could have got carried away.'

'She could, but I certainly don't think she's preggers. She says she wants at least a year to plan the wedding.'

'Ah. Well – maybe she's after his money.'

'He hasn't got any. I keep telling you.'

'Yes, I know you do, but I've also seen your parents' house and to someone who grew up like I did, it does kind of spell M-O-N-E-Y.'

'Maddy, you've got to believe me. We don't have any money. The house is falling down. Anyway, that wouldn't explain him wanting to marry her.'

'I s'pose not. But girls can be pretty cunning, you know. And Charles seems fairly – innocent. And he's not very sure of himself, is he? He told me how he envied me, doing something I loved and was good at. He said he wasn't in the least good at his job, he'd only got it because someone your parents had known had put in a good word for him . . .'

'Yes, well, that is true. But – that applies to loads of people, doesn't it?'

'Not loads of people where I come from,' said Maddy, just slightly tartly.

'Don't start all that,' said Eliza, 'you know it makes me cross. Well, whatever the reason, it's awful. Oh, Maddy, I love him so much, and I'm going to lose him!'

Anyone would think she was interviewing them, Matt thought. It was a bit much really. She sat there, all big dark eyes and thick fake lashes, her brown hair cut in a Vidal Sassoon-style bob, crossing and uncrossing her long legs, totally cool and in command of the situation. Who did she think she was? He felt disconcerted and then irritated with himself. She could be exactly what they needed, he was just being pathetic. He just had to get the upper hand in the interview.

He cleared his throat, looked down at the piece of paper in his hand, to remind himself exactly who she was and what she had to offer. And to buy a little time, hoping against hope that Jimbo would appear.

'Right,' he said, appearing to study the paper closely; unnecessarily, since he knew every word of it by heart. But he wasn't an experienced interviewer, and it gave him something to do.

Louise Mullan.
Marital status: Single.
Born 1943. Education: Ealing County Grammar School for Girls.
O-levels: English, Maths, French, History, Geography, Biology.
Secretarial course, Ealing Technical College.
Typing 70 wpm, Shorthand 120 wpm, Book-keeping.
Previous Posts: since September 1962, secretary Baker & Hilliard solicitors.
Interests: Cinema, Theatre, Netball—

'Netball!' he said, seizing on a point of discussion. 'Isn't that more of a school game than an interest?'

'Not at all,' said Louise Mullan firmly. 'It certainly isn't. I play for the Ealing Ladies and also for a team that meets every Thursday in Lincoln's Inn Fields, legal secretaries. You can play netball to a very high level, Mr Shaw. National championships at Wembley. Do you play any games?' she added.

'No. Not really. Well, a bit of soccer. Yes.'

'For?'

'Oh – just a local team. Just messing about, really.'

'Yes, I see.' She was obviously very unimpressed.

He wasn't even sure that he liked her. Certainly not sure that he could work with her. She made him feel a bit of an idiot. But – she was rather perfect. Pretty. Clever. Well-spoken. Sexy. Very sexy, while being not in the least tarty. And, most important of all, seemed to know exactly what Simmonds and Shaw were about and what was required of her, over and above good shorthand and typing and what she had described in her letter as a good telephone manner.

'You're just starting out on your own, aren't you?' she said briskly. 'So – first impressions, really really important?'

'Really, really important.'

'In which case, you'll never want the office left empty, or the phone unanswered?'

'We won't, no.'

'So.' Pause. 'So say it's my lunch hour and neither of you are here, you won't want me going out to get a sandwich or meet a friend?'

'Well – probably not. No.'

'And sometimes' – another pause – 'you'll want me to work late?'

'Just possibly – sometimes, yes.'

'I'd say not possibly. I'd say definitely.'

'Well – OK, definitely.'

'It's not a lot of money, for all that, you know. Eight pounds a week.'

'Plus luncheon vouchers,' said Matt desperately.

'Which I won't be able to spend half the time. And I'll be taking on a lot of responsibility.'

God, she had a cheek. He had half a mind to tell her the position was actually filled. In fact—

The door burst open and Jimbo half ran in, parked his bowler hat on the hat stand, the only piece of furniture in what would be their reception area, apart from the chair on which Louise Mullan sat, and the tea chest on which Matt was perched, and started pulling off his raincoat.

'Evening,' he said, 'sorry I'm late. Client meeting overran a bit. I—'

And then, almost farcically slowly, he looked at Louise Mullan, absorbed Louise Mullan, and registered rather visibly his approval of Louise Mullan.

'You must be the secretary,' he said, holding out a bony hand.

'Well,' she said, smiling at him sweetly, 'I've come about the secretarial post, yes.'

'Ah. Yes. It's very nice to meet you. I'm Jim Simmonds. Matt – Mr Shaw's partner.'

'Yes, I guessed as much. I was just saying to Mr Shaw that you'd be asking a lot of me for the money.'

'Would we?'

'Miss Mullan has correctly pointed out,' said Matt rather wearily, 'that she would sometimes have to work late. And through the lunch hour.'

'But you'd be prepared to do that?'

'Well – if I took the job on, I would. Yes. I can't see the point otherwise. It's a very important position, it seems to me. Exciting though,' she said, with a re-cross of her black-stockinged legs and a dazzling smile at each of them in turn. 'To be in at the beginning of something. Who knows, you might turn out to be millionaires one day.'

'We – plan to be, yes,' said Jimbo. He smiled back at her. Matt felt irritated without being sure why.

'Anyway – about the money. If you were to offer me the job of course.'

Which she knew they would, Matt thought; she had them by the short and curlies really. Still—

'I'm afraid eight pounds is our top limit,' he said firmly.

'Plus luncheon vouchers, of course,' said Jimbo.

'Mr Shaw has already said that. And I have pointed out I won't be able to use them half the time. It's not a very high salary, you know. Legal secretaries get a lot more,' she added.

'Yes, but this is a really good opportunity for you,' said Matt, 'and the work will be extremely interesting, I can promise you that.'

'I can see that, but I've still got to eat. And pay for my season ticket, and so on. I really don't know—'

Inspiration came to Matt.

'Tell you what,' he said. 'Why don't we pay for your season ticket, how about that? It'll be a real benefit, like your luncheon vouchers, you won't have to pay tax on it.'

A silence. Then she stood up and said, holding out a very pretty hand to each of them in turn, 'Done.'

'Great. Well, I think we'll all work very well together. I can see you've got the makings of a negotiator yourself, Miss Mullan.'

'I hadn't thought of that,' she said, 'but I'll bear it in mind. Well, thank you. I can see it'll be fun. And I really will work very hard. And stay late from time to time if necessary, I meant it. Oh – except on Thursdays.'

'What happens on Thursdays?' asked Jimbo.

'Miss Mullan plays netball,' said Matt.

'Ah. OK. Fine,' said Jimbo, with a grin. 'So when Harry Hyams comes round, we'll have to make sure it's not Thursday.'

'I've heard of Harry Hyams, my boss was talking about him. Famous property tycoon. Is he really a client?'

'Not yet,' said Matt.

'We thought 24 June would be the best date for the wedding,' said Juliet. 'Midsummer Day.'

'Lovely!' said Sarah.

'And – we wondered if – that is, if you'd mind if we had it here?' Charles asked. Just slightly tentatively, Eliza thought.

'Here! How very very nice. Darlings, that would be wonderful. We'd be honoured, wouldn't we, Adrian?'

'What? Oh, yes, absolutely. Marvellous idea.'

'And that's all right with your parents, Juliet?'

'Gosh, yes. They're just thrilled at the idea. And really looking forward to meeting you.'

'And we them. We must ask them here for lunch. Summercourt is always at its best in the summer, all the roses, and we can patch it up a bit—'

'Mummy!' said Charles. 'It doesn't need patching up. Don't be silly. It's beautiful.'

Eliza was having lunch with Fiona Marks, a thin, nervy creature, who talked at such high speed that it was hard to understand her without one hundred per cent concentration. She was the fashion editor of *Charisma*, the new ultra-chic glossy that was a talking point everywhere that autumn. Very feature-led, it was completely different from most women's magazines, and one media commentator had already described it as a journey to another universe. In its first three issues, it had run interviews with Betty Friedan and Gloria Steinem, who talked, among other things, about her infamous stint as a bunny girl, as reported in *Show*, the magazine she had helped to found; there had been a very graphic account of the new 'natural' childbirth, complete with show-it-all photographs; and an article on the death of marriage in twentieth-century life. And its 'Twenty-Four Hours in . . .' slot, photographic essays on life in such disparate places as a casualty department, an East End housing estate and a luxury liner, both above and below stairs, was already being widely copied. It had also run an extremely frank quiz on how intrinsically sexy its readers were, and another on how they viewed drugs (with the clear expectation that they would almost certainly have experimented with at least one and probably more).

'Yes?' said Eliza nervously. Fiona's voice had had a rather businesslike tone.

'Look – I don't know if we can use those dresses, but certainly we'll do the Courrèges-style boots, they're wonderful. But I just wanted to ask you something. Look, how settled do you feel at Woolfe's? I mean, I know Lindy's leaving and you must be a bit worried about it—'

'Oh, no,' said Eliza, carefully airy. 'The person who's taking over from her is marvellous, might not be actually as young as Lindy, but my goodness, she thinks and sees young. I'm really looking forward to working with her.'

'In that case, forget what I was just going to say to you.'

'What?' Eliza stopped in mid-company-line. 'What were you going to say to me?'

'Well, I was going to say I'm looking for an assistant. Lucy is leaving to have a baby. So disappointing and stupid, she was doing really well. Anyway, loads of people are going to be applying, half London actually; but I'd like to know if you'd be interested.'

'Me!' said Eliza.

'Yes, you. Because I really think you've got a terrific eye and that's what I'm looking for above all else. And someone who isn't quite out of the normal fashion assistant mould. I want someone a bit different. *Charisma* being the sort of magazine it is. But if you're really happy where you are—'

'I'm not,' said Eliza and heard her own voice as an odd, high squeak. 'I'm really not. I'd love to apply for the job. Absolutely love it. Please. I mean thank you. Oh, gosh – golly.' She wasn't doing very well here at being stylish and cool. 'I mean, of course, of course I would.'

'OK. Great. It's quite – tough there, you know. They really are determined to do something quite different and the editor, Jack Beckham, isn't one of your fashionistas, he's a proper, old-fashioned journalist, come up through the ranks, got the job because he worked on the *Sunday Times Magazine* launch with Mark Boxer. He actually sees fashion as a necessary evil, to bring in the advertising, he'd prefer to stick to features about class and politics and sex, so every single idea we do has to be sold really hard. And they have to be proper ideas, not just the new hemline or whatever. But I fancy you could cope with all that. Having been in the real world, not the *Vogue/Queen/Tatler* school of fashion. Anyway, let me have your CV—'

'It's pretty unimpressive,' said Eliza, 'I've only ever been at Woolfe's—'

'But you've done so well there. We all love you and you can't say that for many PRs. But I still have to go through the motions of presenting you to the editor, so you do need to apply. And then he'll give you a really tough interview, I warn you. But—'

'Oh, God, it's so exciting,' said Eliza. 'Thank you so much, Fiona, I couldn't be more flattered or excited if you'd – well, I can't think of anything. Crikey. It's just amazing.'

She really must stop saying things like crikey; it made her sound as if she was back in the Sixth at Heathfield.

She got an interview two weeks later. She rather liked Jack Beckham, terrifying as he was; he reminded her of Matt Shaw. He was dark and heavily built, with quite a strong London accent that was clearly genuine – unlike Rex Ingham's – and he looked completely out of place in the rather rarefied air of *Charisma*'s offices. Not that they were too much like those of most of the magazines she knew, full of pretty posh girls in mini-skirts chatting up models and effete photographers. The atmosphere here was much more serious, with a couple of very intellectual-looking men – one the assistant editor – and the features department, which was next to Fashion and twice its size, was full of the sort of girls who had probably, Eliza thought, been to Oxford, clever-looking creatures with wild hair and arty clothes, with voices two octaves deeper than their twittering counter-parts. Their office, moreover, was full not of clothes rails and beauty products, but great piles of books and records and a couple of tape recorders, and the pictures on the walls were not of Jean Shrimpton and Patti Boyd, but Kenneth Tynan and Norman Mailer.

They stared at her rather coolly as she waited in the corridor outside Beckham's office; only one, a tall, aristocratically beautiful creature, smiled at her and said 'Hello'.

Beckham's office was full of smoke; he had a cigar smouldering in an ashtray on his desk and a cigarette in his mouth. He leaned back and studied her.

'So you're Fiona's great discovery. I hear you were a deb or some such rubbish.'

'I was,' said Eliza, 'but that wasn't my fault.'

'Well, I suppose not.' He smiled at her. He had liked that. 'What makes you think you can do this job for us?'

'I don't – yet. It was Fiona's idea. But I'd love to try. I think *Charisma* is amazing.'

'Oh yes? In what way amazing?'

'Well – fascinating. Different.'

'And what's the most amazing thing you've read in it?'

This was a test; she'd prepared for it.

'I think the piece about the down-and-outs. It was – well, it was great. So well written, and the photographs were—'

'Bollocks,' said Jack Beckham.

'I'm sorry?'

'I said bollocks. I bet you don't have the slightest interest in down-and-outs.'

'I—' This was perfectly true; she smiled at him reluctantly.

'Tell me the truth, what really grabbed you?'

'OK, the piece about the cloakroom attendants at all the big hotels.'

'That's more likely. Why?'

'Well because I – I—'

'Go on.'

'I must have met lots of them. And never realised what extraordinary lives they led. And the people they deal with on a daily basis.'

That was a pathetic answer; it made her sound like what she was, a spoilt, upper-class girl.

'Good. I like that. That's what we try to do in all our features. Turn accepted ideas on their heads. Think you can convert that into fashion?'

'I – I don't know. I mean – surely that's Fiona's job. She's the editor. I'd just be her assistant.'

'Yes, yes, but we don't want some crap yes-girl in that job. We want someone with balls. Understand what I mean?'

'Yes, of course I do.'

'I interviewed Bernard Woolfe once. For the *Sunday Times*. Bit full of his own importance, I thought.'

96

'Well, in his world, he is very important,' said Eliza staunchly. She wasn't going to be tricked into bad-mouthing her present boss.

'Tell me why you think so.'

'He's done something amazing with that store. Especially the department I work in. It's the first to have anything like that.'

'Well, maybe. Like him, do you? It'll be very different working for me, you know.'

'I can see that.'

'You can?'

'Yes.'

God, she shouldn't have said that. Now he was going to ask her in what way. But he didn't. He laughed instead.

'You have a certain honesty, Miss Clark. I like that. Now you're not going to get married and have a baby like that wretched Lucy creature, are you?'

'Absolutely not!' said Eliza.

'You sound horrified. I thought that was what girls like you were trained to do.'

'I'm not like girls like me,' said Eliza coolly.

'I shall remember that. Hold you to it, even. Well, we'll let you know. Lot of people want this job, you know.'

'I'll thank God, down on my knees every night, if I get it,' said Eliza to Fiona over a nerve-calming coffee.

'Eliza, if you do get the job you won't have time for praying. We run three different fashion features every issue, you know. And just the two of us. It's not enough.'

'Why won't he let you have any more staff?'

'Because he doesn't believe in fashion. Waste of money, paying girls like us. Now I must fly. I'll let you know the minute I hear.'

Eliza had to wait two weeks; Jack Beckham insisted on seeing every girl who had applied. But he told her he'd actually made his mind up when she first told him she wasn't like the other girls like her.

'Now don't let me down. And no marriage and no babies.'

'Of course not,' said Eliza.

Chapter 11

'Eliza? Jeremy here.'

'Oh – Jeremy, hello.'

'I wondered if you were free this Saturday?'

'Jeremy, I'm so sorry, I'm not. I'm going to go down to my parents for the weekend. With Charles and his – with Juliet.' She couldn't bear to say the word 'fiancée' in association with Juliet; she found the idea of their being married so awful.

'Never mind. Only a party. Plenty more ahead. Enjoy your weekend.'

'Thank you. And you.'

She put the phone down, looked at it thoughtfully. He did seem to be quite – keen.

They had been out together a few times now: he had taken her to Sybilla's, the newest of the new clubs, and to the opening of the wonderful new National Theatre, with Peter O'Toole playing Hamlet – everything he did seemed to be so glamorous. He'd even taken her to the Royal Variety Performance, and she'd seen the Beatles, for heaven's sake, God that had been amazing, they were so funny: 'Those in the cheaper seats clap,' John Lennon had instructed, 'the rest of you rattle your jewellery.'

He was a member of Annabel's in Berkeley Square, so new and smart and impossible to get into – Mark Birley, the owner, was a friend of his, he explained (who wasn't? Eliza wondered) and had given him complimentary membership. They danced for a long time, after everyone else had gone, and when he dropped her outside her flat – he had an incredible silver E-type Jaguar – after kissing her for a long, long time, she felt everything had shifted up a gear.

He was an absolutely perfect boyfriend. She really didn't know if she was actually falling in love with him or even if she was anywhere near being in love with him. She had no idea what that felt like. She'd always supposed she'd know when she did.

But she did like him a lot. And he was so absurdly, ridiculously nice: she hadn't discovered a flaw yet. So good-natured, so charming, so brilliant at saying the right thing and making her feel good. And clever; she could never have fancied anyone who wasn't really clever. And then he was so good-looking as well.

There hadn't been any suggestion of sex – yet. Just kissing, which he did really well. But then he was just such a gentleman, he'd never dream of pushing it, he probably just thought they didn't know each other well enough yet. Which maybe they didn't.

He had a very big job at KDP, he was a Group Account Director, a breed known at the agency as the Lords. 'And a few of them actually are,' Jeremy said, grinning at her. 'Lords, I mean.'

'Yes, I'd heard you'd got a few there. And that you recruit from – what was it, two universities, three schools and four regiments. Is that true?'

'More or less. Yes. It's a kind of neat copyline, isn't it?'

He took his work very seriously, it was one of the things she most liked about him, it wasn't just something he did, to pass the time, like a lot of rich blokes. 'I get a really huge buzz out of it, you know, getting the strategy for the ads right, working with the creative people, selling it to the clients. It's incredibly satisfying. It's like a battle. A lot of advertising terms are military, you know, it's rather intriguing: things like strategy, campaign, operations room, yup, it is a battle. One I want – no, need – to win.'

She liked that too.

He talked a lot about the advertising industry; Eliza became very intrigued by it, and thought she would have liked it herself if she hadn't been in fashion. He loved the intellectual challenge of it, explaining to her the concept of the USP. 'That stands for Unique Selling Proposition. It means it says something very desirable that only that product does, so consumers think they're only going to get whatever it is by buying it.'

'What, like "Persil Washes Whiter"?'

'Absolutely. They've now done research that shows the word associated with Persil is whiteness. It's a con of course, most washing powders make white clothes whiter. Then there's "Senior Service Satisfies", as if no other cigarette did, and—'

'And – I suppose "If you want to get ahead, get a hat"?' said Eliza.

'Exactly. Clever girl. What a lot that did for the hat industry. Well, you'd know about that. Likewise "Top People Take *The Times*". Who wouldn't want to be a top person? You can start, obviously, by buying *The Times*. I tell you, it's powerful stuff. I love it.'

He earned a great deal of money and he had a seemingly limitless expense account; his office was very grand and indeed like no office Eliza had ever seen. The agency was housed in a row of what had been three rather splendid buildings in Carlos Place, just off Grosvenor Square; the chairman was a legendary American advertising guru called Carl Webster – 'Well, Americans invented advertising,' Jeremy said when she expressed surprise.

Lunches, when clients would be entertained in the dining room on the top floor of the agency, with its huge oval table and view across to the square, would often run from midday until six, when a switch would be made to cocktails and plans for the evening.

They were unashamedly snobbish; even the secretaries at KPD were very well-bred. 'They all disappear and we have to get temps in for Ascot week, you know,' said Jeremy. 'And one of the typing tests includes spelling champagne correctly and Bollinger, of course. Then we know they're suitable.'

Only the creative people, recruited from the art schools, were from the other ranks, as Jeremy called them; boys from secondary moderns, quick, sharp, and irreverent, with totally original ideas on design and openly, if jokily, contemptuous of their social superiors.

The other thing that was absorbing Eliza, even more than her romance with Jeremy, was her new job. She absolutely adored it. As well as running around, as general dogsbody at sessions and in the office, Fiona consulted her endlessly and in the most flattering way about ideas, plans, sessions – and what on earth they could do when they went to the Paris collections. She was extremely neurotic, and indeed difficult, and simply keeping her on an even keel was a job in itself.

'Jack's agreed we've got to cover the collections, but he says he simply will not have any crap about fabrics, he wants a proper idea. I can't think of anything. Can you?'

Eliza said she'd try.

'Matt? Matt, this is Charles. Charles Clark. How are you?'

'I'm fine thanks, Charles. Yeah. Good to hear from you.'

'Yes, it's been too long.'

He was a funny bloke, was Charles, Matt thought, persisting in the idea that the two of them were actual friends; it was quite – quite nice, but he couldn't possibly really think it.

'Yeah, it has,' he said dutifully.

'What've you been up to then? Things going well?'

'Pretty well. Yeah, I'd say so.'

'When did you go on your own?'

'Oh – a few months ago. How'd you find that out?'

'Called your old firm. They told me. Congratulations, Matt. Jolly well done.'

'Yeah, well, we haven't made it yet. May end up in the gutter still.'

'I doubt it. I envy you. I'd love to be my own boss. Anyway, I wondered if you could help me, in a more direct way. I'm getting married. Next summer.'

'Yeah? Congratulations. Who's the lucky girl?'

'Oh – don't know that she's that lucky but I certainly am. Juliet, she's called. Juliet Judd. Anyway, obviously we need somewhere to live. A flat we thought, just to start with. Wondered if you could help.'

'Sorry, Charles. Wish we could. But we're a commercial set-up. We don't do residential. But – tell you what, I'll speak to a couple of mates on that side of things, and drop you a line. How's that?'

'Excellent. Thanks, Matt.'

'What areas, then?' As if he didn't know.

'Oh, you know – Chelsea, probably a bit too expensive, but worth a look, Kensington, Fulham even. That neck of the woods, anyway.'

'Sure. Leave it with me.'

'Fantastic. Well, I hope you'll come to my wedding.'

As if, thought Matt. He didn't mean it, obviously. He was just saying it.

'I'd love to have Happy and Nobby too, if I could find them. You're not in touch with either of them, I s'pose?'

'No,' said Matt. 'No, 'fraid not.'

'Shame. We were such a team, weren't we? God, I loved those days. Happiest of my life, in some ways. Well, cheerio, Matt. I'll look forward to getting those names. And let's have a drink one night.'

'Yeah,' said Matt, 'yeah, that'd be great.'

He put the phone down, stared at it, shaking his head. And then realised Louise was watching him and had been listening to the entire conversation.

'We should have a residential side, maybe,' she said. 'I've often thought about it.'

'Yeah, well, you can stop thinking about it,' said Matt, 'there's not the same money in it, and anyway, you need a clear profile in this business.'

'It could be a separate company. I could run it. And there's quite a lot of money in it, actually.'

'Louise,' said Matt, 'I said no. And you have your work cut out as it is, with what you do already.'

'I could have an assistant.'

'Give me strength. If anyone gets an assistant round here, it'll be me. Now, can you find me those files on the Elephant and Castle development I asked for half an hour ago . . . if you're not too busy, that is.'

'All right, all right,' said Louise. 'It just seems a pity to miss an opportunity, that's all. Still it's your decision, I suppose.'

She had a disconcerting way of getting the last word.

Sarah enjoyed the weekend; most of it anyway. It was wonderful to see Charles, she saw less and less of him these days: which was perfectly understandable of course, it was natural that he would want to spend time with Juliet.

But he had been so sweet over the two days; and he did seem very happy. And it had been lovely to see Eliza, of course; they had had the most marvellous walk together on the Saturday afternoon, Eliza chattering all the way. She was so excited about her new job, which did sound wonderful. And she had been out with Jeremy Northcott several times, it seemed.

'But don't look at me like that, Mummy, I do like him and he likes me, we get on together very well but that's all.'

Sarah tried not to think beyond that, but it was difficult.

They all had a very jolly supper on Saturday night, and played Scrabble afterwards; Charles explained to Juliet it was a family tradition.

'It's scrabble or the cinema and there's nothing on.'

Juliet protested that she was hopeless at Scrabble and Charles said he'd help her, which made her cross.

'I don't want you to help me; I'll feel like a child. I just don't seem to be able to see words somehow. I suppose I should read more, I'm so dim really—'

'Darling, you're not dim,' said Charles quickly, and indeed she wasn't,

Sarah thought, she was quite sharp, but she certainly had a very limited vocabulary. After about half an hour when she was doing really badly, she started to sulk and said she'd like to go to bed, she was terribly tired.

'I don't want to appear rude,' she said, 'but I've had a terribly busy week, and I've got a bit of a headache.'

Sarah said of course she didn't appear rude. 'Just have an early night, my dear Charles, what about some cocoa for Juliet—'

'Cocoa would be lovely. Charles, darling, would you mind?'

They started discussing the wedding plans next day, immediately after breakfast.

About the number of guests, how big the marquee should be, where Juliet might get her dress and the bridesmaids' dresses, what colour they should be, whether the caterers should be local, or from London, did Sarah think it would be all right for them to be married in the village church, even though she didn't live there, what her mother had thought of wearing, what would Sarah wear.

She made notes in a pink spiral-bound exercise book into which she had already stuck photographs torn out of magazines of wedding dresses, bouquets, even honeymoon locations.

It was all perfectly natural of course, Sarah thought, that she should be so excited, but she couldn't help feeling rather sorry for Charles, who was clearly dying to get outside and to spend some time alone with his father. Juliet wouldn't allow that, she said she wanted him very fully involved.

No doubt about who would be boss in that marriage . . .

After they had all gone, Adrian went upstairs for a rest – a misnomer for sleeping off an excess of wine at lunchtime, although he did seem to spend an inordinate amount of time resting these days. He was altogether a little subdued, and had even discussed giving up shooting next season. Well, that would be a financial relief at least . . .

Sarah went for a walk and then came back and sat in the kitchen, next to the Aga – it being the only really warm place in the house – and tried to concentrate on the *Sunday Times*. It was difficult; she really couldn't get worked up about the successors to the ailing Prime Minister Harold Macmillan. It seemed very unimportant.

She was delighted – of course – that Juliet and Charles wanted to have their wedding at Summercourt, but it did seem to fly in the face of the natural order of things. She quite liked Juliet – no, no, she liked her very much, she was sweet, and in many ways would be a very good daughter-in-law, but she just wasn't quite what she would have expected Charles to have chosen.

Sarah's dream had once been that Charles would marry an heiress, one who could bring some money into the family, but she had long given up on that idea. Why should a girl with a fortune marry a man who so patently had none. But she had hoped for – well, someone a bit better than Juliet. She was simply – oh, stop beating about the bush, Sarah thought, she was simply not quite their class. She was rather dreading meeting her parents; she could see they would have very little in common.

The phone rang.

'Mummy?'

'Yes, hello darling. Back already?'

'Yes, I had a terribly good run. Anyway, I just wondered if you were all right. I thought you looked a bit tired.'

'Well, I am a bit, of course. But happily so. I thought it all went very well, didn't you?'

'Yes, of course.'

'Well, I don't know, my babies seem to be getting settled. You next, I wonder?'

She knew as the words came out, it was the wrong thing to say.

Eliza was annoyed; she could tell. Worse than annoyed.

'No, Mummy, I am not going to be next, as you put it. I know you think I ought to have a ring on my finger by now, and be all wrapped up in a tulle parcel like Juliet, but I'm not.'

'Well, I'm sorry darling, and I know of course your job is very important to you and all that. But – don't make the mistake of thinking it's more important than marriage and babies. You're twenty-three next year, most of your friends are married and—'

'This is a ridiculous conversation,' said Eliza. 'I'm not my friends and I'm certainly not getting married just because they are. OK? Now I must go. I'll ring you in a few days. Thanks for a lovely weekend.'

'Bye, darling.'

Sarah put the phone down, trying not to feel too rebuffed. Eliza would come round, she told herself. And she was still very young.

Chapter 12

Like millions of other people, Eliza knew exactly what she had been doing when she heard that President Kennedy had been shot. She was in bed for the first time with Jeremy Northcott. For the rest of her life she was unable to think of one event – with its attendant shock and sense of unreality – without the other.

They were in her flat; he had left behind what he described as his favourite scarf – he must have hundreds, she thought – after a dinner party she had given the weekend before, and they were trying to decide what film to see that evening. They were both keen cinema buffs, they had discovered, and it was a toss-up between a rerun of *La Dolce Vita* at the Curzon, which she wanted to see, and *Lord of the Flies*, which he did.

They were spending more and more time together; they enjoyed the same things, they liked each other's friends, they amused, pleased and interested one another; it was all very suitable. And Eliza was very happy. Very happy indeed. She didn't think about what might happen in the future, she was just enjoying the present.

The weekend looked good. She and Jeremy were going to a party on Saturday, and meeting a load of friends at the Pheasantry in the King's Road for Sunday lunch; Charles and Juliet were going down to Summercourt, with the Judds; Sarah had wanted her to go, but she couldn't face it.

'Do you want a cup of coffee while we argue about the film?' she said now, and, 'Do you know, I wouldn't mind,' he said. 'Had one too many G and Ts at lunchtime. Mind if I put the radio on?'

He was a news junkie, always 'catching the news' as he put it. He bought three or four newspapers a day. Eliza smiled at him, then turned her attention to finding the coffee pot; as she did so, she heard a newsreader's voice, '. . . has been shot as he rode in his motorcade through the streets of Texas. It is not yet known how serious his condition is.'

'Who?' she said stupidly. 'Who are they talking about, who's been shot?' and, 'Shush,' said Jeremy, 'I'm trying to hear.'

She stood there, utterly motionless, holding the coffee pot; when she heard the words 'Mrs Kennedy is at the hospital' she sat down abruptly and listened, stunned with a shock that felt personal, as the ghastly story was told. And when finally Jeremy said, 'Dear God in heaven,' she went into his arms, surprised at her need for comfort.

They sat on the sofa in the drawing room, drinking the coffee and listening to the endless reports, repeating over and over again, 'John Fitzgerald Kennedy, the President of the United States, is dead,' first the English voices, shocked and stunned, then the American ones, even more so, reactions from the crowds, first in Texas and then in New York, disbelieving, grief-stricken. They turned on the television, saw the photographs that would become iconic, of the Kennedys arriving in Texas, both untouchably glamorous, both smiling, waving, she in her Chanel suit and pillbox hat, he with his thick hair lifted by the wind. 'It's almost unbearable,' Eliza said, 'look at them, they were safe then, just an hour or so before, oh I'm talking nonsense, sorry Jeremy.'

'No, no, it's not nonsense, I understand, I feel the same, it's like some awful nightmare that we should wake up from.'

The phone rang. It was her mother.

'Darling . . . darling, did you hear the news? Isn't it so awful, so sad, I can't believe it, he was so marvellously handsome and charming, a real breath of fresh air, and she is so beautiful, poor girl, those tiny children and the last baby died, of course, it must have been so appalling for her, sitting in the car with him – oh dear—' Her voice was very tearful.

'I know, it's horrible, it seems unbelievable, such a shock – oh dear – sorry, Mummy, so ridiculous to cry, not as if we knew him.'

'I feel as if we did,' said Sarah. 'Daddy was saying the same thing, he seemed like a friend—'

'Jeremy said that too,' said Eliza, and then cursed herself; she tried to play down the relationship, knowing that every report of every meeting heaped fuel on the fire of her mother's obsession, and sure enough, 'Oh, I'm glad you're not alone,' Sarah said, 'you sound so upset, can he stay there for a while?'

'Probably,' said Eliza, gesturing at Jeremy to pour her a drink. 'I'm not sure.'

'I just spoke to Charles, he said he was very shocked. They were coming down tonight, but Juliet isn't very well, bad tummy ache you know.'

'Oh lord,' said Eliza. Juliet had Periods with a capital P, making an endless fuss, demanding attention from Charles, who was expected to hover solicitously with hot-water bottles, aspirin and sympathy.

'Silly cow,' said Eliza as she put the phone down.

'Who's that?'

'My sister-in-law to be.'

'Eliza, that's not a nice way to speak about a near-relative. Although I do tend to wonder what old Charles is doing with her, I must say. Now – I don't know about you, but I don't really feel too much like going to the pictures now. What would you say to a nice quiet meal somewhere?'

'I'd say, hello nice quiet meal,' she said and grinned at him. It was a familiar joke of theirs.

'OK. San Lorenzo?'

'Yes, lovely,' she said.

San Lorenzo was surprisingly full. People obviously wanted to be with other people. There was talk of nothing else. Who had heard, what they'd heard, how dreadful it was, how appalling for Jackie, who might have done it – it was the Mafia, it was the Cubans, it was the Russians, and each new person or couple who came in had some new piece of information, 'someone's been arrested', 'Johnson's been sworn in', 'Bobby's just met Jackie off the plane', which was shared around the restaurant.

Finally they had had enough. 'Let's go,' Jeremy said suddenly, 'your place or mine?'

'Yours,' said Eliza, 'there'll be at least two giggling girls at mine.'

'Possibly not giggling tonight.'

'You want to bet?'

Jeremy's flat in Sloane Street was rather amazing. It was quite old-fashioned, admittedly, a mass of gilt mirrors and rather grand furniture and a very out-of-date kitchen, but it was luxurious beyond belief, room after room, high ceilings and tall windows, overlooking private gardens: there was a drawing room, a dining room – very grand indeed with dark red wallpaper and a highly polished floor, and a table that easily seated twelve. There was a very ornate bathroom, with an absurdly huge claw-footed bath, there were three bedrooms, the main one leading into

Jeremy's dressing room which actually resembled a small store in Jermyn Street, rows of suits, of shirts, of overcoats, of shoes; there was a small room which he called the snug, where he read and watched television and listened to music, and then there was his study, complete with leather-topped desk, several wooden filing cabinets, a magnificent wooden plan chest and floor-to-ceiling bookshelves. Her first thought when she went there (and her second and third, if she was honest) was how extremely rich he must be. Jeremy had inherited a very large amount of money from his banker grandfather; 'and when his father died, he would get an incredible house in Norfolk, almost a stately home, with vast acreage, a flat in the South of France, and several millions more.'

'Right,' Jeremy said as they walked in, 'you go and sit down. I'll get us a drink.'

He had been very quiet for the last half-hour at the restaurant and totally silent as he drove to Sloane Street; she wondered if she had upset him in some way, it was so unlike him.

Eliza went into the snug – the drawing room seemed rather over-whelming for the occasion – and waited for him rather nervously. He walked in finally with a bottle of champagne and two glasses.

'Goodness,' she said, 'is it really a champagne moment?'

'It could be,' he said and sat down beside her. 'What would you say to champagne in bed?'

Silence, while the shock of it thudded into her head; and then, 'I'd say, hello champagne in bed,' she said and laughed, and he laughed too, and he kissed her, and she stood up and reached for his hand and they went into the bedroom, his sumptuously grand bedroom, and sat in bed drinking the champagne and not saying very much more really and – well then . . .

It was, well, it was very nice. Yes. Very nice indeed. And definitely better than anything she'd known yet. Which wasn't much, of course. Just one other chap after the first. Another drunken country-house occasion. She'd felt terribly depressed after that one, cheap and tarty, and also beginning to think maybe it was her. Being frigid or something. Her friends all claimed to like it, to find it wonderful even. Maddy said she had what she described as gorgeous sex with her boyfriend, Esmond, who was a hatter and very pale and thin, and if Eliza hadn't been told otherwise, she would have thought he was queer.

Anyway, sex with Jeremy was honestly not gorgeous. But it was very, very pleasurable, of course it was, and thank God, she thought, she'd found that wonderful lady gynaecologist who'd put her on the wonderful pill, no more terror about getting pregnant and no more hideous messing about with Things either. He was obviously very pleased about that; 'Real girl-about-town, aren't you, Eliza?' he said, when she told him, and kissed her nose and then turned his attention to the lower parts of her anatomy. And it was all very nice, and not over too quickly; but she just kept waiting for the wonderful, fireworky stuff to happen – and it never did. And that really was a bit of a shock: that sophisticated, experienced, man-about-town Jeremy Northcott should not be able to do better for her than that.

She pretended a bit – she had to really – and he was clearly enjoying it a lot; and when it was over and he rolled off her and kissed her and told her she was wonderful and asked her with genuine tenderness if it had been as good for her as it had been for him, she said, yes, oh, yes, it had been really lovely.

The worst thing of all, she felt, was that he seemed to believe her.

Matt never forgot 22 November either. It was the day he took delivery, as the salesman put it, of his new car. His first car. His own car.

He picked it up first thing in the morning: a racing-green Triumph Herald, with wire wheels and go-faster stripes, and a twin exhaust that roared most satisfyingly every time he put his foot down.

Driving it into work, he felt completely different: smoother, more confident, no longer an inexperienced boy, but a successful young man going to work, carving his way through the traffic rather than waiting to cross the road, warm and comfortable, not standing at the bus stop in the rain.

'I've just parked my car outside,' he said to the first client of the day, looking at a site in Westbourne Grove and, 'I've put my car in the car park,' he said to Louise as he walked into the office, 'the one just two streets up.'

The day seemed to go on for ever; he longed for it to end so he could drive home and show it to his parents and the boys. Take them for a spin.

It wasn't entirely his, of course: the hire purchase company owned most of it, but it was his to drive away, his to look at, his to take down the A3 when he went to pick up Corinne, his latest girlfriend, in Kingston where she lived.

It even had a radio, a Motorola, dead classy, fixed into the dashboard. It had cost another thirty quid, but it had been worth it.

He was halfway along Oxford Street at half past six, changing gear unnecessarily frequently, revving furiously every time he was held up in the traffic, when an announcement cut into the music he was listening to on the Light Programme.

'We have just received news that President Kennedy has been shot as his motorcade drove through Dallas, Texas. He was taken to hospital, where doctors fought to save his life, but he was pronounced dead at 1 p.m. Texas time. Mrs Kennedy is still at the hospital. It is not yet known who was the assassin, but we will bring you further news as it unfolds.'

Matt stopped revving his engine; he felt seriously upset. Shocked, even. President Kennedy had seemed a symbol of a new age where power didn't have to be in the hands of old men. It seemed totally wrong that he should have been wiped out just like that. Just when he was beginning to do some good. It was so – untidy somehow. How and why would anyone do that? He supposed it was most likely some nutter who had it in for him. Or someone from Russia, maybe, or Cuba.

It was very sad: those two little kids, with no dad. And Jackie, that lovely Jackie, so classy, always so well dressed; she reminded him in a way of Eliza with her dark hair and eyes and her long legs.

He wondered if Eliza knew, and what she was doing now . . . And then wondered why he was thinking of her at all.

Scarlett was sitting in her flat, staring at the television. She felt very upset. Absurdly so. She remembered David talking about Kennedy, his exact words: 'We need him. He gives our nation a kind of grace.'

Well, if Johnson took over – and he would of course, it was in the Constitution – there wouldn't be much grace there.

She had sat on the BEA bus coming into London, tired from a flight to Munich and back, staring out into the crowded streets, looking at the people, all visibly moved, at the queues to buy newspapers, at the placards, all reading the same thing, 'JFK Assassinated', feeling rather as if she was watching a film. It seemed so wrong somehow: that someone so young, so promising, such a force for the good, should have been wiped out so easily.

The traffic was very thick; one of the stewards got out of the bus and bought a couple of papers. Pictures showed them, Jack and Jackie, arriving in Dallas, a couple even of them in the motorcade. The bullets had ripped into the car from a warehouse along the route; the president had been killed more or less instantly; a man had been arrested; Lyndon Johnson had been sworn in as the thirty-sixth president; Jackie was flying back to Washington with the body.

When Matt rang her and asked if he could come round, she said she'd love it.

'It's not a night to be alone,' she said, 'silly, isn't it, to be so upset?'

'I don't think so, no,' he said. She wasn't surprised; he could be quite soppy, Matt could; he was a real romantic under his tough-guy exterior. When he fell in love it would be pretty major, that was for sure.

Charles sat in Juliet's small sitting room, in the Earls Court flat she shared with another ex-Roedean girl, listening to the radio in the same state of shock as much of the entire world, and occasionally asking Juliet if she was OK. To which she gave him a wan smile, shifting the hot-water bottle she was holding on her stomach slightly, and sighing. She didn't seem to share his sense of grief and loss. She said it was dreadful of course and terrible for Jackie; but beyond that she was untouched by it.

'I should be feeling better tomorrow, Charles, but if I'm not, can we leave in the afternoon? And you will tell your mother I won't be able to go on one of her long walks, won't you? I'll feel a bit mean, I know how much she enjoys them . . .'

'Yes darling, of course I will.'

'It's so unfair, I'd wanted the weekend to be a success, Mummy and Daddy are looking forward to lunch so much, but of course they're a bit nervous—'

'Why?' said Charles in genuine surprise. Carol and Geoffrey Judd seemed inordinately self-confident to him, especially the golf-obsessed Geoff.

'Darling, don't be silly. They're meeting my future parents-in-law, it's so important, and Mummy's not sure what to wear, she's not really a country person, as you know—'

'She should wear whatever she feels comfortable in,' said Charles, 'we're not going to take her out shooting.'

It was meant to be a joke; Juliet was not amused.

'I should hope not. She'd be terrified, well, I was that time you took me.'

The occasion, a few weeks earlier at a neighbouring shoot, had not been a success. Juliet had walked along looking apprehensive and hostile at the same time, and whenever a gun went off she put her hands over her ears. After about an hour she had said she would like to go back to the house and insisted Charles escorted her; 'I don't want to go the wrong way, I might get shot at.'

Charles, embarrassed and irritated, left her in the house and returned to the shoot, not returning until the end of the day; she had driven herself back to Summercourt and when he finally reached it, having had to sort out a lift, found her sulky and reproachful. He told her she was being unfair and childish, at which she started crying and saying how sorry she was, and she couldn't bear it if he was cross with her, and she wasn't sure if she was good enough for him. She was very accomplished at emotional blackmail.

'Juliet, it's just a family lunch party, for God's sake, so they see the house and meet the parents.'

'Charles, don't get cross with me, you know I'm feeling rotten – Charles!'

But Charles had turned up the radio; news had come in of a man arrested in downtown Dallas.

'How amazing,' he said, 'that they should find him so quickly. I can't quite believe it's down to one man though, I'd have thought—'

'Charles, I think I'll go to bed. If you don't mind. I'll ring you first thing, let you know how I am.'

'Of course. Sorry. It's just that this is so—'

'Yes, I can see, much more interesting than my curse pains. That's fine. See you tomorrow.'

He stood up; she raised a pinched, half-smile of a face to be kissed.

Charles left.

And walked rather heavily down the road, his mind wiped temporarily clean of the assassination of President Kennedy, in a new and rather more personal panic of his own, that he could just possibly have made a rather terrible mistake.

Chapter 13

Things really were looking pretty good, Matt thought. Too good, he sometimes thought; was it too easy? Were they just enjoying beginner's luck? If they were, then best make the most of it. The demand for office space was insatiable. There was still very little in the way of planning restriction, money was easy to get hold of, and very often a site was sold in a day. The ideal was clearly to pack as much office space as possible into a site, plot ratio was the phrase on every developer's lips. 'It's the relationship between the area of the site and the floor area of the building,' he had explained to Louise on her first day, 'and it's all everybody talks about. In other words, the taller the building the better.'

Giant constructions like the Shell Centre on the South Bank and the Vickers Tower on Millbank both rose above three hundred feet. There was no conservation lobby to contend with; the bomb sites were mainly all developed now, so old buildings were simply being bulldozed and a rash of functional glass and concrete boxes rose in their place. There was even a serious suggestion that the Houses of Parliament be demolished and the site redeveloped.

Matt and Jimbo already had almost more clients than they could deal with; they worked increasingly long days, often arriving as early as seven and leaving twelve or even fourteen hours later.

One morning in early December, a tall, rather severe-looking woman walked in. She was about forty, Matt reckoned, wearing a suit with a pencil skirt; she had blond hair drawn back from her face in what Louise afterwards described as a French pleat, very good legs and an extremely posh accent.

She sat down, accepted a cup of coffee and said she was setting up a secretarial agency in London. 'You'll have heard of the Brook Street Bureau, no doubt?'

Matt said untruthfully that of course he had.

'Our agency, which is called Status Secretaries, is very similar, although with one important difference: all our girls will have GCEs and a shorthand qualification not merely in English, but in one other language. As I'm sure you know, there is an increasingly international emphasis in London business life.'

Matt said indeed he was aware of that.

'So I need not just one but several offices, not too big, say about a thousand square feet each one. I'd initially require one in the City, one in the West End, one in Chelsea, and one in Bayswater. We are extremely busy, and struggling to operate out of somewhere totally inappropriate, just down the road from here. Can you help?'

'I'm sure we can,' said Matt, buzzing for Louise. 'Miss Mullan, could you bring in the small offices file. This lady – I'm sorry, I didn't get your name—'

'I didn't give it. Hill, Valerie Hill.'

'Yes, Miss Hill is looking for space for her secretarial agency. Several offices in fact. In – let's see, EC4 or maybe 2, W1, SW3 and W2. I'm sure we can help.'

'Absolutely, especially in the City area. Several very appropriate properties there. I won't be a moment,' said Louise – she really was impressive, Matt thought, not just a pretty face as his father would have said – and was back well inside a minute holding several bulging files.

Valerie Hill was clearly impressed by her. 'What an extremely efficient girl,' she said, 'exactly the type we would be looking to employ. Not that I would dream of poaching her, of course,' she added hastily.

'I hope not,' said Matt cheerfully, 'she's worth her weight in gold. Now let me see – ah, yes – what sort of rent were you looking at, Miss Hill?'

Half an hour later, they were in a taxi travelling to the City; by the end of the day he was preparing draft contracts for two of her four offices.

It wasn't always that easy; but it was seldom difficult either.

Matt had also acquired a flat. It was quite small, but exactly what he had been dreaming of, a studio in an old converted warehouse on the river in Rotherhithe. He heard about it through Mark Draper, who'd made a fortune himself in studio flats; Matt had met him in the Blue Post off St James's Street, a favourite hangout for young men in the property business.

Draper was moaning one day about a flat he couldn't get rid of.

'Building next to it's derelict, that's all that's wrong and I know for a fact your old boss, Matt, Andy Stein, has found someone who's prepared to take it on, just haggling over timing but meanwhile no one'll take a chance on this place.'

Matt looked at it, at the huge if filthy windows, giving onto the river, the reassuringly sound concrete floor, the makeshift kitchen and bathroom and the one huge, brilliantly light, cobwebby room and bought the freehold for £1,500, beating Mark Draper down from £2,000; his mum and Scarlett spent a weekend helping him clean it, his dad made good the windows and Matt himself painted it all brilliant white. It was now furnished, with a double bed – Matt had spent his life in cramped single beds, and besides who knew who might be sharing this one with him – two garden chairs, a card table and a camping stove. A client in the rag trade gave him a clothes rail, and he stored underwear, sweaters and casual shirts in an old leather cabin trunk, complete with exotic travel labels – Cairo, Bombay, New York – that he bought in the Portobello Road for ten bob. He didn't want or need curtains at the windows, he wanted to see the river, all day, and all night, from the first streaks of dawn reflected on the water to the dredgers working through the black waters of night. The rats that scuttled around on the beach below him at low tide troubled him not in the least, nor did the noise of the river traffic, the wailing of police craft, the endless hooting of the tugs and cargo boats. The raw cries of the seagulls pleased him particularly. To him, it was a palace; his pride in it was huge.

He had money in the bank: not much personally, he and Jim had agreed they would stick to their original tiny salaries, but a steadily growing pile in the company account. They had formed a limited company; 'better for tax,' their accountant had said. Simmonds and Shaw Ltd. It sounded great. Sometimes he still had to pinch himself.

He wasn't doing badly, for someone who'd done it all himself.

'Mr Fullerton-Clark! Come in a moment would you?'

Charles smoothed his hair and walked into Mr Sayer's office. His boss was looking stern: very stern.

'Sit down, please.'

Charles sat; Mr Sayer was opening a drawer, reaching into it, pulling out a file, leafing through it. Then he looked at Charles, and his face was very serious. This was it. Definitely.

'Not a bad year, Charles. You got off to a bit of a rocky start, but I have to say, the second half has shown a considerable improvement. Must be married life, or the prospect of it, eh?'

Mr Sayer smiled suddenly. 'Yes, you seem to have pulled your socks up lately. Getting some good feedback from clients. Old Bosey knew what he was doing when he recommended you. Nice chap, isn't he? See much of him these days?'

Charles felt so weak with relief, he thought he might pass out.

'Oh – occasionally, yes. He shoots with my father.'

'Good, good. Anyway, Charles, your bonus – well-earned. Here's the cheque. Keep up the good work.'

'I will, sir, yes.'

'Help with the nuptials, I daresay. Got a house yet?'

'No, not yet. We're looking of course. But my fiancée is extremely particular.'

'Women are, my dear chap. Better get used to it. Anyway – jolly well done and have a good Christmas.'

'Thank you, Mr Sayer. Very much appreciated.'

Back in his office, he opened the envelope, whistled under his breath. This would help with the deposit all right. Although they hadn't even found a house yet. But – it was true, he knew he'd been working better, more profitably since Juliet had been in his life. She'd definitely made him feel more sure of himself. Knowing she depended on him, and admired him, was terribly important. She might be a bit difficult at times, but she often said marriage was the most important career in the world and she intended to be very good at it. 'Looking after you, Charles, that's my job and always will be. And our children of course.'

The sense of responsibility her attitude gave him was quite literally inspiring. No wonder his performance at work had improved.

The invitation arrived three weeks before Christmas. In a very thick white envelope, addressed to him personally. He read it, said 'Jesus Christ' and then 'Jesus H. Christ', put it down, picked it up again, and then leaned it against his telephone and was sitting staring at it when Louise came in.

'Let's see that,' she said, and leaned over and picked it up. She was so – so bloody cheeky, Matt thought, so bossy and nosy; and then decided he was actually rather happy for her to be looking at it.

'My goodness, Matt, what are you going to wear? Can I come?'

116

'No you can't,' said Matt.

'Why not? She's a client, isn't she?'

'Yeah, but she's invited me. Not you, and not Jim. It doesn't say anything about bringing anyone else, does it?'

'Well – no. But I bet you could, they're very casual, these arty types. Go on, Matt, I'd love to go.'

'Louise, I said no.'

'OK.' She shrugged. 'Fine by me. Now please can you sign these cheques, otherwise we'll all be in queer street.'

'Yeah, OK. And ring Mr Thomas, tell him I think we've let his office. But I need the name of his solicitor sharpish. Like within the hour.'

'Course.'

Once she was gone, Matt picked up the invitation again, and sat reading it, smiling foolishly. This really was exciting. It meant she liked him; she didn't have to invite him after all. Not that he fancied her, too much of a little doll. But there'd be dozens of models there, which would be very cool. And photographers and fashion artists – it would all be fantastic.

And – just possibly Eliza. She and Maddy were great friends.

'Come and celebrate Christmas with us,' it said, in big red letters on a bright white card, with a border of alternate knitting needles and studio lights, 'Friday, 13 December, 8 till late. Connaught Design Studios, Paddington Way, W2. RSVP Maddy Brown or Jerome Blake.' And at the top in that arty writing people like her always did, it said, 'Matt. Do come!'

He put it in the top drawer of his desk and kept looking at it all day.

He didn't reply for three days; he didn't want to look too keen. And only when he had, did he start thinking about what to wear. Not a suit: too formal. Not jeans: too casual. Flannels? He couldn't imagine Jerome Blake in flannels. He was getting desperate when he saw a red velvet suit in a window of that mecca for style, Male West One in Carnaby Street; he couldn't really afford it, but he bought it anyway, and a ruffled white shirt to go with it. What his dad would say, he didn't dare think, tell him he looked like a woofter or something.

✿　✿　✿

'I love you and I'm missing you. So much. I'm dreading Christmas. I'll try to call, but it might be difficult. Meanwhile, keep safe and we'll have our own festive season in January. All my love, David.'

All adulterers dreaded Christmas, Scarlett knew. Being forced apart, knowing the other person was not only not with you, but in the heart of their own family, warm, safe, busy, even while pretending happiness, faking jollity. She could hardly bear to think about the Berenson Christmas. It sounded perfect. Everyone, all three families, gathered in Lily's house. The lavish decorations, the huge tree in the hall, fairy lights everywhere; Santa there on Christmas Eve to hand out presents; midnight service; Christmas morning brunch; Christmas night dinner; charades. She really hated hearing about it, but she'd been torturing herself, asking David, dragging it out of him. A lavish, fairy-lighted Christmas, with a house filled with over-excited children and smiling happy adults. Somehow, Christmas in the little house off the Northcote Road, with her parents and Matt and even with the two boys – teenagers now and bored with the whole thing – didn't match up. And how unpleasant of her even to think like that, when Sandra would be working her socks off, baking and decorating and shopping and wrapping presents, loving that she still had all her brood with her. She cared so much about family, about togetherness; what would she say, Scarlett wondered, if she knew that her daughter, her beloved daughter was doing her damnedest to destroy another family, to disrupt togetherness. Well, maybe not her damnedest, she wasn't actually urging David to leave Gaby, and he had never actually said that he would, or not for a long time. He had always told her that until the children were grown – 'which is not so very long, my darling' – he would need to be there, a proper part of their lives.

But he loved her, he told her constantly so. And – she loved him. And finally, she had told him so, on their last meeting, as they ate dinner together in the Ritz, in that corny, over-ornate dining room, the epitome of excess and foolishness, so well-suited to amoral, self-indulgent behaviour. 'Tell me, my darling, darling Scarlett,' he had said, 'how you really and truly, hand on your heart, feel about me. I've told you how much I love you, for God's sake, more than I've ever loved anyone, and often enough, so—'

And in a surge of emotion that contained sadness as much as joy, regret as well as delight, she took his hand across the table and looked into his eyes and half smiled and then heard her own voice shake, as she said, 'David, really and truly, hand on heart and all the other clichés, I love you too. Not more than I've loved anyone, for I've never really loved anyone before; but I certainly can't imagine anything greater than what I feel about you. So – so yes. How's that? I've done it.'

She did love him, and so much that to deny it seemed wrong, a betrayal in itself. Although quite where it would lead her, that admission, she did not dare think.

Matt arrived at the party at half past eight. He knew better than to be early; nothing worse than being the first.

He was the first.

'Matt, hello!' It was Maddy, looking devastating in a gold knitted shift dress; Matt tried not to look at the hemline, which just covered her pants.

'Hello. Yes. Sorry I'm early.'

'You're not, of course. Everyone else is late. Oh – actually, look, you have company, hello Simon – Simon Butler – Matt Shaw. Matt, Simon's an art director at one of the agencies, I can never remember which one, terribly important anyway, CPV isn't it, Simon?'

'No, darling, CDP. Do you mind?'

'Whoops, sorry. Well anyway, lovely to see you. Matt found this wonderful building for us, didn't you, Matt?'

'Oh yeah?' Simon managed a rather superior smile. 'Good work.'

Matt didn't like him at all.

'Anyway, drinks over there,' said Maddy, 'help yourselves, and later, some lovely little cakes will be coming round. OK? Now I've just got to go and do a few last-minute things, so will you excuse me?'

And she was gone.

'Might as well get a drink then,' said Simon, leading Matt across to the drinks. The studio was a mass of flashing strobe lights, and the music was already pounding; the only decorations to the studio otherwise were the great rolls of background paper, daubed with colour.

Matt helped himself to a beer and said, 'Cheers.'

'Cheers,' said Simon. He took out a cigarette paper and began rather ostentatiously rolling his own from a small silver case. Dope, thought Matt; am I supposed to be impressed or something? He knew what the little cakes would be too, of course; and he wouldn't be eating one. He'd heard too many horror stories about those cakes and the unevenly distributed stuff in them; a friend of Jimbo's had ended up with an overdose, hallucinating and trying to jump out of a second-floor window. Matt had smoked a fair bit of dope and quite liked it, although he preferred alcohol; but he avoided harder drugs totally. He knew the smart crowd took LSD and cocaine all the time, but he couldn't afford risking any trouble: not yet anyway. One day, maybe . . .

'So,' said Simon Butler, draining his glass, refilling it instantly, licking his cigarette paper, 'you're in the property business, are you?'

'Yeah, that's right,' said Matt. 'Got a small agency, in the West End, mostly commercial properties.' He looked at Simon, whose expression suddenly changed from tolerant boredom to a broad smile – maybe he was interested – but, 'Suki! Darling! Over here,' and towards them came the tallest, thinnest girl Matt had ever seen, with a pale, pale face and huge black-rimmed eyes, wearing a narrow silk dress that reached her ankles and no shoes. Her feet, he couldn't help noticing, were filthy.

'Simon, darling, hello, how awful to be so early, it was now or hours later—' She looked uncertainly at Matt who smiled and held out his hand.

'Matt Shaw. Pleased to meet you.'

'Oh. Yes. And I'm Suki.'

'And – are you a model?' asked Matt. It seemed a reasonable assumption, given her shape.

'Oh – goodness no, no, I sew at Granny's.'

'Ah,' said Matt, 'yes, I see. Well—'

'Simon, how are things? Give me a little puff of that, would you? And I'll just have some water. Oh – thank you, Matt. Yes.'

'I'm great,' said Simon, 'yeah. Agency's going like a train, got some massive new accounts, we seem to be the only agency who thinks television, you know—'

'Yeah, I do. Exactly. Guy came into Granny's the other day and—'

'Um – what is Granny's? Exactly?' asked Matt. Largely because he was buggered if he was going to be frozen out of this conversation.

They both looked at him as if he had asked what date Christmas was.

Finally, 'Granny Takes A Trip,' said Suki patiently. 'You know. The clothes shop. Down at World's End.'

'Oh – yes. Of course.'

'So anyway, Simon, this guy said he wanted a dress made for a commercial and – oh, Christian darling, hello. How are you? You know

120

Simon Butler, don't you? From CDP? And this is – sorry, Matt, where are you from?'

'Oh – I'm in property,' said Matt and then, turning his back on them, went over towards Maddy. He wasn't going to be patronised by these people. He was not.

Three quarters of an hour later, he wasn't being patronised; he was being ignored. Everyone seemed to know everyone; and they all worked in the fashion or the advertising business, so there was nothing at all he had to say to them – or they to him. They were bloody rude, most of them, smiling rather half-heartedly while he introduced himself and then turning away from him to continue their conversations; a couple of girls made a pretence of asking him what he did, and then realising there was very little they could say beyond that, excused themselves, saying they were going to get a drink and would be back in a minute, and then weren't.

He had drunk quite a lot of beer, but it wasn't helping. He felt totally sober. Sober and extremely stupid. Most of them were posh, but a few were talking an exaggerated cockney; he actually asked one of them where they lived, and got a cold stare and a mumble that sounded like East London – as if anyone would say that who really came from the East End.

He was terribly hot too. He'd have liked to take off his jacket, but he was scared of it being nicked, and anyway, he could see that the ruffled shirt was all wrong. Most of the blokes were in plain white shirts, or even T-shirts, and jeans, some of those admittedly velvet, but black and not, most definitely not, red. Shit. Why had he thought red would be all right? He looked bloody stupid. Twice Maddy had waved at him and asked him if he was OK; and she'd introduced him to her boyfriend, Esmond, who was dressed all in black, black T-shirt, black jeans, and very black hair, and looked as if he was going to die, his skin greyish-pale, and incredibly thin – how did these people all get so thin, Matt wondered, didn't they ever eat anything at all . . .

He was quite nice, asked Matt what he did, tried to find something responsive to say in return and actually remembered he had found the building for Maddy. He made hats, it turned out, and had even sold one or two to Granny's; Matt, seeing his chance to appear as if he knew what was what, asked him if he knew Suki, but Esmond said yeah, he did, they'd been at the College together. Which college? Matt asked, but this was clearly even more than Esmond could stand.

121

'The Royal College of Art,' he said, 'back in a minute,' and walked off after Maddy.

Matt, alone once more, looked at his watch surreptitiously; Christ, it was only quarter to ten. Maybe he should try and slip away, without saying anything to Maddy; but then what would he say to Louise and Jimbo, they'd been so plainly impressed by his being invited to this party, and he'd talked it up himself, could he really make up enough of a story to satisfy them on Monday? Maybe if he had one more drink, followed Esmond over to where he was chatting to another guy, he'd find something to say. But – they were starting to dance now, Maddy had pulled Esmond onto the floor and was beckoning to everyone to join them. Suki was dancing with herself, in some kind of trance, and so were a couple of other girls, glassy-eyed – stoned he supposed, and Jesus, Simon Butler was in a corner, half-hidden by a roll of background paper, snogging with another bloke for God's sake, what on earth was going on, he must be queer, were there a lot of them here then? He supposed the fashion business was full of them, something to tell Louise and Jimbo at least, but, Christ, he really didn't like it – he might leave, in fact, yes, he would when—

'Matt! Matt hello, what a lovely surprise, Maddy said she was going to invite you, you wouldn't get me a drink would you, I'm desperate.'

It was Eliza. She was wearing a black shift, with a large hole cut out of it where her midriff was – in fact, he could actually see her navel, Christ, why were girls allowed to do that sort of thing – and thigh-high black boots. Her hair had grown, it was past her shoulders, and her fringe was so long he could hardly see her eyes.

'Course,' he said and disappeared into the throng, then realised he had no idea what she wanted: well, not beer, but red or white wine, or some of that evil-looking punch, probably laced with something. He picked up a glass of red and a glass of white wine and made his way back to her, half-expecting her to have moved on to another group like everyone else that wretched humiliating evening. But no, 'Oh, thank you, Matt, I'll take the white if that's OK, are you having a good time?'

'Oh – yeah – well you know.' He took a large gulp of the red. 'Don't know many people, but – yeah, I met someone you probably know, Suki someone—'

'Suki! Suki Warrener?'

'Not sure. Probably.'

'Was she stoned? She always is. Cigarette, Matt? No, no, have one of mine. Mad as a hatter, Suki is – talking of hatters, did you meet Esmond?'

'Oh – sure, yes. Very nice bloke.'

'Isn't he? Oh, Maddy, darling, hello, fab party, sorry I'm late, God, look at Simon Butler, God he's such a tart, bit early to be carrying on like that I'd have thought, tiny bit reckless too, but – oh, now who is that in the PVC dress? We had those in for about a day at Woolfe's and then they were all gone, terrific success. And how many Maddy Brown dresses are here?'

'Oh – quite a few. Yes. Oh, God, Suki's passed out, I'd better go.' Eliza drained her glass and smiled at Matt. She did seem to be feeling really friendly.

'Want another of those?' he asked.

'Umm – yes – no – oh, listen it's "She Loves You", absolutely my favourite at the moment. Matt, dance?'

And she took his hand and led him into the dancing.

She danced well, really well. And she knew it. It began as a performance, and entirely by her; she moved into the music, ignoring him, her head thrown slightly back, her body bending, twisting, turning, her hair flying, her eyes shining, she had a smile on her face that was part pure pleasure, part look-at-me self-confidence. And Matt, nervous at first, demoralised by his evening, simply followed where she led. But then – for he knew he too danced well, really well – he began to perform too, oddly sure of himself suddenly, and she, recognising it, her smile now for him, not her audience, her eyes fixed on his, her body following his, every move, every twist, every turn, pushing double, treble beats into every one; slowly everyone else stopped, staring at them, caught up in what was a virtuoso display and at the end, when the music momentarily finished, when the beat changed, they seemed quite alone together, the evening briefly but entirely theirs, and Eliza stood there, staring at him, her eyes huge and shining, breathing heavily, and he stood too, neither of them moving, caught in a kind of sweet shock, frozen in time.

And then of course, things began again, the music went on, everyone began to dance again, people talking, smiling at one another; and there was a shout of 'Eliza' and a tall, blond man was waving at her from the door, and she leaned forward and gave him a quick, half-embarrassed kiss and said, 'Sorry, Matt, I've got to go, we're only just looking in,' and the magic was gone and it wasn't the princess in the story who had changed into a raggedy kitchen maid, but the prince become a nobody once more.

But Matt didn't care; he left quite soon after that, having thanked Maddy, shaken Esmond's rather cold white hand, and even felt emboldened to kiss Suki, who was sitting on one of the sofas, weeping helplessly, he had no idea why: and drove most happily home.

He wasn't quite sure what had happened, but he felt as if things had changed. As if he was – or might become – a rightful person in Eliza's life, rather than someone she was rather self-consciously nice to; and as if she was a rightful person in his, rather than someone impossibly out of reach. He didn't quite understand it; but there was sex in there somewhere, that was for sure.

Chapter 14

She couldn't be – could she? Surely, surely not. They'd been so careful; she always was. She had never risked it, never. Some girls did, she knew; threw caution to the winds, when desire got too much for them, and then spent the next two or three weeks sick with fear. Not her. Her life, her perfectly ordered life was too precious to risk for a few minutes' passion. And she had certainly never allowed any man to take the responsibility, however much they might assure her it would be all right.

But here she was, over two weeks late, with boobs so sore she could hardly bear to touch them.

'I did tell you,' the gynaecologist said slightly reprovingly, 'it's not one hundred per cent. Nothing is. Except abstinence,' she added with a sudden smile. 'Bit late for that, though.'

'A bit,' said Scarlett. 'So – what can I do?'

'One of two things. Have it. Or not have it.'

'I can't have it,' said Scarlett. 'I really can't. Do you know anyone who could – well, help me?'

'My dear girl, of course I don't. It's illegal. And if I did, and I told you, I could be struck off. But there are people. Clinics even. Expensive, but at least not dangerous. To your health, that is.' She buzzed for her secretary. 'Could you send in my next lady, please, Mrs Blake. Thank you. Good morning, Miss Shaw. I do hope things go well for you.'

'Old bat,' said Diana, 'and I bet you anything she's had a couple of abortions herself. Oh, Scarlett. I'm so sorry. You poor thing.'

'Yes, well. My own fault I suppose.'

'Don't be ridiculous! Are you quite sure?'

''Fraid so. The lady toad has laid her eggs.'

'So bizarre that, isn't it?' said Diana absently. 'To think our pee can make a toad ovulate. That is what happens, isn't it?'

125

'It is, yes. I remember my mother saying in her day they injected a mouse with the wee, and then they had to kill the poor thing to see if it ovulated. At least the toad can live on to be used another day. Anyway—'

'Sorry, Scarlett, I'm not helping, am I? What bad luck. Oh dear. You can't – well, you know—'

'What?' said Scarlett.

'Well – might he – marry you? If you told him?'

'Unlikely,' said Scarlett. 'He's married already.'

'Ah.'

'Yes. Bit of a bind.'

'Bit.' Diana was silent for a moment, then said, 'What have you tried?'

'Oh – you know. Castor oil. Gin. Gin and castor oil together. In a very hot bath. That did give me terrible stomach ache; I was quite hopeful for a bit. But – no good. I spent the night on the toilet and in the morning – right as rain. Or rather the baby was. Don't know what else I can do.'

'Look, I'll ask around,' said Diana. 'Some of the girls are pretty clued up, you know. Amanda, for instance. I know she got preggers once. She swore it just sorted itself out but I never believed her.'

Scarlett's heart lifted just a little.

It had been Eliza's idea, their Paris fashion feature. At the beginning of January, when the plans for shooting the collections were being put in place, and Fiona, always highly strung, became tearful on a daily basis.

Jack Beckham had been dismissing her suggestions for weeks. 'I'm not having that sort of predictable crap in my magazine,' he said. 'If you can't come up with anything better than that, Fiona, best not go at all.'

'We have to go,' Fiona wailed, 'we'll lose all credibility as a fashion magazine if we don't. And it hasn't helped that Mary Quant and Jean Muir have both come out and said Paris is dead. Well they would, wouldn't they?'

It was something Jeremy said that gave her the idea; she had told him that she would be going to Paris as Fiona's assistant and he had said, first having told her how proud of her he was, 'Several of my mother's friends go to the collections to order their clothes for the following season. Most couturiers spend their time dressing middle-aged women, once the razzmatazz of the press shows is over. It must be quite depressing for them, I always think.'

Eliza had reported this to Fiona next day, simply by way of a distraction after another tear-inducing session with Jack Beckham, and she had sighed and said yes, it was true, but there were a few young women, 'mostly film stars', who famously bought couture. 'Like Catherine Deneuve for instance, and Elizabeth Taylor and of course Audrey Hepburn is Givenchy's muse.'

'Are there any young ones who aren't film stars, do you think?' asked Eliza, and Fiona said yes, she supposed there must be, millionaires' third wives, that sort of thing.

'Well, maybe we could find one, follow her round all the collections, feature what she liked—'

Fiona stared at her in silence for what seemed like a very long time. Then, 'Eliza, you are a genius,' she said, 'whizz over to the picture library and get out all the files on the Best Dressed Women, that sort of thing. Photocopy any you think look really good, and let's have a look.'

Terrified at the responsibility, Eliza went to one of the big picture libraries in Fleet Street and came back with a bulging file.

'There aren't many young ones,' she said, 'mostly older people like the Duchess of Windsor and Diana Vreeland. There's poor Jackie Kennedy of course – oh and Princess Grace of Monaco.'

'No, none of them would do it, and anyway, Jack would say they were too obvious,' said Fiona distractedly: and then suddenly, 'but here, Eliza, look at this woman, she's gorgeous. Who's she?'

Mariella Crespi gazed at them from the fading pages: a dazzlingly chic brunette, thirty-seven years old, married to Giovanni Crespi – 'he's much older than her, gosh, over seventy, clearly she's an old man's darling' – one of Italy's richest men. 'It says industrialist,' said Fiona. Mariella, who had been a debutante according to the cuttings, and had worked in the art world, had married him on her thirtieth birthday. She had never quite made the top spot on the best-dressed lists, but had appeared on several for the past four years. According to *Woman's Wear Daily*, fashion was her religion and the salons of Paris, Milan and New York her places of worship.

'One day I will make it,' she was reported as saying, 'right to the top. It is my big ambition.'

'It's worth a try,' said Fiona, 'she might think it would be fun and it would up her profile a bit. Let's send her some copies of the magazine and a grovelling letter, and courier them off absolutely straight away – oh, no wait, I'd better run it past Jack, but I know he'll like it.'

He did. Fiona wrote and rewrote the letter seven times and it was parcelled up with the magazines to go to the villa on the shores of Lake Como, which was the Crespis' main residence.

'I'm not very hopeful,' said Fiona, handing the package to Eliza to dispatch, 'but you never know. And it's terribly short notice.'

'I think she'll do it,' said Eliza. 'I just feel it in my bones.'

Mariella Crespi was in bed eating her breakfast of brioche and caffè latte when her maid delivered the package from England. She read the letter swiftly, then started to leaf through the magazines. As she read, her expression, initially cool, became increasingly enthusiastic; after half an hour she pulled on a robe and went to talk to her husband.

He was in his study, dictating letters to his secretary, as he had been for over an hour already, for he still ran his industrial empire with great energy and enthusiasm; when he had finished he would work his way through the long list of phone calls a second secretary had compiled, ignoring the ones in which he felt no interest.

Mariella adored her husband as he did her; she was well aware that people assumed she had married him only for his money, and the assumption was wrong. Of course the money was very nice, and acquired for her everything it ever occurred to her she might want, but she also found him interesting, thoughtful, concerned and of course admiring. He was also, even in his seventies, an extremely attractive and beautifully dressed man; she was proud to be seen on his arm.

The only demands he made of her were that she should be his constant companion, look beautiful at all times and run his houses – in addition to the main residence on Lake Como, there was a small ski chalet in the mountains at Cervinia, and an apartment in Nice.

The story told in the newspaper cuttings of a lovely young debutante, who had met Signor Crespi at a ball, was not entirely correct; she was not in the least aristocratic, but the youngest of five sisters who had grown up in a two-bedroom apartment in a poor area of Milan. When she was sixteen, her widowed mother Nina had looked at the treasure in her midst, the olive-skinned, dark-eyed, full-bosomed beauty, with her mass of shining hair and deep throaty laugh, and entered her for a local beauty contest. Mariella won, and then another and then another and at the age of nineteen was competing at national level.

Signor Crespi was chairman of the judges at one such event and pronounced her the winner. The prize was five thousand lire and Mariella used it to attend a course on the history of art. She gained a qualification and was employed as a guide in one of the smaller galleries in the city, where Signor Crespi was a frequent patron; he remembered her, invited her to dinner, fell in love with her, and in a fairly short space of time asked her to marry him.

It was, astonishingly, a happy marriage. Mariella adorned Giovanni's life, and truly loved him. She was a tender and devoted wife; and, most importantly, there had never been the slightest whiff of scandal.

Her only regret – and it was a deep and sad one – was that he had been unable to give her any children. When they were first married, Giovanni was in his late sixties, and very far from impotent; but as the years passed, it became evident he was equally far from fertile.

Giovanni had only one child, a son, by his first wife, who was a great disappointment to him. Benino was not the high-flyer his father might have hoped for, an ambitious heir to his large industrial empire, but a gentle creature, who at the age of twenty-five had announced he was entering the priesthood.

However, Mariella was a pragmatic creature, not given to regret; she was a successful member of Milanese society and enjoyed it greatly, only occasionally allowing herself to admit to a certain ennui in her life; the letter from *Charisma* magazine therefore fell into it like manna from heaven.

She had appointments that day in Milan, at both Elizabeth Arden and her hairdresser Mario Petris, for the social season – traditionally launched by the opening night at La Scala at the beginning of December – was in full swing; but before setting off, and having sought the permission of Giovanni, she cabled the fashion editor who had written so charming a letter, saying she would like to meet her and summoning her to Il Grande Hotel Milano in a few days' time.

'She'll hate me, I know,' wailed Fiona. 'She'll be horrible, all spoilt and hard and condescending,' but she came back starry-eyed and dizzy with excitement.

'She is just amazing. So, so nice, absolutely beautiful and terribly excited about it all. She loved the magazine and all Rob's stuff, and she'd heard of Daniel Thexton, said she'd seen his stuff in *Vogue*. She's going to go to all the collections and we can talk to her after each one and hear what she has to say about it and then photograph the clothes.'

'But not on her?'

'No, no, of course not, they wouldn't fit her, they're all model sizes, although she's so glamorous we can certainly do some pictures of her outside each house or something like that. She wants as much exposure as she can get. She wants to come to the sessions too, amazingly. I told her they were often in the middle of the night and she laughed and said, "so much the better". And, best of all, because she's an actual client and such a high-profile one, we'll be able to borrow the clothes that bit more easily. It's perfect, Eliza. Really perfect.'

'I know she can't model the actual clothes for the sessions,' said Eliza slowly, 'but maybe – maybe if she wore her own example of whatever designer we're doing, we could include that in some way. Shoot her alongside the model, or separately, but on the same page or spread. Do you think she'd do that?'

Mariella said she would adore to.

She was staying at the Meurice; she invited Fiona for cocktails the evening before the first show. Fiona came back overflowing with excitement.

'Jacques Fath tomorrow. She always orders at least three things from them, she says. And then she's going to Cardin, Chanel of course, Balenciaga, Balmain, Dior – oh Eliza, it's so exciting.'

She dressed by preference at Jacques Fath and Cardin, 'and Pucci, naturally, I adore Emilio so,' but she was not above the ready-to-wear market as well, 'of course I wear Missoni, who would not?'

Most importantly she was nice: good-natured, patient and enthusiastic. ('How does she get to be that way?' Fiona said wonderingly. 'Most of these women are frightful.') When the directrice of Balenciaga told Fiona coldly she could only have the dress that Mariella had chosen at eleven that night, 'Vogue will have it until then, maybe later, you will just 'ave to wait,' Mariella simply shrugged and said, 'Is fine. We will have dinner first. I will bring a very very tight girdle, so my stomach is holded in. Eliza, you must come too.'

She had taken a fancy to Eliza, who she had met in the studios, and who kept her supplied with the Italian Murillo cigarettes she loved, as well as playing cards with her while the hairdresser did her hair.

'I think it's because you're posh,' Fiona said. 'Takes a nob to know one.'

'I'm not a nob,' said Eliza crossly. She spent a lot of time trying to shed this image, in what was supposed to be the new classless society; nothing seemed to work.

'Course you are. If they cut you down the middle, it would say "posh" all the way through, like Brighton rock. Anyway, I'm grateful, anything that keeps Mariella sweet.'

Keeping her sweet wasn't very difficult, Eliza reflected, as they sat chatting in the dressing room of the studio waiting for the make-up artist, presently working for *Vogue*, to grace them with her presence.

'This is all such such fun for me, you have no idea. So much of my life is always the same, day after day after day. One day I will tell you all about it, and then you will understand.'

Eliza supposed living with a man in his seventies must have its drawbacks. Even if he was a multi-millionaire.

Eliza had only seen one show: Chanel. In spite of the savage heat, a poor seat (gained by sheer force and elbowing other people out of the way – 'it's like a rugby scrum,' Fiona said, 'you really do have to fight, I warn you'), an hour-long wait for the start and a thumping headache, she would not have missed it for the world. She was amazed by the length of the thing – over two hours, one girl after another, showing almost identical suits, and completely identical dresses, the differences often as infinitesimal as a change of button – and the solemnity of the occasion, it really was rather like being at some hugely important religious ceremony. What made it work for her really, she had to admit, was the fact that Chanel herself was there, a small, rather forlorn little figure, sitting at the top of the famous spiral staircase, dressed in a pale pink tweed suit and a boater hat, smoking throughout; Eliza hadn't quite believed she would be there, had thought it was some kind of legend. Which Chanel was, of course, a living legend; I shall be able to tell my grandchildren about this, Eliza thought.

There was a huge drama one day which Fiona and Mariella regaled her with later, goggle-eyed: one of the newspapers had smuggled a photographer in, another got wind of it and there was a great chaos as the show was halted, he was identified and thrown literally out of the doors. The newspaper photographers were used to such hardship; the directrices of the salons despised them absolutely and would only allow them to take two pictures after each collection 'of the ugliest girls, and more or less in the dark', Fiona said.

'Move this girl would you?' Evangeline Turner, scourge of the younger fashion writers, *éminence grise* of the couturiers' salons, and fashion editor of the *Daily Post*, waved her hand imperiously at Eliza. Eliza stared at the directrice of the salon. They wouldn't move her. Surely they wouldn't. She hadn't asked to be in the front row; it was Fiona's place – poor Fiona, who was lying in her hotel room with oyster poisoning. And she really hadn't expected to be given it; front-row seats were for the big editors of the big glossies, *Vogue* and *Queen*, and the really prestigious papers, the *Sunday Times* and the *Daily Express*; assistants, if they got in at all, were usually right at the back behind a pillar. When she had gone with Fiona to the Chambre Syndicale office in Paris to get their passes to the collections, the woman in charge looked at them over her extremely stout bosom and told them she wasn't at all sure she could guarantee them admission at all.

'We do not know your magazine,' she said, flipping through it disdainfully, 'I cannot possibly guarantee you any tickets, or even a pass. Come back tomorrow please.'

They left. Eliza was shocked, but Fiona shrugged it off. 'They're so horrible, these people, they're all the same, I sometimes think they must be bred on a farm somewhere, specially for the job. Then they all call themselves the Duchesse of this or the Princesse of that. I'm sure they're nothing of the sort. It'll be OK, Eliza, we'll get passes. And tickets.'

Eliza was trying to resist the efforts of the directrice to eject her from her seat and exiling her to one five rows back, at Mrs Turner's instigation, when Mariella arrived, looking rather flushed in a red silk dress and black fur stole. She kissed her ecstatically. 'Darling. Where are you going? Stay here with me; I want to show you something . . .'

She sat down, pulling a small Cartier box out of her bag. Eliza sank down again, flashing a sweet smile first at the directrice and then at Mrs Turner. Life really didn't get much better than this.

Paris was a revelation to Eliza: about how the world of high fashion really moved, about how crucial it remained to the industry; about the power of the press to make or break a house – however contemptuous the directrices might be; it also made her realise how far she had moved down the professional ladder by her move. At Woolfe's she had been quite a large fish in a small but important pond, now she was a tiny sprat. Her role as assistant was not to attend the shows, but to wait to collect the chosen dresses from each one – booked out to a timetable by the directrices, which could entail anything up to a two-hour wait, take them to the photographic studio, where Fiona and Mariella would be waiting, and then return them, usually to a shower of abuse for being late; she had

132

to organise slots at the studios, taxis, sandwiches, coffee, cigarettes, had to run around quite literally from dawn to dawn with bagfuls of gloves, belts, shoes, hairpieces; on two days they did photographs out of the studio, and she had to hire limos of a sufficient size to double as dressing room for Mariella, who loved it, and the challenges of pulling up her stockings and even once changing her bra while the chauffeur smoked and acted as bodyguard – 'darling this is so much fun'. Eliza had to keep Fiona calm (not easy), wake her up in the morning (even less so), and try to stop her drinking too much at night (almost impossible). But she didn't care; she was happier than she could ever remember, totally involved in everything, she would have scrubbed the pavements if they'd asked her without complaint. And when finally that last day, she found herself in charge of the session, while poor Fiona lay moaning in her bed, directing the hairdresser, choosing the accessories, and then actually daring to argue with Daniel Thexton and his insistence that Mariella put out her cigarette – 'I think a cloud of smoke sort of round her face would look fantastic, let's just try, Mariella, yes, that's wonderful, look Daniel, don't you think?' – and he AGREED! That was tell-her-grandchildren stuff for sure.

She returned home exhausted, went to bed and slept for twelve hours, to be woken by Fiona with the news that Jack had actually said the pictures weren't bad at all; and when Jeremy rang a little later and asked her if she had missed him, realised that she had hardly thought about him from one day's end to the next.

Amanda had been able to help. Scarlett found herself lying in bed, in a very expensive nursing home in the outermost reaches of North London, enduring no more than post-anaesthetic nausea, mild stomach ache – and no longer pregnant. She returned home after twenty-four hours and to work after another forty-eight; she felt rather tired, she told Diana, as they waited for take-off, but otherwise fine, 'and just hugely relieved'.

'Not – not upset or anything?' Diana asked carefully and Scarlett said no, not in the least upset, and why ever should she be?

'Well,' Diana said, 'just take care of yourself, Scarlett, spoil yourself a bit, don't try and do too much. You might feel a bit – a bit—'

'A bit what?'

'Sad,' said Diana.

'What on earth for? I'd be feeling sad if I was still pregnant. I feel a bit poor, mind you, but—'

'Scarlett,' said Diana, 'however logical you're being about this, you have just been through a hell of a mill. You haven't just had a bad curse, your hormones must be in total turmoil—'

'Oh, for heaven's sake. I haven't had to go through anything. Now do stop fussing; will you do the seat-belt checks or shall I?'

'I will,' said Diana.

'Charles—'

'Yes, darling.'

'Do you want to be involved in things like bridesmaids' dresses?'

'Good heavens, no. Leave it to you. Trust you completely.'

'So – you're not even interested in what they're like?'

He knew that tone; it meant – not trouble exactly, but an echo of it, like a far-away clap of thunder.

'Darling, of course I am. Of course. But I don't feel I have anything to contribute, that's all.'

'Well . . .'

'And you're so good at it, all that visual stuff. Bit like Eliza really.'

'I don't think I'm in the least like Eliza,' said Juliet stiffly. 'She and I couldn't be more different.'

'Well – well, I just meant with an eye for fashion. Colour and style, that sort of thing. You know, I really can't wait to see your dress. I'm sure it's going to be absolutely beautiful.'

'It is,' said Juliet, 'but you are going to have to wait – of course. Only a few months, though. Goodness, it's getting close. Now you are all right for the weekend, aren't you? To talk to Mummy and Daddy about caterers.'

'Yes, of course. Looking forward to it.'

He was. Well, he would have been if it hadn't meant staying overnight at the Judds on Saturday. They were perfectly nice of course; very nice indeed. Just rather – well, dull. He couldn't find much to say to either of them; once he'd finished talking to Geoffrey about his golf, which he himself didn't even play, and his company, and Carol about her tennis and her charity work; they didn't chat and they didn't joke, and they didn't know anyone he knew – except Juliet of course – and dinner was eaten in the rather large and cold dining room, even if it was just the four of them, and then Carol and Geoff sat and watched TV and he and Juliet would go out for a drink to the pub. And there was always a huge song and dance about his room, and whether he'd been comfortable and if he'd slept all right. It was rather as if they were at pains to point out that it was his room and where he slept and there was to be no straying from it to visit Juliet. Which was wholly ridiculous, as there would be ample opportunity for him and Juliet to sleep together during the week as they both had flats in London – albeit shared with other people. They were hardly likely to risk the wrath of her parents by doing it under their roof.

But of course they didn't sleep together, because Juliet was determined to go to the altar a virgin and Charles – well, Charles totally respected that. Of course he did. It wasn't easy, in some ways, but in others it quite suited him. He wasn't sexually confident, never had been; he was prepared to wait for the honeymoon when they would both be relaxed and could take their time.

'You look tired,' said Matt. 'Really tired. You OK?'

They were in what Scarlett called her pub, in the Old Brompton Road. She'd been avoiding him for weeks, and he'd been worrying about her, still feeling the old sense of responsibility about her; and she'd finally agreed to meet.

'Yes, I'm perfectly OK,' said Scarlett. But she didn't sound it. She sounded irritable, scratchy. It was unlike her. Maybe she had a headache, or was about to come on or something. Girls did get very odd around that time. The only girl he'd ever known who was always the same, day in, day out, permanently up and running as you might say, was Louise. She was amazing. Really amazing. Just as well really, the way they depended on her . . .

'Well – that's good. Been working hard?'

'Yes, I always work hard. Matt, I'm fine. What is this?'

'Nothing. What you want to drink?'

'Oh – Scotch I think. Yes. On the rocks.'

'Bit early for that, isn't it? You usually have a G and T this sort of time.'

'Yes, well, I don't want one today. I've gone off gin.'

She had too; ever since drinking it neat, lying in that agonisingly hot bath, willing it to do its work, the very thought of it made her feel sick.

'Fine. You go and sit down.'

When he got back, she was studying herself in her compact mirror.

'I don't think I look tired,' she said.

135

'Well – maybe not. I like the hair.' She'd got it drawn back off her face, and up into a sort of ponytail of curls. 'It must have grown fast.'

'Thanks, Matt.' She smiled at him. 'The curls are false.'

'Never! Good match. Anyway, very sexy.' But that seemed to have been the wrong thing to say too; she frowned slightly, shifted in her seat.

'So how're things?'

'Oh – you know. Fine.' She pulled off her gloves, her hands, unusually for her these days, bare of rings; in fact the only jewellery she was wearing was a very simple string of pearls. 'What about you?'

'Yeah, OK. Better than OK, actually, f— bloody brilliant. We are so busy, Scarlett, you'd never believe it. Last night Jim and me was in the office till after one, just catching up on paperwork.'

'Sounds great.'

'It is. The sky's nothing like the limit. We're looking for premises of our own, can't manage cadging off Robertson any longer.'

'Well – that's wonderful.'

Matt and Jimbo had agreed, as they yet again found themselves in the office at midnight one night, that they needed help.

'We can't go on like this,' said Matt. 'I mean it's great that we're so busy, but I'm knackered. What do you think we should do?'

'Take on some more staff. I reckon we need a couple of trainee negotiators. They'd be dirt cheap. And then a junior, maybe, to help Louise.'

'Sounds OK. But we can't fit them in here. We'll have to move. That'll be expensive too.'

'You don't think we could cadge another room off Robertson?'

'No,' said Matt, 'I don't. He's done enough for us. Anyway, it looks bad, us squashed into two rooms in his place. Let's talk to Louise, tell her to look out for somewhere. Once we've done the sums, that is.'

They did the sums, and told Louise their plans.

'Right,' she said, 'you're talking about taking on three people.'

'That's right, yeah.'

'Two trainee negotiators and a junior.'

'Correct.'

'So I'll have help too.'

'Yeah, that's right.'

'With what exactly?'

'Well – what you're doing now. The paperwork. The letters and filing and that.'

'So – they'll be blokes, will they? These negotiators?'

'Yeah, that's right. Two young chaps – already got feelers out—'

'Fine. Well, better be looking for a replacement for me then.'

'What?'

'You heard. I'm off.'

'Now Louise . . .'

'Don't you "now Louise" me, Jimbo Simmonds. How dare you. How dare you bring in some spotty boy lording it about, having to be spoon-fed for weeks, and you'll be expecting me to help him, I daresay?'

'Well – we did think you might, yes. As you're so fab at it all, know so many clients and that—'

Matt had imagined this bit of flattery would calm Louise down. He was wrong.

She stood up and picked up her bag, made for the door.

'Where you going?'

'I'm going home.'

'Louise, it's only half past five—'

'Yeah, and you've clearly forgotten that's when I'm supposed to leave. Not staying here, sending out mailings, hanging around waiting for you, buttering up clients, keeping them sweet, showing them particulars, having my legs looked at—'

'But—'

'You listen to me, you pair of jumped-up barrow boys. I'd say at least twenty-five per cent of the business we've got in the past two months has been down to me. Who suggested Mr Banks looked at the place in Camden Town, who sent Valerie bloody Hill over to that new office block in Chiswick, who found Joe Evans that space in Streatham, you just tell me that. And who missed four out of five lunch hours last week and neither of you even thought of getting me a sandwich? Eh? Well, I've had enough. Quite enough. Valerie Hill'd employ me tomorrow and not just as a secretary either, if I so much as hinted I'd like to work for her. So – I'm off. You're pathetic, the pair of you.'

They found themselves offering her the job of negotiator, bringing her salary up to a thousand – well, they'd started at seven fifty, and she'd picked up her bag again – and told her she could start the minute she found her own replacement. It had been an interesting half-hour.

Chapter 15

'That was just amazing.'

'Good.'

'I can't believe how amazing it was.'

'Pleased to be of service. You're not so bad yourself.'

'Well thanks a lot.' She punched him gently in the chest. 'You're such a romantic, you know.'

'Sorry. You're great too. Fantastic. Very, very sexy. How's that?'

'Better.'

He could tell she was disappointed; that she was hoping for the words. The three words. The ones girls wanted, especially after sex. But he couldn't.

He couldn't because he'd never felt them. Or rather it. Sometimes he wondered if he ever would. He presumed he'd know it when it came . . .

But what he did feel for this one, Gina she was called, short for Georgina, was pretty strong.

She was gorgeous, for a start. Not quite his usual type: light brown hair, long of course, with sort of blond streaks drifting in it. Huge grey eyes. Small heart-shaped face. Full, slightly pouty mouth. Very small, with firm, round little breasts. Great legs. Really great legs. And she was very, very good in bed.

She came a lot too, not just once, but over and over again, yelling each time louder and louder, biting him, clawing at him; and then when it was over, she would turn to him, smiling, with the face of an angel, and tell him she loved him. What man could ask for more?

He had met her at a party, given by a friend of Jimbo's. She had wandered in, alone, looking rather shy – that was a laugh, given what he had discovered about her pretty soon after – and he'd put her at about seventeen.

In fact she was twenty-two, and she worked in a fashion boutique in the King's Road, on commission, she was paid almost no salary. Nevertheless, she made quite a lot of money. She had a pale blue Mini, and she'd stuck transfers of big white daisies on the doors. She lived with six other girls in a flat in Barons Court; she smoked a lot of dope, but she said she'd had a really bad experience with LSD and it had scared her off for good.

She wasn't exactly posh, not like Eliza, but she was certainly a lot further up the class ladder than he was. Or any other girl he'd been out with. She'd been to a private school for a start. 'Only a day school though,' she said, as if that somehow made it quite different, and her mother had a car as well as her father and played a lot of bridge; they lived in Gerrards Cross, in a detached house, and employed not just a cleaner, but a gardener as well. Her father was a solicitor, a partner in a local practice, and her brother John was at university, reading law so that he could go into the firm. It was all very respectable, which made Gina's sexual amorality seem all the stranger to Matt. Scarlett would never have got into bed with someone the evening she met him, as Gina had done with him.

Louise was trying very hard not to lose her temper with Jenny Cox, the new junior. She had personally picked her, thinking correctly that her sweetly pretty baby face, long blond curls and rather unfashionably large bosom would provide an excellent distraction for clients kept waiting to see either her or one of the boys. It was her first job, 'a big chance for you,' Louise had said firmly, and as well as her physical assets Jenny did have extremely good shorthand and typing skills, obtained at Pitman's Secretarial College in Purley. However, she found the telephone a problem and frequently either failed to write down messages, or lost the scraps of paper she had entrusted them to. Two important would-be clients had already rung irately to enquire if their business was of any interest or not; and that morning Louise had discovered Jenny had spent the whole of the week's petty cash on a large, rather ornate white vase and some flowers to fill it with.

'I'm sorry, Miss Mullan,' Jenny said, her eyes filling with tears (and looking even larger and bluer), 'I thought the office looked a bit bleak and it would be nice for people to have something pretty to look at. I read in an article in *Woman's Own* that an attractive office helps morals—'

'Morale,' said Louise after a moment's thought.

'Yes, that's what I said. And—'

'Jenny,' said Louise, 'that might be true, but we can't afford lots of flowers. We have to improve morale in other ways. And anyway, you shouldn't have spent the firm's money without asking us. The petty cash is for coffee and tea and biscuits for visitors. I told you that on your first day. Better to concentrate on them.'

'Yes, Miss Mullan.' The tears brimmed over. 'I'm very sorry. I was only acting for the best.'

'I'm sure. Anyway, just remember that in future. Now, I want you to type a letter and then deliver it yourself, this afternoon; it's to go to Leicester Square and it's very important.'

'Yes, Miss Mullan.'

The phone rang. 'Shall I answer that?'

'Yes, please.'

She picked up the receiver rather gingerly: 'Simmonds and Shaw. Yes. Oh, yes, I do remember, yes. Well – oh, dear I'm not sure. Could you just wait while I ask—'

'Check, Jenny, not ask,' hissed Louise.

'Sorry, while I check. Thank you.'

She put her hand over the receiver and looked at Louise, her face rather flushed.

'I'm ever so sorry, Miss Mullan. They rang on Monday. I forgot. It's about the lunch.'

'What lunch?'

'Um – would it be the A Lunch. Something like that?'

'Let me speak to him,' said Louise, taking a deep breath. The A1 lunch club had been formed by some of the younger members of the property fraternity; it met monthly, in the private room of a pub in Dean Street, with the primary purpose of exercising that new skill, networking. By invitation only, the members pooled information about deals that were going through, city planning, useful contacts. Both Matt and Jimbo had been very excited at being invited to be members; they would not be pleased to hear that Jenny had failed to acquaint them of some important development.

'This is Louise Mullan speaking, negotiator for Simmonds and Shaw. I wonder if you could just – ah. I see. Yes. Well, I'm afraid both Mr Simmonds and Mr Shaw are out all day, seeing clients. So – no, they won't be able to attend. I'm so sorry. I do appreciate that. They were both called out at the last minute, and my secretary was about to ring you. But . . .' she perched on the edge of Jenny's desk, one long leg crossed over the other, and smiled brilliantly at some distant point in the room. 'I would very much like to attend in their place. I am fully acquainted with all our business and I'm confident it would be of mutual benefit. I am a senior negotiator here. I beg your pardon? Oh, no of course I don't mind.' She smiled into the phone. 'I like all-male gatherings. So – yes, I'll hold.' She waited, scarcely daring to breathe. 'Wonderful. Thank you so much. Twelve forty-five, upstairs at the Queen's Head. Fine.'

She put the phone down, smiled at Jenny. 'Now then, Jenny. If Mr Simmonds or Mr Shaw ask you where I am at lunchtime, say you're not sure. You don't know anything about the lunch, all right? And I think that article you mentioned was quite right, and I'm prepared to pay for the vase myself. And I think you should get a notebook out of the stationery cupboard and keep it for telephone messages. Now, can you take the letter I mentioned to you earlier please?'

'Yes, Miss Mullan. Thank you Miss Mullan.'

As Louise left, at twelve thirty, Jenny looked up at her and smiled. 'Have a good lunch, Miss Mullan. And if you don't mind me saying so, I like your hair like that.'

'Thank you, Jenny,' said Louise. She had put her hair up in a French pleat, thinking she would look more businesslike than with it tumbled onto her shoulders. 'Now, don't forget – you don't know where I am. If they ask.'

Jenny looked at her and her eyes widened even further.

'But I don't, Miss Mullan. I can't remember any of what was said on the phone. I never can.'

'Fine,' said Louise, and then added, 'but do start that notebook today, won't you?'

'Oh, I certainly will, Miss Mullan. Thank you.'

Louise got back from the lunch at three o'clock. She was flushed – not with alcohol, which she had been careful not to touch, unlike most of her fellow guests, but with excitement.

Matt looked at her suspiciously.

'Where've you been?'

'At a lunch,' said Louise carelessly.

'What lunch?'

'Oh, you know, one of the A1 property lunch clubs.'

'But you're – you're—'

'Yes?' She smiled at him sweetly. 'What am I?'

He clearly saw a big mistake coming and warded it off.

'You're quite – late. I thought we had a meeting this afternoon.'

'Of course we do. A presentation, isn't it? At three thirty.'

'Yeah. Yeah, that's right. And – did they actually invite you? The A1 people, I mean.'

'Of course. It was a last-minute thing. They had a vacancy and they said they'd like me to go.'

'Were there other – girls there?'

'No, there weren't actually. I didn't mind that at all though. It was very interesting, Matt. There was a lot of talk about planning gain, and also a new property page starting in the *Daily Sketch*. They're having a launch party apparently; I've just rung them to make sure we'll be invited. And the chap I spoke to, he said it was interesting a woman being a negotiator and he wants to interview me.'

'You?'

'Well, yes. I don't think there are any other women working here, are there? Except Jenny of course. Anyway, he's coming round tomorrow.'

'Well I presume he'll want to talk to us as well?'

'Oh, I don't think so,' said Louise, 'he wants to interview a girl negotiator, Matt. You seem to have missed that particular point. But it'll be good publicity for the firm, won't it? Got to go now, get ready for the presentation. See you in ten minutes or so, and you'd better tidy this office up a bit. It looks like a bomb hit it.'

'Yes, all right,' said Matt irritably.

'Eliza! Have you got a minute? And Fiona, if she's around?'

It was Annunciata Woburn, the features editor of *Charisma*. She was dazzlingly beautiful, with a great cloud of red hair and huge green eyes, and was breathtakingly clever; she had a double first in classics from Oxford and was married to Oliver Burton, the author of a much-admired biography of Sophocles and another of Chaucer. They were renowned as one of London's leading media couples and hosted a literary soirée at their house in Highbury every Tuesday evening. Eliza had been amazed to find her at *Charisma*, thinking she was exactly the sort of person Jack Beckham would have no truck with, but he adored her, and even while telling her not to give him any fucking intellectual rubbish, he hung on her words. And she was, to be fair, a brilliant journalist; she had worked on the *Times Literary Supplement* and before that on the *Manchester Guardian*, but she had also been a hugely successful columnist for the *Daily News*, writing first from Washington where she and Oliver had lived for a year and then from Paris. One of her best friends was Emma Northcott, Jeremy's sister with whom she had been at Oxford. Beckham had hired her against everyone's advice and everyone had been proved wrong, very wrong. Annunciata it was who had suggested a feature about strippers' boyfriends, 'so much more original and revealing than talking to the girls themselves', another about the relationship between cooking and sex, and a third about homosexuality and had indeed conducted it herself and then published a savage interview with Henry Brooke, the Home Secretary, over what she called the archaic illogicality – and moreover danger – of homosexuality remaining a crime.

Eliza was so much in awe of Annunciata that she found uttering more than two words in her presence almost impossible. She was forced into it today.

'Oh – Fiona's not here. She's out on appointments. Sorry. Maybe later in the day . . . She did have to make an awful lot of excuses for her.'

'OK, I'll catch her then. You'll do for now though. I'm just trawling the office for ideas, I'm looking for people for a feature which I'm calling The Intropreneurs.'

Eliza tried to look politely interested.

'It's about people, young people, who are making waves from a base of absolutely nothing. And who haven't quite arrived, but are almost certainly going to. Know what I mean?'

'Um – think so, yes.'

'Not been to public school, not been at university necessarily, just bright young people who've got an idea and gone for it. I'm sure there must be lots in the fashion business – but if you know anyone outside it as well, just give me their names.'

'Should I sound them out first?'

Annunciata considered this for a moment; then, 'No, don't think so, because then if I don't use them, they could be disappointed. I'm just getting a directory together for a start. No great rush: any time in the next week.'

'Fine. Yes. I'll tell Fiona, shall I?'

'Please. Right. Like my boots?' She did this, switching from the seriously cerebral to frivolous within the same second.

Eliza looked at her boots: they were softest white kid, with a wide cuff. 'They're beautiful,' she said truthfully, 'they look like Courrèges.'

'They are Courrèges,' said Annunciata.

She was clearly extremely rich as well as extremely clever.

Eliza went back to her office and pulled a sheet of paper towards her. There must be lots of people. Maddy. Esmond. Jerome Blake. She managed ten, then realised they were all in fashion and she wanted to impress Annunciata by being more than a fashion bird-brain. She thought for a bit, then rang Charles, asked if he knew anyone; he said he didn't think so, there wasn't much working-class talent on the stock exchange. Then he said, 'Tell you what, though, Matt Shaw might be an idea. He's a real working-class hero.'

She remembered dancing with Matt at the party that night and smiled. She liked Matt; he was very sweet. Well, maybe sweet was the wrong word. Bit too stroppy and pleased with himself to be sweet. But – quite sexy. Well actually, very sexy. He was certainly an amazing dancer. Anyway, he'd probably be really chuffed. Free publicity. Yes, it was a great idea. She'd call him.

'I love you so much.'

'Do you really?'

He looked hurt. 'Yes, of course I do. Don't you believe me?'

'I – yes, I suppose so.'

'Is there – is there something the matter? Because you've been – not quite yourself, not quite my lovely laughing girl for some little time now. Just tell me what it is, I'll put it right, I swear. I can't bear to think you're not happy.'

As if he could. As if she could tell him. It was too complicated, too difficult. And too dangerous.

To say, 'I was pregnant with your child. And I got rid of it. Just had it – flushed it away.'

That was one of the worst things; wondering what they had done with it, her baby. That minute, more-than-half-formed human being. She had found an article, complete with very beautiful and graphic photographs, about the development of the embryo in an old issue of *Life* magazine, had tried not to even look at it, had found herself studying it compulsively, over and over again. At eight weeks, the age of her baby when she had had the abortion, it had had a completely recognisable human face, jointed limbs, even tiny fingers. Its heart, liver, lungs and sex organs were formed; it had been a very-much-alive human being. And what had she done, as it nestled within her, growing, sweetly safe, towards its birth? Killed it. Had it ripped out of her. Just wrenched away. And . . .

'No, honestly, David, I'm fine. Just a bit – a bit tired.'

She managed to smile at him, thinking what would he have said, or done, if he'd known, and that she'd had no right to take the decision on her own, without discussing it, that it had not been just her baby, to do what she liked with, it had been his baby. He had put it there, within her, they had created it together. He might be terribly angry: which she could have dealt with. Or terribly hurt: which she couldn't.

'Well, I think we can do something about that.'

'Really?'

'Yes. I think we can go on a little vacation. Just the two of us. For a few days, a week, maybe. To Venice, or Florence, somewhere really romantic. How would you like that?'

'I – well I – well it would be wonderful of course. But—'

'But what?'

How could she explain the but? That she was finding it so difficult to cope with everything at the moment, that she woke up most days feeling completely shattered, that she often cried herself to sleep at night – she could hide that for a day or two, while he visited London, but not for a longer time, not day after day. No, it would have to be postponed – while she pulled herself together, got her emotions under control, learnt to cope with what she had done: which had been the sensible, indeed the responsible thing.

'But what?' he asked again.

'Oh – it's just that my schedule is all done for the next month or so.'

'Can't you change any of it?'

'Not really, David. And then I'm going on a course. I'm hoping to move to BOAC, I told you, and—'

'Oh well,' he said, 'it was just an idea. A little later in the year, maybe.' He looked hurt; he could see she wasn't really very keen on the idea. Poor David. And she did truly love him; she hated to hurt him. But – it would be worse to hurt him more.

'I'm sorry,' she said, putting her arms round him, giving him a kiss. 'So sorry. And yes – later in the year would be lovely.'

But she couldn't go on like this, crying all the time, not sleeping. Diana, who had been watching her worriedly for weeks, suggested she ask the doctor for some sleeping pills.

'You look terrible, Scarlett, completely exhausted. What you really need is a holiday.'

'I don't want a holiday. Who do you suggest I go with? My mother?'

'Of course not but—'

'Look, Diana, just leave me alone. I'll be all right.'

Diana looked hurt.

'I'm sorry. I just feel so – so despairing.'

'I know. It's all right, I understand. But please talk to the doctor. I'm sure he could help.'

Scarlett was sure he couldn't, but she was wrong; he prescribed her a month's worth of sleeping pills. Within a week she felt a little better, less exhausted at least, and less tearful. And, even, less angry.

But she still felt physically frail and in need of a holiday.

She checked out some destinations and settled on a tiny Greek island called Trisos, small and peaceful with its one hotel and a tiny harbour.

And it was absolutely – well, words failed Scarlett. Perfect was under-rating it. After a long journey – a flight to Athens and then a long boat trip from Piraeus, she had arrived in a deep grey dusk, was led up to her hotel by the ferryman, fell onto a comfortable if rather hard bed in a small, almost cell-like room – and woke in the morning to a world of dazzling light. She had never seen or imagined anything like that light; it was positively celestial – shining, white, that shamed full noon English sunshine into shadow. Her hotel, little more than a taverna, was one of a cluster of white-domed houses, carved out of the brilliant blue sky; she leaned out of the window and felt the sun not just on her but in her, beating down to her bones, and smiled to greet it. It might only be spring in England and a rainy one at that, but summer had certainly come to Greece.

She sat on the small terrace, framed with trailing begonias, and ate figs and yogurt and honey and drank orange juice and then strong sweet coffee while lizards sunbathed beside her and seagulls whirled and called above her head, and felt she might actually have landed in paradise. Her hosts, Demetrios and Larissa, were charming, with the Greek gift of warmth and ease; she had one of only six rooms, and her fellow guests –

all clearly younger and less exhausted than she – were already gone for the day.

They directed her to the beach, only about two hundred yards away, by way of a tiny meandering path; she wandered down, settled under a straw umbrella and gave herself up to pleasure.

Five honeyed days later, she felt mended again; restored to herself, the feeble, fretful Scarlett gone, she truly felt, for good. She had done very little: swum when she got too hot to sunbathe, sunbathed when she wanted a return to the golden warmth. Somewhere halfway through the day she would wander through the tiny village, with its narrow, white streets, and buy herself fruit, bread, feta cheese and huge, misshapen tomatoes and make herself a picnic, which she ate either on the beach or the small terrace of the hotel. Then – a sleep, on her bed, its muslin drapes saving her from one of the few perils of the place, mosquitoes, and when she woke, another swim, a walk and then the first glass of ouzo at some small taverna or another, and later, dinner which she ate against a background of a million crickets chattering, or so it sounded, and a sliver of moon carving itself out of the dark, still-just-blue sky.

She was enchanted by what passed for a menu: a visit to the kitchen, to see the food on offer and then to choose, from moussaka, wonderful baked vegetables, aubergines, courgettes, tomatoes, and then huge omelettes, and of course fish, wonderful fish, fresh from the sea, brought in that very evening.

One day she hired a boat, a small fishing vessel with a noisy, rather smelly outboard and a tiny sail. Its owner looked about sixty and was, Larissa told her, little more than forty, bark-brown and half toothless. He took her on an enchanted journey to adjoining coves, to tiny islands little more than large rocks, even taught her the rudiments of sailing when a breeze sprang most obligingly up.

Another day she hired a motor scooter and took herself on a journey a little way into the hills – surprisingly green for Greece, 'Trisos is green,' Demetrios told her, 'we, like Mykonos, have much rain in the winter' – and to other small, white villages, slumbering in the heat.

On her last but one day, a man arrived: tall, dark, English, quite young, around thirty she would have said, single – or at least alone. He was rather good-looking, with floppy dark hair and grey eyes fringed with almost girlishly long lashes, and he wore steel-rimmed spectacles. She had tried to be friendly, had smiled at him and asked if he was having a good time as they passed on the terrace before dinner, and he smiled almost anxiously, shook her hand and said he was finding the island delightful, 'as I am sure you are too', but he was clearly phobically private, buried himself rather ostentatiously in his book while eating his dinner and then disappeared upstairs. She supposed he must be taking, like her, a restoratively cheap holiday; it was only when she was leaving, paying her bill, that she learnt from Larissa that he was looking for somewhere to build a house for himself. His name, she discovered, through peering surreptitiously through the hotel visitors' book, was Mark Frost. Very appropriate. She hoped – rather meanly, for what could it matter to her? – that he would not settle on Trisos. He wasn't worthy of it.

Had anyone told her she would be happy to holiday alone, with no entertainment or company whatsoever on offer, she would not have believed them; nor that she would not think of and pine for David constantly, but he scarcely entered her consciousness, and then only as a distant happy presence, no longer a source of bitterness. She felt indeed the opposite of lonely there, surrounded as she was by smiling and friendliness, and her own thoughts and growing happiness; she read a great deal, and wrote a few postcards, but for most of the time she just reflected, and most happily, on the lovely place she was in and what it was giving her. And when her five days came to an end, she felt only a sweet sadness to be leaving; and waved goodbye to the island through smiling, grateful tears.

Eliza was sitting in the Markham pub, in the King's Road, waiting for Matt. She was early; she had arranged to meet him at six, but she had finished scouting round the wonderful stalls of Antiquarius – the magazine was doing a spread on vintage jewellery – and didn't really want to hang around the shops any longer. One of the few disadvantages of working in fashion was that shopping as an activity rather lost its charm. She ordered herself a gin and tonic and was flipping through the pages of the new *Vogue*, when she saw him coming in, looking slightly nervous.

She called to him. 'Matt! Over here.'

'Hello, Eliza. Sorry I'm late.'

He was dressed in a rather sharp suit, and a blue-and-white shirt with a white collar and cuffs. He looked very – well, very cool. And sexy. He was very sexy, she decided. She'd always vaguely been aware of it, from that very first time on Waterloo station – but ever since the party, and

The Dance in capital letters as she thought of it, she'd realised he had whatever it was in very large quantities.

And – what was it exactly? She'd often tried to define it and failed. You knew it when you saw it, that was for sure; the physical unsettling of yourself, the need to acknowledge it, a sudden change in atmosphere from social to sexual. It wasn't looks and it wasn't charm, although it could accompany both those things; it certainly wasn't ease or comfort, indeed it induced a rather raw intensity into a situation . . . anyway, it was standing in front of her right now. She smiled, stood up and on an impulse leaned forward to kiss him on the cheek. And felt him flinch just slightly and wondered if that was shyness or shock – or simply that he didn't find her sexy back. Probably the latter.

She smiled at him, suddenly nervous, and sat down abruptly. 'Hello, Matt. You look very smart. Like the suit.'

'Oh – thanks.' He smiled back at her just slightly uncertainly.

'What would you like to drink?'

'Oh – no—' this clearly threw him, 'I can't have you buying me a drink.'

'Yes, you can. It's on expenses.'

'Oh – OK then.' He grinned at her. 'I'll have a beer please. Well, a – a lager, you know.'

'Course.'

She fetched it and a gin and tonic for herself, and two packets of crisps, settled back in her chair.

'So – how's things?'

'Oh – pretty good. Yes. We've expanded quite a lot, taken on three staff. So there's six of us altogether now.'

'Really? That's very exciting. You've done so well, Matt.'

'Oh,' he said, offering her a cigarette, 'this is only the beginning. I've got bigger plans than this, believe you me.'

'Like what?'

'Well—' He produced a rather nice Colibri lighter; he really was moving up in the world, she thought. The old Matt would have had a box of matches. 'Well, we're hoping to move into the development side. That's our next plan. But – don't know when. So, what's this about then?'

'You see—'

'Eliza! Hello. What on earth are you doing here? I thought you were working late.'

She looked up; it was Jeremy. Jeremy with a couple of friends. Or

149

were they colleagues? Impossible to tell. For some reason she wasn't particularly pleased to see him.

'I am working,' she said, just slightly cool. 'I'm about to tell Matt here about a feature. In the magazine. I'm not sure if you've met. Matt Shaw, Jeremy Northcott. Matt was in the army with Charles.'

'Really?' She could see Jeremy looking at Matt slightly doubtfully. Then he said, 'How do you do.'

'Great, thanks. Pleased to meet you,' said Matt.

'Right. Well, we'll leave you to it. Enjoy your drink.' His companions had moved on towards the bar; he bent down, kissed Eliza's cheek, then hissed in her ear 'clients'. And then more audibly, 'Let me know when you've finished, maybe we could have a bite.'

'Oh – well maybe, yes.' She smiled at him, then turned back to Matt. 'Sorry.'

'That's OK. Who's he, then?'

'Just a friend.'

There was a silence; the bar was quite empty, and Jeremy and his companions were making the usual, rather predictable noises, loud laughter, a joke clearly told, more loud laughter. Eliza felt uncomfortable without being quite sure why.

'Anyway,' she said, 'you'll want to know why I've asked you here.'

'I do rather, yes. '

'Well, you know I work on a magazine now.'

'Oh, right. What's your job there, then?'

'I'm called assistant fashion editor. But I'm just a dogsbody really.'

'Like it?'

'Oh, Matt, I love it. I'm so happy there, I actually look forward to—'

'I know. Monday mornings. Me too. Most important thing of all, I reckon, enjoying your job. It's what you spend most of the time at, after all. Course, most people see it a bit differently. Live for the weekends and that. Your friend Maddy, I reckon she feels the same.'

'I think she does. Well, we're all so lucky, doing such interesting things.'

'Yeah, that's true. My dad, he's a builder, that's really hard, specially in the winter. He feels the cold something – really badly. And one of my little brothers, not so little now, he works for an insurance company, so boring—'

'Haven't you got a sister?'

150

'Yeah, I have. Now she's one of us. Likes Mondays, I mean.'

'What does she do?'

'She's an air hostess. Works for BEA.'

'Goodness. That's very impressive.'

'Yeah. Well, my mum certainly thinks so.' He grinned at her.

'And is your mother impressed by what you do?'

'Yes, she is. My dad, he just worries about it. Reckons I should get a steady job, you know?'

'I think so, yes.'

'Your parents pleased about what you do? I suppose they are.'

'Not really,' said Eliza, laughing, 'they think I should be married. Not working at all.'

'Married! What, to some rich bloke, I suppose.'

'Ideally, yes. Did you know Charles was getting married?'

'Yeah, I did. He asked if I could help him find a flat. Said he'd ask me to the wedding, matter of fact.'

'Really?' She knew, try as she might, there was a touch of surprise in her voice, hated herself for it.

'Yes, really,' he said.

She struggled to put it right. 'Well, that'd be lovely. Although I'm afraid I'll be looking like something out of a Christmas cracker, I'm a bridesmaid, and his fiancée's very keen on frills. Pink ones. Well you won't have to look at me.'

'I think I'd find that rather difficult,' he said and his eyes on her were quite serious suddenly. 'Whatever you were wearing.' And then he flushed and said, 'Another cigarette?' and she took one, flustered herself, surprised at the sudden move of the conversation from formal to personal.

'Thank you,' she said. There was a silence, then, 'And – you're not married? Or engaged or anything?'

'Not likely. I'm married to the job. Wouldn't have time to spend on a wife. I hardly ever go home. I've got my own place now,' he added. 'Old warehouse, on the river.'

'Sounds lovely. Right, let me come to the point. This magazine I work for, *Charisma*, the features editor has asked us all if we can suggest people who are doing well, really well, and—' She stopped suddenly. Careful, Eliza, you'll say something tactless if you don't watch out.

'You're not thinking of putting me in this article, are you?'

'I am, actually. If you'd like it.'

'Sounds all right so far. Tell me more. Who else is in it? You got Charles, I suppose, he's doing all right for himself.'

'No, not Charles. No, it's got to be people working for themselves. With their own companies.'

'Yeah? Right. Well, that's me.' He smiled at her expectantly. 'Anything else?'

'Well – well, yes. It's also about people who haven't been to university, or –or well, you know – public school. That sort of thing.' She was aware she was talking rather fast now. 'Self-starters, I suppose you could say.'

'Oh yeah?' His expression had changed; it was wary, there was no amusement in it. 'You mean working-class heroes, don't you? I keep reading about them – us. Lot of us about. All of a sudden.'

'Really? Well, yes, I think it's because of the times we're living in, don't you – really, really new world, isn't it, completely – completely classless – and thank goodness for that—'

'Eliza!' It was Jeremy again. He was walking to the door with the rest of the party. 'Don't disappear, I want to see you.'

He waved them off, then came over and sank down beside her. He was, she realised, quite drunk.

'God, I'm knackered. Been at it since noon. Bloody hard work. We're off to dinner at Quags now, you wouldn't like to come, my darling, would you? It'd be fantastic if you did, really help—'

'Jeremy—'

'Yuh? Or, sorry, you haven't finished. Don't mind me, I'll just sit quietly for a bit. Can I get you another drink, Matt?'

'No,' said Matt, 'thank you. I'm just leaving.'

'Leaving!' said Eliza. 'But Matt, I haven't finished explaining—'

'You've explained quite enough, thanks. And the answer's no. I'm sorry, Eliza, but I don't want to be cannon fodder for some patronising article about the working classes making good. I don't want to be held up as some sort of cretin from a secondary mod who's doing well in spite of it, and isn't that wonderful, he can actually run a business, even if he doesn't speak properly, he can add up and read and write, and aren't we all just so astonished by that, who'd have thought it, and isn't it great of us to write about him in our very posh magazine.'

'Matt – please – you've got it all wrong.'

'I don't think so. If you want to know, I think the whole idea stinks. It's condescending crap and I don't want any part of it.'

'Look – Mr Shaw.' Jeremy had been listening quite intently, looking at Matt with increasing distaste. 'Could you stop talking like that to Eliza, please? You're being pretty rude, I'd say, and it's completely unwarranted. It might be better if you left.'

'Yeah, I will, I'm going right now. And you two can sit and discuss how ungrateful I am, over dinner at – what was it? Quags? Yeah. Have a great evening.'

And he stalked out of the pub.

'Ghastly chap,' said Jeremy. 'How on earth did you get mixed up with him?'

'Oh, just shut up,' said Eliza, 'you were a lot of help, weren't you?'

'Well, I thought I was, yes. He had a nerve talking to you like that. And the feature sounded like a great idea to me. He should have been bloody grateful.'

'Jeremy,' said Eliza, 'I can't believe how stupid you're being. That's the whole point, why he was so upset, him feeling he was supposed to be grateful.'

'Darling.' He put out his hand, tried to take hers. She snatched it away.

'Don't. And don't call me darling. And you can find someone else to sweet-talk your clients at dinner. I'm going home.'

Chapter 16

'So – it's terminal?'

'Well.' The consultant looked down at his desk. 'I wouldn't say terminal.'

'Incurable though?'

'Er – yes. I'm afraid so.'

'I'd call that terminal. Actually. What can you do for me?'

'Well, there are drugs, of course. Very good ones, these days. Which will delay the – the progress of the disease quite a bit.'

'And – how fast will it progress? How long have I got?'

'Hard to say. It does vary from patient to patient.'

'There must be some kind of an average.'

'Maybe – maybe five years. But I really couldn't say anything very definite.'

'Now look, I don't want to tell anyone yet, how long do you think I can keep it to myself?'

'Not long. A few weeks, perhaps. I'm surprised your wife hasn't noticed anything, to be frank.'

'Well, she has a lot of worries. And I always was a clumsy bugger. If you could give me a prescription for one of those drugs—'

'I could write to your GP, you should be able to get them on the NHS.'

'Please don't. It might get out locally. I'll pay for them until such time as I think my wife can cope with the news.'

He was a brave chap, the consultant thought, watching him as he walked out of the room; dealing with this on his own. Hopeless to think he could keep it from his wife for long though. Poor old bugger. Not a nice way to go.

✿   ✿   ✿

154

'Matt!' It was Jimbo, sounding excited.

'Yeah, what?' He still felt out of sorts about the evening before, embarrassed even, when he'd calmed down. She hadn't meant any harm, probably thought she was doing him a favour. But him: what a wanker. It had changed his view of Eliza, uncomfortably so. She clearly liked the prat, went out with him; how could she? He hauled his mind back to the present with an effort. 'Yeah?' he said again.

'It's Paul Crosse. He wants to meet us. Can you do tomorrow? Around eleven?'

Paul Crosse was an aggressive young developer who had already made a lot of money. More than Matt, much more than Matt. And Crosse had come to them, asking them to find him a building in the Elephant and Castle area; it was developing fast, the ideal location, cheek by jowl with Waterloo, but cheaper. He wanted it simply to develop and then sell on, 'for offices. Many as I can get in'.

Matt had heard of a building that was going begging. It was in an appalling state, next to a bomb site, infested with rats, the roof falling in on one side, with consequent damage to floors and ceilings. Nevertheless, it was a building, it didn't have to be designed or built; it just needed some skilful renovation. And Paul Crosse had said, over a pint after the viewing, that it was what he wanted in a way, but needed more work than he was prepared to take on, and he had his hands very full at the moment. And Matt had said, after taking a deep breath and swig of rather warm beer, that he might be able to help.

'What we could do,' he said, 'is develop it for you. Get it ready for you to sell on. I know that area, I got very good contacts there. I know the planning people as well, of course,' he added, not entirely truthfully.

'And, what'd be in it for you?'

'A cut in the profits,' said Matt, 'say ten per cent. Just an idea.'

Paul Crosse said he'd think about it. And a week later agreed.

'But you'll have to earn it, mind. A weekly report, and a regular site meeting, that's all I want to do with it.'

'That's fine,' said Matt, 'that's absolutely OK. That's how we like to work too.'

'Good. Right then. Now – how about a drink?'

Simmonds and Shaw, property developers, were on their way.

❋   ❋   ❋

Matt walked back to the office on his own; Jimbo had gone on to meet another client. He felt elated, powerful, totally self-assured once more. Today had been special, a huge leap towards the future. He was getting there; he was within grabbing distance of success. It felt suddenly and wonderfully near. And it felt very good. Very good indeed. And it had certainly taken his mind off Eliza.

Things felt slightly less good when he actually reached the office. It was empty, apart from Jenny, who was sitting on her desk, reading a newspaper with a feverish intensity. She looked up at him, and he saw she was flushed, her huge blue eyes brilliant.

'Oh, Mr Shaw,' she said, 'isn't it exciting?'

Matt was slightly surprised she knew about the new deal, but maybe Jim had rung.

'It is, yes,' he said.

'In the paper, I mean, fancy! I think it's wonderful. I've never known anyone be in a paper before. Except when my nan died that is, and the local paper put in about her funeral. That was because she was once the Carnival queen back in the 1930s and . . .'

'Jenny, what's in the paper?'

'It's Miss Mullan, Mr Shaw. Here, look. Only you will give it me back, won't you, I want to show my mum. She'll never believe it. '

'Yes, of course I'll give it back,' said Matt impatiently. 'I'll just – just take it in my office. And I'd like some tea, Jenny, if it's not too much trouble.'

Matt stalked into his office and slammed the door; he felt slightly sick. He sat down at his desk and started to read the article. It was in the new property pages of the *Daily Sketch*; they had all attended the launch a few weeks earlier and while he and Jimbo had spent much of the evening talking to each other, Louise had been circling the room like a hula hoop. And this was clearly the result.

'A new breed of negotiator,' it was headed. 'Not many women make it in the world of property development, but Louise Mullan looks set to shin up the scaffolding any minute now. She started work as a secretary at Shaw and Simmonds, a small commercial agency, less than a year ago and now does up to fifty per cent of the negotiating work herself. An attractive brunette, Miss Mullan smiled happily as she sipped her orange juice. (She never drinks on duty.) "I love my work," she said, "and I think it's an absolutely ideal job for girls. It involves all the things we're best at: spotting a bargain, matching up people and places, and doing a dozen things at once. I think the sky's the limit for us, in the property world."

'So it's hard hats off to Miss Mullan; we wish her all the best.'

As if this wasn't hard enough to swallow, there was then a photograph of Louise, sitting on a pile of breeze blocks in a half-completed building, swinging her long legs, a hard hat perched on her head, and smiling happily.

Somehow, even the thought of the Paul Crosse project and the twenty grand minimum they were going to make from it could not compete with that.

Eliza was sitting in the Palm Court of the Ritz, waiting for Jeremy, when she heard a joyful cry of 'Eliza!' and was smothered in a headily perfumed embrace.

'Mariella! Oh, how lovely to see you. What are you doing here?'

'What would I be doing here? I am shopping.'

It was the loveliest surprise: Mariella was easing herself gracefully out of her red jacket, revealing an exquisitely simple matching shift (Cardin, Eliza thought), slinging it at the hovering waiter. 'I am exploring this wonderful new London I keep reading about. I have already been to the King's Road, and Carnaby Street, where else should I go? This is so wonderful, that you should be here. May I join you for a moment?'

'Yes, of course, I'd love that. Come and sit down.' She called the waiter over, asked for another glass of champagne. 'Mariella – are you here alone?'

'Yes, quite alone. Giovanni had work to do, and he said he could spare me for a few days.'

'I wish I'd known you were coming.'

'I thought of telling you, but I know how busy you are. Anyway, this is extremely nice. I don't suppose you are free for dinner?'

'No – well – no, I really can't. I'm waiting for my – my boyfriend now, we're not even going out with friends or clients, or I'd ask you to join us.'

'*Cara*, I know about clients and how important they are. Tomorrow perhaps? We could eat here.'

'That would be wonderful. Thank you. Now, let me see, you must go to Woollands, the 21 shop and to Woolfe's to New Generation, that's the boutique I helped launch.'

'You? Eliza, you are a wonderful girl, the things you have done. And I have done nothing with my life, not really—'

'Oh, no not really, only married—' She stopped. 'One of the richest men in the world,' she had been going to say but it suddenly sounded rude, as if it implied Mariella was a gold-digger. She saw Jeremy weaving his way across the foyer with a certain relief.

'Jeremy! Over here! I want you to meet my friend Mariella Crespi, from Milan.'

He bent and kissed Eliza, then made a small bow over Mariella's hand – God, he was so bloody charming – and smiled into her great dark eyes.

'How lovely to meet you, Mariella,' he said. 'Jeremy Northcott.'

He was looking particularly gorgeous in a light grey flannel suit, exquisitely cut, and a light blue shirt. She saw Mariella taking him in, approving him, clearly doing more than approve of him.

'It is very lovely to meet you too,' she said.

Over dinner the next evening, she cooed about him for some time.

'So elegant, Eliza, so charming, so good-looking. So very much the English gentleman. You have found, I think, the perfect man.'

'Yes, well he is, I suppose,' said Eliza.

'You suppose! Eliza, you are so English. So stating under, is that right?'

'Understating. Nearly right.'

'And he clearly adores you, too.'

'I – well, I'm not sure about that,' said Eliza truthfully.

'Is he rich?'

'Terribly rich.'

'Well then.' Mariella sat back. 'Truly perfect. You must marry him.'

'I'm afraid that's not quite up to me,' said Eliza. And then in an attempt to change the subject, 'Now, Mariella, how was today? And what did you think of Young Generation?'

'It was very nice. I bought two dresses from Jean Varon.'

'Absolutely my favourite evening dresses in the world. And what are you doing tomorrow?'

'Eliza, you are trying too hard to change the subject. I want to know about Jeremy. Is this a serious relationship? Would you like to be married to this perfect man?'

'I – I'm not sure,' said Eliza. 'Maybe because my job is so important to me – but then Jeremy knows that, and he respects it, he's really interested in my career and he's even a champion of working mothers.'

'Really? Now that is very unusual, for an Englishman, I think?'

'Very. He thinks it's important for women not to waste their brains and training.'

'Yes, I see. Well, so there is no problem anywhere, then?'

'No. Not really. Maybe I just don't love him enough, maybe he doesn't love me enough.'

'Oh, *cara*,' said Mariella, 'if everything else is right, there is enough love. Love grows, with the marriage. Believe me, I should know. It is clear to me that he is quite perfect for you, and he is simply waiting for the right minute. And when he does ask you, I want to be one of the very first to know.'

'You will be,' said Eliza, 'if he does. Now can I see your Jean Varon dresses and all the other things you've bought after dinner?'

She was discovering that however heavily gilded it might be, Mariella did live in a cage. Giovanni might genuinely love her, he might be the soul of generosity, but he wanted her near him almost all the time; and when she was not, he had to know where she was and what she was doing every minute of the day.

'I could never, ever have an affair,' Mariella said, 'Giovanni would find out in days. But I do not wish to have an affair,' she said, with her dazzling smile, 'I love him very, very much, and more all the time. As I told you, love grows. It is probably just as well, in Italy you can be sent to prison for adultery.'

'What!'

'Oh, yes. So you could never book into a hotel under a false name, or anything like that, you have to be terribly careful.'

'Good heavens.'

'But anyway, I love Giovanni, very dearly. No one else is good enough, handsome enough, charming enough. Except perhaps your Jeremy, *cara*! Don't look like that, I am only teasing you. Giovanni is a very difficult play to follow.'

Eliza was constantly enchanted by Mariella's take on the English language.

She thought a lot about Mariella's philosophy of marriage in the weeks that followed: that if everything else was right, love would grow. She wondered if it would work for her. And perhaps more importantly for Jeremy.

'This has been so lovely.'

'Hasn't it? I've had just the best time.'

'No, I've had the best time.' Scarlett leaned across the table, gave him a kiss. 'I love, love, love New York.'

'Me too. Always have.'

'And the Carlyle is just – well, gorgeous. Is it true it was JFK's favourite hotel?'

'Absolutely true. And you know something else, every single US president has stayed in it.'

'Every single US president and me. And you. Oh, David. It's been so heavenly. Thank you!'

'I won't say it was entirely my pleasure; I think that would be a little inaccurate.'

'Certainly would. Very mutual, the pleasure's been. And I love my Kelly bag so much. You are just so generous.'

'Well, I'm glad you love it. Do you know the story about it?'

'No. No, I didn't know there was one. Except that it was designed for Grace Kelly.'

'Not quite. It was designed sometime in the Thirties, I think – but it was named after her because she famously used it to conceal her pregnancy from the paparazzi.'

'What do you mean?'

'Well, she held it across her stomach. So it didn't show. Of course it was very early days, or it wouldn't have done the job. Later on she'd have needed a cabin trunk.'

'Why should she want to stop it showing?' said Scarlett. A knot of hurt had suddenly formed somewhere near her heart. 'She was married to her prince by then, I presume.'

'Yes, of course. But – she was shy, nervous. And women are very sensitive about these things, you see. Something so intensely personal.'

'Is that so?' said Scarlett and she could hear her voice getting harsh. 'Well, I suppose you would know.'

She met his eyes, those amazing green Berenson eyes, and saw them first puzzled, then wary; then his whole face changed, into something carefully and neatly composed.

'Well of course,' he said. 'Is that so terrible?'

'No,' she said, 'of course it's not terrible. I just thought it was a bit –

odd. That a married woman should be sensitive about concealing her pregnancy. But it is a very sweet story.' She smiled with a huge effort. 'Let's have another cocktail and then I want to go out to dinner. You said you'd take me to Sardi's.'

'And I will. I've booked a table. Can you be ready in ten minutes?'

She had been so looking forward to going to the legendary Sardi's; now she wasn't so sure. She felt irritable, disorientated, and she knew why, even as she acknowledged it as unreasonable. Any talk of pregnancy hurt; hurt in a confused, desperate way. To hear it discussed lightly, almost jokily, by David was almost unbearable.

And however often she told herself that what had happened was not his fault, that it was she, if anyone, who had done the wrong thing, she realised, as she combed her hair and sprayed on some scent before rejoining him, she was still dreadfully, painfully angry with him.

Chapter 17

Mr and Mrs Geoffrey Judd request the pleasure of your company at the wedding of their daughter Juliet Carol to Mr Charles Edward Fullerton-Clark at 3 p.m. on Friday 26 June 1964 at Summercourt, Wellesley, Wiltshire.

RSVP Mrs Adrian Fullerton-Clark.
Summercourt, Wellesley.

All in perfect, curvy script on ivory card and 'Matthew Shaw' written in bold black ink at the top. He'd never expected to see his name on anything like that. He'd never really expected the invitation at all, had thought it was just Charles being polite; and especially after the business with Eliza. Which she was sure to have told him about.

There was another sheet of paper inside with a map of how to find Wellesley – obviously that was the entire address, no street name or anything – and a list of local hotels if people wanted to stay. It arrived at the office, together with a scrawled card inside from Charles apologising, 'Sorry, don't know your home address. Please come. It'd be so nice for me. Let me know if you want to bring anyone. Charles.' And then, 'PS Morning dress.'

That would be the monkey-suit number; he was probably the only person they'd had to spell it out to. He couldn't go. He just couldn't.

He kept it in his drawer for a bit, then left it on top of the desk by mistake while he was rummaging in the drawer, where it was spotted by Louise.

'Gosh, Matt, you are going up in the world. First a trendy party, then a society wedding.'

'Yeah, well, I won't be going to it.'

'Why on earth not?'

'Because I don't want to.'

'Matt Shaw, you need your head examined.'

He took it home, and left it on the kitchen table, where of course Gina found it.

'Crikey, Matt, I didn't know you had friends like this.'

'I don't. I never set eyes on the Judds and I won't know anyone there.'

'You could take me. Sounds a bit funny, replying to the bridegroom's parents. Is Summercourt where he lives?'

'Yes.'

'Posher and posher. Why isn't it being held at her parents' place?'

'I have no idea.'

'So how do you know this Charles person, then?'

'We were in the army together. Before he went off and became an officer, that is.'

He could hear the bitterness in his own voice.

'He must be a pretty nice chap.'

'What, to ask me to his wedding?'

'Oh Matt, don't be so touchy.'

'Well, that's what you meant.'

'No, it wasn't, I mean because you obviously don't see him very often and he hasn't forgotten you.'

'How do you know I don't see him very often?'

'Oh, for fuck's sake,' said Gina. 'Let's change the subject. But you should go, you're crazy.'

He didn't reply to the invitation immediately; he wasn't actually sure how to, what words you used. Maybe he could just ring Charles. But then that might lead to an argument and he didn't want Charles to be upset.

Two evenings later, he was having supper with Scarlett and after several stiff drinks showed her the invitation.

'That sounds like fun,' she said, 'or interesting anyway. Actually those upmarket weddings are a bit dull. I went to one last year. It was all over by six in the evening.'

'What, no dancing?'

'Nope. Just the service, then champagne and canapés on the lawn, speeches, cutting the cake and off the bride and groom go. But still nice he asked you.'

'Not you as well,' said Matt.

'What's that supposed to mean?'

'Everyone seems to think it's really good of Charles to invite me to his wedding. As if I was a charity case. Anyway, I'm not going.'

'Matt, that's just completely ridiculous. Why on earth not?'

'Because I'd feel like a charity case. I might drink out of the wrong side of the glass. And anyway, I've fallen out with his sister.'

'How on earth did you do that?'

'It's – complicated.'

'Well, I just might understand if I really concentrate. I'm not that stupid. Tell me.'

He told her.

'Matt, that's awful. I'm ashamed of you, I really am. So childish. How old are you?'

'Oh, for God's sake.' He glared at her, got out his cigarettes.

'You're smoking too many of those things, you know,' she said. 'There's some new research says smoking's very bad for you.'

'Oh Scarlett, give me a break. I like smoking. I couldn't cope without it.'

'Well anyway, I think you should apologise to Eliza or whatever her name is. I really do. I expect she thought she was just doing you a good turn.'

'A good turn! Blimey. Spelling out in print what a deprived background I'd had—'

'Deprived! For heaven's sake . . . All she was going to say, obviously, was that you'd done incredibly well, and you'd done it all on your own, without the sort of advantages lots of people take for granted. What's wrong with that? Absolutely nothing. Rather the reverse, I'd say. And you're so ambitious. Just think of the publicity you'd have got. Couldn't you benefit from that?'

'I don't need that sort of publicity, thanks,' said Matt.

'Well, I think you're just ridiculous. And I also think you've been very rude. What would Mum say if she knew?'

'I wouldn't have thought she'd want to read about my humble background either.'

'Oh, for pity's sake. I can't take any more of this. Let's change the subject.'

'It's not me going on about it,' said Matt, with some truth.

The next morning, he told Jenny he didn't want to be disturbed, smoked two of the cigarettes that Scarlett had suddenly decided were bad for him, and for the second time in his life, made an apologetic phone call to Eliza.

'Darling, don't cry, whatever is it, come on, tell me—'

'Sorry, Jeremy. So sorry. I'll – I'll be all right in a minute.'

'It's not Charles, is it? Charles and Juliet?'

'God, no, I wouldn't cry about that. This is much, much worse. It's— it's Daddy. He's – he's got Parkinson's Disease.'

'Oh, my God. Oh, Eliza, my darling, I am so, so sorry.'

'Yes. It's terrible, isn't it? He's not too bad yet, he hadn't even told Mummy, but he's got a bit – well, feeble and – and shaky obviously, and he dropped one of her precious bits of Spode the other day and it smashed and she lost her temper and started yelling at him, she says she feels so ashamed now—'

'These things happen. I'm sure he understood.'

'Yes, of course. But – well, he told her. That he'd got it. She rang me, she was crying, it was awful. And then there's all the worry about the house . . . I'm sorry, but I'll have to go down this weekend to be with them, I can't go to Norfolk with you, I'm so sorry.'

'Darling of course you must. Don't even give Norfolk a thought. It won't go away, we can go another time.'

She came back on Sunday evening, very subdued.

'It was horrible.' She took the gin and tonic Jeremy had poured for her. 'Worse even than I expected. Daddy wasn't so bad, he was sort of determined but cheerful, Mummy was terribly shaken, trying to be brave. He's not too bad physically, they've put him on some drugs that will help for a while, apparently, but he has got a bit of a tremor in one hand, I can't think why I didn't notice it before, I feel dreadful about it.'

'Darling, that's exactly what your pa didn't want, that's why he was keeping it to himself. Bloody brave, I must say.'

'Isn't it? Bless him. And of course what they're most afraid of is having to move. Apparently the doctor said they should consider moving into a bungalow. Because Daddy will find the stairs very difficult, later on. And Charles started going on about the house falling down round their ears, and how we couldn't afford to get it fixed, said perhaps it would be better to try and sell it and—'

'Could they sell it? Didn't you tell me there was some kind of trust?'

'Well, yes. It's owned by the trustees, but Mummy has Power of

Appointment, which means she can appoint it out to anyone within her discretion and that of the trustees of course. But unless one of us was really rich that wouldn't do any good because the trustees aren't allowed even to mortgage it to raise money for repairs.'

'It sounds like a very badly thought out trust to me. Who set it up?'

'My grandfather. But they could let it, I think. And move. But can you imagine, leaving Summercourt and living in a bungalow. It would break Mummy's heart. "It'll be fine," she kept saying, "as long as we can stay here." And then I said well what about if we both chipped in, me and Charles, we've both got a bit from Granny and Grandpa, that'd pay for quite a bit of work, and Mummy said she couldn't possibly accept it and Charles said of course she could and it would be for our benefit in the long run, when we take Summercourt over. Anyway that calmed them down, and we managed to get onto talking about help and daily care when it was necessary, and they both looked a bit happier. But they seemed so small and vulnerable and lonely somehow, when we left. It's such a nightmare, and I don't know how much we helped at all.'

'I'm sure you did. Look, darling, you know I'll do what I can, don't you? Help you organise nursing for your father, that sort of thing. And as I've said, my GP is excellent, we could talk to him, see if he knows any specialists. And we can go down any weekend you want to. I don't mind. I adore your parents, you know I do.'

'Oh, Jeremy, you're such an angel,' said Eliza, putting her arms round him, kissing him, 'so kind and – well, so good. Thank you.'

Later, staring into the darkness, fretting over the situation, and thinking how extraordinarily nice he was – how did anyone get to be like that? Especially someone as over-privileged as Jeremy? – the words 'too good to be true' kept slipping into her head. That's what he was. Bit hard to live up to, that was the only thing. So, was this love? Certainly seemed to be.

'That wedding,' said Matt. His voice was very casual.

'What, the posh one? Yes, what about it?'

Gina's large grey eyes were suddenly sharp.

'I – well, I've decided to go after all. And I – well, would you like to come with me?'

'Well – I don't know. I might be busy. When was it?'

'It's 26 June.'

'I'll have a look in my diary.'

He knew she would agree and she knew he knew; but she played a lot of games like this.

'Well – I'll have to see what my parents say. They're having a drinks party that evening. But should be all right.'

'Well, don't put yourself out.'

'I won't.'

It was the conversation with Eliza that had persuaded him. She was clearly embarrassed herself by the whole article thing, and said she was sorry if she'd upset him, she really hadn't meant to, it had all been a stupid misunderstanding, and that she'd see him at the wedding.

'You will come, won't you? I know Charles is really hoping you will.'

After that, it seemed rude to refuse.

He was dreading it just the same. He'd been to Moss Bros and hired a monkey suit, the full works, had even been talked into a top hat. He'd never seen such a prat in his life as the one who looked back at him from the mirror.

Gina was very excited about it, and had bought a long crêpe dress from Biba.

She had also borrowed a hat from James Wedge, whom she knew, and told Matt, to his relief, he shouldn't wear the one from Moss Bros.

'It'll be mostly the ushers and so on who'll wear them, well, they won't wear them, just carry them. I wouldn't even worry about gloves, it'll be awfully hot hopefully. Now, have you thought about a present?'

Matt said he hadn't and that he didn't have the faintest idea what to give them.

'OK, well, they'll have a list, probably at Peter Jones. We can just choose something off that, it's really easy. Don't look so worried, Matt, it's going to be fun. I can't wait.'

'Hope so,' said Matt gloomily.

Sarah felt very frightened. A friend's husband had died after four years of Parkinson's and she knew very clearly what lay ahead. Increasing immobility, increasing dependence, a shutting down of life as she knew it; she would be confined to the house, less able to do what she wanted, to make trips to London, and to visit friends. What at the moment were the mildest of symptoms would become, she knew, something quite ugly. Adrian would become depressed, physically feeble, odd-looking, unable to perform the most simple tasks for himself. Eating would be difficult, a social life impossible. With the best will in the world, they would become more dependent on their children, turn into the sort of responsibility she would hate.

But all of that paled into complete insignificance, set against the threat of having to leave Summercourt. That was unthinkable.

Summercourt was a part of her, she belonged to it and it to her. It gave her happiness, interest, and an absolute sense of security; and it would give her courage. She knew that. Somehow, somehow, they had to stay there.

'Matt?'

'Yeah.'

'It's Eliza. Eliza Clark.'

'Oh – yeah. Morning.'

'Good morning. Look – I know I told you it was too late to do that article.'

'Ye-es?'

'Well, it might not be. The editor's decided to put it in a later issue.'

What he'd actually said was, 'Is it too much to ask you to find me someone just a little more interesting than this load of wankers. I don't want to read about a lot of bloody poofs. Hairdressers! Give me strength.'

'So – would you still be interested? I mean, now you understand what it's about a bit more?'

'I – might be.'

'Oh – well, good. Could we – could we do it this week, do you think? If you decide you will, of course.'

'I don't know about this week. Very, very busy this week.'

'Well, that's a shame. Next week really is too late.'

'Well, let me just ask my secretary, might have a corner on Thursday –' he bellowed Jenny's name – 'yes, I could possibly do Thursday evening. Any good?'

'I'll see if the journalist's available.'

'I thought it'd be you.'

'Oh – no. No, it'd be a freelance. Or possibly our features editor, Annunciata Woburn.'

Annunciata! What kind of person called their child Annunciata? Their kind, he supposed.

'That's a shame,' he said, 'I'd much rather talk to you. Can't you do it?'

'Um – well – I don't think so. I'm not a features person. I'm fashion, it's quite different.'

'You still work on the magazine. I really don't want to talk to – well, to anyone else.'

'Right. Well – OK. I'll have to ask, get back to you.'

Annunciata said it would be fine, if that was really the only way they could get Matt, and that she would supply Eliza with a list of questions and then write it up herself, 'so it reads like the others', thus displaying the usual attitude of what Jack called 'proper journalists' to the air-headed fashion girls. Eliza swallowed it without protest; she was too intrigued by the prospect to risk losing it.

'And ask him about photographs. I'd like to do one on a building site or something like that.'

'Yes, course.'

'Is he photogenic?'

Eliza thought of Matt: the thick, dark hair – quite short by the standards of the day, the probing brown eyes, the – well, yes, it was fair to say – the sexy mouth.

'Very,' she said.

'I wonder how I knew you were going to say that.'

Eliza was very impressed by Matt's set-up. He was clearly even more successful than she had thought. Four offices, all very streamlined, in a very good building just off Wardour Street; she was greeted by the most amazing blonde who looked as if she ought really to be on the cover of *Seventeen* magazine, and who made her an excellent cup of coffee and offered her an extraordinary array of biscuits. She was introduced to Matt's partner, Jimbo Simmonds, who was very nice but clearly not the real brains in the outfit; and then another very pretty girl appeared, clearly hugely bright and quite acerbic, who Matt rather pointedly dismissed, but not before she'd introduced herself as their partner, and said if there were any gaps in the information Matt supplied just call her, and gave her a card.

'Quite a harem you've got here, Matt,' said Eliza, settling back into the leather visitor's chair opposite Matt's desk.

'Yeah, well. I'm a great believer in employing women.'

'And not just as secretaries?'

'Course not. Cigarette?'

169

'Yes, thanks. Well, that's a very modern attitude. Not many male feminists about.'

'Oh, I'm not a feminist,' said Matt firmly, 'don't hold with all that. Once a woman's married and has children, I think she should be at home, looking after things.'

'Including her man?' Eliza's eyes danced.

'Yeah,' he said, very seriously, 'yes, I do. That's the natural order of things, isn't it?'

'No working mothers, then?'

'Absolutely not. That's a straight route to society falling apart, as I see it. But – while women don't have any other responsibilities, yeah, I think they should be given a chance.'

'Very generous of you. Right. Well, let's get started.'

'Just before we do,' he said, 'can I read what you write before it goes into the magazine?'

'I'm afraid we don't allow that.'

'Right. Well, in that case,' he stood up, 'the interview's not happening. I'm sorry, Eliza, I'm not giving you carte blanche to write whatever you like about me. I'm not completely wet behind the ears. Either I see the interview or you don't get one.'

'Well, in that case, I'll arrange for you to see it. Of course.' She smiled at him. 'Now, what was actually your first job, and how old were you . . . ?'

'My dear, I'm coming over to do a little shopping and some theatres, and how nice it would be to see you again. Tea at the Connaught one day – would that be possible? I shall be there from 6 June through 10 – on my own, alas, this time, no David – and I hope very much that you could join me on one of those days. Lily Berenson.'

Scarlett's first instinct was to refuse, to tell her she was away on those dates; it seemed very dangerous to meet with her a mere couple of weeks – as it would be – after seeing David. And then with a streak of pure perversity, she decided to say yes. Dangerous it might be, but it would also be rather exciting. And she might – just might – be able to garner from Mrs Berenson some information about David and Gaby's marriage, whether the end was truly in sight, as David kept intimating to her – without actually saying so.

She wouldn't mention the meeting to David; she wondered if Mrs

Berenson might. That would make him very nervous. Well, too bad; it was time, perhaps, for a bit of reality to enter the situation.

She checked her schedule; she was free two of the days. She wrote back and said she would be delighted to see Mrs Berenson on whichever suited her better.

'You look lovely my dear,' said Mrs Berenson, rising to kiss her. 'I like the shorter hair very much.'

'Thank you,' said Scarlett.

'I'm giving myself a treat tomorrow, going to René, you know? To have just a bit of a restyle.'

'Goodness,' said Scarlett, for she did know – who couldn't? – of René, hairdresser to the Queen, to the noblest ladies in the land, and his dazzling reputation.

'I hope he won't do anything too drastic. I'm always a little nervous of new hairdressers, but I'm told he is truly wonderful.'

Scarlett assured her that Rene was indeed truly wonderful, and about as likely to do something drastic to a client's hair as Hardy Amies was to dress one of his in a miniskirt.

'Good. Well, that's very nice to hear. Now, how are you, darling? I want to hear all your news. I was very pleased when you wrote and told me you were working for BOAC. If you ever flew down to the Southern States, I want you to promise me to come and stay.'

'That sounds wonderful,' said Scarlett carefully.

'And I could show you Atlanta, where your namesake lived for much of her life; and of course Rhett Butler came from Charleston. I know the rest of the family would love to meet you; especially the girls. Now did I tell you that Gaby is having another baby?'

Scarlett was pouring out the tea and thinking rather vaguely about Rhett Butler, and how she'd had a crush on him – or rather Clark Gable – when she first saw the film, and Mrs Berenson's announcement did no more than skim across the surface of her mind for a moment or two. And then she thought that she must have misheard, got the name wrong, that it was one of the other wives Mrs Berenson was talking about.

'I'm sorry?' she said politely. 'Who's having a baby?'

'Gaby, dear. David's wife. In December. It's very early days of course, but so exciting, Alicia, their youngest, is eleven, so it's a wonderful surprise for everyone.'

171

It stopped skimming then, the announcement, and settled: heavily, painfully, digging its barbs deep into her, so painfully indeed that she felt it physically, was afraid she might cry out.

She heard a voice, which surely couldn't have been hers, a calm interested voice, saying, 'Really? How lovely,' and then asking most politely if Mrs Berenson would like sugar in her tea, and then how David felt about the baby. 'After such a big gap.'

'Oh, my dear, he is thrilled. Over the moon. He's a wonderful father and he always said he was happiest when the children were tiny. He is definitely the only one of my sons who's been known to change a diaper.'

'Really! How sweet. And is Gaby well?'

'She's very well, yes. She thrives on pregnancy, always has. And in spite of her very busy life, she's happy to put it on hold to enjoy this. "The Post Script", they call him or her. So sweet, don't you think?'

'Very sweet,' said Scarlett. 'Um – could you excuse me just a moment, Mrs Berenson? I have to go to the ladies' room.'

She looked at herself in the mirror in the ladies and was amazed to see exactly the same person who had left her flat an hour ago. She looked slightly flushed, and her eyes were very bright, but there was no sign whatsoever that she was enduring such nightmarish pain. She combed her hair, admiring the shape of her new Vidal Sassoon five-point bob, sprayed herself with the Diorling that David had given her only two weeks ago, and renewed her lipstick. She didn't dare start crying because she knew she would never stop.

Then she went back to the lounge of the Connaught and drank two cups of tea, ate three finger sandwiches and told Mrs Berenson that she had been thinking about her invitation and she thought she might well like to take her up on her invitation to stay with her in Charleston, 'just for a couple of days, I've got a little leave in hand. I'll have a look at my schedule. I would so love to see your beautiful house.'

'My dear, how lovely! David will be thrilled.'

Chapter 18

'Charles is late,' said Eliza, 'I wonder where he is. He said he'd be here by four at the latest and it's – what – nearly six.'

'Oh, I expect he's working late. He said he'd had a lot of extra work to do, before he went away. Now, darling, you do think the flowers are all right, don't you? I'm not sure about the ones in the marquee—'

'Mummy, they're lovely. The whole marquee looks wonderful. Stop worrying.'

'Yes, but it was rather a responsibility, organising them myself. And—'

'It was Carol's decision,' said Eliza firmly, 'she obviously just didn't want to be bothered with them. In which case she has only herself to blame. And given her taste – or rather complete lack of it—'

'Darling!'

'Well—'

Eliza's dislike of Juliet had spread to her parents. Geoffrey Judd she could just about cope with, but Carol – she was so, so awful. So phoney and silly and eyelash-fluttering, just like her daughter. Who she had certainly trained well.

They were both clearly dazzled by Summercourt, especially now it was at its loveliest; the last time Eliza had seen them there together, a couple of weeks before the wedding, they had walked round the house and garden for hours together, 'as if they were learning its every corner by heart, so they could pretend it was really theirs to all their ghastly friends,' Eliza had said to Jeremy; he had laughed and told her she was a snob.

It hadn't been easy for Sarah, planning a wedding while not being really in charge of it. Carol had actually been quite good about it all, Sarah said, and had said she wouldn't interfere. 'And of course Juliet is so sweet, she knows what she wants, but she's not been at all pushy – and Charles has been a tower of strength. Dear Charles. I do hope—' She stopped.

173

'What, Mummy?' said Eliza curiously. 'You do hope what?'

'Oh – nothing. Just that he's happy. What every mother wants.'

'And – do you think he might not be? That Juliet isn't right for him?'

'Darling, I didn't say that.'

'I know. But you meant it.'

'Not really. It's just that—'

'Just what?'

'Oh, nothing. It's not important. How are things with Jeremy, darling? You and he seem very happy together.'

Eliza said things were fine and told her not to worry about Charles and Juliet. 'I think Charles adores her and they'll be very happy. Where's Daddy?'

'Oh – having a rest, I think. Helping me get the house ready has worn him out.'

'I'll go and find him.'

The house was looking truly glorious: dressed up for the wedding with huge vases and jugs of flowers in every room, the garden immaculate, filled with the scent of roses, and the lavender bushes along the terrace just beginning to bloom, a little early, as if they knew it was required of them. Sarah had taken a deep breath and had the drawing-room floor professionally polished; the golden wood reflected the light, filled the whole house with sunshine. It had rained a few days before and she had lit fires in the drawing room and the dining room, fearing they might be needed, and the sweet, haunting scent of wood smoke was everywhere, mingling with that of the roses. Eliza had stood in the hall, when she arrived, absorbing it all, and thinking, as she always did on such occasions, that she loved the house almost as if it were a person. She hoped Juliet realised how extremely lucky she was to have it as a setting for her wedding; but to be fair, she had written Adrian and Sarah a very charming and appreciative letter about it.

And one day, Eliza supposed, it would be the setting for hers.

She went up to the room where her father now slept alone; her mother said his restlessness kept them both awake.

'And I need my sleep. More than ever.'

He wasn't there, but she could hear footsteps overhead on the top floor. She went up and called him; he came out of one of the bedrooms on the long corridor, looking sheepish.

'Hello, poppet.'

'Daddy, what are you doing up here?'

'Oh – just looking down on the garden At the marquee. It looks awfully big.'

'Daddy! Don't fib.'

'Well – as it's you. Don't tell Mummy. But look.'

He led her back into the room where in the corner, at floorboard level, something was growing. It looked like some obscene yellowish-white fungus.

'It's dry rot. I did suspect it was there. But it's one thing to think it, and another to actually confront it. Oh, Eliza, what are we going to do? The house will become uninhabitable in no time.'

'Has Mummy seen this?'

'No. I've just been chipping away at the skirting board. Silly, I know.'

He looked at her and a tear rolled slowly down his hollow cheek.

'Daddy! Darling Daddy, don't cry. It'll be all right, promise!'

'No, Eliza, it won't. We've got no money, and a house that's going to fall down. And I'm not exactly in the pink, physically. I just don't see how we can carry on here.'

'What, you mean—' She could hardly get the words out. 'You mean, sell it? Daddy, no!'

'I – we – love this house so much, Eliza. It's almost – oh it's absurd, I know—'

'As if it was a person. I know. I was thinking that very thing, just now. A much beloved, beautiful person. Part of our family, the heart of it really. It would be impossible to say goodbye to it.'

'Darling one, I think we might have to. I know you and Charles have been very sweet and offered us some money, but I also know it wouldn't scratch the surface. I'm afraid we – Summercourt – is doomed. And maybe – well maybe, we can find someone who deserves her. Anyway, this is no time to discuss such things. She is all dressed up and ready to do her very best for us tomorrow. And she will be greatly admired and we can enjoy that. Now, none of this to Mummy. Not today. It would finish her off, I think.' He smiled. 'She's extremely anxious about everything.'

'I know she is. And – oh, Daddy, we'll think of something. Anyway, Mummy's wondering where you are, wants you to come down. Shall I tell her you're still asleep?'

'No. Just give me a few minutes. Bless you, darling. Don't say anything to anyone about all this, will you?'

'I wouldn't dream of it. Promise.'

It was almost seven when Charles arrived: he looked exhausted but cheerful.

'Sorry, everyone. I got held up in the office. Lot to do before I left.'

'Oh well, I suppose we can't be cross with you tonight. Juliet's rung twice.'

'I'll ring her in a minute. It's been a bit of a week, you know.'

'Yes, of course. Your stag night on Wednesday – how did that go?'

'Oh, it was great. Yes. Jeremy was fantastic. Really good value. He organised most of it. You've got a good one there, Eliza.'

'He's not mine,' she said irritably. People kept assuming that it was only a matter of time before she and Jeremy got engaged, and – he just didn't seem anywhere near asking her. He hadn't actually told her he loved her, not really. He said he loved being with her, and of course she loved being with him, and he'd told her he'd never felt about any girl the way he felt about her: but that wasn't quite the same thing. In fact it wasn't the same thing at all.

It was as if he was feeling his way and – well, that was all right. It wasn't a decision you could – or should – make in a hurry.

And, actually, she felt a little bit the same. If he did ask her, then obviously she wouldn't turn him down. Nobody would.

But – and what was the but? It hovered very vaguely in the background, but whenever she tried to analyse it, she couldn't even work out what it was.

'So, what did you do on your stag night, Charles?' she asked now. 'Hope you didn't get tied up to a lamp post without your trousers, like my friend Nick did last month.'

'Oh – no. Nothing like that. It was quite tame really. Well, I got jolly pissed of course, but—'

'No strip joints? Charles, I'm disappointed in you.'

'Well, I'm sorry. Not really my sort of thing, as you know. ' He grinned. He did look very happy, she thought. Which was all that mattered. And he had a new assurance these days that was very good to see.

'I'd better go and ring Juliet. Then I'll have a good strong drink.'

She heard his voice, kind and concerned. 'Hello, darling. Yes, I know. I'm so sorry. I was working late. No, of course I didn't realise you'd be worried. How are you anyway? Yes, of course I understand.'

Eliza couldn't bear to hear any more. She went out onto the terrace, and breathed in the lovely rose-laden air. It reminded her of her dance, that air, when life had been so simple and her father had been well and Charles had just left Oxford with girls throwing themselves at him, and there had been no bloody Juliet anywhere; it seemed a long time ago . . .

Charles seemed very calm at supper, no pre-wedding nerves visible, and conducted a brisk discussion with his father about the advisability of buying shares in BP; there was much talk of oilfields in the North Sea.

'I'd certainly buy into one of the companies,' he said, 'maybe not BP. Their share price is too high already, but maybe one of the companies who are building the drilling platforms. What do you think, Pa?'

'I'd get into it like a shot,' said Adrian. 'I was reading all about it the other day, sure they're going to find something – don't look at me like that, Sarah, I know my speculating days are over. Interesting prospect though, isn't it? Think what it would do for the economy.'

The phone rang twice during supper: both times Eliza answered it, thinking it might be Jeremy. The first time it was Juliet; she sounded very intense. 'Oh, Eliza, could I just speak to Charles, quickly. I'm sorry if you're having supper. I just feel so – so emotional. I know he can calm me down.'

'Yes, of course.'

'Sorry.'

'Don't apologise. I'm sure all brides must feel pretty emotional the night before their wedding.'

'Well yes, of course. But I have always been rather inclined to go over the top. I can't help it, it's the way I'm made. Mummy's the same, terribly over-sensitive.'

'I'll go and get him,' said Eliza quickly. She couldn't be rude to Juliet tonight of all nights.

The second call was her again. 'Sorry, Eliza, but could I speak to him again? Just to say goodnight, you know? You must think I'm awfully silly.'

'No, no, of course not,' said Eliza. She half-expected Charles to be as irritated as she was, but he jumped up looking rather pleased. It must be love. No other explanation . . .

At quarter to ten, Charles stood up.

'Better turn in,' he said, 'believe I've got a big day tomorrow.'

'Really?' said Sarah, smiling. 'What's that about then?'

* * *

177

She couldn't sleep for a long time. She lay awake, thinking about the next day, about Charles, about how sad she felt to be losing him and to someone so unworthy of him. But – he was so clearly happy: maybe they didn't understand Juliet. Maybe she had lots of qualities they just didn't appreciate. Maybe they hadn't tried hard enough. But they had, they had.

Well, all they could do was hope for the best. Starting with the wedding. It should be fun, anyway. Lots of old friends. And a few new ones. Like Matt Shaw . . .

She was really pleased he was coming; it meant he'd properly forgiven her.

She'd really enjoyed doing the interview with him, not just because it had been Matt, and finding out about Matt, but actually doing it. She'd liked moving the conversation along, flattering him and flirting with him more than he realised. Well, she hoped more than he realised. Probably actually not. God, he was clever. And tough. She'd left him feeling quite – odd. Thinking of the raw, nervy lad she'd met at Waterloo station only a few years ago, and how he'd turned into this cool, hungry, ready-for-anything creature exuding confidence and courage. And sex. You really couldn't ignore the sex. And so yes, his girlfriend would certainly be very sexy too. No doubt about that. Well, that was all right. It was nothing to do with her, what sort of girlfriend Matt Shaw had. Nothing whatsoever.

The church looked wonderful, Sarah thought, huge urns of roses and white peonies on either side of the screen, wonderful arrangements of scabious and cow-parsley on the windowsills, an inspiration of the local florist she had used – 'I thought we should have something natural and countrified' – and white-ribboned bunches of sweetheart roses hung on the end of every pew. And a wonderful arch of white roses and moss over the church door to welcome people as they arrived.

She walked in with Adrian, smiling and nodding at such of the congregation as she knew – at least half: and there was no doubt about it, their half was so much better-looking and better dressed. She'd never seen so much brightly coloured lace in her life as on the Judd side, including Carol's suit, which was a pink that could only be described as hectic. And there were a lot of painfully ill-fitting and new-looking morning coats, obviously hired. A lot of the Judd side were nursing top hats as well, dreadful new-looking grey things; oh, dear, she did hope their friends would all understand.

Charles was sitting at the front, looking dreadfully nervous, but so handsome; and beside him Jeremy, his best man, calm, smiling, utterly at ease. What an asset he had been all day: arriving as promised, really early, his E-type pulling up outside the house just after nine. 'I said I wouldn't let you down, old chap,' he said, clapping a white-faced Charles on the back, kissing Sarah and then taking Eliza into his arms in a bear hug. He really did seem to adore Eliza, Sarah thought; maybe this weekend, maybe the magic of another wedding . . .

As she sat in the bridesmaids' car, feeling pretty miserable really, waiting for Juliet to arrive, Eliza saw Matt. He looked nervous, on the edge of the crowd, but pretty good, she thought; but then all men did in morning dress. What really engaged her rather miserable attention was the girl with him. Who was, quite simply, stunning. Quite small, long, brown, blond-streaked hair, done in sort of Pre-Raphaelite waves, with a great cartwheel of a hat trimmed with a ribbon the same fabric as her Biba chiffon dress. She was, without doubt, the most stylish as well as one of the prettiest in the crowd outside the church. Even Maddy, who had rushed over to say hello, looking stunning in one of her own crocheted silk dresses, and a matching crocheted bonnet, could not compete with her. She was quite pale, and enragingly cool-looking, with a tiny little tipped-up nose, the sort of nose Eliza had always longed for, and the most enormous grey eyes, double-fake-lashed of course and a very sexy mouth, and every so often she tapped Matt's arm and reached up to whisper in his ear, in that way very flirty girls did, and he would smile back at her and nod.

And here she was, dressed from neck to ankle in sickly pink frills, her face heating up to match it – with her ringlets, the twee little basket of flowers they all had to carry instead of ordinary posies and, worst of all, silver pumps. Silver! Why silver? They were slightly too tight as well, and she could feel her feet swelling inside them already.

They hadn't seen her yet, Matt and the girl; but they would, they would, and how, Eliza thought, was she going to get through the rest of the afternoon looking like she did, while that girl, that lovely girl, Matt's coolly beautiful girlfriend, looked like she did? Oh, stop it, Eliza; what did it matter what Matt's girlfriend thought of her? And what was it to her? Nothing, absolutely nothing.

The music was beautiful. Luckily Juliet had claimed that she had no ear for music ('I just know what I like') and had agreed that Charles and Sarah should make the initial suggestions, 'And then Mummy and I'll make the final choice. She's got much more of an ear than I have.'

And Sarah and Charles, both very musical, had had several wonderful meetings with the church organist, John Phillips, who was quite exceptionally talented; he sang with a nationally acclaimed choir and had trained his small village throng with great care and skill and the most extraordinarily lovely music issued from the church, especially at evensong. He had made enough traditional suggestions to satisfy the most conventional of brides, while adding such strokes of genius as having the choir sing "Laudate Dominum" for the signing of the register.

So the music at least would not be commonplace, or even common. Sarah, sitting and listening to John Phillips playing Handel's *Water Music*, and then slipping into *The Cuckoo and the Nightingale* – 'known in the business as "The Cuckold and the Nightingale", he had said with a twinkle – slipped her hand into Adrian's, took a deep breath, and allowed herself to relax. It was all going to be all right. It really, really was.

It was all very – very nice really, Matt thought. He'd never been in such a pretty church in his life – well, he hadn't been in many churches at all, come to that, his parents were not religious and he couldn't really remember being in one since school carol services.

Everyone looked extremely smart, and although it was odd to see such a large gathering of people dressed identically, it was actually rather nice. He noticed a lot of blokes looking at Gina, and felt a rush of pride, almost as if she was properly his. Watch it, Matt, you'll get carried away if you're not careful. Infectious, this wedding business. Louise had warned him of that, when she'd left the office the night before.

'You be careful, Matt, lots of men propose at weddings. Bit too much champagne, all that talk of love and commitment and you find yourself saying all sorts of things you don't really mean.'

A really pretty woman came in, dressed in pale lemon yellow, on the arm of a rather fragile-looking old chap: they sat down just behind Charles. Must be the parents; Matt looked at them interestedly. They looked different from how he'd expected, had an air of gentleness and courtesy about them; they were joined shortly by another couple, who were more what he'd expected, embracing them rather exuberantly, with cries of 'lovely . . . wonderful . . . marvellous . . . so exciting'. The man was rather stout and red-faced and the woman was tall and looked particularly imposing, dressed in dark red silk with a sort of turban hat and rows and rows of pearls round an indisputably wrinkly neck. Every so often she would jump up from her seat and rush to embrace someone in the aisle, braying (there was no other word for it) 'Binky!' or 'Rozzy!' and other such names.

'Must be a relative,' hissed Gina. 'God, this is fun.'

And then the music paused; and then it changed; and everyone stood up, and the bride and her father stood in the doorway of the church, the light behind them, and the choir began to sing Vivaldi's *Gloria*; and the magic that takes over a wedding – any wedding – began to do its work.

Juliet did look really lovely. Eliza had to admit it. Of course, it was difficult not to look lovely in a wedding dress, unless you were a complete fright, and Juliet was an extremely pretty girl. And Charles's face, fixed on her as she walked down the aisle, showed his very clear pleasure and pride.

The dress was exactly what she had expected it to be, a tiered confection of a thing, all tulle and lace, with a full skirt and tight bodice, long sleeves, and a modestly swathed boat neckline. She looked, Eliza thought, exactly like a Disney princess. Her hair was drawn up in a tower of curls, her veil very long, gallantly tended to by four pageboys in blue silk suits, complete with knee breeches; her bouquet was a slightly over-large arrangement of pink roses. The eight bridesmaids wore dresses that were a simpler version of the bride's own – four of them in pink and four in mauve, with white roses in their ringlets. Eliza – relieved at least to be in the pink party, not the mauve – smiling until her face ached, felt oddly lonely, looking at a church-full of people, half of whom were strangers and to whom in some strange way Charles was defecting. Then she saw Jeremy, so absurdly handsome in his morning dress, first grin and then wink at her and she felt much better.

The service was charmingly predictable. Juliet's voice was very firm as she made her vows, Charles's less so, and Eliza's heart lurched as he stumbled over 'till death do us part' and had to say it twice. Juliet, on the other hand, did not seem nervous in the least and the smile she gave Charles when the vicar pronounced them man and wife could have been better described as smug than radiant.

The bridal party had now disappeared into the vestry for the signing of the register. Eliza was sitting on the end of a pink and mauve line on the bride's side of the church. God, the church was hot; she could actually feel sweat trickling down between her breasts, her feet were throbbing, and the back of her neck under the bloody ringlets felt extremely damp. She was sure she must by now be quite hideously red-faced.

She picked up the order of service and began to fan herself with it. That wasn't entirely to her taste either, to put it mildly. Carol and Juliet had designed it between them, and it was pale pink, with a drawing of two wedding rings intertwined on the front linking up with the words 'Charles and Juliet'. Her mother had practically had hysterics when she saw it, and said it just wouldn't do, but Charles, unusually firm, said he liked it, and that it was his and Juliet's wedding, not Sarah's. It made quite a good fan though.

She would give anything for a bit of fresh air, she thought, anything, and then suddenly and shockingly felt like crying. It had really happened, her beloved brother had left her, left all of them really, for a girl who was in no way his equal – not intellectually, not emotionally, who lacked his sense of humour, his style, his charm, his ability to befriend just about anybody; and she felt lost and terribly alone.

And then two things happened: the music changed, and the choir led by the most amazing soprano began to sing the *Laudate Dominum*, and the sheer searing beauty of it shocked her out of her sadness and quite literally took her breath away. And she turned round and, without quite knowing how she could have found him in that crowded church, she was staring at Matt, and he in his turn was staring at her, as clearly moved, shocked even, by the moment and music as she was, and then very slowly he smiled at her, and it was not the cocky, awkward Matt, or even the sexy, self-assured one, it was someone different, one she had not known before, or even suspected he could be, someone warm and oddly gentle; and in that moment, suspended for ever against the music and with the sunshine shafting in the windows of the small flower-filled church, and without her really understanding how or why, the world seemed to shift just a little.

'What a lovely, lovely house,' said Gina.

'What?'

'Matt! I said, what a lovely house. Isn't it?'

'Oh – yes. Yes, not bad.'

A tall, slightly languid man had appeared, grinning rather foolishly at Gina. She smiled back. 'Yes indeed.'

'Good service, wasn't it?'

'Lovely. Specially the music.'

'Jolly pretty girl, isn't she? Old Charles has kept her to himself, I must say. Known her for a long time?'

'No, no, I've never met her.'

'Oh, I see. I thought – well, I thought you must be a friend of hers. Haven't met either of you. Tim Dalton-Smith, at your service.'

'How do you do, Tim. I'm Gina, Gina Barker, and this is Matt Shaw. He and Charles were in the army together.'

'Oh really! What, out in Gib? Jolly good fun that must have been. I only managed Cyprus.'

'I wasn't in Cyprus or Gib,' said Matt, 'I was just with Charles in basic training. I was in the Royal Engineers out in Germany. Just an ordinary old sapper, you know.'

'Oh. Oh, I see.' Tim's face was contorted, struggling to find the right expression. 'Well, that must have been jolly interesting.'

'Yes, it was. Did me the world of good.'

'And you and Charles have stayed in touch, have you?'

'Yes. You could say that.'

'Well, jolly good.' There was a silence; then Dalton-Smith smiled rather uncertainly.

'And what do you do now?'

'I'm in property.'

'Oh, are you now. Well, it's the right field to be in. Growing quite literally. What firm are you with?'

'My own,' said Matt decisively.

Dalton-Smith was briefly silenced. Then he said, 'Oh, I see. Right. Domestic?'

'No. Commercial.'

'Well – well, jolly good for you.' He was clearly nonplussed. Matt wasn't going to help him. 'And you,' he said to Gina, 'what do you do?'

'I'm in the fashion business.'

'Oh? A model, I presume. Sure I've seen you in *Vogue*.'

''Fraid not. No I – well, I run a boutique. In the King's Road.'

'Oh, I say, what fun. Eliza's in the fashion business, isn't she? Edits some magazine or other.'

'Something like that,' said Gina.

There was a silence: then she said, 'I was just saying what a lovely house this is.'

'Isn't it? Glorious. What a setting for a wedding! I came here for Eliza's dance. God, that seems a long time ago. You weren't here, I suppose – er—' He looked at Matt awkwardly.

'No,' said Matt. 'I don't get out much. Not in polite society anyway.'

'That was so rude,' said Gina crossly, as Dalton-Smith made an excuse and hurried off. 'He was only trying to be friendly.'

'Yes, well, that's fine. I didn't want to be friendly back.'

'But why not?'

'He was bloody patronising me. Why should I be friendly?'

'Oh, for Christ's sake,' said Gina, 'I'm off. I might see you later.'

She stalked off; thirty seconds later she was chatting and laughing to a couple as if she'd known them all her life. Matt decided to explore. The house was locked of course; but he was able to see quite a lot of it, squinting through various windows. Into what he supposed would be called the drawing room, for a start: a huge, beautiful room, with a wonderful carved fireplace, shelves in alcoves, containing what was obviously rather special china, and clearly old books, and a lot of very posh-looking chairs and sofas. He walked round to the front of the house. The windows on either side of the great front door – flanked by two quite large stone dogs – showed a hall, bloody great space, with a staircase with an iron rail rising from the centre of it; and as he looked down the avenue, as it curved gently towards the village below, there was a sense of peace and set-apartness that was quite extraordinary.

He glanced to the other side of the house. Set just slightly to its right, below yet another lawn, was an exquisite building, with a glass dome at the top; he walked down towards it, intrigued. It had huge glass-paned doors, which he tentatively tried, but which were locked, tall, tall windows, almost floor-to-ceiling height, and a tiled floor; there were two trees inside, growing almost to the full height of the building, a fan-trained flowering shrub (Matt wasn't sure which kind) on one of the side walls, its blossom fallen with a kind of casual extravagance on the floor around it, and several palms and other plants in enormous pots, set about the room. Well, he supposed it was a room. Or was it a kind of giant greenhouse? There was a large and rather lovely white wrought-iron table in the middle of the room and a couple of matching chairs; otherwise there was no

184

furniture and no further decoration. Except perhaps the sunlight, which filled it, an almost tangible thing; he felt if he could have opened the door he would have had to push against it, as if it was silk. He stood there, looking in and smiling and thinking it was the loveliest place he had ever seen; and thinking too of Eliza growing up with this exquisite thing as part of her everyday life, taking it for granted, careless of its beauty. What a charmed childhood she and Charles must have had, playing in these gardens, walking in the woods just beyond, beauty wherever they looked . . .

'Matt, hello.' It was Eliza. His head was so full of her, he was in no way surprised to see her, had somehow had been expecting her. She smiled at him; she seemed no more surprised to find him there. She was on her own. Like him.

'Are you all right?'

'Yes. Yes, I'm fine. Thanks. Just exploring a bit. Hope it's all right.'

'Of course. Well, certainly for you. Mummy was worried about the riff-raff, as she called it, but—'

'Glad I don't qualify as riff-raff.'

'Matt, of course you don't.'

'This is a lovely place,' he said, quite gently. 'Well, it's all lovely, but this building—'

'Oh, the orangery. Yes, it's very special. I'm glad you like it. It was built at the same time as the house; it's in the original plans. I adore it. We were never allowed in, I think Mummy and Daddy thought we'd smash the glass or something, but one day I saw the gardener get a key from under a flowerpot by the door – bit like Peter Rabbit, you know – and when no one was about, often early in the morning, I would creep down and let myself in, pretend I was a princess and this was my palace.'

'Well, it is a bit like a palace,' said Matt, 'and you are a bit of a princess. By my standards anyway.'

'Am I? Quite a poor one these days.'

'Yes, well, poverty is relative, I suppose,' said Matt, but his voice was easy, gentle, with none of the truculence that so often filled it, and then he said, 'I don't suppose the key's still under the pot?'

'Yes, it is. Do you want to go in?'

He nodded; she smiled at him conspiratorially, and like a naughty child walked over to the corner of the building and retrieved the key.

He stepped in, looked round; the air was heavy with scent and heat.

'I was right,' he said. 'I thought it looked from outside as if you could touch that light, feel it even.'

'Matt!' said Eliza. 'What a lovely idea. I didn't know you were such a romantic.'

'I'm not usually,' he said, 'I feel a bit as if it's cast a spell on me.'

Eliza smiled at him, and then suddenly sat down on one of the chairs. 'Sorry to break the spell, but I have to get these foul shoes off. Too small they are, I'm sure Juliet did it on purpose.' She clapped her hand to her mouth, looking again like a naughty child. 'Gosh, I shouldn't have said that. Sorry.'

'You don't like her?' he said grinning.

'Not terribly much.'

'She seems a bit—' He stopped.

'A bit what?'

'A bit wrong for Charles. Can't say more than that, don't know her.'

'Oh Matt,' said Eliza, 'I could kiss you for that.'

'Well,' he said, 'well, go on. I don't mind.'

'All right.' She hesitated, then reached up and kissed him lightly on the cheek. 'There. Thank you.'

'That's – that's OK.'

And she moved back a step, away from him, and they stood there, in the bright, hot light, staring at each other, half-shocked, rather as they had in the church. He felt suddenly and unaccustomedly shy; and she seemed slightly awkward too, not her usual brisk, bossy self.

'Well,' she said, quickly, 'we'd better go. The speeches are about to begin. Where's your – your girlfriend?'

'Gina? I have no idea. We had a bit of a tiff.'

'Oh, I'm sorry,' said Eliza, 'what a shame. We'd better go and find her, and – and some champagne, we'll be doing some toasting. I can't put those shoes on again, I'll leave them here, come on, if we scuttle down this path here, we can stay on the grass and I won't hurt my feet – oh, better just lock up.'

He followed her, bemused and still feeling half-enchanted, through an avenue of trees and out onto the sunlit lawn; people were moving into the marquee.

'Oh good,' said Eliza. 'Or bad, maybe. We haven't missed anything yet. Now can you—'

'Eliza, my darling girl! I've been looking for you. You look perfectly frightful, may I say. What a dreadful dress. Bride's choice, I suppose.'

It was the woman in red silk with the turban. Eliza leaned forward and kissed her.

'Hello, Gommie darling. Yes, very much her choice. I can't say you've made me feel any better though.'

'Oh, you know I don't mean it. You usually look marvellous. What a dreadful lot. Your poor mother, having them swarming all over the place.'

'I – um, Gommie, this is Matt Shaw. Matt, this is my godmother. Anna Marchant.'

'How do you do?' said Anna Marchant. 'How do you fit in here?'

'I don't,' said Matt briefly.

Mrs Marchant laughed. 'Very good. That woman, the bride's mother, perfectly dreadful. Putting on airs and graces, telling me how she'd just been to a royal garden party. I told her I always turned the invitations down, too many unsuitable people there these days. That shut her up.'

'Gommie, do be quiet. Someone will hear you.'

'Darling, they're much too drunk. Now how is Jeremy? We had the briefest chat in church. So good-looking. And so extremely rich. I bet your mother's getting her hopes up.'

'I – wouldn't know.'

'Of course she is. She's only human. A mother's dream, that young man. And they could use the money, that's for sure. But, it's your life. Not theirs. Remember that.'

'Gommie, *please.*'

'Well, it's important. Anyway, he ought to have asked you by now. It's gone on too long. Or has he?'

'No Gommie he hasn't, and—'

'Well, in my day it was called trifling. Trifling with your affections. Not done.'

'Well, things have changed now,' said Eliza firmly.

'Yes, and not always for the better. Still, just remember what I said. So, why are you here, Matt? Not part of the bride's lot, I'm sure.'

'No,' said Matt, grinning, 'no, I'm a friend of Charles's.'

'Oh really? How'd you meet him?'

'In the army. Doing basic training.'

'Yes, I see. What were you in?'

'The sappers.'

'Good for you. Damn fine lot, the sappers. We'd have lost the war without them. Mulberry harbours and all that. And what do you do now?'

'I'm – I'm in the property business.'

'Eliza, you must bring Matt to lunch one day. I'd like to talk to him some more. I'm thinking of buying some shares in Blue Circle Cement. Good idea, Matt?'

'Um – probably.'

'That's what I thought. Oh, God, here we go, Father of the Bride at the microphone. It'll be dreadful. I need another drink.'

She moved off.

'I'm sorry,' said Eliza, laughing, 'she's so outrageous.'

'I thought she was wonderful.'

'Well, she took a great shine to you. You'd better watch it, she's a frightful flirt.'

'Fine by me,' said Matt. 'She's got terrific legs.'

They moved into the marquee together, brought increasingly close, Matt thought, first by the singing, then the orangery, then by that wonderful conversation. He looked at Jeremy, smug bastard, laughing with Sarah, handing her a glass of champagne: and felt against all the odds a lurch of self-confidence.

Chapter 19

'I've got something – something I want to talk to you about.'

Eliza looked at Jeremy across the table; she felt a clawing at her stomach, a constriction in her throat. Was this it? Finally? And if so . . .

'Yes?' she said. Her voice didn't sound quite as it should. Bit squeaky. It was awful. Embarrassing.

'It's – well, it's pretty exciting really. I – I hope you'll like it anyway. OK, here goes.' He refilled her glass. It wasn't champagne. Which she might have expected it to be if . . . But he had made a bit of a thing about getting some wine he knew she'd love. So . . .

'Well, I've been asked to go to New York for six months. To head up the office there.'

'Oh. Oh, Jeremy.' She smiled. A brilliant, dazzling smile. She could feel its brilliance. It quite hurt. 'Jeremy, that's – that's wonderful. So wonderful. I – well, I – congratulations, Jeremy. Um – how soon?'

'Oh – beginning of September. I have to say I am a little bit nervous. But – well, it's a great challenge. Carl Webster's leaving the London office after five years and returning to New York which, according to him, is going down the pan fast. Not a cosy situation.'

It didn't sound cosy, that was for sure. They'd lost several accounts, including JKL Tobacco and La Roche toiletries; Jeremy was being brought in as overall account director and his brief was to work with Carl, relaunching the entire agency.

'It will be fun,' he said, leaning back in his chair, 'and I will enjoy it, I'm not asking for sympathy – except having to live without you of course – but God, the egos I'm going to have to dance around. The creative people are great, it's the account people who've made a complete horlicks of it all, and morale is seriously bad. First off I've got to decide who's wheat and who's chaff and then see about getting rid of the chaff; there'll be ground glass put in my coffee on a daily basis, I should think. But there will be good aspects, no doubt.'

'Like?'

'Oh – like an apartment on the Upper East Side – that's sort of Knightsbridge-y; excellent expenses of course, and a contractual agreement that I can fly home at least once a month – First Class, natch. And then there's you, of course.'

Oh God. He was going to say it after all. She composed her face again. Took a careful sip.

'I shall miss you terribly. Terribly.'

'I'll miss you too, Jeremy. Of course.'

'But I do want you to come over lots. For long weekends and so on. As well as me coming home lots as well. In fact I think I can swing the fare on expenses fairly often. I really couldn't manage without you entirely. So – shouldn't be too bad. Oh, darling.'

'Yes?'

Maybe even now? His idea of a joke? A tease?

'I do hate to leave just now while you're so worried about your dad and the house and everything. But you know we can talk whenever you like.'

No joke, no tease.

'Yes. Yes, of course I know that. And – congratulations, Jeremy, again. It really is wonderful.'

Well – so what? she thought when finally, finally she was safely home, in bed, with the light out, no longer pretending, no longer having to smile. Exploring how she felt. Which was fine. Absolutely fine. It would be marvellous to go to New York, meet the editors of things like American *Vogue* and *Harper's*, see the New York designers. So it was a huge bonus, really. And it was only for six months. And what would be the point in getting engaged when they weren't going to be together? Probably Jeremy had thought exactly that – although he could have said it. No, the simple fact was that clearly he just didn't want to be tied down at this stage in his life. He had enough to worry about. And anyway – who on earth wanted to get married, when they were flying as high as she was? It was her career that really mattered to her. More than anything else in the world. Wasn't it?

As if on cue, Jack Beckham sent for her the next morning, told her he had just fired Fiona – 'and don't try to defend her, I've had it on very good authority she's been completely off her head for the last three days, and not for the first time, migraine my arse, and it was her fucked up that last session with the ball gowns, not the photographer' – and formally appointed her fashion editor.

They all argued later over who had had the idea first. Valerie claimed it inevitably, Valerie Hill, still one of Simmonds and Shaw's major clients, Valerie Hill who had become a phenomenon in her own right, one of the first female tycoons, constantly featured in the magazines and newspapers, with a chain of offices supplying at least half the upper echelons of the secretarial community.

She had come in one morning to see Louise, who now regarded her as her personal client, about a couple of offices in Ealing. And told her over Jenny's coffee and biscuits, which continued, Louise claimed, to be one of the major contributions to the firm's success, that she could see in the years to come there would be a huge increase in offices in the outer suburbs.

'We'll just have to look further out – well beyond Guildford. In the green belt, even. It can't go on like this.'

Louise was talking to Matt and Jimbo later that day, about the nightmare of the Brown Ban, as it was called (after George Brown, a new minister in Mr Wilson's punitive government) on any further office building in London. 'Half our development work is being stalled for lack of planning permission,' said Jimbo gloomily, 'bloody Labour, thought they were meant to be getting us out of trouble, helping the working man, not putting him out of his job.'

'Well, we're not going to change that,' said Louise. 'And Miss Hill was saying this morning we'd all have to move right out, start building offices in the suburbs.'

'Can't see that,' said Jimbo, 'commercial firms want their feet in central London. They won't want their offices here there and everywhere. So unless you can persuade an entire company to move, it'll never work.'

'I'm not so sure,' said Louise. 'Sun Alliance are doing it, moving everyone out apparently, except for head office. It'd be much cheaper for them, and it'd be nice for the staff, wouldn't it, not having to go into London every day, able to work much nearer home. There's a lot of people moving out of London to live, you know.'

'Yeah, and if they were big firms,' said Jimbo slowly, 'big offices, people would move to work there, like they do to Ford, in Dagenham. I can see that makes sense.'

'Yeah, but that's factories,' said Matt. 'Can't see people moving to be near an office.'

'This'd be a bit like a factory though, wouldn't it?' said Louise. 'Only not manufacturing cars or washing machines, but processing insurance claims or whatever.'

'Tell you what,' said Matt, 'if we could buy some land, and then develop one of these places, ready and waiting for some of these big firms – well, we'd be printing money.'

Jimbo stared at him. 'Mate, you're living in dreamland. You'd have to print a whole lot, just to buy the land in the first place.'

'Not necessarily,' said Matt. 'It'd be much cheaper than land in London. And there's plenty of money around. You just need to have a good business plan, that's all.'

'Well, if you say so. But how'd you know where to buy it, where the firms would want to be?'

'We could work it out,' said Matt slowly. 'It'd be where the public transport was good. The underground, bus routes, mainline stations. Easy as that.'

He sat back in his chair, and lit a cigarette, looking at them very coolly through the smoke. 'This is our way into the big time,' he said, 'trust me.'

The news had broken fast about Eliza's appointment. Next morning, she came in to an office filled with flowers; by lunchtime every vase in the place was utilised, and she had to ask her secretary to go out and buy half a dozen more. Breathy messages accompanied them: 'darling Eliza . . . so thrilling . . . so exciting . . . so well deserved . . . many congratulations': all from people who only days before had been fawning over Fiona. The phone rang constantly, offering her lunch, drinks, even that newest social occasion, breakfast; other fashion writers called in their unique code: 'We've been worrying about Fiona . . . she couldn't go on like that . . . she needs a rest.'

Eliza called Fiona herself, several times; there was no reply. Finally at the end of the day, feeling increasingly wretched, she wrote her a note and ordered some flowers to be delivered to her flat next morning. They were returned, with the message that said there was no reply; later that day Fiona's mother phoned Jack Beckham to tell him that Fiona had been admitted to a psychiatric clinic suffering from a major breakdown. Jack called Eliza into his office to tell her.

'Oh, Jack, that's terrible, I'm so sorry.'

'Don't be,' he said. 'I only told you so you could see how right I was. She obviously couldn't have gone on anyway.'

She thought suddenly – and not for the last time – how like Matt he was.

'Scarlett, it's David.'

'Oh – hello, David.'

'Look – are you quite mad? My mother says you're coming out here to stay with her. You can't do that, you really can't.'

'I don't see why not. It'll be fun. It sounds so lovely. And maybe it'll answer some queries for me.'

'What sort of queries?'

'Well – you know. Like how Gaby can be pregnant, when you haven't slept together for years. Does she have a lover, I wonder? Is it someone else's baby?'

'Of course not.'

'Well – must be immaculate conception then. How amazing.'

'Look, Scarlett of course we – that is I – she— occasionally we – well, we sleep together. It's – it's just—'

'Just what?' A silence. She sighed. Loudly and theatrically. 'Well, this is why I want to come, you see. To answer those sorts of questions. And I do like your mother so much and her house sounds really lovely. And she says so is Charleston this time of the year. So – I'm coming. Sorry, David, if you're not entirely pleased. But you should have thought that something like this might happen. Bye now.'

Something like this. That hurt so much a lot of the time she felt she couldn't breathe properly. Someone else having the baby she should have had. With the man she loved. The baby she didn't have, the baby that had been torn out of her, just to save the man and his filthy, lousy marriage. The baby she had kept quiet about, been so brave about, never complained about. The baby that still haunted her sleep, with its sweet, smiling embryonic face, the baby that she had killed.

What kept her going was the rage. At the lies, the injustice, her own gullibility. How could she have listened to him, believed him, trusted him?

Well – she had. And now she was getting her revenge. A bit of it anyway.

'What on earth is going on in there?'

'I really don't know, I'm afraid. He just seems really angry.'

'Who with?'

'I don't know. Someone on the telephone.'

'Well, who was it? A client?'

'I don't know, Miss Mullan. I don't think so. Well, first some woman phoned, she was ever so posh.'

'Not Valerie Hill, I hope?'

'No, she was called – oh, dear. It was a name I've never heard before. Really unusual. I thought at first she said she was making an announcement about her name, but that seemed to be it. Her name. Seemed to be something like Announcement. Anyway, he didn't talk to her for long. Then he rang someone else. That's who he's shouting at.'

Louise listened at the door for a moment; she heard the words 'bloody outrageous' and then slightly later, 'You made me a promise and in my business we don't renege on such things. Yours is obviously less principled. I'm quite prepared to sue if necessary,' and then, 'Well you'll have to sort it out because I'm not bloody having it.'

There was then a loud noise as the phone was slammed down and a long silence.

'Heavens above,' said Louise.

Rather reluctantly, she went out, to meet a client. When she came back, Jenny was looking rather excited, typing very fast.

'Oh, Miss Mullan,' she said. 'What a morning we've had. That girl came back—'

'Which girl?'

'That girl who came to interview Mr Shaw for the papers.'

'Oh,' said Louise. 'Her.' She hadn't taken to Eliza; she'd thought she was too self-confident by half. Snooty too.

'Yes. She was quite rude.'

'She has no business being rude to you. What did she say?'

'She said, "Is Matt Shaw in there?" so I said what you always told me to say, I said, "Mr Shaw is very busy at the moment but I'll see if he has a moment to speak with you," and she said, "Don't give me all that rubbish, is he in, yes or no."'

'That is rude. So what did you say?'

'I said, "Well yes, he is". And she just barged in.'

'Goodness. And then what?'

'Well, I heard a lot of shouting.'

'What about?'

'Well, she was saying he was pathetic and he should . . .' She glanced at her notepad.

'Jenny, you didn't write it down!' said Louise, grinning at her.

'Well, Miss Mullan, you always say to take notes if it might be important.'

'That's – that's true. So what else did you hear?'

'Well, she said he should stop being so – well it was the f-word, Miss Mullan.'

'Goodness.'

'Yes, stop being so, well so – so effing – defensive, and did he really think they were going to write dis – disappearing things, would that be it?'

'Disparaging?'

'Yes, that's it. Disparaging things about him, and he said he didn't trust anyone in her business and she said she'd begun to admire him, and think he was clever, but now she could see he was a total – total – oh, yes, moron, and it was the last time she'd ever try to do anything for him and then he said he didn't want her to do – well – effing anything for him, he'd never asked her to in the first place, and she'd obviously lied to him and what did she have to say about that.'

'Right. So – then did she leave?'

'No, but I went to the toilet. I felt a bit bad listening any more. And when I came back it was all quiet. So I thought she'd gone and then I thought maybe he'd like a nice cup of tea or something, to calm him down a bit, and a biscuit, you know how he likes his biscuits, so I knocked on the door and there was no reply, and I thought he'd gone out, so I opened the door really quietly, and—'

'And what, Jenny?'

'And – well, he was kissing her. I mean really kissing her, you know. And she was – Miss Mullan, she was most definitely kissing him back.'

Emma Northcott looked at her brother across the table. They had dinner together once a month; it had been an unbreakable rule ever since Emma

195

had come down from Oxford and Jeremy had returned from National Service.

'So – you're off to the Big Apple, then? Told the aged Ps?'

'Yes. Pa wasn't very interested, Ma said she'd be over to stay with me quite often. She's got friends there, you know, and then there are the cousins in DC.'

'Yes, of course I know. Now Jeremy, I want to talk to you about something. Nothing to do with me, I know, but—'

'That's never stopped you before.'

'True. Anyway, it's about Eliza. I presume you've told her?'

'Oh yes. She seemed quite happy about it.'

'Jeremy, what are your plans? For Eliza? Or rather, with Eliza?'

'Well – not quite sure.'

'You do seem very fond of her.'

'I am. Very fond. She's a darling.'

'Is that it?'

'Probably not.' He grinned at Emma. 'I know what you're thinking. And I've been thinking about it too.'

'You have?'

'Yeah, I have. Quite seriously. Maybe very seriously. She's the perfect girl, in lots of ways. Fun, bright – very bright, attractive. We get on incredibly well. I adore her, actually.'

'So?'

'Yes, I know, I know. She probably is the girl for me. And it's time I got married, I know that too.'

'Yes, it really is. And have you thought about how Eliza might be feeling right now?'

'Well – not really. She didn't seem too upset.'

'Jeremy, you are incredible. Have you not heard of female pride?'

'I'm sorry?'

Emma struggled not to sound too exasperated.

'Jeremy, look at it from Eliza's point of view. You've been going out with her, and I presume rather more than that, for about a year. Everyone thinks of you as a couple. Now suddenly you announce you're off to the States, bye Eliza, been fun, see you when I get back—'

'I didn't say anything remotely like that,' said Jeremy half-indignantly.

'You might not have expressed it like that. That's how it looks to everyone, most of all to Eliza. You really have got a hide like a rhinoceros,

Jeremy, I feel quite ashamed of you.'

'But Emma, she's got a career. Just been made fashion editor. She's not going to be bothered about how things look. And anyway, is she going to want an absentee fiancé? We can see lots of each other, I've organised very generous expenses, I thought I'd leave it till I got back, see if we both feel the same way, and then—'

'Jeremy! Eliza could easily be snapped up in the space of six months. I'm sorry to interfere, and of course you're not sure, it's different, but . . .'

'Well – I'll think about it really hard, promise. And I'll let you know if anything drastic takes place. Now – shall we share a Chateaubriand? I'm awfully hungry.'

Charles arrived home on the dot of eight thirty. He was carrying some flowers and looked tired.

'Hello, darling. These are for you.'

'Oh – thank you, darling. They're lovely. I'll just – just put them in water. Nice evening?'

'Yes, very nice, thanks. Just chewing the fat about Gib.'

'Anyone I know?'

'Oh – yes. Sandy Miles, remember? He was one of my ushers. And John Bridges.'

'I remember John. Nice man. And his wife, she was very pretty. Well, dinner's ready, I'll just dish up. I presume you won't want anything to drink before we sit down?' Her tone made it very clear there would be no question of such a thing.

'No, no, of course not. Nice dress, darling, is it new?'

'Oh – yes. I bought it today. At Jaeger. Do you like it?'

'Yes, sweetheart, it's lovely. But—'

'But what, Charles?'

'You seem to be buying an awful lot of new dresses.'

'Well, I like pretty clothes. Is there anything wrong with that?'

'Of course not, darling. And I like to see you looking nice, of course. It's just that – well, we're a bit stretched this month. Bit overdrawn, you know?'

'Are we? My account's all right.'

'I know, darling, but all you have to pay for out of that is your travelling expenses and the food of course . . .'

197

'And my hairdressing, we agreed that. And the char, don't forget. So, quite a lot really. Anyway, darling, sit down and I'll dish up. And then we can talk about the weekend. Susie Short said would we like to go to the Ad Lib. I'd love to go, Charles, I wish we were members, everyone seems to belong these days.'

'Juliet—'

'I hope you like this, it's a new dish I got from *Good Housekeeping*, I know how you love chicken – wine?'

'That would be lovely, although I thought we did agree not every night, not when we're at home together, just the two of us. Still, as it's open—'

'Mummy and Daddy always have a glass of wine, every night, Mummy says it makes a meal that bit more special.'

'Of course it does and it's lovely, but again, rather expensive—'

'Oh Charles, do stop going on about money, it's so boring and that reminds me, I keep meaning to ask you, why don't we open an account at Harrods?'

'I'm a bit wary of accounts, Juliet, I think they're dangerous things—'

'Charles! This is getting very tedious. Now, I bought something else today, at Fenwicks, and I can't wait to show you—'

'I can't wait to see it, darling, either.'

'But you're going to have to wait till bedtime. It's really quite special.' She looked at him from under her eyelashes.

'Right. Well, I'd best eat up, hadn't I?'

'Well, I don't want you rushing my meal. Are you enjoying it?'

'Yes, it's lovely. Really delicious, thank you. You're so clever, darling.'

'Not terribly. I just like looking after you. It's all I ever wanted. I can't wait for when I can do it full-time – don't look so frightened, Charles, I know we've got to wait a bit. Now about this account at Harrods, I've actually got the forms here.'

'Matt, hello, it's Eliza. I've got the copy for you to check.'

'Oh – great, thanks.'

'Shall I bike it over to you?'

'You could. Or you could bring it yourself. In case I have any comments.'

'I do have a few other things to do, I'm afraid,' said Eliza tartly. 'And you can ring me with the comments. Or you could come over here.'

'Er – I don't think so. In this instance I'm the client.'

'I'm not sure that's right.'

'I am.'

'Matt, this is a ridiculous conversation. I'll bike the copy over. And you can ring me with any comments.'

And please, please God don't let there be any. Jack Beckham would go completely insane if he knew this was happening. 'Copy approval is for advertising agencies,' he said, whenever anyone – usually an interviewed actor – requested it. 'They want fucking approval, they can pay for the fucking space.'

She was definitely feeling a bit odd about Matt. These weird things kept happening. Like at the church, and in the orangery, and when they'd had that fight and he'd kissed her. What had that been about?

It had been quite a kiss. She'd literally felt weak at the knees afterwards. Of course it hadn't meant anything; it was just that they got carried away. But – well, she hadn't quite been able to forget about it.

She was going to feel a bit silly seeing him now as well. He must think she was a bit of a tart, as well as all the other things, like snobby and bossy, and full of herself.

Although it had been – well – it had been his idea. Their relationship was very complicated. Not that it was a relationship, of course.

Her phone rang at five. 'Got a few queries. Would you like to have a drink with me, so we can discuss them?'

'No, Matt, I'm sorry, there really isn't time.'

'OK then, I'll just bring this over later and come up to your office. How's that?'

'Matt, no.'

'But I've agreed to save you the trip. And I'd like to see your office. You've seen mine, after all.'

'Matt—'

'I'll be there at seven.'

At six forty-five Jack Beckham put his head round the door of her office.

'Everything sorted for your November pages?'

'Yes. Absolutely.' It wasn't, but she couldn't afford to have him hanging around her office now.

'Just remind me what you're doing for the second feature.'

'Oh – it's these designs from the Royal College. I'm calling it "Why Not?" They're quite revolutionary things, an all-in-one sort of dungaree boiler suit for instance.'

'Sounds hideous.'

'It's not, Jack, it's wonderful.'

'Got any sketches?'

'Yes, they're here – yes, look.'

'Oh, yes. I do remember now.'

'Good, and then some bunny rabbit coats in all sorts of wonderful primary colours, like yellow and blue.'

'That sounds better. Well, keep up the good work. Night, Eliza.'

'Night, Jack.'

Phew. That had been close. Five to seven. He . . .

'Eliza!'

He was back. God.

'I'd quite like to do some men's fashion in the not too distant future.'

'Yes, of course. Me too. Wonderful idea.'

'Good. Not worn by some fairy boys, mind, but red-blooded males – footballers, that sort of thing. Like – well, OK, this chap'd do. Boyfriend of yours? Looking for Eliza, are you? This way.'

Matt walked in. Eliza felt faint.

'Oh – Matt. Hello. Yes. This is Jack Beckham, our editor. Jack, Matt Shaw.'

'Pleased to meet you,' said Matt.

'You look familiar.' He peered at Matt. 'Yeah, I thought I recognised you. You're in our feature, aren't you? The Intropreneurs.'

'Well – I hope so. Yeah. Providing—'

'Great photographs weren't they, Eliza. Terry Donovan, wasn't it? Like him, got a sense of humour. I particularly remember your pictures, Matt, up on that scaffolding. Brave of you, I thought.'

'Yes, well, I'm used to it. But there are a couple of things I'd like to—'

'We're leading on you, as a matter of fact. Double-page spread, picture of you over two-thirds of it, then a column introducing the feature and leading into your interview. And we've got you on the cover as well, small picture that is, hang on, I'll get the dummy. You'll be pleased, I think. Too late if you're not, it's gone to press.'

He disappeared into the features department. Matt and Eliza looked at one another in silence. Then, 'I am not,' Matt said, 'repeat, not—'

Beckham was back. 'Right. Here it is, look.' A small shot of Matt, dropped onto the corner of the cover, captioned. 'The Intropreneurs, the new-style tycoons, talk about life at the top.'

'What do you think about that then?'

'It's – it's not bad,' said Matt, 'not bad at all.'

'It's bloody good publicity, I'll tell you that. You should be grateful.'

'I – I am, yes. Thank you.'

'Good. Well, I'm off, see you tomorrow, Eliza.'

He slammed the door behind him. Matt looked at Eliza. She smiled at him, very sweetly.

'What was it you were saying?' she asked.

Chapter 20

'Darling—'

'Yes, darling?'

'I need to talk to you.'

'About?'

'About Summercourt.'

'Charles, if it's about finding money to fix the roof, we really can't help. We're hardly coping financially ourselves. If we can't afford to go skiing and you're fussing about my clothes budget, then we certainly can't afford to give your parents any money. They've got plenty of their own, surely, and they can always raise some on the house, Daddy suggested that when I mentioned it last time, it's just not fair to ask us—'

'Juliet, I've told you before they haven't got any money, any at all—'

'Well, that's ridiculous, of course they've got money, they're just worrying about their old age, Mummy said Granny was exactly the same, now please Charles, just don't mention it again, I'm finding it very upsetting. I love your parents, of course I do, but it's a kind of emotional blackmail what they're doing – Charles, where are you going?'

'I'm going for a walk,' said Charles. 'I need to think. And please don't talk about my parents in those terms, I don't like it.'

Juliet stared at the slammed front door. She felt rather shocked. Neither Charles nor their life together was turning out quite how she had imagined.

He decided he would ask her. It couldn't do any harm. She could turn him down of course, but then at least he'd have tried. And a few things recently had made him feel, well, differently about her. As if it wasn't all quite as he had imagined. Like – like that moment in the church. And what that wonderful old bird the godmother had said. And – of course – the way she had kissed him back, that morning in his office. He still didn't know quite how that had happened. Why he'd kissed her in the first place. Except that he really hadn't been able to stop himself.

He just wanted to – what? Explore the situation a bit further. That was all.

And so he asked her to lunch, 'to thank you, you've done me quite a big favour, actually, with that article, lot of enquiries'; she said she didn't get much in the way of a lunch hour; and then he asked her for a drink after work; and she accepted.

And thus it was that Matt Shaw and Eliza Fullerton-Clark informed their respective regular dates that they would be working late the following Wednesday; each adding, without any further consultation with one another, merely obeying some rather basic instinct, that they had no idea when they might be back, and not to make plans for dinner.

Every time she thought about leaving Summercourt, Sarah felt like screaming. Not from misery or outrage or even trepidation, but from a sheer blind panic. Summercourt was not just her home, it was where she belonged, where her entire world was centred. Nowhere else was even imaginable; wherever it was she would feel herself a vagrant.

Summercourt gave her strength, courage, comfort; it was like a staunch, serene friend.

And now people kept telling her she must leave it, that it needed the most appalling sounding sums of money spent on it, that she couldn't possibly nurse Adrian there.

The prospect seemed very nearly as dreadful as losing Adrian.

It was very close to unbearable.

If only, if only Eliza were to marry Jeremy. She knew it was wrong of her to think like that, to see Eliza's future in such financial terms, her happiness as something essential to her own, but she couldn't help it. The thought consumed her. And it wasn't as if they weren't in love with each other, they'd be terribly happy. It just had to be a matter of time; and until it happened, she mustn't make any rash decisions. She would just stay calm and wait.

'Emma, it's Jeremy. Look – I just thought I should let you know. I've decided to ask Eliza.'

'Jeremy, I'm so pleased.'

'Yes. I thought this weekend. We're going down to Norfolk together, so pretty perfect really.'

'Absolutely. Well, Ma and Pa will be pleased. Particularly Pa. He's always saying what a lively girl she is.'

'I know. Anyway, I'll have to ask her father first of course. Like to do things properly. Have to dash down tonight, only chance I've got. Eliza's out working or something.'

'Oh Adrian, isn't it wonderful?' Sarah's voice was shaky. She felt slightly dizzy. 'If only he could have stayed, I feel dreadful not giving him dinner.'

'Darling he couldn't stay, he had to get back, he explained.'

'I know. And so sweet of him to come at all, it's such a long way, he really does know how to behave.'

'Indeed he does.'

'Oh, Adrian! It's like a dream come true. Darling Eliza. Oh, how wonderful.'

'He hasn't asked her yet. She might not accept.'

'Adrian! Don't say that. Of course she'll accept. Of course she will.'

'Well, she's a very independently minded girl. And you know how much that job of hers matters.'

'Charles, hello, darling. Are you all right?'

'Yes, Mummy, I'm fine. I just rang to see how Pa was doing.'

'Pretty well,' said Sarah cautiously. 'The drugs really are helping.'

'Good. Well, I was hoping to come down this weekend, bring Juliet, but she's not feeling too good—'

'Oh, I'm sorry – Charles, she's not – not—'

'Mummy, she's got flu.' Charles's voice was heavy.

'Yes, I see. Well, give her my love. Yes.'

'And how are you?'

'Me? Oh, darling, I'm just fine. Feeling very good as a matter of fact.'

'Really? Why's that?'

'Oh – well – just had some very nice news.'

'What's that, then? About the house?'

'Oh – no. I can't tell you, darling. It's not my secret. I'm sure you'll hear soon enough.'

'Mummy, what are you talking about?'

'Charles, I really can't say. Except it's – it's family.'

'Family? Well, it must be Eliza. What's she done? New job?'

'No, Charles, much better than a new job. She's – well, Jeremy's just come down and spoken to Daddy and—'

'No! Good lord. Fantastic.'

'But don't tell anyone, will you? Because you see, she—'

'Mummy, of course I won't tell. Promise.'

'Guess what?' he said to Juliet over the supper tray he had taken her in bed. 'Good news.'

'Well, that makes a change. What is it?'

'My sister and Jeremy Northcott are getting engaged.'

'Gosh. That should stop you all worrying about Summercourt.'

'Indeed,' said Charles, stifling his irritation at this rather inappropriate response. 'Now you mustn't tell anyone because it's not official yet. I hope you're pleased.'

'Of course I'm pleased. If she is.'

'Juliet, I should think she's over the moon.'

'Well, she's very lucky,' said Juliet. Her voice had a distinct shake in it.

'Goodness, Matt. Champagne! How amazing.'

They were in the American bar at the Savoy.

'Yes, well, I've got some celebrating to do.'

'Really? What?'

'Oh, two big new clients in one week.'

'That's great.'

'How about you, any news?'

'I can't think of anything particularly,' said Eliza, 'but I'm happy to share in yours.'

'Annunciata, hello. How nice to hear from you.'

'Hello, Emma. You free for dinner on Friday?'

'Yes, think so, let's just look – yes. Thank you.'

'Good. I've got some quite interesting people coming.'

'You always do.'

'Want to bring anyone?'

'No. Would you like me to?'

'What about your beautiful brother? I've got another advertising bod coming – creative director of BBDO.'

'I'm afraid J's off to Norfolk.'

'Oh, fine. With the fair Eliza?'

'Well – yes.'

'Really? How serious do you think that is? She tries to pretend they're just friends.'

'Well, they most certainly are not "just friends". In fact—'

'No! Don't tell me.'

'I don't know what you mean, Annunciata.'

'Goodness, wait till Jack hears about this.'

'Don't you dare tell him. It's totally under wraps, he hasn't—'

'Of course I won't. Must go, Jack wants me.'

'Jack, you've lost our wager.'

'Which one was that?'

'The Eliza one. She's getting engaged. And I'm afraid I was right. To someone pretty blue-blooded.'

'Oh Christ. Not that tall blond twit?'

''Fraid so. But can you blame her? He is one of the richest young men in England.'

'I really thought better of her. She's not leaving, is she? I couldn't stand it.'

'Well – I hope not. For all our sakes. But—'

'I'll have to have words with her. So, how much do I owe you, Annunciata?'

'Twenty quid. But lunch at the Terrazza will do. I do so love it there.'

'Eliza, I – don't suppose you'd like to have dinner now? I'm starving. Or are you busy?'

'I'm not – not really, no. It sounds lovely.'

'OK. Well, have you been to Inigo Jones? It's in Covent Garden?'

'I have and I adore it. So beautiful.'

'Great. I'll go and find a phone and see if I can get a table.'

'OK. Don't be long.'

Now why had she said that? How not cool. How extremely sort of – of – Juliet-ish.

'I won't.'

He wasn't long; he came back looking rather pleased with himself.

'OK. Done. Ready at eight thirty. So we could have another.'

'What, another bottle of champagne?'

206

'If you like. It suits you, champagne.'

'Thank you. In what way?'

'Well – it's got class.'

'Matt, we'd probably better not get onto that.'

'I didn't mean that sort of class. I meant totally first rate.'

'Right. Well – thank you. You're pretty classy yourself. In a totally first-rate sort of way.'

'You reckon?'

'I reckon. You're clever. And funny. And that's a great shirt.'

'Thanks. I had it made. To my own specification.'

'Really? Where?'

'Chap in Jermyn Street. You know by the time we've walked to Inigo Jones, it will be well past eight. We could just have some more champagne there.'

'OK. Pull me up. Oh, dear. I feel a bit dizzy. Might just go to the loo. I'm sure I look a complete fright.'

'You look lovely,' he said and his voice was very serious.

'Juliet? Mummy. How are you, darling?'

'Bit better. Horrid bug, this, though.'

'Charles hasn't got it?'

'No, no.'

'Any news?'

'Well, yes. Apparently Eliza's going to marry Jeremy Northcott.'

'Goodness. From everything I've heard about him, that should solve all their problems. Stop them worrying you about it. So unfair.'

She felt very – odd. Sort of – well, very sexy. Almost uncomfortably so. She kept fidgeting about in her seat. He noticed.

'You OK?'

'Oh – yes I'm fine. You?'

'Very OK.'

It was odd, being with him when he was relaxed. And when she was relaxed. So often they were fighting. She said so.

'Yeah, I suppose we are. Why do you think that is?'

'Oh – can't imagine. Because you're such a stroppy bugger, maybe?'

'I am not stroppy.'

'Matt, you are very stroppy.'

There was a silence; he picked up his glass and scowled into it.

'And I suppose you're not?'

'I don't think I'm stroppy.'

'Yes you are.'

'OK,' she said agreeably and smiled at him. He stared at her and then quite suddenly smiled back.

'Yes, all right. I am too.'

'Do I make you worse, do you think?'

'Definitely.'

'Why do you think that is?'

'Well, obviously, because you're stroppy. In fact I'm the sweetest, mildest bloke when you're not there.'

'Oh, really? And what would your girlfriend have to say about that, I wonder?'

'I have no idea,' he said, and took another gulp of wine.

A stab of something. Not jealousy, obviously. Just – interest.

'She's very pretty, your girlfriend.'

'Yes, she is.' He sounded rather complacent.

'And – is she clever? Nice?'

'I don't think I want to talk about her.'

'Why not?'

'Because – because it's hardly the way to improve the evening.'

'There you go, stropping away. Now there's a new verb, to strop. So, does she live with you?'

'Good God, no.' He looked horrified. Eliza giggled.

'But you – well, you?' This wasn't very ladylike of her, but she really wanted to know.

'I sleep with her,' he said, and his eyes on hers were very steady. 'If that's what you're asking.'

'Of – of course not.'

'I think it was, but never mind.' He looked round the restaurant, then, as if he had made some kind of decision, back at her. 'Now, while we're getting down to basics, how about you? Do you live with him?'

There was no need to establish who 'he' was.

'Absolutely not.'

'But you sleep with him?'

'That's not a very gentlemanly question.'

'I'm not a gentleman. That's one thing we have established. Anyway, asking me the same question wasn't very ladylike.'

'I didn't actually ask it.'

'Not in so many words perhaps. So—'

'Yes,' she said almost reluctantly, 'I do – sleep with him.'

'OK. That's got that out the way. Any more questions?'

'No. No, don't think so.'

'Good. Did you ever play truth, dare, promise?'

'Course. When I was little. Not since I grew up. Why?'

'Oh – my sister and I used to play it a lot as well. I was just thinking we were being quite truthful with each other. That's always interesting. More wine?'

'Please. Oh, this is so – so nice.'

'Good. It's a burgundy.'

'I don't mean the wine. I meant sitting here, just chatting to you, getting to know you properly. All these years since we first met—'

'Do you remember that?'

'Of course,' she said, surprised. 'Of course I do. It was at Waterloo station, and you and Charles were home on leave and I thought how good-looking you were.'

'Really?' He looked so astonished, she laughed.

'Of course. Ask Charles if you don't believe me, I told him.'

'Blimey. Well. I thought you were pretty good-looking too.'

'There you are then. It's obviously a match made in heaven. Pity we've wasted all this time squabbling.'

'Yes. Um – let's do a bit more truth-telling. What's the most important thing in the world to you, Eliza?'

'My work.' It shot out, without even a pause for consideration. 'You?'

'Sort of the same. Being a success. Making a ton of money. So – work.'

'But do you enjoy what you do so much you'd do it even if it didn't make you rich?'

'Oh, no,' he said with the same lack of consideration. 'I'd find something else that did.'

'Yes, I see. For me it's not the money.'

'Well, it's different for girls. Anyway, they can just marry rich blokes.'

'That is the most terrible thing to say.'

'Well, it's true.'

'OK, so you could marry a rich girl.'

'And do you think that would give me any satisfaction? Even supposing I could. Which I couldn't.'

'Why not?'

'Eliza, don't be bloody stupid. What rich girl would marry me?'

She looked at him, sitting there, so cool and sexy and clever and stroppy and she leaned forward across the table and kissed him, very gently, on the mouth.

'Lots,' she said. 'I should think.'

'Sarah dear, it's Anna.'

'Oh – hello, Anna.'

'I just rang to see how Adrian was.'

'He's doing pretty well, I think. Being so brave.'

'And you're not feeling too down? Worried about the house?'

'No, not really. Actually I'm feeling rather happy this evening.'

'Glad to hear it. Why?'

'Well – I shouldn't really tell you.'

'Oh, don't be so ridiculous. Of course you should and you're going to. I can hear it in your voice.'

'Well – all right. But you're not to tell anyone. Jeremy just came down to see Adrian. A couple of hours ago.'

'What, to ask if he can marry Eliza?'

'Yes.'

'About time too. You think she will?'

'Of course she will. I mean, they're so perfectly suited. So – so happy together. It's just marvellous.'

There was a silence, then Anna Marchant said, 'No wonder you're not worried about the house any more.'

'Anna, that's a terrible thing to say.'

'It may be terrible, Sarah, but it's also true. Isn't it? Oh, don't get me wrong, marriages – our sort of marriages – always have been based on property, and I'm delighted for you. I just worry a little about Eliza going into something like that. She's so ambitious, so clever, and such – such a free spirit.'

'Anna, you're talking as if she's going to be sold into domestic servitude, when she's going to have the most marvellous life.'

'Possibly. Oh, don't get me wrong, I like Jeremy very much, and he was the sweetest child. He's just not very – exciting.'

'Anna, you are in danger of making me quite cross,' said Sarah. 'Eliza is obviously very much in love with him, and I'm pretty sure they're – well—'

'Sleeping together? Well, I should hope so, after all this time, something wrong if they're not. Oh, Sarah, don't mind me. It is wonderful news, and marvellous for you. It's just that I adore my goddaughter and I want her to be happy. Tell her to give me a ring when she has a moment. Night, darling.'

'Goodnight,' said Sarah and slammed the phone down.

'So – suppose you got married. Would work still be so important?'

'Of course.'

'Better not marry me, then.'

'Is that a proposal?'

'Certainly not.'

'So your wife's going to be a domestic slave, is she? Yes, I forgot, you said that the other day.'

'Well, she's certainly going to be at home looking after me. That's for sure.'

'How boring for her.'

'Why? Am I so boring?'

'No, you're not, not at all, but presumably you're hardly ever there. You're out working till all hours.'

'All the more reason to have her home, waiting for me with a good hot meal.'

'Matt Shaw! I can't believe I'm hearing this.'

'Well, you are. I'm not ashamed of it. I think it's the natural order of things.'

'Did your mum stay at home?'

'Most of the time, yeah. She did a bit of cleaning, that sort of thing. Fitted round my dad.'

'And did your dad help in the house?'

'Course not. He paid for it, didn't he? And all the food and that. Why should he wash up as well? Not fair, far as I can see.'

'I – don't know.' She really couldn't find an answer.

'Jeremy – does he wash up and that?'

'Well, if we're eating at home, yes he does. Specially if I've cooked. But he likes cooking too.'

'Blimey. Funny bloke. I suppose it's different for him. Sort of a novelty. I mean, presumably staff and that do it usually. What's he do? Works in advertising, that right? And – does he – does he take his work seriously?'

'Goodness, yes. It's one of the things I really like about him. He doesn't actually have to work—'

'Why not?'

'Well – well, because he just doesn't.'

'Got private money, has he?'

His eyes were very watchful on hers.

'Mmm. What does Georgina do?'

'She works in a shop. A clothes shop in the King's Road, called Silk, Satin, Cotton, Rags.'

'Oh. I know it well. Lovely things. I must go and introduce myself, we didn't really talk at the wedding, tell her we had dinner.'

'I'd really rather you didn't,' he said. 'She wouldn't like it.'

'Why not?'

'Because you're like you are.'

'Which is?'

'So bloody sexy,' he said, and then, 'Ignore that. It's the wine talking.'

'Is it?'

'No,' he said, 'not really.' And he took her hand across the table and pulled it towards him and raised it to his mouth. Turned it over. Kissed the palm. His tongue moving over it. She stared at him, feeling it, feeling it everywhere, and with a thud of shock, in her head and wherever or whatever her heart was, and deep, deep inside her, as if the tongue was in her, probing at her, sweetly uncomfortable. She shut her eyes, opened them again, met his.

'So bloody sexy,' he said.

'Apparently Eliza is engaged to that chap at the wedding, Jeremy Northcott,' said Carol Judd.

'Really?' her husband replied. 'Well that should stop them all bleating about not having any money. I can't stand the way those people carry on as if they were one step from the workhouse.'

'I know,' said Carol, 'and upsetting Juliet, it's too bad of them, when they're obviously completely loaded.'

'I really loved that house of yours,' Matt said. He had asked for the bill; they were on coffee.

'I'm so pleased. It's so special to me. To all of us.'

'Specially the orangery. That was gorgeous.'

'Well, you must come again. See the inside. Come this weekend – oh, no, I'm going away, but – next. I'd love to show it to you properly. You can bring Georgina if you like.'

'No, don't think so. Not a good idea. What about Jeremy, will he be there?'

'No,' said Eliza and she could hear her own voice, very cool, very firm. 'He won't.'

'OK. It's a date.'

'I'd like to see your flat too, Matt. The one in Rotherhithe. It sounds so cool.'

'OK. You can. It's open to the public.'

'Right. So there's the promise. We've done truth. Only thing we haven't done,' she said, smiling into his eyes, 'is the dare.'

'Piers, do concentrate. I've got a bit of news.'

'Yes, all right, sorry. Trying to finish the crossword. What was it?'

'I've just been talking to Sarah. And apparently, Jeremy Northcott has just asked Adrian if he can marry Eliza?'

'Really? Well done her. Can you think of a five-letter word ending in D that bakers and others do daily?'

'Grind, dear. Is that all you have to say?'

'Well, there isn't a lot more, is there. She has done well. He's one of the richest young men in England. Better than her mother managed.'

'Piers, really!'

'Well, he's a nice enough chap, Adrian, but absolutely useless. No money, no drive, got through what was left of Sarah's inheritance. I should think they're both down on their bended knees in gratitude.'

'Yes,' said Anna soberly, 'that's worrying me as well.'

'Well, Matt, it's been so lovely, thank you.'

Eliza stood up, and smiled at Matt, bent to kiss him again, on the cheek this time, and then rather unsteadily walked to the door.

As they reached the street, she turned to him, suddenly thinking she would offer him a lift, for her car was only a few streets away, in the silent reaches of Covent Garden, and saw he was standing stock still, and just staring at her, clearly wanting to say something.

'I've got a dare for you, Eliza,' he said, finally speaking rather slowly and sounding a bit breathless. 'Come back to my place. For a nightcap. You said you'd like to see it.'

And she said, 'What, now?' and he said, 'Yes Eliza, now.' And there was a long silence and then her eyes met his, very steadily and then she smiled at him, and tossed back her mane of hair, and said, 'Dare accepted. OK, Matt. You're on.'

That weekend, Jeremy Northcott went down on one knee in a muddy field in Norfolk, produced a rock of a diamond from his pocket and asked Eliza Fullerton-Clark to marry him.

Part Two

The Marriage

1965

God, she felt terrible. She really felt she might throw up, then and there. All over the registrar's table.

The registrar's table. In Chelsea Town Hall. Not the altar in Wellesley village church.

She looked down; saw her shoes. Her white pumps, with those wonderful red bows on them, that echoed the red bows on her dress. Her short lace dress, not a long, full-skirted satin dress. A very short white lace dress with red bows all down the front.

The ceremony continued; they made their vows, were declared man and wife, exchanged a kiss.

She felt better now, turned, smiled into the room. At their friends. Not a church-full, just a couple of rows; and only a handful of family, mostly his.

They signed the register, stood up, walked out of the room. Out of the room, not down the aisle, not into the church porch but the register-office lobby. And then outside, onto the steps, not into a laughing, loving crowd but a couple of half-interested passers-by.

What had happened to her; what would happen to her? And how could she possibly feel so shockingly, wonderfully happy?

Chapter 21

Autumn/Winter 1964

'Mummy, I've got something to tell you.'

'Yes, darling, we know. And it's so lovely—'

'No, Mummy, it's not so lovely. It's not what you think. Jeremy's asked me to marry him—'

'Yes, darling, we know. He asked Daddy, all very correctly . . .'

'Yes, he told me. But – well, I'm not going to. Marry him. I can't. I really can't. Because I'm not – not in love with him. I'm in love with someone else.'

Who she wasn't – necessarily – going to marry. He certainly hadn't asked her. And she didn't like his views on marriage. She didn't like his views on lots of things. But she did, totally and absolutely and violently, love him. It was extraordinary. Really extraordinary.

It was partly the sex, of course. The sex was amazing. Totally astonishing. She would never have dreamed that a different body could make so much difference. The difference between smiling, easy pleasure and shrieking, frantic delight; between wanting and needing, desperately, desperately needing, so much that she was unable to think about anything else until she had it. Had him. Between comfort and torture; between warmth and tenderness and shocking, sweating near-distress; between saying 'that was lovely' and speechless, tearful stillness.

'Oh, my God,' she had said, when, after the first time, she finally eased, flung herself back from him, gazing at him, fighting for breath, her body still pulsing in a sort of aftershock, 'Oh, my God, Matt.'

'Oh, my God what?'

'Just – oh, my God.'

'I knew it,' he said, and sounded smug suddenly, 'I knew you hadn't. Not properly.'

'Hadn't what?'

'Hadn't come.'

'Of course I had.'

'Not properly. Not how you deserved.'

'Don't be silly,' she said, smiling. 'You can't deserve sex.'

'OK. How you needed. You're so bloody sexy, Eliza, and you were just missing the point. I could tell, you know. You were like – like some sort of half-virgin.'

'That's even sillier. You can't be a half-virgin; it's like being a little bit pregnant.'

'Course you can. You were. Half-cooked – oh shit, I'm no good with words.'

'No,' she said, 'you're not.'

'Well,' he said, after a pause, 'how about this? I love you.'

It was the first time he'd said it.

'Mr Shaw seems very cheerful at the moment.'

'He does, doesn't he?'

'I mean, I just told him Roderick Brownlow didn't want to work with us on the development and he just said, "OK, fine."'

'I know. I heard him.'

'Well, I'm sure it won't last. We'd better make the most of it.'

'It's all over with that girlfriend of his, Georgina.'

'Oh really?'

'Yes, as of Monday morning.'

'Jenny, how do you know that?'

'He told her on the phone. He said he just wouldn't be seeing her any more and that was that.'

'God. What a bastard he is. Fancy doing it on the phone.'

'That's what I thought. And then she started to cry and he said all right, he'd meet her that evening one last time and explain. It wasn't very nice to listen to.'

'Maybe you shouldn't have listened then.'

'Maybe not. But it was the usual problem, I couldn't seem to switch the interconnecting thing off.'

'Jenny, if you're having that much trouble with the phone, maybe you'd better get it looked at.'

'I did, Miss Mullan. The man said there was nothing wrong with it.'

'Well, ask him to check it again.'

'Yes, all right Miss Mullan, I will.'

Everyone was so angry with her. Her parents, in a quiet, damaged, seething way: how could she have turned Jeremy down, when he loved her so much – 'I'm not sure he does, you know, actually', when he could offer her so much – 'but what he's offering is not what I want'; when they had been together for so long – 'I mean, this – this other young man, how well do you know him?' her mother said, her eyes full of tears.

'Not that well. But well enough.'

She could see, of course, what it meant to them.

Jeremy had been what her entire upbringing had been about: what they had worked for, sacrificed for, hoped for, almost prayed for. Turned down for someone and indeed something so inexplicably different, so outside the realm of their own experience, that they saw it as a personal slight, an insult to their social creed. And she could see she had robbed them of something else as well, although they would die rather than admit it.

Charles, who had professed such genuine friendship with Matt, was almost as shocked and nearly as angry. 'It's ridiculous, Eliza, you must see that, an absurd idea, throwing over Jeremy for Matt Shaw.'

'But why?' she had asked, and, 'Just tell me what's so ridiculous about it, Charles?'

'You know very well,' he said, and no, she had said, she didn't,' and he said rather lamely that Jeremy was one of his greatest friends, he had been his best man, for God's sake, and she had said she was very sorry, but she really couldn't be expected to marry someone she didn't love just because he had been her brother's best man.

'Well, I hope you know what you're doing,' Charles said. 'I really don't want you to be hurt.'

Juliet said nothing to her at all.

She saw Emma in a restaurant one day and went over to her table, trying to be friendly, hoping to explain; Emma was curt and cut her short, turned back to her companion very pointedly. Eliza supposed it was understandable, but she was surprised nonetheless. Emma was such a free spirit, so anxious to be recognised as such.

She began to dread bumping into any of Jeremy's friends; they were all very cool with her, clearly feeling, exactly as Emma did, that she had behaved extremely badly. Anyone would think, Eliza reflected, she had been married to Jeremy and two-timing him. Whereas they hadn't even been engaged, and whose fault was that? If he'd asked her earlier, she'd probably be married to him by now. She did try making this point one night at a drinks party to one of his old army friends; it was a big mistake. He looked at her very coldly and simply walked away.

What was that expression? Oh, yes, closed ranks.

Most of her friends, the ones she had grown up with anyway, and gone to school with and shared flats with, were horrified, and told her she'd regret it, and that men like Jeremy Northcott didn't come along very often; though a handful were clearly intrigued, and asked her what exactly it was about Matt that was so special. She knew what that meant: sex. Everyone assumed it was sex and only sex. It had to be the only explanation, for turning down someone as rich and handsome and totally suitable as Jeremy for someone who was – as one of her friends put it – 'from such a different world'. But it wasn't sex – or only partly; it was almost impossible to explain, but the closest was that when she was with Matt, she felt absolutely and completely interested and absorbed by him, on every level and in every way. He engaged her. He engaged her head and her heart and her body and her very self. Life without him was completely unthinkable. It was as simple as that.

Even Maddy seemed a bit shocked. 'Jeremy's so sweet,' she said, 'and he just is so suitable for you.'

'Maddy!' cried Eliza. 'Don't you start! I thought at least you'd understand, I thought you'd be pleased with me, for choosing someone not suitable and predictable.'

'It's not that,' said Maddy. 'It's just that I'm not sure Matt's really right for you altogether. He's awfully different from you, Eliza. As a person, I mean. And in his own way, he's more old-fashioned than Jeremy.'

'Well, that's just totally ridiculous,' said Eliza.

Most of the younger fellow fashion editors thought she was mad, throwing away a prize like Jeremy, 'instead of getting away from all this shit,' said one, and Annunciata and her ilk were coolly amused, implying that they thought Eliza was being silly and immature and didn't quite know what she was doing.

Only Jack Beckham seemed to be on her side, and actually took her out for a drink. 'Well done,' he said. 'Liked that young man, what I saw of him that is, liked him a lot. Not easy, what you've done, though, I can see that.'

Eliza was so touched and surprised she started to cry and then said she was sorry to be so silly; but Jack lent her his handkerchief, and said at least she wouldn't be leaving to have any babies yet.

'Of course I won't be having any babies,' said Eliza, sniffing, 'I've just said I won't marry someone, Jack, not the other way round.'

Anna Marchant, her godmother, invited her to lunch, and instead of launching into the attack Eliza had expected, handed her a large sherry and said, 'I'm sure everyone's been telling you what a terrible mistake you're making. I'm not one of them. I'm proud of you. Too easy to just say yes and do what everyone wanted. Now, don't start crying for goodness' sake. I thought you'd be pleased.'

'I am pleased,' said Eliza, 'of course I am. But it's been so awful, everyone telling me I'm mad or bad or both.'

'Well, I'm not surprised. Nothing to do with them, of course, but people are bloody nosy, and nothing easier than to live other people's lives for them.'

'I suppose so. And of course I've broken Mummy's heart—'

'That's nonsense. She's disappointed, of course she is, and I can see it would be very nice for her, to have you gliding up the aisle with young Northcott. But she wouldn't have wanted you to be unhappy either. Which you would have been if you'd married someone you didn't love. She'll come round, darling. Don't worry.'

'And then there's the house.'

'Oh, I know all about the house, but you can't go marrying someone just to pay for some building work.'

Eliza giggled, then looked more serious again. 'Gommie, there's more to it than that, you know there is. It's so important to her, that house, and with Daddy being so ill, she needs to stay there, if she can.'

'Well, her life would be easier if she didn't, of course, but I know how she feels. We'll sort something out for her, don't worry. What about Matt, he's in the building business, isn't he? Can't he help?'

'I – don't know. He hasn't got any real money, if that's what you mean.'

'Maybe not, but he must know a few builders.'

'Yes, I suppose so.'

'You going to marry him? I liked him very much. Interesting, clever, bit of a rough diamond, but that was the whole trouble with Jeremy, he was too smooth a one for you: not a lot of sparkle. Anyway, you're not answering my question. Are you going to marry Matt Shaw?'

'I don't know,' said Eliza, with a heavy sigh, 'he hasn't asked me, so maybe not.'

'He will,' said Anna Marchant. 'I'd put money on it.'

The one person who'd been completely sweet and nice to her had been Jeremy. It was absurd really; she'd looked down at him, as he knelt there in the mud, and after – actually – a very brief pause, said she was very sorry, but she couldn't, she just didn't love him enough, and then burst into tears; and he'd stood up, put the ring box back in the pocket of his Barbour, put his arm round her and said, there, there, he quite understood, he'd much rather she was honest and didn't marry him now than walked out on him later. They'd gone back to the house and had tea and crumpets in the kitchen, and then she'd said she really thought she'd better go and he'd said yes, probably best, and then he'd actually put her case in her car and kissed her goodbye and waved her off. That moment had probably been the hardest of all; looking at him in her rear-view mirror, so unutterably handsome and nice and – so perfect really, his golden Labradors on either side of him, and the massive house in the background, and she wondered, just very momentarily, whether she had done the right thing. Very momentarily though; and then she drove straight to Matt's place by the river and he was waiting for her, anxious and almost truculent with trepidation, and everything was all right.

She stayed in her own tiny flat in Earls Court, spending most nights with Matt in Rotherhithe, and driving home at crack of dawn to get ready for the day. She had wondered if he would suggest she moved in with him, but he did rather the reverse, pointing out on that first Sunday that it really wouldn't be very practical. 'It's so small here, we'd drive each other nuts. There'd be all your clothes and where'd you put them? I'm falling over mine as it is.' He then added that it was very early days anyway, and they should probably take things a bit steady. Ignoring a stab of raw terror, telling herself she was acting like a caricature of herself, she agreed.

Jeremy left for New York; he even phoned her the day before he left, 'I thought I'd just say goodbye, seemed a bit unfriendly not to and we are still friends aren't we?' Slightly bemused, but grateful, she agreed.

Christmas was – well, it was odd. All right, of course, but odd. The Summercourt Christmas that she had known all her life, the perfectly decorated house, the huge tree, the carol service on the village green, midnight mass, the whole family gathered by the fire for presents, the enormous turkey carved by her father, the evening's charades – all this was barred to her. There was a slightly chilly note from her mother: they obviously couldn't host Christmas this year and were invited to spend it with local friends instead.

'And I really don't feel able to ask if you can join us, under the circumstances, I think they would find it rather uncomfortable.'

'Fucking hell,' said Matt when she showed it to him, laughing, for she knew its absurdity would amuse rather than offend him. 'What am I supposed to have done, kicked a litter of puppies to death? I tell you what, my family wouldn't be uncomfortable inviting you, want to experience a Clapham Christmas? Scarlett'll be there, you like Scarlett, don't you?'

Eliza did like Scarlett, very much; she seemed to have all Matt's virtues and none of his vices. She was good company – although Eliza sensed a sadness underlining the sharp remarks that she couldn't quite pinpoint. She told Eliza she thought she was very good for Matt. 'He's not nearly so pleased with himself as he was. As far as I can see all his other girlfriends have let him walk all over them, I like to see him stood up to.'

Eliza, who actually found it quite difficult to stand up to Matt and more often than not gave in simply for a quiet life, was very pleased by this and resolved to be firmer with him in future.

Scarlett had a very nice flat in Kensington, which Eliza would have priced beyond her air-hostess salary, but then she told herself she didn't actually know what that was; she also had a lot of very expensive clothes, including a fur coat, which she kept telling Matt was rabbit. Eliza, who knew sable when she saw it, was intrigued and resolved to ask her about it when she knew her better.

They spent much of Christmas day in bed; but in the evening, they went over to Clapham and Eliza was introduced to Matt's family. She liked Sandra very much, she was pretty and jokey and had the same sense of style as her daughter, and the two boys were great, but she wasn't so sure about Pete. She could tell he felt the same, was clearly suspicious of her and more than once made a joke about her 'slumming', as he put it. It was clearly a situation that would either resolve itself or not; there was nothing she could do about it.

She was interested to observe Matt in the heart of his family. She had half-expected him to behave differently, but he was exactly the same, bit cocky, quite touchy, very affectionate to his mother.

They drank a lot, watched TV, and after a bit Matt and his brothers and Pete went out to the pub 'just for a couple'.

'Sorry about this,' Sandra said apologetically. 'Pete doesn't feel it's Christmas if he doesn't go to the pub. When they get back we'll play Monopoly if that's all right, Matt's favourite since he was quite a little chap.'

Eliza said she didn't mind at all, and asked Sandra where she bought her clothes, 'I just love that dress, it's completely fab', and then settled down to an evening of Martinis and Monopoly, watching Matt sweep the board – she had a strong suspicion he cheated – and buying not only Park Lane and Oxford Street and a whole lot of hotels, but all the London stations as well. She wondered if he would ever do it for real, and decided that, with him, nothing was impossible.

Chapter 22

'So!' Mariella's huge dark eyes danced at Eliza. 'Tell me, *cara*, tell me all about this new love of your life. It sounds most romantic.'

'He most certainly isn't romantic, I can tell you that.'

'Unlike the noble Jeremy.'

'Well, yes. Yes, Jeremy was really romantic. I mean, did I tell you, he even knelt down in a muddy field to ask me to marry him.'

'And you still said no!'

'I still said no.'

'And Matt – how did he ask you?'

'He didn't,' said Eliza and even to herself her voice sounded abrupt.

'So – you gave up Jeremy, you gave up a fortune, you gave up your family's love—'

'Mariella,' said Eliza, laughing, 'you're making it all sound much more dramatic than it really was.'

'I don't think so. What did I say that was not true?'

'Well – nothing, I suppose. But—'

'Are you living with him?'

'Yes and no.'

'And what does that mean?'

'Well – I spend a lot of time at his place, obviously. But I still use my flat as home. I keep my clothes there, and so on. If he's busy, I stay there.'

'So, he allows you to use his place for sex. And nothing else.'

'Mariella! No. We eat there sometimes. I cook supper.'

'You cook supper! *Cara, cara*, at the very least he should be cooking for you.'

'He doesn't do that sort of thing.'

'And why not?'

'Well – he – he doesn't come from a background where men cook.'

'Giovanni neither. But he often cooks.'

'I don't think we could compare Giovanni and Matt.'

'I would disagree. To me they sound very much the same. Both – what do you say, made by themselves—'

'Self-made.'

'Exactly what I said. Both very married to their work, both with women they are most fortunate to have. I must tell you, Eliza, so far I so much prefer Jeremy.'

'Mariella, you haven't even met Matt.'

'Well, we must put that right. I shall make a special visit. I might even bring Giovanni, he needs some more shoes.'

'That would be lovely. But the whole point about all this is, I didn't love Jeremy.'

'But that does not mean Matt should treat you badly.'

'He doesn't treat me badly.'

'*Mi scusi, cara*, but he does not treat you well. Therefore I think, he treats you badly.'

'No, but you see, he didn't ask me to leave Jeremy. I decided to. It was all down to me.'

'Even so – if he loves you—'

'Mariella, I'm really sorry, I've got to go, I'll be late for Cardin at this rate. See you very soon, maybe tomorrow?'

She was in Paris for the collections, with a horrendously difficult idea to realise. She had regretted having it at all, had tried indeed to banish it from her brain, but she had finally, almost against her better judgement, pitched it to Jack. Jack inevitably had loved it, and had told her that if she managed to pull it off, he would display it as a fold-out extension on heavier paper than the rest of the magazine. Eliza felt quite faint at the thought of both the responsibility of that and the incredible kudos she would gain from it.

Her idea was that instead of the normal run of eight or ten photographs of clothes from all the different designers, *Charisma* would offer its readers just one big picture, featuring the clothes from ten or twelve houses all together. This was, everyone told her, completely impossible. The dragonesses who policed the releasing of garments held rigid timetables, the competition from other fashion editors not only for the clothes but their permitted release was intense, the models were fully booked up to eighteen hours a day.

But she had a plan, and it was to shoot at two o'clock in the morning.

The hours between midnight and six were quiet; all she had to do, she told herself, was a bit of persuasion.

She had booked Rex Ingham to do the shoot; he had sorted out a studio, and she had managed to bribe at least half a dozen models, largely by paying them double their normal fees, but more successfully by promising them future work with *Charisma*. It was the magazine they all wanted to be in at the time, *Vogue* apart, and Eliza was notoriously picky, always after a new girl, a new look.

She had arranged sandwiches, wine, cigarettes and even allowed it to be known unofficially that should the odd spliff appear she would turn a blind eye.

So far, with four days to go, she had only managed to secure three outfits. Most of the *vendeuses* just sneered at her.

By the end of the next day she had hit on another plan: to beg the outfits from all the editors who were doing late-night shoots, promising to return them first thing in the morning. This meant that they would avoid the responsibility of getting the clothes back and enduring the purse-lipped, inch-by-inch examination of each garment by the directrices. Which brought her total up to seven.

Word was getting round that something extraordinary was happening. Models begged to be allowed to join the shoot, Rex was being offered assistants free, ready to do anything, even carry the clothes on foot through the dark Parisian streets, to be allowed to share in the glory; and a couple of the younger, more adventurous houses offered her the pick of their collections.

The day before the shoot she had fifteen models and called Jack. If the picture was big enough, would he extend the pull-out to three pages? It would be a crime to bunch the models together and not show the clothes properly. Jack said he would.

Mariella asked if she could come along. 'I will act as dresser,' she said, 'I long to see this. It will be fun. And also, *cara*, I am a very skilful make-up artiste. I can help with that as well. And – do you have jewellery?'

'Not enough,' said Eliza with a groan.

'I will bring all of mine. It is naturally only the cooked pieces—'

'The what, Mariella?'

'Giovanni says I must not wear my real diamonds, it is too dangerous. They are all in the vault of the bank. But I think you will not be able to tell, in a photograph.'

'Oh,' said Eliza, 'you mean fakes.'

'Exactly. I said, cooked up. That's the English phrase, I was told? But it all looks very, very nice.'

'Mariella,' said Eliza, 'I love you.'

She never forgot 24 January, 1965. For most of the English nation, it was a day of shock and mourning: the ninety-year-old Winston Churchill died early in the morning but for Eliza, the bigger drama was taking place in a large photographic studio off the rue Cambon, in a hubbub of noise, activity, beautiful girls and incredibly valuable clothes. By two thirty all but one of the girls were dressed and made up. Rex was taking Polaroids to check his lighting and work out the composition, 'One long line's just fucking boring, Eliza, I don't care what you say, we're going to have to have some variation in level.'

The assistants stood in for models in the Polaroids – many years later Eliza found one, a fading panorama of fifteen pretty, barefooted, long-haired boys, dressed in jeans and T-shirts, some of them sitting on stools and stepladders, some fooling around, pulling on hats and long gloves, others gazing as haughtily into the lens as the models themselves; looking at it she could almost hear the thud of the Rolling Stones in the background, feel her own excitement and terror. She and Milly sellotaped the soles of shoes, sorted and resorted jewellery and gloves, pinned hems, bulldog-clipped bodices to fit; Mariella and two other girls worked tirelessly on make-up, heated and re-heated Carmen rollers, painted nails, and consumed great jugfuls of coffee. The air was so thick with cigarette smoke that Eliza said there must be no more; there also hung about the place the unmistakably sweet smell of hash.

Only one dress still hung on the rail: the statutory wedding dress. One girl had still not arrived.

'It would be her,' groaned Eliza. 'It just would be. We can't do without. She's the centrepiece. Where is she, for God's sake? I knew it was a mistake, agreeing to her.'

'Which one is it?' said Rex.

'Bloody Alethea Peregrine something or other. Total amateur. But she's just such an aristocrat. She's going to look amazing in that dress. Oh God, where is she? Milly, call the hotel. She's staying at the Castiglione.'

Milly disappeared and then came back looking slightly smug. 'She's on her way. But can someone somewhere please find a radio that we can get the BBC World Service on?'

'Yeah, I got one,' said Rex.

'Thank God. I told her we had one here. She said she wouldn't come otherwise. The thing is,' said Milly, going rather pink, 'you know Winston Churchill died this morning.'

'I know, I know. It's awfully sad. But—'

'Well, Alethea was listening to all the stuff about him in the hotel. She sounded as if she'd been crying.'

'Oh, for God's sake,' said Rex, 'that's all we need, blotchy skin, runny nose.'

'Yes, but I think,' said Milly carefully, 'and sorry to sound bossy, but I think it would be an idea if we all seemed terribly sympathetic. Alethea was telling me this morning she was some kind of distant relation of Sir Winston's.'

'Pretty bloody distant,' said Rex, 'few light years, I'd say.'

'Shut up, Rex,' said Eliza, 'we need Alethea and if pretending she was practically Churchill's favourite daughter and saying how sorry we are will help, then we're all going to do that, OK? Ah—' An extremely tall redhead had come into the room, swathed in black fur, dabbing theatrically at her enormous green eyes. 'Alethea, darling, come in. I'm so sorry, you must be feeling terribly sad. Just sit down here and relax. Rex has got his radio all ready, so you don't miss anything, and then Mariella is going to do your make-up. It's wonderfully brave of you to come.'

'And you,' she hissed to Milly, who was rushing about collecting boxes of tissues, 'you are going to get just the biggest rise I can possibly manage when we get back. You're a star.'

The shoot finished at half past six when Paris was still in darkness; Eliza sat in the emptying studio, high on excitement, gazing at Rex's polaroid and rather irreverently paraphrasing Winston Churchill, that 'this is our finest hour'.

'I want some money,' said Scarlett. 'Quite a lot.'

She hadn't gone to Charleston. What, after all, would it have achieved? Except frighten him, to no real end.

But she could see quite clearly now what common sense should have told her from the beginning. David was never going to leave his wife and children.

He had simply been playing with her, enjoying her, amusing himself; he was the archetypal philanderer, and she should have realised it, recognised him for what he was, instead of falling for all the moonshine like some pathetic virgin. It was her own stupidity that made her angriest, her wide-eyed willingness to believe him, her misplaced selflessness in sparing him the anxiety of the pregnancy, the anguish of the abortion. She should have told him, frightened him, demanded he paid for it, instead of tiptoeing round pretending everything was all right. She thought of all the men she had met during the course of her affair with David, men with whom she might have had fun, found affection, possibly even love itself, had she not held them up to invidious comparison, and refused their invitations, crushed their interest, denied their potential.

She wished she could say she hated David, but of course she did not; love, she had discovered, could not be extinguished with the flick of a switch, the drop of a phone. Love invaded you, and even when it had become the enemy it was not to be easily overpowered.

Had David called her that afternoon, as she sat in her flat, weeping with anger and humiliation and pain, had he begged her forgiveness, said he must see her, told her that he did indeed still love her, she would, she knew, have had difficulty in rejecting him.

But – thankfully, he had not. And in the interim her heart had hardened, had even recovered a little.

And now she had a plan.

The first thing was to make him sweat. That wasn't very difficult. After a silence of about a week, he started calling her. How was she, was she feeling a little better, he'd like to try and explain, what were her plans . . .

She rang off: every time.

Another week: he rang again. 'You're not coming to Charleston, then?'

'Not yet. But I hope to.'

She rang off.

He rang on a weekly basis; he was worried about her, he needed to know how she was, he would like to see if he could help.

She continued to ring off.

He sent her a Christmas card, signed 'Bertie', their code name for him. He missed her; was she well? She threw it on the fire.

Mrs Berenson sent her a card, reiterating her invitation: 'I told David I'd invited you, he was so pleased. The whole family knows about you, how kind you have been to me over the years. Gaby in particular would like to meet you, she says, having heard David talk about you.'

Yes, that would be fun, Scarlett thought; she would enjoy adding to Gaby's knowledge of her.

He called her early in January, to wish her Happy New Year and to ask her how she was. She said she was fine. 'Your mother has just invited me again. Apparently it's lovely there in the spring. And Gaby will be having her baby, she tells me. I could meet him or her. I told her I'm looking at my schedule again.'

Finally, she called him in the office. 'I'd like to see you,' she said.

'Of course, of course. I shall be in London in about ten days. Would that suit you?'

He was obviously, she thought happily, shitting himself. 'Yes, very well. You can come to my flat if you like.'

'Oh, darling,' he said, 'would I like?'

He arrived looking apprehensive, his arms full of flowers, and a small Tiffany carrier bag in one hand.

'Hello, Scarlett.'

'Hello, David.'

'You're looking marvellous.'

'You're looking tired. Is Gaby not sleeping well?'

A pause: then, 'I've been working very hard,' he said.

'Oh dear. Are those things for me? Shall I take them?'

She put the roses in water, opened the Tiffany box, drew out a gold locket and chain.

'That's lovely, thank you. Drink?'

'Yes. Yes please. Bourbon if you have it.'

She had always kept some for him; now she shook her head regretfully. 'I'm so sorry, David, I don't have any. None of my friends drink it. Wine?'

'Yes, very nice. Thank you.'

She poured him a glass of white wine and one for herself, sat down at the small dining table, signalled to him to sit opposite her.

'I want to start a business,' she said.

'How exciting. What sort of business?'

'Travel.'

'Ah. Yes. Well, that would make sense.'

'I hope so. I've got quite a good idea. But I need some capital. About ten thousand pounds.'

'That doesn't sound very much.'

'Oh, it'll get me going. Pay for an office – I've spoken to my brother about that, an assistant's salary, bit of promotion. My idea doesn't require huge investment. It's hopefully word of mouth, and I think I'll get quite a lot of PR. But of course I'd like to ensure I could get some more if necessary. It would be a pity to see a good idea go down the pan for lack of capital.'

'A great pity. So – where do you see it coming from in the first instance? Your bank?'

'Well no. I don't have any security, you see.'

'What about this place?'

'David! I rent it, you know I do.'

'Yes. Yes, of course. Well—'

'No, I think I know where the money will come from.'

'Good. That's splendid. Excellent. Where?'

'You.'

'Me!'

'Yes. Who's got lots of money, I thought, who would like to invest in me? Who could afford to invest in me? And then I thought – who could afford *not* to invest in me?'

'Scarlett!'

'Yes, David?'

'Scarlett, I – I don't have that sort of money.'

'Oh, I think you do.'

'And besides – it would be very dangerous.'

'Really?'

'Well – yes. I mean, I couldn't slip that through on my cheque account. It would have to be formally done.'

'That would be all right. You could be a director if you like. I'll tell you more about it, it's a clever idea, I'm sure you'll be impressed—'

'Scarlett, no, I'm sorry.'

'David, yes, I'm sorry. Otherwise – well, I'd hate to think of Gaby being upset at this point in her pregnancy.'

'Scarlett, this is blackmail.'

She smiled at him, happily.

'Yes, that's right.'

Her idea was a very simple one. Simple and clever. The big new thing was package holidays: to the sun. The English were sick of wet, windy beaches and inhospitable landladies; they wanted to go and lie on golden sands and swim in warm seas and swimming pools. Daunted by the prospect of booking flights and hotels in unknown destinations and complicated foreign currencies, they were being offered something wonderfully simple from the big companies like Thomas Cook: one simple payment in sterling paid for a flight and two weeks in a hotel, including meals. The only extra costs were alcohol and shopping money.

Eliza wouldn't be taking on Thomas Cook, obviously. She would be running a travel club, which would book holidays that were several steps up from fourteen nights in the vast blocks being built all along the Costa Brava.

Members would be assured of smaller hotels, not very grand, all personally vetted – and she would certainly include her small taverna on Trisos. There were already horror stories about people arriving with their luggage at what were, literally, building sites; for their annual fee of, say, thirty pounds on top of the cost of their holidays, her clients would get absolute peace of mind. And the hotels would be asked for a small fee as well, to be included in her portfolio.

It would probably take a little time – and a fair bit of publicity – but she was absolutely sure it would be successful.

All she needed was the initial investment. And she knew she could get that. No trouble at all.

Chapter 23

'I've got to go out, Jenny, I'm afraid. Leave you alone with him.'

'Oh, that's all right, Miss Mullan. He can't kill me, can he?'

'Well he could,' said Louise, 'but I don't think he will. Anyway, Mr Simmonds will be in soon and he'll protect you.'

'I'm not so sure,' said Jenny, 'he's been pretty grumpy lately too.'

'I know. Well, I won't be long. Wish me luck.'

'Where are you going, if Mr Shaw asks?'

'Tell him I've run off with the petty cash'

'Yes, Miss Mullan.' There was a pause, while the blue eyes grew even larger. 'You're not really, are you?'

'Wait and see,' said Louise.

She knew what was upsetting Matt this morning; he'd been to see yet another bank. About financing his office factory scheme. And yet another bank had clearly turned him down. It was all proving much more difficult than he had expected; and as always when crossed, he was unable to see anyone else's point of view.

He had become completely obsessed with his new scheme. Which was, Louise did think, very clever. To offer offices, ready-built, to any large company that might be looking to move out of London. He had established his areas quite swiftly; both to the west of London, the first north, in the direction of Ruislip – splendidly served by the Central line, and the second due west, taking in Slough and Reading – both of which benefitted from not only a very good mainline service, but the large roads, and therefore bus and coach routes, leading to London Airport.

He had spent the best part of two weeks exploring both areas, and finally settled on a place called Barkers Park, due west of Slough. He had found an actual site, big enough for a development of a thousand staff, and established that planning permission was obtainable. It was ideal, in every way; the only thing was the money required – around five to seven million, he said. 'And then the construction costs would be much less than that, about two, two and a half million.'

'Any investor worth his salt'll come across with the money. Trust me, Jimbo, it'll be like taking candy from a baby.'

But it was proving rather more difficult than that.

Louise was not running off with the petty cash, she was going to see a builder, Barry Floyd, who had just completed a ten-storey office block in Vauxhall; Louise had been retained as the letting agent. Floyd had become hugely successful over the previous ten years by the simple process of coming in ahead of time, if slightly over budget, on every project he had worked on. Time being an even more expensive commodity than money, Floyd was greatly in demand and had work scheduled for up to two years ahead. He was still young – only thirty-five, having come over from Ireland ten years earlier to work with his father, Michael, in the familiar expectation that the streets of London were paved with gold. Between them they found a little gold-dust, but then Michael had dropped dead of a heart attack and young Barry had taken over the company and made it a great success.

He was in fine form that morning, and when Louise had made her inspection, he invited her to join him for a coffee.

'I have a little something to celebrate,' he said, as they settled into a rather insalubrious café on the Kennington Road, 'and if I thought you had time I would have invited you to join me for lunch at the Ritz.'

'And I'd have come,' said Louise.

'And would you now? Well, another time perhaps, when I have me indoor shoes with me.'

'Great. And what are you celebrating?'

'Two things. You see before you the chairman and managing director of Barry Floyd Ltd. As from today. My old father must be dancing the jig in his grave.'

'I'm sure he is. Well, that's very good. And what's the other thing?'

'My accountant tells me I am now officially a millionaire. He did the last set of accounts and that is what they show. And what a pity it is that so much of it will be going to that miserable creature in Number Eleven Downing Street.'

'Well – yes. Matt Shaw is always saying the same thing, but there's not a lot you can do about that.'

'You might think that, but now the clever thing, I'm told, might be to find something to invest in. Somewhere to put the money where it would work.'

'What, the stock market, you mean?'

'Well, maybe, but what a dry, miserable old world that is. I'd rather go for a bit of excitement. With the odds a bit higher.'

'Barry, higher odds means higher risk.'

'And what would life be without risk? This whole business is about risk. And I'm getting pretty good at assessing it. I tell you, making money in this business is like taking candy from a baby.'

Louise recognised that phrase. She ordered a bacon butty, purely to gain herself some time, went to the filthy shack at the back of the café which called itself a toilet and did a few sums on the notebook she always carried with her. Then she went back to Barry, took a deep breath, and started to talk.

'You what!'

Louise had often seen Matt angry; she had never been properly frightened by him. She was now.

'You told him! My idea! You just – just gave it away. Jesus Christ, Louise, you might as well have taken the front page of the *Daily Mirror*. You stupid bloody cow.'

'Don't swear at me.'

'I'll swear at you if I want to. What right did you think you had to do that? Why couldn't you have asked Floyd to come in and see me?'

'Because I wanted to seize the moment,' said Louse, only slightly untruthfully, 'everything could have been lost if he'd gone off and found somewhere else to put his money, some other scheme.'

'That's bollocks. You just wanted to muscle in on it like you do on everything. I've a bloody good mind to sack you, right now—'

'OK.' Louise stood up. 'Fine. A month, I think I'm on. I told you David Elstein's looking for a junior partner.'

'Well, he's very welcome to you. No doubt you'll be hawking his confidential business round London in no time at all.'

'Matt,' said Louise, very calm suddenly, 'you've tried every source in London for that money and just met a complete blank wall. And it's because you haven't got any money to put in yourself; or not nearly enough. Floyd's prepared to build at cost. And put some cash in. You'd be able to borrow plenty more on that basis. Look, just talk to him, for heaven's sake. He's looking to invest in something exciting. And he thinks your idea is exciting. Very. Bloody brilliant was what he said. It's the opportunity you've been waiting for. You're just not recognising it because you're so pig-headed and because I've provided it.'

'That's bollocks.'

'It is not boll— oh, Jenny, could we have some coffee please. And Mr Shaw would like some biscuits – those lemon puff ones. Now Matt, just listen and think properly about what I'm saying. It really is the way forward, it would be a joint venture, with the profit shared on completion—'

'Yeah and bloody Floyd would get the lion's share. I'm not daft, Louise—'

'Oh, no, not daft at all. And besides, it would obviously be in a direct ratio to what each party contributed. I'll tell you what would be daft, and that would be not to do it at all. Just out of pure bloody-mindedness. If this project yields anything like what you've been saying, there'd be masses for everyone to share, including Jenny.'

He smiled suddenly. 'Christ. Think of all the bloody biscuits she'd buy. Well, go on. Tell me some more.'

Louise emerged from his office half an hour later. She looked rather drained, but her eyes were very bright.

'Jenny, we're going to have a very big meeting here this afternoon. At four o'clock. All three of us, and a gentleman called Mr Floyd. So some really special biscuits, and I also want you to buy a bottle of champagne. Get the man in the off-licence to advise you, but something French. Here's some cash. But don't tell Mr Shaw yet, OK? Just bring it in when I tell you.'

'Yes, all right, Miss Mullan. I'd best get some proper glasses as well then. And what about some of those really posh cigarettes? The ones in a box?'

'Jenny,' said Louise, 'you know something? We're a team here. And you're a very important part of it.' .

'These are fucking brilliant,' said Jack Beckham.

'I'm glad you like them.'

'I do. Well done. I'm doing the fold-out, as promised.'

'Great.'

He peered at her. 'You all right?'

'Yes. Yes, I'm fine.'

'You look tired.'

'Jack, Paris isn't exactly a convalescent cure. Nor was pulling that off. Of course I look tired.'

'Juliet darling, I wondered if you might like a spot of lunch in town on Saturday. And then how about some shopping, we could go to Harrods. Would you like that?'

'Sounds lovely, Mummy, but for goodness' sake, don't let me spend any money. Charles will start moaning about my extravagance. It's getting very boring.'

'What a shame. Well, never mind, I'll treat you to something. What about a new bag, that old black one was looking a bit shabby, I thought. And you need to look smart, not just for yourself, but for Charles, you're the wife of a successful young man, you know, you owe it to him to—'

'I'm beginning to wonder about the success bit, to be honest. Either that or he's very mean. And he goes on and on about Summercourt and what's going to happen to it, he's going down there on Saturday to discuss it with his parents. He wanted me to go too, but I couldn't face it, it's so depressing.'

'Summercourt? What can possibly happen to it?'

'Well, I don't know, but it's in a pretty bad state of repair, and it seems his parents have got terrible financial problems. It's held in trust for the family, so they can't sell it or raise any money on it.'

'So' – Carol Judd's expression became rather sharp suddenly – 'far from being an asset it's a liability?'

'It looks like it, yes.'

'Well, that's appalling, I don't know what Daddy would have to say. But however it's actually organised, that house will be Charles's one day, his and yours, it's his inheritance. I love imagining you there with your children.'

'Well – I hope so.'

'Of course it will. Mind you, we'll all have terrible financial problems with this wretched new government. Daddy says Callaghan is an absolute brute. He's going to push income tax right up, apparently. And the trade unions will get much more powerful. Daddy's very worried indeed, he says his job will become almost impossible. He's been in a frightfully bad mood ever since the election. Perhaps he should speak to Charles.'

'I really don't think that's a very good idea,' said Juliet.

'Maddy, I need to talk to you. Want to come round to my flat for some pasta?'

'Um – yes. That'd be nice. I'll bring the vino.'

'Sorry but I can't invite Esmond.'

'He won't mind. Why, should he?'

'I – don't know. Matt gets very aerated if I want to go out without him. Or spend an evening on my own. He takes it as a personal insult.'

'And how about if he wants to go out without you?'

'Oh – well, that's different,' said Eliza.

'Why?'

'Well, it's always work.'

'Paris was work, and you said he made a terrible fuss about that.'

'Well – that was for ten days. Anyway, what about this evening? He's out with his new Irish partner.'

'You're not eating much, Eliza.'

'No. I'm not very hungry. Got any ciggies? I've run out.'

'Sure.'

She did seem very edgy, Maddy thought. 'So – what's the problem?'

'Oh, it's – well, it's— my period's late.'

'Oh.' Maddy put her fork down. 'How late?'

'Um – three weeks.'

'Oh cripes. But – aren't you on the pill?'

'Well – yes. I am. Of course.'

'OK, so it's probably just a bit of a blip. It'll sort itself out.'

'Well, the blip is – actually – that I forgot to take them to Paris. Just forgot. In all the excitement and panic and everything. And I thought it wouldn't matter, because I certainly wouldn't be having any sex over there. When I got back, I was nearly due, well in another week, so I thought I'd wait and get it over and then start again.'

'OK. So you were having lots of reunion sex—'

'I – well – yes.'

'Without any contraception?'

241

'Well – yes. I couldn't suggest using something else, or he'd have gone nuts.'

'Hmmm. And so – don't tell me – your period never arrived.'

'Well – no.'

'Cripes. You're a prize idiot, aren't you?'

'I suppose I am. Oh, dear.'

'Have you been to the doctor?'

'No. Anyway, I'd want to go to my gynaecologist, and she's been away. I've got an appointment on Tuesday. Then she'll do a test. I mean – it's probably just worry, holding everything up. It does, you know.'

'Yes, of course. Um – any other symptoms?'

'Well, my tits are very sore. But then they get like that when I'm due anyway. I – oh God.' She lit another cigarette.

'Poor old thing, you are in a state, aren't you? What do you think Matt would say?'

'I think he'd be pretty horrified. I mean, we're not even living together. Yet.'

'But you will be – won't you?'

'I – I suppose so. Anyway, the last thing I want to do is sort of blackmail him into it. Into fatherhood. I just so disapprove of girls who do that.'

'Well, yes of course.'

'I just know he's not ready for it. He's so busy, making his way and everything and he's got some incredible new scheme, but it's a big risk, he could lose most of what he's got – God, he's such a hero, Maddy. When I think of Jeremy, everything just handed him on a plate and Matt's done it all himself, it's extraordinary really, I admire him so much.'

'But – if you are, you will tell him?'

'Oh, yes, of course, I'll tell him. I just hope I don't have to. Probably I'm just – late.'

'Probably,' said Maddy.

Chapter 24

'I hear you've become a client.' Louise grinned at Scarlett. 'I've got a super place in mind for you. Small, but very nice, good area – just in Kensington, in the Old Brompton Road. It's in a mews, really pretty.'

'Sounds great. Can I see it?'

'Course. We can go now if you like. I'm free.'

'Fantastic. Thank you, Louise.'

Scarlett liked Louise: very much. She reminded her of Eliza, except that Louise was tougher, could have taught Eliza a thing or two about keeping Matt in order. Which increasingly he needed; he was becoming more and more arrogant.

It was the twin successes, of course: first with his new business venture, the out-of-town offices and then his conquest of Eliza. And how had he done that Scarlett wondered, when she could have had anyone, like for instance the boyfriend everyone had thought she would marry, rich and charming and handsome. And instead she had chosen Matt. Who was all right, very good-looking if not conventionally charming, and becoming quite, if not very, rich. And much softer and more vulnerable than he'd ever let on. Or rather wanted to let on.

It was lovely, of course, and Scarlett was really, really pleased for him, but still a bit surprised. They had certainly seemed pretty good together, he and Eliza, at Christmas time. But, love him as she did, Scarlett also knew that Matt could be extremely selfish, and oddly old-fashioned in his attitudes, a dead ringer for his father in lots of ways. She couldn't see him enjoying Eliza's meteoric career, for instance. And Eliza was very vulnerable. She was emotionally young for her age in spite of her professional success, probably due to having had a very sheltered and privileged childhood and early life. And while she did quite obviously adore Matt, it was rather too much for his own good in Scarlett's view. She just hoped he adored her back.

243

Louise drove them both down to Kensington in her small green Mini Cooper, weaving in and out of the traffic with skilful impatience, cutting other drivers up, cheerfully raising two fingers to anyone who shouted at or beeped her.

She was feeling very happy this morning; contracts were being drawn up for the new development partnership with Barry Floyd and she was named as a director. They'd tried to elbow her aside, of course – well, Matt had, and he should have been more generous, she reckoned; the partnership wouldn't be happening at all without her.

Anyway, she'd used her usual tactics, talking tough, threatening to leave. Valerie had most fortuitously just offered her the job of deputy managing director in her company, which actually Louise would have hated, dealing with personnel directors and a lot of women all day instead of builders and developers and a lot of men. Louise didn't exactly dislike women, although most of them irritated her with what she thought of as their feeble ambitions and their reluctance to meet life head-on – which was the precise reason she liked Valerie Hill so much – but she was easier with men, the tougher the better, she found them more straightforward to deal with and she perversely enjoyed parrying their attempts to belittle her and put her down. Particularly Matt . . .

She knew she had done extraordinarily well; she loved her job, she made more money than any woman she knew, she had her own flat in Chiswick and a lot of very nice clothes, and she was really extremely happy. Her mother fretted over the lack of men in her life – but Louise remained untroubled by it. Work was what she cared about; she had had a few boyfriends, and had even slept with a couple, but none of them seemed worth investing any time in.

One day, she supposed, someone would come along and sweep her off her feet, but he'd have to be pretty damn amazing, and what was more recognise that she was amazing too. Otherwise – why bother?

She too worried about Eliza – who, now she knew her a bit better, she liked and admired a lot – and Matt's apparent high-handed treatment of her. God, she wouldn't have been kept out of that poncey flat of his if she'd wanted to live there. There she was, this girl, born with a silver spoon in her mouth, as successful in her own field as Louise was in hers, trailing round after him, doing what he said. Not good for him, Louise knew that better than anybody. She probably knew him better than anybody as well, she thought; and understood him through and through, every awkward, arrogant and – just occasionally she would admit if only to herself – endearing, bit of him.

The office she had for Scarlett was pronounced perfect: on the first floor of a very pretty mews building, two rooms, one large, one small, both very light, plus a small kitchenette and loo.

'You can rent the garage beneath if you want it, or you could take it and let it, or just let us do that for you. I'd take it if I were you. Use it for your own car. If your business goes well, you'll want to expand in no time, and if it doesn't it'll be an additional source of income.'

Scarlett said she'd take it.

'Thank you, Louise. Can I buy you a coffee?'

'Oh, no thanks. I've got a meeting in half an hour, back in West One. Can I give you a lift?'

'No, I'm cutting down to the terminal. I'm still employed by BOAC, will be for a couple of months. Which is fine, I get a lot of leave, so I can set things up well and truly. How about a deposit, contracts, all that sort of thing?'

'Oh, we'll deal with that. I'll let you know when we want some money.'

'Well, thanks. Oh, and when I get my travel club up and running, I'm offering a few complimentary memberships. Would you like one?'

'Yes, please! I think it's a great idea by the way. Really clever. You should do very well.'

'Well, I was lucky persuading someone to back me,' said Scarlett, 'couldn't have done it otherwise.'

And she smiled, thinking of her backer, her reluctant, terrified backer, and the tortuous route by which he had arranged for the money to be made available to her. There was an expression about rough justice she seemed to remember; this, she felt, could be better described as smooth.

'Miss Clark?'

'Yes, that's me.'

'Miss Clark, I have Mrs Munroe on the phone for you. She wants to speak to you.'

'Oh – yes. Yes, thank you. Do put her through.'

Mrs Munroe. Mrs Munroe, FRCS FRCOG. Mrs Munroe who held

life-altering information in her hands: both professional and personal. Mrs Munroe, who had appeared almost incredulous that she had been so reckless. Mrs Munroe, who . . .

'Good morning, Eliza. How are you?'

'Oh, fine, yes. Not sick or anything, if that's what you mean.' (She was clinging to how well she felt; everybody was sick when they were pregnant, surely, and she didn't even feel remotely nauseous.)

'Good. Well, that's excellent.'

'Excellent?' Clearly it was all right, the toad hadn't laid any eggs, how fantastic, how . . .

'Sickness is such a curse in pregnancy. Although of course it's very early days for you. It could change.'

Very early days. Oh. Oh, God.

'So – does that mean . . . ?'

'Yes, Eliza, it's positive. I do hope you'll be happy with that. If you want to talk anything over with me, please do. I'm delighted to help.'

'Yes. Yes, thank you, Mrs Munroe. I – well, yes, I might want to do that.'

Was that code for something? Did she want to even let her mind glance in that direction? Oh, God, oh, God. *Oh, God* . . .

'Matt, can we have a talk please?'

'Of course. But not right now.'

'No, of course not now. But – maybe tonight.'

'Yes, sure. What about?'

'Well – about – about—' God, what could she say? Get at least an idea of how he might react? Then, inspiration. 'About my flat.'

'What about your flat?'

'Well – the lease is about to expire and I—'

'Eliza, talk to Louise, see if she's got any ideas. She's got a few residential properties on the side. She knows about leases. Sorry, got to go, Barry Floyd's here.'

'Yes. Yes, of course.'

Well, what had she expected? That he would say, 'oh, don't renew your lease, move in with me'. Or – 'let's get somewhere together'. Not expected that, no. But – maybe – hoped for.

It was a clue at least.

✿ ✿ ✿

'Maddy, hi, it's me.'

'Eliza! What's the verdict, tell me quickly.'

'It's positive.'

'Oh, God. Well – I suppose – anyway, what does Matt say?'

'I haven't told Matt.'

'What!'

'He was rushing into a meeting.'

'Tell him tonight, then.'

'Yes. Yes, I will.'

'Promise!'

'Yes, I promise. Of course.'

'Matt—'

'Yes? God, I'm exhausted. So tired. And starving. Is there anything we can eat? Otherwise, let's go out.'

'Um – well – no, there isn't. But I do want to talk to you.'

'We can talk in the restaurant. Surely.'

'Yes, OK.'

'Meet me in the Soup Kitchen, the one near Harrods, in half an hour, OK?'

'Yes, OK.'

Over a bowl of vegetable soup, she tried again.

'Matt, now can we talk?'

'Oh – yes. All right. What, about this lease of yours?'

'Yes. And—'

'I've been thinking and—' (please, please say, 'and I want you to move in with me . . . and I think we should get a place together') '—and I think you should just renew the lease on that flat. It's very good value, and you're not there much and you'll waste a lot of time and effort looking for somewhere else . . .'

'Oh. Oh, I see.'

'Ask Louise to check the lease, she'll know if it's a good one, OK?'

'Well – yes.'

'Good. Now let me tell you about the meeting we had today, Barry Floyd and I, with his builders, really promising . . .'

She pushed her chair back, and stood up. He stared at her.

'What's wrong?'

'I don't feel too good, that's what's wrong. I'm tired as well, very tired.

I don't want this soup, and I don't want to hear about your meeting, I just want to go home and go to bed.'

'Well, let me finish mine and we'll go.'

'No, Matt, I want to go home to my own bed, OK? In my flat. You just take your time. Enjoy your soup.'

She would have enjoyed it if it hadn't been so serious. She couldn't remember when she last stood up to him like that.

'Eliza, what on earth was that about last night?'

Eliza glared into the phone, heard her voice icy cool.

'It was about me being sick of you never wanting to talk about what I want to talk about.'

'But I told you what to do about your flat. We talked about that first.'

'I know. But – don't you think there might be something else here?'

'Like what?'

'Well – maybe, about us – well, about the – the—' Her courage was failing her. This was not a conversation she should be having. Well, not initiating.

'The what, Eliza?'

'You really can't think what?'

'No, I can't.'

'Then I think you should just try a bit harder, OK? Call me when you've got a suggestion.'

'Eliza, hello, it's Matt. Look, I think I know what you're on about. It's getting a flat together, isn't it?'

'It – could be. Well done, Matt.'

'Yes, it was Scarlett who made me see it.'

'Scarlett?'

'Yes. I talked to her about it, about how you were upset and I didn't know why and she said maybe it was that.'

'Oh, I see. You didn't work that out for yourself.'

'Well, no. Anyway, I just don't think it's a good idea, not yet. Maybe in another few months or so. Thing is, I'm so busy and I haven't got the time to look at places and I can't see why it's not OK how we are. I mean, there isn't a rush, is there, and we're still feeling our way really and—'

'Just fuck off, Matt, will you? I'd hate you to be late for whatever meeting you're supposed to be in.'

She put down the phone and burst into tears.

'Mrs Munroe, I – well, I hope I didn't misunderstand something you said to me.'

'And what was that?' Alison Munroe smiled at her; it was a warm, encouraging smile. 'Try me.'

'Well, you said if I wanted to talk anything over with you, then you would be happy to help.'

'Go ahead. I'll try.'

'Well – well, you see the thing is—' God, this was so hard. So, so hard. When she didn't know what she wanted herself.

'Yes? What is the thing?'

'Well – I – oh, dear, sorry—'

Alison Munroe passed her a tissue.

'That's quite all right. Pregnancy makes one very emotional. I should know, I've had four.'

'Four children! And – and you went on working?'

'I did. With great difficulty.' She smiled again. 'But, you know, you can do anything if you want it enough.'

'How – I mean was – was your husband happy about all that?'

'Oh, yes. As long as it didn't interfere with his much more important career, I could do what I liked with mine. He's a barrister,' she added, with a slightly cooler smile.

'Yes. Well, that's very comforting. I suppose you must have had lots of nannies and so on.'

'Oh, yes. Expensive of course, but I thought it was worth it. I love my job and I'd have been a very poor full-time mother. Now then, what about you, what did you want to talk to me about?'

'Well, you see, my – my boyfriend – I'm not married as you know. I really think he won't want this baby – I mean, we're not even living together properly—'

'Improperly perhaps?' She smiled again. 'Sorry, bad joke.'

'No, no,' said Eliza, smiling back. 'Yes, well, my parents would certainly think so. Anyway, he's going to be totally horrified, I know he is. And I really think – well I – I—'

'Want a termination?'

249

'Yes!'

There. She had said it. She didn't, of course. She wanted to have the baby – somehow – and keep working – somehow – but she wanted Matt to want it too, and that most certainly wasn't going to happen.

'I see. Well, to start with, you know that is illegal, don't you?'

'Yes. Yes, I do. Of course.'

'Now I happen to belong to the Abortion Law Reform group. I believe that in certain instances – such as rape, risk of health to the mother, either physical or mental, and serious financial hardship, abortion should be legalised. I have had women come to me with a fifth, sixth pregnancy, so desperate they'll do anything. I've been unable to help them and I have to send them away knowing full well they'll go to some back-street butcher and quite possibly die as a consequence.'

'Yes. Yes, I see.'

'So I can't help you, I'm afraid. And even if the law was changed, I don't think you would qualify, do you? Not really? I mean, you are young, healthy, well off, you are at least in a relationship, you have a good job, friends, a big family from what I've always understood—'

'Yes, but – but you don't understand what Matt's like. He's – well, he's very difficult. He just wouldn't go along with it. And even if I could twist his arm, make him marry me, he'd resent it terribly. It wouldn't be a good – good start in life for a baby.'

'Eliza, if you knew how many young women have sat there over the years, saying all this, and then come to see me again, a few weeks later, radiantly happy, you'd be surprised. I'd put it at thousands, certainly hundreds. Now the first thing you have to do is tell your Matt, and yes, I'm quite sure he'll be very put out. Especially as you've been a bit – foolish about contraception. But he'll come round. Almost certainly. He'll even, dare I suggest, be quite pleased. Once he's got over the idea. Men do like to know they're potent and fertile and all that.' She didn't actually say 'poor things' but it hung in the air. 'And do it sooner rather than later, as soon as you can indeed.'

Eliza didn't say anything; she just sat, looking at her hands.

'Try to believe me,' Alison Munroe said, 'be brave. How about your boss, do you think he'll be sympathetic?'

'I absolutely know he won't,' said Eliza.

✿　✿　✿

250

'Maddy, you don't know anyone, do you?'

'Anyone what? Who's had an abortion? I do, but I wouldn't recommend it. It sounded hideous. She's lucky to be alive.'

'You don't know anyone who's had the expensive, nice sort?'

'I'll think. Trouble is you can't ask anyone, can you, there's just nowhere to go. The quacks know full well they can't advise you, even if they're sympathetic like yours. Eliza, please, please won't you tell Matt? He might be OK about it.'

'He won't be. I know him very well. Maddy, he doesn't want to share a flat with me; how can I expect him to want to share it with me and a baby? Anyway, he hates babies, he's hardly likely to say "darling, that's fantastic". He's not Jeremy. Not that I'd want to be having a baby with Jeremy, obviously,' she added hastily.

'No,' said Maddy. 'No, of course not.'

Maddy did come up with someone. A make-up artist she had worked with quite often, who had just had a 'frightfully expensive operation, you know what I mean, worth every penny though, I have to say, in for just one night, all over next day. You don't feel a thing.'

Maddy asked her if she could recommend the surgeon for a friend and the girl had laughed and said 'you bet', adding that it was funny how it was always a friend. 'I've got the number somewhere—' She rummaged in her bag. 'Yes, here we are. Tell her to say Margaret Blake-Smith recommended her. That's the code. So they know she's not the police or something. It'll cost her.'

'He'll do it!' said Eliza. 'Soon as he's had my test confirmed. They need to be sure it's genuine, of course. So – towards the end of next week. He's got some clinic in Surrey, out Dorking way. Oh, Maddy, thank you so much. I just don't know what I would have done otherwise.'

'I just hope it's the right advice,' said Maddy gloomily. 'How – how do you feel about it now?'

'Oh – just terrifically happy and relieved,' said Eliza

She certainly wasn't going to tell Maddy she was having horrible dreams and waking up crying almost every night.

'Louise, have you got any good flats I can look at? Round Pimlico way. Or even Battersea, if it's right on the river?'

'I'll have a look. What on earth are you looking at flats for? Not thinking of moving, are you?'

'No, no,' said Matt hastily, 'I wouldn't give up my pad for anything. No, I've got a friend who's moving to London. But it needs to be really nice, two bedrooms at least, maybe three, and a decent kitchen.'

'Oh, right. Well, I'll let you know. And you'll be looking at them for him, will you?'

'Yes. He lives up in the north; he can't keep coming down here.'

'No, course not.'

Pull the other one, Matt. But it was nice; he must really care about her, if he was prepared to move. He loved that place of his.

Well, so far he'd managed to pull the wool over Eliza's eyes, Matt reflected. God, she must think he was one hell of a shit, believing that rubbish about taking it slowly. It had shaken him a bit; he'd be losing her if he wasn't careful. And moved fast. He had felt a bit cautious at the very beginning of course; but now, now he just wanted to be with her. He really loved her. No other word for it. Just – love.

'Mrs Clark? Yes, we have your result and it is positive. So Dr Melrose has asked me to book you in for next Friday. First thing. Please don't have anything to eat or drink after midnight, and come just with overnight things and a packet of large sanitary towels. You'll be leaving the following morning. Please arrange for someone to collect you, you won't be able to drive. And please bring the fee in cash. We don't take cheques.'

Absurdly, the thought of the sanitary towels was the most upsetting thing.

'Matt, I've got to go down to see Mummy and Daddy next weekend. It's their – their wedding anniversary and I must be there. I'm going down on Friday night.'

'Oh, OK, fine. I'm not invited then?'

'No – not this time Sorry.'

'This is great, Louise. He'll like this. Yes, I'll take it. Well, what I mean is, I'll tell him he should take it.'

'Right, fine, OK.'

It was a great flat, in one of the big mansion blocks, right near the river, opposite Battersea Park. A big sunny sitting room, which would take a dining table easily as well, a large kitchen, it needed modernising of course, and two large bedrooms and one tiny one that would do for a study. Eliza would love it. Most important of all, it was empty.

He'd hoped to show it to her that weekend, but she was away. Well, Monday would do. No huge rush. She could go on thinking he was a shit for a couple more days. It would be all the nicer a surprise when she found he wasn't. Well, not such a big one as she'd thought. He might even do something really romantic, like get some flowers in, put them in a big vase on the sitting-room windowsill, and put some champagne in the antique fridge. That was the sort of thing she'd really appreciate.

'Eliza, I still think you ought to tell Matt.'

'Maddy, for God's sake, shut up about it.'

'But he might surprise you.'

'Matt couldn't surprise me, Maddy. Not if he tried for all eternity. I know him too well. Much too well.'

'So – do you think you still have a future together?'

'Oh, I don't know. I hope so. Well, I think I hope so. Oh, I just don't know.'

'I think that flat's for him, Miss Mullan. Him and Miss Clark.'

'Now what makes you think that, Jenny?'

'I just do. And I heard him asking her if she was free on Monday evening and then ordering some flowers to be delivered to it. He wouldn't do that for some man from Yorkshire, would he?'

'Probably not. Nor from anywhere else. Anyway, it's to be a complete surprise, Jenny, and even I'm not supposed to know or have guessed, so don't say anything about it at all, will you?'

'Of course not, Miss Mullan.'

OK, this time tomorrow it would be over. Just twenty-four hours more to go. It helped that she still felt completely normal. Not sick, at all, not even specially tired. Well, a bit tired. She was obviously a natural at it. At pregnancy. Oh, God, she wished she didn't keep crying. It was so stupid. If she hadn't been able to sort things out, then she would really have had something to cry about . . .

She felt very ambivalent towards Matt; she was finding it hard to act normally. Half the time she thought she hated him, just for putting her through this; then she'd remind herself that he had no idea he was putting her through anything; and then she'd look at him, or he'd say something and she knew she didn't hate him at all. God, what a mess. And was she going to be able to forgive him? But – it really wasn't his fault. Or was it? Partly it was, for being such a pig, such a selfish, emotionally retarded, thick-skinned pig. But then she'd known he was all those things ever since she'd met him. Or certainly since she'd begun to get to know him. He was Matt, and she loved him. Was it fair to suddenly expect him to be sweet and tender?

Well, time enough to find out when it was over. Which it nearly was.

'Matt, sorry. There's a hitch on the flat.'

'Oh, God. What?'

'Nothing serious, but he won't take your offer. Wants the asking price.'

'Oh no. I've never paid the asking price for anything. It's against my religion.'

'Well, there's someone else after it.'

'Yeah, I bet.'

'Matt, it's true. I'm the agent, remember?'

'Ah. Yes. Well – it's a lot of money. How long have I got?'

'Well, the bloke's in a hurry. The other one. And the vendor is obviously going to take the higher offer.'

'Bloody hell. Well – well, I think I might take another look at it. I'm not going to just lie down on my back with my legs in the air, I'll see if I can find something wrong, some bargaining point. OK?'

'Yes, OK, but you'd better get a move on. Like you need to decide today.'

'All right, all right. I'll get down there now. Well, this afternoon. That too late? Got to see some money men this morning.'

'I'll say I couldn't get hold of you.'

'Fine. Thanks, Louise.'

'Jack, if you don't mind I'm going to leave a bit early today. I'm looking for locations for the haunted-house feature and I think I might have something. Is that OK? I know you wanted to talk about the summer issues, but this is more urgent.'

'Yes, course. Right, see you Monday morning. Good luck.'

If he only knew what he was wishing her good luck for.

She tidied her desk for the weekend, asked Milly if there were any calls.

'Yes, just one, Eliza. From Matt. He wants you to call him.'

'Matt!' That was odd. They'd said goodbye that morning. Somehow she couldn't face ringing him, telling him yet more lies. She'd be so relieved when this was over. So relieved.

'I can't speak to him now, Milly. If he calls again, tell him I've gone.'

'Yes, of course. Have a good weekend. Hope you find a house. It's such a good idea.'

She hoped it was. It was another of her over-ambitious ones, to photograph nightdresses in a supposedly haunted house. The trick would be to double-expose each photograph so that the model would be followed by, or stood beside, or be running away from, what looked like her own ghost. Rick Wilde, the art director, kept saying it was technically very difficult; but she'd talked to Rex and he said it would be a doddle. She decided it was simply because Rick hadn't had the idea himself.

'I'm sorry, Mr Shaw, but Miss Clark has left.'

'Oh hell, Jenny. Are you sure?'

'Well, that's what her secretary said.'

'Bloody hell.'

'Yes, Mr Shaw. Can I do anything?'

'No. Well – maybe. Look, I'm going out now. If she does ring, can you just tell her to call me in the office. Say I know she's going to her parents, but this is really important. At around five. No, six. I'll still be at the flat at five. Is that clear?'

'Yes, Mr Shaw. I've written it down.'

Eliza went down to her car; her overnight bag was in the back. She looked at it and her eyes blurred with tears. Stop it, Eliza, stop being so pathetic.

She was just driving out through Wandsworth, towards the Kingston by-pass, headed out for Dorking, when she felt a pang of remorse about not ringing Matt. It might be important. His father hadn't been well. Maybe she should . . .

She saw a telephone box, and pulled in.

Yes, it was worth the asking price. Definitely. He'd like to get a bit off, he'd found evidence of a bit of damp round the bathroom windows, so it was worth a try, but Louise was quite sure he wouldn't manage it. Well – if he was going to have to go that far beyond his principles, he'd really want to be sure Eliza liked it. And that she was up for moving in with him. She might not be. You never knew with women. They were very perverse. She might say she wanted to go on a bit longer, as they were.

Well, he'd have to call the chap's bluff. If Eliza couldn't see it till Monday, that was all there was to it.

'Jenny? It's Eliza Clark.'

'Oh – hello, Miss Clark. Yes. Can I help?'

'Mr Shaw rang me about an hour ago. He wanted to speak to me.'

'I'm sorry, Miss Clark. He's not here. He said he knew you were going to your parents, but could you ring him because it was important, and if you did, could you ring again but not at five, because he would still be at the flat at five, but at six here.'

'Right. I see. Well, it's only half past four, so – what flat, Jenny?'

'The one for his friend in Yorkshire.'

'I'm sorry? What friend in Yorkshire?'

'I really don't know, Miss Clark. I don't know any of his friends, and definitely not from Yorkshire. I mean, he doesn't really have that many friends at all, not really, he's too busy for that sort of thing—'

'Is Louise there?'

'No, she's out as well. And so is Mr Simmonds. Well, it is Friday, and he always leaves at four on Friday to go to his fiancée's house, as she's Jewish. He is too, of course.'

'Er – yes. Yes, of course. Well – you don't know anything about this flat, do you? Or where it is?'

'Oh, I've got the details here. Just a minute. Yes. Flat 6, Prince of Wales Mansions, Battersea. Sought-after location overlooking Battersea Park. One reception, three beds, large kitchen, bathroom, freehold – do you need to know the price because I can't make out if it's ten or sixteen thousand, it's really badly smudged on the roneo but that's a big difference, isn't it?'

'It is, yes.' A strange sensation was filling Eliza. Very strange. She felt light-headed and her heart was thudding rather hard. The telephone box, which had seemed very unpleasant, filthy dirty and smelling of tramp, suddenly seemed to be rather lovely. 'And – you say, he'll still be there at five.'

'That's what he said, and he said to tell you he'd be back here at six. Which I'm sure he will be because he's always very punctual.' She hesitated. This was beyond her brief. But then, the article in *Honey* magazine she'd been reading this morning, about how to get ahead, said you had to use your initiative, and surely since Mr Shaw was going to meet Eliza at the flat on Monday anyway, he would be pleased to see her there now. 'Um – I don't know where you are, Miss Clark, but if you're anywhere near Battersea, you might think about popping into the flat. And then if you miss him, you could come back here for six and see him then. I've got some very nice chocolate digestive biscuits in, they're his favourite. I hope you like them too.'

'I do, Jenny, very much.' For some reason, Eliza felt her stomach heave. 'Right, I think that's a good idea, actually I am quite near Battersea. I'll head over there now, should only take about ten minutes. Thanks very much indeed.'

Matt was just slightly disconsolately deciding to leave the flat when there was a ring at the front door. Maybe that was the owner; about bloody time too. He didn't like being kept waiting; time was money. Clearly Mr Flat 6 had too much of both commodities.

'About bloody time – oh, Eliza. It's you.'

'You're so observant, Matt. Yes, it's me. May I come in?'

'Well – yes, if you like. As a matter of fact I – I did want you to see this anyway.'

'Really? Why?'

'I thought I'd get your view on it. Give me your reaction.'

'Well – let's have a quick look. Mmm, great view. Wonderful fireplace. Grotty old kitchen. But lots of potential. Wonder if the fridge works – oh gosh, there's a bottle of champagne in it, did you know? Fancy leaving that behind. And two bedrooms – three really. Yes, it's – not bad. Not bad at all.'

'Only not bad?'

He was looking as she had hardly ever seen him, anxious, even slightly strained.

'Does it matter what I think of it?'

'Well yes, actually it does. I thought if you liked it, I might buy it. But it's terribly overpriced and I've got to pay the asking price, which really sticks in my craw, and so if you don't—'

'Matt,' said Eliza, taking a deep breath, 'have I got things very wrong, and are you thinking of this flat for the two of us?'

There was a silence; God, she thought, I've got it terribly, terribly wrong, now what do I do, flee down to Dorking . . .

'Well – well, yes,' he said, 'I was – thinking about it. As a matter of fact.' He sounded almost sulky. She giggled.

'You're so romantic, you know that? Look, as far as I'm concerned it's worth more than the asking price. Quite a bit more.'

'Oh, no,' he said, 'that's ridiculous. It is absolutely top of the market, I do know that, and—'

'You wouldn't make an exception because you thought it might be ideal for us? For us to live in together?'

'Well, it looks like I might have to,' he said, 'but I'm not happy about it.'

'Oh, I give up,' said Eliza, picking up her bag, pulling out her keys, 'you are just so – so—'

'No, no, don't go. Please. The thing is, Eliza – the thing is, I would like us to move in together. I can't think why you thought I didn't.'

'Possibly because you kept saying you didn't.'

'I thought you'd see through that.'

'And how was I supposed to see through it?'

'Well – I kept telling you I loved you. I'd have thought that made it pretty plain really, what I wanted.'

'Not terribly.'

'Oh. Well, let me tell you again. I – I have decided I'd like to live with you.'

'What about asking me. It's normal to ask people if they want to live with you. Not just announce it.'

'But I knew you did.'

'How?'

'I could just tell.'

'You could have been telling wrong. Ask me. Go on. Properly. Nicely. And stop looking so cross.'

He sighed. 'Oh, this is ridiculous.' He walked over to the window, turned to face her, scowled. 'All right. I love you, Eliza. I'd like you to move in with me.'

'Please.'

'Does that mean yes?'

'No, it means you have to say please.'

He sighed. 'Please.'

There was a long silence; his expression began to change from irritated to anxious.

Eliza walked towards him and took his hands and kissed him on the mouth, very lightly.

'I would like to live with you, you wretched man. And I love you too. Very much, I can't think why. But – there's something I need to tell you and I think I'd better do now it while I'm feeling brave enough and before you sign anything. Um – how would you feel about one of those bedrooms being turned into a nursery?'

Chapter 25

Eliza had never seen him so angry.

'You are what?'

'I'm pregnant. I'm sorry.'

'I should bloody well think you're sorry. After all your fine words. And it's due when?'

'Um – October-ish.'

'So you've known for four bloody months. You had no right to keep it from me. God, I can't believe it. Bloody outrageous.'

'Jack,' said Eliza, 'I'm pregnant. I haven't committed a crime.'

'That's a matter of opinion under the circumstances. I've stuck my neck out, given you this chance and this is how you repay me. Well, you needn't think you're staying on here. Jesus Christ.'

He told her to get out; she sat in her office shaking slightly. Milly came in offering tea; Annunciata appeared in the doorway.

'Eliza, I couldn't help hearing that. I should think the whole office did. It was outrageous. I'm so sorry.'

'Yes, well.' She managed to smile, then suddenly started to cry. 'Sorry. I'm not really unhappy. It was just a bit of a – a shock. He was so – so brutal.'

'He's such a bastard. Well, I think it's wonderful, that you're having a baby.' She walked round Eliza's desk, gave her a hug. 'Congratulations. Don't take any notice of him. I'm about to go and give him an earful.'

'Annunciata, please don't. He'll think I put you up to it.'

'Oh, no, he won't. Anyway, he'll calm down. I can't think why he's so angry. It's nothing to do with him.'

'Well, he thinks it is. Obviously. It is such a shame, because I want to go on working.'

'And you must.'

'No. He's firing me.'

'Bastard! Well, he can't do that to you.'

'Unfortunately he can. He's the editor.'

'Mmm. We'll see. So anyway, are you going to get married?'

'I am, yes. In a couple of weeks actually. Matt says no son of his is going to be born out of wedlock.'

'Oh, it's a son, is it?'

'So Matt says. Anything else would be an insult to his virility.'

'Oh, for heaven's sake. These men. Eliza, ignore Jack. He'll get over it. He can't afford to lose you. It's as simple as that.'

'Jack's fired me,' said Eliza, looking tearfully at Matt across his apartment. They had not yet moved into the flat. 'Isn't that foul?'

'Well, it doesn't matter, does it?'

She stared at him. 'Why?'

'Eliza, you're having a baby. You can't go on working anyway.'

'I'm sorry?'

'Look, there's no way I'm having you working when you've got the baby. You're not leaving it with nannies.'

Eliza felt her stomach lurch.

'Of course I'm going to work. Why should I give it up? I love it, it's really, really important to me.'

'Eliza, that baby is much more important than any job. I want you at home looking after it.'

'You want that? What about me?'

He looked at her, his face very set.

'It's not about you. It's about the baby. For Christ's sake, it's not a doll you've got in there. It's a person, a responsibility, and it's a lot more important than any fucking magazine.'

'I don't need to be lectured about my responsibilities, thank you,' said Eliza.

'It rather seems you do.'

'Oh, for God's sake. I'm going back to my place. I'm tired.'

She walked out and slammed the door. As she walked down the track to the road she heard the door open and Matt's footsteps behind her. He caught her by the shoulders and swung her round. 'Do you know why you're tired? It's because you're pregnant, you're having a baby. It seems I have to keep reminding you of that.'

'Oh, stop it,' said Eliza. 'You're just being horrible and hateful and—'

261

She suddenly burst into tears. She kept doing that; she supposed it was her hormones.

Matt's voice changed. 'Look, come on back in and sit down. I'll make you a cup of tea.'

'I don't want a cup of tea.'

'Well all right. I won't make you a cup of tea. Look Eliza, I'm – I'm sorry.'

She stared at him. He never said he was sorry. Never. 'I – I over-reacted. I – I love you, Eliza. So much. And I'm over the moon about the baby. You know I am. I just – just sometimes wonder if you are too. Come on, come back in, calm down. I don't want you getting upset. It might – well, it can't be good for either of you.'

She sighed, then put her hand in his.

'OK. Thank you. Could it be hot milk instead of tea?'

'Course. And then if you still want to go home, I'll drive you.'

'No,' she said, 'no, I'll stay here. Of course.'

They didn't return to the subject of her working.

It was quite extraordinary, how excited he was about the baby. She was amazed. When she'd told him he'd gone bright red and said, 'oh, my God,' and then again, 'oh, my God,' and then, 'that's bloody amazing.'

They'd sat down on the bare boards of the flat, and he'd asked her how she knew and if she was sure, and when it was going to be: and he just couldn't stop smiling. She'd said she was pleased he was so pleased and he said of course he was pleased, he was bloody over the moon.

He was obsessed by her pregnancy; he'd found a book with some pictures of a baby developing in the womb and kept showing it to her. Did she realise their baby already had a heart, limbs and his sexual organs? That seemed very important to him. Even more important that they were, without question, male sexual organs. A girl child was not even worthy of consideration.

He had asked her to marry him within an hour of being informed about his prospective fatherhood. 'Or rather, made an announcement,' Eliza said, laughing, to Maddy, 'like he does about all his major decisions. He said no baby of his was to be born a bastard, and there was no time to be lost.'

'So what did you say?' said Maddy curiously.

'Oh, I just said that would be lovely. I'd already forced him to ask me properly to move in with him, I couldn't face doing it all again.'

'And – are you really, really happy about it?'

Eliza stared at her.

'Of course I am. I feel like I'm going to burst I'm so happy. I love him, so, so much. Why do you think I did all this, gave up Jeremy and everything? Honestly, Maddy, that is the strangest question.'

'Well, that's fine. Sorry. I just wanted to – well to hear it from you . . .'

'Well – now you have. Anyway, we're getting married in a month, put it in your diary, nothing big, just the families and best friends, Chelsea Reg, and a party afterwards at the Arethusa. That was my idea,' she added. 'I think Matt would have settled for a quick drink in the pub.'

'No he wouldn't. What are you going to wear?'

'Oh – little dress from Foale and Tuffin. Really sweet. Short and white, but I can't do the bridal number, not being up the duff and all. Even though I don't show.'

'And – sixty-four-thousand-dollar question: are your family coming?'

'I don't know,' said Eliza. And burst into the inevitable tears.

She had taken Matt down to Summercourt to give them the news. For the first and last time in her pregnancy, she was sick that morning.

They drove down in her Mini: she knew Matt's new toy, a Lotus Elan, would make her feel even worse.

Her mother greeted them, smiling rather wanly, telling Matt just a bit too graciously that it was very nice to see him again. 'Come through, both of you, Daddy's in the morning room, been having a little nap, he's been so looking forward to your coming, darling. How are you, you look well.'

'Yes, yes, I'm fine, thank you. Bit tired, we're moving, got a flat in Battersea, lovely Victorian mansion block by the river, it's really super, isn't it, Matt?'

'Yeah,' he said, 'yeah, it's great.'

'I'm so glad. Adrian, darling, here they are.'

'Daddy, hello. How are you? You remember Matt?'

'Yes, yes, of course.' Expression had largely deserted Adrian's face; it was the frozen strained look of the Parkinson's victim that struggled to smile. He held out his shaking hand.

'How do you do?' he said, in his new, whispery voice. 'Delighted to meet you again. Heard a lot about you, of course.'

'Nothing too bad I hope,' said Matt, smiling politely.

'No, no, of course not. Good journey down?'

'Yes, it was really easy, thanks.'

'Er – sherry?' said Sarah into the silence.

'Or a beer?' asked Adrian.

'Oh, now you're talking,' said Matt, 'I could murder a beer.'

Eliza watched him being himself at his best, polite and attentive, while refusing to put on any kind of a show, and thought how much she loved him.

She saw him taking in the kitchen, every detail of it, the cold, the peeling paint at the windows, the shabby worn rug on the stone floor, the Aga, the huge wooden table, the jugs of dried flowers, the two cats asleep in the big chair. 'Lovely,' he said, 'a real old-fashioned family kitchen. Very, very nice. Can I stand by the stove, I'm absolutely perished.'

'We couldn't live without our Aga, could we, Eliza?'

'No, Mummy.'

'Do you want a sherry, darling?'

'No, no thank you.'

Matt was very disapproving when she drank; he said he was sure it couldn't be good for the baby.

'Why on earth not?' she had said. 'French women drink at least two glasses of red wine a day and an aperitif before dinner.'

'I don't care what the bloody frogs do,' he said, 'that's an English baby in there and I was reading the other day that alcohol was bad, OK?'

'So – you met Eliza through Charles I seem to remember, Matt?' Sarah's smile was not so much chilly as frozen.

'Yes, that's right. Charles and I were army mates.'

'Oh really? How interesting.' A silence. Then, 'were you out in Gibraltar with him?'

'No, no. Just on the old basic training. But we kept in contact afterwards.'

Another silence. Eliza broke in slightly desperately.

'Yes, and then he helped a friend of mine, Maddy, you remember her from the wedding, Mummy, she's the designer, wore that terribly short sort of crocheted dress and little bonnet, Daddy loved her—'

Adrian's face went into its rictus smile.

'Do remember her, yes. Lovely girl.'

'Thought you would. Anyway, Matt found her the premises where she works. He's in the property business, as you know.'

'That must be most interesting,' said Adrian. 'They're practically rebuilding London, aren't they, I heard on the wireless the other day.'

'Yeah, it's true. And I like to think I'm helping them.'

'I think I rather preferred it how it was,' said Sarah.

A very long silence.

'Eliza, why don't you show Matt round the house,' said Sarah, 'while I heat up the soup.'

'Got a knife?' hissed Matt as they walked out into the hall.

'What do you want a knife for?'

'To cut the atmosphere with.'

'Sorry, Matt. It'll get better, I'm sure.'

'Hope so.'

He was slightly taken aback by the house all over again; she could see that. By its size, as well as its beauty. Despite the fact it was a sorry change from the lovely warm, light-filled place he had peered into at the wedding.

'Very nice,' he kept saying as she led him from the drawing room into the morning room and then across the hall to the dining room. 'Very nice indeed,' as they mounted the staircase, 'God, another one,' as bedroom followed bedroom, 'Crikey,' as they went up to the top floor.

'Yes, and this is why it's such a nightmare,' said Eliza, indicating the collection of bowls in the corner of the old nursery. 'Look, they collect water when it rains. Roof's leaking and they can't afford to fix it. None of us can.'

'Shame. God, this is some place, Eliza. It is really—' He paused. 'Really beautiful. I can see why you love it. But – lot of money.'

'Yes, to put it all right, you mean? Which they just haven't got. It's so horrible, what's happening. But – nothing to be done. Well – let's go down and face the music. Shall we tell them before or after lunch?'

'After might be better.'

After lunch, which wasn't as bad as Eliza feared – her father seemed to like Matt and showed a genuine interest in his work – Sarah suggested coffee.

'Lovely, Mummy. Now – just before you make it Matt and I have something to tell you.'

She saw her mother stiffen, watched her face freeze. Eliza struggled to stay calm.

'What's that, then?' asked her father.

'Well – two things actually. But they are – linked. Matt and I are going to get married.'

'Married!' Sarah's voice rose; the distaste in it was undisguisable.

'Yes, Mummy, married.'

'Well – isn't that rather – rather soon?'

'Not really. And we're very sure about it. We've known each other quite a long time.'

'No you haven't!' Sarah's voice tore into her. 'It's only – what, a few months since – well, since you were in another relationship. Surely you should give it a little longer.'

'No, we don't want to do that.'

'Eliza – please—'

'Please what, Mummy?'

'Don't – don't rush into this. There's no need to get married surely, you could just live together and – and make sure – and—'

'Mrs Fullerton-Clark,' said Matt, and there was a hint of menace in his voice, 'we are sure. I love Eliza very much and I want to marry her.'

'Yes,' said Sarah, with a very faint smile, 'yes, I see.'

'And,' Eliza took a deep breath, 'as well as being sure, there is a – another reason for it. For getting married.'

'Yes?'

Eliza looked at Matt; he was staring at the ground. He clearly wasn't going to say it.

'I'm – well, I'm going to have a baby.'

'A baby! Oh, Eliza, no.'

Eliza quite literally held her breath and counted to ten; she knew she must remain calm, she knew she was imposing a lot on her mother, but at the same time, she could feel the cumulative strain of the past few weeks erupting into rage.

'Yes,' she said finally, 'aren't I – aren't we, Matt?'

'Yes,' he said, 'yes, that's right.'

'Well – I just don't know what to say.' Sarah sat down suddenly at the kitchen table; she was very pale.

'What about – congratulations?' said Eliza, her own voice icy now.

'Yes. Come along, Sarah.' It was Adrian, clearly making a huge effort. 'Congratulations. It's very exciting. Well done.'

He held out his hand to Matt, who took it rather bemusedly.

'Thanks,' he said.

'No,' said Sarah, 'no, it isn't exciting. It's rather the reverse, I would

266

say. I can't pretend I think anything else. I'm sorry. I'm – I'm just going upstairs for a bit.'

'I think we should leave,' said Matt, quite quietly.

Half an hour away from the house, he pulled over to the side of the road and looked at Eliza.

'Well?'

'Oh, Matt. I'm sorry. You were awfully good. Staying polite.'

'It was a bit weird,' he said, 'being regarded as a blight on your young life.'

'It wasn't that bad, Matt.'

'Yes, it was. It was exactly that bad. I wasn't just not good enough, I was totally too bad. Christ all-bloody mighty.'

'I'm sorry,' she said again, 'I'm sure they'll get over it. I suppose – I suppose it was an awful shock. Me being pregnant and everything. I mean it wasn't the sort of thing that they know about—'

'Really? None of your posh friends ever get knocked up? I don't believe it. Unless all those blokes lack balls as well as chins.'

'Matt—' Of course it was true. A couple of girls she knew had had to get married rather more quickly than might have been anticipated and then had surprisingly 'premature' babies. Moreover, she knew if she had told her parents she'd been having Jeremy's baby they would have got the champagne out.

'Look,' she said, 'they will come round. I know they will. Specially when the baby's arrived.'

'Matter of fact,' he said, 'I'm not sure I want them to. And I don't want them coming to the wedding. I really don't. Even if they begged me.'

'Oh, Matt, please! Let's not get into all that. A family feud. Please, Matt. Just for me. Me and the baby.'

'Well – I'll see. Not saying any more than that. Anyway, something tells me they won't even consider coming.'

He was horribly hurt; it took him days to get over it. She felt very hurt herself, and shocked and embarrassed at her parents' behaviour – well, her mother's. She thought she had never loved her father more than when he had held out his shaky hand to Matt.

'Give them time,' she said again, 'and I love you, that's what matters.'

So far there had been a chilly note from her mother, saying she was of course pleased to hear about the baby 'if that's what you want' but she would have to get back to Eliza about the wedding. 'Daddy's health being what it is, I think it's a little unlikely that he could make the journey, but we will have to see how he gets on in the next few weeks or so. He varies a lot.'

Charles had called to say that he and Juliet would be there. Eliza felt a flash of remorse. 'That's really lovely, Charles. Thank you.'

He also made a rather stiff phone call to Matt, congratulating him and with a feeble attempt at humour telling him he was mad, he had no idea what he was taking on.

Matt's family were all delighted; his mother especially so.

She embraced Eliza, patted her stomach tenderly, told her she was a brave girl to take Matt on and said she couldn't wait to have her as a daughter-in-law. Pete was slightly stiff about it, and took Matt down to the pub to give him a quick lecture. 'Getting a girl in the family way, without marrying her, that's not how we brought you up, Matt. It's a big responsibility, being a family man. You can't just pick it up and put it down again, you know.'

'Yes, Dad, I do know. And I'm taking it very seriously. Honestly. I'm marrying her, aren't I?'

'Son,' said Pete, 'that's only the beginning.'

His young brothers were both slightly embarrassed; they said she was much too good for Matt, and then disappeared up to their rooms.

Scarlett's reaction was the most unexpected. She embraced them both, told Eliza she couldn't be more pleased, 'but you will have to keep him in order, you know, not let him run rings round you,' but was clearly also rather upset by something, and suddenly announced in the middle of lunch that she was sorry, she had a bad headache and she was going to lie down for ten minutes if nobody minded.

Sandra went up after quarter of an hour and came down looking worried.

'She's upset about something, she'd obviously been crying, you didn't say anything to her, did you, Matt?'

Matt replied indignantly that of course he hadn't; Eliza was worried that Scarlett might secretly dislike her but when she came down again, looking flushed and rather bright-eyed, she hugged Eliza, said she was sorry, she'd had a dreadful week's heavy-duty flying, and that she was absolutely delighted to have her as a sister-in-law.

❊ ❊ ❊

Sarah was trying very hard to be positive about Matt. She told herself there was no point thinking about Jeremy, or what might have been; nevertheless she found herself doing exactly that a great deal. She felt outraged that her daughter should be throwing away all the work and all the money she and Adrian had invested in her. 'Just for a bit of foolish romanticism. That's all it is. She could have had a golden future, with someone of her own sort and here she is, slumming it with this person.'

Adrian told her she was a snob and that her father had no doubt thought she was slumming it with him. 'Darling, that's just not right. You might not have had any money but you knew what was what. This – this Matt clearly doesn't.'

'Sarah! Darling! Don't start thinking like that, please. It's just not very – very helpful.'

She was increasingly worried about the house; it was still cold and they simply couldn't afford to heat much of it. She had converted the morning room into a sort of bed-sitting room with two comfortable chairs and the television, a small table and a bed for Adrian to use when, as increasingly was the case, she was unable to get him upstairs. She would then go up alone to her bedroom and quite often lie awake for hours, worrying what on earth would become of them.

Charles increasingly urged her to talk to the trustees about breaking the trust and moving into something smaller; she would have hoped he'd be more helpful and positive, Summercourt should, after all, become his one day; didn't he want that, she asked him, almost exasperated, at the end of a long Sunday when they had talked endlessly about it and surveyed the increasing ravages of neglect.

'Mummy, I have to be realistic,' he said, looking slightly hunted, 'I don't have any money, you know I don't, I don't earn a lot, Juliet wants to move into something better than a flat in Chiswick—'

'Which I presume Summercourt isn't?' said Sarah coldly.

'We can't come and live down here, you must see that. I have my job, she has hers, and she would like to think about starting a family—'

'Which should have Summercourt as its home. Charles, I don't understand you, you don't seem to have any sense of Summercourt's place in your life.'

'Mummy, its place in my life feels like an immense drain. Look, please try to understand. I'm sorry, and of course I love it, and I'll be sad to see

269

it go, but it's simply making life harder for all of us, particularly you. We have to move with the times, and face facts.'

Sarah wondered how much of this speech had originally come from Juliet.

In the event they didn't come to the wedding. Sarah wrote a stiff little note saying they could come, 'Daddy's health permitting,' but two days before, she rang to say that Adrian had had a couple of falls and was very badly bruised and with a possibly broken wrist. 'He simply isn't well enough to come, and I don't feel I can leave him.'

Eliza was so hurt and angry she could hardly speak.

'Mummy, it's my wedding day. Surely someone could look after Daddy?'

'No, Eliza, I'm afraid not. I don't think you understand how difficult things are for me. I understand Charles and Juliet are coming, they can represent us all.'

Eliza thought of the loving family she had grown up in and wondered for the hundredth time if they really cared about her at all.

Not even the Marchants could come; they were away visiting relatives in Washington.

'But thrilled to hear about the baby,' Anna wrote, 'and as soon as I get back, we must celebrate, the four of us. Enjoy being pregnant, darling; I never managed it, as you know.'

Eliza was rather sadly trying on her shoes the night before, and trying to decide whether to wear white tights or cream ones, when the phone rang.

'Darling? It's Daddy.'

'Oh – Daddy. How lovely to hear your voice, you're all right, are you?'

'As all right as I'll ever be again.'

'Oh, Daddy. I'm so sorry.'

'Yes, well, this call isn't about me. It's about you. Listen, sweetheart, you have a lovely day tomorrow and I would give anything, anything, to be able to be there and walk you down the aisle. Who's going to do that, for you, Charles?'

'Um – yes,' she said quickly, unable to face explaining that there wasn't any aisle.

Charles had actually offered to 'escort her in' to the room, and she had accepted gratefully. It would be at least someone of her own.

'Good, good. Well, make sure there are lots of photographs.'

'I will, Daddy.' She smiled into the phone.

'And now, don't you worry about your mother. She'll come round. I like your young man, I think he's rather interesting and obviously going far. Take care of yourself, darling, and God bless. I love you.'

She took those words into the room with her next day.

She took other things too: a sense of absolute happiness, and of rightness; and a heart so overflowing with love that when she looked at Matt, smiling at her rather tensely, it was all she could do not to rush into his arms there and then before any more of the ceremony took place.

The lunch at the Arethusa was great fun; Louise, who proclaimed herself honorary best man, made a very funny speech full of affection, Charles made a very touching one, saying how much he loved his sister and how he had always regarded her as his best friend – Juliet's smile at this point became slightly strained – and Pete got very carried away, and made a completely unexpected unrehearsed speech, saying what a lovely girl Eliza was and how proud he was to have her in the family. At which point even Matt was seen to look distinctly moist-eyed. And when Matt himself stood up and declared that he simply couldn't believe how lucky he was to be marrying a girl who was 'so completely special and who I love so completely much, nothing more to be said really', Eliza burst into tears and sobbed for at least a minute on a slightly bemused Pete's shoulder. It wasn't a conventional wedding and nor was it large or lavish; but it was, in the end, an extraordinarily happy one.

Chapter 26

He kept reading it, thinking it would seem better as he got used to it. It didn't.

'Dear Mr Fullerton-Clark,

I felt I should bring it to your attention that your current account is now overdrawn £2,500. This is, as I am sure you must be aware, a very large sum, and goes far beyond the £500 limit we initially agreed, and even the temporary extension to £1,000 which you assured me would be settled within thirty days. Please make arrangements to come and see me as soon as possible to discuss repayments, and in the meantime I regret I shall have no alternative but to return any cheques written on your account. As it is a joint account please inform Mrs Fullerton-Clark of this also.

Yours sincerely,

John Winston

Manager, Sloane Square Branch.

Christ, now what did he do. Two and a half grand, that was an awful lot of money. An impossible amount. How had he done that? Mrs Fullerton-Clark of course had a great deal to answer for in the matter; that cocktail party she'd insisted they gave, not to mention the endless tedious dinner parties, her bloody Harrods account, the holiday she'd booked 'as a surprise' on the joint account, flying – flying for Christ's sake and First Class, to Venice for their wedding anniversary, and then, oh God, the deposit on the house Juliet had found and fallen in love with near Guildford, maybe he could do something clever with the mortgage, now there was an idea. It just crept up, month by month, the odd saving of ten or twenty pounds here and there hardly worth making, so he didn't, but the worst thing was that insane gamble with those shares, which everyone had said were a dead cert – fifteen hundred bloody quid, worth just about a tenth of that now – anyway, he had to think of something. And talk to Juliet.

'But I just don't understand. We're so careful, don't live at anything like the rate of our friends, hardly ever go out to restaurants, still haven't joined the Ad Lib or the Saddle Room—'

'Juliet,' said Charles, 'we are not careful. We' – he longed to say you – 'are quite extravagant. Every month it's the same, spending over what we can afford, I don't want to spell it out—'

'Well, I think you'd better. Otherwise I'll never understand—'

He spelt it out; she listened.

Then, 'Well, you'll have to ask your father. He can make you a loan.'

'Juliet, my father has no money whatsoever. I wish you could understand that.'

'I don't, to be honest. Living in that great house with your mother's grand family—'

'Oh, for Christ's sake. That great house is falling down. There is no money to patch it up. My mother never even puts the central heating on, she doesn't even have a cleaner any more, they're stony-broke.'

She stared at him. 'You don't mean that.'

'Of course I mean it. I don't know where this idea came from, that there was money in my family, I've told you often enough.'

'Well, obviously you didn't make it clear. I don't know what Daddy will say.'

'I don't see what it has to do with your father.'

'Of course it does. You're his only son-in-law, he'll be so disappointed in you. And if you're going to start buying shares, you'd better consult him, he's really clever at it, made a lot of money, although I'd have thought with you being a stockbroker, you wouldn't have made such a stupid mistake.'

'Oh, go to hell,' said Charles and walked out of the house.

He made an appointment to see the bank manager two days later; he asked Juliet, who didn't seem remotely remorseful, to go with him. She refused.

'I don't see why I should put myself in such an awful, humiliating situation. It's not my fault.'

❂ ❂ ❂

Mr Winston was sympathetic. 'I know how easy it is for young people to get into this situation. But I can't allow this to go on, Mr Fullerton-Clark. I'm afraid I'll have to take a charge on your flat.'

'But – it's on the market,' said Charles. 'I've put down a preliminary deposit on a house.'

'Cheaper?' said Mr Winston hopefully.

'Er – no.'

'Well, you'll have to take the flat off the market again. In any case I couldn't possibly give you any kind of guarantee to a building society. My advice to you would be to look for something cheaper, use the difference to pay off your debts. You can't go on like this.'

'Now I want you to listen to me very carefully.' Jack Beckham glared at Eliza.

'Yes. I'm listening.'

'I've decided that I – I was mistaken the other day.'

'Yes?'

'I perhaps shouldn't have said what I did.'

'Right—'

'And – well, I have decided that we'll leave things as they are. That you can stay in the job.'

'Well, that's very nice of you Jack. Er – what happens if I don't want to?'

'Of course you bloody well want to,' he said.

There were, he said, conditions. 'I don't want to hear anything about you being tired. I don't want you to be away. I—'

'Er, excuse me,' said Eliza.

'Yes?'

'Do we convert my office into a labour ward?'

'What?'

'Well, if I can't be away – I mean this baby's got to come out sometime.'

'Don't be so fucking ridiculous. You know perfectly well what I mean.'

'Ah. So I can have a day or two off?'

'You can have a week,' he said, grinning at her, 'possibly with an extension for good behaviour.'

'Right. OK. Well – thank you.'

'The thing is,' he said, 'you're the best fashion editor in London at the moment. Everyone says so. And if I want you here, I suppose I just have to put up with your – your condition.'

'I suppose you do.'

'Now what do I do?' she wailed to Maddy. 'I've got my job back and I'm over the moon of course, and Matt won't let me do it.'

'Has he said so?'

'What, since Jack told me? Of course not. I – well, I haven't told him.'

'You haven't told Matt! Eliza, you know what he's like, he'll be even more livid when he does find out.'

'Yes, all right. I'm just waiting for the right moment,' said Eliza irritably.

The fact of the matter was that she couldn't bear to, in case he simply forbade her to accept. Her job defined her; it was what she was all about. She adored Matt, and she was incredibly happy about the baby: but if she was deprived of her work, a large piece of the jigsaw that was her would be missing.

When Jack had told her she was the best fashion editor in London, she felt literally that she could have flown; she savoured those words, went over and over them in her head, she felt stroked and sleek and dizzy with them. They made sense of it all, the endless pressure for ideas, the tedium of looking at racks and racks of dull, unsuitable clothes, the fights with the art director, the battles with photographers, the absurd demands of models, the racking fear that a session wouldn't go well, that the photo-graphs wouldn't do her ideas justice . . . suddenly none of that mattered. She had done it, she had made it all on her own, she was that most elusive, sought-after, fought-over thing, a success. It was a prize beyond anything she could have imagined. She could not, she would not, give that up. She would manage Matt somehow. Somehow . . .

Mariella was coming to London on a shopping trip, not merely for her, but for Giovanni. Eliza was rather charmed that he bought his clothes in London – it was, Mariella explained, because he was not an aristocrat.

'The old families dress in Italy and the new ones in England. That is how it goes. He has his shoes made in Lobbs, he buys his suits at Henry Poole, he has his shirts made in Savile Row. His ambition is to look like an English gentleman.'

She invited Eliza and Matt to join them for dinner. 'We are staying at the Ritz. I need to meet your husband. Shall we say Wednesday?'

'Wednesday would be lovely,' said Eliza, trying and failing to imagine Matt dining with the Crespis.

It was a surprisingly successful evening; even though Eliza could tell that Mariella was struggling not to compare Matt unfavourably with Jeremy. She herself was very taken with Giovanni, who was tall, charming, and elegant, with thick silvery-blond hair and sculpted features. He was tactile without it being remotely disagreeable, frequently kissing Eliza's hand, putting his arm round her shoulders and at one point patting the tip of her nose when she made him laugh. He told her that their villa on Como was always available to her if she was working in Milan; Matt had mercifully gone to the Gents at this point.

Giovanni clearly adored Mariella and was to be seen constantly blowing her kisses across the table. He spoke perfect English, and had the stamina of someone twenty years his junior, suggesting a nightcap in the bar after dinner and would have, Eliza was sure, taken her up on her offer of a visit to the Saddle Room if Mariella had not reminded him gently that it was already almost midnight and he had an appointment with his tailor at nine.

But the real love affair of the evening was between Giovanni and Matt, who formed a mutual admiration society, trumping each other's stories of early successes, of risks run and dangers confronted, and agreeing that business was the most potent drug in the world.

'Nice chap,' said Matt as they sat back in their taxi. 'Don't know what my dad would say, me consorting with wops.'

'Matt!' said Eliza. 'Honestly, you are so dreadful. Sometimes I think you do it on purpose.'

'Course I do,' he said and grinned at her.

'My dear Scarlett (wrote Mrs Berenson),

I do hope you are well and might consider again a visit here. It is so very lovely and you could meet our newest family member! David and Gaby's daughter, such a beautiful little girl and named Lily, after me. Such an honour! I was just so thrilled, you can imagine. Do come, we would all love to have you.'

This hurt so much that Scarlett, after a sleepless night, called David in his office and told him she needed some more money. She actually didn't, but frightening him was the only way she could find of getting any kind of revenge. It wasn't much but it was something.

Her project was going well; she was doing her research whenever she could and wherever her schedule took her, and had already signed up several small hotels, mostly in France and Italy. In a few weeks, she was returning to Trisos to do the same there.

She had even persuaded a couple of small chic hotels in New York to come into her fold. The city had suddenly become accessible, with David Frost's famous weekly trips, rocketing backwards and forwards across the Atlantic; going there was no longer an impossible or even distant dream.

Just very occasionally she fantasised about sending people to the Southern States, including (obviously) Charleston; now that would really frighten David, she thought . . .

Chapter 27

'Daddy's going to help,' said Juliet. 'He says he can't have me humiliated like this, and he wants to talk to you about making you a loan.'

'Oh. Oh, I see.' He wasn't sure he wanted help from Geoffrey Judd, and he longed to say that it was him being humiliated, not Juliet. But beggars, he supposed, couldn't be choosers. And a beggar was what he seemed to be. Geoffrey Judd certainly seemed to think so.

'I have to say,' he said, glaring at Charles. 'You've let us all down, especially Juliet. Managing your money isn't very difficult, you simply need some self-discipline.'

Charles longed to say it was Juliet who lacked the self-discipline. Instead he looked at his hands and metaphorically bit his tongue.

'What's more, I think we've all been deceived, leading us all to believe you owned that house, all of you, giving Juliet false expectations when it's nothing of the sort.'

This was too much. 'I'm afraid, Mr Judd, you don't understand. The house is owned by a family trust, holding it for my mother and then for future generations.'

'Same difference as far as I'm concerned. And a drain on any resources you may have into the bargain. Well, none of my money is going into it, I can tell you.'

'I wouldn't dream of suggesting such a thing,' said Charles.

'Maybe not, but the fact remains you've got yourself and Juliet into a financial mess, haven't you? My daughter can't have the home or the lifestyle she was very much led to expect. She shouldn't be living in a flat at this stage of her life and nor should you, and you should be keeping her, not sending her out to work every day. She wants to have children, you know, like any young woman; she's not going to get them the way you're going on.'

Just stay silent, Charles, don't rise to this, it won't be worth it, not in the long run.

'Anyway, I'm prepared to make you a loan, to pay off your overdraft, so you can start afresh, get a mortgage on that house Juliet's set her heart on. I'll want a formal repayment plan, but I'm prepared to be reasonable about it, nothing too steep while you get yourself sorted out. How does that sound?'

'That's – that's very generous of you, sir.'

It really was all he could do; the alternative was quite literally bankruptcy, which would mean the end of his job on the stock exchange.

'And I don't want to hear that a penny of it has gone into that house in Wiltshire, do you understand. You go and talk to the trustees; tell them to find some way of putting it on the market. Right. Well, here's a cheque. As far as I'm concerned, it's worth it to see my daughter happy and secure and not fretting over money. In my family, that's men's work. Now let's put together a schedule of repayments, shall we? What salary are you on?'

Adrian had had another fall and broken his pelvis. Sarah rang to say that she knew he would love to see Eliza, 'It's been quite a long time.' Eliza lost her temper and said she would have been down quite often if they hadn't been so hostile to Matt; Sarah said she was sorry, but it had been a terrible shock about the baby.

'Mummy, if I'd been pregnant with Jeremy's baby you'd have been over the moon with excitement.'

'That's not true.'

'Isn't it? Isn't it really?' There was a silence; then Eliza said, 'Well anyway, of course I'll come and see Daddy. I'd have come before if you'd asked me. I just felt so hurt. I can't come this week; next Saturday all right?'

'Yes, I suppose so. I had hoped Charles would be down, but he's very much out of our lives at the moment, I don't know what's going on. Anyway Saturday will do. Of course. And if Matt wants to come, then he'll be—'

'Honestly,' said Eliza, interrupting her, 'I don't think he will.'

But Matt, unpredictable to the last, insisted that he would go with her.

'I don't want you driving all that way on your own. It's not good for you to get too tired and long car journeys are probably not good for the baby, you getting all shaken about—'

'Matt, that baby is safer right now than it will be for the whole rest of its life. It's cushioned in God knows how much fluid, gallons by the look of me—'

'Well, I don't want you having a miscarriage on the side of the road.'

'I hardly think you can prevent that just by being there,' said Eliza, laughing.

Matt's devotion to his unborn child continued to surprise and delight her. He insisted on attending her appointments with the doctor, to her considerable embarrassment; the doctor clearly thought he was some unemployed lunatic who had nothing better to do. He had more or less auditioned all the hospitals and insisted that he would pay for her to have the baby privately if that seemed to be the best option. However, Eliza had established that one of the most highly regarded obstetricians in London, one Professor Anthony Collins, worked at the maternity unit of the Fulham and Battersea, an NHS teaching hospital, where he had established a culture of excellent education on all aspects of pregnancy and childbirth, including one evening which fathers were encouraged to attend, close family bonding and the admission of fathers to the labour ward if both parents wanted that. This was so revolutionary a notion there had even been letters to *The Times* about it. Eliza said hopefully she was sure Matt wouldn't want it, and that he'd faint but he said he wouldn't miss it for the world and that he wanted a grandstand view.

'No,' said Matt, 'no, no, no, no, no. That clear enough for you? I'll repeat it, just in case. No. You are not going to work when you've had the baby.'

'But—'

'Eliza, no. I don't know how you can even think of it. Don't you care about the baby, don't you think you'll love him?'

'Of course I bloody well care about the baby. Of course I'll love it. Him. But I don't see why that means I have to spend twenty-four hours a day with it – him. I love my work too, it's so important to me, and we can get a nanny, the baby will be fine—'

He stared at her for a moment in silence. Then, 'Oh, no. You are not sacrificing that baby in favour of your career. Do you really think photographing a few frocks is more important than bringing up your own child? I've never heard anything so – so disgusting, frankly.'

'Of course it's not disgusting. And I don't think my work is more important than my child. But I just don't see how being away from it –

him – for a few hours a day is so terrible. And I really don't think I'm cut out for full-time motherhood.'

'Oh, is that so. Well, you might have thought of that before you got yourself pregnant.'

'That's unfair!'

'Is it? I don't think so. I tell you what I think, Eliza, I think you're so fucking impressed with yourself and your life as a lady fashion editor, getting your arse licked all day long by all that fancy riff-raff you seem to like so much, you can't face giving it up. I've heard them at parties, and in the office, oh, Eliza you're so marvellous, oh, Eliza darling, what a wonderful editor you are, oh, Eliza you're so clever. It makes me want to throw up. Well right now, I don't think you're marvellous or wonderful, I think you're pathetic and self-centred and attention-seeking with a pretty rotten sense of values, and it's not good enough. Not good enough for the baby and not good enough for me. So – is that quite clear?'

She had walked out after that, and gone to the office, where she had smoked at least five of the cigarettes Matt had ordered her to give up and sworn and cried and talked to Annunciata and rung Maddy, both of whom agreed that Matt was a monster and was not to be given in to and she said of course she wasn't going to give in to him, it would be marital suicide, she would do what she liked with her life and she even went out for a drink with Annunciata to give herself Dutch courage for the evening's battle.

It was a battle and it raged for days, and became very ugly. He told her she was disgraceful; she told him he was monstrous; he told her she lacked a sense of maternal duty; she told him he had no concept of the sort of person she really was; he said if he had, he certainly wouldn't have married her.

'I'm surprised you didn't just get rid of the baby, I really am,' he said, finally, 'since it's going to be such a burden to you. Maybe it's not too late to do that now, Eliza. I'd investigate it if I were you.'

Eliza walked up to him and started to attack him physically, flailing at him with her fists; he stared at her then turned in silence and left.

He didn't come back that night, spent it in the office; but as he sat at his desk, grey-faced and shaking with exhaustion the following morning, staring out of the window, and his misery so evident that even Louise was touched by it, Eliza walked through reception and into his office, shut the door behind her and told him she had decided that she would give up work when the baby was born.

❋　❋　❋

Jenny was having what she called a turnout. This mostly meant taking everything out of every cupboard and drawer in the office and putting ninety-nine per cent of it back again, all to a running commentary on her own progress. She was just debating with herself whether she should keep the envelopes with the windows, probably not, as she very rarely used them these days, ever since Mr Shaw had said they looked tacky, but then they could come in very handy if she ran out of the others, when the phone rang. It was Barry Floyd.

'Is that the lovely Jenny?'

'It's Jenny, Mr Floyd, yes. I don't know if—'

'And is the equally lovely Louise there?'

'I'll just enquire, Mr Floyd, would you mind holding?'

'I wouldn't mind holding anything at all, and certainly not you, my darling, no.'

'It's Mr Floyd, Miss Mullan,' said Jenny. 'He sounds very cheerful. Do you want to speak to him?'

'Well, since he's cheerful, yes, Jenny, I will. Put him through. Barry, hello.'

'Good morning, my darling Louise. And how are you this beautiful morning?'

'I'm fine, thank you,' said Louise, 'but I don't know where you are. It's pouring with rain in London.'

'I'm in London and it looks beautiful to me. Now then. Could I interest you in a tenant today?'

'I daresay you could, yes. What sort of tenant and for where? That building in Holborn?'

'No, not Holborn. This is about Slough. Someone who just might be moving in . . . that direction, just so long as he can find premises.'

'Oh, my God. Barry, that's amazing. Who is he?'

'It's a little outfit – you may not even have heard of them—'

'Oh,' Louise's voice echoed her disappointment. They needed a big one for Slough: a really big one. They would be losing thousands a year in interest alone once the final payments had all been made.

'Still – worth pursuing, I think. Could you see him for a meeting this afternoon on site, do you think? At around 3 p.m. And bring those two boys of yours with you.'

He always referred to Matt and Jimbo as Louise's boys; she liked it, it diminished them rather satisfactorily.

'I'll try. But it's quite a trek out to Slough. And – well, if he's really small, is he the sort of tenant we want anyway?'

'Oh, I think so. Could be. You know how one thing leads to another in this game.'

'Well – all right then. I'll be there.'

'Good girl. You'll like him, he's a real charmer.'

'That always helps,' said Louise.

She asked Matt and Jimbo if they wanted to come; they both said they had far more important things to do, and that a small tenant for Slough would be worse than useless.

'Barry said he was worth pursuing. And it is very important to us, that site.'

'Yes, all right,' said Matt irritably, 'I think I know that without being told, Louise. And of course someone should go, but that's fine, you'll do.'

'Well, thanks for that vote of confidence. And you can jolly well wait till I get back, so we can discuss his feasibility. Barry said he'd want a quick decision if he liked the place.'

'Barry always talks like that. There's no way I'm going to be rushed into letting some wanker take half that space or less, and you can tell Barry that first off.'

'Yes, all right,' said Louise. She went into her own office and slammed the door, saying she didn't want to be disturbed; and got into her car after lunch and set off on the long crawl to Slough.

She had still not returned by half past six; Matt and Jimbo were beginning to grow irritable. Jimbo was expected at his fiancée's home for a family conference about the wedding, now rivalling the D-Day landings in its complexity, as Louise had remarked, and Matt wanted to go and look at a car-park site in the City.

'Give her another half an hour, then we'll lock up and she can tell us about it in the morning.'

At 6.59 precisely they heard the reception door open and Louise came in.

She had what they both called her look on. It was a look that transformed her from sexy, sassy girl to sleek, successful woman; and it settled on her whenever she had pulled off some deal, made some new contact, embarked on some new project. It was hard to define exactly, but it was partly the way she moved, rather more slowly than usual, partly the expression in her eyes, partly a just-supercilious curve to her mouth.

'Oh,' she said, 'hello.'

'Hello, Louise. Bit late, you could have called.'

'Yes, well, unfortunately there aren't any telephones set into the foundations at Slough and the two boxes I passed were out of order. Anyway, it's only seven for Christ's sake.'

'Yes, OK, OK. What was this mysterious client then and is there any hope of a deal?'

'I – think there might be, yes.'

She sat down on Matt's desk, her long legs swinging, pulled out a pack of cigarettes and the small tortoiseshell lighter they had given her for her last birthday and lit one, inhaling hard and then blowing out a great cloud of smoke.

'Quite a lot of hope. Good thing I went, he's going to need quite a bit of stroking. He was obviously a bit disappointed we weren't all there, he'd brought his PR along.'

'His PR!' Jimbo and Matt looked at each other. Small firms didn't usually have PRs and certainly not ones they brought to meetings.

'Yes. She was great. I really liked her.'

'She!'

'Yes. Nothing wrong with that, I trust. Or do you not approve of female PRs?'

'Of course we do,' said Jimbo hastily. 'We approve of female everything. Even developers.'

'Yes. Anyway, her boss, he liked the development, very much, liked the landscaping particularly, and the location of course. Matt, I made sure you got the credit for that at least—'

'What do you mean, at least?'

'Well, even though you were too busy to come.'

'For Christ's sake, Louise,' said Matt, 'who the fu—, who was this client?'

'Have you heard of WireHire?'

'WireHire?'

There was a silence; Matt and Jimbo looked at one another and then at Louise, Jimbo's face red, Matt's white.

'WireHire? You mean – the company that's hot on the heels of Radio Rentals?'

'Yeah, well done. They're very big mostly in TV now, and especially the new colour sets. Which they say are the next big thing. No one's going to want to buy them at the moment, they'll be terribly expensive, but everyone'll want one, so—'

'Shit,' said Jimbo.

Louise smiled at him sweetly.

'Yes, indeed. Well, they want to rationalise their offices, as they put it. As you can imagine, the set-up is huge, nationwide. Having all their clerical staff under one roof will save them zillions. So – they're really keen. Said it would be perfect for them. We'll have to hurry the completion along, of course, and of course you did say you weren't going to be rushed into letting some wanker have it, so as I said to them—'

'Louise, we must have a meeting with them asap. Obviously. Er – who came then, apart from the PR?'

'What do you mean?'

'Well, obviously Bill Laurence wouldn't have come himself.'

'Now why do you think that?' said Louise.

'Well, he's the big boss. He wouldn't have time to visit sites, for God's sake.'

'Do you know, he does. He thinks it's crucial that the head of a company is involved in decisions over where his workforce is to spend its days – its habitat, as he put it; and to meet the people who are creating that habitat. He didn't seem too much of a – what did you call him? Oh, yes, a wanker – to me. Anyway there's no need for you to meet him yet.'

'What? Of course there is.'

'No, no, really there isn't. I explained to him I was a partner in the company and that Barry and I had actually been present at its birth, so to speak, and he was perfectly happy to shake hands on it. Felicity made sure there were some photographs of that.'

'Who's Felicity?' said Matt irritably.

'The PR. Felicity Bristow she's called, jolly posh, Matt, she could have gone to school with Eliza. Anyway, she said the pictures would go into the company magazine and then later on, when contracts had been exchanged, she'd circulate them to the press. So all you have to do for now is sit tight and wait for further developments.'

She stood up, smiled at them sweetly, stubbed out her cigarette in Matt's ashtray and walked to the door. 'Night, chaps. See you in the morning. Haven't you got homes to go to?'

Chapter 28

'I just can't do this, I can't, I can't.'

'Yes, you can. Come on, you have to concentrate.'

'No, no, I can't, I'm so tired, oh, God, here comes another one, oh, my God—'

'Come on, hang on to me. That's it. You can't give up now. You're nearly there—'

'It's all right for you, you bastard, you've no idea what I'm going through. Will you just fuck off, go away.' Tears streamed down Eliza's face; she threw back her head and shut her eyes.

'That's good,' said Professor Collins, 'that's very good. She's getting upset, means she's in transition, any minute now she's going to want to push.'

He had only popped in, as he put it, an hour earlier, to see how Eliza was getting on; he'd become interested in her, having met her in the clinic once or twice, his wife was an avid reader of *Charisma*, and he'd promised that if he could visit her while she was in labour he would.

'Can't guarantee it, I'm not one of your smooth, suited obstetricians, this is an NHS hospital, but I like to see my mothers putting all the theory into practice.'

'Your theories stink,' said Eliza, glaring at him as he walked into the delivery room. 'The breathing doesn't help much at all, I'm completely exhausted, I want some more pethidine, and the only thing that's made me feel better so far is screaming.'

He grinned and patted her shoulder.

'The midwife tells me you've been wonderful. And what about the father, how's he doing?'

'Oh, I kicked him last time he tried to calm me down.'

'Excellent. We men need a lot of that. Bet you wouldn't like to be doing it without him though, would you?'

'No,' said Eliza, 'no I wouldn't and I don't know how people do. Oh, my God, here it comes again—'

'Right. Off we go. One more push and – yes, good, very good, there's the head, now wait, try to relax and again – yes, come on Eliza, now, now, now, yes – yes, there we are – good, good, very good, yes – and – yes! Good girl, well done, well done—'

As Eliza said afterwards, it was a bit like being told how to have an orgasm.

A moment's silence then; the pain gone; the room back in focus; Matt smiling at her, tears streaming down his face; and then, the cry, the raw, triumphant, newborn cry; and then, 'Well done, Eliza. Congratulations. Must dash,' from Professor Collins. And then 'seven and a half pounds, very good, she's beautiful, here, hold your baby, Eliza. That's right,' from the huge smiling black midwife who had cajoled and bullied and encouraged her and cared for her through the long, long night, and she was crying and Matt was kissing her and kissing the baby's head and crying too, and telling her he loved her and then – then –

'Better start saving for the wedding,' the midwife said.

'Wedding?' Eliza peered into the towel that was wrapped round her daughter, her screaming, amazingly beautiful, astonishingly wonderful daughter. 'Oh, my God! It's a girl. Nobody told me.'

'We told you, honey,' said the midwife, 'you just weren't paying attention.'

'Matt, did you realise, it's – she's a girl.'

'I did, yeah. Bit different from a boy in certain departments, I noticed. I'm quick like that.'

'So – is that all right?'

'Course it's all right.' He was bent over the baby, smiling at her, stroking her cheek. 'She's amazing. Beautiful. Can't believe it.'

'But – you don't mind it's not a boy?'

'Mind? Why should I mind? Girls are much more fun. We can have a boy next time.'

'What next time?' said Eliza.

She looked down at the baby in her arms, and the baby looked up at her, and love took hold of her heart and turned and twisted it into a completely different shape. She stroked her daughter's small, dark head and her soft, limp little legs, and tangled her tiny starfish fingers round her own giant one, and the whole world was changed.

They called her Emmeline ('No, *not* because of Mrs Pankhurst,' Eliza said that day, for the first of a thousand times, 'we just like it'). Emmie for short. Their blue-eyed, dark-haired, strong-willed, difficult little daughter. Who had them wrapped around her tiny fingers from day one, who defied routine, who screamed from one feed to the next, who seemed to need far less sleep than they did. Whose father doted on her, whose mother adored her, whose two grandmothers, bonding most happily over the small head, agreed that she looked like both her parents, while each privately knowing that she actually looked exactly like only one of them, and whose two grandfathers, the one wheeled into the ward in a wheelchair, the other swaggering with second-hand pride, shook hands over her, smiling bashfully, and became friends. Pete took charge of Adrian for the rest of his visit, wheeling him out of the hospital and into the pub – 'well, we can't sit there all day can we?' – plied him with the beer he was forbidden and promised to sort out a series of ramps for him at home, so that he could be moved about more easily.

Charles, Jimbo and Maddy were all asked to be godparents, and were all duly moved to tears by the request; friends flocked to Eliza's bedside for the entire seven days she was in hospital, in larger groups every day until Sister said she really must insist Mrs Shaw respect visiting hours and the rule of three visitors at a time – although some of them were so exotic, men in brocaded frock coats, worn over faded blue jeans, or velvet suits in purple or black, and girls in knicker-skimming dresses, thigh-high boots and brilliantly coloured fur coats, that she was reluctant to halt the flow, although she did have to put a stop to the flowers which threatened to engulf the entire ward.

'It's always the same with these bohemians,' she said to the Staff Nurse, 'they don't know when to stop.'

'Just like children, I always think,' said Staff Nurse darkly. 'Spoilt children at that.'

Eliza recovered quickly, and begged to be allowed home early. Sister said she was to do nothing of the sort; 'you feel all right here, I know, but you wait till you get home to the housework and the washing and no one to help with the baby.'

Eliza said rather sheepishly that she was going to have help with all that (a cleaner, a present from her godmother, who had actually wanted to pay for a maternity nurse for a month but Matt had forbidden that – 'I'm not having some starched harridan taking over our baby'), but Sister then pointed out rather sharply that she hadn't actually resolved Emmie's feeding yet and it was a good idea to have that established before getting home.

'And besides, Professor Collins likes his mothers in for a week, building up their strength, and getting some proper rest.'

'I don't want to rest,' said Eliza crossly, 'I want to go home with my baby.'

Four sleep-deprived weeks later, she remembered that conversation and thought she would have paid the hospital to have her and Emmie back.

She wasn't very good at the breast-feeding; Emmie was very slow at latching on, as the nurses called it, and when she finally managed it, it hurt so much that Eliza yelped aloud with pain every time. She longed to put Emmie onto the bottle, but Matt wouldn't hear of it; he had taken in, along with his other pre-natal reading, the fact that babies not only thrived better on breast milk, but it protected them from all manner and kinds of infections and illnesses.

'My mum says you've just got to persevere,' he said, coming home to find Eliza weeping one night over the screaming Emmie, 'and the more you do it, the more the milk flows.'

Eliza said irritably that was all very well, but at the rate she was going, Emmie would probably starve to death while she was persevering, and before the flow ever got going.

Most of the time though, she felt too exhausted even to be irritable; day had blurred into night, one feed into the next. She was frequently still in her nightie at teatime. When she did finally get dressed it was into her maternity clothes; the huge leaky breasts that so totally failed to satisfy her daughter were not to be suppressed under any T-shirt or sweater, her waist still went out rather than in, and her stomach still protruded soggily beneath it. 'Even my thighs are twice the size,' she wailed to Maddy, 'I can't bear to look at them.'

She longed for Matt to come home each evening and then within ten minutes was quarrelling with him; he too was tiring of the noise, the lack of sleep, her exhaustion and the apparent end of life as they knew it.

The cleaner left after the first week, when Eliza lost her temper with her and told her to stop polishing the bloody floor and wash up last night's supper things instead; she thought she might spend the money on hiring a maternity nurse at least one night a week, but it turned out that it was a whole month or nothing, and when she mentioned it to Matt he told her he was simply not prepared to even consider it.

They rowed a great deal; Matt simply couldn't see why Eliza was failing so spectacularly at what seemed to him a fairly simple set of demands. 'All I'm asking,' he said in exasperation as they went into week three, 'is that you'll have a meal ready for me when I get in, and maybe the baby in bed for a bit. What the hell have you got to do all day? And where the fuck have you put my clean shirts?'

That was the night when Eliza discovered there was not a clean or even a dry nappy in the place. Every single one of the two dozen were in the disagreeable-looking and worse-smelling pails in the bathroom.

That was the night when she told him to piss off when he tried to make her smile, told her it didn't matter and they could rip up a towel and use that for a nappy; that was the night when he said he didn't mind any of it, except her being so bloody miserable; that was the night when she told him if he didn't give her a break and look after Emmie one night a week, she couldn't answer for the consequences; that was the night when he told her to pull herself together and that he was going back to the office.

That was the night when she rang her mother and her mother told her to go out and buy some bottles and some Cow & Gate milk powder first thing in the morning.

The next night was the one when Emmie slept as she was supposed to do, from six to ten o'clock and then from eleven to almost five.

Gradually things improved; Matt was cross about the bottles, but grudgingly admitted that Emmie did seem happier. Eliza knocked her life into some semblance of routine, managed to get a meal on the table although not usually before nine or ten, and discovered that great saviour of new mothers, the nappy service, whereby a cheerful man arrived on the doorstep every morning with a neatly folded pile of clean nappies and bore off the heap of dirty ones in a plastic bag. It seemed a much better use for her godmother's money than the cleaner.

They were not of course short of money; Matt was making a lot now and was the opposite of mean with it, but Eliza had had to hit the hard and unforgiving buffers of not having her own supply. She had saved up a bit, but her natural extravagance combined with the beguiling nursery department of Peter Jones had soaked up most of it.

She would not have believed how diminishing and dispiriting it was to have to rely on money she had not earned herself. She had not given it much thought, indeed, until a few weeks before Emmie was born, when she had announced to Matt that she was thinking of changing her car, 'it's only got two doors, difficult for putting the carrycot in,' and he had said, yes, fine, he'd had the same thought, and what about a Ford Capri?

'Matt, I am not driving our child around, or myself come to that, in a Ford Capri, horrible vulgar cars. I thought a Hillman Imp might be nice, or there's a Fiat 124, that's very pretty.'

Whereupon Matt had given her one of his old-fashioned looks and said the Capri might be vulgar but it was very economical and he thought she might like to remember that.

She had been about to say she didn't care how economical it was when the full meaning of what he was saying struck her rather hard somewhere in the centre of herself; such decisions were no longer hers to make. Leaving her job, which she had with an aching heart only a week before Emmie was born, didn't simply mean giving up status, interest, and the utilisation of her talents; it meant that she was about to be answerable to Matt for everything she wished to buy. Money, she saw in that moment of ferocious clarity, wasn't just the means whereby you acquired what you wanted or even needed; money was power, and lack of your own supply, even under the most benign and domestic of circumstances, was a genuine and rather ugly impotence.

Christmas that year was spent at Summercourt with her parents; her mother had written and begged her to come. 'You must try to forgive us for our attitude to Matt, we can see now we were very wrong, and he is so fond of you and clearly a most devoted father and this could be Daddy's last Christmas, certainly I fear his last one at home, and it would mean so much to him, even more than to me, to have you with us.'

To her surprise Matt had said yes, all right, her dad was a good bloke even if her mother did have a poker up her backside, and he could see Adrian hadn't got a lot of time left, 'but just for the two days mind, I'll be climbing those elegant walls by then.'

Charles and Juliet had also said they would like to come for Christmas Day, but would have to leave early on Boxing Day morning as it was Juliet's father's birthday; Sarah was so happy at the turn of events that she went round the house singing for at least two days before working herself into a fever of anxiety about the coldness of the house and the bathrooms in particular and in relation to Emmie, but Eliza said she could bath Emmie in the big sink in the kitchen and she could sleep in their room and they could bring a couple of their own fan heaters to warm it up.

'I'm sure we'll all have a lovely time,' she said, 'don't worry. Matt is looking forward to it, truly. And he's so obsessed with Emmie, he's just happy to be with her.'

'It's odd, isn't it?' said Sarah. 'One wouldn't have expected it,' and then added hastily that she simply meant that men weren't normally obsessed with their babies, 'I'm not saying anything specially about Matt.'

'Yes, well, I sometimes wish he wasn't,' said Eliza gloomily, 'and he'd just leave me alone to get on with looking after her.'

'And – how are you finding it, darling, being at home? With Emmie? Enjoying it I expect, not missing your job too much.'

'Oh – yes, it's – it's lovely,' said Eliza carefully. There was no way she could even begin to explain to her mother how she felt.

Lost. Disenfranchised. Lonely. And confused.

Now that she was feeling better, now that Emmie slept a bit, now that the days had more shape to them, she wanted to be happy, to enjoy it so much; but she missed work horribly. Missed the daily pressure, the tensions, the dramas; missed the joy of having ideas, clever ideas, and then seeing them through, however difficult it might be. Missed the company, the association with people who talked her language, cared what she cared about, understood her ambitions. And – yes, Matt had been right, and she was ashamed of it, but she did miss the praise, the admiration, the acknowledgement of her success, the glossy rewards of her job. She just couldn't help it.

On the other hand, now she had Emmie, it was quite difficult to imagine leaving her. She loved her more than she would have believed she could love anything. She would look at her as she slept, making her funny little twitchy movements, and her odd little snuffly sounds, and marvel at how passionately she felt about her. The day Emmie first smiled at her, she never forgot. She had just fed her and burped her and was sitting looking at her, holding her on her lap, and Emmie's brilliant blue eyes fixed very firmly on hers. She seemed to be concentrating very hard, almost anxiously, on what she was doing, which was looking back at her mother. And then, slowly, her rosebud of a mouth moved into a rather lopsided, but distinctly joyful, smile. All her tiny world, every bit of her effort was in it; it was a great, joyous, evolutionary leap. And Eliza touched beyond anything by it, found tears in her eyes and a great aching rush of love and something close to awe.

She had experienced that feeling once before: the first time she had felt Emmie move. Like a small dusting of sensation, deep in her stomach, that came and went and then, as she wondered what it could be and then dismissed it, it came again; and she thought, with complete wonder, that she wasn't just pregnant, she was a mother, or soon to be one, that there was actually a person growing inside her, not just a cluster of cells or a bobbing embryo, but a small human being, a new member of the human race that she and Matt had created, and she walked round the flat for half an hour, looking down at herself in wonder, willing it to happen again.

She had tried to explain her feelings to Matt, half-expecting him to pooh-pooh it, to tease her; but he looked at her very seriously and then kissed her.

'God, I love you,' he said.

It was at such times that she knew she had done the right thing.

Christmas worked out very well. Her father was incredibly frail and was beginning to find making himself understood difficult; but he was so patently happy to have them there that it was impossible not to feel pleased in return. Pete Shaw had, as promised, been down to Summercourt to install some ramps for his wheelchair, both in the house and the garden, which was a great help to Sarah, and had taken to coming down every other Saturday to take Adrian to the pub.

'Well,' he said to Sandra, 'what a life, stuck in that freezing pile of a place, no one to talk to except Mrs C. and she may be perfectly nice, but she's not exactly a barrel of laughs. He likes a good joke, and we can talk about the war a bit, he was in the army, the gunners, did some pretty brave things, and then I tell him about being at sea, and it's closing time before you know it.'

He had also, he said, nipped up to the top of the house to look at the rooms: 'sodden they are, it's bloody terrifying, thinking what might happen, but doing nothing's really daft, they seem to think it'll all go away if they ignore it. I'm going to tell Matt to have a look, see what he thinks, if anything can be done that won't break the bank. Funny, isn't it, you'd think they was rolling, but Matt says the only money they've got is tied up in the house.'

'They should sell it,' said Sandra, 'buy a little cottage somewhere. Then they'd be in clover. What d'you reckon it's worth?'

'Oh – I dunno. Hundred grand at least.'

'A hundred thousand pounds. Crikey, Pete. What couldn't we do with that?'

'Your dad's so good to mine,' said Eliza on Christmas Eve, as she began the momentous task of unpacking Emmie's things for the two days' stay. 'I'm so grateful to him. Funny, isn't it, they're really quite good friends now.'

Matt said he couldn't see why it was funny, and what the hell was this contraption; Eliza said it was a sterilising unit for the bottles.

'I thought boiling did the job. That looks a lot more expensive. OK, don't give me that constipated look, I'm only kidding. Now look what I got Emmie for her first Christmas. Can't you just see that on her little wrist?'

It was a gold bangle, hung with two discs, one engraved with Emmie's name and one 'Christmas 1965'.

'D'you think she'll like it?'

'Oh yes,' said Eliza, laughing, 'she'll absolutely love it and she'll say thank you so much Daddy, it's beautiful, please will you help me put it on.'

He looked hurt; he couldn't stand being teased about his devotion to his daughter. Sometimes Eliza wondered just how far below Emmie she came in the family pecking order. A long, long way . . .

They put Emmie in the carrycot on wheels and took her for a walk while they waited for Charles and Juliet. Eliza was looking forward to seeing Charles. He seemed to be avoiding her and had become a commuter, leaving London on the six o'clock train to Guildford and their new house, and apparently completely unable to delay for even an hour for a drink. But he was quiet and subdued she discovered, miles away from the charming, funny brother of their childhood and youth; and Juliet had developed an attitude towards him that Eliza really didn't like. She had always been bossy, but now she was quite overbearing, and seemed to have him constantly running round after her, fetching her cups of tea and 'another cardigan, darling, it's so cold here', refusing to go for a walk on Christmas morning, which would have been fine, except that she wouldn't let Charles go either – 'I really don't want to stay here all alone, on Christmas Day.'

Eliza marvelled at Charles's patience, worried about his state of mind and resolved to insist on meeting him when they were all back in London. She was, after all, free every lunchtime.

On the other hand, she had to admit Juliet was very sweet to both Sarah and Adrian, kissing Adrian and making a great fuss of him, telling him she was looking forward to sharing the Mateus rosé she'd brought him that was his favourite wine, and chatting quite animatedly to Sarah, about her job and a new dress and jacket she'd bought to wear on Christmas Day. Sarah was fond of Juliet; they would chat about house décor and clothes for hours on end.

They all went to midnight mass in the village church, apart from Matt who agreed to babysit both Adrian and Emmie; 'How marvellous of you,' said Sarah, looking at him quite fondly. Eliza pointed out briskly that this was the first time ever Matt had looked after Emmie, and Juliet said she thought that was quite right, babysitting was not a man's job. It began to look like a long Christmas to Eliza.

Christmas lunch – 'this is one of your best, Mummy,' said Eliza, smiling at her – was followed by a walk – Juliet agreed to this one, as it was necessarily short – and then presents, followed by tea which nobody wanted and some carol singing by Eliza and Juliet, while Sarah played the piano. Everyone was putting up a very good pretence of being happy, Eliza thought; and who was to say it was only pretence? She had enjoyed her day, Matt had behaved very well, and he and Charles had spent a fair bit of time reminiscing about the army, and he had presented her with an extremely pretty gold bracelet watch, 'in case you got jealous of Emmie's. I've put the date on yours as well.'

'Now,' said Matt, as Eliza stood up and said she was going to bath Emmie, 'I'd like you to come upstairs with me, Eliza. Got something to show you.'

'Goodness,' said Juliet, looking arch.

He led her up to the top of the house, into the leaking rooms.

'My dad told me to take a look at these,' he said, 'shocking sight, isn't it? Tragic really. Why they don't move, your parents, I'll never know. Still, I got an idea. Wanted to see what you thought.'

✿   ✿   ✿

'Mummy! Daddy! Matt wants to talk to you. It's so exciting . . .'

'What is?' said Sarah, her eyes meeting Eliza's. Heavens, Eliza thought, she thinks I'm having another one already.

'Well, thing is, I got quite a big team now, working on my various sites.'

'Ye-es?'

'Yeah. Couple of very good roofers. And I thought, I could send them down here. It's quiet just now, and we're waiting on planning permission on a new development, costs me money for them to be hanging about. So they could come down here, do some work on your roof.'

'Oh, my goodness!' Sarah went bright pink. 'Well, that is so very kind of you, Matt, but we don't have any – enough money for that. I have no idea what it would cost and – I'm afraid we would just have to say no, wouldn't we, Adrian?'

'No, well, I could help there as well,' said Matt. 'First off, it won't be nearly as much money as you might think, we can do everything at cost, and then I could arrange you a loan. Not me personally, my company. We've got a couple of very good bank managers who value my custom, if you know what I mean; it'd be company rates. And if it was too much, I could absorb it, and you could pay me off as you could afford it. What d'you say?'

'I – I just don't know what to say,' said Sarah, 'it is so terribly kind, but we couldn't possibly accept, I'd feel so embarrassed and why should you—'

'Well, I'm married to your daughter,' said Matt, smiling at her suddenly, 'I don't like to see the family house going to rack and ruin.'

'Oh, dear,' said Sarah, and there were tears in her eyes, 'oh, dear, it's so – so good of you. I just don't know what to say . . .'

'You're such a fraud,' said Eliza, as they got ready for bed, 'pretending you're so hard and tough. It's so wonderful, Matt, so generous, I can't believe it.'

'It's you I'm doing it for really,' he said. 'Because it worries you. Because I love you.'

'Oh Matt – I love you too.'

'And if it's not too cold, leave that nightdress off, would you. I want to celebrate Christmas properly with you.'

'Now how can I refuse, after what you've done for us all?' said Eliza, grimacing at the cold as she pulled her nightdress off again.

She woke Emmie; yelling as she came. She simply couldn't help it. Matt grabbed a pillow and put it over her face, but it was still quite noisy. And good. So, so good.

They had only just started having sex again; it was different. She'd dreaded it, had lain there almost shaking when the statutory six weeks were up, and she'd been told at the post-natal that she could 'go back to being intimate'.

But Matt had been very patient, very careful; even so, it took her a while to start responding, wary of pain, of tenderness, of damage even, but when she did, when the half-forgotten sensations began, when she felt the stirring, the wanting of him, when she started moving under him, it became a roller coaster, a wonderful wild rediscovered delight, gathering pace, sweeping her along, carrying her up and up and into pleasure.

'Goodness,' she said, lying back when it was over, wiping the tears that always came on the back of her hand, 'goodness, Matt, I never thought that would happen again.'

'Nor did I,' he said with a grin.

She turned to him now, moved beyond anything at his generosity, filled with love and a certain pride in him, kissing him, pulling him against her, wrapping her long legs round him.

'More than more than?' he said.

That was their private joke; he had once asked her if she wanted sex 'more than anything' and she'd said no, she wanted it more than more than anything.

And – how did you describe that feeling? It was exactly that. You could want lots of things more than anything; but wanting sex, wanting the sweet, shooting, aching, painful pleasure of it, the absolute laughing, crying joy of it, the huge, wild relief and release of it, that really was more than more than anything. Nothing could be better than that. Really and truly, nothing at all.

Emmie woke again; started snuffling and moaning, then whimpering.

'Now look what you've done,' she hissed at Matt.

'I didn't make all that noise. Your fault, your fault entirely.'

'So that means I have to go downstairs and heat up the bottle and sit and feed her in that freezing kitchen? While you sleep?'

'Got it in one,' he said. 'Anyway, you can sit by the Aga.'

She picked up the baby, went down into the kitchen. She waited until she was inside, with the door closed, before turning on the light; and then jumped.

Her mother was sitting at the table, a bottle of whisky in front of her. She was clearly a little drunk. She was also crying.

'Mummy,' said Eliza in alarm, going over to her, putting her spare arm round her shoulders. 'Whatever is the matter?'

'I just feel so – so ashamed,' said Sarah, 'so very ashamed. Of how we – I – have behaved.'

'In what way? Here, take Emmie, I have to put her bottle to warm . . .'

'Of the way we treated you and Matt. When he is clearly so kind and loves you so much. What he's doing for us, with the house – well, it makes everything so much better. I don't know how to make it up to him, I really don't.'

'Oh, Mummy,' said Eliza. 'That's easy. Just tell him what it means to you. He'll understand the rest. He's not nearly as – as difficult as he seems. I'm just glad he could do it for you. Now, I wouldn't mind a drop of that whisky myself.'

She looked round at the scene, five minutes later, as Emmie sucked peacefully on her bottle and she and her mother downed rather large glasses of Adrian's best single malt, and giggled.

'If a health visitor came round now,' she said, 'Emmie would be taken into care. Alcoholic mother and grandmother.'

Chapter 29

She had been afraid that someone might beat her to it, have discovered it for themselves and set up some alternative deal. Or – of course – that it was not quite as she had thought, less perfect, less tailor-made for her purpose.

She need not have worried.

'Miss Scarlett,' said Demetrios, beaming at her as she walked into the foyer, the still blessedly small foyer, a wonderful sweet, cool contrast to the pelting heat outside. 'How very, very nice to see you once more.'

'It's lovely to see you too, Demetrios. Are you both well, you and Larissa?'

'Very, very well. Larissa is having a baby—'

'A baby! How lovely.'

Would she ever be able to contemplate babies again without a catch at her heart?

'Yes. Very soon, in three, four weeks.'

'That's wonderful. So – is she resting?'

'Resting? No, Miss Scarlett, she is busy, busy in the kitchen, busy in the garden, I don't know where she is not busy.'

'Well, I'll catch up with her later. You know why I've come?'

'I do. And we think it is very, very good plan. We would like to join your club after all. If we may.'

They had been wary at first; afraid of losing their uniqueness, their personal running of the place.

'Excellent. We can talk tonight.'

Over dinner in the vine-roofed veranda, watching the sunset, she chatted to them both, agreed terms, told them it would be for the following year.

'I know most bookings are in January, February time, so there's no

299

point doing anything before then. You can go in my next little brochure, and – well, I'm sure you'll get lots of people.'

'Lots of nice people?'

'I can't guarantee it,' said Scarlett, laughing, 'but just let me know about any who aren't and I'll tell them they're out of my club. Oh—' she added, as a tall shadow fell across her view, briefly blotting out the sunset. 'Oh, hello.'

The owner of the shadow looked at her blankly, and attempted a rather anxious smile.

'I don't think—'

'Mr Frost. Good evening. Can we get you a drink? You remember Miss Scarlett, she was here last year at the same time as you. Excuse me. Larissa, can you get some vine leaves, perhaps, and some olives . . .'

'I – well, of course, I—' He looked increasingly bewildered.

Scarlett took pity on him, stood up, held out her hand.

'Why should you remember? I was staying here, on my own, and so were you, but we overlapped by only one night. Scarlett Shaw.'

'Ah. Well – yes, of course. How rude of me.' He took her hand. 'Mark Frost. How do you do, Miss Shaw?'

'Please join me. I'm just chatting to Demetrios and Larissa.'

'Oh – no, I couldn't – that is, no I'm just passing – I—'

Since there was nowhere to pass from or to at the taverna, this was clearly a feeble attempt to escape; Scarlett felt quite sorry for him. He was so clearly excruciatingly shy, it would have been cruel to pursue the encounter. She would make her excuses and disappear to her room; but Demetrios had returned with a bottle of ouzo and four glasses.

'There. We all drink together. Larissa will be back very soon. Mr Frost is building a house here, Miss Scarlett.'

'Oh, so you are building it?' said Scarlett, passing him the glass of ouzo, hoping it would help him feel better. She actually hated the stuff, sipping at it cautiously now so as not to offend Demetrios.

'Yes,' he said, clearly slightly baffled by her question, 'yes, I am.'

'I heard you were looking for somewhere to build,' she said, 'Demetrios told me, after you'd left last year.'

'Yes. Yes, that's correct.'

'And – is it going well?'

'Yes. Very well.'

'How near completion is it?'

'Not very near. They are only just starting work now. So—'

'Perhaps tomorrow, Mr Frost, you could show the house to Miss Scarlett.'

'Oh – I don't think—' He looked as if Demetrios had suggested Scarlett did a striptease.

'No, no, Demetrios,' she said quickly, 'you know I'm leaving first thing. But are you staying here while your house is being built, Mr Frost?'

'Yes. Yes, I am. Not all the time, of course. Just – just when I can get away.'

'Of course.'

She smiled at him; he smiled back, very briefly, his whole persona transformed. He was, she realised, quite exceptionally good-looking in a kind of chiselled way; she had not properly absorbed that fact before, the height, the slenderness, and the floppy dark hair. What she had remembered were the unusually dark grey eyes looking warily out from the wire-framed spectacles. He was wearing a blue denim shirt with frayed jeans and washed-out-looking espadrilles; he was very tanned and when he did smile, his teeth were American-perfect. He could have been a film star.

'So – where's home?'

'England,' he said. Not a very detailed piece of information.

'And you work in England?'

'Yes. Most of the time.'

'But – you obviously love Greece?'

'Yes.'

Scarlett gave up. The thing about people as shy – or, to be precise, unforthcoming – as Mark Frost was that you couldn't make any progress without asking endless questions, and that seemed, after a while, intrusive and impertinent.

'Mr Frost found out about us through a friend,' said Demetrios, as if reading her thoughts. 'Is that right, Mr Frost?'

'Yes. That's right.'

'His friend came here three years ago and he very kindly suggested Mr Frost came to see us.'

There was a silence; Larissa came back and started speaking very fast to Demetrios in Greek. After a few minutes, she stood up and beckoned to him to follow.

'Excuse us,' he said.

Left alone with Mark Frost, Scarlett felt quite panicky, then told herself she was being ridiculous and made one more attempt.

'So, what do you do?' she asked. 'What sort of work are you in?' Trainee Trappist monk perhaps?

'Oh – I – I –' there was a pause, then, 'do research,' he said as if suddenly alighting on an explanation.

'Oh, really? Into what?'

'I'm sorry?'

'Well, I mean what sort of thing do you research?'

'Oh. Oh, I see. Yes. Well – geography, I suppose you could call it.'

'So – are you a lecturer?'

'Not exactly.'

He poured himself some more ouzo, offered the bottle to her. She shook her head. 'No thank you.'

Another silence. Then, 'Filthy stuff isn't it?' he said. 'I observed you not drinking it. I don't like it either, only drink it to please Demetrios. Shall we . . . ?' He looked over his shoulder into the house and then, confident of not being observed, tipped most of the bottle into one of the pots of budding geraniums.

'Probably kill the poor things,' he said, 'but better them than us.'

Scarlett looked at him consideringly; he suddenly seemed a different person. 'Indeed,' she said.

'So – you must like it here a lot. To come back.'

'I absolutely love it. I was afraid it wasn't as special as I remembered, but it was.'

'I always fear the same thing,' he said, not sounding in the least surprised, 'but it always is.'

'You must like it very much,' said Scarlett, 'to be building a house here.'

'Indeed,' he said, and lapsed back into total silence. After a minute or two, she decided her book would be more interesting and stood up.

'I think I'll turn in,' she said, 'I'm leaving early.'

'Ah. Getting Ari the Ferry out of his bed early. No mean feat.'

She giggled, surprised again at this flash of humour. 'Is that your name for him?'

'It is. Well, I discovered his name was Aristotle and I couldn't resist it. I'm part Welsh, you see, and in Wales everyone is Dai the Baker or Jones the Fish. It came from that.' He stopped and looked quite anxious, as if aware he had made too big a revelation. He's afraid I'm going to start asking him about Wales, Scarlett thought. 'Goodnight then,' she said and saw the relief almost palpable on his face. He was a nutcase.

'Goodnight,' he said, standing up and shaking her hand formally, 'safe journey.'

Her last thought was that in the right circumstances, Mark Frost could – just possibly – be quite fun.

'I just – don't like it. I'm sorry.'

'But, Matt, why not? What's wrong with it?'

'He's married for a start.'

'Matt! He hasn't seen her in years.'

'And how do you know that's true?'

'Matt! For God's sake. I don't know, not for sure, but I trust him.'

'Well, I don't.'

'Funny thing to say about your business partner.'

'That's not what I meant and you know it.'

'Oh, Matt. Chill out. I've got an appointment, I'll see you later.'

Driving into Chelsea, playing 'I Can't Get No Satisfaction' by the Stones very loudly, Louise smiled to herself. She did enjoy rattling Matt. And he was seriously rattled by the fact that she was having an affair with Barry Floyd. She would have liked to think he was jealous, but it was a less flattering reason: he felt professionally threatened by it. He thought they'd gang up on him. Which was pathetic really. She was too professional in the first place, and it stung that he might even consider it; and in the second, the partnership was much too successful to put at risk. Barkers Park was going up fast, WireHire were perfect tenants, making stage payments on the dot, agreeing to a bonus payment if the offices were finished ahead of time.

There was no way either of them would want to change the basis of any part of their working relationship.

Their personal one, however, had changed rather quickly.

'I mean, I thought he was pretty sexy,' Louise explained to Valerie Hill, who had become her confidante over the whole thing. 'But I knew about Maura, of course—'

'The wife?' Valerie managed to convey a lot in those two words: that wives were asking for trouble and their husbands fair game if they weren't keeping an eye on them, and were too complacent to worry about what they were up to.

'The wife. Yes. But—'

'Don't tell me, in name only.'

'If living with another man means in name only, yes. And don't look at me like that, it's true. They were married when he was eighteen and she was seventeen. She was in the family way, or told him she was, and then surprise, surprise, soon as they were married, she had a miscarriage. He said he walked straight into it. Well, you would at eighteen, wouldn't you?'

'I wouldn't,' said Valerie. 'So then what happened?'

'Well then, she did have three babies, over the next five years or so, but then when Barry came to London, she stayed behind and then started playing around, got very friendly with this farmer—'

'Louise,' said Valerie, 'are you sure it wasn't him playing around? He doesn't seem too much of an innocent to me.'

'Oh, no doubt he did too,' said Louise. 'I'm not that stupid. But now she's living with the farmer over there, and . . .'

'Don't tell me they're going to get a divorce.'

'No, of course not. It's not an option in Catholic Ireland. And even an annulment is virtually impossible unless you're best friends with the pope. But a lot of people just do what Barry and Maura are doing and get on with their lives. He sends her money, of course, a lot, and besides, the farmer is not exactly poor as far as I can make out.'

'And are you sure this is all on the level?'

'As sure as I could be without going over there and checking it out for myself.'

The fact was that, in spite of her tough talking, Louise wasn't entirely happy about getting involved with a married man. In the first place, she knew that, given the divorce laws in Ireland, it could never lead to anything permanent; and in the second, and more importantly, it was against her rather complex moral code. She really didn't like girls who broke up marriages; in fact she disapproved of them quite strongly. She had grown up in a very moral culture that respected marriage and the family above all things; and she had struggled with herself considerably over taking the affair with Barry any further than their ongoing and very light-hearted flirtation.

But, she was beginning to find her single lifestyle unsatisfactory; she didn't dream of a home and babies, but she was beginning to think she would like to have someone to share things with, not just her leisure time and her bed, but the contents of her head, her thoughts, her plans, her ambitions for herself, someone who understood her and what she was about. The only man who had ever fitted that brief was Matt Shaw; and he was clearly hopelessly in love with someone else – someone who just happened to be his wife and the mother of his adored child.

But she discovered on their very first date that Barry Floyd did fill the brief extraordinarily well.

He'd asked her out to dinner one evening, after they had been to a meeting at Barkers Park, and then made an unapologetic pass at her afterwards ('You know, I fancy you absolutely, Louise, and I just get the feeling you might return the favour, and if you do, well, I wonder if you'd like to take it a little further').

Not wishing to be a pushover, Louise had said that dinner was all well and good, and that yes, she didn't find him completely unattractive, but she wasn't sure how much, or indeed if at all, she wanted to take it even a little further, and that she didn't approve of women who slept with married men; Barry said, his blue eyes dancing, that he couldn't recall having mentioned anything about sleeping, all he'd had in mind was a second date.

'You're a liar, Barry Floyd,' Louise said, pushing his hand from where it was resting on her knee, and struggling to ignore the effect it was having on the area just above it, 'and you are married and don't give me any of that rubbish about how it's in name only, because I won't believe you.'

'So you're just an old-fashioned girl at heart, are you?' he said, and she said if not wanting to put a marriage at risk made her old-fashioned, yes she was.

They had a second dinner. It was even better than the first: just as much fun, but they talked more, about more serious things, the business, the future and, as the wine went down, their own hopes and fears. And he told her about Maura and the state of his marriage.

'I make no apologies for how it sounds,' he said, his blue eyes fixed very seriously on hers, 'which is terribly corny and extremely un- likely to a hugely intelligent girl like yourself. But it's true. I don't know how to make you believe me, Louise, but I would give a great deal if I could.'

'How great a deal?' she said. 'Your stake in Barkers Park?'

'Oh, now, let's keep things in proportion, for the love of God,' he said, laughing, and she laughed too; but afterwards, as she told Valerie, it was when she began to believe him.

'If he'd said yes, I'd have known it couldn't be true.'

She was not, however, prepared to make things easy for him.

'So can we have a third date?'

'I think I could agree to that, yes.'

'And where would you like to go? Your choice.'

'OK,' she said, 'let me see. Um – how about the Ritz?'

'Well, that's easy. I can certainly arrange that. Tomorrow night?'

'Oh, you couldn't arrange it by tomorrow, surely,' she said, 'there'd be the flight and all that sort of thing.'

'The flight?'

'Didn't you realise, sorry, I meant the Ritz in Paris.'

He didn't flinch. 'Well now, maybe we should make it Friday instead,' he said. 'Because we probably wouldn't get the last train home.'

He called her in the morning with a flight booked 'and somewhere to stay, not the Ritz, I can't afford that, not this year, next maybe, but a very nice little hotel on the South Bank. Two rooms if you like.'

'Two rooms of course. This is only our third date. What sort of girl do you think I am?'

'A very sexy one,' he said.

Dinner at the Ritz was spectacular; back in the small hotel, Louise kissed him goodnight at the door of her room, and waved him off down the corridor. After ten minutes, she knocked at his door.

'I don't seem to be able to sleep,' she said, 'I wondered if we could have a bit more of a chat about Barkers Park.'

She arrived back in London dizzy with weariness, and extremely happy; and reflecting on the great foolishness of Maura Floyd. For the time being, she thought, she had found exactly what she had been looking for. And the time being was long enough for now.

She had been speaking the truth when she said she wasn't looking for marriage; as far as she could see, it was a straight and fast road downhill to a place where even if you continued with your career, and earned as much or even more than your husband, he still remained in some mystical way the head of the household, and had to be waited on, fussed over and asked permission if you wanted to be away or even work late.

She had been shocked by Eliza's giving up work; she and Eliza were not close friends, but she liked and admired her, and she was fairly sure it had been at Matt's insistence, and an extremely foolish move. Eliza had changed from dazzling, successful girl to anonymous mother; where, Louise wondered, was the wisdom in that? She wasn't sure which was her strongest emotion, distaste at Matt's behaviour or disappointment in Eliza's; either way, that assuredly wasn't what she wanted.

That was the spring that *Time* Magazine bestowed upon London the ultimate accolade of the title 'The Swinging City', when it became the most desirable place on earth, a modern day Camelot, home of every kind of pleasure. That was the year that photographs of London – often also featuring the new model sensation Twiggy, with her childlike face, her boyish haircut, her spindly body – appeared in every newspaper in the world. That was when everyone fought to get in on the act, when the Prime Minister Harold Wilson was photographed with the Beatles, and the Queen's sister (who had after all married into the Camelot fantasy herself) rocked to the Rolling Stones; when Michelangelo Antonioni chose London as the location for *Blow Up*, his iconic tale of fashionable and degenerate society; when even Paris fashion turned tricksy and trendy, when Courrèges showed girlish rather than womanly models in short white boots and plastic dresses, and Paco Rabanne draped models' forms with dizzily wonderful plastic mirrored jewellery; and that was the time when Eliza thought she was going mad, watching from her self-imposed exile, as every fashion editor in the world battled to find new designers, models and photographers and to give them the freehold of their pages in ever wilder and more imaginative ways.

She would sit in the flat or in the park, Emmie in her pram, leafing through magazines, in an agony of impotence: thinking how differently, how much more creatively, how much better for Christ's sake, she would have shown this dress, those colours, that designer. Occasionally she would go and meet Annunciata or Maddy or one of the other fashion editors for lunch, and come back feeling depressed, disenfranchised, cheated of her rightful place in this dazzling over-the-rainbow world. She told herself it was pathetic, struggled to rise above it, to see it all as so much nonsense set against her new, more worthy role in life, struggled also to see Emmie's achievements – sitting, crawling, smiling toothily – as truly important, so much more so than a few double-page spreads in a magazine, or being crowned fashion editor of the year at some award ceremony. And she knew they were, of course she did; but her pleasure and pride in them were hard won.

'And I'm lonely,' she wailed to Maddy, one of the very few people to whom she would admit any flaw in her new life. 'Matt's never home before nine, and then he's too tired to talk and more importantly listen.'

'Don't you have friends with babies?' asked Maddy.

'Well, yes and no. Lots of acquaintances, girls I used to know of course and they ask me to tea and to meet them in the park, although lots of them have got nannies, it drives me crazy, Maddy, there they are, allowed nannies by their husbands, so they can leave their babies and go shopping and do dinner parties, and I'm not allowed one by mine to do something really important. God, it's so unfair.'

'Have you told him you feel like this?'

'What would be the point? It would be like – like trying to explain to a fly there was glass in the window. And they're so bloody boring, always going on about their dinner parties and which schools the little boys are being put down for. So actually, yes, I prefer to spend my time alone with Emmie. Although I have got one friend,' she added, 'much more interesting. I met her at the clinic.'

'The clinic?'

'Yes. I go there to have Emmie weighed and have her vaccinations and so on. It's the highlight of my week, I tell you.'

'Oh, Eliza—'

'No, I'm serious. Anyway this girl is called Heather and . . .'

'Heather! That's a pretty name.'

'Do you think so? Thanks.'

'Yes. And little Coral, how is she getting on?'

Coral was exactly the same age as Emmie; Eliza and Heather had eyed one another up for several afternoons at the clinic, and with the small class-crossing miracle that only babies can wreak had each recognised something in the other they liked and had smiled at each other and said hello occasionally, but this was the first time they had exchanged more than a few words.

'Oh – bit slow. She hasn't gained much this week. She's been poorly, had a bad cold, and they can't eat, can they, when they're all bunged up.'

'No. Emmie had a cold last month, that spell when it was really windy, you know, and I was so fed up with being indoors, I took her out anyway, and she got worse, in fact she had a temperature, I felt so guilty—'

'Oh, I know, the guilt's awful, isn't it? I put Coral in the bath without testing it properly and it was—'

'Not scalding?' said Eliza in horror.

'No, no, almost cold. Poor little thing, I felt so ashamed but I'd boiled it in the kettle because we've got no hot water, you see, and it wasn't enough.'

'You've got no hot water?'

This was so unimaginable to Eliza she forgot to be tactful.

'Not running, no.' Heather gave Eliza a slightly cool look. 'None of the flats in our house have. We've got the toilet on our floor though, so we're lucky. Girl in the basement, she has to come up three flights every night, she's pregnant, how she'll manage when she's got the baby, I don't know.'

'Poor girl.' Eliza struggled to sound concerned rather than horrified; but horrified was how she felt half the time talking to Heather, who lived in two rooms and a kitchenette and a shared bathroom in one of a row of old houses just off Clapham Common. Heather, whose husband Alan worked in an engineering factory, who had lost two babies before she had Coral and considered herself most wonderfully fortunate; Heather, who had less money for everything, food, rent, and the electric and gas meters each week than Eliza spent on food and petrol for her car; Heather, who was so terrified of Coral crying and the other tenants complaining (Coral was a colicky baby) that she spent half her days pushing her round the streets and some of her nights or certainly her dawns as well. 'Also, Alan works nights quite a lot, and he can't cope with the crying either, he has to get some sleep. It's not so bad now the weather's warming up, but it was awful in the winter and especially when she was really tiny.'

Heather wasn't seeing much of Swinging London, that was for sure.

She was small and pale, with long straight light brown hair and enormous grey eyes, and Eliza found her much better company than her old friends; they chatted a couple of times over a cup of tea served from the antique urn in the clinic, and then one day had walked up the road together towards where Eliza had parked her car and Heather caught her bus.

'Blimey,' Heather had said, eyeing the white Ford Cortina that Eliza loathed and that Matt had insisted on, 'that yours?'

'Um – yes. Yes, it is. Now, why don't I give you a lift, then you won't have to wait for the bus. We can put both the carrycots on the back seat, look, side by side, it's fine, and both sets of wheels in the boot. Come on, hop in.'

She always took Emmie to the clinic in a carrycot because it could be lifted from its wheels and put in the car; the large Silver Cross pram that her mother had bought her didn't actually get many outings. She felt pretty sure that Heather's shabby pale blue carrycot was probably all she had to cart Coral about in. And lifting it off the wheels to get it onto the bus – well, it was hard to imagine how she managed. It was hard to imagine how she managed at all.

Heather never complained, she was quite funny about it all. 'Last night Alan and I went to bed at seven, the meter ran out of electricity and we didn't have any more money, and it's quite cold so it seemed the best thing to do, Coral was quiet, and it was all right till it got dark, and we couldn't even read so – well, yeah. We quite often do that; I expect people think we're having a high old time, but nothing of the sort, haven't got the energy.' She grinned at Eliza. 'Just as well, probably, we couldn't afford another one, Alan's scared to look at me half the time.'

'Aren't you – I mean, couldn't you – well, you know, take the pill?'

'No, I get these headaches and they suggested one of those coil things at the family planning clinic, but it hurt so much when they tried to put it in, I couldn't stand it, so – well, yeah.' She stopped, looked slightly bashfully at Eliza. 'Sorry, you don't want to hear all that.'

'Yes, I do,' said Eliza.

She was shocked by the house Heather lived in; she helped her up the stairs to the second floor, with the carrycot wheels: the dark, dingy stairs covered with linoleum, the light green paint peeling off the walls and the time-switch light going off repeatedly. It was cold, in spite of the sunshine outside, and the stairs smelt bad, a nasty mixture of cabbage and urine.

When they reached Heather's door she looked at Eliza slightly apologetically and said, 'I can't ask you in, sorry, it's all a bit of a mess.'

'That's fine,' said Eliza, 'I haven't got time anyway. Bye Heather, see you next week.'

As she walked back down the stairs, two teenage boys passed her; one of them was carrying a transistor radio, playing some pop music very loudly. She heard them laughing and shouting something as she shut the front door. If they were allowed to make that sort of noise, how could the neighbours complain about little Coral crying?

'It's exactly that, because she's a baby,' said Matt when she told him about it. 'Lot of these landlords don't allow children, any more than they allowed coloureds, she's lucky to have a place at all. That place we're knocking down in Camden Town, no kids allowed there at all.'

'Lucky! Matt Shaw, how can you possibly think someone living like that, sharing a lavatory, no running hot water, is lucky?'

'Because she is,' he said calmly, 'people like her, they have to take what they can get. At least the toilet's on her floor.'

'Matt Shaw, you are such a foul, bloody hypocrite. Going on and on about your working-class credentials, and you sit there calmly telling me Heather's lucky to have a toilet on her floor. How would you feel if that was us, with Emmie living there?'

'We wouldn't be there for more than five minutes,' said Matt.

'Oh, is that right? And how would we get out of it?'

'Listen, Eliza, when my mum and dad got married they didn't have a toilet at all, not in the house. For years I had my bath down the municipal baths twice a week. I survived, as you know. My dad worked his arse off to get that house sorted.'

'Yeah, yeah, I know, and your mum went cleaning. I don't see how that makes Heather lucky.'

'She's got a roof over her head, that's why. It's a starting point, OK? Mind you, she could lose it any time now. Lot of big terraces in Clapham are being knocked down. Getting the tenants out is a nightmare. I feel for the landlords, I really do. All right, all right, only joking.'

'You are disgusting, you know that? And I just hope for your sake you don't have any of those houses, with signs up saying "No children". God, you're a nasty lot, you developers.'

'And what would you do if I did?'

'I'd leave you,' said Eliza.

Chapter 30

It was of course completely ridiculous: to be so completely – well, nearly – defeated by someone else. To be forced to do what that someone else wanted, often in the full knowledge that it was wrong: to hear herself giving in to entirely unreasonable demands: to find herself lacking in all the qualities – like common sense, willpower and even humour – that she had thought she possessed in abundance: to become, quite simply, the sort of person she disapproved of and even despised. But, confronted by this tyrant, this self-opinionated, hyper-confident creature whose wishes were forced upon her by a confusing mixture of icy determination and noisy aggression, she was lost. Defeated. She had no idea what to do.

And every day, it got worse: and Emmie was not quite two.

'No no no no no,' the familiar, almost daily tantrum would begin.

'I'm sorry, but yes yes yes yes yes. Now, do what I say.'

'No!' The blue eyes blazed; a small foot stamped, hard, on the ground.

'Emmie, stop it. At once. If you won't wear your coat, you're not going.'

'I don't want to go.'

'I don't care. You're going.'

'I'm not.' And she drew in her breath and held it, her eyes fixed on her mother in defiance, her face slowly turning bright red.

It was the stuff of nightmares.

Heather's little girl, Coral, was naughty, had the odd tantrum, but Heather could control her quite easily with a mixture of coaxing and threats; she never slapped her.

Emmie could be neither coaxed nor threatened; she did what she wanted, and if anyone tried to stop her, she seemed prepared to die in the attempt. She had twice made herself lose consciousness by holding her breath; she was equally capable of going on hunger strike and not eating for as long as it took. The longest she had managed was two and a half days, after which, of course, it had been Eliza who had cracked, afraid Emmie would become ill from lack of nourishment. Matt, who found the whole thing rather annoyingly amusing, said there was no danger of that, and that Emmie was far too greedy to go seriously hungry; but then he didn't have to see her growing if not faint, certainly a bit listless.

On the other hand, she was an enchanting child when things were to her liking: she was affectionate, interesting, and lively, her speech advanced and her manners charming – all the other mothers remarked on how nicely she said 'thank you' long before her peers did – and she shared her toys with a generous maturity that surprised Eliza, given that she was an only child. She just liked to do things her way.

The doctor at the clinic, where she still went regularly, mostly because they had a mother and baby group once a week, and she met Heather there, talked like the baby books, urging cooperation and reasoning. Sandra advised depriving her of things she did want to do.

'Sandra,' said Eliza, 'she doesn't want to do anything as much as getting her own way.'

She wondered if having another baby would help. She had decided she would like one as soon as possible, she was at home anyway, and it made every sort of sense and Matt was very keen, but she wasn't sure if she would be able to cope.

'Supposing she took against the baby, then what would I do? Nightmare.'

'She won't,' said Matt cheerfully, 'she's not like that. I think we should go for it, Eliza, she'll be at least three at this rate, and that's a big gap.'

Eliza stopped taking the pill for a couple of months, then panicked, as Emmie's behaviour worsened, and went back on it.

'I don't care how big the gap is, Matt, I'll be in a loony bin at this rate by the time I have the baby, and then what will you do?'

'Bring them in to join you,' said Matt.

She missed Charles dreadfully; it was as if he had left her to live in another country. She had seen him only a handful of times over the previous year and a half, at family gatherings, her father's birthday, Emmie's christening, and he had seemed fairly cheerful, slightly sub-dued perhaps, but distant, reluctant to be alone with her, and resisted all her attempts to see him on their own. They had had lunch once at her insistence, but he had been wary of any attempt to get him to open up to her.

'I just don't know what to do about it,' said Eliza to Maddy, 'I know there's something wrong, but he won't talk to me. They've sort of shut themselves off down there, we've only been to the new house once, and then there's another thing, I'd have thought they'd have had a baby by now, Juliet was so keen, and Charles is besotted by Emmie, said he couldn't wait to have one of his own.'

'Well, maybe that's it,' said Maddy, 'maybe she's just not getting pregnant, and they're depressed about it, and don't want everyone asking them all the time.'

'Maybe. I don't know, Maddy, my whole life is filled with things I can't sort out. Charles, my parents, that little fiend I've given birth to. God, when I think how a couple of empty pages seemed like a problem – I didn't know I was born.'

Going to visit her parents, which she did at least once a week, was dreadfully dispiriting.

She was shocked by the constant and ever more swift deterioration in her father; he was losing weight fast and his features were frozen into total immobility. He spent a lot of time sitting in the kitchen doorway, staring out at the garden, seemingly lost to reality; but whenever she arrived, he managed a grotesque echo of a smile and then as she kissed him, would start to cry.

Sarah had to feed him much of the time, draping him in a large napkin, and tenderly wiping his face afterwards; and then she would wheel him off to the lavatory, refusing help.

'He hates it so, feels so humiliated, I promised him I would never let anyone else do it for him and I won't.'

Everyone said he should be in a home, that she really couldn't cope with the sheer physical hard work of lifting and moving him from his wheelchair to his bed and back again, skeletal as his large frame had become, and Anna Marchant – 'darling, we are practically sisters, don't argue' – was paying for a nurse who came in twice a day. It was felt Matt had done enough in fixing the roof for what turned out to be a far higher cost even than he had expected and funding the loan himself – but it was still an extremely difficult situation for her. She was increasingly frail herself and the house was grotesquely unsuitable: but she was not to be moved.

✿ ✿ ✿

Scarlett was at Athens airport with two hours to kill and realised she had nothing to read. The news kiosk yielded (not surprisingly) a lot of Greek books and newspapers, but she did finally manage to find one out-of-date copy of the English news magazine *Time and Tide*. She ordered herself a coffee and sat down in the departure lounge, and was flicking through the magazine when she saw quite a long article on Venice. Venice, which she knew and loved so well . . .

She started to read the piece and found herself instantly and extraordinarily there, and not just in the spectacular set pieces of St Mark's Square and the Grand Canal, but exploring the narrow back streets, wandering from one *bacari* – the small bars that are Venice's speciality – to the next, growing slowly tipsier, discovering the lesser known churches, like the lyrical marble San Giorgio Maggiore best viewed by moonlight, and combing the flea market in the Campo San Maurizio. It was an extraordinary piece of writing.

She looked for the writer's name, thinking she must find more of his – or her – work and saw the article listed at the front of the magazine: by one Mark Frost.

'Oh, my God,' said Scarlett aloud, and she would have dismissed it as an absurd coincidence, but gazing at her intently from the title page, there he was, complete with wire-framed spectacles, floppy dark hair and an extremely solemn expression. 'Mark Frost,' it said, 'one of the finest travel writers around today, and author of *The World's Loveliest Train Rides*, gives his unique and vivid take on one of his favourite cities, Venice.'

Geographical research indeed! Well, she supposed it was in a way.

'Now look, Eliza, and don't start cutting up rough, please, but I'm going to have to cancel our trip.'

'You what! Oh, Matt, no. Please, please no. I've been looking forward to it for so long.'

'I know, I know, and so have I. But we're having trouble with this second development, the one out Swindon way, and I just can't be away at the moment.'

'What about Jimbo?'

'He's up to his eyes in it too.'

'Louise?'

'Eliza, if you think I'd leave this in Louise's hands, you're living in fantasy land.'

'Why?'

'Because she's – she's—'

'A woman?' Eliza's voice dripped venom.

'No. Course not. Look, I've said I'm sorry. I could go mid-November.'

'Oh, that's a really good idea. Be away for Emmie's birthday. Fuck you, Matt Shaw. Just – fuck you.'

She went out of the room slamming the door, her eyes full of tears. Tears of anger and disappointment. She had done so much these two years, tried so hard to be good, and this was his way of thanking her, with this great ton of shit. A fortnight in the sun, he had promised her – well, a week in the sun, in Bermuda straddled by a few days either side in New York; she couldn't remember when she had looked forward to anything so much. Or even looked forward to anything at all.

She went to bed in the spare room that night; when Matt knocked on the door tentatively some time after midnight, saying he was sorry, and he loved her, more than more than, and please to come to bed and let him prove it, she told him to fuck off.

She was still fuming in the morning when Mariella phoned, and so she poured out her story, tearful and angry still. Mariella's reaction was predictable.

'You can come and have a holiday with me, *cara*. I would love it, Giovanni would love it, it is beautiful here in September, and we can do some shopping, I can show you my beloved Milan—'

'Oh, God, Mariella, it sounds wonderful. But I'd have to bring Emmie.' She knew Matt would never agree to leaving her with Sandra for such a reason. Besides, she suddenly didn't want to.

'But of course you must bring her. That would be lovely for me too. There are plenty of people here to help, and we can buy her a new chic wardrobe from Milan.'

'Oh, it sounds so tempting. Are you really really sure?'

'But of course I am sure. Tell me when, and I will be ready for you. And we can teach the bambina to speak Italian. *Ciao, bella*.'

'*Ciao*, Mariella. Love to Giovanni.'

'No,' said Matt when she phoned him, 'no, that is not acceptable.'

'I'm sorry, Matt, but it's acceptable to me and I'm going.'

'I don't want my child left in the care of a lot of wops.'

'What makes you think I'm leaving her in the care of anyone? And don't use that disgusting word.'

'And who is going to look after me while you're away?'

'You can look after your fucking self, Matt. I'm going.'

'My goodness, they were using the most terrible language this morning, Miss Mullan, Mr and Mrs Shaw. She's going away without him and—'

'Good,' said Louise, 'first sign of common sense I've seen from her in ages.'

Eliza had stayed in a great many beautiful houses in her life, and done photographic shoots in many more, but in nothing quite as splendid as the Villa d'Arice. Set in incredible gardens right on the shores of Lake Como, it was actually a small palace, built in 1600, in a style that could only be described as fantasy-classical. As Mariella's (surprisingly modest) Fiat 600 – 'Italian ladies don't drive big smart cars on their own' – drew up in front of it, Eliza let out a yelp of pleasure.

A great white edifice, it was four storeys high, pillared and columned and balconied, with the lake shining before it and the mountains brooding beyond: the sloping lawns leading down to the lake were set with huge trees, only just turning into their autumn colours, and on either side of the house were curving colonnades and wide white terraces.

Mariella had met them at the airport and chattered the entire way to the villa. Giovanni was standing on the steps to greet them, immaculately dressed in slacks and a blazer, his handsome old face smiling. A beige standard poodle sat on either side of him; Mariella's small white poodle Pucci was running to the car. It would have made, Eliza thought, a wonderful fashion shot.

'Eliza, *cara*. Welcome to our home. And this is the *bambina*! Oh, she is so beautiful.' He reached out a thin brown hand to stroke Emmie's cheek, murmuring to her in Italian; Emmie smiled at him, enchanted.

The entrance hall was immense, marbled and chandeliered, with a staircase of great grace and grandeur rising from it; Giovanni led them down an arched corridor, opening on one side onto formal gardens, and into a smaller, but exquisite, *salone*, with a low table set with tea and a display of sandwiches and pastries that would not have disgraced the Ritz. Emmie made for the food, her large blue eyes shining.

317

'Emmie! No,' said Eliza, but a smiling girl in a black dress and white apron moved forward, took Emmie's other hand and led her to a chair where she took her on her knee, swathed her in a large napkin and fed her the cake in bite-size pieces, tenderly wiping her face free of chocolate between each one.

'This is Anna-Maria,' Mariella said, 'she will be helping you with Emmie all the time you are here. She comes with very good – good reviews.'

'References?' said Eliza.

'Yes, perhaps. I hope that will be all right. Of course if you would rather not . . .'

Eliza, feeling she had suddenly come home, said it was very much all right.

Her room was on the first floor, another scene from fantasy land, with silk wallpaper, brocade curtains, a very fine four-poster bed, a gilt and marble desk, a balcony overlooking the lake, and a small room leading from it, furnished with a cot, a highchair, a playpen and a mountain of soft toys. Another door opened to reveal a bathroom with an immense claw-footed bath and enough snowy towels piled up on a low table for a month's stay.

They dined, the three of them, in a room overlooking the lake, dark now, shot with thousands of lights, and the clear sky with millions of stars. Mariella had popped her head into Eliza's room as she was getting ready and told her that although Anna-Maria would sit with Emmie during the evening, if Eliza preferred, she could be with them. Eliza said she would much prefer it if Emmie was not with them and that she was already fast asleep.

'*Bene*. Then we can all have a very lovely dinner. Very, very informal, *cara*, do not dress up.'

Eliza knew what very informal would mean: not black tie. She wore a black silk dress and high-heeled sandals, Mariella was in palazzo pyjamas, Giovanni in an exquisitely cut smoking jacket.

It was an absurdly relaxed evening, given the setting and the constant attendance of staff. They chatted throughout, there were no awkward silences. Giovanni spoke perfect English; Eliza, who spoke no Italian at all, felt embarrassed, and even said so, but he smiled at her and said it was good for both of them to speak English.

Giovanni clearly enjoyed gossip; Mariella chattered away about mutual

318

friends, about clothes and shops, about their summer on their yacht, moored at Portofino.

'Everyone leaves Milan in the summer months,' she said, 'you cannot buy so much as a loaf of bread. It is deserted. The families have to leave, the city is so hot, unbearable even, out here.'

'And the mosquitoes are terrible, you are eaten alive,' Giovanni said. 'Milan is built on a swamp, you see, surrounded by the mountains. People go to the seaside, the country, a few to chalets in the mountains. We have a place there, in Cervinia, but we usually only use that in the winter.'

'And – do you ski?'

'A little. Mostly we just eat lunch.' Giovanni smiled at her, refilled her glass. 'You must think we are very idle. I don't suppose Mariella has told you about her charity work. That redeems us both, I hope.'

'She hasn't, no,' said Eliza, intrigued. 'What charity work, Mariella?'

'Oh – I help other ladies raise money for the poor children of Milan. And once a year, I go to Lourdes.'

'To Lourdes!'

'Yes. I go with some of the Sisters from the convent here, and other volunteers, we accompany the poor pilgrims on their journey. It is a long journey on the train, or sometimes for the very worst cases by ambulance and coaches. They need much help, and some have no families. It is very, very sad at times. But wonderful, nonetheless.'

'Tomorrow, we have a more interesting evening for you,' Giovanni said, clearly in need of a change of subject, 'a few friends, two of them English.'

'English!'

'Yes, there are many English working in Milan. It is an industrial city and an international one. I try to support our motor industry,' he added with a smile. 'Mariella has her Fiat and I have a Lancia. But then in the garage, we have an English Rolls-Royce.'

The next morning, Mariella said they would drive into Milan.

'I have a lot to do, and I think it will be interesting for you. Emmie can come if you wish, we will take Anna-Maria too, and then if the little one gets bored, they can go for a walk.'

Eliza had been to Milan in her work but, moving from hotel to fashion show to photographic studio, had simply seen it as a plain, if stylish, sister to Florence and Rome. Now, she was able to appreciate it so much more, to see it above all as a working, lived-in, sleekly fashionable city: large avenues, lined with balconied houses, with smaller charming ones, little more than lanes, turning abruptly off them, the chic streaks of colour that were the fashion streets, the treasure troves of Via della Spiga, Corso Venezia, Via St Andrea; the sudden glimpses of tranquil, tree-filled private courtyards, opening off the busy streets; the orange trams with their blazing headlights, carving their way through the city; the palazzos, great and small, set so casually among the streets and squares, the wide piazzas, the vast open space occupied by the Duomo, the elaborate wedding-cake-white cathedral, topped by *La Madonnina* – and the great curving colonnade of the most famous shopping street of all, the Galleria Vittorio Emanuele II, leading from it, for another kind of worship altogether. And all of it bathed in the brilliant clear light of autumnal Milan.

And the Milanese women: so chic, so perfectly presented, with their strong features and wonderful hair, a little flashier than their Paris counterparts perhaps, in their exquisitely cut jackets, brilliantly coloured scarves and their high leather boots. It was a visual gluttony; Eliza found herself constantly sighing with pleasure.

Mariella's main preoccupation, it appeared, was preparing for the Milan social season.

'It starts on 7 December, every year, the day of St Ambroeus, the patron saint of Milan. Everyone goes to La Scala, that is the great social event of the year. Always Verdi, although just very occasionally Rossini. Heads of state attend, and very often monarchs from other countries. Certainly from France and Austria, and I think sometimes your Queen? There are pre-Scala parties, the night before, very, very grand, and of course many, many afterwards. So, you see, one needs so many dresses. Today we will visit my dressmaker. And also I have an appointment with Mila Schön, my favourite Milanese couturier. I thought you would be interested in that. But before we start, we will go to Cova for coffee. You will like it.'

Cova was a coffee shop on the Via Montenapoleone, a glut of gilt and pink and marble, with pastel-painted friezes festooned with golden cherubs, and piles of picture-perfect pastries and chocolates. Emmie took one look at the pastries, reached out a chubby hand and said 'for me'. It had been her first sentence, learnt, Eliza said, from her father.

'Everybody comes here,' said Mariella. 'In the morning early you order your coffee and a croissant and stand at the bar. If you have a little time, you sit in the café. We will sit.'

Anna-Maria settled Emmie on her lap and did the napkin routine again; Eliza sat thankfully back and ate two pastries in swift succession and drank a large hot chocolate and then even finished a slice of panettone. Mariella watched her, smiling.

'I was suspicious that your brioche was not enough for you this morning,' she said.

'No, no, it was wonderful,' said Eliza, 'it's just that everything is better than the thing before.'

The day went on. Anna-Maria took Emmie for a series of little walks; they visited Mariella's dressmaker, where she had fittings for six long dresses, three silk, three satin; then to Mila Schön, where she ordered two cocktail suits; then to Sebastian in Via Montenapoleone for some shoes.

'Nothing for you?' Mariella asked.

'No, honestly. I really mustn't. I've spent all next year's dress allowance already.'

'Then I will buy you a little present. Some gloves? Perhaps a handbag? Yes, we will go to Prada. We must walk through the Galleria Vittorio Emanuele, it is very, very important.'

'Yes, I do know,' said Eliza, suddenly anxious not to appear a fashion bumpkin.

'Yes, yes, of course you do, but also it moves between Milan's two great landmarks, La Scala and the Duomo. Come. Look, the little one is asleep in her chairpush. Now there is Rinascente, our great department store. Look at the windows, Eliza, are they not wonderful? They have a brilliant young man dressing them, Giorgio Armani. I think he will go far. Come, to Prada.'

Mariella marched towards Prada, through the great vaulted arcade of the Galleria and ushered Eliza inside. Anna-Maria sank into a chair in one of the cafés nearby.

They knew Mariella in Prada. A great deal of greeting and fast-fire Italian went on; five handbags appeared on the counter with great speed.

'There. You choose, *cara*. You need a bag. The one you have is not worthy of you.'

'Oh,' said Eliza, enchanted by the notion of being worthy of a bag, protested a little longer and then gave up and decided it would be rude not to accept.

The one she chose was a glorious soft pouch of a thing. 'That will hold the kitchen cupboard, I think,' Mariella said. 'Why not something a little more chic?'

'No, this is what I want, please,' Eliza said, 'and I often have to take the kitchen cupboard when I go out these days. So—'

'*Bene*,' said Mariella. 'Then have it, with my love.'

They left, no money apparently having changed hands.

'And now,' said Mariella, 'shall we have lunch?'

'I couldn't eat lunch,' said Eliza, laughing, 'and I think Emmie has had several lunches already.'

'Then we will have an early tea and go home. And prepare for our dinner party.'

The dinner party was fun, conducted for the most part in English, as a clear courtesy to Eliza: the guests included a delightful Italian couple, a fashion editor on Italian *Vogue* called Alessandra, and her banker husband; an Italian woman friend of Mariella's who had once been a dancer, Mariella told Eliza as they waited for her to arrive – 'she married a count and pretends she has forgotten her start' – who was very grand until a few glasses of wine had gone down and then became rather bawdy and even sang a Billie Holiday number at one point, rather well and unaccompanied; and an Englishman called Timothy Fordyce, who worked, it transpired, in advertising. And not only in advertising, but for KPD in Milan.

'I don't believe it,' said Eliza, laughing, 'I had no idea they had a branch in Milan.'

'Oh, they do,' said Fordyce, ' KPD is everywhere. You know the one in London of course.'

'Of course. A – a friend of mine, a great friend actually, worked there, Jeremy Northcott. He's in New York now—'

'Oh, Jeremy. Yes, I've met him a few times. What a charmer. He's running the office there now, meant to stay six months and they won't let him go. Tell me, has he married yet? I heard some English beauty broke his heart, is that true?'

'Um – it could be,' said Eliza.

'The English beauty, Timothy,' Mariella said, 'she is sitting next to you.'

'No! Good lord. Is that right, was it really you?'

'There could have been another one since,' said Eliza feebly, 'I don't know.'

'Well, small world,' said Timothy Fordyce. 'Wait till I see him. I'm off to New York in a few weeks, big agency conference.'

'Well, give him my – my regards.'

'I will. And you're married, are you?'

'Oh – yes. But he's not here.'

She felt confused and rather foolish; it was patently obvious that her husband wasn't there.

'So, what do you do at KPD?' she asked. 'Are you on the account side?'

'Yes. We service all the international clients. There are several English agencies in Milan, as a matter of fact, McCann's, JWT. The art directors are all English too, they despise graphic design at the art schools here, only teach them the classical stuff. And you, what do you do?'

'Eliza and I, we met in Paris,' said Mariella, 'she is a very famous fashion editor.'

'On?'

'A magazine called *Charisma*.'

'*Charisma*! No! Marvellous magazine. Absolutely marvellous. Fashion pages are incredible. Well – clever old you.'

Eliza felt very sad suddenly, rather like Cinderella at the ball, only less fortunate, for where was the prince who could save her and keep her in this enchanted kingdom? Then she told herself she was being ridiculous, and that she wasn't here to mope, but to be amusing and earn her keep.

She fell asleep with the curtains open, a full moon streaming onto her bed. Emmie slept sweetly and peacefully; a note on Eliza's pillow said that if she wanted to stay in bed late, she had only to ring for Anna-Maria when Emmie awoke.

The thought came to her, swift and unbidden, that if she had married Jeremy, her life would be at least a little like this one.

Chapter 31

Quietly, gently, Adrian died. He drifted away from the sad travesty of a thing that his life had become by way of first a minor stroke and then a major one, followed by a heart attack, none of which he was properly aware of.

He had been listening to the news, and heard about the shooting of Bobby Kennedy, and had called Sarah to join him.

'Who could have imagined anything so dreadful,' he said, 'only five years after his brother. What a dreadful thing. And how hard for the family to bear. We've been lucky,' he said, taking her hand, his voice faint, but quite cheerful, 'we've been spared that kind of grief, we still have each other and our – our . . .'

'Children,' Sarah said, into the silence, for he often lost his place in sentences these days, but then turning to smile at him, got nothing in reply but a blank stare; and watched as his head lolled sideways, and his body slumped heavily away from her, still holding her hand.

She sat for a short while, listening quite carefully to the details of the events in the Ambassador Hotel in Los Angeles, recognising the much greater importance of what had just happened in her own kitchen, but not quite yet able to face it and all the procedures that must follow.

And so Eliza heard the news, not as she had always feared by way of a panicked phone call in the middle of the night, but by an almost unnaturally calm one, halfway through the morning; a small, sad voice that was almost unrecognisable as Sarah's, telling her that her father was in hospital and was not expected to last the day.

She and Charles arrived too late to say goodbye to him, and stood staring down at the white empty shell they knew to be, but could scarcely recognise as, the handsome, caring, charming father they had all loved so much.

Sarah was calm, clearly shocked and relieved in equal measure; they spent the rest of the day talking, the three of them, remembering, laughing, crying, reliving what had been the happiest of childhoods and family life, and Adrian's greatest gift to them all.

Matt and Juliet came too, later in the day, but stayed uneasily together on the perimeter of the group; Matt had left Emmie with Sandra.

The funeral, a week later, was wonderful. The little church was full, people standing at the back and even in the porch, the flowers done with particular care by the ladies of the parish, the choir especially well rehearsed, the vicar at full throttle, his rather fruity voice extolling Adrian's courage through his long illness, and his outstanding virtues as church warden, his generosity both with his time and Summercourt's produce (eggs and strawberries) at the village fête, his diplomatic skills as a parish councillor.

Charles, pale and very nervous, spoke of childhood and adult memories of his father and said how greatly his life had been shaped by both Adrian himself and life with him at Summercourt; Eliza spoke briefly but tenderly of her parents' long and happy marriage, and of their wedding in the same church, almost forty years earlier.

'Too short, of course,' she said, glancing briefly at her mother and smiling, 'but they were lucky that it was nonetheless longer than many.'

Sandra and Pete had come, Pete genuinely sad at the loss of his new friend; Sandra had wanted to sit at the back of the church, but Matt ushered them forward. 'Don't be daft, Mum, you're part of this family.'

Anna and Piers Marchant were there, Anna surprisingly subdued, although she came over to embrace Matt and Eliza, telling Matt how marvellous it was to see him and berating Eliza for not bringing him over for dinner, and Piers pumped his hand and said he hoped the whole family realised what a lot Matt had done for Sarah.

'Lucky to have you, dear boy, that's the fact of the matter. See you later up at the house. Share a few jars, eh? Like to know what you think of this Roy Jenkins chappie. Five bob on a bottle of Scotch indeed! Daylight robbery.'

Emmie had not gone to the service; it was felt she was too young and that it would be distressing for her. Eliza had been terrified she would throw a tantrum and demand to be allowed to go, but she seemed to have picked up on the general subdued atmosphere, and was behaving beautifully. She had been left in the care of Charles and Eliza's old nanny, who was, with her little problem, she said, unable to attend long ceremonies. 'Incontinence,' whispered Eliza to Matt, 'but Emmie will be fine with her, they're going to play snakes and ladders and the catering lady has promised to keep an eye on them both.'

But as they walked up the hill, Emmie was standing by the big gates, with large tears rolling down her cheeks.

'I was too sad to play,' she said.

It was perhaps a most fitting tribute to Adrian the family man.

Sarah had wept quite a lot at the service, but afterwards at the party at Summercourt – the drawing room cleaned and tidied by volunteers from the village – she seemed surprisingly cheerful, sparkling her way round the room, thanking everyone for their help and generosity.

'Poor Mummy,' said Eliza to Matt, standing and looking at her, as people began to leave, 'she's still in shock. She'll have to leave now, of course, she can't stay here. And Charles certainly can't afford to keep it, so it really will have to go.'

'But I thought it couldn't be sold. Because of this trust.'

'It can't. Not in Mummy's lifetime. She has this power of appointment thing which means she can appoint it out – that is, say who is to have it – but there still won't be any money to do it up. I know you've been wonderful and done the roof, but it still needs so much more spent on it. I think there are some cousins in Canada somewhere, who could afford to spend money on it. Of course the trustees would have to agree to that. Bit of a poisoned chalice, you could say. And – who is to say they'd do it properly? How we'd want?'

'Now, hang on a bit,' said Matt, 'I may be a bit thick and not used to all this, but if someone else has got the house and they're pouring money into it, why should it be the way you want?'

'Because it's Summercourt,' said Eliza. 'Because it's ours.'

'But it wouldn't be yours.'

'Matt,' said Eliza, 'Summercourt will always be ours. It's part of us.' The emotion of the day and anxiety and grief about the future were beginning to get the better of her. 'Even if someone else was living here. I mean, suppose they decided to – oh, I don't know, put in modern windows so it was warmer. It would be unbearable. And wrong. You don't understand.'

'Too right I don't understand,' said Matt. 'If it was mine, I tell you, I'd put in any sort of windows I liked, and paint the door sky-blue pink if I wanted to. You people really are something else. Eliza, if my dad sold our house, do you think he'd have the right to hang about outside telling the new owner not to paint the front door green just because he liked it red? Course not. I tell you, Eliza, if you think having grown up in a house that you can't afford any more gives you the right to lord it over anyone who can, you got real problems. Now I'm going to get myself a drink and find someone I can have a reasonable conversation with. Where's Emmie anyway?'

'She's with Nanny. Playing snap, last time I looked.'

'Eliza, the old bat's completely immobile. Anything could have happened. I'd better go and check on her.'

'Yes, do. And don't hurry back,' said Eliza. Tears choked her suddenly; she looked at him as he moved off in the direction of the kitchen. He could be such a bastard; he seemed to have completely forgotten she'd buried her father today.

She moved out of the drawing room and out onto the terrace, lit a cigarette; then, feeling calmer, walked a hundred yards away from the house and looked back. It was a beautiful early autumn day; the golden sunshine, slightly misty now, lit the grey walls, smoke rose from the chimneys, people moved behind the windows, the hum of conversation reached her even at this distance. Briefly Summercourt was alive again, but not for long: once today was over it would fade back into its empty, silent state, with her mother alone in it, having lost the one great love of her life and faced with losing the other. It was all nearly unbearable.

A few weeks later, Charles rang Eliza. Could they meet?

'Charles, I'd love to see you. Come over here if you like. Emmie's at playschool now, thank God, and the mornings are wonderfully peaceful.'

'I'd like that. What about Matt?'

'Matt's never here,' said Eliza briefly.

'The marriage is over,' he said, sitting down and sighing heavily. 'Juliet's divorcing me.'

'What?'

If he had told her Juliet was running away with Mick Jagger she couldn't have been more astonished.

'Yes. She's got someone else. Rich bugger, South African, banker. She married me largely for my non-existent money, it seems. Oh, Eliza, I feel such a fool. We've had awful rows, all about money—'

'But – I don't understand. What does she want?'

'A small fortune. Which she was mistaken in thinking she'd found with me. Summercourt, family, the Stock Exchange job – it all added up to huge mistake on her part. And I – I fell for it.'

'Charles – oh, God, I'm so so sorry. How dreadful for you.'

'The worst thing is I really did care about her. She made me feel good about myself. Stronger, more successful. I'm a bit of a disaster, really, Eliza. I'm a lousy businessman, never really up to standard. If anyone should make money, it's a stockbroker. And I lost thousands. I couldn't handle my own wife, stop her spending a ton of money we hadn't got, just stuck my head in the sand and hoped it would be all right. I owe her old man thousands. He had to bail me out twice. I gambled money on the Stock Exchange, money I didn't have, lost the lot; and then – well, I was so bloody miserable I started going to the races with clients, I've always loved doing that, and I started risking money with the bookies. Just to cheer myself up, really, and I did quite well sometimes. But mostly I didn't. In the end we'd have lost the house if Geoffrey hadn't stepped in again. But it was very much a loan and I've got to pay him back.'

'Even though his daughter's leaving you for someone else?'

'Yes, he says she's only going because I've demoralised and humiliated her. Which is true to an extent. I didn't even manage to make her pregnant. She wanted that so much.'

'Oh, Charles. I'm so so sorry. You should have asked Matt.'

'I couldn't have. At least Judd knew I was a disaster. Matt respects me, God knows why. I think so anyway.'

'Yes, he does,' said Eliza.

'Anyway, final straw, I lost my job, told I wasn't pulling my weight. So as of the end of this month, I'm unemployed.'

'But – but—' Her mind was whirling. 'Why is Juliet divorcing you for a start? Why not the other way round?'

'Her old man insists on it, says I've got to do the decent thing, provide grounds. Oh, I don't care too much about that, in fact I might emerge with my dignity intact. Not a cuckold at least. And then she won't ask for anything in the way of a settlement. And her father will pick up the bill for the court costs. That was the deal. I couldn't afford to argue.'

'Charles, that's shocking. So immoral.'

He sighed. 'I know. But – I just want it to be over. Oh, Eliza—' His voice broke suddenly and tears filled his eyes. 'I loved her so much, you know, I really did. That's the worst thing, to think she didn't love me.'

Eliza sat there, her arms round him, unable to comfort him. Finally she said, 'What are you going to do about – about your job?'

'Oh, I've got an idea about that,' he said and he looked slightly more cheerful. 'I'm going to try teaching. I've got a good degree and I can get a job in a prep school, quite easily it seems, teaching history. I'm pretty sure I'd like it. I won't earn much, though; and what with paying old Judd back, I really won't have a bean. Certainly can't help with Summercourt. Matt's been great, hasn't he?'

'Yes, he has,' Eliza agreed soberly. She still felt stunned. Charles her big wonderful brother, turned into a penniless failure. It just didn't bear thinking about. What on earth would Matt say?

Matt was characteristically brutal. 'Not surprised to be honest,' he said, 'I like old Charles, but he's his own worst enemy. Too much of a gentleman, that's his problem. No wife of mine would spend money she hadn't got.'

'Really?' said Eliza.

Her tone was wasted on Matt. 'And he should never have let old Judd take things over—'

'Matt, that's so unfair. What else could he do?'

'Sell that poxy flat for a start, tell Juliet she couldn't have her bloody house, rent somewhere modest and the bank would have met him more than halfway. Well, I'm glad about this teaching lark, I tell you that.'

'Why?'

'I thought you were going to say he was going to ask me for a job. Then what would I have done?'

'Given him one,' said Eliza, 'I very much hope.'

'Yeah, I would. But not the sort he'd have wanted. I don't carry dead wood, Eliza, and Charles would have been no use to me.'

'You are so vile, you know that?' said Eliza.

But something deep in her heart forced her to admit that he was to some extent right.

Chapter 32

It was definitely him. No doubt about it. Sitting there, looking quite cheerful, smiling at the crowd of people in front of him: signing what she presumed was his name, on the books being handed to him.

She would normally never have gone into Hatchards, that smartest and most exclusive of bookshops. Grabbing a paperback on her way through the airport was how she obtained most of her reading matter; but she had seen a new Margaret Drabble novel she hadn't read in the window, and couldn't resist getting it as soon as possible.

She had found that straight away and then thought she might get a birthday present for Diana and was wandering about the shop when someone said, 'Are you looking for the signing?'

She'd said not really and then, in case the signer was someone famous, thought she'd just find out and – well, best get out quickly, Scarlett, before he sees you.

But it was too late; he had seen her and his grey eyes widened with alarm. Which annoyed her. What did he think she was going to do, make a scene, try and claim friendship or something? Arrogant pig, he was.

She was about to turn away and leave the shop, when something very peculiar happened. She could hardly believe it and had to blink and then look again to make sure she hadn't imagined it. But – no: no doubt about it, he was smiling at her. It was certainly not a welcoming grin and he wasn't waving, or inviting her over, but it was definitely a smile just the same. And a very nice one. Almost conspiratorial. And his eyes behind the wire-framed spectacles were unmistakably friendly.

She smiled carefully back, and one of the shop assistants who was managing the queue noticed that they were smiling at one another and came over.

'Did you want to get a book?' she said, indicating a pile of very large and expensive-looking volumes. 'They're over there. It's Mr Frost's companion volume to *My Favourite Train Journeys*. *My Favourite Island Journeys*.

Scarlett was about to say that she didn't want a book, when it occurred to her that he might have included Trisos among his favourites.

'I'll just have a look,' she said, 'thank you.'

'That's all right. And then of course, if you buy it, Mr Frost will sign it for you.'

The book was very large, and very glossy, with colour photographs every few pages; Scarlett picked it up and started rather cautiously looking at the index, which was difficult as it was so large and heavy. She glanced over her shoulder rather guiltily. Mark Frost had stopped smiling and was watching her quite closely. She quickly put the book down and saw to her horror that the assistant was coming back.

'I don't think I want it, thank you,' she said, 'it's not for me.'

'Oh right. But I've just got a message for you from Mr Frost. He said to tell you Trisos was on page seventy-two.'

'Oh. Oh, thank you.' She felt herself blushing. Damn. Now she'd have to look at it again, or it would seem very rude.

She opened the book and there it was. A picture of Trisos, of a trio of white houses, with the sun setting behind them, and a seagull trailing across the sky. She could almost hear it, with its wild, raw cry, feel the heat, smell the herbs. It was a glorious photograph; she smiled and turned to Mark Frost in a moment of pure unselfconscious delight. He smiled again.

'I think,' she said to the assistant, 'I think that I will get one after all. Thank you.'

'Good. It's four pounds nineteen and eleven. I'll take it over to the desk for you. Would you like to pay by cash or cheque?'

'Oh, cheque,' said Scarlett firmly. Nearly five pounds. For a book. She must be mad.

She joined the queue feeling a bit silly; there were only three people in front of her.

'Hello,' he said, when she finally reached the table, taking it from her.

'Hello. It's – it's a very nice book.'

'Thank you. Right now – no, I know what to write—'

He scribbled away, big sloping letters in thick black ink, handed it to her.

'There. Hope that's all right.'

'I'm sure it will be. Yes, well, thank you.'

'Thank you for buying it. Maybe we'll meet there again one day. On Trisos, I mean.'

'Maybe. Yes.'

She left the shop, the book in a large brown paper bag. She was dying to see what he'd written but she couldn't stop in the street to look, it was too heavy and anyway, it was raining. She went into Lyons Corner House at Piccadilly Circus, sat down at one of the tables and opened the book. And smiled with pleasure.

'For Miss Scarlett, from Mark Frost, a neighbour.'

Miss Scarlett. That was what Demetrios and Larissa called her. How nice that he'd remembered. He really was quite – quite charming, in a quiet sort of way. She felt touched, sat there staring at it, at the black ink on the white paper, at the sprawling writing, spelling her name. And then it happened.

One of the waitresses collided with another, both of them carrying cups of coffee: both cups went over the book. The precious five-pound book.

'Oh, madam! Oh, I am so sorry. Oh, how dreadful, how careless of me. Oh, dear.'

One of them dabbed helplessly at the brown-stained paper, smudging the writing into illegibility; the other tried to wipe the table and the coffee dripped into Scarlett's new Fenwick's handbag. She suddenly felt furious.

'Look, just leave it, would you? You're making it worse. Leave it alone.'

'What is this, Doreen?' It was the manager, pompous, fat, red-faced.

'I spilt some coffee, Mr Douglas, on this lady's book.'

'Oh, I do apologise, madam. Very unfortunate. May we offer you a free coffee by way of recompense?'

'Coffee?' said Scarlett, losing her temper completely. 'You call coffee recompense for a five-pound book. Don't be ridiculous. I've only just bought it—'

'Yes, I do see. Very annoying for you.'

'Annoying! It's much worse than annoying. I actually think you should buy me another copy.'

'Oh, I'm sorry, madam, I'm afraid that's not possible Maybe a contribution – please wait.'

He went away, was gone for ages, came back smiling. 'I've just spoken to our regional manager and he says if you'd like to write a letter explaining what happened, he'll consider it and perhaps send you a book token for some of the amount. I'm afraid that's the best I can do.'

'It's a very poor best,' said Scarlett, glaring at him.

'Perhaps, madam,' he said, his face growing more hostile, 'it was a little unwise to open such a valuable book at such a busy time. We do stress that customers should take care of their possessions while they're here.'

'Oh, never mind,' said Scarlett, 'I'll just leave. And not return in a hurry, I can tell you that.'

'That is your prerogative, of course, madam.'

The entire café was now silent, everyone's eyes fixed on her. She picked up her ruined book and left.

Outside she found herself near to tears. Her lovely book with its lovely inscription – ruined. To make matters worse, it was raining much harder and the brown paper bag was getting soggy too and the cover wet.

'Oh – shit!' exclaimed Scarlett aloud and dumped the whole thing in a rubbish bin.

'Was it that bad?' said a voice. 'How very embarrassing.' It was Mark Frost.

Five minutes later they were back at Hatchards. Another book was found, and inscribed, Scarlett protesting helplessly, and slightly quaking at the thought of parting with another five pounds.

'No, no,' said Mark Frost, as she rummaged for her cheque book. 'I get a dozen complimentary copies from the publisher, I never know what to do with them all. I'll bring Hatchards one of those.'

'Thank you again for coming, Mr Frost.' It was the manager. 'Such a success.'

Mark Frost handed the book to Scarlett. 'Now you must excuse me,' he said.

'Of course,' said Scarlett. 'I've taken up far too much of your time already. And thank you so much.'

'Please don't mention it. And – perhaps on Trisos, then? Are you returning this year?'

'Oh – I don't know.'

'I'll be there in October. My house is supposed to be finished then. God, it's taken a long time. Well, goodbye.'

The surprising smile again; and then he was gone. She felt a little odd. Shaken up. As if someone had given all her feelings a physical jolt.

'He's so charming, isn't he?' said the manager. 'And such a wonderful writer, don't you think?'

'Oh – yes. Wonderful.'

'He's gone to meet Mrs Frost now,' said the manager. 'Have you met her? She's the most brilliant poetess.'

'Um – no.'

'Such an amazing woman. And he is so devoted to her. Such a brilliant family.'

Scarlett resisted slamming down the second book with great difficulty.

She walked down Piccadilly, feeling absurdly depressed. Another bloody married man, devoted to his wife. It wasn't fair. It really, really wasn't.

'Eliza, hi! It's Annunciata. Have you heard the news?'

'Of course not,' said Eliza, 'when did I ever hear any news?'

'When I ring you up. Don't be so touchy.'

'Sorry. It's lovely to hear from you anyway. Did the pope elope?'

This was a well-worn joke of theirs.

'Much more exciting than that. Jack's leaving.'

'No! Oh, my God. Where's he going?'

'Back to Fleet Street. He says he can't stand all the hormones any longer. Typical Jack, terribly arrogant, apparently he hasn't even got anywhere to go yet.'

'Wow. So how do you feel about that?'

'Depressed,' said Annunciata. 'It's the end of this magazine as we know it.'

Eliza felt it was the end of her life as she knew it as well. Those heady years when she had been certain of what she was doing and where she was going, when she had owned her own life, had made her own decisions about where she went and when and why, when she had risen to brief and starry success on the most starry and successful of all the publications in London – they were over.

As *Charisma* was over. It would live on, no doubt, for a few – maybe many – years, other editors would arrive and mould it to their own visions and it would be quite possibly perfectly successful, but it would be different. The extraordinary fusion of Beckham's Fleet Street brilliance and belligerence, the slightly effete intellectualism of people like Annunciata and the stunning visual precocity of the art department and indeed Eliza's own, had made of *Charisma* much more than a magazine. It was a phenomenon, watched, wondered at, admired and imitated, a meteor blazing through the Sixties' skies; it was of its time absolutely, both created by and contributing to it and its like would not be quite seen again.

Eliza knew she had been privileged and blessed to have been part of it, it had made her as she had to a small degree made it; but its time, along with the decade that had spawned it, was drawing to a close.

The perfect symmetry would become a memory; and it made her very sad.

Jimbo had given in his notice. Or rather, as Louise remarked with some asperity, he had jumped before he was pushed, Matt tiring of his ongoing absences due to his ever-increasing familial responsibilites. These had come to a head one afternoon when he had been summoned home to look after his small son while his wife took her mother to hospital to have a broken arm set.

Matt who had arranged a big meeting with an important new prospect, was roaring at full throttle.

'So where's that waste of space with nothing between his ears that he calls his assistant?'

'At a site meeting,' said Louise, caught as so often in the crossfire.

'Jesus wept.'

'He might be able to help. Jesus, I mean, not Terry.'

'Not the time for jokes, Louise.'

He walked out of her office shouting for his secretary, a determinedly cheerful girl with stout legs and a steady nerve, who had so far shown no signs of following her three predecessors out of the door of Simmonds and Shaw before the end of their first week of employment, and indeed was about to celebrate her third month with Matt. 'Sally, get Jimbo for me, would you. He's at home it seems. And put it through to my office.'

Louise, walking past Jenny's desk, heard the familiar roaring coming from behind Matt's closed doors and winked at her.

Matt would have been less angry with Jimbo had this been the first time he had fled home at a snap of Roberta's long elegant fingers. But it was the latest in a long series of demands for his presence at bar mitzvahs, birthdays and of course the Friday suppers.

'You're supposed to be my partner, Jimbo, and you're not playing fair,'

Matt said, 'and you might remind Roberta that it's your salary that pays for that house she lives in, two kitchens and all, and she might find things less cosy without it.'

Three weeks later, Roberta called Jimbo to say that Mikey, their oldest child, was running a temperature and was asking for him; Jimbo looked at his life and prospects in his father-in-law's firm, and made his decision.

'I'm sorry, Matt,' he said, 'very sorry.'

'You will be,' said Matt briefly. 'What notice are you on?'

'Six months, I think. But I won't be working it out. Soon as you can let me go, I start with the old man.'

'What old man?'

'Roberta's dad. He's offered me a partnership and a big stake in the firm.'

'Well, that's bloody convenient, isn't it? Overnight, was it, this offer?'

'No,' said Jimbo, 'no, over a year ago. But I didn't want it. Still don't. What I do want is a quiet life and Roberta isn't going to give me one until I join the family firm. Sorry, Matt. But – that's married life, I suppose.'

'A quiet life!' said Matt to Louise. He had most unusually asked her out for a drink. Normally such arrangements in his life were entirely male. 'Whoever gave up everything for a quiet life?'

'I can think of a few,' said Louise. 'My dad for one.'

'Thought your dad was a successful banker?'

'No, Matt, he's just a local manager. He was offered a job at head office, but he decided he liked knowing everyone in the town, making his own decisions about people, getting home to us all at night for supper.'

'Right. Blimey. Where do you get it from, then? Your ambition and so on?'

'My granny,' said Louise.

'Your granny? But she's a—'

'Woman? Yes, obviously. A woman from a different age. When they didn't usually do a lot. But Granny did. She founded a cleaning agency, when she couldn't get a charlady one day, and it was terribly successful. She was running five branches right up to the war. Had to stop then because the charladies were all working in factories, but afterwards she started again. Then she got ill and died of cancer, and Grandpa took the business over and ruined it.' She sat back in her chair and smiled sweetly at Matt. 'So I'm not the first tycoon in the family.'

When she got home that night to her rather grand new flat in Paulton Square, Chelsea, she sat looking over the square, sipping some very nice white wine, and wondering if Matt would now make her an equal partner in the firm in place of Jimbo. He ought to; she had contributed certainly as much as, and arguably a great deal more than, Jimbo. But she had known Matt for long enough to know that this was far from being a certainty.

What was a certainty, however, was how extremely sorry he would be if he didn't.

Victor Johnson looked at David Berenson across his desk. His expression was the mixture of self-confidence and cunning that had made him one of the most successful divorce lawyers in the southern states of America.

'I'm glad you told me all that, David,' he said, 'and under the circumstances, your wife hiring a private eye, it's a pity you didn't before. I think you need to get this girl on side. How does she feel about you now?'

'Not too warmly.'

'Right. I mean, it's a pretty dodgy scenario, if it got out. Especially you giving her that money.'

'I didn't have any choice,' said David defensively.

'No, and you can warn her that blackmail is a crime. But – actually it is checkmate on that one. So, see if you can talk her into at least keeping shtum. Maybe she needs a little more money for her business? Could that be the way forward?'

'It could be,' said David. 'That's very clever.'

'Right. See what you can do.' Johnson smiled his catlike smile. His nickname was not Victory Johnson for nothing.

Eliza asked Matt if he was going to make Louise his partner; he told her he didn't want to talk about it.

'Why?'

'Well, I assume you're concerned with her feminist rights. Making sure she gets them.' His eyes across the table were wary.

'And if I was?'

'You know my views on all that.'

'What, that women don't really belong in the real world? That they're there to breed from and cook and look after you lot.'

'That's a fair summary,' he said.

Eliza had had a difficult day with Emmie and she suddenly felt angry.

'I know you're trying to wind me up,' she said, 'but I still find that offensive. I just don't understand you, Matt. Louise is as important to that company of yours as Jimbo ever was.'

'Yes and no,' he said. 'Viewed from outside, which is important, she certainly isn't. You'd never get a huge deal signed on her say-so. People wouldn't have the trust in her.'

'But you could help change that. If you made her partner now.'

'And why should I want to change it? It's the way the world works, Eliza. You'll never get women running it, never, and I for one don't think they should.'

'Because they should be at home having babies?'

'That's what you're ultimately there for, for God's sake.'

'No, Matt, it isn't. The things are not mutually exclusive. I hate it that you talk like that, I really do. And I hate how it's affected my life and what you've made me give up.'

'I wondered when we'd get round to that.'

The row was long and bitter, only ending when Matt appeared in the doorway of the spare room, where Eliza had retired as she increasingly did, saying he was sorry and he loved her. And that he would try at least to see things more sympathetically, 'although I still think it'd be wrong, you leaving Emmie when she's so young.'

'So I've just about gathered,' she said, but she managed at least the shadow of a smile.

'And meantime, I have a little idea for right now?'

'I'd sort of gathered that too. And what if I don't go along with it . . .'

'I shall try very hard to make you,' he said, 'and if I fail, I'll try some more.'

He sat down on the bed, leaned forward to kiss her. Reluctantly she felt herself respond, and then pushed him away.

His head dropped to her breasts; he began to tease her nipples with his tongue; angry still she pushed him off, but not before the familiar stabbings of pleasure began, the softening within herself; he sensed it and moved his head down to her stomach, began to kiss her there.

'I want you,' he said, 'I want you so much. So much more than more than. I'm so sorry, Eliza. Sorry I'm such a brute.'

She giggled suddenly. 'You don't really think that. That you're a brute.'

'No, of course I don't. But I am sorry to have upset you so much.'

'You always win, don't you?' she said, slithering down in the bed, holding out her arms, 'always, always.'

'So far,' he said.

Afterwards, he told her he hoped she knew how much he loved her. Eliza said she didn't actually and asked him if he realised the only time he told her that was in precisely those circumstances, 'you know, after the row, after the sex, when you're feeling sleepy and soppy,' and he was so shocked that he put the light on, struggled to sit up and stared at her, with an expression of such acute remorse that she laughed.

'That's not true, is it?' he said, and 'Matt, it's totally true,' she said. 'Try saying it at some ordinary time. Like breakfast.'

'I never see you at breakfast.'

'That's true. OK. When we're watching telly.'

'You're always asleep.'

'That's true too. OK, then when we're in the park. With Emmie.'

'I'll try and remember.'

She actually forgot all about it, but the next time they were feeding the ducks in Richmond Park, he suddenly took her hand and said, 'Eliza, I love you.'

'Oh, my God,' she said, touched beyond anything, 'oh, my God, you remembered. Matt Shaw, I love you too.'

'Good. Right, don't expect it every time, will you?'

Jack Beckham had invited Eliza to his leaving party.

Her first reaction to the invitation was surprise that he should have remembered her; her second delight that he wanted her there; and her third a serious doubt as to whether she actually wanted to go.

She had been feeling increasingly demoralised. In theory her life was great; she spent a lot of time telling herself so and most days would see her determinedly setting herself to various tasks – finding the new house that Matt wanted, she'd made an offer on a four-storey beauty in Fulham, quite near the river, checking out schools, taking Emmie to endless ballet classes and music clubs and riding lessons, buying her clothes, and of course seeing her friends. Ah yes. Her friends. The girls with whom she had grown up, middle-aged beyond their years, all braying versions of their own mothers, married to carbon copies of their own fathers; quite often she would feel a sort of claustrophobia, a despair at the life she had found herself locked into, and make her excuses and leave.

Her only real friend was Heather. She genuinely looked forward to their weekly meetings at a mother and baby group and to the picnics and outings to the swings that they shared when the weather was nice enough. She admired Heather more than anyone she had ever met. She was so brave, so cheerful, and a wonderful mother; she never smacked Coral, unlike most of the other mothers at the clinic, or shouted at her, or even got seriously cross.

And every time Eliza dropped the pair of them off at Heather's flat, she looked back at her standing in the doorway with its peeling paint and half-broken handle, smiling cheerfully and waving, Coral at her side, the smell of dustbins and lavatories mingling in the air, especially in the summer, and wondered how on earth she could ever complain about anything.

It was Maddy who told her that of course she must go the party.

'You'll be so sorry if you don't, and anyway it'll be fun, everyone'll be there—'

'Everyone,' said Eliza miserably, 'I don't know "everyone" any more, it's all right for you, Maddy, you're still a star, but me, what do I do every day, poor little woman at home . . .'

'Oh, stop feeling so sorry for yourself,' said Maddy, 'you're coming.'

What really made up her mind was Matt offering to babysit; it was so big a concession that she felt she simply couldn't refuse.

So she bought a new dress and had her hair done and took a taxi from home, feeling like a proper person again, and then had to stand outside in the street for several minutes, gathering her courage to go in.

Once inside, she stood there, absorbing it all, feeling quite drunk just on the atmosphere: the shrieks of recognition, the kisses, the hugs, the bitchy remarks – 'that hair colour almost suits her', 'does that girl really think her legs deserve that dress?', 'time he got a different boyfriend, that one makes him look quite old'.

The air was thick with the smell of smoke, marijuana and expensive perfume; the decibel level of the music and the shrieking was very high.

She scarcely moved for two hours: just stood there being kissed and embraced and given drinks and told how wonderful she looked and how much they missed her.

Jack came over and gave her a bear hug. 'Stupid girl,' he said, 'stupid, stupid cow. I might not be leaving if I still had you here, do you know that?'

'Oh, yes, course I do,' said Eliza.

'Want to work for me on the *News*?'

'I didn't realise you were going to the *News*.'

'I am. Deputy editor, with a special brief on features. Which means fashion. I could pay you four times what you got here. And make you properly famous. The Fleet Street girls are all on the sides of buses these days.'

'Oh Jack, no, I can't.'

'Why not? The dwarf must be nearly at school now.' He called children dwarfs.

'No, 'fraid not. Anyway, I'm planning on another one soon.'

'Oh, Jesus! What for? You can't tell me you enjoy looking after them. More than you enjoyed all this?'

Eliza looked round the room, the teeming, colourful, brilliant room, at the people who made her laugh and excited her and inspired her, the people who thought like she did, wanted what she did, cared about what she did, the people she felt she belonged with, and looked up at him very steadily.

'Not exactly enjoy,' she said, 'no.'

'So – why?'

'Oh, Jack, I don't know. I'm trying to be good. That's all.'

'Waste of a fucking life,' he said, 'if you ask me.'

When she got home, Matt was rather surprisingly still up, watching television.

'Hello,' he said. He looked at her rather warily. 'Good time?'

'Yes, very.'

'You're much earlier than I thought.'

'Am I? Why are you still up? You said you were going to bed early.'

'I know. I – just thought you might want to chat,' he said, 'when you got in. Tell me about it.'

'Oh.' She felt rather disoriented suddenly. This wasn't like him.

'You must – you must miss it,' he said, slightly aggressively. 'I do realise that. I'm not completely stupid.'

'Oh,' she said again. Her sense of disorientation increased.

'I mean – well, I can see it's a struggle for you. Sometimes.'

341

'Yes. It is actually,' she said. 'An awful struggle.'

'Yeah. Well, I just wanted to say that. Let you know I know. And that I – I appreciate it.'

'Oh, Matt,' said Eliza, sitting down beside him, her eyes filling with tears, 'that is just the nicest thing you've ever said to me.'

'Blimey! I don't do very well, in that case. I do love you, you know,' he said suddenly. 'I really, really love you. More than you might think.'

'And I love you,' she said, 'more than more than you might think.'

'That's OK then. Shall we – you know, shall we go to bed?'

'I think that'd be a very good idea,' she said.

It was at times like this that she knew why she had married him.

Chapter 33

Sarah knew she looked dreadful. She felt dreadful too. Odd. Frightened. She was still sleeping badly, still waking every two hours with a jump of fear that Adrian might be calling for her, need her. That she could turn over and go back to sleep seemed – for the time being – an unutterable luxury. Of course she missed him, missed him physically and emotionally, and the house seemed vast and silent – ah, the house. What was she to do about the house? She would have to leave it now; she had no excuses any more. Adrian had left nothing, except some minor debts. She had a tiny pension, what was left from a very handsome portfolio bequeathed her by her father, and the state pension of course. Which would be sufficient to feed and clothe her and fill her car with petrol and pay the electricity bill and feed the Aga; but no more. In the winter the house would be freezing again and she would be living in terror of burst pipes.

She often thought now she was as pathetically poor as anyone living in the council houses in the village – probably more so, and drew a certain amusement from it; but at least the council house tenants could stay in their homes, and the council would fix their roofs. No one would do that for her, the lady of the manor.

No, it had to go; she would see the trustees, see what they would suggest. Not a lot, she feared. But someone had to do something: she was living in an unaffordable prison.

Eliza, flushing and flustered, had said she knew Matt would do more building work, and had even hinted that they could make Sarah another loan; but equally flustered, Sarah had refused absolutely.

'I can't and won't live off you, darling, however kindly the offer is meant, and I can't stay here on my own, it's quite impracticable. None of us can afford to look after Summercourt as it requires; we just have to be brave about it. We've enjoyed it for a long time, and now it must be someone else's turn. We'll find someone who deserves her, don't worry.'

And she smiled brilliantly at Eliza and said why didn't they take Emmie for a walk, before it got dark.

Eliza thought she had never admired her so much.

A meeting with the trustees and Sarah, Charles and Eliza was arranged for a fortnight's time. 'Will you come, Matt?' said Eliza. 'I'd so like you to be there.'

'I'll see. What's the date? No, sorry, got a big meeting at Slough that afternoon.'

'Can't you change it?'

'No, I can't. You'll be fine with Charles. Besides, I might say something inappropriate.'

'Like what?'

'Like I thought putting in modern windows would be a really good idea. Help to sell it, even.'

'Oh, do shut up,' said Eliza. 'You never let anything go, do you? Anyway, it can't be sold, that's the whole point, you know it is. Somehow they've got to find someone who satisfies the terms of the trust. And there just isn't anyone.'

'Sounds like a very badly thought-out trust to me. As I've said before.'

'I know, I know. But there must be some way. The lawyers will just have to find it.'

'Not a lot of use, lawyers, in my experience. One of the reasons my business does what you might call moderately well is having as little to do with them as possible.'

'How well does it do?' asked Eliza suddenly. 'I mean, how much money have you got?'

'Why do you ask?'

'Well – I just thought – I mean, we never actually discussed—'

'Oh no,' he said, 'oh no, I'm not putting my hard-earned cash into that mausoleum. The words good after bad come to mind. And besides, if I did, I'd almost certainly want to do all sorts of things you wouldn't like. No, sorry, Eliza, I'll help do up some little place for your mum, course I will, but that's the limit.'

'Yes, all right,' said Eliza sadly.

Charles said he would buy them all lunch on the day of the meeting. 'I've booked a table at the Savoy, give Mummy a bit of a treat.'

'That's very kind. Can you afford it?'

'Eliza, I want to do it. OK?'

344

Eliza woke up feeling almost frightened.

'I feel as if a great piece of myself is somehow going to be taken away from me,' she said to Matt at breakfast. He told her not to be so melodramatic.

'It's only a house,' he said, getting up and giving her a brief kiss. 'You've got to remember that. I know that's not how you see it, but that's the fact. Got to go now. See you tonight. Does your mum want to come and stay here? You could show her the Fulham house tomorrow, cheer her up a bit.'

'I don't think anything to do with a house would cheer her up,' said Eliza with a sigh.

'No? OK. I've been thinking. I wouldn't mind getting somewhere a bit out of town myself. Lot better for Emmie than Fulham. Brownlow's got some lovely developments going up in Surrey. Detached, big gardens, double garage, all mod cons.'

'Matt—'

'Yeah, private roads, no riff-raff. We'd get a very good price. I've got some brochures here, have a look at them. The best ones have got swimming pools. Emmie'd love that, you know how she enjoys the water.'

'I don't want to look at the horrible brochures for Roderick Brownlow's horrible houses,' said Eliza, 'they make me feel sick. And how you can present them to me on a day like today, I really don't know.'

'Why not? I thought it might cheer you up. You're always saying children should be brought up in the country.'

'Surrey is not proper country,' said Eliza coldly. 'And I won't have Emmie growing up thinking it is.'

'No? Pardon me for living, as Ringo so memorably said. Right, I hope the meeting goes well.'

Eliza dropped Emmie off with Sandra and then went to the Savoy; Charles was waiting for her, looking rather irritable.

'Where's Mummy?'

'She's not coming. Going to meet an old friend instead. There was a message with the front desk here when I came in.'

'Oh. How annoying.'

'It is a bit. I planned this so carefully too. As a treat for her.'

'Never mind,' said Eliza, 'we can have a nice lunch. It is very unlike

345

her though. Well, she's not herself. We can't expect her to be. How are things, Charles? You look much better, I must say.'

'I feel it. And I've got a job in a nice little prep school near Esher. Start at half-term. I'm looking forward to it. So apart from paying off millions to the Judds—'

'Are you really?'

'Well, not millions. Thousands though.'

'It's so unfair,' said Eliza.

The meeting was set for three. When they arrived, they were greeted by Digby Ward, the manager of the trustee department. If you had asked a casting director, Eliza thought, to find you someone to play the manager of the trustee department of a private bank, Digby Ward would have been your man, He was tall, white-haired, slightly over-gracious in his manner, wearing morning dress, and with a habit of rubbing his hands together repeatedly as he spoke.

'Mr Fullerton-Clark, Mrs Shaw, how delightful to see you here. Do follow me to the boardroom. May I offer you some refreshment? Tea, perhaps?'

'Tea would be nice. Is our mother here?'

'No, not yet. She has been delayed.'

'What! Oh, really. This is too bad. How much delayed?'

'Only about fifteen minutes. My assistant, Mr Fleming, has prepared some notes for the meeting. I will ask him to bring them in so that we can go through them before your mother joins us.'

They were shown into the boardroom, dark, book-lined, heavily furnished, with green-shaded brass lamps hanging over the table. In front of each place was a folder, with a picture of Summercourt on the front – 'this is going to be worse than I imagined,' Eliza thought – and 'Family Trust, entailing Summercourt, Wellesley, Wiltshire' written underneath it.

She started to flip through it. The first page outlined its history, its planning, construction, its lands and properties (and the sale of most of them) down to the rather stark details of the present day.

'Summercourt is presently occupied by the Hon. Mrs Sarah Fullerton-Clark, Mr Adrian Fullerton-Clark having died a few months previously. It is entailed to a discretionary trust, set up by Mrs Fullerton-Clark's father, Sir Charles Cunninghame.'

'I have the deeds here, if you would like to see them,' said Digby Ward, and 'Yes please,' said Eliza and Charles in unison. And the lovely things were produced, great pages of waxy parchment, with exquisite cursive writing in thick black ink, covered in great red seals, the complex language made further inexplicable by the script, but still certain words and phrases were familiar . . . 'Summercourt, situate in the parish of Wellesley in the county of Wiltshire . . . large house . . . freehold . . . two hundred acres . . . with pasture . . . stables . . . orangery . . . woodland . . . two tenant cottages . . .'

There was the trust document too, the Instrument, astonishingly still laboriously written out by hand in 1936, detailing the strictures of the trust, putting it into the ownership of the trustees, while forbidding them 'to raise security on the house by way of mortgage,' and Sarah's absolute Power of Appointment, 'lasting in accordance with the royal lives clause'.

'What does that mean?' said Charles.

'Ah,' said Digby Ward, 'it means that the period of the trust would end on the death of the last living descendant of the monarch of the time the trust was settled, plus a period of twenty-one years after that. King George V was on the throne when your grandfather entailed the property; as our dear Queen is still so young, you will appreciate there are many years for the trust still to hold.'

'Well – yes,' said Eliza. She was looking at the signatures on the document, 'Charles Cunninghame Bt', 'Sarah Fullerton-Clark', sundry witnesses from the bank, 'signed sealed and delivered'. It all seemed so archaic, so disconnected with the reality of today and its problems; and she thought of the passion that had engendered it, her grandfather's patent mistrust of her father, and wondered about the occasion of the signing, whether her mother had been willing or wretched, agreeable or anxious as she scrawled her rather schoolgirlish new signature, and whether she could have imagined for a moment what difficulties it could lead them all into.

'So, you haven't found a way we can actually sell the house?' said Charles. 'No way of going against these terms?'

'Sadly not. I thought you realised that.'

'I did. But I also thought we had come here to find a solution. To keep Summercourt from becoming derelict and ultimately a ruin. Which it undoubtedly will unless something can be done.'

Eliza winced; it was like hearing a beloved person diagnosed with a terminal illness.

'Of course. And it is extremely difficult to see what can be done. The house is too small to be opened to the public in order to raise money, in too much disrepair to let – and even that would be against the terms of the trust, of course, were the tenants not to be known to and approved of by your mother.'

'Well, all right,' said Charles, 'is there really no way we can at least raise a mortgage so that my mother can do some work on the house?'

'Sadly not. I confess to feeling a certain responsibility in that it is this firm who drew up the terms of the trust. Had I been a partner at the time, I would have pointed out the shortcomings.'

'There's nothing to be gained by going down that road,' said Charles, shortly. 'And – what you're saying really is that this is stalemate. We have nowhere to turn.'

'That would certainly have appeared to be the case,' said Digby Ward.

Eliza looked at him sharply. 'Would have?'

'Indeed.'

'So you have found a solution? Is that what you're telling us?'

'It's possible. As of today, as a matter of fact.'

'Well – what is it?' Her voice sounded suddenly silly and squeaky, even to herself.

'A – person has come forward. With the necessary funding available—'

'What sort of person?' said Charles. 'Acceptable within the terms of the trust?'

'The person could be made so. It's rather complicated.'

'I don't understand. Did my mother know about this, and if so why—'

'Not until today. Ah, Mrs Barton – is Mrs Fullerton-Clark here? Yes, excuse me, please, just for a moment. I must go and greet your mother.'

He went out, closing the door behind him.

'What on earth is going on?' said Eliza staring at Charles. 'Oh, God. I'm scared. Mummy could have warned us, she must have known something was up.'

The door opened again, and Digby Ward came in.

'Your mother won't be long,' he said. 'Now there is something that I must warn you about, before we go any further. I am asked to tell you that this solution could – I only say could – result in some things being done to the house that you might not find acceptable.'

'What sort of things?' Eliza spoke slowly; something was stirring in the very back of her mind, something unsuspected, something quite unthinkable.

'Well – there is talk of – er, modern windows being installed. And possibly even a – let me see.' He consulted his notes. A very discerning observer would have noticed his lips coming close to twitching. 'Sky-blue pink paint on the front door—'

'I suppose we don't have any right to—' began Charles.

'Oh. My. God,' said Eliza, and she was smiling now. 'The bastard! The bastard! Charles, you know who it is, don't you? It's Matt!'

Matt it was indeed; and he came in with Sarah, grinning, looking even slightly sheepish; and Sarah was flushed, half-laughing, while at the same time clearly embarrassed to be confronting her children with something so totally unexpected.

'The thing is, darlings, I knew nothing of this until yesterday afternoon. Matt called me and asked me if I could meet him here early today—'

'You bastard!' said Eliza. 'Straight after telling me to look at horrible mansions in Surrey.'

'If this hadn't worked,' said Matt, 'that would have been an alternative.'

'Not to me it wouldn't! It was mean and hateful and – and cruel and—'

'Eliza!' said Sarah. 'Matt has been the opposite of mean, I do assure you.'

And he had.

Sarah had agreed to appoint the house out to Eliza, thus terminating the trust. What had made this financially viable as a solution was that Matt had paid Sarah 'something called an inducement, it sounds a bit dodgy doesn't it, but it's a legal loophole, anyway, it's very, very generous' of twenty thousand pounds – Summercourt's market value given its appalling condition.

'This would enable your mother to buy herself a smaller, more suitable property,' said Digby Ward, 'and then Mr Shaw has also agreed to provide the wherewithal to do the house up, make the necessary repairs—'

'And install modern windows,' said Matt with a grin.

'That will of course be impossible, Summercourt being Grade 1 listed,' said Digby Ward. 'I do hope you will forgive that little joke, Mrs Shaw.'

'I forgive you,' said Eliza, 'not my husband.'

'My lawyers are drawing up a deed of gift of a half share right this minute,' said Matt. 'Now, something else I'd like to say: bit hard on you, Charles, all this, and I'm sorry. But – you've said often enough, you didn't want it, couldn't cope with the expense, and at least it'll be in the family.'

'No, no, that's true,' said Charles, 'and oddly, I don't see it as hard. I see it as a marvellous solution. If it was going to someone outside the family, I would mind very much, but as it is – well, I think it's fine. I really mean that,' he said, smiling gently at his mother. 'I'm not just being noble. I really do feel that.'

'Yes, but Charles dear, if – when you get married again, you might have a son,' said Sarah anxiously. 'You might feel rather differently.'

'Well, if I do, that will be my problem,' said Charles, 'and I shall try to deal with it graciously.'

'Charles, as far as I'm concerned,' said Eliza, 'Summercourt will still be home to you as well as me. And I'm sure Matt would say the same.'

'I would. Of course. And – Sarah – you don't have to move out. You can stay there, long as you like. We're hardly going to be living there full time. I'm sure I speak for Eliza as well, don't I, Eliza?'

Eliza nodded; she felt very emotional suddenly. She got up, went round the table and, careless of any embarrassment she might cause, put her arms round Matt and kissed him.

'I love you,' she said, 'and thank you. And you're not that mean and hateful. Not really.'

And so it was that on one particularly lovely August evening that year, the new owner of Summercourt – for that was how he regarded himself – drove down to view it, with his wife and daughter, there to meet his mother-in-law who had arranged a picnic supper in the orangery, always his favourite part of the house.

A bottle of champagne sat in an ice-bucket on the picnic table; Sarah asked Matt to open it and then went very pink.

'I have something to say Matt,' she said, raising her glass to him, 'and that is that I feel extremely fortunate at the turn of events, of course, but I also feel extremely ashamed of myself over my behaviour when Eliza first brought you to meet Adrian and me. You're the best son-in-law I could have wished for and I'm only sorry I couldn't see it then.'

She had obviously been rehearsing this little speech and when it was over she started to cry; Matt told her not to be so silly and that he wouldn't have thought much of himself as a prospect for his daughter. 'If

I'd come asking to marry Emmie, I wouldn't have given myself the time of day.'

'Well,' Sarah said, 'if there's anything I can do, to show my gratitude . . .'

Matt told her not to worry about it, but after supper when Emmie sat sleepily sucking her thumb demanding stories, he said yes, now here was a thing, if Sarah really wanted to show her gratitude, she could put Emmie to bed so that he and Eliza could be alone together for a while.

Sarah led Emmie off towards the house, and Matt turned to Eliza in the dusk of the conservatory evening and said, 'I love you Eliza,' adding that he couldn't recall them having had a row, whereupon Eliza said she couldn't either, and she loved him too, and maybe they could reverse the usual order of things . . .

'You mean – you want to – do it now?'

'I do. I want it more than more than.'

'What – here?'

'Here.'

'And then, since we're doing everything the wrong way round, do we have to have a row?'

'We can if you like,' said Eliza, 'but it's not compulsory.'

'Oh, God,' he said, and he reached out and took her hand, and kissed it and then pulled her towards him, the intense expression on his face that he only wore on such occasions, 'Oh, God,' and then, 'the floor's a bit hard. Won't you mind?'

'I might,' she said, 'but it'll be worth it. Don't you think?'

'I can't think,' he said, 'I can't think about anything. Get your knickers off, Eliza. Quick.'

It was not the most romantic of phrases, but then romantic phrases had always irritated her.

In the house, sitting by the open window of her bedroom, Sarah heard some wild, strange cries coming from the direction of the conservatory and hoped they hadn't shut some poor creature inside it, and resolved to send them back to check when they came in. But they were a long time, wandering the grounds, she supposed; and by the time she did hear them on the stairs she was too sleepy to care.

Chapter 34

There is no such thing as overnight success. Success takes years, sometimes decades, of planning, foresight and investment. It demands huge courage, a steady nerve, a hard head and massive reserves of determination. It allows no room whatsoever for self-doubt and it is also based to a degree on luck.

There is, however, once or perhaps twice in a lifetime a congruence of opportunity, good fortune, experience and skill that provides a sudden and increased impetus, thrusting players into a new and higher gear, and a kind of Midas touch moves into play.

This happened to Matt Shaw with the take-up of the first two office parks and the development of a third; he was making a great deal of money – although no one knew quite how much, not even Eliza. But he was dealing in large developments rather than single buildings, he was revered and admired, written about and photographed, his methods studied and analysed, his personal history trawled for clues. And he was the perfect subject, still a year shy of his thirtieth birthday, working-class and good-looking; even quite famously now, the owner of a beautiful country house. Journalists couldn't get enough of him.

It was an extraordinary time for those who worked with and for Matt, and even more extraordinary for his family. He was generous in giving credit where it was due, frequently praised Louise – and even the now-departed Jimbo, on occasions – and paid several quite fulsome tributes to Eliza, but the fact remained that the credit was for the most part his, and he knew it. Louise had pulled off more than one coup on her own, but she did it from the security of Matt's framework just as Jimbo had capitalised on and exploited opportunities that Matt had created.

Against all the odds, however, the effect of all this success was, initially at least, beneficial. The truculence created by his modest background combined with his searing conviction that it was an injustice that should be righted, eased considerably; he became less tense, and better-tempered; less dismissive and more tolerant; he listened more and shouted less.

'It's really funny, isn't it?' Jenny said one morning to Louise. 'Not being worried what sort of mood he's going to be in.' And then added that she quite missed it really and she wondered if it was going to change again.

Louise told her that she should make the most of it while it lasted.

Eliza felt the same. The break in hostilities between him and the rest of the world was, she felt sure, temporary. It was nice, but was not to be trusted; rather in the manner of one of those over-bright summer mornings that offer the first wispy clouds by breakfast, and lowering dark skies by lunchtime.

But so began – she realised, looking back – one of the happiest periods in her life. She was still restless, still lonely – for the kind of company she craved at least – still bored; but Matt's saving Summercourt had made her see how much he loved her. He had done it primarily for her, and she knew it. And consequently, knew that all his demands, all the personal sacrifices she had made, were actually worth it.

Nevertheless, he did love the idea of owning Summercourt, as well as the place itself. His owning it, he felt, was so pleasingly inappropriate. It was the sort of house that spoke of breeding, of sophistication, of taste; Matt would have been the first person to cheerfully disclaim any pretension to any of them. Just the same, he had the money to buy it and restore it, as its former owners, so well endowed with those qualities, could not, and that fact, that slap in the eye for the Establishment, made him very happy indeed.

It was costing him a small fortune, as he liked to say – with its implication that he could find several even larger ones should he so desire – and the expenditure of every pound of that fortune made him feel sleekly self-satisfied.

Matt was also very happy – when he thought about it. The least analytical of people, he was only aware of uncomfortable emotions: rage (frequent), stress (more frequent still), envy (now rare). When he was feeling none of those things, it could be presumed he was happy. He had the things he had always wanted: money, status – and Eliza. His love for Eliza surprised him at times: born that day on Waterloo station, it had never faded, never failed. From unapproachable creature, a world

353

removed from him, she had moved towards him through the years, and was now almost unbelievably at the centre of his life.

It was not a comfortable relationship still: he found her frequently enraging. There had been women over the years who, he could see, would have made him more comfortable, more at ease with life, less challenged. Eliza was disruptive, demanding, restless, and very critical. He had no opportunity of growing complacent so long as he was with her.

Sometimes when they quarrelled, and more seriously than usual, he would glance at least in the direction of life without her, and found himself faced by an abyss so vast, so terrifying, so ugly he would literally close his eyes and turn away.

She was what she was, with all her imperfections; and he could consider no other.

His honeymoon with the rest of his immediate world was, however, coming to an end and very fast. In a way that Eliza could very well have predicted.

For he called Louise into his office one morning and told her he had offered Barry Floyd Jimbo's partnership in the firm: without consulting her, looking in her direction, or considering that he might offer it to her. She found it hard to believe in the cruelty of it. In the sheer, blind, callous, careless cruelty.

She listened in silence as he told her. Then, as she had never ever done in all the years of provocation and injustice, knew she was going to break down.

And said that she wanted to be alone and shut the door; and put her head on her arms on the desk and cried and cried.

It was Jenny who first went in, who had listened to the sobs, in an agony of sympathy, her tender heart wrung, Jenny who had asked Matt what was wrong and if there was anything she could do, and was told to do what she liked; Jenny who put her arms round Louise, and told her to hush and fetched her some water and then sat down beside her and drew her head onto her soft, comforting bosom, which might have been created for exactly such a purpose, and waited there until the sobs subsided, and was told that she had been kind, very kind but Louise thought she would go home for the rest of the day.

What hurt Louise most was what she clearly was to him. In spite of everything, all the loyalty, the thought, the care, the hard, hard work, the near-inspirational ideas, she was still simply the sassy girl with good legs who had walked in the door and been hired as the company PA. There she was, preserved, a sexy dolly bird, for the rest of their time together; everything else that she had achieved had clearly been seen as some kind of happy accident made possible by Matt and Jimbo's generosity, and the opportunities they could offer her, and nothing to do with any talent that she might have brought to them. A considerably greater talent – and commitment – than Jimbo had shown, particularly latterly.

And – just as bad, worse possibly, was Barry, who had accepted the offer, shaken hands on the deal and not even thrown her a word of warning, or sympathy, or insisted that she should at least have been aware of it, before going off to meet some developers in Manchester for the day. That was a truly, truly dreadful example of Men, in all their arrogant, God given superiority, At Work.

At some point in the afternoon, Jenny called and said that Matt would like to speak to her.

'I said I'd try, Miss Mullan, ask you if you wanted to speak to him, but I told him I didn't think it was very likely.'

'You tell him you were right, Jenny. I don't want to speak to him.'

'Of course, Miss Mullan. Are you feeling a little bit better?'

'No, not really,' said Louise.

Later, much much later, the phone rang again and it was Barry. Louise told him to fuck off.

'And just before you do, may I say I always thought Matt Shaw was a bastard: I had a slightly higher opinion of you. How wrong I was.'

First thing next morning, a huge bunch of red roses arrived, with a card that read 'I love you, and I'm sorry. Barry'. Louise instructed the florist to send them to the offices in Wardour Street, scrawling over the words with a heavy 'Really?'

She stayed at home for another two days, gathering her strength; and then called them to say she was coming in to see them.

They said all the predictable things, that they really valued her input to the company but that it was a man's world, and there was no way she could do the job that Jimbo had and Barry would; that they would create a new role for her within the company, with a new title, like New Business Director, give her more money, give her a swanky new office.

'Well, that's extremely generous of you.'

She saw the two of them glance at one another, clearly thinking that she meant it, that they had done it, pacified her, won her over. Driven by a wave of anger, she stood up, walked over to the door.

'Let me tell you, you pair of bigoted, self-centred chauvinist idiots, I wouldn't go on working with either of you if you paid me a million pounds a year. This is the last time I shall set foot in this office. And don't think I won't play very dirty if you try and hold me to my contract or tell me to keep my hands off the clients. I can think of several who'd rather work with me than you. WireHire for a start.'

'I think you should be very careful about all this,' said Matt. 'Whatever you might say, there are legal restraints in place.'

'Oh, for God's sake,' said Louise, 'I suppose you think I'm not capable of realising that either. Anyway I'm having lunch with a guy from the *Mail* tomorrow. I think I can persuade him to write a really nice piece about me and what I've achieved, and your pathetic, antediluvian attitude and how I'm looking for a job. I'm going now. Barry, please don't bother trying to contact me. I'll decide when or rather if that happens, OK?'

'Oh, Christ,' said Matt, as she swept out. 'We'll have to think of something pretty damn smart. And – what does antediluvian mean?'

'Before the flood,' said Barry.

'Right. But I'll tell you something,' Matt added, 'I'm not going to be held to ransom over this, Barry, and I imagine you aren't either.'

Barry, who had spent most of his life avoiding conflict by the simple deployment of his charm, found himself in the interesting position of having to make a choice between Matt and his career and Louise and his personal life. Matt, slightly to Barry's own surprise, won.

Louise, having checked out her contract and removed her personal possessions from the office, had left without further discussion of any kind. They tried to tell themselves they didn't care.

'I think you're quite mad, both of you, and I think you'll be very sorry,' said Eliza, when Matt finally told her what had happened. She had a feeling he might not have done even then, had she not called the office one day, and found his phone answered by someone who sounded rather like Louise, but who informed her that no, Louise had left three weeks earlier.

'Rubbish,' said Matt. 'She wasn't up to a partnership, and that's all there is to it.'

'Really?' said Eliza. 'We shall see. I'd put money on us hearing quite a lot about Louise Mullan in the future. I shall miss her. I always enjoyed chatting to her. I presume it's all over between Barry and her?'

'I believe so, yes,' said Matt shortly. 'It was never going to work anyway. Not long-term.'

'Because he's married?'

'Well yes, but also because she was far too ambitious. Not wife material.'

'Oh, for God's sake,' said Eliza. 'Do come into the real world, Matt. Not that I'm in it either,' she added with a sigh. 'And it'll be another twenty years I suppose before I even qualify for entry, if you have anything to do with it.'

She rang Jenny to find out Louise's new number.

'I'm sorry, Jenny. Very sorry. To hear she's gone. Please give her my love and tell her if she likes to call me, I'll always be very happy to hear from her.'

'I will, Mrs Shaw. Thank you.'

'She's so nice,' Jenny said, reporting this conversation to Louise. 'What a time she must have with him, I feel quite sorry for her, even with all she's got, the money and that.'

'Jenny, so do I,' said Louise.

Two weeks later, having worked out her statutory notice, Jenny left also, and moved into the temporary office Louise had set up in her flat. Both Matt and Barry were at a complete loss without her.

Barry moved into Louise's old office, feeling a certain sense of discomfort; he missed her on both levels, but – at gunpoint – he would probably have said more in her professional capacity than her personal one. She had always been rather challenging as a girlfriend, but as a work colleague Louise had been inspirational. Bossy, demanding, sharp, confrontational – and inspirational.

Matt agreed they had lost a lot by her departure; while adding that there would be a lot less emotion and turmoil around without her and that their day-to-day professional life was certainly simpler. And that no one was irreplaceable.

Barry wasn't quite sure how much he meant it.

✷ ✷ ✷

The following spring, Eliza became pregnant again. Slightly anxiously, but very happily. Emmie's behaviour had slowly begun to improve and she felt – just – brave enough.

Matt was extremely pleased. 'This one will be a boy,' he said, 'I know it,' and when he had had a few drinks, would lie with his head on Eliza's stomach talking to the baby.

'You in there,' he would say, 'you listen to me. We're going to need each other, you and me, protect us from your mother and sister. Don't worry, I'll look after you, make sure they don't boss you around too much. You take care now, son. See you soon.'

It was very sweet really, Eliza thought. Sweet and, like so much to do with Matt, unexpected. His unpredictability was one of the things she most loved about him.

'I have some good gossip,' said Annunciata.

Eliza and she were having lunch; they did so quite often, now that Eliza had more time on her hands – 'Well, for a bit,' said Annunciata, on hearing about the pregnancy, 'you're mad, you know that? You keep saying how much you miss it all, and then you go and lock yourself away for another ten years or whatever. It's that husband of yours who locks you away, I appreciate that, but even so—'

'I know,' said Eliza, 'but I don't approve of only children. Anyway, tell me the gossip.'

'Jack Beckham's got the editorship of the *News*. Frank Fergusson's been threatening to retire for years, and he's finally done it.'

'He'll be a hard act to follow,' said Eliza. 'I love that paper. It's so clever, broadsheet wearing tabloid clothes. I bet Jack's over the moon.'

'He is. I had lunch with him the other day, and he told me. In between criticising *Charisma*, saying how it's gone downhill, and telling me I should get a proper job.'

'Is he going to offer you something?'

'Don't know. Hope so. I've had women's magazines really. And anyway, where could I go after *Charisma*. Carthorse after the Lord Mayor's Show, that would be.'

Eliza called Jack to congratulate him.

'Thanks. Want to join me?'

'Um – I'd love it but—'

'Don't tell me. You're having another baby.'

'Actually I am.'

'Silly cow,' said Beckham briefly, 'I could make you a star, Eliza.'

'Well, that would be lovely,' said Eliza after a rather long moment's pause while she envisaged what being a star in Fleet Street meant: your name in lights, your photograph on posters, a huge salary . . . 'but I can't. Maybe one day.'

'Maybe. If I can catch you in between confinements. You call me if anything changes, OK? How's that dinosaur of a husband of yours?'

'Pretty dinosaur-like,' said Eliza.

Mark Frost was sitting on Demetrios's and Larissa's veranda, dutifully sinking a bottle of the hated ouzo while admiring their son Stellios, who was toddling around eating stuffed vine leaves with great aplomb.

'And this time next year,' Demetrios said, 'we hope there will be a sister for him.'

'Good gracious,' said Mark, 'how very impressive. Now tell me, Demetrios, has Miss Scarlett been out here recently?'

Demetrios said she hadn't, but her club had worked very well for them, 'all such very, very lovely guests', and that they were hoping she would be out very soon.

'Now the other thing,' Mark said, 'is that I would like to bring my mother out here shortly, to see my house. I think she'll like it, but in case she doesn't it would be nice if she could stay here.'

'Mr Mark, I hope she will not like your house too much. You know how much we enjoy to have the famous Mrs Frost staying here in our hotel.'

Chapter 35

It seemed the happiest, the sweetest, the most hopeful of days. A hot day in early August and she'd been having a picnic in Richmond Park with Heather and Coral; she was only in London and not at Summercourt because she'd had an appointment at the hospital.

Everything was fine, they said, she was twenty-four weeks, the baby was developing absolutely according to the book; her blood pressure was a bit high, perhaps . . .

'You'd have high blood pressure,' Eliza said to the midwife, 'if you lived with my husband.'

'Oh, they all say that,' the midwife said, smiling. 'Just the same, be careful; take it a little bit easy.'

'I'll try.'

She couldn't ring Heather, because she only had the payphone in the hall, so she just went round on the off-chance. Heather greeted her at the door, looking pale and tired. She said a picnic sounded really nice.

'Good. I've bought the food already, I hoped you'd be able to come.'

'We got sick of the swings, didn't we, Coral? All the bigger children there, now it's school holidays, it's a bit rough for her. Everything all right at the hospital?'

'Yes, fine, thanks.'

'You're so lucky. I'd give anything for another, but Alan says not till he's got made up to works manager and we can look for a different place. Maybe with a garden. Trouble is,' said Heather, settling Coral in the back seat of Eliza's new car – a bright yellow Renault, and her pride and joy – 'it's made us nervous of doing anything, you know, case I do get pregnant. And then of course, that spoils everything, I can't relax and he realises and—'

'I think you should have another try with the pill,' said Eliza, 'they're much better now, lower dose of hormones, you might be OK.'

'I'll try,' said Heather.

It was a beautiful day, the sort that England occasionally does so well. The sky was cloudless, the sun hot, and there was a slight heat haze hovering above the bracken.

They found a small stream and helped the children dam it; ate their picnic, played hide and seek, and then lay down in the sun while Emmie taught Coral how to paddle, as she put it.

It was all very idyllic.

And then: 'Ouch,' said Eliza.

'What's the matter?'

'Tummy ache. Oh, that's better. Must have got in a funny position.'

'You sure?'

'Yes, honestly. It's fine now.'

'When are you going back to your mum's place?'

'Oh – tomorrow. I want to spend the rest of the summer there.'

'In the country? How lovely,' said Heather, without a shred of rancour in her voice, 'wish my mum lived there.'

'Yes, it's nice,' said Eliza. She would have given a great deal to invite Heather down to Summercourt, but she couldn't. It might spell the end of their friendship, an unbridgeable chasm. So stupid. So unbelievably stupid.

'Um – Eliza.'

'Yes?'

'Can I ask your advice about something? I'm in a bit of bother – money bother.'

'Oh. Like what?'

'Well – like a few weeks ago, I just ran out of money. I couldn't wait till Tuesday, you know, when I get my family allowance and I didn't dare ask Alan, because he's just put my housekeeping up, and he gets so cross when I can't manage—'

Eliza, who couldn't imagine how anyone could manage on Heather's housekeeping money, sat up and looked at her.

'And?'

'And well, the lady at the corner shop, she lets you get things on tick. If you've – you know, run out. So I had to do that, get a few things, just for Coral, some fruit, you know how she loves her fruit, and some cornflakes and—'

'Heather, it's all right; you don't have to justify what you spent to me.'

'No. Anyway, it was ten shillings before I knew it. Of course I paid it off the minute I got next week's housekeeping. Only that meant I only had four pounds ten left and it wasn't enough. So I had to borrow again from Mrs B. And it just – went on. And now I owe her a pound and it's happening every week, and I don't know what to do. It's just getting worse, and I can't sleep for worrying about it. So – do you think I should tell Alan, ask him if I can have a pound to pay her back?'

'No,' said Eliza briskly, 'I don't. He'll be cross with you and he shouldn't be and it's not fair. I'll give you a pound, Heather—'

'No, Eliza, you mustn't, that's not what I meant and I couldn't let you.'

'Yes, you could. Look—' Somehow it had to be said. 'Look, you must realise, Heather, we're not – not exactly hard up.'

Heather was silent.

'I could give you a pound and not notice it.'

'Could you really?' The hope in her voice was unmistakable; then she said, 'No, Eliza, honestly I couldn't. Don't, please, even offer it. I'd feel – feel so bad.'

'All right,' said Eliza, 'I'll just lend it to you. You can pay me back when Alan's got his new job. Please, Heather, it's so stupid not to. You lying awake and worrying about a pound that I'd probably waste on a new T-shirt for Emmie, when she's got—'

'Dozens,' said Heather and laughed.

'Not exactly. But lots. Now look, here you go, take it now.' Eliza took out her wallet, a present from Matt for Christmas and (carefully covering the Gucci logo with her hand) pulled out a pound note.

'Go on, Heather, it's yours until you can pay me back. I – oh God, there it goes again.'

'What?'

'My tummy. Feels like cramp.'

'We'd better get back,' said Heather, anxiously, 'just in case.'

For some reason, Eliza didn't argue with her.

She helped Heather up the steps as always, there were no carrycots these days, but Coral had her dolls' pushchair and two dolls and Heather had her big leather shopper which she'd filled, gratefully using Eliza's pound. The children were trailing behind, and as Heather reached the top of the steps of the house, Coral tripped and fell, grazing her knee, and started to scream for her mother.

'Oh, darling,' said Eliza, scooping her up and carrying her up the steps, handing her over to Heather, 'there you are, there's Mummy. Come on,

Heather, let me come up with you. Emmie, you stay there and look after the dolls.'

It all took a long time; as she turned to wave goodbye to them, the pain came again. Harder and a little longer. By the time it had happened the fourth time, just as she reached home, she realised, while not wanting to, that there was a pattern to it.

She called her GP; he told her to rest for an hour and then if it was still going on, to ring the ante-natal clinic. After an hour, and two more contractions, she rang; the clinic told her to time the pains and if they continued, to come in.

'Is baby moving around much?'

'Um – yes, think so,' said Eliza, feeling as she spoke the reassuring dance of the baby in her uterus. Surely nothing could be wrong if he was jumping about like that . . .

Another pain: she began to feel frightened, and rang Sandra, asked her if she would look after Emmie, and drove over to Clapham, very slowly and carefully, ignoring Emmie's fractious whining, asked Sandra to ring Matt and warn him and then drove in a growing panic to the hospital.

She walked into the ante-natal clinic, shaking, remembering and marvelling that only a few hours earlier she had run in, carefree and unafraid, offering breathless apologies for being late and simply looking forward to the rest of the now-darkening day.

They did all the usual things, so slowly and carefully she wanted to scream: checked her blood pressure, her pulse, her urine and put her to bed in a cubicle in the ante-natal ward.

The pain was getting worse; she said so, and they said they would bleep the registrar. She lay there, timing the pain, willing it away; it wouldn't go. The baby was still moving, but slowly and more feebly, as if it was frightened, as she was.

She stroked her stomach, talked to the baby. 'Stay there,' she kept saying, 'stay there, little one, stay safe, let me look after you. Wait a little while longer.'

By the time the registrar came she was crying.

Matt arrived white with fear and sat by her, holding her hand as they checked her, monitored her pain, and palpated her stomach.

'He's moving around all right,' said the registrar, 'doesn't seem too bothered by all this.'

But his eyes were just slightly evasive.

'That's fine,' said the midwife, listening intently to the small trumpet pressed to Eliza's stomach, 'good strong heart there. No need to worry about him.'

But her smile was just a little bit too bright.

By eight o'clock the contractions were coming every five minutes. The registrar came again, and said she should be moved to the labour ward.

'I'm sorry, Eliza, but that baby's coming, and we have to do the best we can.'

'Could it – could it be alive?'

He smiled, patted her hand.

'It's alive right now, that's all we know. But it's very, very tiny, the lungs are underdeveloped, it's a difficult situation. Right, off we go.'

It hurt, as much as delivering Emmie; she was surprised. They offered her gas and air, but she refused; she wanted to be totally aware of what was happening. They urged her to do her breathing as she groaned and sweated and struggled with the pain but she found it impossible, it was something that went with hope and courage and she felt neither. And she half welcomed the pain, feeling punished for whatever she should or should not have done to save the baby.

The small, perfect creature slithered out of her just before midnight; it was Matt, standing holding her hand, who told her what it was, the longed-for boy.

'He's beautiful,' he said, 'a beautiful baby.'

He was alive, the beautiful boy, wailing if not yelling, but still quite impressively; so far so good, the registrar said, smiling at Eliza. She was allowed to hold him for little more than ten seconds, and then he was gone, gone to lie within his other, substitute womb, an incubator in the premature unit. She didn't cry, just gripped Matt's hand, closed her eyes and did what all mothers do when their children are in danger, and whether they acknowledge it or not: she prayed.

She was to do a lot of that in the days to come.

They wheeled her into the maternity ward; a couple of mothers were feeding their babies and smiled at her.

'What did you have?' they said.

'A boy,' she said, too weary and overwhelmed to say more.

'Lovely,' said one of them. 'I don't care what people say, boys are just that bit more special.'

364

And hers was more than more than special; she closed her eyes against the rush of tears.

She lay awake all night. Towards dawn she managed to get up and stagger to the nurses' desk.

'Mrs Shaw,' said one of them, a probationer, 'you shouldn't be out of bed.'

'I want to know what's happened to my baby.'

'I'm sure he's fine,' she said.

'Really?' She stared at her.

'Yes. Why shouldn't he be?'

'Because he's twelve weeks early, that's why, I'd have thought you'd know something so basically important—'

Her voice sounded harsh even to her; the nurse flushed, looked at Eliza, embarrassed.

'I'm sorry. I didn't realise.'

'Well, perhaps you should check on your information before you give it out. Upsetting people—'

'Mrs Shaw,' said another nurse, 'let's get you back to bed. I'll check on your baby and let you know if there's any news.'

There wasn't any news, except that the baby was still alive.

'He's doing well,' said Staff Nurse, adding, lest Eliza might grow too hopeful, 'considering the circumstances.'

'Can I see him?'

'Of course. We'll take you down there later. And meanwhile, I'd like you to try to express some milk – colostrum anyway.'

'He's feeding!'

'Of course he is. You can't starve babies, Mrs Shaw, you should know that. Does them no good at all.'

The morning – a thunderous August version – suddenly seemed brighter, her heart lighter.

Matt arrived, silent and tense; she smiled at him.

'So far – so good. He's still all right. I've even had to try and express some milk for him.'

'Good,' he said, but he didn't seem reassured.

They wheeled her to the premature baby unit. She said she would walk, and tried to prove it but collapsed, nauseous and weak, halfway along the corridor.

Their baby was the smallest there; so tiny, so desperately tiny, with a head that looked too big for him, and scrawnily thin limbs. His skin

365

seemed transparent and almost shiny, the veins showing painfully through it. He wore only a nappy; there was a tube through his nose.

'Oh,' said Eliza, 'oh, that must be so uncomfortable for him, why does he have that?'

'He can't suck properly,' said the nurse in charge of him, 'and the tube leads down to his stomach.'

'I see. And – how – how is he?'

'He's doing well. Considering.' They all said that. 'He's breathing OK, at the moment, but his lungs are very underdeveloped. He may need help with that later.'

'Is he asleep?' she said, frightened by his stillness.

'Yes, he is now. But he has been awake, moving around.'

'Really?'

'Of course. He was moving before, in the womb, wasn't he?'

'Yes,' she said, remembering those strong, thrusting wriggles, and felt like crying. He had been so safe then: she had thought.

'So – what might happen next?' asked Matt.

'We just wait. The next forty-eight hours are pretty crucial. But every day is a bonus. So far his liver function is good, that's very important, he's showing no signs of jaundice and—'

'Look,' said Matt, 'look, he's waking up.'

The baby moved restlessly, turned his head, slowly opened his eyes. Milky-blue unseeing eyes

'Oh,' said Eliza, 'look, Matt, he's looking at us. Oh, baby, I want to hold you so much.'

'I'm afraid that's impossible,' said the nurse, 'he has to stay there for a long time yet.'

'I do understand. Can I – can I touch him in there?'

'Of course. Look, there are some holes in the side of the incubator, bit like portholes. That's how we feed and change him. Put your hand in there – that's right.'

She put her hand in very gently; it looked vast next to her baby, half as big as he was. She stroked his skin, his smooth vein-y skin; it was wonderfully warm. She moved her hand near his, tried to lift it, then pulled back.

'I'm afraid to disturb him.'

'No, it's all right. Put your finger under his hand, that's right. Don't be frightened.'

'Oh,' said Eliza, as the minute hand rested on her finger, 'oh, my God.'

God was much in her head over the next twenty-four hours; she prayed relentlessly and silently, sitting by the baby for hours at a time, willing her strength into his. Matt grew restless and miserable; she understood and sent him away.

'I don't mind, honestly. Go and get some rest or do some work, you'll be better. There's nothing you can do here. Come back this evening. I'll be fine.'

'If you're sure.'

'Of course I'm sure.'

'Have they said anything about why—' he said.

'No, nothing. I keep asking them, they say it's just one of those things.'

'So – nothing you – we – could have done?'

'They said not.'

He nodded, bent to kiss her. 'I'll be back later.'

She watched him going down the corridor away from her, guiltily relieved. He looked older suddenly, old and exhausted and somehow collapsed in on himself, the cocky striding creature that was Matt quite gone.

'Does he have a name?' the nurse asked.

'No. I suppose he should have.'

'It would be nicer for you.'

'Of course.'

'Can we call him Charles?' she said when Matt came back that night.

'Yes. Of course. Whatever you want.'

He obviously thought it was unnecessary, a bit of foolish optimism; she felt angry suddenly.

'Matt, you've got to stay positive. He's going to pull through, I know he is. And he has to have a name.'

'Fine. Call him Charles, then.'

'Right, Mrs Shaw. Time to express some more milk. I've got the pump.'

'I'm so pleased he needs it.'

'He certainly does. He's a lively little thing.'

'Is he? Is he really?'

Staff Nurse smiled her cautious smile.

'Yes. He is. But he's got a long way to go.'

'Of course. I understand.'

Baby Charles, as they called him in the unit, survived his second night; Eliza watched him through much of it. She was supposed to be in bed, but she crept out of the ward which she couldn't bear anyway, full as it was of enormous crying healthy babies, and smiling, smug mothers, complaining cheerfully about the pain of their stitches and their engorged breasts, and made her way to the premature unit. Baby Charles was sleeping when she got there: very still.

'Don't worry,' said the nurse, seeing her face, 'he's been awake, he's had some milk.'

They understood every fear that went through her; she felt very close to them, absolutely a part of their team.

They let her stay however long she wanted.

She looked around the other babies in the unit: all bigger than hers, all doing well, it seemed. The largest, a pair of twins, together in their incubator, weighed four pounds each.

'They'll be leaving us tomorrow, going up to the ward,' said the nurse.

Baby Charles weighed just under two pounds. It seemed impossible that he would ever be as big as they.

He woke, she put her hand in the incubator and stroked him, lifted his hand with her finger, persuaded herself he had responded.

'I love you,' she said, over and over again to him, 'I love you so much.'

She wanted him to know that, whatever happened.

On the third morning, she woke to find her breasts filled with milk, leaking onto her nightdress. She felt pleased, illogically hopeful, that it was a good sign.

Sandra came in to see her, bringing Emmie. 'She's missing you, Eliza, I thought it was best.'

'Of course. Hello, darling.'

Emmie hugged her, hurting her tender breasts. 'Where's the baby?'

'He's in a special place, where they're looking after him until he's bigger.'

'Can I see him?'

'No, I'm sorry, you can't.'

'But I want to.'

'Darling, no.'

'I want to see him.' Her clear little voice rang through the ward; Eliza could see the other mothers staring at her, exchanging pointed glances that said 'spoilt brat'.

'Emmie, darling, in a few days you can see him.'

'I want to see him now.' Her eyes brimmed with tears. 'He's my baby brother, why can't I? I won't hurt him, I'll be very careful.'

Eliza felt her own tears rising. 'I know you will darling. But—'

'Emmie, no,' said Sandra gently. 'The baby's not well enough for you to see him.

Emmie was silent, but clearly upset; Eliza didn't have the strength to comfort her.

'I think it might be best if you went,' she said apologetically.

'Of course. Say goodbye to Mummy, Emmie.'

'Bye, Mummy.' She gave her another kiss; then, 'Why did the baby come out too early?'

'I – don't know,' said Eliza, 'nobody does.'

'Did you do something? To make it come out?'

'I don't think so,' said Eliza, trying to sound brave, but the stinging tears filled her eyes again.

'So why?'

'Emmie, darling, nobody knows.' She reached for a tissue.

'Emmie,' said Sandra, 'you're not helping Mummy. Why don't we go to the swings?'

'OK.' She skipped out, without looking back.

'Thank you for looking after her,' said Eliza, 'thank you, Sandra, so much.'

'It's all right, my love. She's no trouble, really. You take care now. Try to rest. Baby'll be all right, I'm sure of it.'

'I – hope so.'

She looked after them, Sandra leading Emmie by the hand. She managed her awfully well, Eliza thought. Better than she did. She was a lousy mother altogether, it seemed; couldn't handle the child she'd got, couldn't maintain the one in her womb . . . She pulled the curtains round her bed, and started to sob.

When Matt came back, they sat watching Baby Charles for a long time. She told Matt to do what she did, touch him, lift his tiny hand; he shook his head.

'I might hurt him. He's so tiny.'

'You won't hurt him, Mr Shaw,' said one of the nurses, 'go on, touch him, it's good for him.'

He looked at her, then grasped Eliza's hand and very slowly and

369

cautiously put the other one into the incubator, stroked the baby's head; she watched it, the large, male hand, incongruously strong, reaching out to his son. And realised that Matt's eyes too had filled with tears. He saw her looking at him and half-smiled, embarrassed.

'Sorry.'

'Matt, it's OK. You can cry.'

'I – I – oh, God,' he said, staring into the incubator. 'Oh, God, he's so helpless.'

In the morning, her breasts aching with their load of milk, she made her way down to the unit; the nurse looked at her warily, clearly feeling awkward.

'Hello, Mrs Shaw.'

'How is he?'

'He's – not quite so well.'

She felt sick.

'What's wrong?'

'I think you should talk to the doctor. He's developed a slight liver infection.'

'Oh, God. Well, where is he, where's the doctor?'

'He's on his rounds, he'll be back soon.'

'But I want to see him now.' She heard her voice rising. 'Please get him.'

'I'm afraid I can't do that. He won't be long. Please try to be calm.'

'Calm! You tell me my baby has a liver infection and the doctor won't talk to me and then you tell me to be calm—'

'The doctor will talk to you when he gets back. Which won't be long. Now excuse me a moment please, I have babies to feed.'

'Sorry,' said Eliza, suddenly shocked at herself, 'I'm so sorry. I—'

'That's all right.'

She sat down by Baby Charles, her heart pounding, an odd echoing roar in her ears. He looked the same. Well – maybe he didn't. He was very restless; his movements were different, somehow quicker, almost twitchy, and smaller.

'Don't,' she whispered, 'don't get sick, don't, stay well, stay strong, please, little one, stay well.'

Her helplessness was almost the worst thing.

The doctor was very honest.

'I'm afraid his liver function isn't so good. It happens with these babies.'

'And – so?'

'Well, he could get jaundiced, and of course it increases the danger of a haemorrhage.'

'A haemorrhage?'

'Yes. Into the brain.'

'Oh, no,' said Eliza, 'oh, no, please no.'

'I'm sorry. But it hasn't happened yet. It may not. It's just important for you to know that it might.'

'Yes, of course.'

'But how do they know?' said Matt. She had rung him at the office, and he had arrived within twenty minutes.

'Oh – just blood tests, I think.'

'Could they be wrong? Should we get someone else to see him?'

'No,' said Eliza, 'no, of course not. These are the very best people to be looking after him.'

'How do you know that? I think we should get another opinion, just to be sure.'

'Matt,' said Eliza gently, 'this isn't helping. Please stop it, please.'

He argued for a while, and she knew why, it was because he felt it was something he could do: rather than just watch and wait. He even asked the doctor – quite politely – if he was sure, if there might be some mistake, some treatment the baby could be given. And the doctor, charmingly and patiently courteous, said that there was no mistake, that there was no treatment.

They resumed their vigil, watching Baby Charles and his helpless, feeble movements.

He died twelve hours later. It was a haemorrhage into his brain, they said, a very big one, he couldn't have survived it. And nor would they have wanted him to, they were told, he would have been helpless, a baby for ever.

'I would though,' said Eliza, tears streaming down her face, 'I would have looked after him, I would have loved to, don't say we wouldn't have wanted it.'

They let them hold him, once they knew it was hopeless. The nurse wrapped him tenderly, so tenderly, in a shawl and handed him to Eliza; she sat staring down at his tiny face, peaceful now, feeling his warmth, feeling him alive. She lifted him, kissed his head, stroked his cheeks, took the tiny frond-like hand that she had held so often now, and kissed that too.

'It can't be true,' she said to Matt, 'he can't be dying, he feels – feels like a baby, an all-right baby.'

He said nothing, staring at the baby in silent shock.

'Take him, hold him.'

'No. No, I can't.'

'Matt, you must. It's important.'

'I'm so afraid of hurting him.'

'You won't. You really won't.'

He took it, the tiny creature in his blue blanket – how sweet, Eliza thought, that they had even found that for him, the right-coloured blanket – and sat cradling it. A tear splashed down on the peaceful little face, and then another: Matt's tears. 'Sorry, son,' he said and wiped them tenderly away. Eliza slid her hand into his and rested her head on his shoulder, gazing at the baby. Time passed, but they had no idea how much of it. They only wanted to be with their baby, sharing what was left of his life.

He left them with a small turn of his head towards Eliza, who was holding him once more, and a soft, long sigh; and then they realised with something that was shock in spite of everything, that all his movements had stopped, and the faint strength they had still felt in him, was over.

The staff were wonderfully kind and gentle, said they could stay and be with him for as long as they liked; for a while it seemed the right thing to do, but then slowly it felt wrong. Matt went to find a nurse and she came back, stood very still for a while, and then said softly, 'Shall I take him now?'

'No,' said Eliza, suddenly fierce, holding the baby closer to her, 'no, don't take him, not yet.'

'I won't.'

The nurse went again, and the scene was repeated twice before they could bear it; before slowly, falteringly, Eliza felt able to pass the baby over. It was a dreadful moment, when finally he left her arms; when she stood staring at him, his tiny face dully still now, quite different – and she realised how truly alive he had been, a real baby, her baby, their baby, taken from them so cruelly and so wrongly: a piece of true and awful injustice that anything so perfect, so ready for life, could actually be dead.

'Stop,' Eliza said, as the nurse turned away with the baby, 'wait—' and then, as she turned back, 'let me say goodbye just once more.'

She did not take him, then, but bent over him, kissed his head for one last time and then he was gone, gone from the room, gone from their lives and from his, taking all that he had promised with him.

They held a funeral for him in Wellesley village church. It seemed important, made him important, a real person who had lived, however briefly.

They laid him in a small white coffin, with a spray of white roses on it, and put inside it a letter Eliza had written to him, telling him how much she loved him and how she would never forget him or his short, important life.

Matt, white-faced but dry-eyed, carried the coffin alone into the church, Eliza walking beside him, and they stood holding hands, through the short, painfully sweet service. There was only the family there, Scarlett, fighting back tears, Sandra and Pete, Sarah, and Charles who said he was so proud that the baby had been given his name. It was felt to be too much for Emmie to cope with; she was left with one of Eliza's friends.

They sang no hymns, but the organist played very beautifully and at the end, Eliza read the lovely Gaelic blessing, that felt so appropriate:

'May the road rise gently at your feet.
May the sun shine warmly on your face.
May the wind be always on your back.
May the rain fall softly on your fields.
And until we meet again
May God hold you in the palm of his hand.'

How she got through it she never afterwards knew and she broke down once, but for the rest of the time her voice remained strong and steady and as Matt picked up the coffin again at the end of the service, she bent her head over it and kissed it and even smiled as she said, 'Goodbye, little one.'

And then she could be brave no longer and ran ahead of Matt out of the church through the graveyard, and was found by Charles, leaning on a tree, literally gasping with pain, and looking with huge trepidation at the thought of the rest of her life.

Chapter 36

It wasn't what she wanted. In fact it was pretty well the opposite. But having done ten presentations in ten virtually identical boardrooms to ten groups of stony-faced and/or patronising board members, she felt she had no choice. At least he knew her, knew her track record, and had some respect for her abilities. Just the same it was potentially pretty humiliating.

She called him in his office and invited him to lunch. After a lot of predictable innuendo, about how she must be very busy shopping these days, he said he was free the following Monday, 'but it'll have to be fairly quick, very busy at the moment and where did you have in mind?' The slightly stunned pause – albeit brief – when she said briskly 'the Savoy Grill', was worth enduring every one of the innuendoes.

'You girls really do get everywhere these days, don't you?' he said finally.

'And further every day. Twelve forty-five all right? I'd say one, but I've got a three o'clock myself.'

Round one to you, Louise, she said to herself, putting the phone down.

She was waiting for him when he got there. Because she ate there on a regular basis with her journalist friend Johnny Barrett and he gave it lots of good publicity, the maître d' knew and liked her and had agreed to give her one of the best tables. She had attracted a lot of attention as she walked across the room; she was wearing a black trouser suit, a white ruffled shirt and very high heels; the four men at the next table were patently intrigued by her and who her companion might be. Probably expecting some kind of sugar daddy, she supposed.

She whiled away the ten minutes Roderick made her wait studying the city pages of the *Evening Standard*, and managed to appear so engrossed that the waiter who had brought him over gave a small cough and said, 'Your guest has arrived, Miss Mullan.'

'Oh,' she said, standing up, 'sorry, Roderick, just keeping up with the markets, you know.' She offered him her cheek. 'How are you?'

'Fine thanks,' he said. And then, eyeing her up and down, 'You look very nice.'

'Thank you. Your usual?' and then as he nodded, 'Gin and tonic,' she said to the hovering waiter, 'large. And a Virgin Mary for me, please.'

'What the hell's a Virgin Mary?' he asked, sitting down.

'I'm surprised you don't know. I discovered it in New York.' She had never actually been to New York but he couldn't possibly know that. 'It's tomato juice without the vodka. Keeps the head clear. Now let's order straight away shall we, and then we can concentrate.'

He ordered pâté and then 'beef from the trolley', she asked for a tomato salad and a steak au poivre. 'Rare. And then, Roderick, you can order the wine if you like, but the 1952 Château Cheval Blanc, it's a St Émilion' (she'd got this from Johnny Barrett) 'is amazing.'

'Right,' he said, a certain respect in his eyes she hadn't really seen before, 'but I'll take a look for myself if you don't mind.' He started thumbing through the leather-bound encyclopaedia the Grill presented as its wine list, and said, 'So what are you doing with yourself these days? Must be odd to be unemployed. Or are you enjoying it?'

'I wouldn't be,' she said briskly, 'if I was. But I'm not.'

'Oh, really? You and Matt kissed and made up, have you? I thought you would, sooner or later.'

'Matt and I have not made up, as you put it,' said Louise, 'and are most unlikely to do so ever again. There are however other ways of working in our business than as an undervalued partner.'

'Of course. So – are you looking for a job, Louise, is that it?'

There was an expression in his eyes she couldn't quite analyse; but it wasn't hostile or dismissive. That had to be something.

'No,' she said, 'no, I'm not. Oh, look, here's the sommelier back. What are you going to order?'

'Well – let's see.' He flicked over a couple of pages then said, 'Tell me, would you recommend the Cheval Blanc '52?'

'An excellent choice, sir, if I may say so.'

'Right. Well, in that case, let's have it. I presume it's *chambré*, all that sort of thing?'

'Of course, sir. I do assure you you'll enjoy it very much. But no doubt you're familiar with it? It's a favourite with many of our more, shall we say, discerning clientele.'

God, thought Louise, I'll throw up in a minute.

'Right, we'll go for that then.'

The sommelier gave a small bow, took the list. 'I'll have it brought to the table, sir.'

'Thank you.' The first course had arrived; Roderick gave Louise a very slightly shamefaced grin. She met his eyes rather coolly.

'I'm glad we've made a good choice of wine,' was all she said, and then: 'So have you seen Matt? Since – the – well, since the baby died.'

'I have, yes,' he said, and added, surprising her, 'Poor bugger. Awful thing to happen. He was very cut up about it.'

'I see Scarlett from time to time, his sister, you know, she's a friend of mine. She says Eliza has been in a really bad way, not sleeping. Spending a lot of time in the country with her mother. Well, at weekends anyway.'

'Ah, at Matt's famous pile.'

'I don't think it's exactly Matt's,' said Louise, 'it's part of Eliza's family trust. As I understand it.'

'Yeah, yeah, but we all know it was Matt's money saved it, OK? And what Matt pays for, Matt's bought.'

'I suppose so. Oh, now look, here's the trolley so let's just – oh, and the wine.'

There was a lot of fussing, of choosing meat near the bone, of sniffing and tasting; finally, Louise said, 'Right. Let's get down to business. I know you haven't got long and neither have I.'

'I thought you didn't want a job,' said Roderick slowly.

'I don't want a job. I want some backing for a project.'

'You want backing! From me? I suppose you think I'm some kind of a soft touch. Louise, you should get into the real world, girl. Go and talk to an investment bank, they're the ones with the money.'

'I did. They all turned me down.'

'Yeah? They obviously thought it wasn't a good enough proposition.'

'No, they thought I was a woman.'

'Uh-huh. Well, fair enough. You can't argue with that.'

'I know. But I thought they'd have the nous to see beyond it.'

'Clearly not.'

There was a silence; then Louise said, 'Don't you even want to know what my project is?'

'Well – OK. Don't want to appear rude. Seeing as the lunch is on you. On you go then . . . But I'm telling you, Louise, I don't have any money available for investment. Everything I've got goes straight back into the company.'

'OK. You've made that pretty clear. Anyway – it's hotels.'

'Hotels!'

'Yes. The industry is absolutely booming, growing by the day. London's full of tourists. Has been ever since the Swinging London thing. And there aren't enough hotels. It's simple. The American market alone is massive, I was talking to Scarlett about it the other day, they flock here in thousands. Her clientele is the boutique end, but she sees the frustration of people trying to find places to stay. And how far out they have to go to find anywhere. All income levels too, I've got some figures if you're interested . . .'

She reached for her briefcase and the folder she'd prepared for him, a full set of statistics, the number of hotels in London, the number of tourists visiting annually, the consequent potential, expressed in investment terms, and a list of possible sites. She put it on the table; he didn't pick it up, but he was silent. That was good. She had his interest. She could tell.

'The thing is we need to act fast. There's such pressure on sites. It's going to get more difficult, with these bloody conservationists getting a hold. I mean Covent Garden, what a fantastic place for a hotel that would be. But I heard all those trendies who live and work around there, actors and artists and so on, are preparing a campaign to save it – God knows what for. Something pretty useless, I expect. And of course the thing about hotels is you can build up and up. It's a big plus; you're offering people views over the city. Look at the Hilton in Park Lane. Something like four hundred and fifty rooms, twenty-eight storeys. How's that for plot ratio? So pressure on space is less of a problem.'

'You know the Queen opposed that place, don't you?' said Roderick, grinning. 'It overlooked her back garden. She didn't like it one bit. Well, I'm not saying it's not a good idea, Louise; to be honest I'm impressed.'

'Look at the figures, Roderick. Go on.'

'I told you, I don't have that sort of money, I mean what are you looking for, hundred K or are we into really fancy money?'

'I reckon we could make a start with a million. It'd have to be that, because of the site cost. It'd have to be central.'

'A million! Louise, you're insane. I'd have trouble laying my hands on fifty grand right this minute.'

'Roderick, I'm not asking you to put up the money. Just to front the venture, with me as your partner. I told you, the bankers only turned me down because I'm a woman. One of them more or less said so. There's so much money out there still, it's growing on trees. We could get the capital I need tomorrow, with your record.'

He was silent for a moment, then he said, 'No. Honestly. I got enough on my plate, and I don't know anything about the hotel business, it'd be crazy.'

'No one's asking you to get into the hotel business; all we're doing is providing the buildings. Then we sell them. Or build them under licence.'

Another silence. Then, 'No, it's just too risky. Sorry.' He looked at his watch. 'Now we've only got fifteen minutes left, so why don't we talk about something else. Like where we're going on our holidays. We're off to Florida in a couple of weeks, fantastic place apparently . . .'

OK. Time for the trump card.

'Well – OK. If that's your final word.'

'It is. Absolutely final.'

'You do know, I presume, that the government doesn't agree with you.'

'What are you talking about now?'

'They're giving a tax incentive, or it might be a grant, my accountant told me this morning, to assist in the development of hotels just because of exactly what I'm talking about, the shortage. It's going to be in the press tomorrow, apparently. Oh, well. I'll just have to find someone else. Pity. But I will. I'm not giving up.'

Roderick put down his wine glass, and waved at a passing waiter.

'Can I see the cigar list?' he said, and then turned back to Louise, picked up the file and started leafing through it. 'What sort of structure were you thinking of with this company, then?'

When Louise got home, she called Johnny Barrett.

'I'm going to have a really nice little story for you in a day or two,' she said. 'Thanks for the tip about the wine. And you will run the piece about the hotel grant, won't you?'

'Do I get lunch at the Savoy and a bottle of the St Émilion?'

'No. Two bottles.'

'OK. I'll see what I can do.'

'Johnny—'

'It's all right, honeybunch. It's already in proof, I'm looking at it now. And a little bird told me the *Sketch* was doing it too.'

'Oh, my God. Johnny, I love you.'

Eliza really didn't know what the worst thing was. Sometimes it was reliving Baby Charles's birth. Or his death. Or the funeral. Or the ongoing, savage guilt. Or people not knowing what to say, stumbling around the subject. Or people not mentioning it, being bright and cheerful as if nothing had really happened. Or telling her how wonderful it was that she had one healthy child at least, that was one of the particularly worst things, as if the baby had been a new dress or a car or something, that she could perfectly well manage without as she had one already. Or being tired absolutely all the time, deep, deep, bone-weary-tired. Or not wanting to do anything, not go out, or stay in, or see people or not see people, work or not work.

Being told that something would cheer her up, make her feel better, was particularly worst. Because she didn't want to feel better ever; if she felt better, she would be betraying Baby Charles, he would really be gone, it would really be over. While she was so unhappy, while everything hurt so much, he was still real.

Matt found her behaviour and her constant weeping very trying, she could see. He had been as heartbroken as she when Baby Charles died and for the first few weeks afterwards. But he was busy and he was preoccupied with problems at work, and he took refuge in them, as Eliza couldn't, and she watched him through a haze of resentment as he visibly began to recover and resume something approaching normal life. He tried extremely hard to be patient, she could see that, and to cope with her grieving, but misread her reactions to his suggestions that they should go out, go to a film, go on holiday even, as rejection; as for sex, there just wasn't any. It had been such a panacea in their lives always, such a happy ending to so many rows; but she shrank from even the gentlest approach, feeling a kind of physical outrage that he could intrude into not only her sorrow, looking for some kind of happiness with her, but her body, her poor, failed, exhausted body.

She took to going down to Summercourt at the weekends with Emmie, leaving London on Friday night, and coming back late on Sunday afternoon; he joined her at first, but then, finding the same bleakness in her there as in London, he started to drive down later and later on

379

Saturday, or even Sunday morning, and for the past two weeks had not been at all.

Sarah tried to help with advice, sympathy, and practical action, offering her services as babysitter if Eliza wanted to go out with Matt, or spend a weekend with him in London, but she met only with blank rejection and a declaration that she didn't understand.

Finally, after Eliza was particularly snappy with her one afternoon, she said, 'Darling, I'm sorry to tell you this, and I do feel desperately sorry for you, and I can see your grief is frightful, but you can't go on behaving in this way. You're damaging your marriage, Matt is genuinely trying so hard to understand and help—'

'That's really extremely nice of him,' said Eliza, 'I mean, he is actually my husband, it was his baby too who died, and now everyone seems to think I'm selfish, because I'm so miserable and ought to be making more of an effort for him. How he can still even think about his bloody deals and where he's building what I don't know.'

'Eliza,' said Sarah patiently, 'Matt is a man. Of course he's sad and extremely so, but he can't possibly feel the loss as intensely as you do. He didn't carry the child, or bear it, he wasn't physically affected by it. And I think he's trying very hard to be supportive. You're just not trying to meet him even halfway. And he does also have an obliga-tion to continue to make a living for you all. For us all,' she corrected herself.

'Oh, for God's sake,' said Eliza, 'save me all that old-fashioned claptrap. Honestly, Mummy, Matt can do no wrong these days, can he, ever since he saved Summercourt. I never thought to hear you defending Matt against me.'

Sarah said no more, just walked out of the room; Eliza glared after her, and refused to eat the supper she had cooked, saying she'd have a sandwich upstairs.

Sarah went to church next morning and prayed for patience.

Eliza went through the weeks in a daze, taking Emmie to her new school, going home again, lying down on her bed and crying until she could cry no more. There was a great deal that had to be done in the new house, they had moved only a few weeks before Baby Charles had been born, but she had no heart for it; rooms remained unpainted, curtains unmade, and books and pictures sat on the floor, stacked against the walls, as even commissioning shelves and replacing ripped-down picture rails seemed completely beyond her.

Quite often she didn't have to pick Emmie up from school because she was constantly being invited out to tea, which was a help in a way because she didn't have to look after her or amuse her, and no one seemed to expect her to ask their children back, but it made her days longer and lonelier still.

Emmie loved school, she was happy and popular; which was just as well, Eliza reflected, as she wouldn't be having much fun otherwise.

She found it hard to be affectionate with her, and worse, she was horribly, physically bad-tempered, pushing her away if she interrupted her from trying to read or write letters, and even slapping her at times. They had standoffs, as Emmie told her she was horrible and she hated her and she would tell her she was a naughty, nasty little girl and it was time she learnt to do what she was told.

And then she did the really awful thing and realised that she actually did need to get some help from somewhere, somehow.

Matt would have died rather than admit it, but he missed Louise a lot. At a time when he was in any case depressed not only by the death of his son, but the loss, temporarily at any rate, of any happiness in his marriage, he felt his whole life under assault. Barry was great, he was fun, he was a very hard-working and generous partner; but he was pretty two-dimensional. Also he didn't have many ideas, and he didn't do the kind of quirky sideways thinking that had always been Louise's strength. A lot of her ideas had been impractical, and over-ambitious, but they had kept on coming; her brain was tirelessly fertile.

He had been shocked when he heard she was going into business with Roderick Brownlow, partly because she had always been so hostile to his particular brand of sexual chauvinism, and partly because he felt she was too clever for him.

And why the hell couldn't she have mentioned her hotels to him? They had reputedly acquired their first site, with planning permission, on the southerly edge of Regent's Park; he heard that even before it hit the press from Scarlett, who seemed to be seeing a great deal of Louise.

'She's a wonder, that girl, all that electric energy,' Scarlett said, 'she's going to make a killing with that company.'

'Yes, all right, all right,' said Matt. 'She couldn't have done it without all the contacts she made here over the years.'

'Of course not. I realise that. And I'm not taking sides, either. But you must miss her.'

It was true, and he missed Jenny dreadfully as well; he had already hired and fired three receptionists in the space of six weeks. Jenny's dazzling prettiness, her gentle manners, her immense desire to please, even the simplicity of her thought processes, had done a lot for the atmosphere in the outer office. He could hardly bear to walk down the biscuit aisle at the supermarket. That bugger Brownlow had better be treating her well.

He felt guilty to be able to think about work at all; but had his eye on a new prize, a very fine row of houses in Clapham, just off the common. Owning Summercourt had increased his appreciation of architecture, but this was too big a plot to waste on aesthetic considerations. He could replace them with a huge block of flats; and the nutters, as Barry called the conservationists, hadn't yet reached far out of central London. It would make him a new fortune; he had lost none of his fervent ambition, and it certainly helped to take his mind off what was happening at home.

'Mummy's horrid to me,' said Emmie, 'she doesn't like me any more.'

'Oh, darling!'

Sarah looked at her; she was beginning to recognise Emmie's manipulative talents, but the small face was genuinely sad.

'Darling,' she said, 'of course Mummy likes you. She loves you very much.'

'Well, why is she always cross, always shouting at me?'

'Emmie – Mummy is very unhappy at the moment. You know the baby died, the one that was in her tummy, and that has made her so sad that she can't think about anything else. She can't sleep, so she's always tired, and that's making her a bit – a bit bad-tempered.'

'It's not a bit,' said Emmie, 'it's very and always and all the time. Anyway, I haven't died, she shouldn't be that sad.'

'I know, darling. And she does still love you.'

'She's always smacking me too,' said Emmie.

'Oh, I'm sure that's not true, Emmie. Perhaps just when you've been a bit naughty.'

'No, it's all the time, even when I'm good. Don't you believe me?'

'Well—' Now what did she say?

'You just notice. You just listen and watch. You'll see.'

'Yes, all right, darling. I'll notice. But I'm sure you're wrong.'

'I'm not wrong. I'm not, not, not wrong.'

'I'll notice, Emmie, promise. Now what about some nice eggy bread?'

It was an icy, sparkly October Saturday. Eliza had arrived with Emmie the evening before, pale, touchy, but bearing a peace offering for her last outburst, a huge bunch of white chrysanthemums.

'Thank, you darling,' was all Sarah had said. 'Er – no Matt?'

'No, he's gone to some stupid conference in Manchester. He never used to go to conferences. It's so he can get away from me.'

'Darling, I'm sure that's not true.'

'Mummy, it's true. And I don't blame him, I'm so bloody miserable all the time, I must be awful to live with.'

Sarah gave her a hug and didn't pursue the subject, but over supper, she said very tentatively, 'Darling, I wonder if you've considered having some help.'

'What sort of help? Do you mean see some shrink or something? No, of course I haven't. I'm not mad, Mummy, I'm just very unhappy and with very good reason. That's for people who have some kind of problem.'

'Well – don't you? You are depressed—'

'Yes, but you know why. For God's sake, don't you start, Maddy said the same thing.'

Good for Maddy, thought Sarah.

'Did she? And—'

'I haven't spoken to her since.'

'Eliza—'

'Oh, this is stupid. I'm going to bed. I'm going to try to sleep late, so if Emmie gets up, could you keep an eye on her please?'

'Yes, of course. But—'

'Night.'

But in the morning, she was down in the kitchen before Sarah, making herself a cup of tea, looking exhausted.

'Bad night?'

'They're all bad,' said Eliza briefly.

After breakfast, Emmie suggested they went to the village shop to buy some sweets.

'No,' said Eliza, 'you eat too many sweets.'

'I'll take her,' said Sarah.

'Mummy, no. Don't try and undermine what I say, please. Emmie, if you get me your storybook I'll read to you.'

'I don't want a story.' The storm was beginning to gather. 'I want to go to the shop.'

'Well, we're not going. And that's that.'

Emmie came over to her and pushed her. 'You're horrible.'

'I am not horrible, Emmie. I'm simply trying to stop you eating too many sweets. We could go for a walk if you like.' She sighed. 'To the woods.'

'I want to go to the shop.'

'Emmie, we are not going to the shop. Is that clear?'

'I hate you.'

'That's a horrible thing to say.'

'It's a true thing,' said Emmie, 'I hate you.'

Eliza shrugged and picked up her coffee.

'I'm going into the drawing room to read. Come and find me when you want a story.'

'I hate you,' said Emmie again. 'You're horrible to me.'

Eliza walked out of the room, feeling her temper soar. She went into the drawing room, and sat down on the chair by the fire. It hadn't been lit and the room was very cold. Why did her mother have to be so mean with everything? Matt had put in central heating, for God's sake, she must have it set very low.

She looked down at her hands; God, they looked awful. Nails all broken and uneven, one of them bitten down to the quick. She'd been proud of her nails once, had regular manicures. What an extraordinary thing to care about. Same with hair. Who could go through all that rubbish, just to look good? Crazy.

She couldn't concentrate on her book, and picked up a copy of *Tatler* instead. That had been another world, when she had been in *Tatler* endlessly, a happy, happy world. When she had been able to sleep and not hurt all the time and – shit. She hurled it aside and picked up the *Telegraph*; there was an article on one of the women's pages about working mothers and a photograph of one of the girls who she had done the season with, beaming complacently, holding a baby in white fluffy lace, and with two other small children at her side.

'The Honourable Mrs Archie Sissons,' said the caption, 'with her family. Asked what she thought about working mothers, Mrs Sissons said, "I see my work as raising a large and happy family. That's the only work I value. I can't understand how women can put work before their babies. Archie and I plan at least one more."'

'Stupid bloody cow,' said Eliza to the photograph, 'smug, stupid cow, wouldn't we all like that,' and realised that Mrs Sissons's plump face had blurred and she was crying, as she did so much of the time, and . . .

'Mummy, please can we go to the shop? Please?'

'Emmie, I said no. Now stop it. And don't fiddle with those ornaments, you'll break one of them . . .'

'You're horrible,' said Emmie and came over to her, raised a small foot and kicked her on the shin. She had outdoor shoes on; it hurt.

'I hate you and I hate that stupid baby, I'm glad he died.'

Afterwards Eliza remembered very clearly thinking that the words 'red mist' did actually describe rage; she saw the world through a bright, agonising light. She raised her hand and hit Emmie, hard, on the face. Emmie fell, catching her head on the edge of a low table.

And lay there staring up at her mother, her huge eyes shocked and dark, a trickle of blood oozing from the corner of one eye; then she covered her face with her hands and started to scream.

'Just shut up,' shouted Eliza, 'shut up, shut up—'

'What is going on – oh, my God.' Sarah had run into the room. 'Emmie – darling – Eliza—'

And then she scooped Emmie up in her arms, and half-ran with her out of the door.

Eliza followed her, shaking, thinking she might throw up.

'No great harm done,' said the cheerful doctor at the local hospital, following Sarah and Emmie out to where Eliza was sitting in the Casualty waiting room. 'Just one stitch below her eyebrow, and she was very brave. It'll be a bit swollen for a few days, but it's fine. She told me how it happened . . .'

'Oh,' said Eliza, 'oh yes?'

'Yes. These accident things occur all the time at home, don't they?'

'Yes,' said Eliza again. She presumed it was only a matter of time before the social workers came and took Emmie away from her.

'Right, keep her quiet for the rest of the day, she'll be fine. Perhaps some extra sweeties, Emmie, eh?'

They drove home in silence, Emmie sucking her thumb on the back seat. She was very subdued. They passed the village shop and Eliza asked her if she'd like some sweets; Emmie shook her head.

Once home, Sarah laid her down on the sofa and then fetched her a drink and a storybook. Eliza hovered in the hall, trying not to panic, trying not to scream. After half an hour Sarah came out.

'She's asleep,' she said, 'I'll just fetch a blanket and then I think we should have a talk, Eliza.'

'Yes, of course,' said Eliza.

'Right,' said Sarah, 'I'm not going to reproach you, I can see I don't need to. But I hope now, Eliza, you'll recognise what a terrible state you're in and how much you need help. God knows what you might do next.'

'Yes,' said Eliza, humbly, 'yes, I do. Oh, Mummy, I feel so – so totally ashamed. I'm sorry, so, so sorry. And what Matt will say, I don't know. Have her taken away from me, I should think.'

'Yes,' said Sarah, 'I think he might. If he knew . . .'

'What do you mean. You're not suggesting I don't tell him? Mummy, I'm not that much of a monster . . .'

'No. Nothing to do with me. It's Emmie. She was completely hysterical while the doctor was examining her, screaming and screaming, "Don't tell Daddy, don't tell Daddy, please, please don't tell Daddy." Nothing would calm her until I promised I wouldn't. What you say or do is of course up to you.'

'I don't understand,' said Eliza, 'I really don't.'

'She saw it as her fault. She said she kicked you. On the leg, twice. With her shoes on.'

'Yes,' said Eliza, looking down rather surprised at her leg, which was indeed developing a mild swelling and bruising of its own, 'yes, she did. But that was no reason—'

'Of course not. And she said she didn't hate you, she loved you, and she hadn't meant to hurt you. And that she said a horrible wicked thing to you . . .'

'Well – she did say something quite – quite strong,' said Eliza, 'but she's only a little girl, for God's sake.'

'Indeed she is.'

Emmie woke up about an hour later. She appeared in the kitchen door-way, sucking her thumb, and walked over to her mother, took her hand.

'You won't tell Daddy, will you?' she said. 'Not what I said.'

'Emmie, I think I should—'

Emmie started crying again.

'No, no, don't, please don't. Don't tell him any of it, please, Mummy. Don't tell him.'

Eliza took her onto her lap and sat cuddling her, shushing her, telling her not to worry, that Daddy would understand.

'You're not to tell him,' said Emmie, 'if you tell him, I shall run away. Promise me.'

'Well,' said Eliza, 'I promise not to tell him yet. We'll talk about it some more. But I'm sorry, Emmie, so, so sorry I've been so horrible lately. I love you so much. I really do. Would you – would you like to go down to the shop now and get some sweets?'

'Yes, please,' said Emmie, and she smiled, her sudden, rather fierce smile. 'Now. Straight away.'

Eliza went to fetch their coats. She didn't meet her mother's eye. But later, while Emmie was up in the old nursery, playing with the dolls' house, she said, 'Mummy, I don't quite know how to handle this. Of course Matt ought to know what I did. It was awful, dreadful. But he'll want to go over it all with Emmie, so I'll have to choose my time and my words very carefully. She really is in a terrible state. Thing is, she and Matt adore each other, and he'll never hear a word against her, always takes her side against me, thinks she's absolutely perfect. I think she wants to keep it that way. That's my explanation for it, anyway.'

'That's a very sophisticated thought process,' said Sarah.

'Not really. Pretty basic instinct.'

'Well, you must do what you think best. But—'

'Yes, and I know what that should be, I just don't know how to handle it. And she ran away before a few weeks ago, she was missing for over an hour in London, same thing, she told me she hated me and she was going to live with someone else. I didn't take any notice till I called her for tea and found the house was empty. I've never been so frightened. I rang the police, everything—'

'Where was she?'

'Just wandering about, in and out of the shops, up and down the streets. She actually got lost, and then a friend, thank God, was driving along, recognised her, brought her home. But she was very cool, said she would do it again if I wasn't nicer to her or if I told Matt. She was very firm about that.'

'And—?'

'Well, I didn't,' said Eliza, avoiding her eyes. 'I was so terrified of what he'd say, like that I was an unfit mother or I should be in a loony bin or something. Things are quite – quite bad between us. He's even accused me of doing something stupid and bringing the – the miscarriage on.'

'Oh, my darling!' said Sarah. 'I'm so sorry.'

'Anyway, I knew it was wrong, not to tell him, but – well, I didn't. And I did try harder to be nice to Emmie for a bit. Oh, Mummy, I feel really frightened. It's so, so awful. But very first thing, on Monday morning, I'll find a shrink, I promise. I'm obviously going mad.'

But later, as she lay wide awake as always in the small hours of the morning, she reflected not only on her own shortcomings but on Emmie's power to manipulate and her steel-strong will. It was quite frightening: it really was.

Chapter 37

It wasn't fair, it just wasn't fair; here she was with her life in order at last, everything going well, the company a success, making money, and this had to happen.

'My dear,' Mrs Berenson wrote, 'I have some very sad news. David and Gaby are to divorce. It seems they haven't been happy for a long time, and they see this as the only solution. I am devastated, as we all are. I don't suppose you remember David very well, you only met him once as far as I can remember, but I can tell you he is the most sensitive man and is deeply upset by what has happened. I shall be over in the New Year and will hope we can share our usual tea at the Connaught then. With my love, Lily Berenson.'

Actually, Scarlett thought, reading and re-reading this letter, trying to define how she felt – shocked? pleased? sorry? outraged? – the one thing that could be reliably acknowledged was that David and Gaby hadn't been happy for a long time. No truly happy marriage would allow for a long, adulterous relationship within it. That was what she had always believed, how she had justified her affair with David; if Gaby had made him happy, then he might have flirted with her, might have taken her to bed even, but it would not have gone on as long as it had. She had no real picture of Gaby, no idea of what she was like: the darling girl of Mrs Berenson's imagination, the perfect mother, the adoring wife, or the cold distant creature of David's, controlling and greedy.

Perhaps she would learn more over yet another of those life-changing teas at the Connaught; and meanwhile, she would simply wait. She wasn't sure what for – a visit from David? A phone call? A letter? Or nothing? Probably the last, she thought, for she knew she had angered and antagonised him hugely, and with good reason. Blackmail was not an attractive crime.

And perhaps she should be fearful of him; for now freed from the reason for it, and his own silence, might he come back for retribution?

It was a wonderful moment: in its own way. It didn't exactly make everything all right, everything never would be all right again. But the escape, from the fear that she was going mad, and even some of the guilt, was intense, and she sat staring at the calm, gentle face of the psycho-therapist, feeling stupid with relief, and asked her to repeat the words, just to make sure she hadn't imagined them.

'Of course,' said Mary Miller, smiling and understanding at once why she should be asked to repeat herself. 'I said, had your gynaecologist ever suggested that you had post-natal depression? Because to me it seems really rather – likely.'

'No. Well, I never went back to her, there didn't seem any need.'

'In which case I think perhaps you should, and ask her yourself. I am not medically qualified, but – well, apart from all your very natural grief, think of the physical trauma you've been through. Six months of pregnancy, it takes its own toll, birth, and from what you say, it was an extremely painful experience, with no attendant joy or hope to see you through it, your milk coming in, which you say was one of the worst things of all, and it must have been cruel indeed; and then the complete exhaustion that follows any birth, again without any happiness or satisfaction to help you, and what sounds like a very demanding child to keep you from resting as you needed. I would say your body has as much to do with your problems as your mind, Eliza. How did you feel after Emmie was born?'

'Oh, I had quite bad post-baby blues, lasted longer than I expected—'

'How long?'

'Oh, I don't know, couple of weeks. But no, nothing like depression.'

'Post-natal depression can be cumulative, getting worse with each child. Now we can continue with these sessions if you like and I would hope that would be helpful, but first—'

Eliza made an appointment to see Mrs Munroe the moment she got home, and sat in her consulting room the following morning, hearing the wonderful words repeated.

'I think that is a very likely diagnosis, and I only wish you had come to me before. Everything you describe, the insomnia, the rage, the weeping, it all fits. Of course you have also lost a baby, I don't for a moment diminish that as a cause of unhappiness either, and I think your session

390

with Mrs Miller sounds very helpful. But I am going to write to your GP immediately and suggest you are prescribed some antidepressants.'

'Oh, no!' wailed Eliza. 'I shall feel such a failure taking them, I really don't approve of all that stuff, and now I know—'

'Eliza,' said Mrs Munroe firmly, 'you are not a failure, and it would be extremely foolish not to take them. You are physically ill, your body needs help. Now please – otherwise, I wouldn't like to answer for the consequences.'

And so it was that the very next day, tentatively, nervously, but still flooded with relief, Eliza embarked on a course of Trazodone. Within a week, she was sleeping well, and by the second she could feel, day by day, the baffling and frightening sensations of despair shifting from her. She still cried for Baby Charles, but she felt in control of herself and her emotions once more, she was less exhausted and she could find some sense in life and even began to enjoy simple things again, going to Summercourt, making progress on the Fulham house, and looking for a pony for Emmie for Christmas – as instructed by Matt.

She even began having conversations with Matt again, talking about the baby and how he felt about it now, and that was hugely helpful, as he felt less rejected by her and less alone in his own grief. They even managed some sex, a poor, frail shadow of its early noisy self, but as they each quietly reflected, it was a beginning.

She did not, however, tell him about what had happened with Emmie that dreadful day in the drawing room; she decided that had been the actions of the other Eliza, the poor, mad, sickly Eliza, and what would be the point? She had begun afresh with Emmie and indeed with him and with every day it felt better to leave it. Some things, as she said to her mother, were best left buried. And her mother, relieved beyond anything at the change in her, was inclined to agree.

She still avoided certain things: social gatherings were beyond her, and she hated the bossy, pushy mother mafia at the nursery school gates, saying 'sorry, double parked' whenever anyone tried to engage her in conversation. The mafia thought they understood and continued, mercifully, to invite Emmie to parties and to tea.

Heather had been the only person she really wanted to see in those early dreadful days; Heather had lost two babies herself, and had been quietly kind, concerned, and helpful, and would come round to the house, not as overawed by its size and opulence as Eliza had feared, taking

Emmie out when Eliza lacked the energy to walk to the park, or was crying so hard even Emmie became alarmed. She had provided Eliza's link with sanity and she owed her more than she felt she would ever repay.

But she had been avoiding Eliza recently, making excuses not to see her, saying she was too busy or too tired to go to the park or to have her in to tea; baffled, anxious, slightly hurt, but thinking that perhaps she had foisted too much of her grief on her, Eliza went round to see her at lunchtime one day.

Heather appeared at the door, looking listless and pale. 'Oh,' she said, 'oh, hello.'

'Heather,' said Eliza, alarmed, 'what it is it, what's the matter?'

Heather said nothing, just started to cry.

'Oh now, come on, you can't cry. That's my job,' said Eliza.

Heather managed a feeble smile. 'Got a tissue?'

'Yes, of course. I knew there was something wrong. Can I come in?'

'Yes. Yes, of course. Sorry.'

Eliza followed her upstairs, into the dingy room. 'Cup of tea?'

'No thanks. You have some. I've – I've gone off it.' She met Eliza's eyes reluctantly.

'Oh,' said Eliza, and it was as if the ground had dropped beneath her. 'Oh, Heather. I see. You're pregnant.'

'Yes. I'm pregnant,' said Heather with a huge, heaving sigh. 'I'm sorry, Eliza.'

'Sorry?' said Eliza, crushing, stifling the fierce shot of jealousy. 'Don't say sorry, Heather. Is that why you've been avoiding me?'

'Yes. Yes, it is. I just couldn't face telling you. I thought it would be so – so terrible for you. Oh, God, excuse me.'

She rushed out of the room and into the toilet on the landing and came back a few minutes later, ashen, tears in her eyes.

'It looks like it's terrible for you, not me,' said Eliza. 'Did you really think I was so mean-spirited I'd not want to see you because of it? Heather, you're my friend, you've saved my sanity last summer. I'd do anything for you, anything. I'm sad you felt like that.'

'I didn't. Well, not exactly. It just seemed so – so ironic. And cruel. You losing a baby you wanted me so much, me pregnant with one that we really don't want at all. That's not exactly right, but that we can't cope with.'

'Well, I think that comes under the heading of life,' said Eliza. 'Matt says it's shit and he's right. Now come on, tell me all about it.'

'There's not much to tell,' said Heather. 'Alan's really bad-tempered with the worry, and me being so sick, and we'll have to move now and I can see we should, but we can't find anywhere. Not that'll take a baby. And this flat is at least cheap. It's a controlled rent, do you know what that is?'

'I – think so,' said Eliza carefully. (Controlled rents and the iniquity of them formed one of the main subjects of Matt's rants. '. . . people living in places, pre-war rents, can't put them up, can't get the tenants out, it's completely wrong . . .')

'But it's terrible living here now,' said Heather. 'The roof's leaking now and old Mrs Foster on the top floor, she's finally had to go to live with her son, and the other toilet is leaking too, and often blocked.'

'Oh, God. Poor you. Look, I'll go and get Coral for you, Emmie's out to tea. I'll pick up a few things from the shop. And have you tried peppermint tea for the sickness? Or camomile? I'll get you some of both. And don't start rummaging for your purse, because you can give it to me some other time, OK?'

'OK,' said Heather, leaning back with a sigh, 'thanks, Eliza.'

Eliza fetched Coral from playschool, and then whizzed her round the supermarket, buying her what were clearly luxuries, biscuits, squash, fruit yogurts, crisps.

'Emmie's so lucky,' said Coral, 'having a kind mummy like you.'

'Oh Coral,' said Eliza, with a sigh, 'your mummy's much kinder than me. Now how about some Rice Krispies? D'you like them?'

She took Coral back to the flat, cooked her tea and made some camomile and then peppermint tea for Heather to try. Heather said they were both disgusting and managed a feeble smile.

'Right. I'd better go. Her Highness will be waiting for me. But I mean what I said, Heather, I really would do anything for you, anything at all. I mean it.'

She went to collect Emmie and transport her from one large luxurious home to another, reflecting yet again on the iniquity of life.

'A drink, Miss Scarlett?'

'Oh – Demetrios, yes please. How lovely.'

She was spending the last sweetly warm days of late autumn on Trisos; she had wanted to be alone, to think.

393

'Lot of bookings for next year already, Miss Scarlett. We're thinking of extending the house.'

'Oh, Demetrios, is that wise?' She had visions of some hideous modern adjunct. 'Don't spoil it.'

'No, no, only just a little courtyard at the back, and maybe two, three rooms round it. I asked Mr Frost what he thought, he said we should talk with his architect.'

'That's a good idea. But isn't he rather expensive?'

'No, Miss Scarlett, very, very cheap.'

'Oh.' She was surprised. 'Has he been here this year, Mr Frost?'

'Oh, a lot of time yes. He is writing new book.'

'And – was Mrs Frost with him?'

'For a week, in the spring. She does not like the heat.'

'Right.' Bit of a funny place to build a house, then; he must spend a lot of the summer on his own . . . why did she care about Mrs Frost, for God's sake.

'She is wonderful lady. Very, very clever. She is poet. She talks not very much.'

That must be a quiet household, Scarlett thought. How dull . . . but at least it was a household. Which remained just a tantalising mirage in her own life.

She was thirty now, and she wanted marriage, a home, babies. She sighed, finished her drink, looked at the moon, rising over the dark, dark blue sea, cool, clear, huge, almost near enough to touch. But of course she couldn't; it was far, far away. Rather like the husband and home she wanted.

Maybe, that was all she was doing, crying for the moon.

Chapter 38

Mariella had invited Eliza to stay with her in Milan that autumn, to cheer her up after the death of her baby, and Eliza had clearly longed to accept. Matt however had refused to allow it.

'He says it is term time, and I must be here with Emmie.'

'I thought her *nonna* would look after her. You poor angel. Really, I am surprised Matt doesn't want you to have a little holiday. He must realise you are tired and sad.'

'He does. But he doesn't understand how coming to you might help. And he's unhappy too, and I – well, I suppose – oh dear – sorry, Mariella—'

Mariella could hear the tears in her voice and felt a rush of sympathy and sorrow – and rage towards Matt.

'Perhaps,' she suggested, 'I should speak to Matt myself?'

'Absolutely not,' said Eliza, horrified. 'That really would do no good at all.'

'Well, I am not pleased with him. Not at all. You must tell him so.'

'Maybe,' said Eliza.

That afternoon Mariella went into Milan for some fittings for the coming season; feeling a little tired afterwards, she went into Cova for some hot chocolate and a pastry. She never ate the pastries, or not more than a tiny mouthful, but they were so delicious, and just looking at them on her plate made her feel happy.

As she sat there, sipping the chocolate, nibbling at the crumbs, surrounded by her shopping bags, she heard her name. She looked up. It was Timothy Fordyce.

'Timothy! How very lovely. Come, sit down, share my *cannoncino*, I have already eaten more of it than I should.'

'Lovely for me, too, Mariella. Thank you. How are you?'

'Oh, you know, so very, very busy, getting ready for the season.'

'I can see. Obviously a heavy afternoon,' he said, grinning, gesturing at the bags.

'Come, sit down. How are things at the agency? The *fattoria inferna*, as Giovanni calls it.'

'Very good! Not too infernal just now. Actually, very busy, hardly got time to lunch. Got one of the big guns coming over from New York beginning of December. In fact I think you know him, seem to remember his name coming up at that splendid dinner you gave that time when your English friend was here, Jeremy Northcott, nice chap.'

'Jeremy! Yes, of course. I would very much like to see him again.'

'Well, you must. We'll have dinner one night.'

'Oh, that would be so delightful. Thank you, Timothy, how very, very kind. Now, let me order you a *cioccolata*?'

'You can indeed. It looks wonderful. *Grazie.*' He smiled at her. There was a great deal of admiration in that smile, she noted. Good. She would use that, as she always did, when the need arose.

'*Prego,*' she said, smiling back.

'Eliza.'

'Yes, Matt.'

'Look—' He was clearly finding whatever it was difficult to say. 'It probably would do you good to go away for a few days. I know I should have taken you, but I've been so busy.'

'Yes, I had noticed.'

'So – maybe, I thought – you could go a bit later. At the end of term. Emmie breaks up quite early in December, I think, and then you could take her with you.'

'Well, I don't know if that would suit Mariella,' said Eliza coolly. 'She's a very busy woman.'

'Oh Eliza, come off it.'

'There are more ways of being busy than covering the country with concrete.'

'Yes, all right, but I don't count buying frocks among them. Look, I'm trying to help. To be – nice.'

'I – I know. But I don't think you understand. Getting away would be so lovely—'

'Getting away from me, you mean.'

'No, Matt, of course not.'

'Well, that's what it looks like. From where I am.'

'You are so self-obsessed,' she said, 'you know that?'

'And you're not, I suppose. Look – oh, what's the use. You do what you bloody well want, you usually do.'

And he stalked out of the kitchen.

She hesitated for a moment then followed him.

He was standing in the drawing room, staring out of the window.

'Matt.'

No reaction.

'Matt. I'm sorry.'

He turned round; his face was flushed and his eyes very brilliant.

'You really are not the only one hurting, you know,' he said and his voice cracked slightly. 'I know it's worse for you but—'

'I know. And I am sorry. Really sorry. I shouldn't have said that.'

'No, you shouldn't, Eliza, we've got to stop being so hard on each other. It isn't helping.'

'I know,' she said, 'I know. But I feel you don't even like me any more. I don't know what I've done.'

'You've shut me out,' he said. 'You're so bloody hostile . . .'

'Matt it's not me being hostile, it's you. I just want—'

'What?'

'For things to be better again. Oh, we've had this conversation too many times.'

'Probably.'

She walked up to him, stood very close. He looked down at her, his expression blank.

'Please,' she said, 'please, Matt. Let's not give up.'

He didn't answer, just kissed her rather perfunctorily and walked out of the room.

That night, he wanted to have sex with her; wearily, she gave in. He could sense her reluctance. Afterwards, he turned away from her and sighed, a deep, heavy sigh.

'I'm sorry,' she said, after a moment. 'So sorry, Matt. I just can't – don't—'

'Want me any more?'

She hesitated.

'Not just now, no. I can't help it. Mrs Miller says it's quite natural, it's—'

'You've been discussing our sex life with that bloody shrink?' he said. 'Well, that's great. Marvellous. All I need.'

'Matt, I tell her everything. It's important in the whole process. How I feel about myself, my life, how I feel about Emmie—'

'What do you mean, how you feel about Emmie? Why should that need talking about?'

Eliza felt a pang of fear. That had been unwise . . . 'Well – it's hard to explain,' she said carefully, 'and it's fine now, but being so unhappy, so exhausted, I felt I was failing her as well as everybody else. And she is so demanding, you must admit.'

'She seems like a normal little girl to me. And your life, what's wrong with that, I thought you were feeling better since you've been taking those pills. Because – oh, let's stop this. I can't cope with any more.'

'Where are you going?'

'Downstairs, to do some work. It's a bit more rewarding than making love to a limp fish.'

'I hate you,' said Eiza.

'That's fairly obvious,' he said and went out, slamming the door.

In the morning they made up.

Uncomfortably, uneasily, but it was better than not doing so.

'I'm sorry,' she said, coming first with it as always, 'so sorry. I'm trying very hard. And I'm sorry about the sex specially. And sorry, that you don't like me telling Mrs Miller. But – I feel I have to tell her everything, otherwise it doesn't – doesn't all work together properly. I'm sure in time it'll all be fine again. I just feel so – so – unsexy.'

'I can tell,' he said and managed a grin. 'I suppose I'm a bit – jealous. That you can talk to her and not to me. Never mind the subject matter.'

'But we have been talking. More. Haven't we?'

'I suppose so,' he said and sighed. 'I'll hang around a bit longer.'

'Please, please do.'

'And it seems we must both try a bit harder.'

'Yes. Yes. We must.'

'So, I'll let you go to Milan to stay with your terribly busy friend—'

'Matt!' she said. 'You'll let me go to Milan, indeed! You're a feminist's nightmare.'

'Good,' he said. 'Now go and get my pipe and slippers, and look sharp about it.'

Eliza did something she'd thought she would never do again: she giggled.

✿   ✿   ✿

398

Mariella said a visit early in December would be excellent.

'And it is the beginning of our social season, as you know.'

'I do know. That's wonderful. Thank you, Mariella.'

And then Mariella called Timothy Fordyce at KPD Milan, and suggested he and his wife join her and Giovanni in their box at La Scala. 'Callas is singing *Traviata*, it should be very beautiful.'

'Wonderful, thank you, but in that case, let us do dinner. Oh – no, that won't do, it's the week Jeremy Northcott is here.'

There was a silence; and then, 'Well, he must come with you,' said Mariella, her voice a soft, sweet coo. 'That would be truly delightful.'

Perhaps she could teach Matt a lesson . . .

'My dear, you look wonderful. Truly wonderful.' Lily Berenson smiled at Scarlett, kissed her fondly.

'Thank you. You look pretty good too, Mrs Berenson.'

'Yes, I suppose I'm fairly well. Of course this wretched business with David has taken its toll. I feel so angry with her.'

'With Gaby?'

'Well yes, dear. David would have been prepared to struggle on, try again, for the sake of the children—'

'Oh really?'

'Yes. He's always put his family first. But Gaby has proved herself very selfish. There is another man, as I suspected, even though she has no intention of actually setting up house with him. She will have the children, she is a very good mother, if nothing else, and David couldn't possibly cope with them. He's away such a lot. She told me she puts a lot of blame for the marriage break-up down to that. I was very shocked.'

'Really?'

'Of course. I did point out to her that the extremely comfortable standard of living she has always enjoyed was down to David and his hard work, but she couldn't see it.'

No longer a darling girl, Scarlett thought; how swiftly things had changed for Gaby. Poor Gaby. She could have told her a thing or two about David and the unselfishness of his absences . . .

'Well now, my dear, how about you? How is your business going, such a very clever idea.'

'Oh, it's going pretty well,' said Scarlett. 'I'm doing quite a bit in the States now, I've got a couple of hotels in San Francisco, and—'

'I keep telling you, dear, you should consider Charleston. It's exactly your profile, especially in the spring. There are several small hotels that I think would suit you, in fact I think I'm going to speak to David about it tonight—'

'David!'

'Yes, dear, he's here with me. Just overnight in London, then he's flying over to Paris. He knew I was seeing you this afternoon, but most unfortunately he had several appointments, so he couldn't join us. I wonder if dinner might be a possibility for the three of us—'

'Oh, no,' said Scarlett, panic rising in her throat, 'no, I'm busy tonight, Mrs Berenson. Sorry.'

'What a pity. You couldn't make breakfast, I suppose?'

'No. I've got an early morning meeting.'

'What a hard-working girl you are. Now you see, I think if Gaby had had a career, it might have been better, she would have been less inclined to think about herself all the time. She is a very self-centred woman . . .'

Poor Gaby, Scarlett thought again, the times Mrs Berenson had berated one of the other daughters-in-law for working and leaving the children with a nanny; mothers-in-law were obviously a pretty big factor in a marriage.

As she was leaving the Connaught, a taxi pulled up; it had David in it. She turned and made her way to the Ladies and sat there at one of the dressing tables for ten minutes, shaking slightly. David still had the power to disturb her sexually and indeed emotionally; he was so bloody beautiful, damn him. Beautiful and dangerous.

Later, in her flat, she was settling at her desk when the phone rang.

'Scarlett?' It was him.

'Yes.'

'I was hoping to catch you this afternoon. I came back earlier than I had said. I was hoping to take you by surprise. I knew you'd never see me of your own volition.'

'No. I wouldn't.'

'Scarlett – you know my marriage really is over now.'

'I heard that Gaby had come to her senses. Yes.'

'Well, you can interpret it how you will. Perhaps at last you will accept that what I told you was true, that she really didn't care for me in the least.'

'And – little Lily? Was she conceived in an uncaring moment?'

'Scarlett, please. Of course I slept with Gaby occasionally. I had to. We were married, for God's sake. These things happen.'

'You said they didn't.'

'I know. But I was so afraid of losing you.'

'Oh, David, please.'

'Well,' he said, 'I still love you. I always will. Remember that, Scarlett. Don't throw it away without at least a little glance backwards.'

'I'm tired of looking backwards, David,' she said. 'I need to look forward now instead.'

Just the same, after she had put the phone down, she sat staring at it, thinking about him and their time together; and it was the first time she had smiled as she remembered it.

Heather was very low. She was sick and very tired now, with her pregnancy, her inconvenient, unwanted pregnancy. Alan was increasingly bad-tempered and depressed.

'And Coral doesn't like her school, says she's still being teased. How about Emmie?'

'She's OK. Would you like to bring Coral to tea tomorrow?'

'I don't think I can. I've got to do something about this toilet and the landlord says he's sending someone round tomorrow. Of course he wouldn't say when, so I've got to stay in all day, and I know what'll happen, I'll go out to collect Coral and he'll come then, and then they'll have an excuse.'

'I'll collect Coral for you,' said Eliza.

'Oh, Eliza, would you? That's ever so kind.'

She was very early to pick up Coral, so she parked and then dashed into a newsagent for a paper to read; the only one they had was the *Daily News*. Jack Beckham's paper. He'd hired some fashion writer called Katya Rowlands and turned her into a star. Her waiflike face was indeed on the side of the bloody buses. Every time Eliza saw her, she felt sick.

She looked at her column, and had to admit it was pretty good. Not brilliant, but pretty good. Style was a bit arch, but the content was good.

She turned the page quickly, skimmed over an irritating interview with the twenty-one-year old Prince Charles saying how careful you had to be choosing a wife who was going to be Queen one day – talk about stating the obvious, he was hardly going to pick up someone off the street – and tried to concentrate on the gossip column instead. She hardly knew anybody mentioned; that depressed her as well. Oh, Eliza, what have you come to? An embittered old has-been, that's what.

She was almost late in the end to pick up Coral at the gates. She drove her home, and found poor Heather coming out of the lavatory looking green.

'Sorry,' she said, 'still can't stop being sick.'

'Don't apologise, you silly girl. Has the man been?'

'No, not yet. He—'

A man appeared on the stairs just below them.

'Mrs Connell? I've got a note there's some problem with the toilet. What would that be then, perfectly all right when I left last time.'

'It's the same problem,' said Heather, 'it's leaking.'

'That's very odd. I'll have another look but – God, it stinks in here.'

'Yes, it does,' said Eliza, shooing Heather back into the flat, shutting the door on her. 'That's because it's not flushing properly. The whole system needs replacing.'

He dumped his bag of tools on the floor.

'Qualified plumber, are you?'

'No. I just know faulty workmanship when I see it.'

'You've no right to say that. This toilet was perfectly all right when I left it. These people' – he gestured at Heather's door – 'misuse things. Don't clean up properly.'

'I very much doubt that. This lavatory is used by four families, it needs to be in proper working order.'

'Oh, yeah? You one of them?'

'No,' said Eliza, 'I'm not. But I do know that binding a cracked pipe with a dirty cloth is hardly a long-term solution.'

'OK,' he said, picking up his toolbag again, 'you fix it then, since you're so clever.'

Eliza felt slightly panicky; she seemed to be depriving the tenants of even minimum attention to their problem.

'Look,' she said, 'who do you work for, who's your boss? Couldn't you get him to authorise a proper repair?'

'My instructions are to do what's needed,' he said, 'and that's what I do. Now am I going to be allowed to get on with it, or are you going to stand there, telling me my bloody job?'

'Yes,' said Eliza hastily. 'Yes, of course you must do what you can.'

For the first time in her life, she had seen for herself the total indifference shown by the powerful towards the powerless; it shocked her.

Chapter 39

'That is just so – so dreadful. I can't believe it. Please, please tell me it's not true.'

'Why so dreadful? It will be fun, we will all have a lovely time together.'

'But—'

'I'm sorry if you think badly of me. I thought you would be pleased—'

'Mariella, how can I be pleased? Jeremy – here, in Milan! And not just here, but having dinner with us. You could have warned me at least.'

'*Cara*, I am sorry. I really didn't think it was such a big – big deal.'

'Well, it is. I feel a bit like not coming . . .'

'Eliza.' Mariella's voice dropped its expression of abject innocence and took on a tone of steely determination. 'Eliza, of course you must come. It will seem very, very rude if you do not. Timothy Fordyce and his wife, Janey, it is they who are taking us to dinner. And do you really want to miss Callas? All Milan will be there – it is such a wonderful occasion—'

'All Milan and a bloody Englishman.' Eliza hesitated. There was clearly nothing she could say to change things. And what did it matter? Really? She was being ridiculously immature. All that was going to happen was she would see Jeremy again and it would be fun.

'Sorry, Mariella,' she said, 'I'm being stupid. It all sounds lovely. But can we go shopping? I need some better shoes. And do you really think what I've got is grand enough?'

'For Jeremy?'

'No, of course not. For La Scala.'

'Eliza, Le Smoking by Yves Saint Laurent is smart enough for any-where. I wanted one for myself, but it does not suit my shape. You will look extremely chic. But yes, perhaps, some new very, very high heels. We will go this afternoon. We will leave Emmie behind, I think, with Anna-Maria.'

✿ ✿ ✿

Alone in her palace of a room, unpacking Emmie's things, she wondered why she was so horrified at the prospect of seeing Jeremy. It wasn't as if she'd dumped him last week. Or even last month. And he hadn't given everything up in his grief, and gone to live in a monastery. He was a hugely successful corporate figure: CEO of KPD New York. And still extremely rich.

Of course, it would never have worked if she had married him. There had never been any real fire in their relationship (she tried not to think of the problems the fire in her relationship with Matt had caused).

What was worrying her was how she might feel about Jeremy after all this time, whether there might in fact be more of a fire than she thought.

And however much she loved Matt – and she did, she did – the magic had inevitably faded. There had to be an easing of emotion, a blunting of desire, however strong the relationship might be; and you would hardly be human if you didn't welcome, however briefly, the dance of a flirtation, the disturbance of an attraction, the flickering of intrigue.

Jeremy could clearly offer that: and that was unsettling. Not to mention scary. Very scary indeed.

'No! No, I won't. I want to come with you.'

'Emmie – darling, I won't be long. Anna-Maria will play with you, however you want, you know she will.'

'I don't want to play with Anna-Maria. I want to go shopping.'

'Look, suppose I bring you a present back. It's going to be such a dull afternoon, trailing round the shoe shops—'

'I don't want a present, I want to be with you. Why can't I come? I'll be really, really good.'

'Emmie—' Eliza stopped. There was no reasoning with Emmie when she was in this mood; and besides, she couldn't afford to antagonise her at this stage in the trip; she needed her cooperation for three more days, culminating in the night at the Scala when she really would not be allowed to come.

'Well, look. If we take you today, will you promise to be very, very good? And then maybe we can take you for hot chocolate and a pastry afterwards. But I don't want any complaining, Emmie. Is that a deal?'

Emmie understood deals. She smiled at her mother, a sweet, gentle smile, the huge dark blue eyes innocently wide. 'It's a deal.'

※　※　※

Milan, getting ready for Christmas, was at its fairy-tale best; strung with lights, across the street and down the lamp posts, the shop windows rich and luscious, gold and silver settings for sparkling evening dresses, glittering rich-coloured jewels. Especially wonderful to Eliza's eyes were the food stores, butchers' displays of boar, deer, hare, hanging pheasants still in their fine feathers, fruit and vegetable stalls, stacked high, and the *pasticcerie*, their windows works of art, and on every corner, flower stalls, offering huge ready-dressed bouquets and great bowls and vases of roses, lilies, and lush thick greenery. For Milan Christmas was the winter solstice, the ancient Roman feast day; less sentimental than London with its endless Santa Clauses and galloping reindeer, more adult, more concerned with sensual pleasure.

Even the nativity scenes in windows or in front of churches, were works of art, beautifully carved, life-sized shepherds, wise men, Mary and Joseph and the baby all exquisitely presented.

Everyone was in furs, leopard, sables and mink, with huge fox-fur collars, and even mink collars on the cashmere and camel coats of the men.

And woven into this dazzling throng were the gypsies, hundreds of them, raggedy and dirty with their sleeping babies – 'they are drugged,' Mariella said disdainfully – thrusting sprigs of heather, muttering curses. Some sat on pavements and in doorways; the Milanese stepped round or over them, never breaking off from their conversations for a moment, or handing over any money.

Emmie skipped along wide-eyed between Mariella and her mother, the faithful Anna-Maria trailing along behind.

'Can I have some new shoes?' asked Emmie. 'I want black patent ones, with square ends. Like Katy's.'

'Who is Katy?' asked Mariella. 'I think she has good taste, square ends are very, very fashionable just now.'

'She's my best friend. At the moment.'

'Do you often change your best friends?'

'Yes. Lots of times.'

'Good girl. I also.'

'Is Mummy your best friend at the moment?'

'But of course. And very, very often. Whenever I see her. She is a very good best friend, your mother.'

'Mine too. At the moment,' said Emmie.

They passed the dazzling windows of Rinascente: Emmie's eyes glowed.

'Can we go in there?'

'No, we're going to buy my shoes,' said Eliza.

'Please!'

'Emmie,' said Eliza warningly.

'But it's fun in there.'

Mariella spoke to Anna-Maria who nodded and grasped Emmie's hand.

'Emmie, *carina*, you go with Anna-Maria, she will take you round the store. We will meet you in one hour in Cova and you shall have a *millefoglie*. You will like that very much.'

'But I want you to come—'

Mariella's eyes became nail-hard and Anna-Maria pulled at Emmie's hand. Eliza had seen the look.

'Emmie! Remember the deal.'

'OK.'

An hour and several dizzyingly high-heeled shoes later, they walked, swinging the bags, and giggling, to Cova.

'Now. Where are they? Not here yet, I think.'

'No,' Eliza felt a slight heave of anxiety.

'We will order the *cioccolata* and the *millefoglie*,' said Mariella, sinking down at a table, 'and they will be here very soon. Now, let me look at the last pair of shoes, the ones with the diamond straps, I think they are the ones – ah, here is Anna-Maria now.'

Anna-Maria, yes: a white-faced, wild-eyed Anna-Maria. Alone. No Emmie.

She rushed up to Mariella, spoke through almost hysterical sobs. The slight heave in Eliza's stomach became a major turbulence. Mariella turned to her. She spoke carefully and slowly.

'It seems Anna-Maria cannot – cannot find Emmie. She said she was there one minute and gone the next. In a very short time.'

Gone. A five year old, in the middle of a foreign city. Where she didn't speak the language. A city teeming with people, where a child could be – could be—

'God,' she said, and again, 'God.' She thought she might be sick. Don't panic, Eliza, she can't be far away, someone will be taking care of her, Italians love children, little girls don't get lost in the middle of the afternoon in broad – only it wasn't broad daylight, it was dusk, almost dark.

'Ask her where she last saw her,' she said, trying to keep her voice calm.

More terrifying, incomprehensible Italian. Eliza swallowed.

'It was in Rinascente. Anna-Maria just turn her front for a moment and Emmie was gone.'

They went back to Rinascente, all of them. To the children's clothes department, where Anna-Maria had taken her, Eliza sobbing, and terrified. The wilful, manipulative Emmie had been entirely replaced in her head by a small, frightened child in danger. She kept thinking of the gypsies, with their angry curses: suppose they had taken Emmie, she had been fascinated by them, she would have gone . . .

'Was here,' Anna-Maria said, indicating a line of smocked, embroidered dresses. 'I look away for one minute – and gone.'

'You should have held her hand,' said Eliza, 'you should have kept holding her hand.' Her panic had risen from her stomach into her throat.

'She would not. She pull away. All the time.'

She mustn't get angry with Anna-Maria. She mustn't. It wouldn't help.

Mariella, who had vanished, returned, looking smug. Maybe she'd found her, Eliza thought. Maybe she had some news.

'That is done. The announcement – any moment. They say they will find her in no time, they always do. They say go to toy department.'

They went to the toy department; it was thronged with overdressed children and fur-coated mammas and *nonnas*, laughing, shouting in Italian. She began to feel hysterical. Why couldn't they speak English, for God's sake? If Emmie asked for help, no one would understand her. She'd be frightened, lost, crying – anyone could take her . . .

Eliza was sobbing now; Mariella took her by the shoulders and shook her.

'Eliza! Be calm. We will not find Emmie this way. She is a clever child. We must think, think properly. What did she want this afternoon?'

'Just – just come with us. And get – get—'

'Oh, yes. The shoes. There she might be, I think. And they will have heard the message. Come, *cara*, courage.'

She held out her hand; Eliza was now sobbing uncontrollably. The fur-coated women looked at her with a mixture of disdain and sympathy. As long as she lived, Eliza thought, she would never again let Emmie out of her sight. And never, ever buy a fur coat. How she hated fur coats. If she never found Emmie, she would have to kill herself; she would climb up to the top of the Duomo, and throw herself off it, it would be the only thing she could possibly do . . .

'Here. Here we are. Bambini. And – there now. What did I say? There she is, your clever little daughter. A fashion editor-to-be.'

And there indeed she was, a security guard at her side, sitting and smiling, not in the least upset, on a tall chair, rather like a throne, surrounded with patent leather shoes of every shape and colour. An amused shop assistant, clearly expecting that any moment a fur-coated someone would come and claim her, was helping her to try them on.

'Emmie,' shouted Eliza, across the room, 'oh, Emmie, Emmie, I've been looking for you everywhere, where have you been, oh my darling, darling—'

Emmie heard her name, turned round, proffering two small feet, one in black patent, one in red.

'Which do you think?' she said.

Later, much later, when they were safely home, with both pairs of shoes, the red and the black, bought by Mariella against Eliza's express instructions – 'She deserves them, *cara*, she is so clever, finding them, you should be proud' – Emmie was put to bed early as a punishment, told there would be no story that night, no more outings to Milan, and no Christmas presents for her on Christmas day.

'What do you think Daddy will say, when he hears what you did, that you ran away from Anna-Maria like that?' asked Eliza.

'I don't know,' said Emmie, her voice implying very clearly that she didn't care; but later when Eliza, softening, read her a story after all and tucked her up, she said, 'Perhaps Daddy will be cross with you instead. For not staying with me.'

And she smiled very sweetly at her mother, put her thumb in her mouth and turned away from her.

The next day was beautiful. Eliza spent it with Emmie, roaming the grounds of the villa, playing hide and seek, eating a rather chilly picnic by the lake, as Emmie wanted (and then warming up in the house afterwards with hot chocolate, brought them by a remorseful and forgiving Anna-Maria), helping Emmie do a picture in crayons of the back of the house with the miniature maze, to show Matt, and finally watching the sun go down on the mountains.

Mariella was in Milan, putting the final touches to arrangements for a dinner party for forty she and Giovanni were giving the following week

408

and collecting her hairpiece from Mario Petris, her hairdresser, to wear the next night at the opera.

Eliza felt anxious for the first time in her life about her appearance; she had not come across such formality, such splendour, even among the grandest parties in the grandest houses in England that she had attended in her coming-out year. But Mariella looked at her, at the dress rehearsal she had insisted upon, the epitome of chic simplicity in her Yves Saint Laurent dinner jacket, and the new, high diamanté-strapped shoes, her hair cut simply and falling to her shoulders, and said she would be the belle of the balls.

That night, Eliza rang Matt; he sounded as he always did on such occasions, irritably surprised.

'I'm fine, no need to worry about me. I'm working my arse off as usual, hardly left the office—'

'I hope you're eating something,' said Eliza carefully.

'Yes, yes, course I am, having dinner with Scarlett tomorrow, she seems to think I'm incapable of feeding myself, I don't know why, she never bothered before you and me were together.'

'I expect she realises I wait on you hand and foot and you've forgotten how to cope on your own,' said Eliza.

'Yeah, well, I'll put her right there. You having a nice time, then?' he asked, clearly with an effort. 'How's Emmie?'

'Emmie's fine. Do you want to speak to her?'

'Yeah, put her on.'

She did so rather nervously, fearing Emmie might go into an elaborate description of her adventure of the day before; she'd decided the only thing was to let her tell Matt about it and then correct her version if necessary, rather than the other way round. But Emmie didn't mention it at all, merely talked about the day they had spent at the villa – 'it's like a palace, Daddy' – and the new shoes Mariella had bought her.

'I'm being very good,' she finished. 'See you soon, Daddy. I miss you.'

Maybe she really did think she'd been very naughty and she didn't want Matt to know about it; that would be the best outcome. It was an increasingly familiar scenario. God, she was clever, Eliza thought, watching her in rather alarmed admiration.

'OK then,' she said, when she got the phone back, 'I'd better go, this is costing a fortune. I'll see you the day after tomorrow.'

'Yeah. Teatime, you said? I can't meet you, sorry, got a meeting.'

'There's a surprise.'

'But it'll be good to have you back,' he added, clearly catching the edge in her voice. 'Bye till then.'

'Bye, Matt. I miss you.'

'Bye, again.'

'Was that your husband you're missing?' asked Mariella.

'Yes,' said Eliza, holding back a sigh. 'I think he's missing me too.'

'He didn't say so?'

'No. He's not romantic. Not like Giovanni. Words aren't his thing.'

'Well,' said Mariella, 'words are not everything.'

Thursday dawned very still and misty.

'I hope the *nebbia* does not come,' said Mariella.

'What's that?'

'The fog. It is very, very disagreeable. It paralyses the city. You can't get out, you can't get in.'

'Oh,' said Eliza, feeling a sliver of alarm, 'and does it often come?'

'In December, yes. We are in the middle of a big bowl, you see, with the Alps on either side, and if the wind is in the wrong direction, it settles upon us. In fact, I think perhaps we should leave a little early. We do not want to miss the opera.'

'No. But – we'd be able to get back all right? Tonight?'

'Oh, yes of course,' said Mariella, 'it cannot stop us getting back.'

Eliza had no option but to believe her.

They left at four in the big Lancia.

Mariella had arranged for them to change at the Hotel Grande Mizzoni.

'It is only a tiny room, all the big ones and the suites have of course gone, but at least we will have some privacy.'

Emmie had been left in the care of Anna-Maria and in case of trouble Bruno, Giovanni's valet, whom she adored. She was very good when Eliza said goodbye to her, made the minimum of fuss and was clearly far more interested in the supper she was to eat with Bruno in the kitchen than her mother's departure.

Milan was indeed blanketed in fog: not the dark smoke of London, but a swirling grey haze, the Christmas lights and street lamps, and the golden Madonna at the top of the gingerbread Duomo all but swallowed by it. Paolo, the chauffeur, dropped them outside the hotel, said he would pick them up at six.

The Hotel Grande was a study in ostentation: mirrors, arches, marble statues, gilt; the tiny room described by Mariella was about the size of a large flat. Eliza was ready long before Mariella, who had imported her hairdresser and a make-up artist; she and Giovanni sat and had a glass of champagne.

'You look most beautiful,' he said, smiling at her, 'and in a very special way. I am proud to be with you.'

Eliza tried to remember when she had last felt so much appreciated.

Mariella appeared, unbelievably lovely in cream brocaded silk, her cloud of dark hair piled high and studded with jewels, her great eyes shining beneath what Eliza reckoned was at least a double row of eyelashes; she heard Giovanni actually catch his breath before rising and kissing her hand.

La Scala was floodlit, a golden glow of splendour, shining through the mist; waves of limousines came and paused and went again, discharging their dazzling cargoes. The opera started at seven, but first Milan had to meet, kiss, flirt, flaunt itself.

Eliza followed Mariella and Giovanni up the wide winding staircase. She lost them swiftly in the huge crush of people, all so wonderful-looking, the men, the dashingly romantic-looking Italian men, in dinner jackets, the women in brilliant colours, their hair piled high. And their jewellery, stunningly bold and beautiful, great ropes of pearls, sculptured twists of gold and emerald, jet and ivory set in silver, and diamond earrings, bracelets, watches. She wanted to stand still, just to gaze at them, but was borne majestically upwards to the great Arturo Toscanini foyer, where the scene was doubled – no, quadrupled – in the huge, gilt-studded mirrors.

She was enchanted, drunk by it, and when she reached the bar she felt no longer nervous of meeting Jeremy, he had become merely an adjunct to this evening of visual feasting.

Which was just as well, as he wasn't there.

'Last saw him dashing into the Hotel Grande to change,' said Timothy Fordyce, shaking her hand. 'He'll make it. He's never late.'

'But always very, very near it,' said Eliza, laughing.

'I'd forgotten you knew him,' Fordyce said. 'Now, Eliza, this is my wife, Janey.'

Janey Fordyce was rather understated in a little black dress, but she was sparkly and pretty, her looks English rose, with blond hair and large blue eyes.

411

'How do you do, Eliza. I've heard lots about you – of course.'

'We never stop talking about her, that's why,' said Mariella. 'Eliza, champagne?'

People came and went, flowed towards them and retreated; all charming, all stylish, all clearly very, very rich. There was much talk of which crowned heads had attended the opening the week before and who had met which of them; and much gossip about Callas, who had been replaced by Jackie Kennedy in the life of her lover, Aristotle Onassis.

'They say her voice is not what it was,' said Giovanni, 'but I think it is still incredible. I heard her sing *Tosca* not so very long ago; it was an amazing experience.'

'But *Traviata* will be so beautiful tonight,' said Janey, 'my favourite opera of all. So exciting to be with you, Giovanni, and in the best box in the house, the royal one apart.'

'The most exciting thing is to have you in it with us,' said Giovanni, taking her hand and kissing it and then bowing just slightly.

The first warning bell went and then the second. Still no Jeremy.

'We shall have to go,' said Giovanni, 'we will tell them to show him up to the box.'

The view of Scala from the box made Eliza feel quite literally dizzy. And awed.

'Oh, my God,' she said, 'it is so amazing. It's all boxes, no seats . . .'

'Nearly all,' said Giovanni, 'there are the stalls as you see, and the *loggione* above.' He waved his hand towards them, the equivalent, Eliza presumed, of the Gods. The boxes were on three sides of the theatre, stacked in great golden and red tiers, the stage directly ahead.

They settled, Mariella insisting she sat in the very front; still no Jeremy.

'Very naughty,' said Timothy Fordyce, 'I'm so sorry, Giovanni.'

'It is OK. I hope they will allow him in, they may not now.'

'Serve him right,' said Eliza. Absurdly, along with Fordyce, she felt responsible for what appeared to be a very English rudeness.

The opera was of course beautiful. Eliza was not very musically literate, but the searing heartbreak of the story and the soaring beauty of the music left her oddly tearful. She sang, flirted, laughed with Violetta, felt herself in love with Alfredo; and then as Violetta sang alone in her parlour, musing upon a possible romance with Alfredo, something most unfortunate happened. Eliza started to cough. It was quite a genteel cough, and the first time it was all right; Mariella smiled at her sympathetically, touched

412

her hand, no one else took any notice. But then – again. Louder. Not only did their party hear it, Mariella frowning slightly; she saw someone in the adjacent box glance along. And then, at a particularly poignant moment in the aria, a third cough rose in her chest; there was only one thing to do. She stood up, holding her breath, her hand over her mouth and almost burst out of the box and then ran down the stairs out into the ground-floor foyer where she coughed, loudly, uninhibitedly, almost joyfully, her eyes watering, fighting for breath. One of the uniformed lackeys came forward, enquired if she was all right; she managed to smile at him, nod, and make her way slowly to the Ladies' room, where a kindly attendant fetched her water, stroked her back, and handed her a towel.

It had all only taken five minutes, and then she was perfectly all right again, make-up repaired, breathing quite normal, cough gone.

Clearly she could not go back to the box; but she could wait outside, it would be the interval in *cinque minuti*, the kindly attendant told her. She thanked her, put a hundred lire in the saucer, and made her way up to the third level, where she knew the box was. Only – which box? The doors were all numbered but she had no idea what the number was, had just followed Mariella and Giovanni while goggling at her surroundings. She tried to be calm, to think. Clearly, the box had been more or less central – but that could account for any one of five doors. She was just standing uncertainly outside one of them when she heard footsteps behind her. She turned with relief, thinking that whoever it was might be able to tell her; and there, even more handsome than she remembered, smiling at her in that so familiar here-we-are-you-and-me-alone-in-the-world way, was Jeremy Northcott.

'Eliza! How lovely! How wonderful you look! How are you and are you lost?'

She stared at him, stared and stared, literally unable to speak. The floor heaved slightly beneath her three-inch heels; she felt as uncertain, as foolish, and as dazzled as she had done all those years ago, the first time she had set eyes on him at Brad's; and he seemed as glamorous, and as sophisticated. The light from the chandeliers seemed to fade and brighten, several times.

And then, as reality returned and he continued to smile at her and she continued to stare at him, she knew. Of course she did . . . And she could see that he did too.

413

Chapter 40

It was incredibly stupid of her; she could see that. Probably the most stupid thing she had ever done. She deserved the most awful retribution and it would probably come.

But here she was, having a long conversation with David, albeit on the phone, as she had sworn she never would again; she had no idea where it might lead, she only knew that it had been an oddly healing experience. And although she had vowed she would never, ever go to bed with him again, she really, really would not, she heard herself agreeing to possibly – just possibly – seeing him, the next time he was in London.

'Matt, it is you, isn't it? Hi!'

It was Gina. Looking very little older and really very good, in one of the new black maxi coats and fur Dr Zhivago hat, her thick fringe just appearing underneath it, her grey eyes sparkling at him.

'Hello,' he said. He'd forgotten how extraordinarily pretty she was.

'How are you? It's really good to see you.'

'I'm fine. Yes. Great.'

'Successful, I gather. Can't stop reading about you. Millionaire Matt. Got your twenty-seven yet?'

She'd remembered. How he was determined to have at least twenty-seven million by the time he was thirty-nine, like Harry Hyams. He was touched.

'Not quite. You don't want to believe everything you read in the papers.'

'I'd believe anything I read about you, Matt. Anything.'

He'd also forgotten how flirty she was; how she could put a sexy slant onto everything.

'Well – you know, it's gone pretty well.'

'Yeah? And how's your wife?'

'She's great. Yes. Thanks.'

'A good few years now, isn't it? Old married man. You don't look it, Matt, you look just the same. Same old Matt. Or rather, same young Matt.'

He'd also forgotten how nice it was to be flirted with.

'What are you doing?'

'Oh, got my own boutique now. In Kensington Church Street. It does pretty well. Biba brings the punters down that way, and then they wander.'

'Yeah, I see. Well, I'm glad, Gina, really glad. And are you married?'

'Divorced. If you're ever down there, come in and see it. It's called Dressing Up. Two down from Bus Stop. Eliza will know. Here – take my card.'

She pressed it into his hand; and managed to make even that a provocative gesture.

'I'm not – not often down that way,' he said hastily. He felt awkward, almost shy.

'It doesn't have to be often.' The grey eyes were amused. 'Just the once.'

She'd recognised how he felt and was using it. He'd liked that. He'd forgotten that too.

'Right. Well, lovely to see you. You're looking pretty good yourself, by the way.'

'Thank you. Date then? At the shop?'

'Date,' he said and grinned.

She smiled, reached up and kissed him.

'Till next time. Lovely to see you too. Bye, Matt. For now.'

'Bye,' he said. He had no intention – ever – of visiting Dressing Up. She was too bloody disturbing.

'Are you all right?' Jeremy Northcott said.

'Yes. Yes. Of course. Thank you. Sorry. Just felt a bit – dizzy.'

'It is terribly hot. Would you like some water?'

'Oh – no. No, it's fine—'

'Is that why you're not in the box?'

'Um – no. I started coughing. In the middle of an aria.'

'How ghastly. That's happened to me. Here.' He rummaged in his pocket and produced a packet of Tunes. 'They make you breathe more easily. If you remember that particular jingle.'

'Yes,' she said, smiling, taking one, 'of course I do. Goodness, how welcome.'

'I always take them to the opera and to concerts. Keep forgetting and then they melt and stick to my pockets. Not good for the old DJ.'

'Oh Jeremy,' she said, 'it's so nice to see you. How – how are you?'

'I'm fine. In disgrace though, I should think. Now I know you're with the Crespis – I didn't before this afternoon when Tim told me. Are they absolutely furious with me? I just got lost in that infernal fog.'

'Oh, not really. I think they'll understand. But – oh, now listen.' Waves of applause reached them from the auditorium.

'Sounds like we could go in,' he said, 'not a proper interval now, is it?'

'No. But do you know which box?'

'Yes, Tim's scrawled it on my ticket. Look. Come on, let's go in. We can talk over dinner.' They opened the door of the box to a second surge of huge applause as the curtains swung down. Jeremy smiled. 'Is that for us?' he said, then, 'Mariella, Giovanni, can you ever forgive me?' He bowed over Mariella's hand and kissed it. 'I am so, so sorry. I got lost in the fog. And then of course I couldn't come in, until now.'

Giovanni stood up, shook his hand. 'Welcome, dear friend,' he said, 'we and Milan should not have subjected you to the fog. It is we who should ask for forgiveness. Let me give you a glass of champagne.'

Ice bucket, champagne and flutes had appeared from apparently nowhere.

'Thank you. How kind. Mariella, how very beautiful you look.'

'Thank you,' she said, 'how kind you are. Come, sit by me.'

Which he did, and as he did so, brushed her hand, momentarily; and she looked down at their hands, and then at him, her brilliant eyes somehow embracing him; and then bent her lovely head over the programme discussing with him what he had and had not missed, occasionally glancing over at Giovanni and, when she saw that he was engrossed in conversation with the Fordyces, addressed the full force of her beauty and its sexual power in another direction altogether.

A love affair was indeed born that night in the Crespi box at La Scala, taking the most extraordinary hold as the music surged and surrounded them and the tragic story told on the stage below found a most haunting and unpredictable echo. And the fog, holding them all captive in the city, disallowing escape, enforcing intimacy, played no small part in the drama that was to come.

Returning to an empty house, with nothing to eat, Matt suddenly felt lonely. He should never have let Eliza go, or at least insisted on a two-day visit instead of four.

He wondered what she was doing; having dinner with the Crespis no doubt, laughing and joking, drawn out of her depression, while he, stuck here without her, went into one.

Suddenly he wanted to speak to her; and why not, he thought, there was a telephone for God's sake; he would ring, calling overseas wasn't very difficult these days. They could have a chat and he would feel better.

He went into his study, sat down at his desk, dialled the operator and asked for the Crespi number. There was a slight delay, it seemed, about half an hour, some problem with the line, but then he should get through. He pulled some papers out of his briefcase and tried to concentrate.

Milan was by now completely fog-bound, with no chance of leaving; Eliza was close to panic. She was away from Emmie, whom she had left with comparative strangers, one of whom had already managed to lose her in Milan, and she quailed from the thought of Matt's reaction to the whole story.

'Can't we even try to get back?' she said to Giovanni, close to tears. 'I really want to—'

'Eliza, you do not know our fog. It is very, very bad. Tomorrow, perhaps, it will be gone, but tonight we must stay here. Try not to worry,' he said, smiling his sweet smile, 'all will be well.'

Mariella was dismissive of her anxieties.

'Emmie will be fine. You can speak to her, you can speak to Bruno, you can speak to Anna-Maria.'

'But she's only very little, she might be frightened—'

'Did she sound frightened? When you called earlier? She seemed to be having a wonderful time.' She was growing bored with the whole Emmie situation. 'Eliza, there is nothing we can do. If we try to get home, we will probably be killed. Please try to accept it.'

'Mariella,' said Eliza, determined to be firm. 'She's only five years old. She's in a strange place with strange people. Of course your staff are good, I don't doubt it. I'm just worried about her if she wakes up in the night or—'

Janey Fordyce, who had been listening, put her hand on Eliza's arm.

'It's very dangerous, the fog, Eliza. It really is. Now the thing is, where will you all stay? Mariella, you and Giovanni are very welcome to stay with us, in our apartment, but I don't think we can find room for Eliza too—'

'No, no, we can use the room at the Grande,' said Mariella, 'and Eliza can stay with you. There. That is settled. Now – shall we go to dinner?'

'We will,' said Giovanni, 'but first Eliza and I will go and make a telephone call, so that she can reassure herself about her daughter. It is very worrying for her, Mariella, and I do not like to see people worried.'

'But—' began Mariella and then stopped, put on her sweetest smile and said, 'of course.'

It was the first time Eliza had seen the true balance of power in that relationship and it intrigued her. The conversations with both Bruno, who said he and Emmie had played cards after dinner and she had then told him a story, and Anna-Maria, who was sitting by her small bed as she slept, were reassuring; Eliza relaxed a little.

'And now,' said Giovanni, 'would you like to try to speak to your husband? To reassure him that you are quite safe?'

'Oh – no, thank you,' said Eliza with a shudder. 'He won't for an instant be worried about me, he doesn't know there's a fog after all and there's no way he'll try to call. No, the best thing is to leave him in blissful ignorance, Giovanni. I'll call him tomorrow when I'm back at the villa.'

'*Bene*. Then let us go and enjoy our dinner.'

It took forty minutes to get to the restaurant from La Scala, limousine crawling after limousine in the thick fog.

'We'd have done better to walk,' said Timothy.

The restaurant, Lisander, was so beautiful that Eliza felt she must have strayed back onto the set of *La Traviata*, with rows of tables, each with their own little white-shaded lamps, and filled with flowers. 'You should see it in the summer,' Janey Fordyce said to her, 'somehow they bring the garden inside, wisteria trailing everywhere, you would love it. A million romances must have begun here.'

'Only a million!' said Mariella, laughing. 'I do not think so.'

And then she organised them all very efficiently, placing herself next to Giovanni on one side and Jeremy on the other. And flirted with both of them quite outrageously. It was a bit like, Eliza thought, looking in on a *ménage à trois*.

❁ ❁ ❁

'Hello! Hello! Is that the Villa Crespi?'

'*Si signor, si,* Villa Crespi is here.'

'Can I speak to Signor Crespi, please?'

'Signor Crespi not here, sir.'

'OK. Signora Crespi then.'

'The *signora* is also not here.'

'Oh. Oh I see. Well, is my wife there? Mrs Shaw? Surely she must be there, it's—'

'One moment, *signor*, please.'

What the fuck was going on? Where were they all? Pretty bloody rude leaving Eliza on her own. And she was obviously there, she wouldn't have left Emmie at night surely, it was eleven thirty Italian-time . . . bloody wops.

'*Signor*. Good evening. Is Sebastiano here, butler to the Crespis. Can I help you?'

'Well, I hope so,' said Matt, 'I'm calling from England, I want to speak to my wife, Mrs Shaw . . .'

'Oh, I am so sorry, *signor*. They are all away, in Milan.'

'Away? What do you mean?'

'At the opera, *signor*. At La Scala.'

'Oh – right.' He did remember hearing something about La Scala and how worried Eliza was about what she would wear. 'Will you ask my wife to call as soon as they get back?'

'They will not be back tonight, *signor*. I am sorry.'

'Not back? Why the hell not?'

'Well, sir, because of the fog. There is a very bad fog here tonight, *signor*. They will not be able to come back. It happens often here, the fog at this time of year. It is very, very dangerous to try to drive, to travel.'

'Well – well . . .' Matt felt himself held in a fog of his own, a dangerous, bewildering, angry fog. 'Well – is my daughter with them? Because if she is—'

'No, *signor*, your daughter is quite safe with us. We are all taking great care of her, you must not worry, she is asleep, Anna-Maria is with her all the time, and she is very, very happy. What a dear little girl she is, so beautiful, so talented, so intelligent—'

Sebastiano's musings upon Emmie's virtues and beauty were interrupted.

'Well, she'd better be bloody well safe,' said Matt, 'and the moment, the moment my wife gets back, you get her to ring me, all right? When will that be?'

'*Signor*, it is impossible to say, I am sorry, the fog sometimes lasts for a day, sometimes two. But I will get a message to Signor Crespi first thing in the morning—'

'You bloody well get a message to him tonight,' said Matt, 'I want to know my wife is safe and when she'll be back with my daughter, is that clear?'

'*Si, signor.*'

Sebastiano put the phone down disdainfully, feeling it had assumed the persona of the ill-mannered foreigner who had been berating him and after a few minutes' thought, dialled the number of the Hotel Grande and asked to be put through to Signor Crespi.

On hearing he was not there, but out at dinner, Sebastiano decided there was no more he could do. Nothing made his master angrier than being pursued in his leisure hours unless it was to do with his beloved wife. He left a message at the Hotel Grande, asking Giovanni to call him when he came back if it was convenient, as Mr Shaw had been asking for his wife, and left it at that. The whole thing was rather ridiculous and nothing that could not be resolved in the morning.

The Fordyce apartment was grander than Eliza had expected, decorated *alla Milanese*, with endless gilt mirrors, heavy draped curtains, lavish flower arrangements, and every spare inch of wall covered in paintings – landscapes, miniatures, portraits, still lifes, many of them quite crude.

'It's a company apartment,' said Janey. 'I wanted to anglicise it, but we're not really supposed to. I've got used to it now and we're going back to London in six months, so—'

'Will you be pleased?'

'Oh yes, I think so. It's wonderful here, but it's a bit – intense. And we're neither fish nor fowl, not visitors, not Milanese, and there's no place like England, is there?'

Eliza agreed that there was not. She lay awake for a long time in her four-poster bed, complete with gilt cherubs, worrying about Emmie and thinking about Jeremy, how extraordinarily nice he was, how extremely attractive still and how much easier her life would have been if she had married him.

✿ ✿ ✿

When Giovanni got back to the hotel, and was told there was a message from Sebastiano, and that Matt had been asking for Eliza, he decided that at one in the morning, he had no stomach for trying to make complex phone calls. It had been a wonderful evening and there was a little anxiety like the mildest dyspepsia somewhere within him, he knew not why, and he wanted to be alone with his Mariella and try to sleep. The morning would take care of itself.

Chapter 41

'Matt? Is that you? Is everything all right?'

'Yes. How about with you?'

'Oh, absolutely fine, yes. Everything's great. Emmie's having a lovely time and so am I and we're both looking forward to—'

'To what? What are you both looking forward to? A reunion?'

'What, with you? Yes, that's what I was going to say, we—'

'So you're together are you?'

'Well – not this minute, no. I'm in Milan. But we're on our way back, just leaving in a few minutes.'

'Which is where exactly, if I might ask?'

'Well – in an apartment. Belonging to friends of Mariella and Giovanni—'

'And why are you there?'

His tone was quite easy, he sounded almost cheerful. Careful Eliza, steady; it might be all right yet.

'Well, you see – last night—'

'Ah, last night. And where were you last night? Exactly? Without Emmie?'

So he knew. He'd found out somehow.

'The thing is, Matt, we were in Milan, at the opera. You know I told you about that. And we got completely cut off by the fog. We just couldn't get back. It was impossible, dangerous. I'm staying like I said, with – with friends of Mariella and—'

'You were staying with people you don't know. And leaving Emmie with people she didn't know. It all sounds rather messy.'

'She did know them, Matt, of course she did. Anna-Maria has looked after her before and she's spent lots of time with Bruno – that's Giovanni's valet—'

'You left Emmie alone with a man. A strange man, a bloody foreigner—'

'Matt, don't be ridiculous. He's not a stranger and she loves him, he always plays with her when we're here and—'

Janey appeared at her bedroom door; she looked flustered.

'Eliza – Mariella's—'

'Sorry, Janey, can you just give me a minute. Matt, the thing is—'

'I don't want to hear what the fucking thing is,' said Matt, 'I want you home, both of you, tonight, is that clear? So you just get out of that apartment with your smart friends and back to Emmie and then straight on to the airport. And I don't want to hear about any fucking fog holding you up. I'm sure Giovanni can find a way out of it. In his private plane perhaps. I remember him talking about that rather a lot at dinner. I'm going to the office now and I'll want to hear from you pretty bloody soon about your arrangements.'

'Matt—'

The phone went dead; Eliza sat staring at it, a crawling fear invading her stomach.

'Eliza.' Mariella pushed past Janey into the room. 'Eliza, it seems Matt phoned the villa last night. Sebastiano called to tell us. For some reason the messages did not reach us.'

'Really?' This seemed unlikely.

'Yes, really.' Mariella's eyes were wide with innocence. 'I am so sorry—'

'Well, it's unfortunate,' Eliza said, driven past courtesy. 'Matt is absolutely furious with me, especially of course leaving Emmie behind—'

'*Cara*—'

'No, let me finish. And he's ordered us both back tonight. So maybe you can help me find a flight – otherwise he'll divorce me, I should think.'

'Of course he won't,' said Mariella, her voice a soothing purr, 'he is just annoyed that you are enjoying yourself and he is not—'

'Mariella, he's really angry and I'm scared—'

'You should not be scared of your husband,' said Mariella airily, 'that is not good for you.'

'Well, I am! I've got to get back. So—'

'*Cara*, there are no planes. Not today. Not tomorrow I think, either.'

'No planes! But—'

'Eliza, look out of the window. No plane can fly in this. We must stay, it is the only safe thing to do.'

'No, no, I must get back to Emmie at least. She's only five, I know she was all right last night, but she needs me. Please, Mariella, can we try at least?'

'I will call Giovanni, see what he says.'

Giovanni said they might be able to leave at lunchtime, that the fog was clearing a very little. 'But he also says no plane will leave Milan today, or even tomorrow. I am sorry, *cara*, it is just one of those things. Matt will understand, I am sure. Perhaps Giovanni could speak to him.'

'I'd rather he didn't,' said Eliza and burst into tears. Mariella left in a huff to return to the Hotel Grande and Janey was left trying to comfort Eliza.

'I'll ask Tim, see if he thinks it would be possible to get back to the villa.'

Tim was reluctant; he knew the dangers too well and he didn't know the road.

Eliza spoke to Emmie who sounded happy, but distinctly less cool, and told her she wanted her to come back.

'Darling, the minute I can I will. Is it foggy there?'

'Terribly,' said Emmie. 'We can't see the garden even.'

Shaking, Eliza rang Matt at midday; mercifully he was out at a site meeting. Mandy, Jenny's replacement, sweet and helpful, asked if she could give him a message.

'Tell him I rang and I'll ring later. When is he back, do you think?'

'I would think about four hours, Mrs Shaw.'

So she had four hours. To get back to the villa. She began literally to pace the floor.

Shortly after one, the phone rang; she heard Janey answer it.

'Oh hello, Jeremy. Yes, she's here. Hold on.'

'Eliza! Hello, darling. I hear you're in a bit of a pickle. Look the fog's thinning out a bit, and I've asked Giovanni to call the villa, see how it is out there. If it's really better, Tim and I are prepared to get a car from the company's fleet, man with local knowledge, and see what we can do.'

'Oh, Jeremy,' said Eliza, bursting into tears. 'You are marvellous!'

'Not really. I like a challenge. Especially when there's a lady in distress involved. Now then, you sit tight and I'll call you the minute I've got some news.'

Why hadn't she married him? Why, why, why?

But she knew. As she had at La Scala. It would have been wonderful, easy, luxurious, and fun. And – emotionally dull.

However hateful Matt was, however critical and bad-tempered and difficult, he still brought her alive: in every possible way. Jeremy had never, ever, been able to do that.

Which was a terrible shame, but . . .

At two he rang again.

'It's now or never. Once it's dark, we'll really be up the river without a canoe. Ready?'

'Of course!'

She rang Matt again, knowing he would still be out, but she wanted to show she was trying.

'Tell him I rang again, will you, Mandy, and that I'm on my way back to the villa.'

They reached the villa at six; it was a long and hazardous journey; twice they skidded and once nearly hit a tree, but the driver was skilful and knew the road, and the fog was less dense the nearer they got to Como, with a breeze coming in from the lake. By the time they arrived, they could actually see the lights of the house from the gates. Eliza, who had been sitting in the back, silent and tense, next to Jeremy, reached for his hand and squeezed it and then leaned forward and kissed the back of Tim Fordyce's rather thick neck.

'I'll never forget this, either of you,' she said, 'never, as long as I live.'

An hour later they were sitting with Emmie in the kitchen, all four of them drinking hot chocolate; Emmie was actually on Jeremy's knee, squealing with delight as he opened and shut his legs endlessly, pretending to drop her. She had taken a great fancy to him; and he rather had to her. And what would Matt have to say confronted by this scene, Eliza thought.

The driver had decided to stay the night as well, which meant Tim and Jeremy would have to; Tim had agreed with a worried Janey that a return journey in darkness was not wise.

'It's going to be better tomorrow,' she said, 'or so the forecast says. I'd much rather you came back then.'

They dined rather well, the adults on osso buco, prepared by the cook and Emmie on pasta, served to the four of them in the small dining room. Emmie was high on excitement and pleasure. 'After this,' she said, 'can we play a game?'

'Emmie, no,' said Eliza, 'it's nearly nine o'clock and I must ring Daddy one more time.'

'Well, after that, then?'

'Emmie, I said no.'

'But you've been away from me.' The voice became querulous, rising in volume.

'That's true,' said Jeremy. 'I'll play with you, Emmie, even if your mother won't. What did you have in mind?'

'Hide and Seek,' said Emmie.

'Sounds fun. But we'll have to do it in pairs, we'll get really lost in this great big house if we're not careful.'

'Oh, God,' said Eliza, and then giggled. And then, in a rush of amusement and relief at at least having Emmie back, 'Talk about a compromising situation.'

'What's compromising?' asked Emmie.

'Fun,' said Jeremy, his face deadpan and winking at Eliza.

She had called Matt both in the office and at home, every hour since they had got back. Mandy said he had come back and she had given him the messages but that he hadn't asked her to try to ring Eliza back. Even now, at eleven o'clock – ten in England – there was no reply.

'He's clearly worried to death,' said Eliza, sharply angry herself; and refilled her glass with the very nice Chianti they had all been drinking, and went off with Timothy Fordyce to look for Jeremy and Emmie. Tomorrow would have to take care of itself. And so would Matt.

Matt received the news from Mandy at five, just after he got back to the office: Eliza wouldn't be back that night, and possibly not the next.

'But she said she was on her way back to the villa and would be with Emmie tonight,' said Mandy. 'Shall I try to get a line through to her, Mr Shaw?'

'No, thanks,' said Matt, 'no point. Make me some coffee, please. And I don't want—' He stopped. No need to reject biscuits; with Jenny's departure the biscuit tin had left as well. On the whole it was a relief.

'Yes, Mr Shaw.'

He sat at his desk, sipping the coffee, contemplating yet another solitary evening. It was not a nice prospect. Matt had never cultivated friendship for its own sake; he saw it as a waste of time. Eliza and his work were all he had ever wanted. Eliza was failing him. So – thank God for work.

He was rummaging in his wallet for the card of a potential client, whom he'd sat next to at a lunch that day, and who had said he was looking for new, larger premises for his company, when Gina's fell out. Matt turned it over, looked at it thoughtfully, half-smiling as he read the words on the back in her rather childish writing. 'Don't forget! Lots to show you.'

No, Matt, don't even think about it. She's trouble, and you don't need it. Not that sort. You've got enough.

He pushed it aside and found the card he'd been looking for and dialled the number. It was a direct line, and his lunchtime companion, the CEO of a large insurance company, was clearly pleased to hear from him.

Matt told him he had a shortlist of available premises for him; 'I'll bike it over tomorrow.'

'Great. Or—' There was a pause. 'I'm actually free and on my own in town tonight, we could meet for a drink.'

The drink led to hands shaken on a deal, then dinner, and Matt arrived home after midnight.

Next morning he spoke to Eliza; she was very sorry, she said, but although the fog was lifting, there were no flights until the following day.

'But I'm with Emmie, at the villa, it was a bit hairy, the drive, but we made it, and she's fine, and we will be back tomorrow.'

'That's extremely good of you. Don't rush on my account.'

'Matt—'

'Sorry, Eliza, I've got to go. In your own time. Bye.'

He arrived in the office tense with rage. How could she? How could she just sit there in that fucking palace and tell him she was sorry but she had to stay there another day? And expect him to be impressed she had made an effort to get back to her own child? How could she, how dare she . . .

He roared for coffee, pulling out his diary. And saw, tucked into yesterday's page, where he had discarded it, Gina's card.

He arrived at Scott's Piccadilly, as she had suggested, just after six. He went over to the bar, looked at the menu, pulled out his cigarettes. He had a pleasant sense of playing truant, breaking rules. Which was ridiculous, of course. He was only having a drink with her, for God's sake. He ordered a large gin and tonic, carried it over to a table in the corner, settled down behind his *Evening Standard*. She was late; but then she always had been.

He enjoyed it all for about five minutes, then began to get irritable. He couldn't stand people who were late, it was so bloody arrogant, wasting other people's time. Five more and he was ready to leave; he'd just go to the Gents and then leave a message with the barman . . .

He was washing his hands when he heard the door open; he didn't even look up. He was trying to decide whether to go out for a meal or find something in the fridge. He'd—

'Fuck off, will you!'

Someone was goosing him. No two ways about it. Some poof, he supposed.

He swung round. Someone was indeed goosing him. But it wasn't a poof.

'Hello, Matt. I won't, if you don't mind. I'm quite enjoying myself; I'd forgotten what a neat little arse you had . . .'

It was Gina. Looking ravishing, laughing, reaching up to kiss him.

He'd forgotten how outrageous she was, how sexy. He'd forgotten what outrageous and sexy felt like.

'Gina,' he said, kissing her hastily back, 'you'll get us arrested.'

'For what?'

'Indecent behaviour in a public toilet?'

'Matt, it's not public. And I'm not being indecent, not any more. Pity, but . . . I just walked in by mistake, thought it was the Ladies. Who's going to arrest me for that?'

'There might have been someone else in here.'

'There might. But there wasn't. Anyway, let's go and get a drink, I'm desperate. Now, how long have you got? Because I've got the whole evening . . .'

They had, of course, gone out to dinner. There didn't seem much reason not to, as Gina pointed out.

'You've got to eat somewhere, Matt. And so have I. And neither of us have anyone to eat with. Except each other. So, where shall we go? San Frediano's? It's such fun there.'

'Gina, I don't think that's a very good idea.'

'Why not?'

'Well – someone might see us. Someone who knows us.'

'So what? Eliza's in Milan, for God's sake. Her idea, as far as I can make out, and with her friends. What are you supposed to do, sit at home eating bread and milk? And then sort out the laundry?'

She made that sound slightly insulting, reduced him to wimpish domesticity.

'No, of course not,' he said, 'no, let's go there, good idea.'

Someone was there who knew them: not a friend of Gina's nor a friend of Matt. But a friend of Eliza's, Jerome Blake, the photographer whose studio was in the same building as Maddy Brown's, together with his model girlfriend. He watched them, saw Matt tense at first, slowly relaxing into laughing, talking ease; watched the girl, sex on legs, with her low-cut clinging dress, her smoky come-to-bed eyes, teasing him, flirting with him, whispering in his ear, and then as the evening went on, picking up his hand and playing with the fingers, resting her head briefly on his shoulder, and then as they left, in their coats, putting her arm round his neck and pulling him down to kiss quickly on the mouth. And then a taxi pulled up and whether both of them got into it or only one, he was unable to tell.

Chapter 42

London looked at once more cheerful than Milan and less appealing. The sun was shining, to be sure, and the sky was blue; but the shop windows, the garish Christmas lights, the endless Christmas trees, looked tawdry and clichéd.

Eliza did however feel much more cheerful, somehow leaving behind her the clawing remnants of her depression over the baby, full of optimism and plans.

She arrived back at the house mid-afternoon, and spent the rest of the day playing with Emmie, cooking dinner, tidying up Matt's appalling squalor, washing her hair, and changing, nothing fancy she decided, that would look as if she was trying too hard, just jeans and a shirt. She bathed Emmie at six and put her into her pyjamas and dressing gown, but told her she could stay up until Daddy got home.

'Unless it's really late.'

'What's really late?'

'Oh, Emmie, I don't know. About eight o'clock.'

'That's not really late. Ten is really late. And in the villa we were playing till eleven—'

'Emmie, I don't want to hear about the villa. That was quite different. We were on holiday. At home eight is late for you. You're tired and anyway—'

'I want to see Daddy,' said Emmie, her small face setting firmly against her mother. 'I've missed him.'

Eliza started to argue, then gave in; the little girl could always go to sleep on the sofa, and Matt would be pleased to see her whatever the time was.

She'd rung him to say she was home and he said he couldn't say when he would be. He sounded cool, but not hostile. Maybe it would all be all right. She'd bought him a new wallet from the marvellous Prada – God, if

430

only there was one in London – and a new tie from Dior. There was nothing else she could do.

The biggest danger was that he would hear that Jeremy had been there at the villa. She couldn't possibly enlist Emmie as accomplice; she would just have to tough it out.

He got home just before eight; she went out into the hall to greet him, her stomach heaving.

'Hello,' she said, reaching up to kiss him.

'Hello,' he said. He didn't kiss her back, but he didn't brush her away. His expression was impossible to read: blank, neither hostile nor welcoming, his eyes oddly wary.

'It's – so nice to see you.'

'Daddy!' A small thunderbolt hurled itself across the hall and into Matt's arms, covering his face with kisses. 'I missed you so, so much. I love you so, so much.'

'I missed you too, Emmie. It's lovely to have you home. What did you do? I want you to tell me all about it.'

'I had a lovely time and I've got a present for you. I got it at the airport.'

'The airport!' said Matt, laughing. 'That sounds a bit last minute to me.'

'No,' said Emmie, 'it's a beautiful picture. Of the Duomo.' Her pronunciation was perfect. 'I chose it specially for you. It's got a gold frame and everything.'

'Gold! It sounds wonderful. Where is it?'

'In my bedroom. I'll get it.'

She ran up the stairs. Eliza's eyes met Matt's. To her surprise he was smiling at her. Emmie's greeting had broken the chill.

'She's wonderful, isn't she?' he said.

They all ate supper in the kitchen; Matt admired the picture and to a lesser degree the wallet and the tie.

'So,' he said to Emmie, 'tell me what you did, and was it fun?'

'Some of the time,' she said.

'Only some of the time?'

Eliza froze.

'Yes, some of it was boring. Anna-Maria's very boring.'

'Really?'

'Yes.' A huge yawn engulfed her face.

'Emmie,' said Eliza, 'what about bed?'

'No, not till I've shown Daddy my new shoes.'

'New shoes!'

'Yes, I'll show you. And a new dress. Wait there, Daddy.'

Eliza waited for her return, feeling sick.

But, 'Mariella bought them for me,' was all she said. She was clearly more remorseful than she had let on about her Milanese adventure.

'And I've got another picture for you,' she said, producing it from her small flight bag. 'One I did. It's of the villa. Look. This is the back of the house, here. That's a fountain.'

'Fountains! For God's sake.'

'Yes, and that's a maze. A – a minty maze.'

'Miniature, darling. We loved that maze, didn't we, Emmie?'

'It's a very good picture, Emmie,' said Matt.

'Yes, the man said so too.'

'The man? You mean Mr Crespi?'

He refused to move into Italian even in the most minimal way. Eliza sat, her fork poised, her mouth dry with terror.

'No, not him, the other man—'

'What other man?'

This was it then: the end of her marriage.

'The man who looked after me.'

'Oh,' said Eliza, relief surging through her, 'oh, you mean Bruno. He didn't really look after you, Emmie, Anna-Maria did, didn't she?'

'Bruno was much nicer. Bruno was fun.'

'Bruno is Giovanni's valet,' said Eliza, 'he and Emmie hit it off rather.'

'I see. So what else did you do with Bruno?'

'Played snap. I taught him, he didn't know. And ate in the kitchen, with him and Lucia.'

'Lucia? Another servant?' asked Matt.

'Yes. The cook.'

'Dear God in heaven. So – what's this blue stuff? The sky? I thought it was foggy?'

'No. It's the lake. And it was only foggy when Mummy went to the theatre. Till then it was really nice.'

'And what else did you do?'

'Oh – I don't know.' Emmie had every child's dislike of being interrogated. 'Will you come and read me a story?'

'Of course I will.'

They disappeared, Matt without a backward glance at Eliza. No prizes for guessing who his favourite person was.

'Welcome home to you too, Eliza,' she said, and started clearing the table.

He was gone a long time; when she went up to find him, he was stretched out half-asleep on the bed.

'Think I might sleep next door,' he said standing up hastily, avoiding her eyes. 'Got a very early start.' And moved into the spare room. She didn't argue, in fact she was grateful, she felt exhausted and very tense. Well – so far she'd got off very lightly. But it was without doubt odd.

Several very chilly days followed, Eliza lurched from anxiety to relief, then hurt and all the way back again. He wasn't even acting suspicious. Just – odd. Working late – which meant at least there was no more questioning of Emmie. But very, very distant, and very, very cold.

On Saturday, she had to take Emmie to a party after lunch; when she got back, he seemed to have disappeared. She looked in the sitting room and the study, and sighed, assuming he had gone out without telling her. Then she heard his voice calling her.

'Eliza! I'm up here.'

He was in the bedroom, in bed. Naked. Sitting up and grinning at her, half-embarrassed.

'Oh,' she said, 'oh. I thought—'

'What did you think?'

'I thought – well, you didn't – didn't like me any more.'

'Now why on earth should you think that?'

'You haven't exactly been acting pleased to see me.'

'Eliza – look, sorry if I've got it wrong, but it was you went off to Milan, saying it would cheer you up, you who were late back; I'm a simple sort of chap, that didn't exactly tell me you wanted to be with me.'

'I'm – I'm sorry but—'

'Look,' he said holding out his hand to her, 'look, I think it's starting again time.'

'But—'

'Eliza, I'm sitting here stark bollock-naked. Waiting for you. Can't spell it out clearer than that. Why do you have to argue about everything? Emmie's out, we haven't really spent any time together since you got back. Don't you want to come and join me?'

She looked at him, feeling almost with surprise a rush of tenderness,

433

and then of desire, the wonderfully powerful clenching deep within her that she had almost forgotten, suddenly longing to be held, kissed, stroked, played on.

'Oh,' she said, 'oh, yes, Matt, I do. More than more than, I do.'

Later, lying beside him, her body still throbbing, but sweetly released, for the first time since the summer, she lay smiling at him, her eyes exploring his.

'That was so lovely,' she said.

He looked at her very seriously.

'Was it really?'

'It really, really was.'

'Well, hallelujah!' he said. She looked at him sharply, fearing irony, but he smiled suddenly.

'Welcome back,' he said. 'And I don't mean from Milan. Although it obviously did you good. I have to admit that.'

'Thank you. And yes, it did,' she said, thinking that in a million years he would never understand how or why, and how dangerous such an explanation might be.

'Love me?' said Matt, rather absent-mindedly kissing her shoulder.

'Yes,' she said, 'yes, I do. You?'

'Oh I love me too,' he said.

She remained terrified of Matt finding out about Jeremy; but as the days went past, Emmie said nothing more about Milan, and as it receded from her memory behind the excitement of Christmas, Eliza began to relax. She felt wonderful, the last remnants of her depression gone, alive and even sexy; welcoming Matt into bed and herself, again and again, soaring higher and higher with release and relief until Matt complained, laughing, that she was wearing him out. They were happier than they had been for months, and that was enough for both of them for the time being.

And certainly too much to risk by confronting another matter, a suggestion from Jeremy, as she had chatted to him and Timothy over breakfast following the hair-raising drive to the villa, as the unfortunate Bruno was borne away to play snap with Emmie once more.

'So, you having a good time?' Jeremy had asked. 'What are you doing, work-wise?'

'Nothing,' she said, and then quickly, too quickly, 'I didn't want to. Not while Emmie was small. I think she needs me at home.'

'Most admirable. Not what you used to say.'

'No. I know. But – I'm not who I used to be.'

'I think you are. In some ways.' He smiled at her; she smiled easily back. 'Anyway, now she's at school?'

'Yes.'

'So you'll be wanting to go back.'

'I want to,' she said, 'but Matt – that is I – we're not sure—'

'And perhaps you'll be having other babies.'

'Yes,' she said, 'perhaps,' and as always happened at such a point in the conversation, the tears came, try as she might to stop them, and one fell rather dramatically on the tablecloth, followed by another.

'Sorry,' she said, 'so sorry, Jeremy.'

Timothy cleared his throat and excused himself, hurried off; living abroad had left his English reserve untouched, she thought, and would have imagined that of Jeremy too, but, 'Tell me about it,' he said gently, and she did and he was sweet and kind, and seemed to understand; but when she said she had been quite depressed, he said, 'Maybe working would do you good.'

'It – might do. Yes. But – hard to organise. Matt's very against nannies. And the school day isn't very long.'

'Mmm. There's one thing you might consider. If you fancied it. It's something I inaugurated in New York and suggest they do in London.'

'What's that?'

'Well, we employ a fashion consultant, who works with a creative group on a project. Once they've decided whether an ad is going to be TV or press, she advises them on what they'd be wearing. And then sources the clothes. And goes along to the shoots. Books the make-up artists and sometimes the models. How does that sound?'

'Utterly wonderful,' said Eliza.

'And it is absolutely not a full-time job. Maybe two days a week. You're pretty well qualified for it.'

'I was,' said Eliza with a sigh. 'I've been out of it for five years, Jeremy, don't forget.'

'Oh, you'd catch up in no time. And they'd love you, having been in the forefront of it all. You'd be perfect. Think about it.'

'But – why should a complete stranger of a creative director want to hire someone suggested by you. I mean, London and New York, pretty far apart. Surely.'

'Well, yes. But I am coming back to London. Early next year. Had enough of New York, it's been fun, great fun, but I want to come home. And Ma's died, you may not have heard? Pa's a bit lost.'

'Jeremy, I'm so sorry.'

Some other information was volunteered by Jeremy that morning: he had been conducting a long, if slightly on–off, affair with a New York divorcee.

'I seem to specialise in such arrangements,' he said, smiling at her. 'We were very happy together, but her life is in New York, she won't come to London. And no, I'm not remotely upset about that. Now, straight away after Christmas, call me. OK? Don't forget.'

She would not forget. No danger of that. Whether she actually would do it was extremely doubtful. Her truce with Matt was far too important to her.

It arrived by a rather circuitous route: a letter addressed to Miss Scarlett, c/o Demetrios on Trisos, enclosed in an envelope sent by Demetrios to her office address.

She opened it, puzzled, pulled out the contents, read it several times over and then set it on her desk, and sat smiling at it.

'Miss Scarlett (it said on the top in the thick black bold handwriting)
  Bristow and Baring, Publishers, request the pleasure of your company at a party to launch the publication of *Favourite French Journeys* by Mark Frost.
  6 p.m., The Gondoliers Room, Savoy Hotel. 20 January.'

Goodness. He must quite have wanted her to be there. To have gone to that much trouble.

How exciting. How interesting. How . . .

Then she remembered Mrs Frost. No doubt she would be there. Well, it would be interesting to meet her, she supposed.

It would also be interesting to go to a publishing party. She'd have to ask Eliza what to expect. And what to wear.

She pulled a sheet of her headed paper towards her (Scarlett Shaw, Exclusive Travellers' Club) and wrote to tell them that Miss Scarlett would be delighted to accept their kind invitation. Now at least he would know her address. And she might even get a bit of free publicity in one of his articles in the *Daily News*. So – who cared about Mrs Frost?

The day before they left for Summercourt for Christmas, Eliza and Emmie went to visit Heather and Coral. They hadn't been there for a while, and Eliza had been worrying about them. She hadn't been much of a friend to Heather, had failed her entirely over her landlord; she felt guilty. They had brought them presents – an Amanda Jane doll for Coral with lots of clothes, and a huge, thick knitted cardigan for Heather. Eliza had a pretty shrewd idea that the flat wouldn't be any warmer this year than last. She'd also brought a bottle of port for Alan. All men liked port and it wasn't a flashy present, not like champagne.

'Now look,' she said to Emmie warningly, as they pulled up outside, 'you are not to talk about how we've been to stay in a palace.'

Emmie gave her a withering look.

'Of course I won't,' she said.

Sometimes, Eliza thought, she didn't give Emmie enough credit. She was actually a rather amazing little girl.

Heather opened the front door, looking exhausted.

'Hello,' she said, 'it's so lovely to see you. Come in. If you can face it.'

The house smelt bad. Coral was clinging to her mother's legs, suddenly shy. Emmie was having none of it.

'Come on,' she said, grabbing Coral's hand, 'we've got a present for you.'

'Emmie,' said Eliza, 'it's a Christmas present. Not for today.'

'I want to give it to her today. Then we can play with it.'

'I think that sounds like quite a good idea,' said Heather apologetically. 'She's so sick of all her toys.'

They went upstairs. The room looked smaller and more dingy than Eliza remembered. Heather had obviously made a great effort, and there was a small tree in the window and some home-made paper chains strung on the picture rails, but it was cold, and there was a damp patch on the ceiling that Eliza hadn't noticed before.

'Yes, it's new,' said Heather, 'from the sink in the flat one floor up. They've gone actually, taken the bribe, and I keep asking the landlord to turn the tap off completely, but he says it can't be done.'

'Oh, Heather. Any progress?'

'Only with this,' said Heather, patting her bump, 'growing very nicely, he is. We can't find anywhere else, Eliza, and I think we may have to bite the bullet and go and live with Alan's mum. Old witch, I really— I mean,' she said hastily, seeing that Emmie was listening, 'I mean she's really kind, but there's not much room. I don't want to go there, I really don't.'

'What about your mum, any better?'

'No, she's only got a two-bedroom flat, in one of those new high-rise things, you know, and I couldn't live there, not with two children.'

'Oh dear,' said Eliza, helplessly. She thought of the house in Fulham, with its five bedrooms for three people. It was ridiculous. 'Have you got your name down for a council house?'

'Yeah,' said Heather with a noise that was half-sigh, half-laugh, 'and I should think we've just risen from the very bottom to nearly the very bottom. They said two years minimum and I know what that means.'

'I'm so sorry,' said Eliza, 'and how do you feel?'

'Tired. Not being sick any more, thank goodness. But Alan's so bad-tempered, and saying he doesn't know how we're going to manage. Nor do I. Oh, I'm sorry, Eliza, sorry to be such a misery. How are you, are you feeling any better?'

'So much better,' said Eliza, 'yes. I've even stopped dreaming about him, about Baby Charles. Of course I still feel very sad but I can cope with it now. And it was you set me on the road to recovery, it really was . . . people keep asking me if I'm going to have another, but I just can't face it. Not yet. I'm even thinking of going back to work. Not full time but – well, something's cropped up that would be wonderful.'

'What does Matt have to say about that?'

'I haven't told him,' said Eliza simply.

They stayed for quite a long time; Eliza had brought some mince pies, which Emmie loved, and some chocolate digestive biscuits which she knew Coral did, and they all sat and munched them and it was all really quite festive. Then the gas fire went out.

'Oh, God, that meter, I know it's rigged,' said Heather. 'I put in loads of shillings just before you came. I'm sorry, Eliza. I'll put some more in—'

'Give it to me,' said Eliza, taking her purse, 'I'll do it. I know where it is, out in the hall. God, is that a police car I can hear? I'm parked really badly, Heather, could you have a look—'

They all rushed to the window; Eliza seized her own purse, went out onto the landing, and stuffed the meter with as many half-crowns as it would take, including two of Heather's to throw her off the scent.

'Right,' she said, going back into the room, 'done. Should last for a bit, hopefully. Now where were we?'

'You said we could play snap again before you went,' said Coral.

'Oh yes, of course we can. Actually – have you got Happy Families?'

'Scarlett?'

'Oh – David. Hello.'

She tried to sound cool and unwelcoming, but it was difficult.

'I just called to say Happy Christmas.'

'Right. Well, thank you. Happy Christmas, David. What are you doing?'

'Oh – spending it with my family of course. Should be fun.'

'Would that include your clever brother?'

'On Boxing Day, yes. I'm going down to their ancestral pile.'

'What are you doing?'

'Oh, it's very much all pulling together for Christmas. Mother insists on everyone being there and I think that will be good for the kids. But after that I'm heading for London. You wouldn't – wouldn't consider seeing me, I suppose? Just for a drink?'

Scarlett took a deep breath and said she really didn't think so.

'Look – I only want to see you. I've missed you so much, Scarlett. Can't we be friends at least?'

Scarlett could feel herself quite literally weakening; she fought it down.

'I don't – I don't see how we can.'

'Why not? That was the best thing about our relationship – well, one of the best things, I can think of a few others. We had a wonderful friendship, we had fun, we talked about everything under the sun.'

It was true; they had. She remembered those conversations, those long, funny, fascinating conversations. She hadn't had many like that since.

'Well,' she said finally. 'I'll – I'll see. I might be away. I'm considering getting into the skiing market—'

'Oh, marvellous idea. Maybe I could help. I know Gstaad really well. And Cortina d'Ampezzo.'

'Oh,' she said, tempted beyond endurance, 'oh – well, perhaps. Call me, when you get to London.'

'I will. I really have missed you. I wish you'd believe me.'

'I'll try,' she said lightly. 'Bye, David. Enjoy your family Christmas.'

She put the stress on the word family and hoped he wouldn't miss the irony.

'Bye, Scarlett. Enjoy yours.'

She put the phone down and sighed. Bastard he might be. Bastard he was. But the fact remained she had spent some of the happiest times of her life with him. It was very tempting . . .

Chapter 43

A lunch is the most dangerous of assignations. It presents a charmingly innocent face, a guileless smile; it takes place in daylight, in the presence of many others; it ends with a seemly return to the workplace, to the home, to workmates, to spouses.

It teases, to be sure, it makes light, flirtatious promises, it amuses; an invitation to it charms, flatters, even intrigues. But it does not threaten; the mention of it does not alarm.

Thus, 'it's only a lunch,' Eliza Shaw told herself, as she drove to meet Rob Brigstocke, the new creative director of KPD at the Guinea in Burton Lane; 'it's only a lunch,' argued Scarlett Shaw as she walked through the frosty sunshine to the Grosvenor House Hotel on Park Lane for an unexpected assignation with David Berenson; and, 'it's only a lunch,' purred Mariella Crespi as she stepped into her limo outside the Pierre Hotel and directed it to the Plaza just across the road – for she did not want her hair to be blown about, nor her nose turned red when she was to sit across a table from Jeremy Northcott . . .

Why was she doing this, why? Eliza wondered. Was she quite mad? What kind of self-deluding recklessness had seen her agreeing to meet Rob Brigstocke that day; to arrange for Emmie to be out for tea lest it overran; to get her hair cut, to buy some new boots, and stand in Smiths for an hour, flicking through *Vogue* and *Queen* and *Nova* and *Charisma*, lest she should have missed out on some vital new fashion trend or look? When they had had the happiest Christmas at Summercourt, when she had never felt more hopeful about her marriage, when the fear of Emmie mentioning Jeremy's name and describing their stay in Milan, the game of hide and seek, had all but disappeared and she and Matt had even begun to talk tentatively about starting another baby 'maybe later in the year'?

But Jeremy had sent her a note in the New Year, saying he hoped she was feeling better and that she might like to consider his proposition, as he called it.

'You'll be getting a call about it,' he said, 'but of course, no pressure of any kind. Just say no, although we would all be the losers for it. It was lovely to see you. Hide and Seek was a particular joy. I've missed you a lot. Much love, Jeremy.' All written in his black-inked scrawling hand, and signed off with a couple of large kisses. She couldn't bear to throw it away; so clearly did it speak of all that she had left behind, professional success, fun, and the sheer joy of being professionally valued. She hid it in the base of her Carmen roller set. Matt would never find it there.

And then waited for the call. If it never came it would be a relief. Of course.

Rob Brigstocke rang her in the middle of January. He sounded slightly wary.

'I'm told by the big white chief you could help us. He says I should talk to you. Over lunch perhaps.'

'I'm not sure if I can help you,' said Eliza, 'but talking is always fun.'

It was only lunch.

The Guinea and the Piggy was rather dark, quite small and much beloved by the advertising trade in general.

'Eliza Shaw,' she said to the maître d'. 'I've come to meet Rob Brigstocke.'

'Ah, Madame, I remember you as Eliza Clark, don't I? The fashion editor?' he asked, smiling at her. She was enchanted. Somebody hadn't forgotten her.

'You do,' she said, 'very clever of you. Lovely to see you again. Anyway – is Mr Brigstocke here?'

'He is not. I am so sorry. Would you like to wait at the table—'

'Oh – yes, all right. No message?'

He shook his head.

'Can I offer you a drink?'

'Oh – yes, please.' She might as well enjoy herself, cost the agency as much money as possible. 'Do you do champagne by the glass?'

He shook his head regretfully. 'I am so sorry. I could get you a bottle—'

'Oh, why not? Veuve Clicquot if you have it.'

She was beginning to feel cross, and more herself than she could remember for years.

She had bought the *Evening Standard* and was reading it engrossed, thinking what a brilliant fashion editor Barbara Griggs was, and on her second glass of champagne when Rob Brigstocke finally arrived. She heard him before she saw him, a public school accent, roughed up to suit the current trend, 'Eliza? Eliza Shaw?', and looked up rather slowly, anxious to show him she didn't expect to be kept waiting. What she saw was – well, it was pretty good: thick, dark blond hair, a slightly boyish face, covered in freckles with rather heavily lashed hazel eyes – he'd have made quite a pretty girl really, she thought, and wondered if he was gay.

She looked at her watch; it said five to one. She waited for his apology; it didn't come.

'Yes,' she said, 'I'm Eliza Shaw. Are you Rob Brigstocke?

'Might I be someone else?'

'Well yes, actually,' she said. 'Considering you were meant to be here twenty-five minutes ago. You could be a messenger. A substitute lunch companion. A—'

'Sorry,' he said, sounding completely un-contrite, 'I was held up by some queen of a photographer.' Not gay then.

'You could have phoned the restaurant.'

'I could, but I didn't. I thought that would waste more time. Anyway, I see you have made yourself at home.' He indicated the ice bucket and the champagne.

'Yes. Well, are you going to stay? Or have you got to go back to your photographer?'

'No, no, he's gone.'

He sat down and looked at the bottle, lifted it out himself. She liked that too; she could never get that waving the waiter over, as if pouring the wine was some kind of mystic art.

'I can see you like the best,' he said, filling one of the white wine glasses to the rim and sipping it thoughtfully.

'Yes, I do.' She was certainly not going to apologise, if that was what he expected.

'That's something. We need the best. I believe you know Jeremy Northcott quite well.'

'Yes, I do. Quite well.'

'He says you're what we need. I can only take his word for that, of course. Especially as he hasn't worked here for five years, and, as I understand it, neither have you.'

'Look,' said Eliza, feeling her temper rising. 'I didn't ask to have lunch with you. You rang me. Jeremy suggested that, as far as I can understand it, none of it's my fault.'

'Yes all right,' he said, sounding half-irritated, half-amused. 'I was just making the point that I need to reassure myself that you're what we need. That I run the department, not Jeremy. It's down to me who I hire. If you're right then that's great. If you're not . . .' He shrugged. 'No hard feelings, I hope. Got any examples of your work on you?'

Eliza felt a flicker of rage, which grew into a hot white flame, soaring through her. How dare he insult her like this? She, who had been acknowledged one of the finest fashion editors in London, if not the world? How could he not have at least done his homework, looked up some old issues? How could he imply she was only under consideration because she was some kind of past girlfriend of the boss? And how dare he not even show her the most basic courtesy of turning up to lunch on time?

'If you don't want to talk to me, Mr Brigstocke, that's absolutely fine, it makes no difference to me. I didn't ask you to get in touch with me and I certainly didn't ask Jeremy Northcott to put me forward.'

'Now look,' he said, 'be reasonable. I'm perfectly prepared to consider you for this job. But given that you didn't even think to bring any of your work with you—'

'Ye-es?' she said slowly.

'And that Jeremy didn't give more than the slightest clue as to the sort of skills you could bring to the table—'

'Yes?'

'Well, you must see I'm being asked to take an awful lot on trust.'

'No,' she said, 'no, not really. Because I would have thought you would have been professional – and actually courteous – enough to do some research on my work yourself, before putting me through this farce. Probably best if I go now, actually, not waste any more of your time. Or mine, come to that. Very nice champagne, thank you—'

'I don't think I had much choice in that either,' said Rob Brigstocke.

'If you'd been here on time, as I was, you'd have had plenty of choice,' said Eliza, standing up, 'but you weren't and you don't seem to feel you have to apologise for that either. Will you tell Jeremy what's happened or shall I?'

'No doubt you will,' he said, 'you seem to have his ear.'

'That is a repulsive thing to say,' said Eliza, 'and I do assure you, I wouldn't consider working for you now if you offered me a thousand pounds a day and unlimited supplies of Veuve Clicquot. Good afternoon, Mr Brigstocke.'

She walked out, rather pleasingly aware that the other occupants of the restaurant had greatly enjoyed their exchange.

David had said he would book a table for one o'clock; Scarlett was there at quarter past, determined to make him wait, only to find a message waiting for her to say he was desperately sorry, he'd been delayed but there was champagne at the table and he'd be there by one thirty.

She was tempted to walk out, and indeed as the clock said one twenty-eight, she looked up from the file she had been pretending to study, and stood up – to see Mark Frost standing in front of her.

'Miss Scarlett,' he said, smiling in apparently genuine pleasure, 'how lovely to see you. How are you and have you been to Trisos lately?'

'No,' she said, flustered, 'no, I haven't, sadly. Just too busy. But I'm hoping to make a trip pretty soon.'

'I too. Perhaps our paths will cross.'

'That would be – be nice. How is the building project?'

'Oh – almost there. I'm rather thrilled with it all as a matter of fact. I've got some photographs here.' He rummaged in the battered briefcase he was carrying. 'I'd like you to see them. I feel we are united in our ambition to see Trisos preserved as much as possible, and as we like it.'

'Oh – yes. Yes, I do feel that so much. That would be nice.'

'Are you lunching alone?'

'No, no, just waiting for someone. You?'

'Meeting my agent. But apparently she's going to be late. May I sit down for a moment?'

'Yes. Yes, of course. Would you like some champagne, it's here to stop me feeling cross.'

'Is it working?'

'Not entirely.'

'Right. Well – I think not for me. Drinking at lunchtime never agrees with me. Now, here we are. Look. What do you think?'

She looked, at a lovely wide, white construction with the requisite domed roof over one half of it, the other half flat – 'I intend that to be a terrace, so I can sit and look at the sea. And down here, look, this will be the garden, small of course, but big enough to sit in and grow bougainvillea and here, you see, I am going to plant a vine, to make a sort of arbour – do you like it?'

'I think it's absolutely lovely. Really. So simple and – and so – so – Greek. Oh, dear, sorry, what a stupid thing to say.'

'Not at all, the very nicest thing, actually. I want it to look Greek. I'm pleased you think so. Anyway, next time you're there, do – oh, I'm sorry.' He stood up, knocking the photographs onto the floor. 'So sorry.'

Scarlett looked up; David had arrived. She had forgotten the sheer pulse-speeding, knee-weakening force of David's presence, the size of him, the power, his blond almost-perfect looks, his sexual magnetism. He was wearing a pale grey flannel suit and a fine cotton shirt that almost exactly matched his eyes, those extraordinary green eyes, the legacy from his mother. He was smiling, easy, his eyes moving over Scarlett, appreciating her. He was carrying a rather overdressed parcel.

'Let me help,' he said, bending to pick up Mark's photographs. 'Lovely place. This wouldn't be your Trisos, would it, Scarlett?'

Scarlett saw Mark look at her swiftly, clearly surprised by the adjective. 'It's hardly mine,' she said as coolly as she could.

'Well, it's lovely. What a great house. Is it yours?' he said to Mark.

'It will be, yes, when it's finished.'

'I have heard so much about that place. Scarlett does love it so. Scarlett, I am so, so sorry to be late. Unforgivable. But you look as if you are putting the time to good use.' He held out his hand to Mark. 'David Berenson.'

'Mark Frost.'

'And – has Scarlett invited you to lunch in my place? I could hardly blame her. I cannot stand people who are late, so rude, so offensive even, I always think. It implies the other person's time is of no value. When I know how hugely valuable Scarlett's is.'

'David, it's fine. And no, of course I haven't asked Mark to join us, but I did offer him a drink.'

'Of course. Mr Frost, do please sit down and have a drink with us – we'd love that, wouldn't we Scarlett?'

'No,' said Mark, 'no, no, I – that is . . .'

'Scarlett, these are for you,' said David, handing her the parcel, clearly impatient with his awkwardness. 'Truffles, your favourite.'

'Thank you,' said Scarlett briefly.

'Mr Frost – please do join us.'

'David, Mark is having lunch with his agent.'

'His agent? Sounds intriguing. What do you do, Mark?'

'I – I travel a bit—'

'Oh, oh, I see. You're in the same business as Scarlett, are you?'

'David, Mark is not in the travel business. Well he is, but not like me. He writes books, travel books—'

'Oh, but how marvellous! I adore travel writing. Rebecca West, one could read her for ever, and Jan Morris and I never leave home without Paddy of course—'

'Paddy?'

'Paddy Leigh Fermor. You know his work? Yes, of course you do. And you write under your own name – can't say I've read any, but I'll certainly look out for them in future. Scarlett my dear, if you move up a little, I can sit next to you, and Mark here can have my chair – tell me, Mark, have you written about the States? I come from Charleston, the Southern states are all so lovely, but we think the Carolinas win the prize – I've been trying to persuade Scarlett to take her business there for years.'

'I'm sorry,' said Mark, by now sounding desperate, 'I must go, I see my lunching companion coming now, do excuse me.' He made a half-bow to Scarlett, then turned to David. 'Very nice to have met you.'

And then he did what could be best described, Scarlett thought, as scuttling off to the other side of the restaurant.

'Odd chap,' said David, sitting down, kissing Scarlett briefly on the cheek.

'He's not odd, actually, he's very nice,' said Scarlett, pulling her head away, 'and he's a wonderful writer, very highly thought of—'

'I'm sure. No need to sound so defensive. But he's obviously very shy. Now, let me refill that glass and maybe we should order and then we can relax. It's so good to see you. Love the dress. That colour is wonderful on you. Oh, Scarlett.' He reached for her hand, kissed it. 'Thank you for agreeing to this. It's so very – generous of you.'

He raised his glass to her, smiled into her eyes. She felt irritated, upset, couldn't think of anything to say. She had only just managed to regain her cool by the time her main course had arrived; to cut into his fulsome chatter about his mother, about Charleston in the fall, about . . .

'Goodbye – Scarlett. Goodbye, Mr Berenson. Nice to have met you.'

He was leaving: a very short lunch, obviously.

'Bye, Mark.'

'Goodbye, Mr Frost. I'll look out for your titles. A treat in store I'm sure.'

What in the name of heaven had she been doing with him? With that appalling, slimy, smarmy creature with his blow-dried hair and his platitudinous observations and his patronising complacency? 'Never leave home without Paddy' indeed. What a cretin. Surely, surely she couldn't like him? If she did – well, he struggled against the concept.

'So – what was it you particularly wanted to talk to me about?' asked Scarlett.

'You're wearing my bracelet,' he said, ignoring the question.

'Yes. I like it.'

'That makes me very happy. And maybe hope that you've forgiven me.'

'No, David, it just means I like the bracelet.'

She did; she'd sold a lot of the other stuff he had given her, to raise money, but the charm bracelet – something had stopped her parting from that. Too many memories.

'So,' she said again, 'what did you want to talk to me about?'

'Ah. Yes. Well, it's complicated. Even a little delicate. I – I hope you're going to understand.'

'David, do get on with it,' Scarlett said. She was beginning to feel a little uneasy.

'Well – well, Scarlett, it's the divorce. My divorce.'

'Ye-es. Isn't it over yet?'

'Well, we tried to make a go of it. For the kids. I thought I'd told you.'

'No, I don't think so.'

'But – impossible. So now it's happening. And God, I don't know how to put this.'

'Try telling it how it is. As they say in your country.'

'Yes. OK. It's just that, as you know, I'm divorcing Gaby on grounds of infidelity. That was how we agreed to do it. She wants to carry on living exactly as she has done, with all the considerable goodies she's grown accustomed to, but without the tedium of having to accommodate me in her life. And although naturally I want to see the children well-provided for . . .'

'Yes, of course. Your mother tells me family is everything to you.'

'Indeed.' He smiled at her, gloriously unaware of the irony of this. 'It is. But you see – well – if she knew that I had also – also—'

'Been screwing around?' said Scarlett, smiling at him sweetly.

'Scarlett! I like to think we had something a little better than that. A lot better than that. You know how much you mean to me—'

'Not really, no. I know how much you said I meant to you. Bit different, from where I'm sitting—'

'Oh, dear.' He sighed.

She realised there were beads of sweat on his forehead. She took another large sip of champagne.

'OK. I'll come to the point. My lawyer says if Gaby was to even suspect that I've been having an affair, she would take me to the cleaners. And it could all get very ugly.'

'I don't see what I can do about it.'

'Scarlett – you can. You can – can – not talk about us.'

'David, I'm not going to talk about us. I never have and I don't see why you should think I ever will.'

'Yes, but – but you see, it's the money.'

'What money?'

'That I – er, invested in your business.'

'Who's going to know about that?'

'Unfortunately, my lawyers have to. And my accountant. Because they're going through all my assets with a fine-tooth comb. And – they spotted a thirty-thousand-dollar discrepancy. The shares I sold to – to make the money over to you.'

'Oh. Oh, I see.'

'Yes. And they say it's inevitable they'll appear in the accounts. Because it's quite a lot of money.'

'Ye-es. And—'

'I have to concoct something. The best thing would be to say it was a business start-up. Can you tell me exactly how you explained the money to your accountant?'

'I said it was from a private source. Which it was.'

'Yes, of course. Did you name the – the source?'

'No, of course not. I didn't have to. As it came in in dribs and drabs.'

He relaxed suddenly. 'Thank God. That's marvellous.' He smiled at her. 'Here, have some more champagne.'

'No, thanks. I've had enough. I'm still a little confused.'

449

'Ah yes. Well, the thing is, you see, if you had named me, I'd have been in the doodoo. Caught out big time. So I'm so, so grateful to you. What a clever girl you are.'

'Now just a minute, David. All this is about, this lunch and everything, is finding out whether you were going to get caught out in your relationship with me.'

'Of course not. It was so `I could see you, discuss our friendship for the future—'

'Our friendship. I thought we had a little more than that.'

'Darling, of course we did. But for now – until the divorce is through – it's very, very important that that is how it is. How it's seen. Well, if it's seen at all.'

'OK. So the most important thing about me in your life is that nobody knows about me. In case it costs you some money.'

'A lot of money. And a much uglier divorce, yes. But when it's over—'

'David, I don't find that very flattering, actually. That really does reduce me to a bit on the side. You always used to say that when you and Gaby did actually separate, then we could be together. Now suddenly everything's different. Because it's going to cost you money. That doesn't give me a very warm feeling inside. In fact it confirms the opinion I had formed of you over these past years that you were one huge, extremely offensive shit.'

'Scarlett – darling—'

'No, David, not darling. God, I feel sorry for Gaby suddenly. Being married to you. You know, your mother's always wanted us to meet, said how well we'd get on. Suddenly I rather fancy that. A long cosy chat with her. I think we'd have a great time.'

'Scarlett – don't play games, please—'

'What makes you think I'm playing games?'

He looked at her, very intently, and realised she was serious, and his demeanour changed almost in a moment.

'Right. In that case, I have something else to put to you.'

'Yes?'

'You actually obtained that money from me by a criminal process. Blackmail is a crime, Scarlett, under whatever circumstances you committed it. And I don't think it would look very pretty in court. If you do talk to Gaby I shall have nothing to lose. And therefore I can reveal that you blackmailed me, took advantage of my vulnerability, at a time when my marriage was breaking up, when I was hoping to repair it—'

'You can't do that! It's a filthy lie.'

'Scarlett, you did blackmail me. And a good lawyer, and I do have a brilliant one, can present you as a cheap little gold-digger on the make. It won't do your reputation in the business world any good. And you might very possibly have to give the money back. So – checkmate, don't you think?'

'This is what I think,' said Scarlett, very loudly, and she stood up, looked around the dining room to make sure people were looking. 'I think you're even more of a bastard than I'd realised. Which is saying quite a lot. Now, I'm going to leave you to enjoy your divorce in the bosom of your family undisturbed, so you can relax. Thanks for the champagne; I don't think I want any more. Why don't you have it?'

And she pulled the still half-full bottle out of the ice bucket and tipped it over David's head.

'So, Jeremy. This is very – very nice.'

She was looking, of course, incredible. Red maxi dress, wonderfully sexy, in soft jersey, high-heeled black boots, hair drawn back from her face, her huge eyes fixed on him, her lips just slightly parted. Her purpose very clear. He didn't have a chance really. And – did he want one?

She had called him out of the blue, had said she was in New York for a few days' shopping, that Giovanni had stayed at home in Milan, he was tired after the Christmas celebrations. Could they have lunch, she wanted to see him.

And he had wanted to see her too, still disturbed, shaken indeed, by the flare of attraction – and more – that had begun at Scala that night. Nothing was said, no contact made beyond the occasional social kiss, embrace, farewell, but he had felt its insistence, its refusal to be soothed, sent on its way.

Love, real love, in all its unquestioning, troubling determination, had eluded Jeremy thus far in his life. He had felt great affection, sexual attraction; he had enjoyed several relationships, and been seriously engaged by a few. But there it had ended; and he had come to think that that was all he was to know or even be capable of. But he wanted it; and he wanted it more as time went on.

He did not lack for contact with beautiful and intelligent women – it was just that they were never absolutely suited to him, and to the complexity of his life and its demands. And this included Eliza, as he very well knew, more clearly than ever now.

And here was one of the most beautiful women in the world, seeking him out. He knew what she wanted, and he wanted it too; but he knew he could not supply it, could not even dream of supplying it. Jeremy was that rather unfashionable and even rather dull creature, a good man. He had made a rule all his life to reject any course of action that he felt to be morally unjustifiable. And a relationship with Mariella, however enticing, clearly came into that category; and so he refused to consider it.

Even so, while shaking his own head at himself, telling himself he was a fool and a reprehensible one at that, he had said, yes, lunch would be delightful . . . trying and failing not to see beyond it and its purpose. It was, after all, only lunch . . .

He smiled at her now. 'It is. Very nice. But you're not eating anything.'

'Yes, I am. I have eaten my salad and one of my eggs Benedict. That is quite a lot for me.'

'Half an egg Benedict actually. What do you usually eat for lunch?'

'Oh – I don't know. A little fresh pasta. With pesto, or perhaps some sauce *pomodoro*. Maybe in the summer some asparagus. Eating is not important to me.'

'I don't believe you. I've seen you tucking into tiramisu.'

'Tiramisu is different. Tiramisu is more like a beautiful melody or – or making love.'

'Mariella! What a ridiculous thing to say,' said Jeremy laughing.

'Well, perhaps. But I could not pass a tiramisu by. My mother made the most perfect tiramisu. Better even than they serve in Bagutta. Have you eaten their tiramisu?'

'I – don't think so.'

'Then you must. We will enjoy it together, next time you are in Milan.'

'Mariella, I don't think I shall be in Milan again for a very long time.'

'Oh, but you must. You can always stay with us.'

'Well, perhaps. Now, I want to know more about your mother.'

'Oh, I loved her so much. She was a very, very wonderful woman. We had no money, no money at all, but every day was happy. She cooked us delicious food, she made us lovely clothes, the house was full of music, she sang, all the time, she had the most wonderful voice.'

'Can you sing?'

'Oh, no. Not at all. I am note deaf.'

'Tone deaf,' he said, smiling.

'Eliza does that.'

'What?'

'Corrects my English. How did it feel, to see her again, after all this time? I think you loved her very much.'

'I'm not sure that I did,' he said. 'I adored her, we were terribly happy together but love – in that sense – I don't think so. If I had been sure, then I would have married her, long before she met Matt and all our lives would have been very different.'

'I do not like Matt very much,' said Mariella. 'I think he is unkind to her. He will not let her do what she needs to do, he would not let her come and stay with me when she was so sad after the baby died, he will not let her work, they quarrel a lot. I think, he thinks only about Matt.'

'Well, I don't know,' said Jeremy, smiling. 'Eliza is quite good at looking after herself, doing what she wants. Or she used to be. But I'm sorry if she isn't happy. Very sorry. She seemed fine in Milan. Except of course over the baby.'

'Yes, but, you know, there was more problem over that—'

'Oh, dear. Poor Eliza. Married life is difficult, I understand.' He smiled at her. 'You and Giovanni, now, do you quarrel? I'm sure not.'

'No, we do not. Never, never.'

'And – you are happy with him?'

'Oh – yes. I'm happy. How could I not be?'

'Well – no, I can't imagine.'

'You are so diplomatic, Jeremy, but I know why you asked. You think Giovanni is an old man, not a companion for me, maybe not even a sexual companion – and you would be right. Of course.'

'Yes, I see.' He felt disturbed by this. It had been what he had suspected, but not that she would address it so soon and so directly.

'Now you are shocked,' she said. 'I do not mean to do that. I was trying to explain. You do not have to have everything to be happy, just the right things. Giovanni loves me, very, very much. And I feel quite, quite safe, all the time. And he has the right things too; he has me for the rest of his life, in his house, taking care of him, loving him, wherever he goes, and that is all he asks too. But now, all of a sudden, there is you. So . . .' she paused, smiled very directly into his eyes.

'Mariella.'

'Yes?'

It had to be done, said, now. Before things went any further.

'Mariella, I don't think I can do this.'

'Do what, Jeremy?' Her expression was puzzled.

'Please, Mariella. Don't insult me by playing silly games. I can't – do what you want. I can't have an affair with you.'

'Don't you want to?'

The dark eyes filled with pain, the lovely mouth trembled. God, she was a master of this. Or rather a mistress.

'Of course I do,' he said, 'I want it very much. It is agony for me to sit here and – and say this. But – I can't do it, Mariella. I like Giovanni too much. He has given me his hospitality, his friendship. I can't deceive him, I can't take from him what he values more than anything on earth.'

'But Jeremy, he would not know. It would not hurt him. '

'I would know, Mariella. I'm sorry. I can't.'

She stood up; she was going to walk out, he thought, possibly throw something at him and in a way he hoped she would. It would make things easier.

But, 'I go to the bathroom,' she said, 'I will be back.'

She was gone a long time: ten, fifteen minutes. Jeremy sat, reflecting on the treasure he had rejected, hardly able to believe it of himself.

And then she returned; stood behind his chair, bent over him, put her arms round his neck, kissed him on the cheek. She smelt amazing, a thick, rich perfume, and when she sat down again, she was smiling, her eyes very bright, her make-up perfect, her hair absolutely in place.

'Oh, dear,' she said, shaking her head at him, 'oh, Jeremy. Would it not be just my bad luck to fall for a perfect English gentleman. Why could I not have found a – a – what should I have found, Jeremy?'

'A cad,' he replied, smiling. 'I think that's who you should have found. A bounder. A rotter. Who would have rushed you off to bed, as I so long to do, without another thought. That's what you should have found.'

'Oh, no,' she said, 'I do not think so. It is you I want, dear gentleman Jeremy. So much, so very much. Well – perhaps. One day. I shall not give up, you know. I am not proud. And I always get what I want in the end.'

'Is that so?' he said, struggling to keep his voice light, and, 'oh yes,' she said, blowing him a kiss across the table, 'that is really, really so.'

Chapter 44

'Miss Scarlett! How nice of you to come.'

Scarlett smiled at Mark Frost. He really was so charming, she thought; and he was attractive too, with his shock of brown hair and those grey eyes peering through his steel-framed spectacles.

And it was nice of him to greet her. She'd actually been feeling horribly out of it, her confidence was at a low ebb anyway, the exhilaration of tipping the champagne over David Berenson's head having worn off after about half an hour, leaving her weary and wretched. In fact she had very nearly not come at all; except that Mark Frost's PR had been doing a ring-round on the last morning and Scarlett had been out and the party being in her diary, the secretary had confirmed and she didn't want to let him down after that.

Although – it would hardly have mattered, the room was packed and every single person there seemed to know every other person and they were all talking loudly and confidently about books and publishers and even agents . . . 'Actually the only one I really liked was her first . . . aren't those new Penguin covers just the most amazing works of art . . . I really think you should move on, they're turning out absolute rubbish . . .' and although smiling rather distantly at her, as she walked slowly past with her glass of champagne, or tried to infiltrate a group, they were the opposite of friendly.

'Anyone here you know?' Mark Frost said now.

She shook her head. 'Not really.'

'Right. I thought you might know a few of the travel journalists. Come and meet Chrissie Morgan, she's on the *Daily Sketch* and quite tame, really. How's your venture going?'

'Oh, pretty well.'

'Good. I asked Demetrios last time I was there, but he's very discreet, always pretends he doesn't know anything about it.'

'I don't think he's being discreet,' said Scarlett laughing, 'I think he really doesn't. I do hope his extension isn't going to spoil the taverna though.'

'Oh, I don't think it will. Not now I've got my architect on it. He and Larissa did have some dreadful ideas, but we've sorted him out. It cost me a bit, between you and me, but it's worth it, from my point of view, keeping the island as it should be.'

'Oh,' said Scarlett, 'oh, that explains it. Demetrios said your achitect had done it and he was very cheap. I thought that was a bit unlikely.'

'Yes, well, not a word!'

'Of course not.'

'Now – Chrissie, meet Scarlett Shaw. She's the brains behind a wonderful travel club, you've probably heard of it—'

'Mark.' It was one of the extremely posh publishing girls. Eliza would have been at home here, Scarlett thought. 'Mark, time for your speech.'

'Oh Christ.' He went quite white; it was the first time Scarlett had seen any hint of the original Mark Frost, the silent, withdrawn person she had first met in Demetrios's hotel.

'Poor Frosty,' said Chrissie, looking after him as he was borne away, 'he really does hate it. Speaking, I mean.'

But he spoke charmingly and amusingly, with some rather fulsome praise for his editor, his publisher, and his agent, and a funny story about how he had heard two ladies in Hatchards discussing the 'Islands' book and saying what a pity he hadn't included the Isle of Wight.

'He's such a star, isn't he?' said Chrissie Morgan. 'So funny and so charming.'

'Yes, he is. I didn't think so when I first met him, he hardly said a single word.'

'No, that's his way. He hides behind this sort of Trappist veil until he's decided he really likes you and then he drops it, just like that. It's quite disconcerting really.'

Scarlett felt rather flattered.

'Have you met Mrs Frost?'

'No. No, I haven't.' She felt promptly recalled to reality.

'She's amazing.'

'I thought she'd be here.'

'No, apparently wheelchair access is difficult here.'

Wheelchair! So he was married to an invalid. How extraordinary, then, to build a house on a remote Greek island. Perhaps he liked getting away from her . . .

'So – your travel club – tell me about it,' said Chrissie. 'I'm doing a piece on the smaller agencies, and I might be able to include it.'

Scarlett left with a signed copy of the book, a kiss from Mark Frost and a sense of considerable achievement.

She just wished David Berenson could have seen her, being chatted up by one of the foremost travel writers of his day.

'Things have got worse here, Eliza. Much worse.'

'Oh, Heather, I'm so sorry.' Eliza felt a pang of remorse. It was mid-January and she had been round to see Heather – now seven-and-a-half months pregnant – for the first time since Christmas, and found her in despair.

'It's not me this time, it's poor old Mr Carter upstairs. You know, he's the widower, can hardly get up and down those stairs at all. Anyway, yesterday morning, a bird got in through the hole in the roof and flew into his face. He panicked and tried to fight it off and then slipped and fell down three or four steps. If I hadn't heard and found him, I don't know what would have happened. Poor old thing, I got the ambulance and he'd broken his hip. Coral and I went to see him in the afternoon in hospital and he was much more worried about what would happen to his room and where he could go when he came out.'

'Poor old chap. How sad. Anyway, I'll come over again tomorrow with Emmie,' said Eliza.

'Oh, would you? Coral is so bored, poor little thing. Getting her to school is all I can manage at the moment, and it gets dark so early—'

'Course I will,' said Eliza and then, struck by a thought, 'have you got a TV?'

'You're joking! No, of course we haven't.'

'Right. Well, we'll be there straight after school.'

Emmie said she didn't want to go to Coral's house, it smelt.

'That is not Coral's fault and she and Heather need our help. Oh, and how would you like to give Coral our old TV, the one in your playroom? She hasn't got one. We can get you a new one.'

'I would. It's a nice idea.' She could be so sweet sometimes.

Heather was so overcome at the sight of the TV she burst into tears.

'I can't take that, Eliza.'

'Of course you can. We want you to have it, don't we, Emmie?'

Emmie nodded. 'Yes, we really do—'

'It will make such a difference,' said Heather, wiping her eyes. 'One of the reasons Coral gets teased at school is because she doesn't know about all the programmes. She'll love it so much. But – oh, dear, Alan will go mad. And he'll go on about the licence, I know he will. He's always said we couldn't afford that, even if we got a telly.'

'Well, he'll just have to go mad. And I'll pay for the licence, tell him it's all for Coral's benefit. You haven't found anywhere, I suppose?'

'No, of course not. We've decided to go to Alan's mum, we've got no choice.'

'Oh, Heather. I'm so sorry. Oh, don't, don't cry. Emmie, take Coral into the bedroom, start a game of snap, we'll join you in a minute.'

'Come on,' said Emmie, holding out her hand to Coral, 'let's go next door. How's Amanda Jane?'

She seemed far ahead of Coral now in every way; and they had been born the same week. That didn't seem right either . . .

'Matt, have you got any cheap flats? I mean really cheap?'

'Not a lot of money in cheap. To buy or to let?'

'Oh, to let.'

'Shouldn't think so for a moment. Why?'

'Well – you know about my friend. The one living in this awful place in Clapham, her and her husband and their little girl, and she's having a baby in a month or so. And they've got to get out, and they can't find anywhere. There's a few months left on their lease, but after that – it's pretty hopeless. And it seems to me what the landlord is trying to do is make their lives so impossibly awful they'll have to leave anyway. Like he's not mending a blocked loo, stuff like that. I just thought you might know of somewhere. Even for a bit. It doesn't seem fair.'

'I've told you before, Eliza, people create their own circumstances. Look, I didn't have any silver spoon in my mouth. I worked like stink, round the clock, nobody helped me, I just got on with it. Who are these people anyway?'

'Matt, for heaven's sake. You haven't been listening to me. I've told you about Heather before. She – she's been a really good friend to me. And I'd so like to help her.'

'You're asking the wrong person. Sorry. Now I've got to go, I'm late already.'

'Bastard,' said Eliza aloud as he closed the door. Well, she wasn't going to let it go. Somehow, she was going to see justice done. She owed Heather too much not to.

That afternoon, she had to go to the dentist. Sitting in the waiting room, she reached for a newspaper someone had left behind. It was the *Daily News*.

She sighed and flicked through the pages. Jack was doing a brilliant job. The news coverage was superb and there was now a full page of analysis called 'NewsWatch' added onto both home and international events.

Very good gossip column – Jack had always had a penchant for gossip, and knew its importance to even the most cerebral paper – and, God, this was a fascinating article: 'A Tale of One City', it was called, written by a journalist called Johnny Barrett, who was billed as the paper's Man of Property. It wasn't just about the property trade, though, it was feature-based, about two families living what Barrett called either side of the Cultural Divide, the intellectual Georgian squares of Islington, and the more traditional, old-money scene of the mews and mansion blocks of Chelsea. She could see Jack's hand in this too; but she loved the way Barrett wrote, sharply and perceptively, catching the nuances of the two different styles of talking, dressing, entertaining. This wasn't about property, it was what property was about: people, and what they made of it, and it of them.

It was that very hour, while the dentist was drilling agonisingly into a tooth which he had declared nerveless, that the idea began to form . . .

'Susan,' said Matt. 'Get Andrew Watson on the phone, will you?'

'Yes, Mr Shaw.'

'And let me have any lists of letting agents on file, as well. The bottom end of the market.'

'Yes, Mr Shaw.'

'Hello, Louise. How are you?'

Eliza was meeting her mother for lunch in the Trattoria Terrazza, the just still-fashionable Italian restaurant in Romilly Street. Sarah had been low after Christmas, missing Adrian more than usual, and Eliza was treating her to a couple of days of shopping and general self-indulgence.

Exactly the sort of day she herself hated, but it wasn't a hardship and she wasn't exactly busy.

Louise was sitting at a table with a man: a young, rather attractive man. Good. Maybe she'd found someone to replace the perfidious Barry Floyd.

'Oh – hi, Eliza. Yes, great thanks.'

'How go the hotels?'

'Oh, pretty good,' said Louise. 'Planning permission's the big bogey, but I'm sure you never stop hearing about that from Matt.'

'Unfortunately not,' said Eliza. She looked slightly questioningly at the young man and smiled; he smiled back at her.

'Johnny Barrett,' he said, holding out his hand. '*Daily News.*'

'Oh, I'm sorry,' said Louise. 'Johnny, this is Eliza Shaw. Married to my ex-colleague, Matt, you know?'

'I do indeed,' said Barrett. He had a north-country burr to his voice, and very direct grey eyes. Eliza liked him. 'How is the great man? I'm always trying to persuade him to do a proper interview but he hates the press. As you probably know.'

'I do, I'm afraid. He's fine, thanks. And you won't believe this and I know it sounds really corny, but I was reading a piece of yours the other day. About the great divide, North and South London. I thought it was awfully good.'

'Thank you. That's very kind. I like to inject some personality into my stuff, brings it to life a bit.'

'Yes, it certainly works. I know Jack Beckham very well,' she added, lest he should think she was some kind of fawning groupie, 'I used to work for him, long ago.'

'Really? That was in his magazine days, I presume?'

'Yes. He – oh, there's my mother, I'd better go and meet her. Lovely to see you Louise,' she said, 'give my regards to Roderick.'

'I will, Eliza, thank you.'

'And – lovely to meet you,' she said to Barrett.

'Likewise. Here.' He rummaged in a scruffy, over-loaded wallet. 'Here's my card. If you can ever persuade your husband to do an interview with me, just let me know.'

'I will,' she said, smiling, 'but I know he won't. Bye.'

460

Chapter 45

It had been a sweet revenge to hear him stuttering out an apology and practically begging her to come in to see him after all – clearly Jeremy had asked how the lunch had gone; and part of her still wanted to say that she really wasn't interested and put the phone down. But instead she heard herself agreeing to go in to see Rob Brigstocke at KPD in a week's time, bearing her cuttings book.

Advertising agencies were very different from magazines, she thought, following Rob Brigstocke down a light, bright corridor, thickly carpeted, with stylish prints on the wall, and firmly closed doors labelled things like 'Creative Resources', 'Library' and even 'Executive Meeting Room 1' and 'Executive Meeting Room 2'. She thought wistfully of her first glimpse of *Charisma*, and the long corridors there, but with paint peeling and scuffed lino floors, and doors opening onto untidy offices. She wasn't ever going to feel at home here.

Not that it mattered, because she certainly wasn't going to be here.

'Right. Here we are. This is my office.'

He opened the door. This was better, more familiar even: a huge window overlooking Grosvenor Square, a blessedly cluttered black desk, one of the new tractor-style chrome chairs, and in one corner a huge plan chest, in another a Grant Projector – the near-magical machine, by which pictures and type could be projected, made bigger or smaller, and moved around a dummy page at will – and every available bit of wall covered with posters, notes, campaign spreads, framed award certificates, polaroid photographs.

'Oh,' she said, smiling with sheer pleasure, 'this is lovely.'

She moved towards a set of photographs. 'I made a collage of all my covers from the polaroids,' she said. 'One of my most precious possessions.'

'Yeah?' he said. His face was still a little cool, but his voice was amused, even friendly. 'I did the same with all my campaigns that didn't make it.'

She laughed.

'That's a nice one. Like it.'

He liked her cuttings; she could tell. He started looking at them rather disdainfully and then he turned the pages more slowly – he had very nice hands, she noticed, as if it mattered – and actually read some of the copy. He didn't appreciate, of course, the logistical triumph of the Paris all-in-one picture spread, but he liked the haunted house, liked the Mariella feature. 'This is brilliant,' he said, smiling at her. 'I love it. God. The magazine should have hung onto you. It's nothing like this now.'

'Thank you,' said Eliza. She reflected on how swiftly dislike could reverse; she was even finding Rob Brigstocke at that moment quite seriously sexy.

He took her out round the office to meet some of the creative people, told her what accounts they all worked on, and which she might find herself involved in. There was a cosmetic account, a very stylish flooring account – 'this needs serious fashion input' – a perfume account, and a hotel.

She felt herself getting excited, having ideas; she liked the people, funny and fun and infinitely serious about what they did, all the things she missed so much.

'Well,' Rob said, shaking her hand in reception, 'cheers. Thanks for coming in. I'll call you. But – first off – you'd be interested, would you?'

Eliza said she could be, struggling not to show how desperately interested she already was. And then spent half the journey driving back to Fulham telling herself first that it would still be very difficult to persuade Matt; and then that it was outrageous that she should be having to persuade him at all.

Three days later Brigstocke called and made her an offer: the job of fashion consultant, two days a week, rising to three as and when necessary; a salary for those two days more than she had been paid full time at *Charisma*; and as far as she could make out, absolutely unlimited expenses. She had stood in the hall, listening to what sounded like an invitation to enter some enchanted kingdom, and heard herself saying well, she would think about it. And let him know in a day or two. And heard him sounding first surprised and then impatient and telling her he would need to know very soon, as there were several other people he wanted to approach; and longing more than anything to say oh no, no, don't, please don't even think about approaching them; and then he rang again, and said if she hadn't made her mind up in the next twenty-four hours, the job would be gone; and she realised she really would have to talk to Matt about it.

Mariella had been only mildly disappointed at the failure of her mission. She wanted Jeremy Northcott, and very badly, more badly indeed than she had ever wanted any man, and this was not just sexual greed, not just a demand for romantic attention, it was altogether more tender, gentler, more intense than anything she had experienced before. With the exception, of course, of what she felt for Giovanni.

Mariella was not actually promiscuous at all; she loved Giovanni, very much, and she had married him for that reason. His money, the glorious house, the clothes and jewels she had acquired were genuinely of secondary interest: had she not felt physically and emotionally attracted to him, she would not have married him. He was the centre of her world; he gave her things she could not have dreamed of, to be sure, but he also showed her tenderness, gentleness and deep admiration. Always intelligent, she became under his tutelage cultured, socially adept, well-read. Their life together was indeed charmed; but it was not simply because of their wealth. It was also because they were, quite simply, good to one another.

And in the early days of their marriage Giovanni was a sensuous, imaginative, tireless lover; he taught her more than she could teach him. He combined sexual skill with emotional; he could catch her unawares, at inappropriate times, and they had made love in a great many more places than their vast, deep bed and as night fell over Como. Few men of seventy could claim to have seduced their wives on a small sailing boat tossing quite dangerously in a summer storm, or behind the door of a walled garden, as their guests strolled just outside, waiting to be called to dinner.

But as his eightieth birthday dawned, Giovanni's sexual powers had begun to dwindle. In three years, his impotence was total. And Mariella had kissed him and said she never wanted to betray him, never wished to sleep with anyone else; and he had said how much he loved her and fallen asleep. And she had meant what she had said with all her heart.

But she was highly sexed; and with the best will in the world she became restless, fractious, snapping at Giovanni as she had never done, until she had wondered if it might be better for both of them if she sought – just occasionally – distraction elsewhere. And then, wonderfully, there

463

was Jeremy, who instilled in her an emotional longing as well as a physical one. And even while she was shocked at herself, that she could feel such a thing, she yearned to have what she had never had: a love affair in the truest sense, with a young and beautiful man.

Well, she always got what she wanted. In the end.

'Eliza? It's Jeremy.'

'Oh – Jeremy! How lovely to hear from you, where are you?'

'In London. For a few days. Just casing the joint. I'll be back permanently next month. Look, I've talked to Rob Brigstocke, and I hear he's pretty impressed by you. Wants you to join us, in fact.'

'Yes,' she said, 'yes, I – I know. It's wonderful. I'm completely, completely over the moon.'

'I hoped you would be. But he also tells me you haven't accepted the job yet. Look, I know you've got problems with Matt, and the whole childcare thing. But two days a week – surely you can make that work. We really do want you. We think you have a lot to offer the agency—'

They thought she had something to offer. She was a proper, desirable person again, not just an inefficient, ineffectual mother, but a professional woman, in possession of a talent. She could still *do* it.

'I – oh, it's not Matt,' she said, taking a deep breath, 'honestly. I'm not that much of a little woman, Jeremy. It's just that I heard of this wonderful nanny and I was just waiting to see her before I committed myself. But – well, it looks like she's agreed, so – yes. I'd adore to take the job. It sounds wonderful.'

'Marvellous! I'll tell Rob. He'll be thrilled. Now, what about lunch? To seal the deal?'

'I'd love to have lunch. Please, please, please.'

They settled on a date the following week. He was off to Norfolk for a few days – 'see Pa, all that sort of thing. So I'll have lots of exciting news about country life as well.'

'I would actually like to hear it,' said Eliza soberly, 'it'd be lovely. So – so normal.'

'My father, normal! Hardly. You can come with me if you like.'

'Oh, I wish I could. Matt would be really thrilled. But give my love to your father; tell him how sorry I am. I did write to him about your mother.'

'Sweet of you. I will. OK, then, next Thursday. Shall we make it the Caprice? For old times' sake?'

She put the phone down and sat staring at it, feeling alternately wildly happy and violently sick. She couldn't renege on that now. Whatever Matt said . . .

'No,' said Matt. 'I thought we agreed that for at least her first year at school, Emmie would need you to be around.'

'But Matt, it's only two days a week. Your mum could look after her, she'd love it. And I get so bored now, with Emmie at school all day, I've got a brain and it's just rotting away, doing nothing, I want to—'

'I get very bored with these cries of anguish about your brain, Eliza. Your brain could be put to perfectly good use doing things with Emmie and even with me, come to that.'

'You?' she said. 'I really don't see what you could ask of me, Matt, that requires my brain. I don't actually recall you ever wanting to go to the theatre, or discussing books with me. Asking what's for dinner and telling me what developments you've instigated in the past twenty-four hours seems to be what might pass for intellectual conversation on your part. As for Emmie, I spend a lot of time reading to her, and playing with her, and I resent the implication that I don't.'

'Yes, all right,' said Matt, 'and don't you think that's rather more important than what length of skirt might go with what sort of shoes or whatever other lofty matters you seem to find so enthralling. And besides, what about the discussion we had the other night, on the possibility of our having another child one day. I presume that wouldn't be even under consideration any more if you took this job, far less important.'

'You are so vile,' said Eliza, holding back the tears with a huge effort, 'and that is completely unfair. I just can't believe you can be so arrogant and so – so old-fashioned. You live in a time warp, do you know that? Forever Fifties Man, with a wife in a pinny, waiting for you to come home so she can wait on you.'

'Chance would be a fine thing,' said Matt and stalked out, slamming the door after him.

God, he knew how to hurt her. He had a genius for it. Why couldn't she ever think of ways to hurt him back? She was always left gasping, like a fish on a hook. And he was so bloody complacent, acting as if he was doing something of real importance with his life, when a lot of the time, what he and his kind did was actually pretty destructive. Knocking down perfectly good and beautiful old buildings and putting up square concrete blocks in their place. Like that row of houses in Islington there had been all that fuss about recently – he'd won the battle of course.

Driving Emmie to school, still fighting down the tears, she felt fiercely, and yes, all right, childishly intent on revenge. She had tried so hard, given up so much, waited so long for what seemed the perfect opportunity – and he still wouldn't move to meet her even quarter way. It wasn't fair; it just wasn't fair.

She stopped to buy some milk on the way back and Johnny Barrett's card fell out of her wallet.

She sat staring at it, thinking about him, thinking about Matt and the way he always won, and about people like Heather who always lost: and suddenly the wonderfully simple idea was born.

Chapter 46

Scarlett couldn't remember when she last met a single man, either unmarried or divorced; there just weren't any, unless you counted one boozy travel agent, who had asked her to go away with him and sample some of the hotels on his books, and one very sweet boy who worked for one of the Hilton chain, who was, he told her over dinner, a virgin and, as the double brandies went down, so frightened of his first encounter that he always became impotent. Sometimes she thought of life with David, and the wonderful sex and the fun, and wondered if she had been crazy to finish it at all.

She tried to comfort herself, telling herself her life wasn't all bad; her business was doing extremely well, and she had made a lot of money – although hardly comparable with Matt's millions – but on reflection it was the only source of happiness or self-satisfaction left to her.

And so she did what she always did when things were bad; she planned a trip to Trisos, having first ascertained from Demetrios that there was absolutely no question of Mark Frost being there. She needed to be alone.

'Hello, Johnny Barrett. Oh – hello. Yes, of course I remember you. Never forget an appreciative face. Nice to hear from you. What? Well, I'm always interested in ideas for a piece. Want to outline it now? And then I can put it to the editor, if I think he'd like it. Yes, sure, go ahead.'

Jeremy Northcott was very pleased to be back in London. The New York years had been incredible, and he had certainly learnt a lot about advertising – God, the Americans were good at it. He had met most of the gods of the game, David Ogilvy, English himself of course, Bill Bernbach, who founded Doyle Dane Bernbach, and broke the mould of the WASP tradition in Madison Avenue; the dazzlingly beautiful Mary Wells, the first woman to head up an agency; he had dined with them, heard them speak at conferences, and had learnt to value above all in advertising the rising sales graph. It had been a tremendously privileged experience and he was aware of being hugely changed and enriched by it.

But he had missed the old country, was homesick for its gentler ways, and his friends there, the customs and attitudes that he had grown up with, and he was impatient now to bring the sharp, edgy competitiveness of New York to London.

He found, of course, that there had been great changes; press ads had become more ambitious, broader in scope – there were a lot of corporate ads for the textile industry – and the TV commercial had become another art form, with creative directors on ego trips, vying for awards, making what amounted to mini films. Humour was crucial (in this Jeremy felt London led the world) and there was a craze for series ads and a build-up of personalities: for Hamlet cigars, 'cars built by robots', and of course the ongoing saga of Katie, the Oxo mum.

The creative director was a comparatively new animal. Rob Brigstocke, Jeremy felt, was destined to be one of the greats, but right now needed to be taken down a peg or three.

Jeremy was that rare creature in advertising, someone acceptable to both the account and creative teams. He was a lateral thinker; under him, creativity flourished and billings increased; and people enjoyed their work. That, he felt, was his greatest challenge: keeping everybody properly involved.

He arrived back from Norfolk for an intense three days before returning to New York for the last time; his secretary, Lucilla Fellowes, who was still at the agency, returned to her role of company wife with huge enthusiasm, making sure he had his favourite coffee, filling his (temporary) office with flowers and Bollinger champagne, running his diary and dovetailing meetings, and booking him into his favourite restaurants. It was as she checked the final arrangements for those few days that she realised he had slipped in a lunch without telling her: Eliza (his diary said in his huge scrawl), Caprice, 1 p.m. On the same day Lucy had with great difficulty managed to arrange for the CEO of Cumberland Tobacco to lunch in the boardroom with Rob Brigstocke, creative director, Michael Rushton, head of research, and Jeremy; she asked Jeremy if she could change the lunch with Eliza to drinks that evening.

'Well, if it's OK with her. She might not be free. Tell her it will be

Bolly. That should swing it. Otherwise – maybe dinner? It's up to her. But I'm sure she'll understand about lunch.'

Lucilla Fellowes had rung Eliza twice now about the change to the lunch date, and got no answer; the third time, she decided she would have to leave a message on the answering machine.

Lucilla left her message, covered up her typewriter, put on her coat and went home to cook dinner for her barrister husband.

'Matt, hello, it's me. Look, I'm in a bit of a fix; I've had my car towed away – what? Well, I left it on a double yellow. Only for a minute – well, ten actually – and I'm waiting at the pound now to get it back. Yes, I know, I know I'm an idiot, and I'm very sorry, but it's taking ages, and I'm going to be late to pick up Emmie. She's out to tea. I don't suppose you could do it, could you? Since you're coming home early anyway. Well, you said you were. Yes, you did, you said you were shattered, and you really needed an early night and you'd better because I've made you a fish pie. Anyway – do you think you could possibly pick Emmie up? Oh, Matt please, I never ask you and it's only in the next street and you like the mummy, it's that blonde called Susannah with the big tits. Yes, Parkham Street, number seven. Six o'clock. I'll be home by six thirty latest, and supper's all under control, you might turn the oven up to five – what, no I know you're not my housekeeper, but it would be helpful – yes? Oh, thank you. Thank you, Matt, very much. Must go, there's a queue to use this phone.'

'That's not a bad idea,' said Jack Beckham. 'Like it. It'll have to be fleshed out, of course, we need names, the landlord identified, all that stuff, but – yes. Time we ran a Rachman-style story. Haven't had one for ages.'

'My – my source was very anxious to protect the tenant. They're very afraid of recriminations, the whole thing backfiring.'

'Yes, well, they can't come whining to the press and then expect everything to be done their way.'

'They haven't exactly come whining,' said Barrett, 'and I don't want to drop them in it.'

'Johnny,' said Beckham, his voice developing the edge that his staff dreaded, 'I'm struggling to turn you into a big name. Thought that was what you wanted. You're not on the local rag in Bradford any more. You can't afford to be queasy. Now, I see this as a spread, with plenty of quotes and another case study or two. If it's half-good I'll trail it the day before. OK?'

'OK,' said Barrett.

Matt and Emmie arrived home just after six. Matt had had a rather irritating conversation with the blonde, big-breasted Susannah, who had tried very hard to press him into joining their wine-tasting group at Hurlingham.

'We all have such fun, meet once a month, only about twenty of us. And then dins afterwards, the restaurant's not half bad these days. Do think about it, be terrific to have you with us.'

What was it with these people? Didn't they have work to do?

Emmie demanded a drink and a biscuit and sat swinging her legs on a stool, chattering about her day, how she had got a star for her sums, and been top in spelling; Matt dutifully turned up the oven and then poured himself a large gin and tonic and went into the study.

The answering machine was blinking. He switched it on.

'Mrs Shaw, hello.' The tones were cut-glass finishing school; God, he hated voices like that. And their owners. 'This is Lucilla Fellowes, Jeremy Northcott's secretary. Mr Northcott is very sorry but he wonders if you could change lunch on Thursday to a drink, after work. He says to tell you, it will definitely be Bolly. Or possibly, dinner, if you could make it. If you just give me a call in the morning and let me know, that would be super. Thank you so much.'

He was so shocked he turned it back to listen to it again; as he did so Emmie wandered in.

'He was my friend,' she said as the message ended.

'What?' said Matt, turning to her. 'Who was your friend?'

'That man the message was about. Jeremy. He was at Mariella's palace when we stayed, he played Hide and Seek with me and Mummy.'

Chapter 47

'Louise? Johnny Barrett here. Look – I'm writing a piece about wicked landlords. Yes. That's right, thought you must know a few. Anyway, it's to do with an idea that friend of yours, Eliza Shaw, put me on to.'

'Really?' Louise felt an unpleasant crawl somewhere deep in her stomach.

'Yeah, some friend of hers, living in some tip in Clapham, part of a row she says, landlords letting the place go to rack and ruin to get rid of them all, doesn't sound a very likely friend for the upmarket Mrs Shaw, but still, she's taking me there to meet her. Anyway, I need to know who the landlord is, obviously, get a quote and that. I thought you might be able to help.'

'Oh – no,' said Louise, firmly. The crawl had burrowed deeper. Unless there were two rows of houses in Clapham with landlords desperate to get rid of the tenants . . . Oh, there were probably half a dozen, you're being neurotic, Louise. Still, she absolutely didn't want to be party to anything that could backfire. How many times had Matt told her what a small world it was? 'And Johnny, I really think it would be better if you didn't use that particular connection.' She knew she was sticking her neck out; but she was surprised Eliza was so naïve as to get involved with anything that might backfire on her. Unless she wanted it to, of course.

'What?'

'Yes. An awful lot of people would be hurt by it. Quite badly.'

'Want to explain?'

'No. I really don't. But – well, that's all I have to say. And I certainly can't help. I'm sorry.'

'OK.'

'OK, you won't ask me any more or OK, you won't write the piece?'

'What do you think? Bye, Louise.'

Barrett put the phone down. This was clearly a much more intriguing story than he'd first imagined. Surely, surely it couldn't be Matt's property and Eliza didn't know about it? Or did know about it? It was a case for some very serious sleuthing. And he could start in the morning when he and Eliza went to meet this poor unfortunate bird in Clapham.

'Matt! Emmie! Hello. I'm home. Bloody cops. I had to practically kiss their backsides to get my keys back. Where are you?'

He came out of the office; his face was white and his eyes very dark. Eliza looked at him uncertainly.

'Hello. You all right? You look—'

'No,' he said. 'I'm not all right. What the hell is going on?'

'What? What are you talking about? I don't understand—'

'Jeremy Northcott,' he said, 'who you're having lunch with apparently. Or a drink of Bolly, how delightful. Or even dinner. And who I now learn, just coincidentally, was in Milan with you. Emmie told me all about it, how you played hide and seek together. How nice, how very nice for you all. What the fuck are you playing at, Eliza? What are you doing—'

'Emmie, go upstairs,' said Eliza quickly, 'see if you can be a big girl and get yourself ready for bed. I'll be up in a minute.'

Emmie didn't argue; she looked at her parents, her eyes large and thoughtful, and then walked out of the room. Eliza closed the door behind her and turned to face Matt.

'You shouldn't use language like that in front of Emmie,' she said.

'I'll use what fucking language I like in my own house. And don't try to change the subject.'

'Matt, it's not what you think,' she said, 'it really, really isn't. It's—'

'Is that so? Well, whatever I think, the fact remains you're clearly seeing him. Having dinner with him in London. Staying with him in Milan. How odd that you didn't mention it. And how did you keep Emmie quiet about it all this time? What the fuck is going on?'

'I'm not having dinner with him,' said Eliza, 'I was going to have lunch. To discuss the – the job.'

'What job?'

'The one you said I wasn't to do. In your sweetly generous, liberated way.'

'Oh, for Christ's sake. Don't start that, please. You didn't say he was at the agency when you told me about it. I thought he was in New York.'

'He has been in New York. He's only just back. The only thing he's had to do with all this is tell Rob Brigstocke to call me.'

'Oh, is that so. Just as he comes back? Well, that certainly settles it. You will not set foot near that agency while he's there.'

'Matt, I sometimes wonder which century you think you're living in. Have you never heard of equal rights?'

'Equal rights! Is that what you call it? Playing around with your ex-lover behind my back, at the first opportunity? And passing it off as some wonderfully fortuitous career move? Oh, Matt, it's such a wonderful opportunity, oh, Matt, it's only two days a week. How many days does it take for Northcott to get into your bed? And – and now I find out he was in Milan. On this therapeutic trip that was supposed to console you after the baby. How carefully was that planned? I suppose you and your friend Mariella cooked it up between you. And you took Emmie along, presumably as some kind of cover. Jesus, Eliza, I wouldn't have believed it even of you.'

'Shut up,' shouted Eliza. 'Just shut up. How dare you talk to me like that. How dare you insult me and Jeremy too, come to that. I had no idea he was going to be in Milan, none whatsoever. He was there on agency business, there's a branch there, and he only came to the villa because of the fog.'

'Oh yes, the fog. The wonderfully convenient fog that prevented you from coming home. I don't quite see how he could have got to the villa in the fog when it was supposed to be so bad you were stranded in Milan.'

'He – he organised a car for me to get back next day, because I was so worried about Emmie. A colleague of his came too. Timothy Fordyce, you can check it if you want to, if you don't believe me.'

'And who would I check it with, to get an honest answer? Northcott's minion, your friend? If the lot of you told me my name was Matt Shaw I wouldn't believe them. I don't think I've ever been so disgusted by anything in my life.'

The door opened, Emmie looked round it. She seemed less sure of herself than usual.

'Mummy?'

'Yes, darling.'

'Can I watch TV?'

'No, Emmie, you can't. It's bedtime. I'll come up and read you a story.'

'I want Daddy to.'

'Right. Well – Matt? Would you like to do what Emmie asks?'

He took Emmie's hand and walked out of the room without another word.

Later she heard him come downstairs and go into the study; when she tried the door it was locked.

Louise had, most unusually, slept badly. She was worried, without being quite sure why, about the Barrett article and Eliza's involvement in it. Not that it was anything to do with her, but there was a chance that it might be the same site that she remembered, and if it was then the tinderbox would be well and truly set alight. But – surely to God, Eliza must have thought there was a danger of a link with Matt, and have checked it out? She'd worked as a journalist, for God's sake. Although glossy magazines and Fleet Street sharks weren't quite the same thing. And she had an uneasy feeling she'd spurred Barrett on, rather than putting him off the piece. So should she warn Eliza? And if so how?

Then she thought of Roderick; he was more likely to know about the terrace, which one it was.

But Roderick Brownlow was away on a skiing trip and had left his secretary strict instructions that he wasn't to be disturbed by anyone.

Feeling by now extremely stupid, Louise rang Eliza's home number. It rang and rang; and then Eliza's clear voice asked her to leave a message on the answering machine. Well, that wasn't on. Matt might hear. It was all getting terribly complicated . . . Louise decided she had done as much as she possibly could and returned to her own problems.

'Is that Johnny Barrett?'

'Yes, it is.'

'Oh – Johnny. Eliza Shaw here. The thing is, I'm very sorry, but – I think I'd rather you didn't go ahead with the article after all.'

She had been worrying about it in the night: that it might be traced back to her, that it would, after all, be casting a slur on Matt's profession. However much he – and it – deserved it, she simply couldn't afford to risk upsetting him any further.

'R-i-ght. Any particular reason?'

'Well – um, the girl in question, she's quite pregnant, as I think I told you and she's just rung to say she's not feeling too good and she's been worrying about the piece, even though I know you promised not to put her name in and –well, I just think it would be better all round if we – we forgot about it. I'm so sorry. To have wasted your time and everything.'

This was so unprofessional, she thought. If Jack Beckham heard about it, that would be her done for. You just didn't cancel an interview you had set up on the morning it was to take place, especially for a national newspaper. But . . .

'OK.' He sounded pleasant, not annoyed, not put out even. 'I can understand that. She must be very anxious, she's in a difficult position, and I really don't want to pressure her. Not in her condition.'

The old-fashioned northern expression made her smile.

'That's so kind of you. I'm so sorry.'

'It's all right. I'm not one of your ruthless, door-stepping kind of journalists. I like to sleep nights. Don't worry, Eliza, I've got something else to put on my page this week. But – if you change your mind, or your friend decides she does want to talk to me, just let me know, OK?'

'Yes, of course. And thank you so much for being so nice about it.'

She rang off weak with relief. Thank God. Most journalists would have been totally furious and at the very least bawled her out. Heather would be relieved too, she really hadn't been very keen. If only she could ring her; she didn't have time to go round today, she'd have to drop her a note. What a nice man. It had been worth looking a bit silly; just to have one thing less to worry about.

Barrett put the phone down and looked at it thoughtfully. He'd been right, there was much more in this than met the eye, or rather ear. He wasn't quite sure how he was going to find the unfortunate pregnant woman, but he'd faced greater challenges. A Victorian terrace in Clapham, just off the Common, falling into dereliction: it would clearly involve a bit of legwork, and it was unlikely to be the only one, but it shouldn't be impossible. As for the landlord, Louise was right; he did have plenty of contacts. And a short list might contain a clue, a recognisable name. It was almost better this way; he could follow the story at his own pace and in his own way.

He went to see Jack Beckham to tell him the story wouldn't be ready for the paper this week, but that he had a cracking one about the new Covent Garden proposals to put in its place.

✻　✻　✻

Jeremy was very understanding too; he said he was sorry and that Rob Brigstocke would be very sorry as well, but of course she must do what she felt right, and that they could have lunch any time that suited her. And if she changed her mind about the job, or had any other ideas that might suit him or the agency, he would always be pleased to hear from her.

Matt was rather less accommodating.

'Can you give me one good reason why I should believe you?' he said, his eyes hostile in his white, exhausted face, as they talked far into the following evening.

'No,' she said, 'I can't. Except that I'm giving up what seems to me to be the perfect job, simply to please you. Which might even mean I still love you. Isn't that worth anything?'

He was silent; then he looked at her.

'It's worth a lot to you, I can see that. Yes. But you see, I find it so hard to understand why your work means so much more to you than Emmie and me do. It hurts me so much.'

'Matt, it doesn't mean more to me than you do. That's ridiculous. It means there's more to me than just – just looking after Emmie and you. I'm sorry. But it does. The person you fell in love with was about more than that. Working, doing something I'm good at, is so much part of me.'

He was silent.

'Matt, you love what you do. Would you give it up to care for Emmie and me? If I asked you, if I was earning enough money?'

'No, of course not. Don't be ridiculous.'

'So – what's the difference?'

'It's my job,' he said, 'to look after you.'

'Matt, that is such crap. You were doing it – and loving it – long before you even set eyes on me.'

'Yes, but now there is you,' he said. 'I can't help how I feel.'

'And how is that?'

'That it's right for me to look after you. And for you to be at home looking after me and the children.'

'We don't have children though, do we?' she said soberly. 'We have one child, and she's at school, all day, every day. If – if Baby Charles had lived, it would be different. But he didn't. And the thing that hurts me so much, is that you should think I would have an affair with Jeremy Northcott. I don't love Jeremy and I never did. I realised that when I fell

476

in love with you. More importantly, I would never, ever betray you. I just wouldn't, Matt.'

'You deceived me though,' he said. 'You hid the fact he was in Milan.'

'Yes, and why do you think? Because I knew you'd never believe me, that it was all completely innocent. That's pretty ugly, from where I'm sitting. Love is about trust. Do you love me still, Matt? Do you?'

There was a silence; then he said, 'Why do you think I care so much, what you do? Of course I bloody love you. You're everything to me, you and Emmie. Everything. More than everything.'

The funny thing was, she still believed him.

She lay staring into the darkness that night, still hurting, still half-resentful, reflecting on what she had given up that day and wondering quite what for. She would not have believed once that Matt, and loving Matt, could result in what was literally self-sacrifice, and she could only hope that it was, in the long run, right for her and her life. There seemed no certainty in any of it. And that made her very, very sad.

That weekend they went to Summercourt; Eliza had not been there for a while and she had only to see the iron gates, the gentle incline up to the house, its charmed outline against the sky, the woods and meadows beyond, and she felt healed and comforted. It was extraordinary how much she loved that house; more than anyone else in the family, she felt. And at least Matt had done that for her, made it possible to keep it.

Sarah had made soup for lunch and her own bread. They all sat in the kitchen, looking out at the frosty February landscape and chatting quite easily; and afterwards Emmie dragged them off to see her adored new pony, Mouse, and Eliza and Sarah helped to groom her and then Eliza gave Emmie a lesson, refusing to allow her to canter because she still couldn't kick the wilful Mouse into a trot, but had to be led. 'You've got to let him know you're in charge, Emmie, it's the whole secret of good riding; that and trusting him to look after you. Now come on, try again, kick him hard, that's better, really hard. Good girl, good girl, well done . . .'

And Matt, who found all things equine intensely boring, even when Emmie was involved, went off for a walk on his own, and came back looking almost cheerful, talking about thinning out the trees a bit to let the new young ones grow, and Eliza thought happily how he too was becoming properly involved with Summercourt and its care; and they ate an early supper with Emmie, and played an endless game of Ludo, and then after Emmie had gone to bed, and Sarah had gone to her room,

Matt and Eliza sat in a peaceful silence by the fire that he had lit in the drawing room watching a terrible play on the TV and then found themselves in bed by ten o'clock, just lying in one another's arms, not making love but finding themselves early in the morning turning to one another in a sharp, intense awakening, and Eliza thought that truly Summercourt did exercise a sort of magic and if nothing else could save their marriage, being there perhaps would.

Chapter 48

'Good afternoon, Miss Scarlett. What are you doing here, in this particularly unlovely airport?'

'Oh – hello. Yes. Well – I'm on my way back from Trisos, to London.'

'And I am on my way to Trisos, from London. There is a certain symmetry in that I suppose. How was it there?'

'Lovely. Quite chilly, but lovely.'

'Did you look at the house?'

'Yes, it's amazing, Mark. Truly amazing. That stone spiral staircase up to the terrace roof – inspirational.'

'I thought so. I'm glad you like it. I'm actually moving in in May and I'm going to have a lavish housewarming party. I shall hope very much to see you there.'

'Oh. Well – that'd be very nice – but—' She thought of his launch party, all those snooty, clever people.

'No buts, Miss Scarlett. I insist. It wouldn't be at all the same without you. It would hardly be a party at all.'

'Mark, that's just silly.'

'I'm not being silly. It wouldn't. I mean, think about it. Larissa. Demetrios. Possibly Stellios. Ari the Ferry, Ari the Poison as well, of course, hopefully without that truly disgusting wine he produces, Stavros' – who hired out the scooters – 'and me. Surely you can see we'd need you.'

'Oh,' she said, smiling now, for she had not liked the vision of the London literati descending on Trisos at Mark's behest. 'I thought you meant a – you know, a proper party – people from publishing—'

'Scarlett! I thought you would know me better than that. I cannot imagine anything worse. Oh, now I have to go, get a taxi down to Piraeus, I shall miss the big ferry. Goodbye for now.'

'Bye, Mark. Have a good trip. Hope it's calm.' For the crossing could be extremely rough and even the goats – inevitable passengers on the small ferry – got seasick.

She looked after him smiling, thinking how nice he was, and what a shame he was married – and as she settled into her seat on the plane, how odd that Mrs Frost had not been named among the guests at the house warming.

Twenty-four hours later, Mark sat on the veranda with Demetrios and Larissa, admiring the new baby, and hearing how Miss Scarlett had been not very happy at all and they had more than once heard her crying in her room late at night.

'We think she has no boyfriend still, so sad,' said Larissa.

Mark agreed that it was very sad; but reflected that if it meant whatever relationship Scarlett had had with the blow-dried blond bugger was over, it was an excellent thing and a big relief to him at least. He wondered if he might try to see her in London.

Meanwhile, 'I want to speak to you,' he said to Demetrios, 'about constructing some ramps up the steps for my mother's wheelchair . . .'

Mariella found out about the party by accident: a very lucky accident, as she said. She was in New York for a few days, ordering some clothes and shopping and had offered to take a friend to dinner at Elaine's. The friend was charmed and impressed; 'I've wanted to go there so long. Did you know Woody Allen met Mia Farrow there?'

Mariella said she didn't, but she wasn't surprised. 'Everybody meets everybody here. I love it. And she is so wonderful, Elaine, so bigger than life. Those flower-covered dresses she wears, so vulgar and all those gold chains. I will book a table and we will have a wonderful evening. See how many famous faces we can see.'

However, there wasn't a table the following evening; Elaine's was full. Mariella was not one of the vast number of people who would have been told this anyway, or turned away at the door, she was one of Elaine's pets.

'We have a big party tomorrow night, Signora Crespi. I am so sorry.'

'Oh, that is so sad. I am not a large person, nor is my friend, could you not find us a tiny table in a corner?'

'I'm afraid not. Lunch perhaps?'

'Ah. Yes. We will come to lunch. Thank you. Not so exciting perhaps but – it will do.'

She and her friend had a very good lunch, eating the fettucine dish that Jackie Kennedy had famously cooked to Elaine's recipe, and were drinking their coffee when a tall, incredibly thin blonde woman walked in looking distracted, demanding to see Elaine. She was told Elaine was not available.

'It's about the seating plan for this evening, I wanted to leave the place names with her and to make sure they were put out before Mr Northcott's party arrived.'

'And you are?'

'Mr Northcott's PA.'

'I can do that for you, Madame.'

'Are you sure? They must be right, it's quite imperative, I would really like Elaine to do it personally.'

'I will do it, Madame. If you just give me the seating plan . . .'

'Come, *cara!*' said Mariella to her friend, jumping up, 'we must go. I have a great deal to do.'

The Summercourt effect had not lasted. They were hardly inside the door before Matt was checking the answering machine, standing over it, listening to it intently, and then rifling through the post. Eliza felt a flash of hurt.

'You don't trust me, do you? You really don't.'

'I don't know what you mean.'

'Matt, you're checking up on me. Just to make sure that Jeremy hasn't rung, that there aren't any love letters lying on the mat—'

'You're being neurotic, Eliza. The purpose of an answering machine is to take messages in the owner's absence. I merely wanted to see who might have rung.'

'Yes, sure. Well, now you know. Two of my friends. Women, so that's all right. Unless you think I might be about to become a lesbian, of course.'

'Don't talk in that disgusting way, Emmie might hear.'

'She's heard you being pretty disgusting already, in my view. Oh, for God's sake, Matt, give it a rest. I'm going up to bath her.'

'It was you not giving it a rest. I'm going to do some work now, some of us have more to do than picking quarrels.'

'If I had more to do,' cried Eliza, her voice cracking with pain, 'I maybe wouldn't be picking quarrels, as you call it.'

'God give me strength,' said Matt. 'I thought we had heard the last of

481

that one for a while at least. You go to bed, Eliza, I'll be very late. I'll go into the spare room.'

'And bloody well stay there,' she said and set off up the stairs.

Waking in the morning, alone in the bed, she realised she was still hurting. When she got down to the kitchen, there were the messy remnants of toast-making and a note saying 'I'll be late tonight.'

And this was meant to be a marriage.

Reflecting that if marriage and motherhood were genuinely to be her life for the foreseeable future, she must pull herself together and put a one-hundred-per-cent effort into it, Eliza called Matt mid-morning to hold out a rather well-worn olive branch, and ask him if he really had to work late and if not, then she would cook proper dinner for them both, rather than the soup-and-sandwich supper she could leave out for him otherwise. He wasn't there, and so she left a message to call her; an hour later, Mandy rang and said she was sorry, Mr Shaw was out of town, but he had asked her to say that he would have to be late and not to wait for him for dinner. Stung that he had not even bothered to call himself, and feeling particularly lonely, Eliza rang Maddy and invited her to have supper with her.

'I need an injection of gossip, I'm going crazy.'

The phone was ringing as Eliza arrived home after school with Emmie and a small friend; she shot over to it but the answering machine had cut in. As so often when a caller unused to such things was confronted by it, there was a long silence, and then a voice said 'oh, doesn't matter,' and rang off. It had sounded like Heather, but she couldn't be sure, the voice was echoey and distorted; Eliza decided she would go round and see her in the morning, just in case, she could hardly go now, and addressed herself to settling the little girls in the playroom and making their tea. If it was important, Heather would surely ring again.

Heather sighed; she had no more change, and anyway, she needed every last penny for the meter. She would try again tomorrow. And it was perfectly all right about the article, she was sure. She just thought she ought to tell Eliza.

Eliza and Maddy were settling happily into gossip mode in the small sitting room when a key turned in the lock and Matt walked in.

'Oh,' he said, 'oh hello.'

'Matt – hello. What are you doing here?'

'I live here, I thought,' he said. He was clearly making an effort to sound light-hearted, but it didn't quite work.

'I thought you were going to be late.'

'Yes, well after your rather touching phone call, I made an effort, got back early, here I am. Evening, Maddy.'

'Hello, Matt.'

'Well, how lovely.' Eliza got up, gave him a kiss. 'You must join us, of course.'

'That would be charming,' he said, a slight edge to his voice, 'but I can see you're having a girls' evening, I won't intrude. I'll just have something in the study, Eliza.'

'Matt, don't. We'd like you to be with us, wouldn't we, Maddy?'

'Course.'

'Come on. Sit down, chat to Maddy while I cook the pasta.'

After about an hour of stultifyingly awkward conversation, with Matt sitting silent and half-sullen, Maddy left, clearly embarrassed; Eliza turned on him in a fury.

'That was so rude. Maddy was my guest and you couldn't have been less friendly to her, didn't even try to join in . . .'

'Eliza, I can't do all that stuff. It makes me feel even thicker than I look. I offered to go to my study, you had to insist. I suppose she'd come to commiserate with you over the job,' said Matt, 'show solidarity with – what is it, oh, yes, the sisterhood.'

'Don't be silly,' said Eliza, struggling to sound calm. 'She'd just come for a gossip. About, you know, the business, what she's doing, all that sort of thing.'

'Why is it always that lot you want to see? From your old life? You just can't tear yourself away, can you? What about some new friends?'

'I have new friends, thank you, I just don't particularly want to spend the evening with them.'

'Because?'

'Because they're not interested in what interests me.'

'And she is?' he said indicating the chair where Maddy had been sitting. 'A woman with no children, just obsessed with the business as you call it, banging on about all those poncey designers and photographers, that interests you, does it? Nothing else? I thought – I hoped,' he said, 'after our last little upset, you were really going to throw yourself into it, forget all that rubbish—'

'It is not rubbish,' she shouted, 'it's what I care about, what I want to be doing—'

'Oh, so you don't want to be at home, looking after Emmie, you're just doing it out of some sense of duty. You really want to be back out there, having your arse licked. You're not really going into this wholeheartedly at all, are you?' he said. 'You're just biding your time, softening me up, waiting for the next opportunity.'

'That is so unfair—'

'Is it? I don't think so. It seems very fair to me. Oh, I'm going to do some work. I'm sorry I've spoilt your girly evening.'

'Yes,' she said, 'you have. Totally.'

Chapter 49

He finally picked up the phone, took a deep breath.

'I – well – that is, I wondered if you'd like to have dinner one night,' he said. 'Nothing – nothing grand, more like supper really.'

He had put it off several times, finding excuses: he was too tired one day, too busy the next, a bit low the third. He needed to feel his absolute best to do it right.

He had often wondered why he was so pathologically shy when it came to relationships. He could, after all, be charming and amusing when he was on show: a different person altogether. But the combined terror of looking foolish and being rejected was too much for his rather fragile ego.

He had only been in love twice in his life: first with his childhood sweetheart, who had turned her back on him and gone off with the rich, smooth heart-throb of the Upper Sixth; and the second time with a sweet, gentle, funny girl who had demanded nothing of him except that he loved her in the way she loved him. They had been engaged for only six months when she had found a lump in her breast; she had died exactly a year later, leaving him utterly broken both in his heart and his head. Since then, and for over ten years now, he had not ventured into a new relationship.

He could not have told you what it was about Scarlett that appealed to him so much; she was lovely, of course, and she had a glamour about her which he liked. And she was clearly very clever and successful in a business that was notoriously tough and cut-throat and didn't suffer fools in any way. But those were all qualities that would normally have frightened him off. And while she was very intelligent, she was far from well-educated and not well-read – which would normally have troubled him, not for any intellectually snobbish reasons, but because it precluded so many sources of conversation. He had decided that what drew him to her was her vulnerability, which lay beneath the gloss and the glamour and the success; like him, he felt she was not personally secure and that personal happiness had eluded her. And if she was looking for it in people like that idiot at lunch that day, no wonder.

Whatever the reason, he was sufficiently drawn to her to risk an invitation to dinner . . .

There was a long, rather unnerving silence. Then she said, 'Mark, I don't think so. I'm sorry. You must know the reason, you really must. But thank you. And it's very flattering, Goodbye, Mark. I'll – I'll see you on Trisos.'

'Yes, of course,' he said, longing to ask her what was this reason that he must know. And wondering how he could ever feel easy on Trisos again, were she around.

'Oh, shit,' said Scarlett, close to tears, looking at the phone, now replaced on its receiver. 'Shit, shit, shit.'

It was so long since anyone she fancied and liked so much had asked her out. But she wasn't risking that again.

'Fuck,' said Mark Frost, feeling utterly wretched, looking at the phone as he replaced it on its receiver. 'Fuck, fuck, fuck.'

It was so long since he had fancied and liked anyone enough to ask them out. But he wouldn't be risking that again.

Suddenly, with frightening speed, Eliza and Matt seemed to have moved into a new, strange country; a silent, unsmiling land, filled with suspicion and a lack of warmth or even courtesy. They moved around, wary of one another, he staring at her with cold, blank eyes, her expression resentful and defiant. Day after day.

He went to work, came home very late, went into his study and then to bed. The spare-room bed.

With Emmie he was himself: greeting her with hugs and kisses, talking to her, playing with her, reading to her, taking her out to the park. Emmie had begun to notice the coldness and the blankness, did her best to ease it. She tried to set up conversations, said, 'Will Mummy come too?' when Matt said he'd put her to bed, or take her to the swings. It was precociously touching; it did no good.

Eliza was in despair.

❊   ❊   ❊

Johnny Barrett was writing his 'wicked landlord' piece. He, in the end, had found the terrace quite quickly; there were only two that fitted the description, and after spending a couple of hours in his car outside each of them, and watching a pretty, heavily pregnant young woman walking gingerly down the steps of one of them with a little girl, and then returning half an hour later carrying shopping, he felt confident he had found Eliza Shaw's friend.

He went over to her the second morning and smiled.

'Excuse me, but can I help you with that shopping? It looks very heavy and those steps seem pretty treacherous to me.'

She flushed, clearly embarrassed.

'Oh – no, no, it's perfectly all right. I'm fine.'

'Well, I don't think it is. Look – come on, just to the front door. It's all right, I'm not some kind of mugger, I promise I won't try and come in.'

'Well – it would be nice. Thank you.'

'These steps are a death trap,' he said, kicking at one of them; a shower of plaster fell onto the one below.

'I know. We've tried to get the landlord to fix them, but he never does. He never fixes anything, as a matter of fact, the place is a tip inside.'

'Going to be worse when you're trying to get a pram up and down the steps.'

'Yes, well, we won't be here then. We're looking for somewhere else, but landlords don't like babies, so we may have to – sorry, you don't want to hear all this.'

'Yes, I do. Don't be silly. I'm very sympathetic as a matter of fact. My sister's in the same fix. She and her husband have been trying to find somewhere for months, they live up north, Manchester way.'

'Really? Well, I suppose a landlord is a landlord. Out for all they can get. And babies put other tenants off.'

'Seems so. Look – I think I'd better come clean. Johnny Barrett, *Daily News*. Your friend Eliza Shaw told me about you.'

She looked alarmed. 'Oh – goodness. I thought – Eliza said you'd decided not to do the article after all.'

'I had. But to be honest with you, seeing what my sister's going through made me keen again. I really think these people shouldn't be allowed to get away with it. It's not right. Look, you wouldn't like to tell me a bit more now, would you?'

'Oh – I don't know. I don't think so. I don't want to get into trouble and while we're still living here—'

'Of course not, but like I said to Eliza, no names.'

'Really?' Her large grey eyes met his. 'It would be completely anonymous?'

She was very pretty, he thought. And very vulnerable.

'Completely. And you'd only be one of several stories. Look – there's a café down the road. Why don't I take you there and you can tell me all about it.'

'Rob? Rob Brigstocke?'

'Yup, speaking.'

'It's Eliza Shaw here. Look – if that job's still going, I'd really like to talk some more about it.'

'Oh – right. Well – well, yes, we haven't found anyone else yet. Got a couple of people to see, but – how about lunch?'

'That'd be very nice.'

'Good. Thursday? Berkeley Grill, one o'clock. I won't be late this time.'

It had come to her suddenly, as she lay awake night after night in an agony of resentment and misery that she really could not miss out on the perfect career move any longer, just to please him; pleasing him seemed absolutely impossible.

And there was no way he could actually stop her, after all.

'Matt, hi. It's me.'

'Oh – Gina. Hello.'

'You don't sound very pleased to hear from me. It's been a while.'

'No, no. I am . . . sorry. I – well, yes, of course I am. How are you doing?'

'I'm doing pretty well, thanks. Very well, actually. Which is why I'm ringing you.'

'Oh yes?'

'Yes. I'm looking for new premises. To open a second shop. I thought you might be able to help.'

It annoyed him when people thought he was a sort of glorified estate agent.

'Gina, I don't handle that sort of thing. Sorry.'

'Oh – OK. I just thought—'

'Well, you thought wrong,' said Matt shortly.

'I'm sorry,' said Gina. Her voice was sharp; it cut through Matt's misery.

'No, no, I'm sorry. Got a few problems at the moment.'

'Anything I can help with?'

''Fraid not. No.'

'Well – you know where I am, Matt. If you need me.'

It worried him that he knew where she was. He hoped nobody else did.

Jack Beckham told Barrett to stay after the evening conference. He was holding the first draft of his article.

'There's not enough here,' he said, 'too much sentimental clap-trap. This isn't fucking *Woman's Own*. What's this girl's name, for a start?'

'I – said I wouldn't give that.'

'Well you need to give it, OK? And we need facts and figures, and I've told you, we certainly need the name of the developer, and a quote from him. Otherwise, we could have made it all up.'

'Yeah, but—'

'Look, I've told you, I'm trying to make a star journalist of you. I thought that was what you wanted, when you came down from that one-horse town. Maybe I was mistaken, maybe—'

Johnny Barrett said OK, and that none of that would be very difficult. And told himself that he had done his best to protect Heather, after all, she hadn't been stupid and she had certainly known she was talking to a journalist.

Now, the developer.

'Eliza, hello, it's me, Heather. Look – I thought I'd better tell you, I talked to that journalist after all. He turned up at the house and – well, he was really nice, just like you said, and he bought me a coffee and I quite enjoyed it.'

'Right. Did he say when it might go in?'

'No, he didn't. But he did promise not to put any names or addresses in and—'

'Good. Well I'm glad you told me, that's great. I'll try and get round later in the week, have to go now. Take care.'

'Johnny Barrett? This is Eliza Shaw. Look, I hear you talked to my friend.'

'To Heather, yes.'

'I wish you'd rung me first. I did want to be there.'

'Not necessary, Eliza. I don't know why you thought you needed to be. She's very bright. Very sweet.'

'Yes, OK, but – you won't put her name in, will you?'

'Now what was the deal, Eliza? And what do you think I am?'

'A member of Fleet Street,' said Eliza. 'Please don't, Johnny, please.'

'You're insulting my integrity,' he said and rang off.

Susan came into Matt's office with a typed list.

'What's that?'

'You asked me to find some low-rent flats, Mr Shaw. I've got a few, all very nice; shall I leave them with you?'

'Oh – yes, please. Thanks, Susan.'

Perhaps this was what it would take to please Eliza, at least a bit, show her he wasn't all bad, break the awful frozen impasse. Although why he should want to, he didn't know. She so clearly despised him and everything he stood for . . .

Barrett's third call revealed the name of the landlord of the Clapham terrace, and of the developer who had bought the freehold.

'And here's a thing,' said his informant, 'it's a subsidiary of Matt Shaw's company. Probably a tax dodge, very clever.'

'Matt Shaw? Are you quite certain about that?'

'Course. Ask him, why don't you?'

'I think I'd better not,' said Barrett.

'Hello, Louise. How you doing?'

'Oh – pretty well. We seem to have got planning permission on the new hotel. Nice story for you, we've seen off the arty brigade.'

'Yes? Well, not for me this time. Look – just checking something, is SureFire Development an offshoot of Matt Shaw's company?'

'Yes, it is. But it's perfectly legal, nothing worth writing about. Why?'

'Oh, nothing,' said Barrett. 'Just doing a round-up, you know.'

✿   ✿   ✿

490

'Louise? Eliza. Look have you heard from your friend Johnny Barrett lately?'

'Funny you should say that, but yes. About an hour ago. Asking me—'

'Asking you what?'

Louise told her.

'Oh Christ,' said Eliza. 'Jesus Christ.'

'OK,' said Jack Beckham, 'this is pretty good now. Well done, Barrett. We'll make a journalist of you yet. Lawyers seen it?'

'Yup.'

'Because it is strong stuff.'

'Yeah, I know. But they said as long as there was no doubt about the landlord – and it's definitely him, and anyway, I got a quote out of him—'

'Good. We'll run it tomorrow. With a trail on the front page. Now – this crap about Covent Garden. Can you believe it, they want to turn it into some kind of fancy shopping area, with cafés and jazz bars. The old porters'd be turning in their graves.'

Eliza even tried to get through to Jack Beckham; it was no use. The story was just too good.

Matt was out that night at a dinner. She sat at home with Emmie, feeling increasingly sick. At eleven o'clock, she called the cab service she and Matt used and asked them to go and get a first edition copy of the *Daily News* from Waterloo station.

Opened it, shaking so hard, and gulping with fear, that it took long minutes to find the feature.

The property feature: across two pages.

'Millions Made from Misery', it was called; and underneath that, in only slightly smaller type, 'The landlords who make lives hell'.

It was after midnight when Matt got home; he'd been to a trade dinner and been made much of. It had soothed his damaged ego, made him feel less of a failure: in fact, rather the reverse.

He'd expected Eliza to be in bed but when he walked into the drawing room, as she insisted on calling it, holding his nightcap of whisky and ginger, she was sitting on one of the sofas.

'Hello,' she said.

'Hello. You're up late. Emmie all right?'

'Yes, yes, she's fine. Fast asleep. Matt—'

'I've got some news for your friend by the way, the one who hasn't got anywhere to live. Found her a couple of very cheap flats. In good buildings.'

'Oh, God,' she said and then, 'that's very – very good of you.'

'Yes, well, it might help to persuade you I'm not actually the devil incarnate. What is it, you look as if you've seen a coachload of ghosts.'

She was holding something: a newspaper.

'What's that, then?'

'It's tomorrow's *Daily News*. I – I sent out for it. There's something in it. Something you won't like. And – oh, here, read it—'

He read it; it didn't mean very much at first, just words on the page. Until he came to a name: a familiar name. And an account of how the owner of the name had made millions – and the methods he employed to enable him to do it.

He put the paper down, very slowly. 'Well?' he said.

'Matt, it was my fault. I didn't realise it was anything to do with you. But I told the journalist about Heather and the other tenants, I just didn't – didn't think, I tried to get it stopped but – I couldn't, I'm so, so sorry.'

'You bitch,' he said, 'you stupid, arrogant little bitch. You think you know it all, don't you, with your fancy friends and your fucking oh-so-important career. You really do despise me and what I've done, don't you? And now you're rubbing my nose in it. Very attractive. Have you ever considered that everything, everything you have, including that fucking pile down in the country you care about so much, is down to me?'

'Matt, no, no, I don't despise you, that's the last thing I feel, I think it's amazing what you've done, I admire it so much—'

'So much you publish a lot of filth about me, and the people who work for me.'

'I didn't publish it Matt, don't be ridiculous. I just – just—'

Her voice tailed off.

'You just alerted your Fleet Street friends to it, said do write about this, it's shocking, isn't it, what my husband gets up to, isn't that about the size of it?'

'No, no, Matt, it isn't, I had no idea it was anything to do with you, how could I have . . .'

'It was my business, though, wasn't it? The business you look down your aristocratic nose at. Have you even thought what this might do to me, me and my colleagues and my clients, come to that? How it will diminish me, do me harm?'

'Yes,' she said, very quietly, 'yes of course I have. And I'm sorry—'

'Oh, you are? Well, that's mighty good of you. You ruin me professionally, we won't go into the personal damage, and all you can manage is tell me you're sorry—'

'Matt! Of course you're not ruined. You're being ridiculous. It's very unfortunate, of course it is, and I'm terribly sorry. But it will be forgotten in a couple of days, you know it will. You're over-dramatising things and—'

She stopped. He had walked towards her: his face was white, his eyes black pinpricks in it, his mouth working almost as if he was going to cry. 'Don't you tell me I'm being ridiculous,' he said, 'just don't. How fucking dare you?' And then very, very slowly it seemed, he raised his hand and hit her hard across the face and then again, knocking her head from side to side.

'You bitch,' he said finally, and there was a break in his voice, 'you stuck-up, arrogant little bitch.'

There was a long silence, while Eliza stared at him, disbelieving what had happened, shaking not with fear but shock; then she recovered herself, pushed back her hair, faced him down.

'Well,' she said, 'so there we have it. Is that the best you can manage, knocking your wife about? And I had hoped to have civilised you a little. But you're still the same ignorant working-class boy, aren't you, Matt? In spite of all your millions.'

Matt said no more, simply turned and walked out of the house.

Several hours later, and extremely drunk, he turned up at Gina's flat.

He sat drinking black coffee, telling her everything, all the ugly brutal truth as he saw it.

'I don't know what to do,' he said, and two tears rolled down his face. He brushed them off, embarrassed. 'Sorry.'

'It's OK.'

'She just seems to want to destroy me. She hates me. And I – I – sorry . . .'

'Matt, it's OK. Really.' She went over to him, put her arms round him, stroked his hair.

'Perhaps you should think about divorce,' she said.

Chapter 50

He had apologised, of course. The following day, his face white and set, unable to meet her eyes, while studying her face for the damage he had done, genuinely ashamed and remorseful, had said he was sorry, that he should not have done it. He asked her if she was all right; she said she was. And that was the end of the conversation; it had not been referred to between them again. And he was still quite clearly ferociously angry with her, in spite of the remorse.

She felt very odd about it, confused, shocked. To have behaved so badly that it induced violence and from someone who had once loved her so much; it had clearly been very bad, that behaviour, and the blows something she had deserved, had almost earned.

She could not tell anyone, anyone at all; could not admit to any of it, simply said she had fallen down the cellar steps, to explain her swollen face and mouth, her black eye, and struggled to bury the memory and the fear – and the shame.

It haunted her, the memory, she lived it over and over again; it rose up not only in the night but harshly and unexpectedly during the day, as she drove her car, stood in the shower, walked down the street, threatening her, an excursion into another place, dark and ugly, where she could never have imagined herself to be.

It had not made her afraid of him, she felt instinctively he wouldn't do it again: and she knew he would never ever hit Emmie. He was simply not a violent man. Which made her own shame worse.

She had no idea what to do next; reconciliation seemed impossible, continuing as they were worse. She felt helpless, suspended in time, moving through the days in a senseless, confused lethargy. It was very frightening. Life as she knew it was lost to her.

Matt, struggling with conflicting emotions of his own, shame, shock,

494

almost unbearable anger, was also hugely fearful of the effect of the article on his business and his professional reputation. But the property community saw the story for what it was, as they viewed it at least, a gross distortion by the media, heaped upon their already unpopular shoulders, presented as they were as pariahs of society, impenetrable obstacles placed between decent people and the housing they deserved. And the public simply read, digested and then moved on into their own mantra that they were all the same, these developers, but there was nothing you could do about it, and went on their way.

But his sense of betrayal at Eliza's hands remained deep and bitter.

For the first time, Eliza was grateful for their lack of social life; there were no embarrassing comments to be endured at dinner parties at least. Sarah of course had seen it, and called her to say carefully that she was sure it was all lies and that Matt would never do such awful things; and Charles's reaction was very similar.

'Jolly hard on old Matt,' was all he said to Eliza and slightly duplicitously, she agreed.

The person who suffered most from the article was Heather; frightened and angry at Eliza's betrayal as she saw it, she refused to allow her into the house when Eliza arrived on her doorstep the next day.

'You promised, Eliza, you promised me. You said there would be no names, we wouldn't be identified. I thought we were friends—'

'Heather, we are friends, please don't say that.'

'That man lied and lied to me and you told me—'

'Heather, I know he did and I'm so, so sorry. I told him to leave you alone, I told him I didn't want him to do the story—'

'Well, why didn't he leave us alone then?'

'Because – because the press doesn't work like that. They're all sharks, they can't be trusted and—'

'But you've worked with these people. So why tell him about us in the first place? And how did he know where we were? Did you give him this address?'

'No, of course not. Well – well – I told him you lived near Clapham Common. And that it was a terrace of big Victorian houses. I suppose after that he just did a lot of legwork. Watched you coming out, recognised you from my description—'

'So you described me to him? Funny way of keeping him away—'

'Heather, please! All I said was you were a young mum, and you were pregnant.'

'Well, I'm sorry, Eliza, I don't want even to discuss it any more. Alan is so angry, he won't even speak to me, Coral's having a horrible time at school, they're calling her slummy, and we're definitely going to have to go and live with Alan's mum now.'

'No, Heather, you're not, look, try these, a couple of much better places that actually Matt found for you, phone them, please.'

'I don't think so. I don't think anything to do with Matt would be a good idea at the moment. We had actually found somewhere quite promising, but the landlord told Alan this morning it was off the market. I wonder why. And now I'm terrified of the landlord turning up here and just putting us out on the pavement—'

'Heather, he can't do that. Believe me.'

'I'm a bit sick of believing you, Eliza. Anyway, we're moving up there next week. I can't even have my baby at the hospital I know and trust. And it's all your fault. Oh, just go away, Eliza, please, and leave me alone. There's one law for people like you in this country and another for people like me, and I should have known better than to trust you.'

'Well – will you at least give me your new address, so I can keep in touch?'

'No. Now excuse me please I'm very busy.'

And she shut the door in Eliza's face.

Eliza went home and wept; and then wrote to Heather and told her if she ever changed her mind, she would always be pleased to hear from her. Heather didn't reply.

The atmosphere in the house was horrible. They hardly spoke, Matt went to work, came home very late, refused food, refused anything, just went to his study and then to bed. She lay awake half the night, every night; several times she had knocked on the door of his room. 'Please go away,' he said, his voice polite but very final. Or sometimes, 'Please leave me alone.'

Only with Emmie was he himself, greeting her with hugs and kisses, talking to her, playing with her, taking her out to the park. At first Eliza though this was his way of returning to normality, an overture via Emmie, but he continued to ignore his wife, to behave as if she wasn't there.

If Eliza spoke, he ignored her, if she tried to follow them upstairs he said, 'would you prefer to take her?' and the same thing on proposed outings, to the swings, the river, even, most dreadfully, to Summercourt for the weekend.

'I'd like to take Emmie down to Summercourt,' he said, the first time. 'I presume that's all right.'

'Yes, of course,' she said, and it was still at the stage when she was hoping he would relent, that things would be normal again. 'When shall we go?'

'I don't want you there,' he said, 'I'll take her on my own.'

That was terrible, that he should put this awful impenetrable barrier round Summercourt too. Even for one weekend.

'But I want to go,' she said, 'please.'

'Of course,' he said and she looked up, sharply hopeful, but, 'you can go next time,' he added, and he walked out of the room.

She had to explain then to her mother; Sarah, while upset, didn't understand, thought it was just a row.

'Don't worry, darling,' she said, 'he'll get over it. Just humour him, that's what I always did with your father. And don't worry about Emmie, I'll see she has a nice weekend. And – who knows, I might be able to talk him round. What was the row about? Not that silly article surely, that was nothing to do with you . . .'

Eliza said she didn't want to talk about it.

The weekend while they were there was endless. She stayed in the house alone, didn't want to see anyone. It meant explaining too much.

Her mother phoned after the weekend, interestingly cheerful: 'Honestly, darling, you must be exaggerating. He was very much himself, I thought, very sweet and polite to me, and so wonderful with Emmie. He does adore that child, Eliza, I've never seen quite such a besotted father. I'm not sure it's good for her. I didn't mention anything about a row, of course; but when I asked him how you were he said you were fine. He seemed very relaxed altogether. Oh, and he insists on my having the room next to mine turned into an en-suite bathroom; doesn't that sound wonderful?'

'Very – wonderful.'

'Of course he dressed it up, as he always does, said it was only to improve the overall value of the house, but I know it was still largely for my benefit. I mean, he's not going to sell it, is he?'

'He can't,' said Eliza. 'It's in our joint names.' But anxiety suddenly flickered through her. There were only two ways Matt could really hurt her: through Emmie – and through Summercourt. That would be – but no. No, he couldn't. However angry he was. He wouldn't.

And then it happened; after two more weeks of the absolute hostility and disdain, as she struggled to remain calm and outwardly cheerful in the face of it all, she received a formal offer of a job with KPD.

'Sorry to have been so long getting back to you,' Rob Brigstocke said when he called, a wonderful bright warmth breaking into yet another bleak morning. 'Had to get a few things rubber-stamped. Hope that's OK.'

'Oh – yes. Yes, of course. Marvellous.'

'Good. So when do you think you might start? Is the nanny you found still available? I know that was an important part of the mix.'

'I'm – yes, yes, I think so.'

She felt her mind racing; why not? Why bloody not? If Matt was never going to speak to her again, she had to do something to help herself. And this was just about the perfect something. But – what would he say? What might he do?

'You do what you want,' he said that night. 'You always do. What are you going to do about Emmie, have her adopted?'

'Matt! Don't.'

'Don't what?'

'Don't say such awful things. Please.'

He shrugged.

'I've been thinking,' she said, 'except for the school holidays, she'll be at school most of the time. After school, I could do exactly what I do now, if I have to, and ask your mum to look after her. I'd pay her, I wouldn't expect her to do it as a favour – and Emmie loves her so much. What would you feel about that?'

'I don't want anyone else looking after her,' he said. 'You're her mother, that's your job.'

She felt a flare of anger.

'Matt – don't be so bloody unreasonable. You don't mind your mother looking after her if I'm at the dentist or have to sort out something to do with the house. What's the difference?'

He was silent.

'And then in the holidays, maybe she could go down to Mummy at

498

Summercourt. For two days a week. Surely that would be all right. She's stayed there with Mummy lots.'

'Your mother's not up to it,' he said, 'I was watching her when I went down there, she can't even pick her up.'

This was undeniable.

'OK. Well, maybe your mum could have her in the holidays as well. Just for two days a week. Why don't I ask her? See if she likes the idea.'

'I've told you,' he said, 'I don't want Emmie left with anyone. She's your responsibility, not my mum's.'

'Matt, you're being so unreasonable. So absolutely unreasonable.'

'Really?'

'Yes. Yes, yes, YES.' She was screaming at him. 'No one, no one in their right minds would refuse to agree to this.'

He stood there, staring at her across the room, with the same, awful blank anger; she felt quite frightened, as if he was going to hit her again. Then quite suddenly he said, 'You do what you like, Eliza. Like I said, you always do. Just don't expect me to agree to it.'

'And – what does that mean?'

He shrugged.

'Work it out for yourself. But I don't want Mum involved.'

'Oh,' she said, taken totally aback. 'Why?'

'I just don't,' he said.

Maybe he was afraid she would confide in Sandra, Eliza thought, maybe he had talked to her himself; unlikely though, he was terrified of confronting his parents with any kind of emotion.

Eliza switched her mind to her current problem: something had to be done about caring for Emmie. She started calling agencies. And that led her to Margaret.

Margaret was actually working for one of the other mothers at school, who was looking to share her with someone. She was a sturdy girl from Birmingham who had taught in a nursery school for five years and seemed the absolute opposite of the sort of nanny who Matt would have objected to. Emmie liked her, and she clearly liked Emmie, although Eliza could see she would be firm, would be able to deal with her tantrums and her manipulative ways. Eliza offered her the job.

Matt said he didn't want to interview Margaret, but then at six o'clock on the evening before Eliza was due to start work, he demanded to see her, and said he wasn't prepared to allow Emmie to be left in her care until he had.

Eliza felt there was too much at stake to argue, and managed to get hold of Margaret, who was just sitting down to supper; she was clearly surprised, but agreed to come over, if Eliza could collect her.

She sat stolidly relaxed, good-naturedly answering Matt's increasingly absurd questions: 'What would you do if there was a fire, do you prefer looking after girls to boys, have you got a boyfriend?' Her rosy, pleasant face showed no irritation or surprise, even when he suddenly said did she know that he didn't approve of working mothers and that Eliza was returning to work very much against his will.

'I think children are best with happy mothers,' she said, 'and happy mothers are best for children. And some mothers are happier working.'

Matt nodded and said she must excuse him now; he had a lot of work to do and disappeared into the study.

Eliza drove Margaret home; when she got back, she went into the study and said, very nervously, would it be all right for Margaret to look after Emmie; he said he supposed so, but he would like to remind Eliza again that what she was doing was in direct opposition to his wishes and that he was going out.

And in the morning, Eliza got up an hour earlier than usual to wash and blow-dry her hair, got dressed in one of her new maxi dresses and her new pink suede Biba boots, made up her face with her new Mary Quant paint box, delivered Emmie to school and told her to be good for Margaret and that she would see her at six o'clock, and then turned her new, souped-up Mini Cooper in the direction of Carlos Place and, more nervous than she would ever have believed, returned to the world of work.

She had expected to spend the first few days at least in a state of trauma, at once unable to cope with the job and fretting over Emmie; in the event, she found herself so instantly happy and absorbed, so soothed by being appreciated and valued and even talked to, for God's sake, and so delighted once the first day was over at finding Emmie contentedly playing Ludo in the kitchen with the estimable Margaret that she was even able to bury the nightmare events of the past few weeks and turn her face determinedly, for part of the time at least, towards what seemed like a new beginning.

Or at least what she hoped was a new beginning.

'Matt, hello. Look, I'd like to see you. It's been so long.'

'Scarlett, I'm terribly busy.'

'I daresay you are, and so am I, but I'd still like to see you.'

'Have you been talking to Eliza?'

'No. No, of course not. Haven't heard from her for ages. How is she?'

'Fine.'

His voice was dismissive; not one to pursue then.

'Right. Well, can I buy you a drink?'

'OK. But I'm not very good company at the moment.'

Scarlett said she didn't want good company, she just wanted to see him.

'Mum says you're avoiding them, you're certainly avoiding me, I just want to make sure you're OK.'

'Scarlett, I'm OK. Believe me.'

'I want to see for myself. Tomorrow OK?'

'Yes, all right,' he said wearily.

'My pub, seven thirty. Don't be late. And – will you be bringing Eliza?'

'I won't be bringing Eliza, no.'

There was that same odd note in his voice.

He walked into the pub in the Old Brompton Road looking terrible: white, drawn, and he had obviously lost weight.

'Hi, Matt. You do look very – tired.'

'Well, I am tired. Probably the reason.'

'Everything OK business-wise?'

'Yes, perfectly OK, thanks.'

'And how's Emmie?'

'She's fine.'

'Good. Well – can I get you a drink?'

'Yes, thanks. Large whisky.'

He downed it in one; she watched, half-shocked.

'Matt, are you sure you're OK?'

'Yes, I'm quite sure. What is it you want to talk about?'

'Oh – nothing much. I'm a bit low. Strikes me you are too. Want to talk about it?'

'No.'

'Well, I'll talk about mine. I need to, really. And there's no one else who'd listen, Mum and Dad would have a fit. Several fits.'

Silence.

'OK. Here goes. I've made a complete hash of my life,' she said quickly, as if it would make it all easier. Complete.'

Matt listened, horrified. She didn't spare herself. There'd even been a child – or rather a termination. Which she'd never told this bloke, this absolute wanker, about. And she'd had to cope with it all on her own. Had never told anyone.

'I'm so sorry, Scarlett,' he said, and then again, 'so sorry. I wish you'd felt you could tell me.'

'Well – wouldn't have helped.'

'Might. I could have given you some good advice. Like sending him round to me, so I could beat him up.'

'Oh, Matt. That wouldn't have helped. It's all right. I went into it with my eyes open. I should have known better. And advice, who takes advice? Especially the sort you don't want to hear.'

'As long as you're rid of him now. And yes, you're right. Advice is pretty useless. It's so bloody easy to live other people's lives for them. I should know.' He sighed, felt the tears at the back of his eyes, the treacherous tears he shed every night, shocked at himself for his weakness, unable to staunch them, biting the pillow lest a sound might escape. 'I – I'm just going to get another drink. You?'

'Yes, please. Vodka and tonic again. Lots of ice. I learnt to love ice in America. It's such a lovely country. Matt – sorry, but are you really all right?'

'Not really,' he said, 'but best not to talk about it. Like you, I want to deal with it on my own for now at least. No one can help.'

'OK. I won't press you. But when you're ready—'

'Yes, thanks.' He managed to smile at her, went to get the drinks; when he came back he sat down in silence again, staring into his glass.

'Sorry, I'm not very good company at the moment.'

'Oh, Matt,' she said, putting her hand on his arm, 'what a pair we are. We used to be able to help each other; it's gone a bit past that now. But for what it's worth, I'm so fond of you, you know. And glad you're around.'

He felt the tears rising again. Shit, what was the matter with him? He was acting like a bloody girl.

He rummaged in his pocket for his handkerchief, blew his nose hard.

'Sorry. Getting a cold.'

'Matt, God, you're crying. Matt, what is it, whatever is it, is it Eliza?'

'I am not bloody crying,' he half-shouted. 'I've got a bloody cold. Now look, I really must go. And please – please – any serious problems, in future, please come to me. I know I'm only your kid brother, but I can still look after you, OK?'

'Yes,' she said, very soberly, 'yes, Matt, I know. I should have done. But I thought you'd be shocked and I couldn't face that. And you – well, you know, I'm always here. We must look out for each other, Matt, you and me. And at least you've still got Eliza—'

Only he hadn't, he thought, walking swiftly out of the pub, after kissing her goodbye. He hadn't got Eliza. It was over. The sweet, sweeping, heady love and love affair were over. And he had to make the most of what he had left.

And make sure he kept it.

Chapter 51

The job was – well, it was wonderful. Eliza couldn't remember when she had last had such fun.

The lines of command were very clear initially, but Rob increasingly referred to her on models, rather than to the fearsome Babs Brown who ran the bookings department at the agency, and there had been quite sharp words exchanged between them. And although Rob chose the photographers, he began to discuss the choice with Eliza beforehand. If she felt he was making a serious mistake – such as when he wanted to use the dreamily romantic Sarah Moon to shoot some dazzlingly sexy poolside images and she would have chosen Helmut Newton – she would say so in no uncertain terms.

Her relationship with Rob was at once combative and relaxed.

They found each other amusing, professionally admirable and sexually attractive. He was unmarried, 'for the third time' as he put it cheerfully, but ran a string of affairs with one devastatingly beautiful girl after another. Eliza, as she told him with a heavy sigh over one too many glasses of wine one night, was married, and wasn't running anything, least of all a sex life. He leaned over and kissed her on the mouth in a rather disturbing way when she said this and told her if she ever felt like extending their relationship, he would be delighted.

She laughed, as she was not really supposed to do, but stored it away for future reference. It all soothed her insecurity, eased her self-distaste; she felt she was waking up and coming not so much back to life as discovering a new one.

It was very odd: to be so happy and so unhappy at the same time. While she was working, absorbed, confident, excited, surrounded by the kind of people she most admired, she was happier than she had been for years. And while she was at home, with a husband who appeared to dislike her, who certainly didn't trust her, she felt an abject failure and was very very unhappy indeed.

It wasn't easy doing the job in two days a week: especially as she could never be late home, or even start early as sometimes was required. Margaret wouldn't have minded coming in early, she knew, although she couldn't stay late, she had an invalid mother to care for, but Matt simply wouldn't have tolerated it. And looking at the clock, sometimes, if they were having a prolonged meeting – and oh, God, how many of them were in the afternoon – seeing the hands apparently fly round at twice their proper speed, she dreaded the moment when she would have to say, 'I'm sorry, but you'll have to excuse me,' knowing that the people she worked with found it at best irritating and at worst unprofessional.

It was Margaret who made the suggestion, as Eliza flew in breathless and panicking one night, saying, 'Sorry, sorry, sorry, meeting overran, it's so hard to get away, and it looks so unprofessional—'

She stopped. As if Margaret would understand that. But.

'Mrs Shaw, I've told you before, you mustn't worry so much. I do have to get home to my mother, so I can't stay very late, but I could always bring Emmie to you at the agency, if you were stuck in a really important meeting. That would buy you at least another half-hour, and—'

Eliza stared at her, wondering how someone so apparently stolid could possibly understand not only her job and how much she wanted to excel at it, but the need to deceive Matt, and in a most subtle way. 'Margaret, you are a genius,' she said, finding it hard not to hug her, 'that would be so brilliant. Next time I'll ring you. Actually, in the traffic it would take at least forty-five minutes. That's wonderful. And then – well—'

Then, she thought, she could sort of imply Emmie had been at a party or something: if Matt was home. He usually wasn't, of course.

The plan worked brilliantly; Arabella, the girl in reception who worked late anyway, was enchanted to have care of the famous Emmeline, and the very first evening asked her if she'd like a cocktail while she waited for Mummy.

'Yes, please.'

'Right. Well, I can make a pink cocktail or a green one. Which would you like?'

'Pink, please.'

'It was raspberry cordial and soda water,' Arabella explained when

Eliza came down, 'she loved it. And then she helped me tidy up the magazines, didn't you, Emmie? She's so sweet, Eliza, and so bright. She can have a job here whenever she likes.'

The only problem was it worked so well that Eliza was tempted to do it every time . . .

'Miss Scarlett, you must forgive me, but I have made a mistake. Mr Frost will be here in just two days' time. I thought he said two weeks, but—'

'Oh, Larissa, no. Oh, that's – that's quite difficult.'

'Miss Scarlett, why, do you not like him? Did you have a quarrel?'

'No, no, Larissa. And I do like him. But – well, I – oh, you wouldn't understand. Is he – is he coming alone, do you think, or with –with Mrs Frost?'

'Oh, alone, I think. Yes.'

'In that case, then, I must go. I know I've only just got here, but it – I – we can't be here together. I'll go and see Ari, ask him to take me back tomorrow first thing. I'm going to bed now, I'll see you in the morning.'

Larissa looked after her sadly. She was such a lovely person and Mr Frost was such a lovely person, and perhaps, in time, they might become friends. No, not friends, more than friends. Of course Mrs Frost was very frightening, but Miss Scarlett would be able to manage. A person who ran their own business should not be frightened of a mother.

The first thing she had to do was try to keep Miss Scarlett on Trisos for at least one more day, so that they could talk; and if possible two, so that after the talk when Mr Frost arrived, they could talk together.

That meant a visit to Ari the Ferry; Larissa pulled on her shawl and set off down the hill towards the little harbour.

Scarlett woke to the sound of rain; damn. Well, it would make leaving Trisos less painful.

She set off for the harbour, pulling her small suitcase – her still-packed suitcase – behind her. Demetrios and Larissa had been nowhere to be seen; presumably busy in the kitchen.

She knocked on Ari's door; he came out looking slightly sheepish.

'Hello, Ari. Are we all set?'

'Oh, Miss Scarlett, we not go. Not today. I am so sorry. Weather too bad. Big wind, big rough. But tomorrow, we can go tomorrow?'

It meant he would have to collect Mark from the big ferry and drop her off at the same time. Well, that would be all right. They didn't need to meet.

'Hello, Larissa. How are you?'

'Very well, Miss Scarlett. Your breakfast is there, for you, on the table.'

'Is Demetrios around?'

'No, he goes fishing, Miss Scarlett.'

'Fishing! I hope he doesn't get caught in the storm.'

'I, too, Miss Scarlett. I did not want him to go at all, there is too much to do here—'

The weather really couldn't be too bad if Demetrios was going fishing.

'I have to stay another day,' she said, sitting down at the table, spooning honey into the yogurt. 'Ari won't go today. I can't understand it, look, the sun's coming out, it's as calm as can be.'

'So you can have a nice day here?'

'Yes. I'll try.'

Larissa looked at her. It was now or never.

'Miss Scarlett, have you ever met Mrs Frost?'

'No, Larissa, I haven't.'

'She is very, very nice lady, Miss Scarlett. Nothing to worry you.'

'I'm not worried about her, Larissa. I'm sure she's delightful.'

'And very, very clever too. And she has been so kind to me always, brings me things for Stellios and Tina.'

'Yes, that's lovely. Larissa, I really want to do some reading, so if you'll excuse me—'

'Yes, Miss Scarlett. Sorry, Miss Scarlett. But—'

Scarlett picked up her yogurt and her coffee, and said in a voice Larissa had not heard before, 'I think I'll have breakfast in my room. Excuse me.'

Larissa looked after her sadly. This wasn't going as planned at all.

'Well, that was a right royal fuck-up.' Rob Brigstocke walked into Eliza's office and scowled at her. She'd styled a session for a shoot yesterday and hadn't seen him since; he'd seemed jumpy all through, but he often was and she'd put it down to the fact it was a new client, a big one, a sports-car manufacturer.

'What? Didn't they like the pictures, didn't they like the clothes? I knew I should have got some more in reserve.'

'Darling, calm down. Not yesterday, that went like a dream. No, stupid bloody art director brought the wrong roughs to the presentation today, made me look a complete fool. Eliza, you're as white as a sheet, what's the matter with you?'

'I – I thought it was my fault, that I'd messed up—'

'You really are a bundle of nerves, aren't you? Silly moo. I told you, the clothes were fabulous.'

'I know but—'

'Come and sit down here.' He patted the sofa in the corner of his office. 'You really mustn't worry so much about things. You're a star and I couldn't manage without you. Drink?'

'Oh – no. I've got to go home in an hour, I daren't start drinking.'

'That hubby of yours really does rule you with a rod of iron, doesn't he? Silly bugger.' He looked at her thoughtfully, then smiled. 'OK, I've got a better idea. Really calm you down. Here—' He rummaged in the drawer of his desk, came back over to her with a packet of cigarette papers, and a small silver foil package.

She felt a stab of total panic.

'Oh, Rob, no, not here, we can't, someone might come in—'

'If they do, they'll want to share it. God almighty, Eliza, it's only hash. Haven't you ever seen Billy Porter snorting cocaine before a big presentation?'

'No,' she said irritably, 'of course I haven't.'

'OK. But this will do you good. Come on, have a puff. Make you feel much better—'

'Well—' Slightly reluctantly she took the joint, sat looking at it.

'Eliza, it won't bite you.' He leaned forward and kissed her. 'Come on, baby, loosen up. Just for me.'

'Oh – oh, all right.'

She took a puff, rolled it round her mouth, looked at him laughing at her, and inhaled deeply. And again. Waited. And it was – well, it was amazing. She had forgotten how quickly it worked. She felt all at once cool, calm, clear-headed. And relaxed. So relaxed. So in control of her life. She looked at Rob and smiled; a sweet, happy smile.

'This is great,' she said.

'Told you so. And no way hubby will be able to detect that.'

After that they shared a joint quite often, if they'd been working together.

That afternoon Scarlett went for a walk; she struck up right through the village, and walked along the high rocky path; she sat down, looking out to sea, the sun warm on her face, listening to the gulls crying, and thought how sad it would be if she could no longer come here.

She went back down a different path and found herself outside Mark Frost's house; intrigued, she walked round it, peering in the windows, admiring it, the wonderful stone floors, the vaulted ceilings, the spiral staircase. She climbed the steep back garden, and found she could get onto the roof terrace; it looked directly over the sea, across the houses below. Lucky Mark. And lucky, lucky Mrs Frost.

'Miss Scarlett, hello. You want to go in, have a look?'

It was Demetrios. She felt foolish, as if she had been caught trespassing. Which she supposed she was.

'I am to plant some things here, on the terrace. You go in, Miss Scarlett, have a look. I show you round. Come in, come in.'

He showed her round. It was lovely, cool and calm, filled with light, an absolute refuge from the world.

'This is kitchen; this living room; this terrace for vine. Come upstairs, come, come. This is bathroom, this Mr Frost's bedroom, this bedroom for Mrs Frost—'

'Oh,' she said, and then again, 'oh.' Of course they would perhaps need separate rooms, her being an invalid, but – the whole length of the corridor apart?

'Anything wrong, Miss Scarlett?'

'Oh, no. No, of course not.'

'She will come this summer, Mrs Frost, and I hope it will be good for her. The sun helps. Poor lady, she suffers so—'

'Yes, what exactly does she suffer from, Demetrios?'

'She has trouble with her back. So she cannot walk. For many, many years—'

Many, many years? That sounded a bit – odd. Old.

'What, from childhood?'

'Oh, no, I think only the past ten, maybe fifteen years. But for many years before that, she was on the sticks . . .'

The sticks . . . fifteen years in a wheelchair . . . what . . . how . . . no, no . . . could it . . . surely not . . . but . . .

'Demetrios? Um – how old – how long – well, how old is Mrs Frost, would you say?'

'She was sixty just one year ago. Mr Frost wanted to bring her here for her birthday, but she was not well enough.'

'I – I see.'

Sixty. So – what an incredibly, absurdly, amazingly – and – well – wonderfully stupid thing. Not Mrs Frost the wife at all. Not the brilliant, kind, poetry-writing, not-frightening, not-worrying wife. But Mrs Frost the mother. The brilliant, kind, poetry-writing, not-frightening, not-worrying mother.

'We're going to shoot this in Scotland,' said Rob Brigstocke, 'fancy a trip to the Highlands?'

'Madly,' said Eliza, 'but there's no way I can come.'

'Pity. The client thinks you're the best thing since sliced bread. Hugh's coming, of course.' Hugh was the very sweet, if slightly old-womanish account director.

'Well then – you certainly don't need me there.'

'Eliza, we do. It would give Hugh confidence, he's very nervous about this one, and he really likes you. Not to mention everything you've done already for this campaign. Bloody good. Getting your mate to knock up some of the clothes, those tam-o'-shanter beret things were a stroke of genius, and the roller skates, using those twins—'

'I can't quite see roller skates in the Highlands. We were going to have them skating down Park Lane.'

'No, no, this is Scottish knitwear we're talking about. It does have to be recognisably Scotland. But the roller skates will do exactly what he needs, make Craigie stuff look young and zappy instead of the century-old brand it is. It'll be fine, there are roads running across all those moors, they're not just heather, much easier to shoot there than in Park Lane.'

'That's true. Who's doing the pictures?'

'Rex Ingham.'

'Rex? Oh, you lucky things, you'll have such fun.'

'Yes, we will. Well, come and join us. The offer's on the table. We'll only be away two nights, hardly a round-the-world trip.' He offered her his pack of Gitanes; she shook her head.

'They're too strong for me.'

'Oh – OK. Want some of the other sort?'

'No, no, I'm late already, I'll have to hit the road in five minutes.'

'Going out somewhere?'

'Afraid I've just got to get back home, bath time and all that, dinner to cook.'

He looked at her consideringly. 'Not a lot of fun in your life, is there?'

'Of course there is,' she said indignantly, 'I have lots of fun. I love working here and I love being with Emmie, and – and seeing friends and going down to our house in the country—'

She stopped. It sounded pretty lame.

'That it?'

'It's plenty for me.'

'What do you and Mr Shaw do for fun?'

She met his eyes and then looked away; and felt a dreadful heavy sadness.

'Not very much,' she said, struggling to sound cheerful, and even slightly amused. 'Not very much at all. Maybe I'll have one of those cigarettes after all.'

'Good girl.'

But as she drew on the cigarette and exhaled again, he leaned forward, and removed it from her lips; and then kissed her.

'We could have lots of fun together,' he said.

So – now what did she do? Now that Mark, lovely, gentle, shy, sweet, funny, perfect Mark – now that he wonderfully wasn't married, now that she could like him, could enjoy him, could talk to him, could be with him – how did she let him know all that, without looking a complete and utter fool? And in more ways than one, for she certainly couldn't rush up to him, saying you'll never guess what, I thought you were married, now I know you're not will you take me to dinner after all – it would look crass, utterly crass. And he had probably thought David was her boyfriend. And then – surely she should have heard of Mrs Frost. As she was so famous. He would think it terrible, stupidly ignorant that she hadn't. All those clever people who surrounded him at his publishers and at those parties and bookshops – whatever would they make of someone who had so little idea of who Mrs Frost was they could think she was Mark's wife and not his mother. It was awful, dreadful, and getting worse. Her original euphoria was fading; she felt helpless, tossed about by Fate; it wasn't fair, it just wasn't fair.

Probably best to go back as planned next day. It would look very – very strange if she just hung around, waiting for an opportunity to talk to him. And what would she say? She had refused his invitation to dinner –

uttered no doubt at some cost, through his anguished shyness; he would not ask her again. He would be as embarrassed as she was, would probably want to avoid her altogether, stay in his house, waiting for her to leave. Yes, best to go. Cut her losses.

The morning was brilliant blue and gold; the sea was very calm.

Weary after a wretched night, Scarlett stood on the jetty waiting for Ari. After fifteen minutes she grew impatient and went and knocked on his door; no reply.

'Ari is not well.' It was Demetrios, emerging from the little house. 'He cannot go, Miss Scarlett. I am sorry.'

'But – but Demetrios, I need to leave. And – and Mr Frost needs to arrive. What shall we do?'

He shrugged. 'Both of you must wait.'

Scarlett stalked back to the house, told Larissa not to disturb her under any circumstances, and settled in her room to read, fighting to stay calm; she had scarcely opened the book when she heard the familiar throb of the heavy diesel engine of the ferry.

'Oh – oh, no!' She went to the window; sure enough the ferry was chugging out to sea.

'Larissa! Demetrios! For heaven's sake, the ferry's going, why didn't you tell me?'

'Miss Scarlett,' it was Demetrios, 'Larissa tells me you say not to disturb you.'

'Yes, but not so I missed the ferry. I just can't believe this, it's ridiculous, totally ridiculous, and I thought Ari was ill—'

'He felt better, and he thought to go. Excuse me now, Miss Scarlett, and don't worry, you can go tomorrow, it is only one night—'

One night. With Mark Frost in the same house. God. God almighty.

She heard the ferry coming in just after four; she had told Larissa she didn't want any supper; she would just have to stay where she was until it was time to get the ferry in the morning. She couldn't risk bumping into him.

She heard him coming into the house, talking to them; heard him leaving to go up to his house, then coming back again at supper time, heard a cork being pulled, heard the clink of knives and forks on plates. She felt increasingly beleaguered, and stupid.

She became increasingly aware of a need to pee; hardly surprising, she'd been locked away for hours. If Mark didn't leave soon she'd have to brave the corridor; and the dining area was at the bottom of the stairs. If the door was open . . . no, she'd have to wait, it was too much of a risk.

But her bladder grew more and more excruciating. She felt quite desperate. And then she looked at the window; although her room was on the first floor at the front of the house, it had been built into the hill at the back and was more or less at ground level. She could climb out easily.

She opened the window cautiously and looked out; absolute silence and stillness. She slithered out and ran gratefully to the nearest bougain-villea bush . . . although why she was looking for shelter she had no idea, there was no one to see her. Probably because there was a full moon and it was light as day, she felt very exposed. She pulled down her pants and . . .

'What on earth are you doing?' It was Mark Frost.

It was such an utterly ridiculous question that she giggled.

'Well,' she said, after completing her task, standing up, and pulling up her pants again, 'you've got to guess. Do you think I was (a) writing a letter, (b) sunbathing, or (c) having a pee?'

And then she felt stricken at having laughed at him. 'Sorry, that was very rude of me, I'm so sorry, Mark,' and turned and walked back towards the open window.

And decided that the more dignified option was to walk round to the front of the house and go in the front door. And set off at a brisk pace to do exactly that.

At which point she felt a hand on her shoulder, and turned, and he said, clearly trying not to laugh himself, 'If you're going in that way, Scarlett, I think you should pull your skirt down. It's tucked into your – your knickers. Just thought you ought to know.'

'Oh,' she said, desperate now to regain a little dignity, and fumbled with her skirt; and then something extremely unexpected happened and he said, 'Here, let me help,' and she felt his hand smoothing out her skirt, pulling it out of her knickers and setting it straight; and then he said, 'Let me escort you to the door,' in a very formal voice.

'No, no, it's fine,' she said, 'I can see, it's very light. It's the moon I suppose.'

'I suppose it must be,' he said politely; and she thought there I go, saying another stupid thing, he must think I'm half-witted.

There was a silence and she stood there, not knowing whether to move or not now and he suddenly said, 'Since things can't possibly get any worse . . .'

'What do you mean?'

'Well, since you're in love with someone else, and you refused my invitation to dinner and you're dashing away from the island the minute I get here and you dislike me so much—'

'Mark—'

'I would just like to say I think you look very beautiful in the moonlight.' There was a pause and then, 'And also that you have an extraordinarily attractive bottom.'

'Oh,' she said, and then, taking a deep breath, 'oh, Mark no, no, you are quite wrong and things could get much, much worse.'

'In what way?' he asked and followed it with a sigh of some magnitude.

'I might never see you again, that would be much worse, and since you've been brave enough to compliment me in that rather personal way, I want to tell you, that I am not in love with anyone else, and I wanted to accept your invitation to dinner more than anything I can remember, and I don't want to leave the island tomorrow or indeed for as long as you are here, and the thing is I thought that you were married and—'

'Married!' he exclaimed, staring at her. 'What one earth made you think that?'

'Well— well, you see, I thought that this Mrs Frost I kept hearing about was your wife. Not your mother. Dumb, that's me.'

'Oh, Miss Scarlett,' he said, very slowly, 'that is so, so stupid. Wonderfully, brilliantly stupid. Come here and let me kiss you.'

And she stood there, being kissed by him and thinking however shy he might be, he had certainly managed to learn how to kiss, on and on it went, and Larissa, glancing out, saw them and called Demetrios over and indicated the pair in the moonlight and said whatever 'I told you so' was in Greek, and how clever she had been to know that if they could only keep Miss Scarlett on the island until Mr Frost arrived, it would work its magic and all would be very well.

Chapter 52

Marriages do not suddenly drop dead; they expire slowly, from a thousand cutting words, a million misunderstandings, from an unwillingness to apologise to a willingness to take revenge. There is a dawning, slow at first then gathering pace, that things are not as they were and moreover not as they should be, that responses are not what is hoped for, that disappointment is more frequent than delight, that resentment is more persistent than forgiveness, all remarked upon and brooded over and then stored angrily away. Desire dies, affection withers, trust becomes a memory.

But there has to be a catalyst, a final piece of havoc, that sees the whole edifice finally crumbling, that makes forgiveness unthinkable and happiness finally an impossible memory; but it is still the rot beneath that makes for that final collapse.

For Matt and Eliza, struggling along in savage resentment and outraged despair, aware of the hopelessness but fearful of the alternative, and lost for what to do, the end when it came was shockingly swift.

Eliza was watching *The Magic Roundabout* with Emmie when the door opened and Matt walked in. He nodded at her briefly, bent and kissed Emmie.

'How's my best girl?'

'Fine, thank you,' said Emmie without looking at him.

'You're home early,' said Eliza, tentatively.

'Yes, I've come to pack.'

'Pack! Where are you going?'

'To Manchester for a couple of days.'

'What for?'

'A conference.'

'You didn't tell me,' she said, struggling to sound friendly and interested. 'What sort of conference?'

'A property development conference. I didn't think it would interest you, given your contempt for what I do. Anyway, I must get on if you'll excuse me, I'm going up on the sleeper.'

'What, tonight?'

'Yes, tonight. And therefore I have to pack. Unless of course you'd like to do it for me. But I imagine you're too busy.'

Eliza turned away without saying any more; she felt the usual surge of anger. Matt could go away at literally a moment's notice, without warning, without the need to make any arrangements, leaving her on her own. Not that that made any real difference, she reflected; she might as well be living in the house without him for all the contact there was between them. But she was not able to even contemplate two days away to do her work. It was so unfair. So totally unfair.

'Mummy! Mummy, look, I can jump like Zebedee, watch . . .'

It was bound to happen sooner or later of course: the world in which they moved, Louise and Matt, was not a large one. Nevertheless, confronted by his name placed next to hers at the table at an awards ceremony, Louise felt momentarily panicked, unsure of what either of them might say or do.

She was as usual the only woman; she was just shaking out her napkin when she saw him approaching the table, but too engrossed in conversation with someone to have seen her. By the time he had sat down himself, he had realised his escape was impossible.

'Hello,' she said, trying to achieve eye contact and failing, as he reached for his glass of water without looking at her, 'fancy seeing you here. Small world.'

'Yes,' he said shortly. 'Very.'

'How are you?'

'Fine.'

'How is that building in the City going?'

'Very well, thanks.'

Louise turned to her neighbour on her other side; he couldn't be worse, she thought.

Ten minutes of appallingly patronising conversation later, she discovered she was wrong. Donald Miller was the managing director of a cement company, and asked her how it was working for Roderick Brownlow, 'with, not for, we're joint managing directors', how it was going, 'pretty well, third hotel going up now, on the Bayswater Road, on the edge of Hyde Park', and told her how nice it was to have a lady at such luncheons. He finally managed to flick a small splodge of prawn cocktail off his fork and onto Louise's blouse; he turned a violent puce.

'Oh, I am so sorry, Louise, may I call you Louise, what my wife would say I dare not think. Here, let me help.'

He started dabbing at her shirt with his napkin; the stain was perilously near her bosom. She tried to smile. 'Please don't worry.'

'No, no, I insist, here, let me call a waiter, see if we can get some water and—'

'Here.' It was Matt's voice; he was proffering his napkin, dipped in his water glass. 'This should help'. She took it gratefully and dabbed at the stain.

'It's great to see you again, Louise,' he said then, deliberately loud, 'and I'm very interested in how the new hotel is coming on. Will it be ready for the summer tourist trade?'

'I'm afraid not,' she said, surprised he should ask such a thing, when the hotel had hardly begun its construction; and then realised he was smiling at her.

'Thank you,' she hissed, giving him back his napkin and turned, relieved, away from Donald Miller, 'thank you so much.'

'It's OK. I thought you deserved a break. I must be getting soft in my old age. Seriously, how is the hotel coming on? Ready for next spring, I suppose. That's a very good site.'

'Yes, hopefully. I had a rival for it, you must have heard.'

'I did. I was pleased you won.'

'Thanks.' It was – actually – nice to see him; she smiled at him.

'How are things with you, Matt? Apart from your new City skyscraper?'

'Oh – pretty good, yes. Increasingly hard to find sites for redevelopment now, as you must know. Only thing that's safe is office development. All these grants for improving old places. Absurdly generous, they are, the government, with taxpayers' money, all those bloody do-good councils. It's certainly changing London all over again. You find posh people in the most unlikely places. Like Islington.'

'Yes. Or even Fulham . . . How – how is Eliza?'

'She's all right,' he said shortly.

Not a good time to discuss the return to work that she'd heard about then.

'And Emmie?'

'Emmie's fine. Doing very well at school. And I've got her a pony, down at Summercourt, she loves him, loves riding. Very good at it.'

'Really? I was so sorry about that piece in the *News*,' she said suddenly. It seemed best to come out with it, rather than let it lie between them. And while he was being friendly. 'I hope you didn't think it was anything to do with me.'

'I have to say it crossed my mind,' he said. 'But then I decided it wasn't your style.'

'No, no, it wasn't.'

'Well – blood on the tracks, I suppose. How's Roderick?'

'He's OK. Very good to work with. How's Barry?'

She hardly thought about him these days; that was revenge of a kind in itself. To be able to dismiss him so easily.

'He's all right. Louise – I'm – sorry you were so upset about – about the partnership.'

Not that he hadn't offered it to her; just that she had been upset. But – that was quite something. For Matt, a huge olive branch. A whole tree in fact.

'Well – also blood on the tracks.'

'Yes, indeed.' He sighed. 'There's a lot of it about.'

'What – blood? On the tracks?'

'Yeah.'

He didn't enlarge upon it; and in any case, the interminable speeches prior to the presentation of the interminable awards had begun. Matt was presenting one of them; he did it rather well, she thought. As soon as he had sat down again, he leaned towards her and kissed her briefly on the cheek.

'Got to cut and run. Mind you behave now and don't run off with Mr Miller.'

'I won't. Nice to see you, Matt, I'm pleased we're friends again.'

'Yes, me too. Bye, Louise.'

She looked after him as he wove his way across the room. There had been something different about him. Still touchy, still argumentative; a bit down, clearly. But – as well as that? He seemed less arrogant. Less sure of himself. Yes, that was it. Interesting.

'Rex, hi. Lovely to see you. Rob said you were coming in. He won't be long, he's stuck in the dining room with a prospective new client. He'll be in a terrible mood when he does get out, I warn you, presentation started at nine this morning, and then lunch—'

'Isn't he quite often in a terrible mood?' said Rex.

'Yes, I suppose so.' She grinned at him. 'I'm just good at dodging them.'

'Yes, I heard you and he were great buddies.'

'Did you now?' said Eliza, not sure whether to be pleased. The last thing she wanted was rumours going round London about her and Rob Brigstocke. If Matt heard anything like that . . .

'Yeah. Don't look so alarmed, nothing unseemly. Just that you're two minds with a single thought. Anyway, you enjoying it here?'

'Oh, Rex, I love it so much. It's heaven. After all those years mopping up mess, and dealing with temper tantrums.'

'Sounds a bit like a creative department,' said Rex, laughing. 'It's really nice to see you, Eliza.'

He grinned at her; he was very sweet, she thought. 'Eliza,' said Rob's secretary, putting her head round the door, 'message from Rob. He's going to be at least another thirty effing minutes, his words not mine, so why don't you and Rex go out and have a coffee or something and come back in forty-five?'

'OK,' said Eliza, 'we will. Thanks. Come on, Rex, licence to play.'

'I don't know about you,' he said, 'but I rather fancy a drink. Bit more fun than coffee.'

They walked down to Browns Hotel, ordered a bottle of champagne.

'You should come with us, you know, it's going to be fun. You know we're shooting near Balmoral, we've found the perfect spot, on the moors, with the castle in the background.'

'Yes, of course I know,' she said gloomily.

'It's going to be a gas. And only two nights. Why not?'

'Oh – Matt wouldn't let me.'

'What? Am I hearing this right? Christ, Eliza, hasn't he heard of women's rights?'

'He calls them women's wrongs.'

'Things not good between you and Matt?'

'Yes, of course they are.'

He shrugged. 'OK. It's nothing to do with me. But I don't believe you.'

'Why not?'

'Eliza, I can remember how you were when we were all starting out.

When you were at *Charisma*, just an assistant, but still so sure of yourself, what you wanted, even when you were taking sessions for Fiona and should have been completely out of your depth. You were brilliant, Eliza, we all thought so. We still do.'

Eliza suddenly wanted to cry. She knew why; he had brought her back to those heady days when she had been happy, sure of herself, successful, when they had all been so young and she had first been with Matt and he had seemed so utterly sexy and totally what she wanted, and it had all been so perfect and exciting and wonderful. Where had that gone, where where where?

'Hi, you two. Is that a private party or can anyone join in?' It was Rob; he sat down beside them and took Eliza's glass of champagne and drained it. 'Mmm, nice, let's get another of those. We can have our meeting here. Now then, Rex, have you managed to talk Eliza into coming to Scotland with us next week?'

'Actually,' said Eliza, and it was as if someone else was speaking for her suddenly, 'actually, yes, he has. I've decided to come.'

Chapter 53

The sun was very warm up on the moor. Surprisingly so. Eliza pulled off her sweater and lolled back, leaning on her elbows. The sky was intensely blue, the view all around breathtaking, a vast wooded valley, the mountains beyond still topped with snow. There was a constant sound of running water from endless small streams, and far, far above, curlews wheeled and cried. Balmoral lay half-hidden in the trees.

'Wine?' said Rob Brigstocke.

They were all there on the Scottish moor, having a picnic, Rob, Rex, the twin models, Hugh Wallace and her. The shoot was going well; the polaroids looked wonderful. There had been a slight problem, when they'd realised that the twins couldn't be roller skating with the castle behind them, sunk in the valley as it was, but they'd got some great shots of them whizzing down the track laughing, past a bemused looking trio of Highland cattle who had most conveniently placed themselves on the verge; Eliza had thought Rob would have a coronary with excitement when they ambled into view.

'Jesus fucking Christ,' he yelled, 'Rex, Rex, get over here, quick and you two, Pinky and Perky, it's you I'm talking to, OK, concentrate, that's what you're paid for, get in the truck, Hugh, you drive them twenty yards up and then, girls, jump out and just skate down towards us, past them. And don't fuck it up, those animals won't wait around for a reshoot.'

The twins, aristocratic creatures whose real names were Hattie and Tilly, didn't seem to mind the rather unflattering nicknames Rob had bestowed upon them or the insults he threw at them constantly.

After the cattle had removed themselves, they had found a field full of sheep, and a local farmworker, as bemused as the cattle, but anxious to oblige. He had corralled a couple of rams and showed the girls how to hold them by their horns and stand astride them – 'that looks fucking brilliant,' yelled Rex, 'hold it, hold it' – and then drove his Land Rover truck along the track, with the girls standing up, laughing in the back, amidst a crowd of sheep.

'We've done well,' said Rob, reaching for a sandwich, 'three fantastic shots already, and it's only lunchtime. Well done, girls.'

'We still haven't got the shot the client's expecting,' said Hugh Wallace gloomily. 'The one with Bamoral behind the girls.'

'Oh, shut up, you miserable old bugger,' said Rob, 'these shots are far better than that, far more original. Just stop fussing, Wallace, the client is going to be over the moon when he sees these. But we'll do the boring old Balmoral thing as well, don't worry. OK, come on, let's get moving again, before the light goes. Eliza, can we have the red kilts now, and I think those funny spat things you found . . .'

Eliza climbed into the back of the van, starting sorting through the rails, pulling clothes out, directing the girls what to wear. God, this was fun. Such fun. Forty-eight hours – no, more than that, three days – of working, being with adults, and her favourite breed of adults too, with no need to clock-watch, to get ready her excuses to leave, just to be able to immerse herself in the job in hand, and then at the end of the day, to laugh and drink and eat and gossip and no one glowering at her, or criticising her, or making her feel guilty – she really couldn't believe it was happening.

It had been comparatively easy to organise, actually; astounded at her calm, she simply told Matt she was going away for a few days the following week, it was work, she had to go, it was very important. She arranged for Margaret to stay the two nights, together with her invalid mother, and for Sarah to come up and live in the house; she even told a couple of the mothers from school she was going away, and Emmie's teacher too, so that any problems that Emmie might have, she would be surrounded by people she knew and loved.

Matt said she wasn't to go, wasn't to leave Emmie; she said she was going to, no matter what he said.

'I don't remember you consulting me about your business trip this week. And what are you going to do? This is about my work and it's very important to me and it will be the first time I'll have left Emmie in nearly six years—'

'Might I remind you of Milan?'

'Oh, yes, Milan,' she said and her voice was thick with contempt, thicker even than his. 'Yes, I forgot that, how I left her in Milan in a friends' house for an evening while I went to the opera with only three people in charge of her. Dreadful. Matt, I'm going. I'll be back on Friday afternoon, almost as soon as Emmie gets home from school. She'll hardly know I've gone. Now please excuse me, I have to pack.'

She had rung home each evening, every morning; spoken to Margaret or Sarah, been assured Emmie was fine, was going out to tea, that Margaret had taught her to knit; had spoken to Emmie herself, who had told her she missed her, wanted her to come home, even put a sob into her voice in true Emmie style and then said she had to go, Margaret was waiting to take her to the park.

The second evening, they all had dinner at the hotel, a rather grand establishment in Ballater, and got extremely drunk. Even Hugh Wallace joined in, demonstrated a fine line in dirty jokes, and then recited a whole string of absolutely filthy limericks. Eliza threw in one of her own of those for good measure – and then was surprised when Hugh suddenly said, 'I'd like to propose a toast. To Eliza.'

'Oh,' she said, astonished at being singled out in this way, 'goodness, how nice, but why me?'

'Because you've brought such wonderful style to the session. I know the client was immensely reassured when he heard you were coming, as indeed was I. And also because I know it wasn't easy for you to leave your domestic commitments. We all really appreciate it.'

'Hear, hear,' said Rob, raising his glass and grinning at her, 'we do. To Eliza.'

'Eliza!' said Rex, and 'Eliza', said the twins in unison, adding 'super clothes' and 'marvellous ideas' several times.

And Eliza sat there, savouring the entirely unfamiliar sensation of being admired and appreciated, smiling slightly foolishly and thinking that whatever unpleasantness lay at the other end of the London to Scotland railway line it had been indisputably worth it.

Margaret was sitting in her room reading after an early supper when she heard Emmie call out and then, almost at once, start vomiting; calmly cheerful, she had put her in a bath, changed her bed and put her back in it in a clean nightie; fifteen minutes later it happened again. This time Sarah heard what was going on and appeared; the third time, Matt put his head round the nursery bathroom door.

'She looks terrible,' he said, 'very hot, anyone thought to take her temperature?'

Margaret looked at him and said that vomiting didn't usually go hand in hand with a fever, but that she would take it anyway; the thermometer read one hundred and two.

'Right, well, I'm turning in,' said Hugh Wallace, 'we've still got one shot to do in the morning, haven't we, outside Crathie church, and I imagine we'll be starting pretty early.'

'Yeah,' said Rob, 'we need to catch the dawn light. Down here, what time do you reckon, Rex?'

'Oh – six should do it. Yeah, I'm definitely off to get my beauty sleep. I'm fucking exhausted. What about the rest of you?'

The twins said they would be going up right away as well; Rob ordered another bottle of champagne.

'I think she's probably just got a bug,' said the doctor, 'but she does seem a little disorientated. I'd give it another hour and then if she's no better, I'd get her along to Casualty. She could become seriously dehydrated—'

Sarah looked at Emmie, lying on her pillows, her eyes closed, her face flushed and then at Matt, and spoke the unspeakable.

'I wish Eliza was here,' she said.

Rob and Eliza were sitting on the deep sofa in front of the fire; she felt happily exhausted and said so.

'Or maybe you're exhaustedly happy,' said Rob.

'Maybe. It's been such fun. I've enjoyed it all so much.'

'Us too. Nice of Auntie Hugh to propose that toast to you.' He looked at her and grinned. 'You look much better for your break from domesticity. You should do it more often. It clearly suits you.'

'I don't think I'll be able to do it again for a long time,' she said with a sigh.

'Really? Why not?'

'Rob, you know why not.'

'I really don't know what keeps you with the bugger,' he said. 'He's obviously not very nice to you.'

'Now how can you tell that?'

'It's bleedin' obvious. You're pale, thin, quite jumpy. Not exactly overflowing with happiness and fulfilment.'

'Yes, and you're a great expert on relationships, of course.'

'Well, I'm certainly experienced. You're so lovely,' he said suddenly, reaching out his hand and touching her cheek, 'and so fucking loyal. You haven't said anything mean about him, haven't complained once. I think you're a bit of a star, Eliza Shaw. And I fancy you something rotten, you know that?'

'Don't come over all stud creative director on me.'

'Why not? I am a stud creative director anyway. And in stud creative director language, I think you're incredibly sexy and I have a very strong urge indeed to get into your knickers. Right now, as a matter of fact.'

'Rob – don't be – don't spoil everything,' she said. 'Please.'

'Now why do you think I would spoil everything?' he asked. 'Do you think we wouldn't have a very nice time? Because I know we would. I'm not asking you to marry me, Eliza.'

'No,' she said, laughing, 'although on your past form, I don't think anything would surprise me—'

'Well,' he said, leaning forward, kissing her on the cheek, 'I'm not. Not this time. But I think you should try to overcome your moral scruples, just for one night, and just enjoy yourself. Have some fun.'

'Yes, but—'

'Eliza,' he said, bending over her, moving his mouth onto hers, slowly, carefully, determinedly, his tongue working at her and somehow deep, deep within her as well, and it took all her strength and determination to pull away from him and say, while hearing her own voice feeble and uncertain, 'Rob, no, no,' and 'Oh, yes, yes,' he said, 'come on, Eliza, let's go up to bed. You want it just as much as I do, you know you do,' and suddenly it was gloriously, headily wonderful to be desired again, rather than repelled and rejected, and so fantastically uncomplicated and joyful, and it was true what he said, she did want it, in a harsh, hungry, needy way that she had almost forgotten, and she heard herself saying, as she pulled herself away from him, her eyes fixed on his, her mind on him and what he might do for her, 'Yes, yes, I'm going up to my room now, don't be long,' and then with no further thought of how insanely reckless she was being, of the risks she was running, taken over by a sort of madness that wanted her to be herself again, young, and sexy, and sure of herself, instead of somehow dying slowly, frigid and frightened, and without being sure how she got there, she was lying in the bed naked, waiting for him with a sort of crazed intensity, and there was not a thought in her head that she might be doing anything wrong, or even unwise . . .

'Her pulse is very fast,' said Sarah. 'He said to take her to casualty if she was any worse. And I think she is. Margaret, what do you think?'

'I do think she's dehydrated,' said Margaret. But I don't actually think it's at a danger level.'

'How are we supposed to know when it is?' said Matt. 'And anyway, I thought you were a nurse?'

'No,' said Margaret patiently, 'I'm not.'

'Well, you've got the job under false pretences then. I remember seeing on your application that you were a nursery nurse.'

'Mr Shaw, that is not quite correct. I did a nursing course, which is not the same thing as being a medical nurse, I do assure you.' She smiled at him; anyone else would have hit him, Sarah thought. Emmie was breathing very fast, she was very pale, and she was whimpering now and saying she had a headache. It was very frightening.

'I'm getting the bloody doctor back,' said Matt, 'make him earn his keep. How dare he bugger off home, when a child's so ill, it's bloody outrageous.'

The sex was wonderful; Eliza was quite shocked at herself. Transformed as she was into a shrieking, shouting harpy, clawing, biting, laughing, crying, her long legs wrapped round Rob, her back arched, her head thrown back, her entire body consumed by her orgasm, making her body sing as she thought it had quite forgotten.

And as she came down, slowly, sweetly, exhaustedly, as she pushed back her damp hair, and smiled rather shakily into Rob's eyes, he smiled back at her with a certain triumph.

'I told you we'd have fun,' he said.

Matt came back into the room.

'He's on his way. Bloody irresponsible, he should never have left. He says he'll come down to the hospital with us—'

'That's kind,' said Sarah.

'Not at all, it's his job.'

Sarah didn't like to say that in sixty years of being a patient and the mother of patients, she had never known a doctor agree to a second house call in one night and then to accompany a patient to hospital. 'Er – Matt. I think perhaps we should ring Eliza. Don't you?'

'Why?' he asked and his expression was so filled with distaste for the notion Sarah was shocked. 'She can't get here; she's five hundred bloody miles away.'

'Yes, but – if Emmie's really ill . . .'

'Emmie is really ill. There's no if about it. And her mother should be here. But she bloody isn't and ringing her up isn't going to help. So—'

There was a ring at the door; it was the doctor.

He came in, looked at Emmie, said he thought she was no worse, possibly a little better, but that she should be taken to hospital just the same.

'Let's not take any chances.'

'Of course we're not taking any bloody chances,' said Matt. 'I'll carry her, you can drive, doctor. You two,' he turned to Sarah and Margaret, 'you can come if you want to.'

They both said they would come.

Matt bent down and picked up the half-sleeping Emmie, enfolding her in the bedclothes; there was such tenderness, such care in the gesture, Sarah felt tears in her eyes. What a mass of contradictions he was, this husband of Eliza's; she saw suddenly and for the first time what difficulties Eliza must face, living with him, probably on a daily basis, his bad temper, his abruptness, his near-rudeness indeed, his perfectionism – and his adoration of this precious only child.

They went downstairs slowly; Emmie's small face had been more peaceful, but suddenly and without warning, she woke up, frowned and said, 'Mummy, I want Mummy.'

'Mummy's not here, darling,' said Sarah gently, smoothing her hair back, 'she's away, don't you remember, she'll be home tomorrow.'

'I want Mummy, I want to see Mummy, I want to talk to Mummy, please, please—'

She was becoming agitated now, her breath faster still; Sarah looked at Matt over her head.

'We could ring Eliza,' she said. 'If Emmie is getting so upset, maybe talking to her might help.'

'I don't see why,' said Matt shortly, but the doctor turned and said, 'I think that's a good idea, the child's agitated which doesn't help and we won't be able to call Mrs Shaw from the hospital. Another five minutes won't make any difference.'

'OK,' said Matt. He sank down on the hall chair, holding Emmie against his chest. 'We're going to call Mummy, sweetheart, you can speak to her on the phone. Would that be nice?'

Emmie nodded listlessly; he dialled the number; they all sat there, watching him; heard the phone being answered the other end.

'Crathie Hotel.'

'Mrs Shaw please,' he said. 'Room – what's her room?'

'Twenty-one,' said Sarah. 'Room twenty-one.'

'Room twenty-one please,' said Matt into the phone.

'I need to pee,' said Eliza, surfacing from her deep, sweet, post-coital slumbers, 'and maybe you should go back to your room. Rob? Rob, wake up—'

'Yeah, yeah, OK, in a minute, go and have your pee—'

Faintly embarrassed, which was absurd, Eliza reflected, given her behaviour an hour earlier, she pulled the thick door of the bathroom firmly shut.

So she didn't hear the phone ringing; if she had she would have told Rob not to do what he did instinctively, half-asleep as he still was, not to pick it up, not to hold it groggily to his ear and not, when asked who the hell he was, to say 'oh shit' and then 'oh fuck' very loudly indeed.

Part Three

The Divorce

1971

It had come on a day she was at home. Not working. Well, obviously, otherwise it couldn't have been accomplished.

A lovely early summer day. They were going to Summercourt at the weekend. Emmie was with a friend for tea.

She'd made some soup for supper; she'd sorted the laundry; she'd tidied Emmie's toy cupboard.

She couldn't be faulted. Not today anyway.

There was a knock at the door. That would be Harrods.

It wasn't.

'Mrs Shaw? Mrs Elizabeth Shaw?'

'Yes. That's me.'

'I have got some papers for you.'

'Papers?'

'Yes. Please look through them and then sign the acknowledgement where indicated.'

'What sort of papers?'

'You have to look at them yourself.'

She took the package he was holding out to her. A large white envelope.

She ripped it open, pulled a sheaf of papers out. Glanced at the top sheet, perfect typing on very white paper.

Didn't take in the words. Not really. Clearly a mistake. Looked at the man, puzzled; he had turned away, was studying the street.

Looked again. The words hadn't changed.

Divorce Petition.

Divorce? Petition? No. Couldn't be.

'In the matter of the Petition of Matthew Peter Shaw,' it said and underneath that, 'and Elizabeth Sarah Shaw.'

He couldn't have sent this. He couldn't. No matter what. Not without – without . . .

She looked again.

Divorce Petition, it said, issued by Morris and Foster. Solicitors for the petitioner. She felt dizzy suddenly, walked backwards into the house, sank onto the hall chair.

The man realised she had gone in, stepped forward, put his foot in the door.

She stared up at him.

'Please look through all the papers,' he said, 'and then, as I said, sign this acknowledgement.'

'What?'

'Look at all the papers, please.'

Page two was worse.

'This petition is issued by' (it said) 'Matthew Peter Shaw (the Petitioner). The other party to the marriage is Elizabeth Sarah Shaw (the Respondent)'.

It went on. Four pages in endless repetitive legal language. Ending with something called the Prayer. That 'the said marriage may be dissolved'.

And then – beneath that, unspeakable. Obscene. Terrifying.

'That custody of the child may be granted.'

Custody? CUSTODY!

She shut her eyes. Opened them again. Someone was shouting, shouting Emmie's name and crying at the same time.

It was her.

Chapter 54

The worst thing was the fear. The fear of moving on, moving on from the present where at least the territory was familiar, the misery recognisable, into a future where nothing was even imaginable. He had clung to what he had, what he knew, foolishly, desperately and for a long time; but he had come to feel it held nothing for him, had no more to give him.

He would wake at two in the morning, sweating, sleep lost, with only the endless awful repetitive questions in his head: what had happened, how had it started, could it have been stopped? While knowing it couldn't. Not now, not ever. His marriage was over, and he wept many of those mornings, heavy, heart-racking tears as again and again he forced himself to face it.

For, he felt, Eliza had not only betrayed him sexually, and undermined him professionally, she had mocked him, belittled him and ignored his most fundamental beliefs. It was too late, far too late, for any kind of reconciliation; he was in another country altogether, a strange, hostile, lonely place, where happiness had died finally and love was an almost laughable memory.

He would have given all that he had to have stepped out of it again, that country, to be back where he knew who he was and what he was doing, where he felt strong and confident and generous, rather than weak and timorous and bitter. But there was no way back. And of all the things Eliza had taken from him, his sense of self was the greatest. He had lost not only Eliza but the person he had thought himself to be.

He had left only Emmie, dear to him beyond anything, and it was Emmie now he had to keep, somehow, safe and for himself.

In that thought there was comfort: and there was also revenge. The greatest revenge he could imagine.

❖　❖　❖

'I would say you're pretty sure to get a divorce on grounds of adultery. But whether you'll get custody of the child is quite another. I should advise you now, Mr Shaw, it will be a very dirty nasty battle and one I'm not at all sure you could win.'

Ivor Lewis looked at Matt across his large desk; he was larger than life, six foot two, sixteen stone of aggression; grammar school and red-brick university, expensive, and reputedly unbeatable in the divorce courts. For this reason alone, Matt was shaken by his last statement. He had assumed Lewis would tell him there would be no difficulty in what he wanted to do.

'Why do you say that?' he said.

'Because your daughter is six years old; a judge would have a natural sympathy for that fact alone, and the great natural empathy between a mother and her young child. Who will care for her? Do you propose to give up your job?'

'No, of course not,' said Matt.

'Well, then to me that implies nannies. An absentee parent.'

'She's looked after by a nanny now. Against my wishes.'

'So why suddenly the change? Why does a nanny's care become acceptable? Does the nanny work full time?'

'Well – no. Two days a week.'

'Mr Shaw, I'm afraid that's not even a comparable situation, as a judge would see it. You, quite clearly, would be leaving her in the care of someone five days a week. Do you work a nine-to-five day?'

'No,' said Matt, irritable at Lewis's apparent lack of understanding of the professional world. 'Of course not. I run a huge business, I work all the hours God sends—'

'OK. Would you be prepared to work a nine-to-five day in future?'

'Absolutely not. It would be impossible.'

'In that case – I don't think you've a very good chance of getting past the first post.'

'Look,' said Matt. 'There's something here I don't think you understand. My wife isn't a fit mother to that child. She does a lot of things that I'm very unhappy about. If you can't help me then I'll find someone who will. Because, believe me, I have to get Emmie in my care.'

'Or out of your wife's?' Lewis looked at Matt very directly. 'Will you be acting in the child's interest, or against your wife's? In other words, is this ambition primarily driven by a desire for revenge? Because, believe me, that child will suffer, if things get nasty. And they will. She's old enough to understand what Mummy and Daddy are doing to one another. And to her. She could even be questioned by the judge himself, I've known it happen.'

'Questioned?'

'Yes. "Who would you prefer to live with, Mummy or Daddy?" Not publicly. He would take her to a private room. But he would ask her a lot of questions. Very difficult questions, for such a young child.'

'I wouldn't allow it.'

'You would have to. Would you really be prepared to put your daughter through that?'

Matt stared at Ivor Lewis and Ivor Lewis stared back. Then Matt said, 'As I see it, I don't have an option.'

'All right.' Ivor Lewis pulled a sheet of paper towards him and picked up the sharpest pencil Matt had ever seen. He smiled at Matt suddenly, a carefully conspiratorial smile.

'Very well. And in spite of all that I have just said, it is also a fact that your wife will start ten points down at least for having committed adultery. So let's see what we can do. Exactly on what grounds do you consider her unfit to be a mother?'

Sarah was out in the garden when Eliza's call came. It was an endlessly lovely June day, one of a long, golden string, warm and mellow and full of birdsong, from the early dawns to the late twilights; a sweet, peaceful day it was, and seriously at odds with how she felt. Eliza and Emmie were due to arrive in time for supper; and with the best will in the world, she was experiencing something close to hostility towards her daughter.

The scene she had been forced to witness that night, a few weeks earlier, had been horrific; watching Matt's anguish, his white, shocked face turning slowly red in anger, hearing his voice cracking with pain and rage as he said, 'Tell Eliza she can fucking get down here fast, Emmie's extremely ill, should she care;' watching the doctor and poor Margaret wretchedly embarrassed, following Matt out of the house, trembling herself now, driving after him to the hospital; sitting waiting, terrified, as he and the doctor disappeared somewhere into the inner workings of the Casualty department; and then seeing Matt coming out again without Emmie, hearing his curt, 'They're keeping her in, but only as a precaution. I'll stay here, you get along home.'

She had felt only sympathy and heartache for him.

Matt, who had showed her nothing but generosity and kindness, had been hurt beyond endurance by her own daughter, and unless there had been some very serious misdemeanour on his part which Eliza had never informed her of, he didn't deserve this.

As he turned and walked away from her; Sarah thought she had never seen anyone look so broken in her entire life.

'Mummy! Mummy, something – something so awful—' Eliza's voice was thick with sobs. 'I – I can't come. Not tonight. Oh, God, you don't know, you just don't know—'

'I don't know what, Eliza?' Sarah tried to keep her voice neutral, not too brisk.

'Matt – Matt – oh, God—'

'What do you mean, Eliza? Calm down, darling, you're not making any sense.'

'He – he's just presented me with – with a divorce petition. And it's not just that. He's – he's trying to get custody of Emmie. He wants to take her away from me. What am I going to do, Mummy, tell me, you've got to help me, what on earth am I going to do?'

'Oh, Miss Mullan, it's so sad.' Jenny's huge blue eyes were brimming over with tears.

'What is, Jenny?'

'Mr Shaw, he's divorcing Mrs Shaw.'

Nothing could have prepared Louise for how she felt then. Or rather for the confusion and conflict of how she felt. That in itself was a shock: more of a shock than the news.

'He's what! Jenny, how do you know that?'

'Well, I had to ring the new secretary there about those files you asked me to, and she said she didn't know if she ought to release them, and I said they were your personal files, and she said she'd have to ask and then some junior' – she spoke the word with deep disdain – 'rang me back and said she'd got them and she was quite friendly and I asked her how she was getting on, and started telling her about the old days and the fun we used to have, and then she said she wasn't sure if she ought to tell me, but Mr Shaw was getting a divorce. She said he was in a terrible mood all the time and I said that was nothing new—'

'Jenny! Anyway, go on.'

'And apparently, he's going to try and get the little girl.'

'What! Emmie! But how could he? Men never get custody. And – and—' She stopped.

'I don't know, Miss Mullan. It is awful, isn't it?'

'Yes, Jenny, it is. Really awful. Poor Eliza. And actually – poor Matt. Oh, dear. Could I have a coffee please? Nice and strong.'

'Yes, of course, Miss Mullan. And a biscuit? I've got some really nice custard creams with sort of flaky pastry—'

'No, Jenny, no biscuit, thank you.'

'I don't suppose that new person gets nice biscuits in for Mr Shaw,' said Jenny.

'Possibly not,' said Louise. She went into her own office and sat staring out of the window. She felt, above all, deeply upset: despite the completely inexplicable confusion, a confusion she crushed, repeatedly and determinedly, refusing even to examine its roots. Matt had adored Eliza, she was the centre of his life, what on earth could have gone wrong? And he was basically a good man, fiercely passionate about his family. Eliza must have done something pretty dreadful for him to go down this route; maybe that article – but no. You wouldn't divorce someone for that. He must be in an appalling state of rage if he was really considering fighting for custody of Emmie.

She spent much of the day fretting over whether or not to ring him and finally decided to do so. The worst thing he could do was put the phone down on her.

It was so truly shocking. And so desperately sad. And she did feel rather confused about it herself.

Eliza was trying to calm down, think clearly, form a plan even; but she was finding it terribly difficult. Panic consumed her, all the time. She felt beleaguered, alone in a completely alien, hostile environment. Even her mother seemed less than one hundred per cent behind her, telling her she wasn't totally surprised about the divorce even if it was a shock about Emmie, pointing out that she hadn't exactly been behaving well.

'God knows what possessed you, Eliza, to do what you did up in Scotland and I certainly don't want to hear any explanations—'

'I don't know either, Mummy. I can't – I can't believe I did what I did.'

She had stayed at the house trying to recover some semblance of herself, on the dreadful day the petition had arrived, waiting for Matt to come home; she rang the mother with whose child Emmie was having tea, and asked her if she could possibly keep her until the morning: 'I'm so sorry, but I've got the most terrible migraine, and my husband's away, it would be such a help . . .'

She spent the evening trying to do all sorts of normal things: trying to read, trying to eat, trying to watch television, but whatever she did the terrible griping fear invaded her, and she roamed helplessly from room to room, up and down stairs, standing at the window, watching for Matt's car. Afterwards she wondered why she had been so sure he would come home at all.

He finally arrived after twelve; she was sitting on the stairs waiting for him. She was shaking, dry-mouthed; she felt nothing except fear: not of him, but of what he was doing to her.

He looked at her and nodded briefly.

'Hello. I thought you'd be in bed. Or out, of course.'

'Matt – Matt, please. We have to talk. Discuss this.'

'I don't think there's anything to be discussed,' he said. 'It's too late for talking.'

'Matt, I've been trying to talk to you for weeks.'

'Really? I hadn't noticed. Anyway, the petition said it all. I want a divorce. I can only imagine you do too. I also want Emmie. I'm not quite sure how you feel about that.'

'How do you think I feel? Don't be so ridiculous. And let me tell you, you're not going to get her.'

'Oh really? Your behaviour would have seemed to indicate that you'd be quite happy not to have her any more. That she's become a burden to you.'

'You – you bastard,' she said, standing up, 'how dare you, how *dare* you talk to me in that – that horrible way?'

He shrugged. 'It would seem to be true. Please let me past, I want to go to my room. Where is she now, by the way, I don't want her waking up and being upset.'

'You don't – don't –' she had heard of the red spots of rage before your eyes; she saw them now, blinding, flashing, like her mythical migraine '– you don't want her upset. So you do this to her. Drag her through the courts. Tell her she has to live with one of us, rather than the other—'

'Oh,' he said, 'it will be me she lives with, you can be sure of that.'

Eliza stepped forward, raised her hand to strike him. Strike his cold, complacently hostile face. Dropped it again. She mustn't descend into violence. She mustn't. It was dangerous.

'I would like to know,' she said, struggling to keep her voice level and calm, 'I would like to know why you are so sure of that.'

'Didn't you read the petition?'

'Of course I read it.'

'Well, then. It's all there. But let me remind you. How you neglect her and go out to work against my wishes. And leave her – overnight, mind – in the charge of strangers in a foreign city while you are out socialising, while leading me to believe she will be with you at all times. How you allow her to be around people I disapprove of. How you diminish me publicly – and, by implication, in her eyes. And then of course there is the small matter of your morals, your adultery—'

'You're mad,' she said, pushing down her fear. 'As if any of that makes me an unfit mother.'

'I disagree,' he said, 'and my solicitor disagrees also. Anyway, we shall see what a judge makes of it.'

'A judge, any judge, would know it was a pack of filthy lies—'

'As I said, we shall see. Now, where is she?'

'With a friend. Staying the night.'

'Would you like to tell me why? So that you could go out with your friends, your lovers—'

'No, you bastard. For the very reason you were so concerned about, so that she didn't have to witness this – this hideous, filthy garbage.'

'It's you who's making it hideous, Eliza. I'm very calm. And – which friend, do I know the family?'

'Yes, of course you bloody know them. The Millers. She's about three streets away.'

'You told me she was with "friends" in Milan. I don't think that was quite the case, was it? She was with your friends' servants. People unknown to either of us.'

She suddenly felt violently nauseated; seeing how everything from now on – and indeed in the past – could be misconstrued, twisted. Her legs felt shaky; she sat down again.

'Matt – Matt, please, can't we—'

'No,' he said, 'we can't anything. "We" don't exist any more. You've killed "we", Eliza. I would prefer never to see you again, but,' he shrugged, 'I have to think of Emmie. So, for now—'

'I hate you,' she said. 'I absolutely hate you. I don't know how you can do this.'

'You might ask yourself how you've done what you have to me,' he said very quietly. She looked at him, saw the pain in his face and in spite of everything felt a stab of dreadful remorse.

'Matt, can't we – that is – I didn't—'

'No,' he said, 'I told you, we can't anything. Except separate our lives and as soon as possible.'

She was silent; then, 'Are you moving out?'

'No,' he said, 'not at the moment.'

'So – so I have to move out? Of my own house?'

'My house. No, of course not. I'm not that unreasonable. You can stay.'

'Matt, please,' she said, staring at him, hearing the horror in her voice. 'You're mad. We can't – can't stay here together. Not if you're really going to go ahead with this.'

'Of course I'm going ahead.'

'So what do you want me to do?'

He looked at her and there was absolute disdain in his eyes.

'I really don't care what you do,' he said.

'OK. I'll go to Summercourt. In the morning.'

'If you wish. Will you be taking Emmie?'

'Well, of course I'll be taking her, you bastard.'

'I could be forgiven for wondering. You might have been leaving her behind. To see some more of your – er, friends.'

'Shut up!' She was screaming now. 'Shut up, SHUT UP.'

'You will be back on Sunday night?'

'Of course I will. She's got school on Monday.'

'You have proposed taking her out of school before, if you remember. In order to go to Milan. To – to cheer yourself up, as I recall.'

'Matt,' she said, her rage stilled into pain, 'you know why I wanted to go to Milan.'

'Remind me. Shopping? The opera? To meet another, earlier lover?'

'It wasn't,' she said very quietly, and tears began now, 'it was because of the baby, you know it was, you know perfectly well, I was depressed and—'

'And of course I wasn't. I was perfectly happy. Or that was what you chose to believe.'

'I can't stand this,' she said, 'I can't stand it any longer. I'm going to bed.'

'If you do go to Summercourt,' he said, 'please get Emmie to ring me on Sunday.'

'What?'

'I would like to speak to her. To be sure she's all right. Quite happy. And actually with you. Not left with – what do you and your mother call them? Oh, yes, the villagers. So feudal.'

This time it was too much for her. She felt the bile rising in her throat, and made the lavatory just in time.

When she came out, shaken and tear-stained, he had gone to his room.

'You need a solicitor,' said Charles, when she called him, 'a good one. I'll do a bit of research.'

'Thank you. Oh, Charles, I'm so scared, so, so scared.'

'Try to keep calm. He'll have a very tough time getting Emmie away from you. No judge would rule against you. You're an exemplary mother.'

'Oh, sure.'

'You are. You've given up your career to look after her. At Matt's express wishes.'

'Until now.'

'What, for two days a week? Leaving her in the care of an excellent nanny?'

'And sneaking off up to Scotland and committing adultery with a work colleague. I don't think so.'

'Well,' he said after a long pause, 'let's see what a solictor has to say about it.'

It was an uncomfortable weekend; Summercourt didn't work its usual magic. She paced the house and the garden, trying to crush the panic, the terrible sense of foreboding, trying to tell herself it couldn't happen, that she wouldn't lose Emmie, that no judge would rule against her. Telling herself, over and over again. And trying very hard to believe it.

Chapter 55

Mariella had done it. Finally. After years of hard graft.

She was at the top of one of the best-dressed lists. In *Women's Wear Daily*, the bible of the fashion trade. Probably the most important list of all. And she was therefore, all over the papers as well, the *New York Times*, the *Daily News*, and even *The Times* in London.

She received the congratulations of her friends, and the press, graciously but modestly: 'It is nothing,' she said, 'just a little lucky moment.'

She knew of course it was nothing of the sort; a huge financial investment, an absolute dedication to her cause, a most careful attendance at the openings, the premieres, the charity dinners, the semi-private parties. Always slim, always glowing, hair and make-up perfect, dressed with wit and panache as well as perfect taste, always charming, always smiling, a shimmering star: the very brightest, for however brief a time, in the heaven she had set her sights upon.

Giovanni was less discreet, telephoning the world, throwing an impromptu party at the villa, boasting about her, showing her off.

A party was to be thrown for her in aid of one her favourite charities, by the American magazine, *US Flair*, to celebrate her triumph: in New York, at the Metropolitan Museum, long the home of such affairs.

All fashionable New York was to be there, of course: the fashion press, the designers, the photographers; but friends were invited too, from Milan, from Paris, from New York – and London. Among whom – of course – were Eliza Shaw and Jeremy Northcott.

'Mariella, darling, so, so many congratulations!'

'Eliza, *cara*, thank you. I am not a little bit pleased.'

'Oh, you mean you are a very big bit pleased! And so you should be.'

'Thank you, darling. Now you must, must come to the party. I will not hear of anything else.'

'I'm afraid you have to hear of it, Mariella—'

'Now *cara*, I cannot celebrate this without you. You helped make me more famous and I insist, insist you come. You can bring Matt, of course, I would not expect you to come without him, to leave him a hay widow—'

'Grass, Mariella, grass.'

'Well, but grass is young hay. Is that not right?'

'I suppose it is,' said Eliza, 'but anyway, I'm afraid he won't come either. And there's something I have to tell you, I've been putting it off, because I can't bear to talk about it, even to my friends but he's – he's divorcing me. I'm afraid I – well, I had an affair, Mariella. Well, not even an affair, just a – a—'

'A one-night lay,' said Mariella and she laughed. 'Good for you, *cara*. How he does deserve that.'

'Well,' said Eliza, thinking how apt this mis-translation was, 'he certainly doesn't think so. And I've done a lot of other horrible things too.'

'I cannot believe that—'

'No, you have to. Horrible things, things I'm really ashamed of. Anyway, he's divorcing me and – and – oh, Mariella—' Her voice was shrouded suddenly in fright and tears. 'He's trying to – to get Emmie.'

'What? He is mad. How can he get her, how can he make anyone think that is right?'

'Well – he's working very hard on it. And actually, Mariella, I have to ask you, and it's a big favour, will you be one of my witnesses?'

'You will have to produce witnesses,' Philip Gordon said. He smiled at her gently. 'It's essential.'

'Witnesses?' said Eliza. 'Witnesses to what?'

'To your suitability as a mother. Several, in fact, who can speak up for you, give the lie to all the things your husband is citing as evidence to the contrary. Mrs Shaw – here—'

He pushed a large box of tissues towards her. He always had one, ready for the first meeting with a client.

Eliza blew her nose, wiped her eyes and smiled a watery smile at him. She liked him. Very much.

He had been recommended to her by a friend of Charles's: 'He appears very sweet and gentle, but don't be fooled. He's tough as the proverbial old boots and he gets – usually – very good results.'

Philip Gordon was a partner in a well-known firm of lawyers just off

Chancery Lane. He was grey-haired, blue-eyed, slim and beautifully dressed, in a dark grey suit, a blue shirt that matched his eyes, and the red, navy and brown striped tie of the Old Wykehamist.

'We like to live over the shop,' he said to Eliza, taking her coat.

'Sorry?'

'The Royal Courts of Justice. Just over there.' He pointed out of the window.

'Oh, I see. It looks very grand from here.' She felt rather alarmed. 'Would – would this case really be held there?'

'Oh, yes. Now – coffee? Or tea?'

'Coffee, please.'

'Excellent. I do like clients who want coffee in the afternoon, not just mid-morning. My preference precisely.'

He was very charming, Eliza thought; she suddenly felt a little better.

'Right,' he said, when the coffee had arrived. 'Now let's see. I've read your husband's affidavit, of course, and I must say it's very aggressive. Gloves off from Day One. These allegations about your being an unfit parent; now I'm sure you can defend them and we'll go through them in a little while, one by one, but my first instinct on this is that several of them hardly hold water. Your going out to work – pretty standard these days, I'd have thought. But the other thing I would like to propose today, only for discussion of course, is that we should consider not defending the divorce petition, and putting all our energies into the custody case. Do you think you could defend the charge of adultery? Or would you want to?'

'Well – no,' said Eliza, living yet again the horror of that moment, of a naked, shaking Rob, handing her the phone across the bed, saying 'it's your husband'. 'But – wouldn't that immediately make me the guilty party?'

'It would, insofar as you were admitting adultery, but not to the other charges, alleging your unsuitability as a mother. Do you think the – the other party would agree to your doing that?'

'I'll have to ask him, but I – I think so,' she said, reflecting on Rob's reaction when she called him to say what Matt had done.

'Stupid bloody idiot,' he said. 'Well, I'll do whatever you want, Eliza.'

'Good. So there is no – no emotional complication?'

'I – that is – no,' she said, blushing. One of the worst things was the way she had been forced to view herself: as a slut, a good-time girl, sleeping with someone she hardly knew. She felt deeply and horribly ashamed of herself . . . maybe Matt was right . . . she didn't deserve to have charge of Emmie.

'Good. Then we simply fight the custody case only. I think you might do better that way. Judges get very weary of listening to couples bitching about one another, for want of a better expression, wasting several days of court time.'

'Would that get it over more quickly?' said Eliza.

'It could. Yes.'

'Because it's so awful, what's happening now, living with him in the same house, sort of pretending to Emmie – to my daughter – absolutely ghastly, you can't imagine. I don't know why he's doing it, when he obviously hates me so much. Why doesn't he move out into a flat or something?'

'I'd quite like to move out,' said Matt, to Ivor Lewis.

'Why?'

'Because it's absolutely bloody awful, living there in the same house, pretending to my daughter—'

'It's a ghastly business, Mr Shaw. Look. You're fighting for custody of that child because you say your wife is an unfit mother. You move out of the house, what do you think that says?'

'I – don't know.'

'Think about it. It implies you're happy to leave the child with her, in her care. Not a good point in your favour when it comes to court. Presumably you're anxious that she's going to neglect her further, leave her with unsuitable people, continue to undermine your parenting wishes—'

'Yes, of course I am.'

'So you shouldn't walk away from all that. Look – are you concerned that the child is in any physical danger. Has your wife ever struck her, to your knowledge? Because if she has—'

'No,' said Matt sharply, 'no, I'm absolutely confident of that. She just – well, she wouldn't. It's out of the question.'

'You wouldn't care to – check up on that?'

Matt stared at him.

'How, for Christ's sake?'

'Ask your daughter?'

'Absolutely not. It would be an appalling thing to suggest to her. It would frighten her.'

545

'Not if there had actually been violence. Children keep very quiet about it, you know, they feel ashamed, as if it's their own fault. And of course that there might be retribution from telling on Mummy or Daddy.'

'No,' said Matt, 'Eliza would never do that. And if she had, Emmie would have told me. She's quite – quite manipulative. In her own way.'

'Right. Well, anyway, I would advise you not to move out. Stick it out, Mr Shaw. Hopefully it won't be for too long. Has your wife suggested moving out?'

'No. No, she hasn't. Apart from anything else, she doesn't have any money, couldn't afford a flat or anything.'

'I thought she half owned your country pile?'

'It's a legal nicety. I paid for it, through the nose. To save her bloody family from penury. Or what passes for penury to those people. Her mother had to break a family trust to enable me to do it. Nice woman, we get along very well. She doesn't approve of Eliza working, for a start.'

'I'd like to look at the agreement,' said Ivor Lewis. 'If you don't mind. And – do you suppose the mother could be persuaded to appear as a witness for your defence? Because that would be a very powerful point in your favour.'

'Oh – no, I don't think so,' said Matt. 'Blood thicker than water and all that.'

'Well, if she's not going to be a witness for you, she'll certainly be one for her daughter. We can cross-examine in court. You never know. Something might come up.'

'Darling,' said Jeremy. 'Sleeping on the job, so to speak. What a silly girl you are. Dear, oh, dear, Eliza, what a mess.'

'Yes. I know. I'm sorry Jeremy. So sorry.'

'Don't apologise to me, sweetie.'

'Well, it was while on agency business so to speak. And you must think so badly of me. It's not as if I was passionately and deeply in love with him. He's just – just a mate really. I thought better of myself, I really did.'

'We all do things that take us by surprise sometimes,' said Jeremy, 'that we thought we wouldn't be capable of.'

'Not you, Jeremy, surely? You're such a gentleman, always so – so perfectly behaved—'

'I try,' he said and sighed suddenly.

'What have I done, Jeremy? It's an awful thing that someone who once loved you so much, and thought you were wonderful, despises you and wants to hurt you . . . you've no idea how frightened I feel, the thought of losing Emmie is just – well, I don't know what I'd do. It's the one thing I don't think I could bear. I thought Baby Charles dying was the worst, but losing Emmie—' She started to cry.

'Oh, my darling, you really have had such a cruel, horrible time, haven't you? It's so unfair and you're so lovely.'

'I'm not very lovely,' said Eliza, sniffing, wiping her eyes on the back of her hand. 'I'm bad. I've been really bad. You don't know—'

'Unwise, maybe. Hardly grounds for custody though.'

'It depends on the judge, my solicitor says. Jeremy, you wouldn't be a witness for me, would you?'

'Darling, of course I will. But – I'm the person who tempted you back to work. And who was your lover for a long time. Not sure your barrister would find that very satisfactory.'

'Maybe not. Oh, God, what a mess. What a filthy, horrible mess. If I could only go back a year. So much of it was me being brattish, Matt being stubborn—'

'Is it really too late now?'

She looked at him and sighed. 'Oh, Jeremy, yes. Of course it is. Absolutely too late.'

Chapter 56

'Now you are not to be frightened, and remember I love you.'

She hadn't got used to that yet. The sheer pleasure not just of hearing the words, but the way he spoke them. Very, very simply, and quietly and as if he was half-surprised himself to be saying them. Which, actually, he said he was.

'I've led a very sheltered life, romantically,' he said with a slight sigh, that first night, as they talked almost into the dawn lying in her bed, astonished at what was happening and its swiftness.

'You could have fooled me, Mr Frost,' she said, stretching luxuriously, her body still half-shocked at the new, gloriously sweet discovery of him.

'Well – of course there has been the occasional encounter. Since – since Catherine.'

'Who died?' she said quietly.

'Yes,' he said, more quietly still. And then, 'I mean – I do like – well—'

'Sex?' she said, and smiled at him.

'Yes. But what just happened to us wasn't exactly sex, was it? It was making love, in the truest sense. It was me, the whole of me, telling you I wanted you, the whole of you. It was – it was lovely,' he said, kissing her gently. 'Thank you.'

'My pleasure. So – tell me about this sheltered life.'

'Well – as you must have realised, I am rather – shy. I'm not sure why, I was just born that way. It's hard to describe, it's a kind of fear, I suppose. Of being judged and found wanting. A feeling you're safer just with yourself. And quite early I discovered the best way was to stay just with myself. I was an only child, and I liked it. I dreaded every effort people made to help me as they saw it, to suggest friends, to invite me to play with other children, parties were a nightmare, I just stood in corners, watching while terrible mothers said "come along, Mark, join in the fun".'

'What about school?'

'Oh, I didn't mind school at all. School was all right, I had a role to play, I knew what I was meant to be doing and I could just get on and do it. I was quite – clever, I did well, got scholarships, things like that—'

'Did you go to boarding school?'

'No. My father thought I should go, but my mother wouldn't allow it and what my mother said went.'

Scarlett had been afraid of that.

'But day school was fine, it was a very academic place, there were other little swots, so, yes, I managed school, I did it quite well. It's why I can give talks at those book launches and things, it's having a clear role to play and playing it. But sitting next to some strange woman at dinner, expected to chatter and be interesting – oh, God. So just a couple of dalliances, over the past years—'

'I can't imagine you having a dalliance,' said Scarlett.

'Well – in both cases, they did the dallying. Very determined. Again, it meant I had a role to play, and they were both very nice, very attractive. It wasn't difficult. And then – nothing. Till I met you. I saw you that first day, here on Trisos, all brown and beautiful and wild-haired, and everything lurched. I felt – physically unsteady. I thought you were the most desirable thing I'd ever seen.'

'Goodness,' said Scarlett. 'Rejecting every effort I made to talk to you, scuttling away as fast as you could—'

'Oh, I know, I know. But there was no role for me with you, clearly. Sophisticated, successful, independent woman – what truck could you have with me? It was very alarming.'

'Well, lots of truck now,' said Scarlett happily, leaning over and kissing him, 'lots and lots of truck.'

'Indeed. And the most lovely thing about you for me is that you are part of Trisos and how I feel about it, I could never think about it from that moment without thinking also of you.'

'That's the nicest compliment I've ever had.'

'I can't believe that. You must have had a great many in your time.'

'Only a few that ever mattered,' she said.

They talked about David; it had to be confronted and simply. She was brutal, did not spare herself. Even about the baby.

Mark listened quietly, only interrupting when she told him about the blackmail.

'How marvellous,' he said, 'what an absolutely correct thing to do.'

549

It was a novel interpretation; but she liked it.

She stayed a week: as she had planned originally. A wonderful, sun-drenched week, as they explored one another and their lives, and wondered that it had taken them so long to come this far. They were at once impressed and delighted by one another; every day a delight of discovery.

On the last night, as she prepared to leave Trisos, he told her he loved her.

And now she was to meet his mother.

Scarlett Shaw, half-educated, ill-read, ex-air hostess for God's sake, being presented to this amazing woman who wrote poetry, who addressed festivals and lectured undergraduates, and not just in the ordinary course of things, not as a mere acquaintance, but as the object of his very great affection, as Mark put it – God, she loved his way with words – and by her only son. God, it was terrifying. She would have nothing to say, she would do the wrong things, she would fail the test completely, and Mark would abandon her . . .

And what did you wear to meet such a paragon of intellect? Did you look trendy or classic, did you wear colour or try to blend into the background?

'Oh, God, oh, God,' she wailed to her wardrobe mirror, looking round at her bedroom, littered with every sort of combination of clothes. And thought of the words of Eliza, whose sartorial opinion she had always relied on, 'when in doubt dress down', and she put on a little black dress and a long string of pearls, and some mid-height heels and very little make-up, and went out to slay the dragoness.

Who was a fairly pleasant surprise. She looked rather like Mark, with the same clear-cut features, the same grey eyes, and what had clearly once been the same dark hair, only thickly interwoven with grey and drawn back into a chignon. Her clothes were a little poetess-like, to be sure, a long skirt, a heavily embroidered Russian-style blouse, buttoned high on the neck, and a silk befringed shawl round her shoulders. She was pale, and very drawn-looking, no doubt because of the constant pain, but her smile when it came was dazzling. She lived in a rather dark large flat in Bloomsbury – where else could it be? Even Scarlett knew Bloomsbury was the centre of female literary London – every wall lined with books, every surface covered with papers. She was cared for day-to-day by a companion called Dorothy, who seemed both efficient and patient, and whose role was clearly not as subservient as Scarlett would have expected, she argued with her mistress quite frequently and eloquently indeed; but she was clearly fond of her and of Mark. 'She's like a rather strict nanny,' he confided to Scarlett afterwards.

Mark had brought some special teacakes from Fortnums which his mother loved, and Scarlett had brought flowers, a rather over-large bouquet she realised, which could have been interpreted as vulgar. But Mrs Frost received them graciously, handed them over to Dorothy, and told her to sit down and 'let me have a look at you'.

She proceeded to scrutinise Scarlett quite closely, for what seemed a long time, then she nodded as if satisfied and said, 'good,' as if she had passed some inspection. Which she supposed she had.

'Mark told me you were very pretty: he was right. And what do you think of him?'

'Oh! Oh, I think he's wonderful.'

'Do you? Well, he's certainly talented. Have you read his books?'

'Most of them.'

'And how do you find his social skills? A lot of people find him rather dull.'

'How rude of them to say so,' said Scarlett. She felt surprised at this attack.

'Oh, my dear, most of my friends are rude. Outspoken anyway. I am myself. Anyway, I'm glad he amuses you. He amuses me too. And you met on Trisos, I understand. Lovely place. I adore the Greek islands. I always wanted to do what Mark is doing and make a second home there. But my husband – now he was a dull man – couldn't understand it. Preferred the Home Counties,' she added disparagingly.

'Oh,' said Scarlett, 'oh, I see.'

'But Mark has been wonderful and taken me there twice. I'm going this summer, to see this marvellous new house he's built. Have you seen it?'

'Yes, and it's wonderful. Absolutely wonderful.'

'Good. Now, Miss Shaw—'

'Oh, please call me Scarlett.'

'Very well, but only if you call me Persephone.'

'Oh, I'd like that. What a pretty name.'

'Yes, it is, rather a lot to live up to though.'

'Yes, of course,' said Scarlett carefully. She had no idea who Persephone was and why she should be such a lot to live up to.

'You don't know, do you? You should. She was the goddess of spring. You obviously haven't studied mythology.'

'Mama,' said Mark warningly.

'No, I haven't,' said Scarlett firmly. 'I haven't studied much, I'm afraid.'

There was a silence. Then Mrs Frost said, 'I believe you've achieved a lot of other things, though, and I must respect that I suppose. And you could argue that what matters is achievement. In whatever field. I'm not sure I agree. Still . . . Well done. She's perfectly nice, Mark,' she added as if Scarlett was no longer there, 'I like her. Now – where is that wretched Dorothy and where is our tea.'

Later, as Scarlett recovered over a stiff vodka and tonic in the nearest pub, Mark said, 'You did so well. I was so proud of you. I was terrified you were going to pretend to be what you so clearly are not, and she'd have hated that.'

'Mark,' said Scarlett, 'I never pretend to be what I'm not. It doesn't work. I learnt that long ago.'

'And it's one of the reasons I most love you,' he said. 'And now shall we go back to my place?'

'That could be a very nice idea. And I'm glad I've cleared the first hurdle.'

'With furlongs to spare,' he said.

Eliza, staring at the letter, or rather at the bottom of the second page, felt rather sick.'

'I thought I should let you know our terms . . . charges will be calculated by reference to the time spent by me and other fee-earners dealing with this matter . . . this will include advising, attendances, dealing with papers, correspondence, telephone calls and travelling time . . . my own charge-out rate is at present fifty pounds per hour . . . my assistant's charge-out rate is thirty pounds per hour . . . I estimate that handling your divorce case will take at least fifty hours of my time, and possibly more of my assistant's, taking into account with yourself, meeting and interviewing witnesses, briefing a QC, attending court . . . our charge may therefore be in the region of, and certainly not less than, four thousand pounds . . . I will review this with you as necessary . . . in addition all expenses incurred will be added to the bill . . .'

'Shit!' she said aloud. 'Shit, shit, shit.'

'Naughty Mummy.'

'Sorry, Emmie. Yes, very naughty Mummy. Don't say that at school, Emmie, and don't, please, say it in front of Daddy, all right? He wouldn't like it.'

'Daddy says rude words too, sometimes. But you say more.'

. . . Right. Let's add that to the list of misdemeanours, shall we, your honour? The mother persistently uses bad language and has taught her daughter to use it as well . . .

'Come on then, finish your breakfast and then go and clean your teeth or we'll be late.'

'I was late two times last week.'

'Were you?'

'Yes, those two mornings you were crying and you said you just had a cold, I was late.'

. . . And there's another. The mother delivers the child persistently late to school . . .

'One day I was so late that my teacher asked me what had happened and I told her that you were crying and that you'd even told me not to clean my teeth so we wouldn't be even later—'

. . . And another: the mother frequently tells the child not to clean her teeth; the dentist reports considerable decay as a result . . .

'Well, there's time for you to clean them today. Go on, Emmie, get a move on.'

Emmie went upstairs; Eliza sat reading the letter again and then again, as if willing the words to change. They didn't.

Four thousand pounds at the very least. She didn't have four hundred pounds, not that she could call her own. There was, in her own bank account, eighty pounds, and when she had paid Margaret, there would be twenty pounds. Shit indeed.

A new reason to panic, she thought, to add to the other, darker fears.

She asked her mother – 'I'm so sorry, darling, I'd help if I could'; she asked Charles – 'Sorry, Eliza, still being stung for a hefty amount by Juliet every month.' She even, heart thudding so loudly she felt he must hear, tried to talk to Matt about it.

'I don't have any money, you know I don't, how can I possibly pay for solicitors and barristers and courts, it's so ridiculous—'

'You should have thought of that,' he said, 'before you started on this.

Why don't you ask one of your lovers, Northcott's got plenty of money, I'm sure he'd love to help. Or your friends in Italy. Or even that art director, they earn a lot, don't they?'

'I hate you,' she said, 'so much.'

'I know you do,' he said. And walked out of the room.

With only ten days to go before the party in New York and a week before they were due to leave Italy, Giovanni developed a very nasty cold. Which in turn developed into bronchitis, and then a more generalised infection, and his doctor advised him very strongly against making the trip; alarmed by the speed with which he had felt himself become ill, he acquiesced and told Mariella she must go alone.

Mariella, equally alarmed, said she would not go, would not leave him; he said – of course – that the party was of immense importance, not only to her and her guests and the entire fashion world, but to the charity that was about to benefit by thousands of dollars.

And so – genuinely reluctant – she agreed, although only with the proviso that he was recovering: which, by the day before her departure, he most undoubtedly was.

And so, while still protesting most volubly, Mariella agreed to go alone.

Matt had – finally – told his parents. Their initial sympathy made him feel embarrassed and even foolish; but when he had moved onto his plans to get custody of Emmie they became almost hostile.

'What?' said Sandra. 'You're going to – to try and take Emmie away from her?'

'Yes, that's right.'

'Matt! Is that really a good idea? It could get very nasty, surely. I mean I can see it's dreadful what Eliza's done, it makes me feel really – really sick, but poor little Emmie, have you really thought what fighting over her would do to her?'

'I think it would be better for her in the long run than leaving her with Eliza.'

'But Matt, she's – she's been a good mother, whatever else she's done. I always thought that.'

'What, leaving Emmie while she goes to work, running off to meet her lover pretending she's on some photographic session—'

'Well, I know, but – look, love, don't you think you should take this a bit more slowly? I mean, every marriage goes through rough patches, but you get through it, you know and—'

'Mum, she's completely betrayed me, I can't get over that.'

'I didn't say over it, love, I said through it. And I do think you should try and think of Emmie, poor little mite, and how she's going to feel, however it turns out.'

'Too right,' said Pete. 'If you really care about Emmie, you'll try and put it behind you. I know Eliza's been playing away, and I can see that's bloody awful for you, I'd want to send her to kingdom come myself, but these things happen, and Emmie and her life with the two of you as a family is more important than your hurt pride.'

This was probably the longest speech Matt or Sandra had ever heard Pete make; they both stared at him in silence. Then Sandra said, slightly nervously, 'He's right, Matt, you should try to see it differently, for Emmie's sake.'

'Well,' said Matt after a silence. 'I know where I stand now then. I won't be coming to you for support or help again. Thanks, both of you. I came to ask you to be witnesses for me, speak up for me, say I'm perfectly able to look after Emmie—'

'But Matt, how could you? When you work so hard, such long hours . . .'

'Oh, for Christ's sake!' he shouted, 'if my own parents won't come down on my side, who will? What a waste of bloody time this has been. Thanks for nothing.'

He walked out and slammed the front door; the little house shook. Sandra burst into tears; Pete got out his tobacco pouch and began to roll a cigarette, his invariable response to any difficult situation.

'Oh, Pete,' said Sandra, pulling out a handkerchief, wiping her eyes. 'What have we done? Poor, poor Matt.'

'We haven't done anything,' said Pete, 'it was never going to work. She's nice enough, but she sees the world differently.'

'Pete! You're talking rubbish. And all that class stuff is old hat—'

'Now you're talking rubbish,' said Pete. 'Class is in your bones, it's what makes you what you are, and it's no use pretending it doesn't. Still, no point arguing about that now, we've got to support him, course we have. He won't get Emmie, not in a month of Sundays, but we can't fail him, we're his flesh and blood after all. I'll go and see him tomorrow, tell him so. Best leave him to cool down now.'

❊　❊　❊

But Matt wasn't cooling down; he was shouting at Gina.

'My own parents can't see it. They think all she's done is sleep with someone else, they can't see any of the rest of it.'

'Well, even if all she'd done was sleep with someone,' said Gina carefully, 'it would be quite bad. I'm surprised they're not on your side over that.'

'Well, Mum is. Dad said I should grow up, put it aside for Emmie's sake. When it's Emmie I'm doing it for, Emmie I want to keep safe.'

'Yes of course,' said Gina soothingly, 'of course it is.'

'And I will get her, I will.'

'Of course you will. What's the latest from your solicitor?'

'He's very confident,' said Matt. 'Very confident indeed.'

'Well – good. What did he think about my idea, you know, to call the psychotherapist?'

'I – I haven't talked to him about that yet.'

'Why not, for God's sake?'

'Because I'm absolutely sure she'll be on Eliza's side, talk about her depression, make me look bad.'

'She might produce her as a witness.'

He stared at her. 'I hadn't thought of that.'

'Of course she might. For the very reason you just said, about how depressed she was, explain a lot of her bad behaviour away.'

'Oh God. God Almighty, what a mess. Give me another whisky, would you?'

'Yes, of course. And Matt, why don't you stay the night, you've had an awful lot to drink.'

He stared at her. 'Stay the night? Are you mad? What do you think she'd do with that if she knew? Of course I can't stay the night. I don't like coming here really—'

'Well, thanks.'

'No, I mean it's dangerous. I mean no one would believe we weren't having it away.'

'No,' said Gina, with a sigh, 'no, I don't think they would.'

Chapter 57

'I think it's time we thought about briefing a barrister,' said Philip Gordon.

'Oh. Oh, yes, I see.'

More money. Terrifying amounts of more money. If solicitors were expensive, how much more would a barrister be?

'Um – does it have to be a very – a very top-of-the-range barrister?'

'Now why do you say that? You don't have unlimited resources, is that it?'

'Well – yes, actually. That is it.'

Philip Gordon smiled at her. She wondered if he'd smile if he knew she had no resources at all.

'Well, that's all right. I was going to suggest we talked to a junior initially, just to discuss the case, timing and so on. I've got someone in mind, nice chap, you might find him a bit abrasive, but very good for a junior—'

'Timing?'

'Yes, the length of time the case might run. We'll go along to the courts and the judge will hear what the case is about, what's involved, and he'll set a timetable, say you need three days, or a week or whatever, maybe in a couple of months' time, if there's a lot of evidence and shilly-shallying to go through, and a date will be agreed on. And that will be set in stone. The judge will be sitting there, and he'll say, right, I've got the husband's statement, and yours is yet to come, and there are going to be six witnesses each—'

'Six?' said Eliza, hearing her voice rise in terror, 'I haven't got six.'

'I was simply pulling a number out of the air. Anyway, that's when we can decide whether we need a junior or a senior barrister, or possibly both . . .'

'So – we'll be in court twice?' said Eliza. 'With two barristers?' This was getting worse and worse.

'Yes, possibly, but this first one is a very minor affair. And you'll get a feel for the courts, find them less terrifying when the real case takes place. Now there's something else I want to talk to you about. You've mentioned you were very depressed after you lost the little baby—'

'Yes. Yes, I was.'

'Would you say you were clinically depressed?'

'I'm – not sure. My doctor put me on antidepressants.'

'Right. Well, we might ask him to present his evidence. Or at least give a written statement.'

'Why? What good would that possibly do? Matt would just say it proved I was unhinged and not fit to look after Emmie.'

'Not necessarily. It could win you quite a bit of sympathy.'

'Oh. Oh, I see. Well – well, I also saw a psychotherapist. She counselled me for weeks and weeks.'

'We could ask her as well. How would you feel about that?'

'Um – I'm not sure.'

'Think about it. Whatever you decide. I think it would be a good idea. But she could well plead confidentiality so she might not do us a lot of good. Now this meeting with the barrister – how are you fixed on Monday or Thursday? He could come in around twelve and then we could have a bit to eat afterwards, if all goes well.'

'You mean if we like each other? Thursday'd be good, I'll put it in my diary. What's his name?'

'Toby Gilmour. As I say, nice chap.'

Eliza was halfway home when she realised that she couldn't possibly ask Mary Miller, her psychotherapist, to give evidence for her in court. Witnesses were always cross-examined, and she had told Mrs Miller absolutely everything. Including that she had once hit Emmie. So hard that she had had to go to Casualty and have her face stitched . . . If that came out, she really would be doomed.

'Matt, hello, this is Louise. How are you?'

'Very busy. Just going into a meeting.'

'OK. I just wondered if you'd like to have a drink sometime? Like tomorrow evening, I'm free?'

'Oh – no, thanks. No, I really haven't got time, Louise. Sorry.'

'Matt! Come on. I've heard you're not exactly having the best time.

You don't have to pretend, Matt. It's me, Louise, remember? Old times in the office, Jenny, biscuits, all that sort of thing. Come on. I'll pay.'

She could almost hear his grudging smile;

'Oh – all right. But I can't be long.'

'You really are a charmer, you know that? Well, today or tomorrow?'

'Oh – tomorrow.'

'Fine. American Bar at the Savoy, OK? Six thirty.'

'Seven'd be better.'

'All right, seven it is. I can hardly wait.'

'It was your bloody idea.'

'Matt, joke!'

'OK, OK. See you tomorrow.'

He would have said it was the last thing he wanted to do; but when he was in the cab, on the way to the Savoy, he realised he was quite looking forward to it. Life was so filthy at the moment, he felt like jumping off his new skyscraper half the time, home was hell, every evening an ordeal, being icily polite to Eliza, especially when Emmie was around because they both knew if they let it crack for a moment, the rage and the hostility would break through; making excuses to Emmie why they could never do things together with her, watching her sometimes sad, sometimes playing on it, putting it to her advantage, playing off one against the other . . . it was horrible.

And then everyone kept tiptoeing round him at work, no one mentioning it, and putting up with his bad temper; and then Gina was so bloody pushy with her Sympathy and her Understanding – you could hear the capital letters – although he needed a bit of that, even his parents kept urging him to reconsider, that had really been a blow. He'd been horribly hurt.

But at least Louise knew him inside out, he didn't have to pretend and he could tell her to back off if it threatened to get heavy.

God, he'd known her a long time – nearly as long as he'd known Eliza – and certainly a lot longer than he and Eliza had been together. He thought of the first time she came into the office, all long legs and big eyes, summing them up in a moment, making her claims, striking her deals – and then continuing to do so, for almost a decade.

You had to respect her, he thought, and what she had achieved; and it was the real thing, what she did, a lot more impressive than photographing frocks . . .

He looked terrible, she thought, as he walked into the Savoy; far worse than he had at the lunch. He must have lost at least a stone, and his face was gaunt and devoid of colour. He was obviously suffering a lot. And – wouldn't want to talk about it.

'Hey, Matt. You look great,' she said, standing up, kissing his cheek briefly. Funny – all those years working together and the number of times they had exchanged even the most platonic embrace could be counted in single figures. However excited they were, however amazing the deal, or landmark they crossed – first really big contract, first million in the bank – she and Matt had never done more than grin at one another and perhaps give one another a thumbs up.

'Sorry I'm late. What are you drinking?'

'I'm not yet. I was waiting for you . . .'

'I said I was sorry.'

'That's OK. I just love sitting around, looking as if I've been stood up. Martini? That's what this place is about.'

'Yeah, why not?'

She was looking very good, actually, he thought. She'd got her hair cut in that new way, in layers, a bit like Eliza's, only shorter, and she was wearing a red dress that although it was quite long swung open from the hips when she sat down, so that her legs were still well on display. She did have very good legs. She looked altogether expensive and sleek and successful; he saw several of the men in the bar looking at her, and felt an emotion that at first he couldn't analyse and then recognised – again from the early days with Eliza – as a certain pride at being with her.

'So,' he said, sipping at the martini – he'd rather it had been an ice-cold beer, but never mind, the alcohol content was probably higher and he needed that – 'So, how are things?'

'It's all pretty good. Got my sights on a spot in Chelsea – just on the edge of the park – for my next hotel. Americans will love it. Near the barracks, near Harrods, near the Albert Hall – perfect.'

'Think you'll get it?'

'Not sure. Bit of an auction going on at the moment. But I'm pretty determined so—'

'You'll get it,' said Matt and he meant it. 'You always do.'

'I appreciate your faith in me,' she said. 'And you, how's it working out with Barry? Is he good enough?'

'Providing I'm there too,' said Matt, 'you know what I mean?'

'Yes, of course. Same with Roderick.'

'I heard you might be breaking away from Roderick.'

'You did?' Her dark eyes became blank. 'Well, that's very interesting.'

'True? Or just a rumour?'

'Matt Shaw, if you think I'd tell you, of all people, something like that, you've lost the plot seriously.'

'That means it's true then.'

'No, Matt, it doesn't. It doesn't mean it's true or not true, it means I'm not going to tell you.'

'Don't you trust me?'

'Professionally? Of course not. Why should I?'

'Not even for old time's sake?'

'Least of all for that, Matt.'

For the first time in months Matt realised he was enjoying himself.

'Same again?' he said nodding at her glass.

They parted, slightly unsteadily, with another brief kiss, four martinis down, and agreed to do it again in a week's time.

There is temptation and there is serious temptation and then there is temptation almost beyond endurance. This came to Jeremy Northcott as he sank into a chair in the lobby of the Upper East Side apartment that remained at his disposal until the end of the year, kicked off his shoes and loosened his black tie, having got home from the reception for Mariella Crespi that evening. He had watched her as she stood smiling and looking utterly ravishing in a black crepe Pierre Cardin sheath dress, her hair pulled back in a chignon, being kissed and embraced and congratulated for over an hour; he had kissed her himself, breathing in her rich, heady perfume; he had chatted to her briefly and then waited patiently while she circulated the room ushered by M. Cardin himself and the director of the charity; he had sat not quite near enough to her at a dinner for the chosen few at Elaine's; and danced with her only once when they went on to Studio 54 at two in the morning.

And now it was four, and he had a breakfast meeting at eight and he was debating whether or not to go to bed at all, when there was a call from the porter to say there was a lady to see him, and he said she should come up and listened to the whirring of the elevator as it approached him, rather as the condemned man might listen for the steps of the executioner approaching his cell, and as she stepped out of it, looking excited, nervous, almost tentative, holding a hooded cloak round her – 'I think no one saw me, I left the hotel by the service exit' – and then slipped the cloak off and held out her arms to him, he thought there could hardly be a man in the universe who could resist such an invitation.

Chapter 58

'Darling, I hear from your mother that you need some help.'

'Well – well, yes, I do. But—'

'Then you must let me give it to you. Let's not be silly about it. I am able to help, I want to help, so will you please let me help?'

Somehow Eliza had never thought of the one person who really did have plenty of money and whom it would be acceptable to take it from.

'So, what do you say?'

'Yes, Gommie, that's what I say. Yes, yes, yes. And thank you. But—'

'No buts. Come and have tea this afternoon, and tell me how much you need and all about it. It sounds ghastly, darling, and quite ridiculous, he'll never win, but I feel so sorry for you.'

Anna Marchant had lived in the same house in Knightsbridge all her married life: one of a terrace, furnished in a wonderfully opulent deco style, all mirrored sideboards, bronze figures and chinoiserie. She opened the door to Eliza and held out her arms.

'Come in, darling,' she said, enfolding her in a rich blend of Chanel N° 5 and Balkan Sobranie Russian cigarettes. 'Oh, you look so tired. Let me take your coat. Tea, darling? Champagne? Cocktail? I've sent Piers out so we can talk properly. He is such a bore these days, nothing to do and just wants to muscle in on all my fun. Just as well I don't have lovers any more. That's my story anyway.'

Eliza, feeling better already, said tea would be lovely, and sat down on one of Anna's rather uncomfortable chairs.

'Right,' Anna said, returning with the tea tray, 'tell me all about it.'

'Silly idiot,' she said, when Eliza had finished, 'I thought he loved that child. Not enough, that's all I can say, and I hope your barrister's making that point. If he really loved her he wouldn't be putting her through this. I don't know what's the matter with you young people today, one affair

,and it all has to be over. All this ridiculous confessing and soul-baring, such a waste of time and money . . .'

'I didn't actually have to confess,' said Eliza ruefully.

'Well, no, maybe not. Bit unfortunate, but you could hardly be blamed for it, silly young man shouldn't have picked up the phone . . .'

'Gommie, really! Oh, it's so nice to see you.'

'Nice to see you, darling. What a nightmare for you. And having Matt still living in the house. Why on earth is he doing that?'

'God knows. It's so horrible, the atmosphere's awful. He's working very late mostly, which is the only thing that makes it bearable. But I can't afford to move out. And anyway, he's so protective of Emmie, and obviously I'd want to take her, I just can't think he'd agree to it.'

'He can't not agree to it. He doesn't have custody of her. You can do what you like. What about going to Summercourt?'

'No, because she has to go to school. Anyway, it's less disruptive for her if I stay. It's probably best to hang on. It shouldn't be more than a few months, the solicitor says.'

'Your mother seems to be inclined to see his point of view,' said Anna thoughtfully, 'very odd, I thought.'

'Well, she's very fond of him. And of course I've behaved so badly, and she minds that.'

'Badly! One night in six years or whatever it is. Good God, I call that grounds for sainthood myself. One thing I'll say for Piers, very good at turning a blind eye, I remember being caught in flagrante one afternoon in the House of Lords, your friend Rex Ingham's father as a matter of fact, old fool forgot to lock the door, some stupid bugger had to tell Piers of course, he never said a word.'

'Oh, Gommie! You're so naughty,' said Eliza, laughing. 'Anyway, back to Mummy, it's not just that, she really disapproves of me working, she always did, and of course Matt's been incredibly generous to her, over Summercourt and everything—'

'Yes, but he can afford it, become extremely rich I gather. You're still working, I hope?'

'Oh God, yes. Just the two days a week, but it saves my sanity.'

'I did rather like Matt myself,' said Anna thoughtfully, 'tough, clever, and very sexy of course—'

'Yes. All the reasons I fell in love with him. Oh dear. But I shouldn't have married him. We're too different. Or – maybe we're too alike. I

564

don't know. Our views of the world are certainly very different.'

And then she suddenly burst into tears. 'I'm sorry. I just feel so – so hopeless about everything. And so ashamed of myself. Oh, not so much sleeping with Rob, well not really—'

'What are you ashamed of, then?'

'Oh – I've just been horrible to Matt, made him hate me, and he really didn't deserve it, and we used to love each other so much, and it's all my fault, or mostly, I've just—'

'Darling, some of it was your fault, of course, and some of it was his. It's called marriage. You mustn't berate yourself so much, it won't do you any good. Now do let's talk about jollier things. Like your work, that's always interested me. It's Jeremy's agency, isn't it, I hope that doesn't have any unsuitable implications.'

'God, no. We really are just friends. Best friends probably—'

'Dangerous to be best friends with a man,' said Anna briskly, 'in my experience anyway. Unless he's a fairy, of course.'

It was true, Eliza, thought, returning home feeling a great deal happier. Work did keep her sane. Not just because it was fun, but because it was so absorbing. She walked in through the great revolving doors in the mornings and into the agency foyer, a different person, with the old familiar happiness at suddenly knowing what she was doing, completely committed.

Of course everyone had heard about her and Rob, it was too good a story for him to keep to himself although Hugh, who had clearly been rather shocked, had told him he had to; anyway she'd had to run the gauntlet at the agency, been petrified the first time she'd gone in afterwards, but apart from a couple of the account people, no one had seemed especially interested; she'd been teased a bit but it was so much the sort of thing that went on all the time, especially on sessions, and everyone knew what a stud Rob Brigstocke was, laying everything that could lie down, as one of the innumerable models he had slept with had memorably put it, and indeed among the girls at the agency Eliza found she was an object of surprise and admiration, rather than opprobrium.

'I suppose it's because they see me as an old married has-been,' she said to Maddy, as she sat among the multi-coloured mountain in Maddy's stockroom that was her autumn collection.

'Yes, well, you are,' said Maddy with a grin. Eliza grinned back. It was so lovely to have Maddy back in her life; with the best will in the world they had drifted apart, nothing in common, nothing to say to one another. How odd it was, Eliza thought, that her best friend for years had not been another person in the fashion business, obsessed with colour and style and trends, but an impoverished mother living in a squalid flat whose knowledge of the fashion business began and ended with whether her coat would last another winter. Well, that was what motherhood did, forging its own unbreakable bonds; she missed Heather horribly still.

'The agency have asked me to set up a series of lunches,' she said now, 'key people in the fashion business, so the creative people and even some of the clients can meet them. Will you come to the first one? It's in the boardroom, in three weeks' time. I'm a bit nervous and it would be lovely to have you there.'

'Of course, I'd be honoured,' said Maddy, 'who else is coming?'

'Oh, Jean Muir. Bill Gibb. Darling John Bates. Should be fun.'

'It sounds wonderful,' said Maddy, 'thank you.'

'I hear they're briefing Toby Gilmour,' said Ivor Lewis.

'Is he a barrister?'

'Yes. And – not a lot to worry about there, I'd say. He's a junior. I suppose they're fighting shy of the big boys, too expensive. Oh, he's clever all right, very old school, bit arrogant, but – nothing like we've got. Bruce Hayward – that's our man – will hang him out to dry.'

'Good,' said Matt. Wondering why he felt just a stab of unease. And stifling it.

'Now look. I've been thinking. We need to go quite hard on her lifestyle. These advertising agencies, from what I've heard, very sex and drugs and rock and roll. Do you think there was anything like that going on there?'

'Probably.'

'Right. Well, we need to get someone as a witness, someone she works with. Can you suggest anyone?'

'Not really,' said Matt shortly. 'I tried not to get involved.'

He had a sudden sharp memory of Eliza sitting at supper, and trying to interest him in her new job, her face alive as it hadn't been for a long time; it had made him so angry, hurt him so much.

'Right,' said Ivor Lewis, 'I think we try to find a witness. All right with you?'

'Absolutely,' said Matt. 'Yeah. Whatever it takes.'

The sense of unease was still with him. Buzzing round his head like a fly. It wouldn't go away.

'Matt, I need to talk to you.'

It was Scarlett; she had her determined voice on. He knew that voice and what it meant; had done since the second week at primary school when she'd told him he must stand up to the bullies, otherwise there was nothing she could do.

'Scarlett, I was just going home.'

'Well, stop off here on the way. It's important.'

He knew better than to argue. 'OK, but I can't be long.'

'It won't take long.'

She was waiting for him with a bottle of his favourite whiskey – Irish variety – on the coffee table; whatever it was, she clearly thought he needed softening up. Or something.

'Just a small one,' he said, 'something tells me I need to keep a clear head.'

She shrugged.

'So – what is it, Scarlett? What do you want?'

'Matt—' She hesitated, then reached for a cigarette, offered him one; he saw her hand shake slightly as she flicked her lighter on. She was clearly nervous: interesting.

'Matt, I – I want you to drop this divorce and this whole case. Or at least think about it, very hard.'

'What!' He wouldn't have anticipated that, from her of all people; he pulled on his cigarette, inhaled hard.

'Yes. Please, Matt. It's not too late.'

'It's far too late.'

'No, it isn't. Just think about it, at least.'

'Scarlett, you really don't know what you're talking about.'

'I do. I really do. Look, I've seen divorce, don't forget. Very first hand. With David. The ugliness, the way it distorts and destroys whatever is left.'

'Nothing's left, Scarlett.' He sighed and leaned forward, poured himself another glass of whiskey.

'Yes, it is. Oh, it probably is too late to save the marriage. I can see that. Although I suspect a part of you still must love Eliza. You adored her, all those years. I'll never forget your wedding day, ever, how you looked at her when the registrar said you were man and wife.'

'Scarlett—'

'Just – please, Matt – just think, really hard. You'll make everyone so unhappy. Including Emmie. And everything you've had with Eliza, every good thing, and there has been so much good, you know there has, along with the bad, it will all be wiped out and – and made ugly and horrible. And Emmie will have to live with that, if you go down this road.'

'Scarlett,' he said, his voice very quiet, 'it is too late. We've both changed, so much. Said and done the most dreadful things to one another . . . we can't go back now. Can't salvage it.'

'Even for Emmie?'

'It's for Emmie I'm doing all this, as you know perfectly well.'

'Matt! You're not doing it for Emmie, you're doing it for yourself, for that bloody great ego of yours.'

'That's an unbelievably filthy thing to say. Jesus, I can't believe this. I was going to ask you if you'd speak up for me in court, I can see there's no future in that one—'

'No, there isn't. I couldn't.'

'Great. Well, nothing like kicking a man when he's down. Thanks for nothing. I can't believe you've come up with all this claptrap.'

She struggled to keep calm.

'Matt,' she said, very quietly. 'All right, divorce Eliza, if you must. But – this custody thing, it's so awful, it has to hurt Emmie, much, much, more than the divorce, can't you find some way round that?'

'Of course not,' he said, and he sounded genuinely astonished. 'I told you, it needs to be settled, we have to sort something out.'

'Yes, of course you do, but in this way? This hideous, public, mud-slinging way? With every sordid detail thrashed out in court, possibly reported in the papers—'

'Of course it won't be reported in the papers!'

'I wouldn't be too sure about that. Exactly the sort of thing people like reading about over their cornflakes, two high-profile self-centred adults fighting over an innocent little girl. A very intelligent little girl, moreover, who loves both of you so much. It will be horrible for her, vile.'

'It will not be horrible for her,' he said, 'she won't know about it, not the bad stuff, you don't know what you're fucking talking about, Scarlett—'

'Please don't swear at me.'

'I'll swear if I want to, you brought this up and it's fucking outrageous, it's nothing to do with you, nothing whatsoever—'

'Yes it is,' she said, 'it is to do with me, because I care about Emmie—'

'And I don't, I suppose?'

'Not as much as you say you do, no, I just don't understand how you can be putting her through this. She's a little girl, she's the completely innocent party, that's the phrase isn't it, and you're just making her a pawn in this hideous game of revenge you're playing—'

'It is not revenge,' he said and his voice was icily, terrifyingly calm, 'I want her to be safe, I want to see that she's properly looked after and safe—'

'No! You don't! You want to win her, and win this horrible fight, and you know something, Matt, win or lose you've lost anyway, because you're ruining her life for her. Doesn't matter about yours, doesn't matter about Eliza's, but it does matter about Emmie's—'

'You are totally out of order,' he said, standing up, 'and I'm going.'

'Good. And don't come back.'

Matt drove rather carefully home. He'd had at least one too many whiskeys; when he got there, it was late. The house was in darkness, apart from a light in the study.

He went in very quietly, opened the door; Eliza was asleep, on the sofa with the TV still on. She was wearing jeans and a T-shirt; her face in repose looked younger, more vulnerable. He stood looking down at her, and it hurt, even that, seeing her as she had been, when they were happy. Happy and hopeful. He had removed all the pictures of her from his desk, for the same reason. He just couldn't bear to look at the past. At the happiness.

She woke up suddenly, and saw him, and just for a moment, she stayed there, held in what had been, her eyes soft, pleased to see him. And then she was back, back in the present, and so was he; and she turned away from him, picking up her coffee cup, standing up, walking to the door, brushing past him.

'You all right?' he said, and then, 'how's Emmie?'

'We're both fine,' she said. 'Please excuse me. I want to go up to bed.'

'Fine. But at some point, we have to have a conversation about Summercourt. You'll remember the terms of the trust no doubt—'

'Yes, of course I do.'

'I wonder if it will be possible for you to pay me your share of the value, which would now be something in the region of twenty-five thousand pounds.'

'Matt, you know perfectly well I couldn't do that. I couldn't give you five thousand. Or five pounds, probably.'

'Right. Well in that case, I shall have to buy your share. When the divorce is final.'

'I will never let you do that,' she said, 'never.'

'I shall go to court and get an order for sale and I shall win.'

'Matt, you can't do that, take Summercourt away from me, it's not yours, it belongs to our family.'

'Well, unfortunately your family was unable to afford it. Oh, don't worry, your mother wouldn't be homeless. I'm very fond of her, as you know. I'd buy her a nice little cottage nearby. So that she could stay in touch with her friends. But I'm very seriously considering selling the place.'

'Selling it!!'

'Yes, I don't think I want it any more. I bought it for – for—' He stopped. Looked at her. And the years rolled away, just for a moment, and they were both back there, back at that day, laughing over the sky-blue-pink door and the modern windows, and her realisation that he had bought it for her, and she remembered kissing him in the lawyers' boardroom and telling him she loved him. And they remembered too, each knowing the other was remembering, the night in the orangery when he had taken formal possession of the house – and of her. And they stared at one another quite shocked at the vividness and the happiness of that memory: and then it was gone and the bitterness and the anger and the power games were back.

'Well, it's worth a lot, and—'

'Matt, you've got so much money—'

'Not quite as much as I did have. Times are becoming harder in my business. In every business, you should read the papers occasionally, it's all to do with the price of oil. And anyway, I always really rather fancied Surrey, so much more convenient and easy to get to on Friday nights . . .'

'Matt, you couldn't,' she said and her voice was little more than a whisper, 'you couldn't sell Summercourt, even to hurt me.'

He said nothing; she sighed heavily and stood up.

'I'm going up to bed,' she said, 'I've had enough.'

He watched her as she went up the stairs, a skinny, almost childish figure, and that was like the past again too, and he closed his eyes against the pain and sat down in the study, on the sofa where she had been, and fought down the grief.

Scarlett was wrong; he didn't still love Eliza. And nor did she love him. The love they had felt for one another, so strong, so joyful, so good, was gone, it had died; they had killed it between them, and it had become a still, cold thing, quite lifeless, with no shreds of warmth or happiness left, and there was no hope for it, no hope of bringing it back, of reviving it, and all they had left of it were memories, and they were not enough.

And the pity of it, the dreadful sadness overwhelmed him entirely, and he sat there, not even weeping, just filled with a terrible remorse for what he had done not only to Eliza, but to himself as well, remorse and shame and an equally terrible bitterness for what she had done to herself and him.

All that he had left now was Emmie; and with every day he became determined to keep her.

'Eliza Shaw, Toby Gilmour.'

'How do you do?' said Eliza.

She had been wondering, to the exclusion of almost everything else, what he would be like, this person who would quite possibly hold her future, and indeed Emmie's future, in his hands. A person of infinite importance to her. Her initial impression was not overwhelmingly good: primarily of someone who was not going to be very sympathetic. But then – was she looking for sympathy? Probably not.

'How do you do,' said Toby Gilmour. His voice was at once clipped and quite deep; it would be liable to sound impatient, that voice, she thought.

He was tall and dark and extremely slim, with brilliant dark eyes, and heavy dark eyebrows, and a smile that came and went so fleetingly that it would have been easy to miss it. She would have put his age at early forties.

He was dressed very well, she noticed – was she ever going to stop thinking clothes mattered so much? – in a beautifully tailored dark grey suit, a slightly surprising pink-and-white striped shirt, and even more surprisingly, Gucci loafers rather than the obligatory lace-ups. Clearly he too thought clothes mattered. Absurdly that seemed a point in his favour.

'Coffee?' asked Philip Gordon.

'Yes, please,' said Toby Gilmour.

His voice was very nice actually, she decided. A bit like Jeremy's but heavier. A sort of actor-y voice. Well, barristers were supposed to be actors manqué.

They sat down at Philip Gordon's low table and Toby Gilmour started immediately spreading notes and papers across it, not waiting for any further niceties; he had good hands, she noticed then, and on his wrist was a very beautiful, classic gold Cartier watch, the sort of watch she most liked, clearly decades old, and the cuffs of his shirt were fastened with heavy gold, plain cufflinks.

'That would be lovely,' said Eliza.

'Right. All well with you, Toby?'

'Yes, yes, fine, thank you. Busy, of course. Tristram keeps us up to the mark. But that's good.'

'Indeed,' said Philip and then, turning to Eliza, 'Tristram Selbourne is the senior QC in Mr Gilmour's chambers.'

'Oh,' said Eliza, 'oh yes, I see.' For God's sake, she thought, say something half intelligent, you sound completely witless. And managed, 'What a wonderful name.'

'Yes, isn't it? It's said if it hadn't been his real name he would have made it up,' said Toby Gilmour.

'Yours isn't too bad,' said Eliza, surprising herself. 'For a barrister, I mean.'

'Well – that's good to know,' said Gilmour briskly, with one of his fleeting smiles; she felt immediately silly. 'Now, if we could just review your case so far—'

Concentrate, Eliza, for heaven's sake, concentrate. This is your future at stake, not a party. And he was obviously not keen on small talk . . .

'So I think that's about the size of it,' said Philip Gordon, 'any questions for us, Toby?'

'A few, yes. Do we have a date for the preliminary hearing?'

'I got it just this morning. I haven't had time to tell you yet, Eliza. A fortnight's time. I checked with your clerk, Toby, and you're free. Eliza, all right with you? Your husband can make it.'

'Oh – yes, of course. It will have to be, won't it?'

'Not absolutely essential, but wise,' said Toby Gilmour briskly. He managed another fleeting smile. 'Now, Mrs Shaw—'

'Please call me Eliza. Mrs Shaw makes me feel old.'

'Eliza then. Now, you're not defending your adultery, I see.'

'No.'

'Probably wise, under the circumstances. And that makes the custody case at least a little more clear-cut. Now your witnesses – you have, let's see – well, your mother, not too good, I mean, forgive me, I'm sure she's a delightful woman—'

'She is actually, yes,' said Eliza defensively.

'I'm sorry. I was going on to say that a mother is not an ideal defence witness. As you must see. A tendency towards bias.'

'Well – yes.'

'Now, your friend Mariella Crespi. Tell me about her. What does she do?'

'She lives in Milan. She's married to a very rich man, she – she doesn't do a lot, she's a sort of – of society lady, she just hit the best-dressed list.' She stopped. Aware that Mariella didn't sound hugely impressive. 'I've known her for a long time though,' she said lamely, 'and she knows everything that really took place in Milan, how I was looking after Emmie properly, how she was never left with strangers, not the pack of lies my husband claims.'

'And she'd come over here for the case?'

'Oh yes, of course. I've asked her.'

'Good. Then there's your nanny, Miss Grant.'

'Yes.'

'Is she quite articulate?'

'Yes,' said Eliza, irritated by this slur at the nanny class. 'Very.'

'Well, they aren't always. Now Mr Gordon has a couple of medical people, your gynaecologist and a psychotherapist, both with queries against them. Have you spoken to them?'

'My gynaecologist has agreed.'

'And the psychotherapist?'

'I've decided I don't want to call her,' said Eliza.

'Really? Any reason why not?'

'I – I just don't want to. I – I told her a lot of things I – well, I'd be embarrassed about, really very – very personal stuff.'

'Mrs Shaw – Eliza.' The dark eyes were expressionless as he looked at her. 'This whole thing is going to get very personal. I think you have to be prepared for it. It's a dirty business, what you're getting into—'

'I didn't get into it,' said Eliza quickly, 'it's all Matt's – my husband's choosing.'

'Of course. But – but I would like you to reconsider calling your psychotherapist, Mrs Miller, isn't it? I think it might be of great benefit to your case—'

'I really don't want to,' said Eliza flatly.

'Well, we can come back to her if needs be,' he said. 'Anyone else?'

'I'm hoping to get a couple of friends, mothers from Emmie's school, to vouch for me, say I'm a good mother. But—' She stopped.

'I can imagine. They're perfectly happy until you tell them they'll have to appear in court. Then they panic.'

'Yes. I did have one friend, who I know would have done it, spoken up for me, she knew me right through the whole awful thing with the baby—'

'But?'

'I've lost touch with her,' said Eliza, realising how feeble this sounded.

Her one really good friend. So good that she had no idea where she lived or what her phone number was . . .

'You could try and find her.'

'Yes. Yes of course.' She was beginning to feel very defensive.

'What about your colleagues at work?'

'Well – Jeremy Northcott, he's the boss of my agency, very establishment, he would speak for me I know, we've known each other forever, since I was – well, since I was very young. In fact at one point I nearly became engaged to him. Only I'd met Matt—' She stopped. 'Is that bad or good?'

'Clearly, it was bad for Mr Northcott,' said Philip Gordon, in an attempt to lighten the atmosphere.

'No, I meant him being a witness. Bit biased, that sort of thing. Like my mother. Anyway, he was in Milan as well, he helped me get back to Emmie after the fog, so that would be another person in my favour—'

'Well, we can consider him. Any others? At the agency?'

'I'm afraid they're all a bit – a bit unreliable.'

'In what way exactly?'

'Well.' She flushed. 'You know, their lives are one long party, they—' She broke off. What if they asked Rob to be a witness, and it emerged that she smoked dope with him. God, was there no end to all this . . .

'Perhaps you could try to find someone who might be, shall we say, sober enough to speak up for you.' Toby Gilmour looked at her as if he was finding her rather unsatisfactory. She was being hopeless – as she seemed to be at everything these days. Then she remembered that she was the client, and therefore paying, and met his eyes very directly.

'I'm absolutely confident I can,' she said.

'Good.' He looked down at his notes, paused and said, 'Mrs Shaw,' he seemed to be having trouble with 'Eliza', 'forgive me for asking this, but was there ever any violence in your marriage?'

She had been waiting for this one for a long time. Wondering when someone would ask her.

'Yes,' she said, 'yes, there was.'

They looked at one another: just fleetingly. Then: 'Could you tell us about it?'

'Emotional violence, plenty of it. And verbal. Horrible rows, endless fights.'

There was a silence; then, 'Right,' said Toby Gilmour. 'Of course one would expect that. But nothing physical? That was all?'

'It was quite enough,' said Eliza. 'Believe me. Quite enough.'

There. She hadn't lied. She had told indeed nothing but the truth. Not the whole truth, perhaps. But it seemed to have worked. They appeared satisfied, nodded, made notes. She was glad to have done that. It was a sort of run-through if she was ever asked in court. Because she still couldn't bear to admit it. Not yet. Maybe, if it made all the difference between keeping Emmie and losing her. But not now, not yet . . . it was too horrible, too ugly . . . on both their parts, what she had said as well as what he had done . . .

'Very well,' said Toby Gilmour, after a few more questions. 'I think that's all for now. Thank you. I'll start preparing my brief, and Philip can fill in any blanks, I'm sure. Although I will almost certainly need to speak to you again. I have your number here.' He stabbed the top sheet of the pile of papers. 'And if not . . . See you in court, Mrs Shaw.' He didn't smile. He didn't look at all happy.

'Eliza,' said Philip after a long pause, 'what are your plans for lunch?'

'Oh,' she said, 'oh yes, lunch.' She had forgotten this was on the unwritten agenda.

'I – I don't think I can,' she said, quickly, very quickly. She really had had enough of Gilmour for now; he made her feel foolish, tongue-tied, completely uncool.

'Pity,' said Philip. 'Well – how about you, Toby, are you free?'

'Yes, I am as a matter of fact,' said Gilmour, 'that would be very nice. Thank you, Philip. Mrs Shaw – Eliza – I'll be in touch. Thank you for your time.'

'Oh – no,' she said, politely, 'thank you for yours,' thinking what an absurd thing to say, that, and what a lot of her money – or rather Anna's money – would be going to pay him for it.

'May I say,' he added, surprising her for she had thought the meeting quite over, 'your case is an interesting one also. I'm glad to have the opportunity of working on it.'

'Well, I'm pleased to hear that,' she said, and then before she could say or do anything still more ridiculous, grabbed her bag, said goodbye to Philip and walked out of the office. What a complete idiot he must think she was: a total, total idiot. And did she really want to work with him? Or were all barristers as abrasive as that?

'Well,' said Philip Gordon, as they heard the secretary say goodbye, heard the door of the outer office close, 'what do you think?'

'I – thought she was very attractive,' said Toby Gilmour, looking at Philip and smiling briefly, 'very intelligent as well. I liked her. I would say incidentally there probably was some violence. Which she's not prepared to admit. Perhaps further down the road . . . But – I would say this is far from an open-and-shut case. Yes, the child is only six, which will clearly count in Mrs Shaw's favour, but the adultery – very messy. And there's clearly some history of mental instability—'

'What, after the child that died? Surely—'

'If she won't call the shrink, her husband undoubtedly will, and I've heard he's got Bruce Hayward as his barrister. I don't need to tell you he's savage in cross-examination. I'll have to look into it all much more thoroughly of course but – well, I hate to say this, and I'd love to handle it myself, but I think you should at least consider briefing Selbourne. She's going to need some very strong advocacy – she's not going to be impressive in court, there are too many areas she's obviously nervous about – interestingly so – and more importantly, we don't want them to think we're a pushover, that our team is not properly heavyweight. I'm afraid that's what my advice would be.'

'Well,' said Philip Gordon, 'I appreciate your honesty. I'm glad you like her at least. So do I, very much. There's something very vulnerable about her. Let's go and have some lunch, shall we? I've booked a table at Simpsons. Pity she couldn't join us. But we'll be able to speak more freely at least.'

'Now Emmie, come on, we've got to go. Otherwise we won't get to Granny's till it's really late.'

'That's all right. She won't mind.'

'She might not, but then you'll be so late going to bed. And tired tomorrow. Too tired to ride Mouse.'

'I won't.'

'Well, you might. In fact, if you don't really hurry up now, I shall ring Gail and tell her not to have Mouse ready for you to ride until Sunday.'

'I can get Mouse ready myself.'

'No you can't. Emmie! Do what you're told. Or I shall get really cross.'

Emmie's eyes met her father's and recognised defeat.

'I'll just pack my shoes.'

'You've already got three pairs of shoes in there. You're as bad as your mother.'

'I want to bring my special shoes. My lost shoes.'

'Emmie, if they're lost how can you bring them, for heaven's sake?'

'No, they're not lost. I was lost when I bought them. In Milan.'

'What do you mean, you were lost?'

'I got lost,' said Emmie patiently, 'when Mummy went shopping. I was with stupid Anna-Maria.'

'Well, you weren't lost then.'

'Yes I was. I didn't want to stay with her. So I went shopping by myself.'

'You – you what?'

'I went to find some shoes. By myself. She was stupid, she was talking to her friend.'

'But – where was Mummy?'

'She was with Mariella. Shopping for herself.'

'Just a minute, Emmie.' Matt sat down on the small chair by Emmie's desk, his eyes fixed on hers. 'You went shopping alone in Milan? Without anyone with you?'

'Yes. It was fun.'

'And Mummy let you?'

'She didn't know. She was with Mariella.'

'So how long were you lost?'

'Oh – a long, long time. I went to the toy place first, and looked in there. Then I looked at some party frocks. They were so pretty, all frilly. And then I saw the shoes.'

'And you were all alone, all this time?'

'Yes. I tried some on, I liked lots of them. When Mummy came, I had two pairs on. One on one foot, one on another.'

'And was she – had she been looking for you?'

Emmie shrugged.

'Yes, I think so. She was very cross,' she added, tucking the shoes into her small case.

'I bet she was,' said Matt.

Chapter 59

'So – what are we going to do?'

Jeremy looked at Mariella across the vast expanse of his bed. She was lying quite naked, one arm flung out, the other tucked under her head; her hair was splayed out on the pillow. The beauty of her body had taken him almost by surprise; he had somehow expected a few small imperfections, but there were none. And – what it could do, that body! Strong, athletic, ingenious: he had been astounded by its power, its passion, its near-fury in the pursuit of pleasure. And had found himself taken into a new country altogether by it; a bewildering, intense place, that he had not, he realised, properly known before. And was this love, at last, he wondered, lying beside her after the first time, did love work this wonder whereby physical pleasure increased a hundredfold, where desire became sweeter, exploration more joyful and release quite astonishingly triumphant? He told her this, as they lay there, shocked into stillness; that he felt changed, filled with new emotions, opened himself to her as he had never thought to do; and she listened, tenderly quiet, not the same Mariella at all that he had known for years, but someone wiser, sweeter, less self-concerned. 'I will not ask you how you feel,' he said, 'if it was different for you, for I would be afraid of the answer, afraid it would be no.' And, 'Don't be afraid,' she said, her eyes huge with tenderness, 'but don't ask it, just the same. It is best unspoken, I think. Safer that way.'

That was when he asked her what they should do. And when she said she didn't know.

And when she left New York next day to go home to her husband there was nothing resolved between them whatsoever; and Jeremy, disturbed and subdued as he had never been in his life, walked round Central Park for hours, reflecting that this could not be just an affair, that he could never deceive Giovanni in so dreadful and shocking a way, but that life without Mariella was suddenly completely unthinkable.

Philip Gordon was becoming increasingly and most pleasurably involved in Eliza Shaw's divorce case. He loved this stage of the game; when you ran it like a roller coaster, preparing witnesses, taking statements, and there were good days when everything seemed to be going well and you were getting evidence and having ideas, and then there were the other days when it all seemed to be going wrong and a witness would come out against you and another would say they weren't prepared to appear in court, and the whole thing gathered momentum, and time raced and the adrenaline soared and for a while you managed to set aside the fact that lives were being shredded and saw it only as a quest for victory. Your victory.

'What we're going for is sole custody and care and control. He's looking therefore for day-to-day care and allowing the mother some access,' said Ivor Lewis. He was having lunch with Bruce Hayward, QC, the scourge of erring wives across the land. 'The mother is going for joint custody, but Mr Shaw feels that she isn't fit to share in any major decisions about the child's future and, quite apart from that, the inevitable conflict would simply be bad for the child.'

'Yes, yes, that's all very well,' said Hayward, 'I hope he's aware how difficult that's going to be. Is he really able to offer the child a home as good as the mother can? He's clearly very fully employed and from what you tell me of Mr Shaw he's hardly likely to stay at home and look after her. What sort of set-up can he offer? The child's not yet six, any judge will award care and control to the mother, unless she is proven grossly unfit. I mean, he'll have to employ a nanny and it's surely one of his beefs against the mother that she's going out to work and employing one, and that's only for two days a week. We need something a lot better than this if I'm even going to take the case on. He's living in cloud cuckoo land. Joint custody, best he can hope for, and not sure about anything else.'

'Ah,' said Ivor Lewis. 'Well, you're right on the face of it, of course—'

'What's that supposed to mean?'

Bruce Hayward was tired and he had a long afternoon in court approaching; he didn't like Ivor Lewis, thought he was a tiresome upstart, grammar-school boys never quite up the mark in his experience and—

'There seems quite a good chance of actually proving the mother grossly unfit.'

'Oh, really? What's she doing, running a brothel?'

'Not quite. But I've had Jim Dodds, you know him, best private eye in the business, doing a bit of work for me and there's quite a lot of gossip about her at the advertising agency.'

'Ah, well, that sounds rather more encouraging,' said Bruce Hayward, 'tell Dodds to carry on with the good work. We might talk to the receptionist and maybe this artist chap, see if we can get them as witnesses—'

'Art director,' said Lewis.

'Art director, artist, they're all the same, all in love with themselves, disappearing up their own orifices.'

'Indeed,' said Lewis. It seemed to him that this was a pretty fair description of Bruce Hayward's opinion of himself.

'Let's talk about your witnesses, shall we?' said Philip Gordon. 'We still haven't got nearly enough.'

'Sorry,' said Eliza with a sigh. 'I don't quite know what I'm supposed to be doing. Or rather what they're supposed to be doing.'

'Well, it goes like this. We need to present a nice three-dimensional picture of you. The good mother, who is devoted to her child and her welfare, and then the very talented lady who takes her work seriously, isn't just playing around, making a few bob and amusing herself. So – friends, relatives, work colleagues, anyone who can vouch for your good name. We have the lady in Milan, she's clearly very important, and your mother of course, but – not really enough.'

Eliza sat down and drew up a list. And while fretting over its shortness, suddenly had an inspiration and rang Jack Beckham.

That afternoon, leaving Maddy's workshop, she bumped into Jerome Blake.

'Lovely to see you here, how are you?'

'Oh – I'm fine. Yes, everything's really good, thank you.'

'Well, I know it's not,' said Jerome, giving her a kiss, 'and I'm sorry. But it's very nice to have you back in the real world. I hope KPD know how lucky they are.'

'I think it's me that's lucky,' said Eliza, 'but they're being very nice to me. Can't say any more than that.'

'So they should be. You know me and my camera are always at your disposal, don't you? I'd just love to work on that cosmetic account, you know the Japanese one, any hope of that, do you think?'

'There could be, yes. I'll talk to Rob about you. I have put your name to him several times. But – you know what he's like, he has his favourites, of course.'

'Yeah, yeah,' said Jerome with a grin, 'including you, we hear.'

'Jerome!' said Maddy. 'Don't be tactless.'

'Sorry. But what the hell, anyway, sauce for the goose and all that . . .'

'What do you mean?' asked Eliza curiously.

'Well – well, maybe I'm speaking out of turn, darling. But I assume the blonde's got quite a lot to do with all this?'

'What blonde?' said Eliza.

'A friend of mine,' said Eliza rather breathlessly on the phone to Philip Gordon, 'says he saw Matt getting into a taxi with a blonde girl, very late one night. Apparently they'd been in the same restaurant as him, and they were obviously very – very friendly, kissing and so on at the table, and then . . . What do we do, Philip, about that? Shall I say anything to him, or—'

'Absolutely not,' said Philip Gordon, 'I'll think about that one for twenty-four hours. It could be quite a nice little card for us to play, could affect his whiter than white image. Would your friend be a witness for us, do you think?'

'I – I don't know. I could ask him.'

'Of course, it's not exactly catching your husband in flagrante but it's still what would be deemed inappropriate behaviour.'

She felt very odd at the thought of Matt being with someone else. Which was totally absurd, of course, given her own behaviour, given how much she hated him. But – yes, she was jealous, she had realised, examining her feelings, even now, jealous, unbearably hurt, at the thought of him being physically – and worse, emotionally – close to someone else. He was her husband, her lover, what had he done to whoever it was, how had he talked to her: and especially as it had been before the real horror started.

'Anyway, yes, could be very useful,' Philip Gordon was saying. 'And – you're still all right for Friday, are you?'

'Yes. Yes, fine. Looking forward to it.'

She wasn't, of course. He was taking her to see Tristram Selbourne, the senior QC at Toby Gilmour's chambers. Philip had told her, very gently, that Toby felt she needed 'a very big gun indeed'. That had really upset her. Not just that Toby wouldn't be handling the case himself – obviously he didn't want to work with her – but that he felt her case was pretty hopeless. But it had to be done.

'My daughter's just told me,' said Matt to Ivor Lewis, his face dark with anger, 'that she got lost in Milan. She was left with some servant while my wife did her own shopping, and she just wandered off and the girl didn't realise. Mind clearly on other things. Emmie was wandering about the shops all alone for hours, in some bloody foreign city, she could have been kidnapped, anything could have happened to her, and nobody realised, as far as I can make out, for quite a long time.'

'Really?' said Ivor Lewis. 'Good God. If it's true, that will certainly help our case. It sounds appalling. Can you check it out? Make sure the child isn't making it up.'

'Of course it's not true. Well—' Eliza faced him across the room; she felt physically weak. Realising what she was really up against, the power of his rage and his hatred. It was horrible. 'I – that is – she did wander off, yes.'

'And you didn't even notice?'

'I was – I mean, I wasn't with her, it was while Anna-Maria was looking after her—'

'So how long did it take before you decided to interrupt your shopping and look for her?'

'Matt, this is so unfair. She went off in the care of the maid, with Anna-Maria, and we all arranged to meet in half an hour. Next thing I knew, there was Anna-Maria panicking—'

'Well, I'm glad somebody was. So Emmie was all alone in a foreign city, where nobody speaks English for – how long? Long enough to come to harm, that's for sure.'

'Matt, stop it.'

'You are disgusting, do you know that? Quite disgusting. Not fit to be a mother. Well, you can be sure you won't be for much longer—'

'I think it's time to consider marriage?'

'Marriage!'

'Yes. You know, nuptials, holy wedlock, that sort of thing. Or don't you? Don't look so surprised, we've been anticipating it, so to speak, for several weeks now.'

'Anticipating? Oh, is that what you call it?'

'It's what the Victorians called it. At least I believe it was the Victorians. Anyway, my dearest love, what would you say?'

'I would say yes,' said Scarlett, leaping out of the bed, 'yes yes yes yes. Oh yes.'

'Right.'

'But – don't you think it's a bit soon? I mean, we haven't known each other properly for very long, and—'

'Scarlett,' said Mark, 'tell me some of the things you love. Really love.'

'Oh, now let me see. Well, you.'

'Apart from me.'

'OK. Trisos.'

'Yes. Very good.'

'Fast cars.'

'Excellent.'

'Champagne.'

'Fine.'

'Um – eggs with Marmite soldiers dipped in them.'

'OK. That'll do. Getting a bit silly. Anyway, how long did it take you to decide you loved them?'

'No time at all. Instant love at first whatever.'

'Well, then. And have you changed your mind about any of them?'

'No.'

'Then I rest my case. Why should you change your mind about me?'

'It's a bit different,' said Scarlett, laughing.

'I don't see why. Love is love. It's about absolute emotional happiness. Which I believe we have found. Listen,' said Mark, and his grey eyes were very serious now, moving over her face with great tenderness, 'you are the heart of my life. I want you to be there always. Please say you will. Dear, dear love, say you will.'

'Oh, Mark,' said Scarlett, 'I do love the way you talk. So much. How could I live without that? Of course I will. Thank you.'

'And we will be married on Trisos, of course.'

'Of course.'

'In the autumn after the tourists have gone and before the bad weather arrives.'

'And after this wretched divorce of my brother's.'

'And my mother can write us an epithalamium.'

'What's that?'

'Wait and see.'

It was wonderfully odd to be so very, very happy.

Chapter 60

'Well, my dear, you are going to be very lucky not to lose this case. Very lucky indeed.'

Eliza, close to tears, stared at him: at Sir Tristram Selbourne QC, who she had been introduced to that day at Toby Gilmour's insistence; everyone had told her how marvellous he was, including her godmother who was clearly impressed – 'that ghastly old fruit with halitosis? Sheer genius, darling, if anyone can do it he can' – and she had walked to his chambers with Philip Gordon with hope in her heart.

It was a beautiful day, the sunlight slanting through the trees of New Square, in the heart of Lincoln's Inn, dancing off the brass door plates, with their lists of august names, Selbourne's included, people strolling slowly through it, engrossed in conversation, others rushing breathlessly past them, clutching files, and in more than one case, wigs – but only barristers' wigs, she noticed, none of the long variety belonging to judges, but then they had special lockers at the Law Courts to keep them in, or so Philip Gordon had told her – and God, she thought, looking at him, how absurd he would look in his wig, this odious man, with his red, self-satisfied face, his full, lisping lips, spraying saliva as he spoke – Sir Tristram Selbourne QC.

Toby Gilmour sat in on the interview, a slightly disturbing presence, his face an aloof blank as he looked at his master: how did he work under him, do what he bade him, follow his lead? Was it possible to be a gentle, courteous barrister, she wondered, or was the job description necessarily abrasive and arrogant?

But the hope had left her heart quite swiftly, as he sat talking to them, in a way that was at once patronising and self-satisfied, sitting at his desk in the lovely tall room, with its wooden shutters and stone fireplace and ceiling-high bookcases: a lot of tutting he did, and a lot of head-shaking and sighing as well, pushing pages of notes aside, reaching for books, flicking through pages, underlining passages, before finally sitting back and smiling at her and giving his verdict.

She had managed to stay calm, not to rise to the occasional bait: 'surely you must have been aware of the dangers of feeding information to the press . . . odd, to have a child brought to the office at the end of the day . . . of course you do realise, admitting adultery is all very well, and you don't seem to have an alternative, but it won't be considered responsible behaviour, you know . . .' and even, unforgivably, 'that must have been difficult for you, losing your baby.'

Not difficult, she had wanted to scream, but hideous, horrible, unbearable; yet she had managed to remain calm and say yes, it was very sad, very sad indeed.

'And would you say you became – shall we say – unstable at that point?'

'No,' she said, steadily, 'no, not unstable. Distressed, of course.'

'Distressed or distraught?'

'Sir Tristram, I was not distraught. But very, very unhappy. It would have been very odd, I'm sure you would agree, to have been otherwise.'

She heard Gilmour rustling papers at this point and turned to look at him; his brilliant dark eyes were fixed on her, and she thought she could read not exactly admiration in them but at least some slight degree of approval. For the first time, she felt she might grow to like him.

She stood out in the sunshine, when they had said their goodbyes to him and to Selbourne, breathing in the fresh, warm air, looking round the lovely square with its tall houses, all occupied by barristers and solicitors, its central paved garden, its lush trees, and feeling closer to despair than she had been since the whole dreadful business began.

'Shall we—' said Philip Gordon, indicating one of the seats in the centre of the square, and she said yes, and followed him and sank down rather feebly and managed to smile at him.

'You did awfully well,' he said.

'I did?'

'You did. Held your own, refused to give any ground. And he's on your side: imagine what he must be like across a courtroom—'

'Ye-es.'

'I wouldn't worry too much about what he said, that you might lose.'

'Really?'

'No, no, they all do that, it's to make themselves seem even more impressive when they win, this seemingly impossible case turned over by their oratory. If he will take the case, and if your – your funds will meet his very high charges, then you will certainly have the very best hope of winning.'

'Yes. Yes, I see,' said Eliza, and sat there, feeling the sun on her face, and thinking about Tristram Selbourne, snide, slithery, spluttering Tristram Selbourne fighting her case, her rather fragile case, but based as it was on such virtues as integrity and courage and love, and thinking then of Toby Gilmour and that flash of approval, and she suddenly heard herself saying quite clearly and firmly, 'You know, Philip I don't think I want him to take my case. Even if he is willing. I think I want Toby Gilmour to. In fact, I'm quite, quite sure.'

She returned home exhausted: after a long argument with Philip Gordon, during which he had told her that in all honesty he did agree with Gilmour that it was a very difficult case, that she had possibly not more than a fifty per cent chance of winning, but that, should she retain Tristram Selbourne, the odds would rise dramatically in her favour. She had said that while Philip undoubtedly had her best interests at heart, she could not contemplate being represented by him, that he would distort and destroy what little she did have to offer, and that funds were not actually a problem, indeed her godmother who was meeting her costs had been very enthusiastic about the possibility of Selbourne being her barrister but she wanted Toby Gilmour and that was all there was to it.

She went into the kitchen and made herself a cup of tea – Emmie was out at a party, as usual, what she would give for Emmie's social life! – and heard the phone ringing in the hall.

She went out and picked it up and said 'Hello?', afraid that it would be Philip Gordon with more arguments; but it wasn't, it was Toby Gilmour.

'I just rang,' he said, his voice, his quick, impatient voice making her nervous again, 'I just rang to say thank you. I hope you've made the right decision, and obviously I am pleased and flattered. And I will do my utmost for you, as I hope very much you know.'

'Yes,' she said, 'thank you.'

'But I do feel nonetheless that you should know it won't be easy.'

'I realise that. As Sir Tristram said, I would be lucky not to lose it.'

'Well, you see, there I would disagree with him. If you don't lose it, Mrs Shaw, luck will have very little to do with it. If you don't lose it, it will be because we, and I include you, will have done an extremely good job.'

'Oh – right. Yes. Well – I'm sure we will. Goodbye then, Mr Gilmour and thank you for ringing.'

He was a bit – odd. But really very, very nice.

Jeremy Northcott had led a charmed life. He had never known financial anxiety, professional failure, social apprehension, or even the mildest depression, for he had been blessed, along with all his other advantages, with a sunny and equable nature. He ran his life, both personal and professional, with considerable ease; he was endlessly clever with people, making the dull feel interesting and the interesting more so.

He was frequently heard to say that his main job in running one of the biggest and most succesful advertising agencies in the world was to keep everyone happy: and when people said there must be more to it than that, he would smile and tell them to try it.

'Not easy. Not easy at all. But fun.'

And indeed in a business where people were devious, greedy – for both fame and money – and self-regarding, it was not easy at all, but he managed to achieve it to a large extent. Under him people worked not only extraordinarily hard, but very happily so; they felt appreciated as well as rewarded, involved as well as ambitious.

Now for the first time, in falling in love with Mariella, he found himself at once happy in a way he had never known before, and yet lost, helpless and genuinely wretched; and for the first time also he could see no answer to it. Had it been simply an affair, a physical experience, he could have ended it; but it was not, for she had taken hold of his heart, and he of hers. And had her husband been harsh, disagreeable or in other ways unworthy of her, then he could perhaps have set thoughts of him aside; but Giovanni was charming, affectionate, a man in love himself and, besides that, a generous host and a good friend.

Therefore, it must end, this joyous, wonderful thing that he had found at long last in his life; he knew that, as surely as he knew anything, it could not continue, he could not continue to deceive a gentle, vulnerable old man, by depriving him, albeit without his knowledge, of the greatest of all his treasures.

And end it he would: and it had been agreed between them, while each of them lacking the will to do so – just yet.

'I am in London, just for a few hours, just a small, small meeting, and then no more . . .'

'I'm in Paris next week, for two days, let us meet, darling Mariella, one last time . . .'

'How can we not be in our lives together, when I love you so much?'

'How can I say goodbye to you for ever when it tears my heart out to say it for a few hours?'

'I love you, dear, dear Gentleman Jeremy.'

'I love you, my darling Signora Crespi.'

'Just one more time.'

'Just one last time.'

It was dreadful, awful, the pain. And the guilt. And the tantalising, shocking happiness.

It had to end. He had to end it.

'I've got some very good news, Matt,' said Ivor Lewis.

'What's that, then?'

'They've dropped Selbourne.'

'Really?'

'Yes. I imagine his fees were too high. They've gone for the junior. Toby Gilmour. Very bright, but none of Selbourne's substance. Obviously.'

'As you said before,' Why did he feel like this? Uneasy? Uncomfortable?

'So Hayward will slaughter him. Slaughter the lot of them. We'll win. It's a foregone conclusion.'

'Well – that's good. That's very good.'

'You OK, Matt?' Louise looked at him across the table.

'What? Oh – yes. Yes, fine.'

'You seem a bit – distracted.'

'Of course I'm bloody distracted. I've got a bid in on a ten-million-contract, and a divorce case starting in earnest on Friday.'

'Yes, OK. It's not my fault.'

'It's your fault you're here. I didn't suggest dinner.'

'Right. Well, in that case you're on your own. Enjoy it.'

Louise stood up, picked up her bag and stalked out of the restaurant. Matt looked after her, hesitated, then got up and followed her, caught up with her outside on the street.

'Louise! Don't be so bloody stupid. I was only – only—'

'Only being rude and arrogant and self-obsessed. So what's new. It gets very tedious, Matt. I was actually in need of a bit of a diversion myself. So I'm going home to watch *Emergency Ward Ten*. Much more interesting.' She raised her arm, hailed a taxi.

It pulled over and she leaned in. 'Paulton Square, please. Night, Matt. Have a good evening.'

He watched her go; she hadn't changed. Still the same stroppy, self-opinionated Louise, tough as all get out . . .

He walked back into the restaurant, sat down at the table, pulled his notes out of his briefcase; they stared back at him. They didn't seem to be making a lot of sense. And now he'd got this long evening on his own. He looked at his watch. It was only eight. He couldn't go home, Eliza had asked bloody Maddy over. Who wasn't just her friend, she was On the Other Side, in capital letters. Funny, how everyone was on one side or the other now. Like – well, he could hardly bear to think of the latest development on that one. And once it was over – then what? Then – the sides would be more rigidly drawn up than ever. It would never be over, actually. Never. They had thrown up this barrier and it was getting higher every day. It would never come down. It was like the Berlin Wall. With one side losing sight of the other.

He suddenly wanted to hang onto his side for as long as he could.

'Louise?'

'Go away, Matt. I'm busy. Washing my hair.'

'Oh, for fuck's sake. Listen – I'm – I'm sorry.'

'You're what?'

'I'm sorry.'

'I thought that was what you said. God, Matt. That's a first. How long have I known you?'

'Too long probably,' he said and he smiled into the phone. 'So could you – hold the shampooing? For half an hour? I could bring a bottle of wine.'

'I don't feel like wine. I could do with a cup of tea though. Yes, all right. Come on round. Oh, and could you bring a nice packet of biscuits? I'm hungry. Lemon puffs, perhaps, for old times' sake?'

'God give me strength,' he said. 'Look, tell you what, I'll make us an omelette.'

'I'll put the kettle on. Then it's over to you.'

Louise put the phone down and smiled at it. Then she patted it. Round to her. Most definitely.

He turned up looking wretched. 'Hello. I've got eggs and some French bread, and I will make the omelettes. But I'll need a drink.'

She poured him a whisky; he sank onto her new cream cord sofa, and nodded at it approvingly.

'Very nice. Heals?'

'Yes.' She'd forgotten how he cared about such things; it was so rare in a man.

'Oh, God,' he said, drained the glass in one go and put his head in his hands.

'Matt – look, I do want to help, but – what exactly is the matter with you? I mean, apart from the obvious one?'

'Sorry. I should have told you in the first place. I just got punched very hard below the belt by my own family.'

'Tell me now.'

'No, let's eat. Give me another whisky and I'll do it.'

He made the omelette; she took a bottle of wine out of the fridge.

'Let's have this, you can't eat an omelette with whisky.'

'I can eat anything with whisky. But – that does look nice. For a person who doesn't like it much, you do buy good wine. Shall I open it for you?'

'For Christ's sake, Matt, don't start treating me like a woman. I can actually turn a corkscrew. Now, tell me what the matter is. What've your family done?'

'Only my sister. She's turned traitor in a big way.'

'Really? I like Scarlett, she's great.'

'I thought so too. Anyway, she read me a filthy great lecture about how I was hurting Emmie, and told me it wasn't too late to stop the whole thing—'

'Ye-es—'

'Don't tell me you agree with her?'

'Well – I – do worry about Emmie, as a matter of fact. Quite a lot.'

'Oh, for Christ's sake,' he said.

'But – go on. I won't say any more. Yet.'

It had shocked and hurt him beyond anything when he heard: Scarlett was going into the witness box for Eliza, hell bent, as he saw it, on queering his pitch.

'I can't believe it. The disloyalty of it. I thought we were mates. We were mates. Always.'

'And – to help Emmie, you say?'

'Yes. She says Emmie will be better off with her mother than me, and she feels she's got to do what she can to help make it possible.'

She noticed he'd started calling Eliza that, rather than by her name; presumably to de-personalise her, make her easier to demonise.

'The thing is,' he said, 'apart from kicking me in the balls, she could have really helped my case. I need people to say I'm a good father, and the only one I've got doing that is Mum. Who you could say was hardly an ideal witness. Bit biased, you could say.'

'You could, I suppose.' She was silent for a bit; she looked at him. He was so thin, and horribly pale, and there was a lot of grey in his hair. She thought of the young Matt, so strong and tough and tenacious, and so sure of himself and where he was going, with his dark good looks and his cocky charm. How had this happened, how had he turned into this wretched, hollow-looking creature? And even though she knew a lot of it was down to his own folly and stubbornness, she felt her heart turn over with sympathy and – and, well, sympathy.

'I just need someone else,' he said, 'not even Dad will do it. And I can see why, I'm not stupid, I'm a man, as they're all so keen on telling me, and she's a little girl and I work all the hours God sends, and – but I'm going to change, Louise, I'm going to be home every night by six and I'm going to read her stories and not go out to dinners, and I've found this very good nanny, an older woman, highly qualified, much better than that Margaret creature, and in the school holidays, my mum's going to be there too, and I'm going to take a lot of time off—'

'Matt, can you really do that? Can you really cut your hours and never be away from home and—'

'Don't you bloody well start.'

'Sorry.'

'No one fucking believes me. No one. Except the lawyer and I pay him to.'

Louise was silent for a moment, then picked up her glass of wine, walked over to the window and looked out. And then she turned round and faced him and said that if he would like her to, if it would help, she would go into the witness box for him, and that she felt she knew enough of him for her words to count.

When he had gone, clearly as shocked and surprised as he was grateful, and as near to lost for words as she had ever seen him, she poured herself another glass of wine and sat down and thought for a long time about what she had done, and why she had made the offer. And to feel deeply thankful she had managed to keep her counsel, and not tell him, in the inevitably high emotion of the moment, why she had done it.

For how stupid that would have been, how crassly stupid, after fighting it down for years, all those long, heady, confrontational years, where she had followed him and argued with him, and admired him and hated him and beaten him at his own game and never, ever allowed herself to recognise how Louise the person felt about Matt the person, had put up a steely barrier indeed between herself and her feelings about him. For what good would have been served by doing otherwise? If ever a man had been in love with a woman Matt had been in love with Eliza. And it had only been then, that evening, moved beyond anything at his hurt and his resolve, and making what was really a rather reckless offer, for what did she know, really, about Matt's performance as a father, that she had finally been forced to admit to herself how much, actually, she loved him.

And she went back into the kitchen and sat down and poured herself a cup of the now-cold coffee and sat licking her finger and picking up the crumbs of Matt's French bread from his plate and eating them one by one. Which was probably about the closest to intimacy, she reflected, as they were ever going to get.

Chapter 61

'I've got some really good news – at last,' Eliza smiled almost proudly at Philip Gordon, 'on the witness front.'

'Good,' he said. Cautiously. She knew he was worried about her situation in this area.

'It's my friend, Heather. The one who moved away, one who really can vouch for me being a good mother. Well, I hope so. She's written to me.'

She still couldn't believe it; seeing her letter lying there, on the mat. She hadn't realised it was from her, of course, written as it was in a schoolgirl hand, and in a small, flimsy envelope, but once she had thumbed through what seemed some rather more impressive missives, invitations to fashion shows and parties and a letter from Emmie's school saying she was doing well and would be moving up into the third form in September, she tore the small envelope open. And stood there, reading it, saying 'Oh, my God' over and over again.

Dear Eliza

I am very sorry I haven't written before, but my life has been quite busy lately and I wasn't sure at first about writing at all. I have a little boy, called Bobby, he is so gorgeous, Coral loves him and isn't jealous at all. He is quite big and sleeps well and the birth was a complete doddle, he practically fell out and I nearly had him in mum-in-law's front room, wish I had, and spoilt her carpet for her. Anyway, we're not there any more, thank goodness, we've got a very nice council house, I can't believe it, with a garden, quite small, but big enough for Coral to play and have a swing. The waiting lists are much shorter out here, and with two children we went to the top.

I've been doing a lot of thinking, Eliza, and I feel bad about how I left things. I can see now, it wasn't your fault, just a chapter of accidents, and you wanted to help. It was difficult for a bit, but Alan has got over it now, as well as me, and you did us a favour in a way as we could say we'd been hounded out of that flat.

Coral still talks about Emmie and I often think of our happy times together and I just wanted to say if ever you were in this area, it would be lovely to see you. We've even got a phone. Alan doesn't like me using it, but this is the number, Watford 4694.

Love, Heather.

Eliza managed to find herself in the area the very next day, and she and Heather and Bobby went out for lunch in a café and Eliza begged her to come and speak up for her at the divorce.

'I just need you to say I was a good mother and loved Emmie and always looked after her well. Because we were friends for such a long time, and it was when she was little, and also at the time I had the baby, it would really mean something. Will you, Heather, please?'

'Oh, I don't know about that,' Heather said, 'it sounds very scary.'

'It might be,' said Eliza truthfully, 'but if you think that's scary, think what it's like for me, facing losing Emmie.'

'I can't believe he wants to do that to you,' said Heather. 'And to her for that matter, poor little thing. It's really shocking. How can he say all those things about you, they're just so untrue—'

'I know. Please, Heather, please! I think in the first instance' – God, she was beginning to talk like a lawyer herself – 'in the first place, a written statement from you would do. It might be all that we needed. Will you think about that, please?'

Heather said she would, but she'd have to ask Alan, and he might act up a bit; 'might think we'd be back in the papers.'

'Of course you wouldn't,' said Eliza, touching wood surreptitiously under the table; Philip Gordon had warned her that with Matt's high profile in the business world, and her own media-based career, it was a very real possibility.

'You said that last time,' said Heather with a grin. 'Don't worry, I'll do my best to talk him round. He's so pleased with himself, having a son, honestly, men are all the same – oh, sorry, Eliza, I'm sorry, what a stupid thing to say—'

'Heather, it's OK. I've kind of got other things to worry about now.'

'I know. Poor you. It does sound so awful. Anyway, Alan's much less grumpy these days, he's up for promotion next year and that plus the house, you should hear him going on about our spare bedroom and what sort of mower he's getting for the lawn. The lawn! It's a little bit of dead grass the size of our living room in Clapham.'

'Oh, Heather,' said Eliza, 'I do love you. It's so nice to be friends again.'

All this she announced to Philip Gordon, who was hugely delighted, and said he knew Toby Gilmour would also be very pleased.

'Yes, and also more good news: we know who the blonde is.'

'The blonde? Oh, the one in the restaurant?'

'Yes. She's called Georgina Barker, she's an ex-girlfriend of Matt's. Jerome, my photographer friend, recognised her from an article in the *Sunday Times* magazine, she runs a boutique in Kensington.'

'She could well be an important witness,' said Gordon. 'Very good, Eliza. The tide seems to be turning just a bit. In our favour.'

'Not before time,' said Eliza. 'I was beginning to feel like Queen Canute.'

Alan Connell, Heather's husband, said she wasn't to appear in court under any circumstances; but he did agree to her giving a written statement as long as he could approve it.

'Well, that's marvellous,' said Philip, at their final meeting before the hearing. 'I'll go along and see her next week, and invite him to sit in on the interview. How would that be?'

'Could I – could I come along?' asked Eliza.

'Possibly best not. Keep it professional,' said Gilmour.

'Oh – all right. But do you think it matters that the article – the one Matt was so angry about – was about her?'

'No, no. Why should it?'

'I feel everything matters at the moment,' said Eliza gloomily, 'you know, like I have to be careful not to pick my nose . . .'

'Oh, now that would be very serious,' said Toby Gilmour. 'In court at any rate.' He actually winked at her; it was the first time she had seen a side of him that was remotely humorous.

After the meeting, he escorted her out onto the street and offered to get her a taxi.

'I think I can do that for myself,' said Eliza, amused by this rather archaic chivalry.

An empty cab was moving towards them; she put two fingers to her mouth and gave an ear-piercing whistle. The taxi pulled in.

'That was rather good,' said Gilmour.

'I know. I learnt it when I was a fashion assistant. First rule of the job, being able to get a taxi at any given moment, even in Oxford Street in the rush hour. Where are you going, Mr Gilmour, can I give you a lift?'

She'd expected him to say no, but: 'I'm heading for Chelsea.'

'I'll drop you off.'

'Thank you. Very kind. So how are you feeling about the hearing tomorrow?' he asked, settling in beside her.

'Oh – fine. Not worried at all, obviously. I just think I might vomit every time I think about it.'

'I have to say, that would be worse, even worse, than picking your nose. Do try to make it outside the courtroom at least. In both cases.'

'OK.' She smiled at him. 'It's nice to joke about it, it makes me feel better.'

'I wasn't joking,' he said, and his face was totally serious. She stared at him; he stared implacably back. Then, 'Well, certainly the vomiting. You could pick your nose very discreetly if you really have to. No, seriously, how do you feel?'

'I just told you.'

'Well, better that way round. Cocky clients, not ideal. But honestly, tomorrow won't be anything much. No difficult questions even. We'll arrive, find out what court we're in and what judge and wait.'

'What, you've no idea? I thought—'

'No, 'fraid not. They very often get allotted the morning of the case. I'm going to a dinner tonight, you can sometimes find out on the grapevine, but I wouldn't bet on it. It does help to know if you've got some fusty old disciplinarian, or one of the new, quotes compassionate close quotes, ones. You can angle your presentation accordingly. But, again, less important than next time.'

'Won't it be the same one?'

''Fraid not. You might think that, but no. Anyway, then we sit and wait for a bit on some excruciatingly uncomfortable stone benches, and we see the other side sitting on theirs and nod politely.'

'Could we nod rudely?' she said, encouraged by his earlier hints of humanity.

'I'm not sure how you would nod rudely, I'll give it some thought tonight. But a frosty smile probably better, never goes amiss. In our profession developing the frosty smile is one of the first things we learn, bit like your taxi whistle.'

'OK.' She was liking him increasingly.

'Then we all go in. It's a court like one you've seen a hundred times on TV. The judge up on the bench. Us all ranged below him, gazing up respectfully. No wonder they enjoy their jobs so much. And then they will present their case, say what it's about, that it's an uncontested divorce and an application for custody, and present the relevant papers, we'll do the same, both sides will say that they have several witnesses to call and the judge will harrumph about for a bit, and then say right, well, six witnesses each, so that's going to take a bit of time and then we need to have time for the law—'

'What does that mean? I thought this was the law?'

'It means legal arguments, a sort of recitation of the whys and wherefores, and then of course, they allow time for the summing up, that can take a while in a case like this, and the judge might say he would want to talk to the child—'

'WHAT!' Eliza's voice was almost a scream. 'Emmie in court! No, no, surely, surely not, no one mentioned that.'

'Well, yes, it is a possibility. But don't worry, not in the witness box, he would talk to her in a side room, I thought you realised that.'

'No. No, I didn't. How absolutely horrible – I—'

'I'm sorry. It's not absolutely a foregone conclusion, in fact sometimes when it's an open-and-shut case, he won't.'

'But this isn't. Hopefully. Oh, God. This gets worse and worse. Do you think Matt knows this?'

'I don't know. I would have thought so, yes.'

'He's kept that to himself.' She was silent, fighting back the tears, picturing the scene, tiny Emmie confronted by the judge, in his long wig; then she suddenly giggled.

'What?' said Gilmour, smiling.

'I was imagining Emmie cross-examining the judge back. Which she probably might. Sorry. Not funny.'

'I'm sure it would be,' he said, politely brisk. He obviously found it beyond his imagination. And probably considered it inappropriate as well.

'I'm sorry,' said Eliza, pulling out a tissue and wiping her eyes. 'I didn't mean to be flippant about it. But – it was such a shock. It's all such a shock. Every day seems to bring a new one.'

'Yes, of course,' he said rather abruptly, and just as she had decided not to say any more, that she was back in her idiot role in his eyes, he added, 'It's all very difficult and distressing. Of course it is.'

'Yes,' she said and then, encouraged by this flash of humanity, 'All this – this pulling apart your marriage, the way you used to feel for someone, and then dragging up bits of evidence—'

'I know,' said Toby Gilmour, surprising her. 'Everyone finds it so.'

'Of course to you, it's all in the day's work—'

'To a degree, yes. But not entirely,' he said and then, his voice at its most impatient, 'I do know something of what you're going through. I was divorced myself two years ago. I can remember every ugly moment.'

'I'm sorry.'

Eliza looked at him; he was staring out of the taxi window, his face bleak.

'Did – do you have children?' she asked.

'No. Thank God. I can see how much worse that makes it. Anyway, I really shouldn't be talking like this. Very unprofessional. Old Selbourne, he's been divorced three times.'

'I'm surprised.'

'Why?'

'Well, that anyone would marry him in the first place. Oh, dear, that was very impertinent of me. Sorry.'

'That's all right,' he said, but he didn't smile. She had obviously offended him, overstepped the mark, when he had been trying to make her feel better; after all, Selbourne was his boss.

'I'm sorry,' she said again.

'It's all right. Please don't apologise.'

The cab had slowed down: 'What number, guv?'

'Oh, that block there. Yes. Thank you. Goodnight to you, Mrs Shaw – Eliza, I'm sorry, I keep forgetting. I'll see you in court.'

He got out, his face blank and aloof. She looked at him, thinking she had blown it totally now. He must think her . . .

He suddenly leaned into the cab and smiled. 'Try very hard not to' – he's going to tell me not to worry about it, she thought, and I shall scream – 'pick your nose please. Until we're outside again.'

And he was gone, up the steps and through the doors of one of the redbrick mansion blocks in Lower Sloane Street; she sat looking after him, trying to sort out how she felt about him, whether she liked him or whether she didn't. God knows how he must view her from his lofty, brilliant barrister position. A dimwit fashion stylist, going through a messy divorce; her only discernible talent wolf-whistling . . .

Toby Gilmour closed the door on his flat and leaned back against it, smiling. She really was rather lovely. Very attractive. And funny. And engagingly self-deprecating. Which was odd, because from all accounts she was a brilliantly successful fashion editor. Well, that was the divorce effect. He should know.

'I'll just say no, I won't be a witness,' said Gina. She confronted Matt's rage calmly. 'You can, you know. Refuse. Unless the judge thinks there's a real reason to call you. And why should he? He'll probably ask you what our relationship is about and you can tell him the boring, unbelievable truth. You'll be under oath, so they'll have to believe you. Oh, God.'

'What?'

'Four more weeks or whatever without any nookie. It's getting very tedious.'

'Oh, for Christ's sake,' said Matt.

Sometimes she really wondered if it was going to be worth it.

'Matt!'

It was late; he'd been out, with a client, he said. She wondered if it had been Gina. She hadn't even confronted him with that one. The solicitors had, and that was all that was necessary. She really, really didn't care.

'Yes?' he said, walking into the study.

'We have to talk about Emmie. I didn't realise until today that the judge might want to question her.'

'Then your solicitor has been very remiss. He should have warned you of that.'

'Warned me! You talk as if it was my fault, the whole awful thing—'

'Isn't it?'

'No,' she said: and then, her voice rising, 'No, no, no, it isn't. It's yours, your idea to do this, to take her away from me – or from you – to force her to live with one or other of us, growing up confused, torn in half, not sure who she's supposed to love, who can tell her what to do, how to behave—'

'That will be me,' he said, 'make no mistake about that.'

She bit back any retort. This was too important. 'Well, but Matt, don't you think we ought to prepare her? Poor little girl has no idea what's happening, or rather what's about to happen, surely if you love her so much you ought to face that fact, and we ought to talk to her, together, tell her, talk to her about it—'

There was a long silence; then he looked at her, and his face wasn't harsh or hostile any more, it was exhausted and infinitely sad and he said, 'Yes. Yes, you're right, of course we should.'

'Mariella, my darling, darling love, thank you for all of it. It's been so lovely. So very, very lovely.'

'Jeremy, *carissimo*, I love you so, so much. Can't we – maybe – just a little while longer, next week I am in Rome, we could have one last wonderful meeting there, and then—'

'No, Mariella. No, we can't. We agreed, you know we did, we promised one another and – and Giovanni, I suppose, although he doesn't know it, and we have to keep that promise. It's the only thing to do, we can't go on like this, it's so . . .'

'Yes, yes, I know. You are so, so good. So much more good than me.'

She sighed, a huge, heavy, tear-filled sigh; they were lying in bed in Jeremy's apartment, had been there for what they had promised one another would be the last time, and now that the dawn was working its way most insistently into the room, the harsh, unforgiving dawn that would part them, they shrank from the task ahead.

'It was the nightingale and not the lark,' said Jeremy suddenly, reaching out, tangling a great lock of her hair round his fingers, raising it to his lips and—

'What? I did not hear anything.'

'Shakespeare, darling one, Shakespeare, Romeo and Juliet. Like us, they had to part at dawn, like us they dreaded it, denied it had really come. Oh, Mariella.'

'Oh, Jeremy.'

She turned to him, clung to him, weeping; he could feel her sobs, feel them in his own body, how could they do this, it was cruel, so cruel. How could they bear it, how could he bear it, so little happiness together, so much pain to come.

'I go now,' she said suddenly, and sat up, turned her back on him and went into the bathroom; appearing again, in a few moments, pale and tearstained, looking as he could never have imagined her, un-chic, tousle-haired, dressed in jeans and a T-shirt, her face stony, her eyes hard with resolve.

'I will not kiss you, or we will be here forever. I love you, I love you, dear Gentleman Jeremy, and – and goodbye. Thank you for loving me.'

And she was gone, swiftly, shutting the bedroom door after her, not even looking back; and he heard the front door slam, and she was gone, out of his flat, out of his bed, out of his life, and he turned back into the bed, and buried his face in the sheets that still bore her perfume and her imprint and the sweet, raw smell of sex with her, and he saw a hair, a long dark hair, and realised it was all he had left of her, and buried his face into his pillow and wept as he had not done since he was a small, small boy, shuddering, desperate sobs; and thought how hard it was, this grief, born as it had been from sheer joy, the joy hardly out of its infancy, that there could be no comfort for it from anyone, for who, knowing the circum-stances, would think they had any right to it? And yet it was as harsh and as cruel as one born of bereavement, perhaps harsher in its own way, for they were without one another, longing for and needing one another, while knowing with the touch of a phone, a scribble on a page, they could be together again. And yet could not.

And then finally, exhausted, he got up and showered and dressed in one of his hundreds of beautiful shirts and one of his dozens of beautiful suits and drank a strong cup of coffee and walked all the way to Carlos Place, blind and deaf to everything, and pushed through the doors of the agency which was still blessedly empty and went up to his office and stood staring at it as if he had never seen it before.

And then the day began, and he went through it, a smiling, charming automaton, so filled with grief and loneliness he had no real idea what he was doing; and no one, no one at all, could have begun to guess the depth of his misery and how his life seemed utterly devoid of any kind of purpose whatsoever.

Chapter 62

It was over. That bit at least. The whole thing seemed like a dream now, walking with Philip Gordon into that vast Victorian Gothic building with its great wrought-iron gates that she had seen a hundred times, on the news and in corny old films. She followed Philip and his pretty, posh assistant, Sarah, into the huge cathedral-like atrium, with alcoves on either side where people huddled, having clearly urgent conferences, and barristers berobed and bewigged strode about looking important. Nobody seemed to be smiling. Rather curiously, large glass cases contained life-size models of judges and Lord Chief Justices down the centuries, dressed in the requisite wigs and robes. It was all totally – what? Terrifying. That was about it.

A glass-fronted, double-sided noticeboard stood just inside the cathedral entrance, with details of the day's cases; and there it was, pinned up, Court number 31, Mr Justice Harris, Shaw vs Shaw. That was her; and how had that happened, that her marriage, her really rather amazing marriage, entered into with such happiness and love and hope, had become Shaw vs Shaw and sent into Court number 31 to be dismembered by Mr Justice Harris? She felt her eyes fill – God, she must stop weeping all the time, it was pathetic – brushed the tears impatiently away, got out a hanky and heard a crisp voice, 'No bogies, please!' and there was Toby Gilmour, not quite smiling, looking oddly older and more important in his gown and his wig.

'All right?' he said and she nodded and managed to smile. 'Good. We're lucky in Harris, nice old chap, quite benign. Pity we won't have him next time. He'd be ideal. Still – you OK?'

She nodded.

'Good. The others are here, upstairs already. We've got a bit of time, want to see round?'

She shook her head; it seemed a bleak suggestion.

She followed them up a large stone curving staircase – everything seemed to be stone or marble – which opened onto a wide balcony overlooking the huge, empty space; 'this is one of the few places you can actually have a meeting,' said Philip, 'you see people balancing enormous files containing millions of pounds' worth of information on windowsills or this balustrade; there's one windowsill if you get there early enough which is pole position, it's actually got a seat and somewhere to put your files, only we're too late. Which doesn't matter, because we don't need to have a meeting.'

He smiled at her and she managed to smile back; they were both being so nice, she thought, working so hard at cheering her up . . .

They seemed to know everyone; they were constantly stopping to say good morning to people and ask them how they were. Her main emotion, apart from terror, was a sort of astonishment at this strange new world she found herself in, so different from anything she had ever known, so cold and muffled and restrained, and she could have been in another country altogether; and yet outside, just beyond the gates, was Fleet Street, noisy, drunken, gossipy Fleet Street, one of the places she knew and loved best in the world.

They stood there for a while and then, 'Might as well go along,' said Toby Gilmour, 'my pupil is meeting us there,' and she followed them again down a long corridor with a vaulted ceiling and panelled walls, with doors leading into the individual courts. 'This is where the family courts are – and look, there are the rooms for the Lord Chief Justice – and oh, yes, there they are, outside Court 31, your husband and his cohorts.'

Her husband; again she thought, he's my husband but now he's also Shaw and I'm Shaw and we're versus one another and how and why . . .

'Morning,' said a rather large, bruteish-looking man to Philip, who smiled graciously and said, 'Good morning, Mr Lewis. You know Toby Gilmour, of course?'

'Yes, morning, good to see you.' He nodded to Eliza, held out his hand. 'Ivor Lewis.'

'Good morning,' said Eliza. Her own voice sounded very clear and firm to her; she felt relieved. She'd been afraid it would wobble.

'This is my assistant, Maureen Gunn. And our QC, Sir Bruce Hayward,' said Ivor Lewis.

Bruce Hayward clearly considered himself far too important to speak; he looked disdainfully at them all. He was much older than Gilmour;

probably about as old as Tristram Selbourne, Eliza thought, approaching sixty, but taller, thinner and much less fruity.

'And you two don't need any introductions, of course,' said Ivor Lewis, clearly with an attempt at humour, indicating Matt rather awkwardly. Matt managed something approaching a smile. Eliza stared back blankly. And thought, two hours ago, we were in the same house, having baths, cleaning our teeth, making tea . . .

'Ah,' said Philip, 'here comes the judge now. Good morning, your honour.'

Mr Justice Harris acknowledged this with a gruff 'morning' and an inclination of his head, and swept into the courtroom followed by his minions. And closed the door.

'Now we wait,' said Gilmour, 'shouldn't be long.'

And then they were in there, and it was even more like a film set with Mr Justice Harris sitting on his bench, beneath a lion and a unicorn carved in wood – it was all wood in here, no longer stone and marble, with every inch of wall, it seemed, covered in books – and some rather lovely art nouveau hanging lamps, Eliza noticed, surprised that such a thing should even impinge on her consciousness.

She and Matt and their legal teams sat on benches below him, and sundry important-looking people bustled about, clerks, she supposed, and a typist who settled herself immediately under the bench.

Mr Justice Harris had a rich but almost quavery voice, a long pale face and an oddly sweet smile – when it showed. He looked over the courtroom and all the people in it, a sweeping, interested survey . . .

'Very well,' he said, 'let us begin.'

It was over in less than an hour; Mr Justice Harris listened courteously to what was put before him, occasionally with a sharp glance at whoever was speaking, and once or twice at Matt or Eliza, and then opined that it would be a whole week's case and that they would need at least six weeks to have it in shape as he put it. 'You will be required to have all your witness statements, medical reports you may want to rely on, documents, letters lodged in a month's time. Your solicitors will then prepare your case. So I suggest the first week in July for the hearing commencing on, let me see, Monday the fifth and that date will be in the court diary and cannot change. I hope that is clear.'

There was a murmur of 'Yes, My Lord', and then the clerk of the court told them to rise and Mr Justice Harris swept out, without a further glance at any of them.

'Come along,' whispered Philip Gordon, taking Eliza's arm, and she looked at him, slightly bewildered, feeling she wasn't quite sure who he was, or indeed who she was, and they left the courtroom ahead of the others, and found themselves suddenly and rather wonderfully out of the building and into the sunshine, by way of a side entrance, and thence into New Square.

Eliza's legs suddenly felt rather weak and she sank gratefully onto one of the seats and looked at the four of them, who were all looking at her in various degrees of anxiety, and said, 'Oh, dear.'

And Matt, having refused the offer of lunch and its attendant post-mortem with his legal team, and loathing the air of complacency draped almost visibly around them, said he had to get back to the office and went and picked up his car from where he had left it in Covent Garden and drove very fast out of town, quite where he had no idea, merely struggling to escape from the demons which had attached themselves to him so firmly in the courtroom that morning; he bought himself a couple of beers and parked in the gateway of a field, and sat there for a long time, drinking and thinking; and then, as the long afternoon became evening, he turned the car back towards the city, while wondering slightly desperately where he might find further distraction.

The person who would have done that most effectively, of course, was on her way to Summercourt with her mother; Gina, he knew, would be waiting for him, with food, drink, the sympathy that was beginning to enrage him, and the ongoing offer of sex; and Louise had told him if he wanted to drop by she would be in and pleased to see him.

They both waited, and for a long time; but he did not come to either of them, merely phoning briefly to say he was tired and going home.

And he walked into the silent house, filled as it still was with the ghosts of happiness and laughter, and sat with only the whisky bottle for company and wondered at the folly of both of them, him and Eliza, that they had thrown that happiness so wilfully and stubbornly away, and what, if anything could have halted them before it was too late. Which it now so indubitably was.

Chapter 63

'Scarlett, this is Persephone. I would like to see you, as soon as possible. And please don't tell Mark.'

Oh, God. This was it. Mark had told her they were engaged, and she was obviously displeased. He had been very quiet when he got back from the interview, and refused to say anything, except that yes, it had gone fine.

'And did you tell her we wanted to be married on Trisos?'

'Yes, of course. And it was fine.'

'And did you ask about writing the – the—'

'Epithalamium? Yes.' An epithalamium, it transpired, was a poem celebrating a marriage.

'And is she going to do it?'

'Yes, I think so.'

It was like being back with the Mark Frost she had first met. And he stayed with them for several days. And now . . .

'Ah, there you are. Lovely flowers but actually next time, I'd rather have chocolates. If you don't mind.'

'Oh, all right.'

'Dorothy, put these things in water, would you? And bring us some tea.'

Scarlett sat silent. She had obviously fallen far from favour.

'Cake?'

'No, thank you.'

'You should eat more. You're very thin.'

'I like being thin,' said Scarlett firmly.

'Very well. If you think you look better that way.'

'I do.'

She was beginning to get the measure of Mrs Frost. She was a bully and you dealt with bullies by facing them down. But . . .

'Now, I'm not going to tell you I'm pleased about this marriage because I'm not.'

'I see.'

'Not particularly, at any rate.'

'Why not?'

'Oh, you're a very nice girl, and I like you very much. But—'

It would be hard for her to say that Scarlett wasn't Mark's intellectual equal. But she probably would.

'But you are simply not Mark's intellectual equal.'

'Mrs Frost—'

'Persephone.'

'I'd rather call you Mrs Frost for the time being. If you don't mind.'

'Please yourself. And do go on.'

'No, you go on. Tell me why that means I shouldn't marry him.'

'Oh, my dear girl, it's so obvious. That you ask that question proves what a mistake it would be. I'm sure everything is hunky-dory now. Lots of lovey-dovey talk, lots of sex, lots of excitement.'

'Yes, that describes it pretty well.'

'But in the years to come, then what, eh? When you've stopped gazing into one another's eyes and so on, what are you going to talk about?'

'What we talk about now, I expect,' said Scarlett.

'And that is? Certainly not the subjects that truly interest him.'

'Which are?'

'Oh, my dear girl, if you have to ask that's extremely indicative.'

'Of what?'

'Of the yawning chasm between you.'

Scarlett digested this for a moment; felt the tears rising; crushed them; and said, quite quietly, 'You must excuse me, Mrs Frost. I don't have all afternoon, I have a business to run.'

She saw herself out; as she passed through the hall she saw Dorothy hovering in a doorway, and could have sworn she saw an expression of approval on her pinched, pale face, and even the shadow of a smile.

Safely in a café about half a mile down Kingsway, she burst into tears; the proprietor, a sentimental old Italian, insisted on supplying her with a cappuccino laced with sugar for free, patted her hand and told her she was *bella, bella, bella*. It didn't exactly solve Scarlett's problem, but it made her feel better for a while at least.

Just the same, and in spite of her rage and indignation, she knew Mrs

609

Frost was actually right; and when Mark rang her that night, she said she was very sorry, but she had a lot of work to do, and that it would probably extend into the next evening as well; clearly hurt, he said he would wait to hear from her, he wouldn't bother her again. And maybe, she thought, it would be better for both of them if neither of them ever bothered the other again; and that Mrs Frost did after all know him a great better than she did and that she was perfectly justified in her claim that she Scarlett was not Mark's intellectual equal by a very long way. And that was – arguably – no basis for a marriage. Or certainly not a happy one.

The roller-coaster ride went on and on. A particularly interesting one it was turning out to be, Philip Gordon thought. Matt's sister was going to appear for Eliza; that must have been a big blow for him. It would shatter his confidence, surely; at this stage of the game, that was good. And then Eliza reported he had an erstwhile business partner appearing for him. 'I thought she hated him. And what does she know about his parenting skills? Weird.'

It was, a little.

A brief note, in her unmistakably foreign-looking writing:

'Giovanni is coming to London when I come to be a witness for Eliza and he has suggested you join us at the opera on the Wednesday night. Please, please tell him you are to be away, I could not bear to see you. M.'

Jeremy read this through eyes blurred with tears. And understood and felt the same and told Lucilla he wanted to make a trip to New York the week of Eliza's custody case.

'Jeremy, you can't. I'm sorry. It's the week of the European conference, you know it is, and all the CEOs are coming to London, it's been in the diary for months. I've fixed meetings, dinners, the opera—'

'The opera? Which night?'

'The Wednesday. Jeremy, you can't have forgotten, it's *Traviata*, oh, dear, you're so tired aren't you, you need a break so badly. Why don't I clear the diary for the following week, and book you into that hotel on St Bart's you like so much?' Lucilla's large brown eyes looked at him with concern; he managed to smile at her.

'No, no, don't worry, I don't want to go then, too hot. I might take myself down to Norfolk though, that week, if you could see your way to facilitating that. Bless you, darling.'

Now how in God's name did he tell Mariella? He could hardly write. And he had to warn her, say when he would be at the opera house. Maybe, maybe – yes, the one person in the world he could trust . . .

'Oh, Jeremy, darling, darling Jeremy, I'm so sorry. How sad, how dreadfully, dreadfully sad. For both of you. I can't imagine how much it must hurt.'

'Unbearably,' said Jeremy with a heavy sigh.

'Oh, God, what a tragic story. And also a wonderfully romantic one. But of course you would be too good to let it go on. I think Mariella might just manage it, she's not used to sacrifice.'

'She's been marvellous,' said Jeremy, swiftly defensive of his love. 'So wonderfully brave.'

'Sorry, and yes, I'm sure she has. God, it's an operatic plot in itself. Yes, of course I'll write to her, I'll be terribly discreet, I'll wrap it all up in fashion gossip and I'll just say you'll be at the opera house on the Wednesday and you asked me to tell her. She'll understand and then she can ring me if she wants. Poor Jeremy. You look so tired.'

'I am tired,' he said. 'Unhappiness is very exhausting. I've never known it before.'

'Not even when I broke off our engagement?'

'My darling, I'm afraid not. This seems to be my first experience of love. I hope that doesn't offend you.'

'Of course not,' said Eliza, giving him a kiss.

Four days later came a phone call from a distraught Mariella to Eliza. 'Please, please tell Jeremy, that is the night we too are going to the opera. Tell him I beg him not to come.'

'I'll try. But it's work, they're clients, I can't see . . . but I'm sure he'll try. Oh, darling Mariella, you must be so unhappy and I'm so sorry.'

'I have not known how to be unhappy before,' said Mariella simply.

Eliza felt she could hardly remember not being unhappy. And frightened too, more so every day. She kept looking at Emmie, as she sat on her swing laughing at her, or cuddled up to her watching children's TV, or kicking Mouse determinedly into a dozy trot, or telling her sleepily at bedtime that she loved her, and she was the best mummy in the world, and thinking that if she did lose her, she wouldn't even want to live any more. But – it was beginning to seem more and more likely.

Philip and Toby had called her to a meeting and said they really thought a robust judge, 'which he will be, Eliza, almost certainly', would want at the very least to read her psychotherapist's report and that they would like to discuss the whole matter with her. 'She will need your permission to waive confidentiality, you see.' Eliza was silent.

'Eliza,' said Philip gently, 'if you refuse, you will not only alienate the judge, who can still compel Mrs Miller to release it on grounds of contempt of court, but it will look very much as if you have something to hide.'

'Yes,' she said, 'yes, I'm sorry. And I – I will. But it could be very bad for me – us. You might want to give up on me altogether.'

'May I say,' said Toby Gilmour, half-smiling, 'that speaking personally, but I feel confident for both of us, I would never do that. It is quite simply unimaginable. And you're talking to a man, you know, who has seen the very worst of human behaviour. Now come along, let's get it over and done with. And if it's really so dreadful that I do actually feel shocked, I shall eat my wig. How's that?'

And she had told them about it without sparing herself, her gaze fixed firmly to the floor, and when she had finished there was a silence and then Toby Gilmour said, 'My dear, dear Mrs Shaw', and she could hear the smile in his voice, 'or perhaps now I am getting to know some of your most intimate secrets, I could manage Eliza – look at me.'

She did so; with great difficulty.

'Now,' he said, 'listen very carefully please. What you've described to me – us – is, of course, unfortunate, under the circumstances. It is also absolutely understandable, and was provoked and quite considerably so, both by your having lost your baby and by Emmie, who is clearly manipulative and very sophisticated, and you shouldn't be quite so hard on yourself. If everyone who lashed out once or twice at a child were fingered, I suspect most of the nation would be under the scrutiny of the social services. Nevertheless, your husband will no doubt make excellent capital of it, and we will have to be very fully prepared for that. Now, let's begin at the beginning, shall we? I think the best thing we can do is approach Mrs Miller, and ask her if she would be agreeable to our going to see her.'

* * *

Four unhappy days and a lot of thinking later, and having shed many tears and seen in many sleepless dawns, Scarlett made up her mind and rang Mrs Frost and asked her if she could come and see her. Her voice dripping with charm, Mrs Frost invited her along that very afternoon. Scarlett said that afternoon was not convenient, but the following one would do very well; after a brief struggle, Mrs Frost gave in.

She wore this time not a discreet dress, but a suit in blazing red, the skirt distinctly shorter than she normally wore, and the heels her highest pair; she carried a large bouquet of roses. She rang on the doorbell, stalked past Dorothy with a brief nod, and went into the drawing room where Mrs Frost sat in her wheelchair, looking more than usually stern. They glared at one another for a moment, then Scarlett said, 'I brought you some flowers. I know you may not be entirely pleased—'

'Not in the least.'

'But my mother brought me up not to arrive empty-handed. She isn't very intellectual either, but she has very good manners.'

'I'm pleased to hear it,' said Mrs Frost.

'Anyway, I have come to continue the conversation I had to terminate the other day. I apologise for that.'

Mrs Frost nodded; her eyes were bright with either apprehension or anticipation, Scarlett couldn't be sure which.

'I think we should get straight to the point, not waste time on social niceties.'

'I agree.'

'Yes. Now as I recall, you were asking me what we talked about when we were alone together.'

'I did indeed.'

'Right. Well, here is your answer. We talk about him and we talk about me. We talk about what I do and we talk about what he does. We talk about what we're going to have for dinner and who is going to cook it. Now all those things seem to me pretty important, just as important, I would propose, as the things you think we should be talking about. Which I presume are literature and art and the meaning of life. Actually we have got onto the meaning of life.'

'Really. And what do you think it is?'

'We're not sure yet,' said Scarlett firmly, 'it's an interesting ongoing discussion that we have. All the time.'

'Huh.' It was impressive, what she managed to put into that sound.

'And you see, there are plenty of people in his life who are his intellectual equals, but he's still fallen in love with me. I'm what he wants. With all my shortcomings. I think you have to face that.'

'What about his friends, eh? How can you communicate with them?'

'Actually,' said Scarlett, 'he doesn't have many as far as I know. He's too shy. He really is very shy indeed, isn't he? I wonder why and whether anything could have been done to help him when he was a small boy. I do think it possibly could, but it clearly wasn't. I expect you were too busy. Still, he's got me now, and maybe I can help.'

'I doubt it very much,' said Mrs Frost.

'Well, we shall see. Anyway, back to his friends. The ones I've met are very nice to me. They quite often want to talk about my company. It seems to interest them a lot.'

'Extraordinary. And your friends, does Mark have conversations with them?'

'He hasn't met many of them. I haven't told anyone about us yet, not my family, not anyone really.'

'"Nor" dear, "nor". Not "not".'

'That is really rather rude,' said Scarlett, hanging onto her temper with a great effort. 'Extremely rude in fact. I don't know why you think that just because you write poetry it's all right to insult me. It's quite beyond my limited intellectual capacity.'

'Yes,' said Mrs Frost, surprising her, 'yes, I can see it was rude. I apologise. I still think, if you're proceeding with this marriage, you're making an appalling mistake.'

'Obviously I've given it very careful consideration, since our last conversation,' said Scarlett, 'and equally obviously of course you have a point. I am not Mark's intellectual equal and I never will be. I do accept that.'

'Oh, you do?' said Mrs Frost. 'That's progress of sorts, I suppose.'

'Not really, because, do you know, I'd worked it out anyway. I'd be pretty dumb if I hadn't, actually. But I sort of think it doesn't matter. Because I'm good at things he isn't good at, and I think between us it'll work pretty well.'

'Well, it's a view,' said Mrs Frost.

'It certainly is. And we are going to get married because we want to get married. And moreover, we want you to be there. Well, I don't, to be honest. But Mark does. He adores you. And he's very good to you, I think.'

'Yes, that's true. But I can't give it my blessing. You can marry him if you like, but it will be against my wishes and without my presence.'

'And what good will that do you?' said Scarlett, increasingly surprised at herself and reflecting that however much David Berenson had sapped her self-confidence, it didn't extend to her relationship with Mark. 'None at all. Mark's not going to not marry me. And don't correct my grammar, please. He'll just marry me feeling unhappy, wishing you were there. And he'll find it hard to forgive you. He has this vision, of us being married on Trisos, with you reading the epithalamium, you see I can say it and I know what it is, and I am trying to become better educated. So if you don't do that, and you don't come, not only will I know you're mean and vindictive, but more importantly he will too. Which is not what you want, I imagine. If you do come and you do write it, only I will know. Well, actually I'll know you're not. And he can continue to think you're a saint. Which I also know you're not. So – your choice, Mrs Frost. Over to you.'

There was a long silence; then Mrs Frost suddenly put her hands together and clapped them sharply, several times.

'Very good,' she said, 'very good indeed. Well, you may be uneducated, but you're certainly not stupid. You may go now. I'm tired and I'm giving a poetry recital tonight at the Festival Hall. I'll think about what you said.'

Scarlett left, hoping devoutly her confidence in herself was not misplaced.

Two days later, Mark walked into Scarlett's office beaming happily, holding a large white envelope. It contained a sheet of white parchment paper, covered in perfect cursive writing. 'The epithalamium,' he said, 'it's beautiful. And my mother tells me she thinks she can arrange to come to Trisos for our wedding after all. She is a wonderfully brave and generous woman.'

'She is indeed,' said Scarlett. 'I must send her some chocolates.'

Chapter 64

'I'm sorry. I'm sorry, I'm sorry, I'm sorry.'

Emmie felt if she kept saying it, they might change their minds. She was so terribly afraid the whole thing was her fault, because she'd been so naughty; and a lot of the time she was so frightened she could hardly breathe.

It had been so horrible, that night, when they'd talked to her and told her what they were going to do: live in two houses, one each, with her living in one or the other.

'But why?' she kept saying, trying not to cry. 'Why not the same house like now, it's nice now, why do we have to change it?'

And they'd gone on and on about how they didn't get on very well any more – 'yes, you do,' she said, beginning to cry, 'yes you do,' but no, her mother said, they were arguing a lot, a bit like Emmie and her friends argued, and that made them miserable, and they thought it would be better if they lived in different houses.

'It wouldn't be better,' she said, trying now not to cry, because very often they got cross with her if she cried when she wanted something and told her to stop being a baby, 'it wouldn't be better, it would be better if you stopped arguing and lived in the same house. That's what you tell me when I do it, with Alice and Hattie and people, to stop arguing and make up friends and I do.'

'It's not quite the same thing, Emmie,' her father said and she told him that yes it was, it was exactly the same thing, you could stop arguing if you really tried; and then her mother said they had really tried, and she said no they hadn't, and anyway, she hadn't seen them arguing and she didn't believe them.

'Please,' she said, starting to cry again and this time not being able to stop, 'please try again. I don't want to live with just one of you, I don't, I don't, I want to live with both of you.'

616

'But Emmie, you will live with both of us,' her mother said, 'just one at a time. Like – like the weekends. That's all right, isn't it, at the weekends?'

'No, not really it isn't all right. I always want both of you, and it's not the same. Please, Mummy, please, Daddy—' and she had faced them both, and she was crying so hard now she couldn't even see them properly, 'please try again, please, please.'

And then her father said, very quietly, 'I'm sorry, Emmie, but we can't,' and her mother said, 'You heard what Daddy said,' and she was angry then, and shouted at them, and told them she hated them both and didn't want to live with either of them, and ran out of the room and up the stairs to her playroom and grabbed Mouse Two, the soft cuddly horse she took to bed every night, and went into her room and got into bed with her shoes on, and pulled the bedclothes right over her head and shouted at them over and over again to go away and that they were horrible.

Next day was even worse; she kept hoping they'd suddenly laugh and say 'we were only pretending' but they were both very serious and she saw her mother cry quite a lot as well.

She went to school, but it was very hard to think about anything else, and she didn't even want to go out to play and suddenly in the middle of reading she was sick, in a great horrible puddle on her desk, and Miss Barnes took her out and helped her wash her face and rang home, and her mother came to fetch her and she drove her home, saying 'I'm sorry Emmie' to her, over and over again.

And then a few nights later, when she was in bed, she heard the worst thing of all, which was her parents shouting at each other and then her mother running downstairs and her father making an awful sort of choking noise and she realised he was crying and she couldn't believe it because men didn't cry, and she ran downstairs to find her mother and said 'come, come quickly, Daddy's crying,' and her mother said of course he wasn't crying and she said yes, he was and she pulled her mother upstairs and they stood outside one of the bedrooms and the noise went on inside, and her mother just looked at her and didn't do anything, and Emmie tried to go in, but the door was locked, and she started to shout 'Daddy, Daddy, let me in,' and finally he opened it, and picked her up and said 'Emmie, I'm sorry,' and there were tears on his face and that was almost the most frightening thing of all, that a grown-up man could actually cry, and she said if he was sorry to stop arguing with Mummy and he said she didn't understand and put her down again, and ran down the stairs and out of the house.

That was when she began to be afraid it was her fault; that they were arguing about her, because she was often so naughty, and she asked her mother if they would be able to stay in the same house if she was good all the time, and her mother gave her the same awful, sad look her father had and said, no, she was sorry, they wouldn't.

That weekend, at Granny's house, it had been all right for a bit and Granny had been so kind to her, and she rode Mouse a lot and felt much better and her mother seemed happier, too, and she thought maybe they'd changed their minds; but when she asked her grandmother if she knew about them living in different houses, she said yes, she did, and she was very sorry about it and then Emmie realised it must be true.

And when it was time to go home, she really couldn't bear it any longer and she went up to the lavatory on the top floor and locked herself in and said she wouldn't come out until her mother had promised to make friends with her father; but she didn't, and they both, Granny and her mother, kept banging on the door telling her to open it, and she wouldn't, but in the end, Mr Horrocks arrived, she could hear his voice outside, and there was a lot of banging and pushing and pulling and when the door finally came off, she was standing on the lavatory, screaming, staring at them, and her grandmother said, 'Oh, Eliza, this is dreadful, what have you both done?'

'I'm sorry, Mr Gilmour – Toby, but I need to see you very urgently. Philip's out of town till Wednesday and this can't wait, it really can't . . . one of his assistants has offered to bring me down to your chambers . . . I want to stop this awful case, I want Matt to have Emmie . . .'

Chapter 65

Toby Gilmour had, until that morning, felt fairly ambivalent towards Eliza Shaw. He had found her very attractive, from their first meeting; he had grown almost fond of her over the weeks, the long, hard emotional weeks, as the case was prepared and she grew paler and thinner and lurched from fear to confidence and back to fear again, and yet still somehow managed – almost always – to be charming, to thank him for everything, to invite his opinion; he had felt a rather unusual degree of sympathy as she recounted, with her own particular brand of courage, the sad and sorry details of the downfall of her marriage, with its horribly familiar procession from struggle to misunderstanding to disillusion to hurt pride and sense of injustice; and on to rejection and entrenchment and thus to reckless revenge; but she was at the same time hugely irritating, with her tendency to keep things to herself, her capacity for self-blame, and a general lack of grasp of the legal processes and the way he was trying to conduct the case. She was also not in any way the type of woman he usually admired; he liked them highly educated, crisply intellectual and in a career path that he recognised, not dizzy and flippant and, while clearly hugely intelligent, doing a job that was by any standards lightweight.

But when she arrived at his chambers, white-faced and tear-stained and trembling, accompanied by a rather nervous articled clerk, and seemed about to collapse into the doorway, he had found himself almost unbearably moved by her. And as he put his arm round her shoulders, thinking only to calm her and soothe her and lead her into his own room, he realised that he was actually coming to a sense of involvement with her that was both unprofessional and dangerously beguiling.

The assistant had followed them in and hovered nervously, clearly uncertain what to do; Eliza looked at Toby anxiously.

'I thought – I thought we could talk alone.'

'Mrs Shaw, I can't discuss your case without a representation by your solicitor, however urgent; it would be rather – rather unethical. I might even be struck off by the Bar Council. Unfortunately, Mr Cowan can't stay for very long, he has another appointment, but he can hear at least some of what you have to say and report back to Philip Gordon.'

'Oh – all right.' She was clearly thrown by this, irritated even; but then he said quietly, 'I'm sorry, I really can't talk to you on your own. Mr Cowan, do use that table, I know you've got other work to do. Let's begin, and see how we get on shall we? Coffee?'

'Yes, please.'

'All the other barristers are in court, including Sir Tristram, so we shall be undisturbed. I will put the kettle on.'

She had imagined that to be a figure of speech, but there was a small ante-room beyond his office, a kitchen of sorts containing a Calor Gas ring, a kettle, a tin of tea and another of coffee and a miniature fridge.

'They don't like it, they claim it's a fire risk, but I want to have my coffee when I want it, not wait for some girl to finish typing a letter or even a difficult bit in her knitting pattern, so I insisted. Tea or coffee?'

'Oh, coffee I think. I've been awake most of the night.'

She looked as if she had, he thought, with eyes that were heavy and dark-ringed, and she had clearly dressed without any thought at all, no sign of her usual style, simply jeans and sneakers and, over a plain white T-shirt, a rather scruffy denim jacket.

'Good choice. Much more restorative. Now, go and sit down and drink this, it's very strong.'

'Thank you.'

And she went over to a deep leather sofa, and sank into it and put her hands round the mug and sipped it gratefully.

'It's lovely. Thank you.'

'Good. Now tell me what all this is about.'

And stumbling over her words at first, then more certainly, she had begun to talk.

It had been the last straw; having to get Mr Horrocks to take the door off its hinges, recognising the extent of Emmie's misery, so great that nothing, no bribe, no sympathy, no loving words could even begin to ease it.

Emmie had been hysterical for a long time, shivering and screaming that she hated them all, except Granny, she wanted to stay with Granny, she wouldn't go back to London, why should she when they were so stupid and horrible and wouldn't listen to her and what she wanted; and after a long time, Eliza said, 'All right, darling, I expect you can stay, but I must ring Daddy first.'

'Why?' Emmie shouted. 'Why do you have to ring him, I thought you didn't like talking to each other any more,' and Eliza had said, 'I know, darling, but Daddy will be worried and he'll need to know where you are.'

Matt had been surprisingly subdued when she told him; then asked to speak to Emmie, who refused.

'I don't want to talk to him, or you, I want to stay here with Granny and you go away by yourselves. Go away, go away, go away, I hate you.'

And so it was agreed that she should stay at Summercourt for the final few days of her parents' marriage and their peculiarly hideous mechanics, be spared the endless phone calls, the closed doors, the 'Emmie, not now, darling, we're very busy talking to people'.

Eliza had driven up to London, having taken her farewell of a sullen, swollen-eyed Emmie, castigating herself and weeping, a rather dangerous presence on the road, but by the time she reached Fulham she had made what felt like, then, a completely final and constructive decision. She would give Emmie to Matt, on condition she had reasonable access and the quarrelling ceased; at least then Emmie would know where she was, the fighting and the bargaining would be over, and they would all be able to go forward rather than sideways into this hideous ongoing tangle of recrimination and distortion and injustice. Emmie would grieve, but it would be over; there would be no danger of it reaching the papers, for her to read when she was older, and she would learn to accept – as children always did – the status quo. It would be the least she could do for her, after tipping her small, secure world into chaos, and it would be amends of a sort for the wrong she and Matt had done.

She sat there now, occasionally taking a sip of coffee, her voice very shaky, her eyes frequently filling with tears; after a while Gilmour got her a box of the client tissues from his cupboard, and she sat pulling them out one after the other and discarding them on the floor in a way which would have irritated him beyond endurance in the normal run of things, but this was clearly not normal – and told him what she had decided.

'It's too cruel, what we're doing to Emmie. It's horrible. I don't know how Matt can go on with it, I really don't. She's beside herself, so confused and really, really upset – last night she shut herself in the loo at Summercourt, Mr Horrocks, he's the housekeeper's husband, had to take

621

the door off its hinges. She's still there, with my mother, she says she hates us both, and I would too, if I were her. I do hate us both anyway. Oh, God—'

She threw her head back, and tried to catch back a sob; she failed.

'Sorry. Anyway, I just think if I give in, if I say to Matt he can have her, as long as I can see her lots, it'll be settled really quickly and we can all calm down and she'll get her new little life and it will be difficult for her, but not as bad as this endless quarrelling and telling her we're doing it so we'll all be happier soon. God, if I hate that solicitor of Matt's for one thing, it's him making Matt stay in the house with me, it's so cruel, so perverse.'

'Quite standard though,' Gilmour said, compelled even in this hour of trial to explain the law to her in all its workings, 'it happens all the time, clients are advised not to leave the matrimonial home – Mr Cowan, I know you've got to go, thank you for your help, can you see yourself out?'

The clerk scuttled gratefully off. Gilmour smiled. 'Proprieties observed. I'll get one of my pupils in to join us in a minute.'

'If he has to. Anyway, then at least I can move out, I suppose Matt will want the house, but I don't care, I never liked it, we bought it when – after – oh, God, sorry.'

'After your baby died?'

'Yes. How did you know that?' she said, staring at him.

'I didn't. Call it male intuition. We are not entirely emotionally illiterate, you know, we men. Even we legally trained men.'

'No, I see.' She felt confused. 'Well – well, like I said, he can have it, and anyway, Emmie should be in it, it's her home, so that's best, and this new nanny he keeps telling me is so wonderful can move in – it shouldn't be a new one you know, it'll be terrible for her, I might try and insist on Margaret staying – and I think then she'll be better quite quickly. Emmie, I mean. No danger of any crusty old judges asking her awful things, like who she wants to live with, and as long as I can have Summercourt, then I'll be all right and I can have her there at the weekends. I can go back to work more days, and once I know how many days Matt's going to allow me, I'll – I'll work round – round – oh, God, it's all so – so horrible –'

And then she was crying hard, and looking at him in a sort of beseechment, as if he could make things better.

'I'm not going to get her anyway and there'll be all this horrible filthy stuff coming out about me in court, most of it not true, but who will believe that, not even you probably, I mean, what must you think of me, smoking pot in the office, like I told you and sleeping around and hitting my child – oh, shit – how did I get into this, how, how, how? I've been so stupid, so epically stupid and selfish and cruel and—'

She looked at him then, met his eyes, thinking how cheap he must think her, how genuinely unfit to be a mother, hating herself, and he put down the cup he had been holding, and stood up and she thought he's going to show me the door, tell me he's dropping the case, he's just realised what an awful creature I am; only what he actually did was come over to the sofa and sit beside her: and leaning forward, studying his hands, began to talk.

'Listen,' he said, and his voice was slower, more patient than she had ever heard it, as if he was contemplating each thing that he said very carefully, 'I can't let you do that. I think what you have just said shows the most generous and the bravest and the kindest heart I have met for a long time, and you deserve to get your little Emmie on the strength of it alone and if only Solomon was here now, he would most surely award her to you. But he is not and therefore you must make do with me.

'Now then, let's take it from the top. In the first place, the quarrelling wouldn't stop, because you would still be, the two of you, on your own, working things out on your own terms, and after a very short time it would be worse than ever. People – and I am afraid this is one of the first lessons I learnt – do not change, and the fundamental problems in their lives do not change unless some fairly radical things happen. You say Matt can have her as long as he agrees that you can see her fairly often. Eliza, who will decide what fairly often is, and who will make you agree on it? While you are both so hurt and Matt is so angry?

'You say if Matt says you can have Summercourt you'd be all right, but what makes you think he would, if a judge doesn't order him to? From what you say, he was very generous to purchase it at all, so he will wonder why he should give it to you now. He might, in the first flush of relief at getting Emmie, but then he will think about it and all the money he has invested in it and I think he might very well change his mind. You say you'll try and insist on Emmie's present nanny staying, but again, you would be powerless and Matt would do what he thought best for her; he is very against Margaret, who he sees as part of the way you have decided to run things. And yes, no crusty old judge, asking her what she wants, but who will decide in his absence? I fear you think that suddenly you and

Matt will become good and reasonable friends, but you won't. Once you've got over the nobility of your gesture and Matt the generosity of it, you'll feel as resentful as hell, believe me, and he will take advantage. And he won't quickly settle on some nice, fair distribution of days for you to have Emmie, so that you can get your work life in order, he'll quibble and fiddle and argue, you'll actually find it very difficult.'

'Yes, but—'

'No, no buts. I know what I'm talking about. That's what you pay me for.' He smiled at her, then asked, 'More coffee? I could do with some.'

She nodded.

'Right.' He disappeared into the small kitchen again; she heard the kettle boiling, heard him rummaging for clean cups. He was being very nice. Nicer than she would have believed him capable of.

'I'm nearly finished,' he said, coming back to the sofa. 'The thing about the law, Eliza, is that it is of course very expensive and very dictatorial but it thinks for itself and for you. And then makes rules, which have to be obeyed. You can't argue with it. The week in court will be dreadful for you, I don't deny it, dreadful for all of you, and I am hoping of course that the judge won't ask to see Emmie, but we have to face the fact that he might. But when it's over, you will know where you are, and Matt will know where he is and that will be it. You will have to do what you are told, sort out your lives as directed and it will be no use Matt saying he's changed his mind and he only wants Emmie at the weekends or he wants her every weekend, or whatever, because he can't. Any more than you can argue for her, beg to have her more. Whatever happens, and however unhappy you are, that will be it. The law creates order. Do you see what I mean?'

'Just.' She sniffed loudly. 'Sorry. But—'

'Listen to me. You and your husband are two very strong-willed people. You are both angry, disappointed, hurt, vengeful, you both love Emmie, you both want Emmie. If you dispatch all of us legal bods now, where do you think you'll be in a week's time? Exactly where you were, only probably much, much worse.'

She was silent, not even looking at him.

'Now, I am fairly confident you will get generous access at the very worst, and I am still hopeful at least you may get custody. Although it will be a very tough week for you, of course. I've seen a hundred wives, with their lives dragged into the gutter, their behaviour misinterpreted, their good intentions distorted, all in the cause of winning the case. The law is of necessity gladiatorial as well as orderly. And the portrait Mr Hayward will be painting of you will not be pleasant. Jezebel will appear a saint, for those few days, by comparison with you, as will Messalina, the lady who slept with the regiment. Wife of poor stuttering Claudius.'

'Oh, don't,' moaned Eliza, 'it's not funny.'

'It's not meant to be funny,' he said, but he was smiling nonetheless. 'I am merely trying to tell it how it will be. And perhaps cheer you just a little. But you will survive. Because you are quite astonishingly strong. Not to mention brave. Now – have I managed to persuade you not to go down the rather dangerous path you seemed to be wandering towards earlier this morning? Because, and I hope you will believe me, it is for your own sake that I wish to divert you from it and not mine. Even though clearly I would benefit in some ways, not least—' He stopped.

'Not least what?' she said, and there was a charge in the atmosphere that she recognised and in spite of everything was excited by and there was a silence and then, and she could feel him drawing back from something, 'Not least the chance to conduct your case,' he said, his voice brusque again. 'It is, as I said, an exciting prospect.'

'Well – I'll think about what you said. Of course.'

'Please, Mrs Shaw, Eliza, do more than think about it.'

'Yes, I will, I will. Oh, God. Look, it's late. I'd better go, I'm supposed to be at work, holding meetings, organising a fashion shoot.'

'There you are, you see,' he said, 'you're still able to think about your work in the midst of all this tumult. I'm amazed by that. As I said, you are astonishingly strong. Now – can I call you a cab? Or will you rely on your whistling skills?'

'I'll be fine,' she said, 'thank you. But could I use your phone, call the agency—'

'Of course.'

He escorted her to the door of his room when she was finished. It was busy now in the chambers, people rushing about, looking important; she felt half-reluctant to leave the intense, personal space they had inhabited.

'You've been very kind,' she said, 'I don't know why you should spare me all that time.'

'I am not entirely inhuman,' he said, and then, quickly as if he knew he would not say it otherwise, 'and besides, you – you invite kindness.'

'Oh,' she said and then, astonished at herself, reached up and kissed his cheek.

'Thank you,' she said. 'Thank you –Toby – very much.'

Chapter 66

Matt had gone down to Summercourt to see Emmie. He had been afraid she would be hostile, refuse to talk to him, but when he got there, and found her sitting on the terrace with Sarah, drawing, she flew into his arms, with cries of 'Daddy, Daddy', and covered his face with kisses.

'How's my best girl?' he said carefully.

'Fine. This is for you.'

He looked at it, blenched. It was a picture of a little girl with long hair, standing in between a man and a woman, and in front of a big house.

'It's me, with you and Mummy. That's Summercourt. Granny said it was lovely.'

'I did,' said Sarah, speaking for the first time. 'Hello, Matt. Coffee?'

'Please.'

He sat drinking it, Emmie snuggled onto his knee, occasionally reaching up to kiss him.

'Can we go and see Mouse?'

'Whatever you like.'

Sarah watched them going off, her hand in his, looking up at him, chattering, occasionally resting her head against his arm. Her heart ached for both of them. All three of them.

An hour later, Matt was still leading Mouse round the paddock; Sarah knew how it bored him, how the whole pony thing baffled him, but she had seen him do this so many times, just as he sat helping Emmie to polish tack for hours on end, and patiently read to her from some exceedingly tedious pony magazine. He loved her so much, she thought, so very much, he would quite literally have died for her; how dreadful it was that such love, such tender, selfless love had to be turned to an act of harsh selfishness.

They ate lunch together on the terrace. 'I have to go soon, darling,' he said to Emmie, as she fed him ice cream, giggling. Normally such behaviour would not have been tolerated; and that was another thing, Sarah thought, Emmie would become spoilt now, as they vied for her favours, discipline would grow lax, rules would be waived: and she was naughty enough as it was . . .

'That's a shame. Are you going home to Mummy?'

'To our house, yes.'

'I wish we could live here always,' she said, her small face serious suddenly. 'It's lovely here. You and Mummy and Granny and Mouse and me. It would be really, really nice. Can't we do that, Daddy?'

'I'm afraid not, poppet. Mummy and Daddy have work to do. We have to be in London.'

'But sometimes then? You and Mummy together.'

'I'm afraid not, Emmie, no. We've explained to you, we—'

And then she jumped up, her small face working, huge tears in her blue eyes, and said, 'I hate this. I hate you. Why not, why, why, why?'

'Emmie – darling—' He reached for her; she pushed him away.

'Don't. I'm going back to Mouse. Mouse and Granny, they're the nicest.'

And she was gone, running, her long hair flying, a small victim of their war; Matt sat watching her and dashed his hand across his eyes. Sarah noticed, reached out and patted his hand.

'Leave her,' she said, 'leave her to me. She'll be all right.'

Driving back to London, filled with a new and savage remorse, Matt felt suddenly very afraid. Suppose he lost, now; suppose Eliza did get custody? How could he stand it, a life without Emmie there, every day? It would be unbearable, he would go mad. He felt half-mad now; he was driving dangerously, well above the speed limit, weaving in and out of traffic. He pulled over, sat trying to calm himself, running over the case, his case. He was doing well, Ivor Lewis was very confident, he said; they had superb witnesses, an excellent case. But there were things . . . things he had never told Lewis. Knowing it was crazy, but too afraid to confront them. About Gina. About hitting Eliza. That more than anything haunted him now: not just that it might come out, but that he had done it at all, that he was the sort of man who could hit a woman, and therefore a child. A man who should never, ever be left alone with a child, let alone be allowed to take it away from its mother.

But – Eliza had never told anyone; he knew that. She bore her own shame about it. And Gina was the only other person on earth who knew. And had sworn she never would tell. But – she did know; she could change her mind.

Matt pulled out his cigarettes, lit one with hands that shook. How had he done that, hit his own wife? How? How had he done any of it, made Emmie so unhappy? But it wasn't just him – was it?

'Would it be asking too much to spend an evening with you?'

'Oh, don't know – very busy—'

'Matt, I've been propping you up for months, it feels, trying to help you through this thing, and all I get is the bum's rush every time I ask for a morsel of acknowledgement. I mean, clearly there's no future in looking for gratitude, but—'

Matt felt suddenly remorseful. Gina had been bloody good, incredibly patient, accepting his explanation that he couldn't go to bed with her until the case was over because he would be compromised if anyone found out, which, while true, was a wonderfully useful cover for the real reason. This was that he just didn't fancy her any more; her sexual self-confidence, her overt sensuality, her greed in bed, all the things that had first attracted him to her had cloyed into something heavy and enervating, that induced the opposite of desire. He had an uneasy feeling that if he tried to have sex with her he would fail; and that was frightening for more reasons than one. She just knew too much; he dared not alienate her. Afterwards – well, she could do him no harm afterwards.

'I'm sorry,' he said. 'Yes, let's have dinner. I'll come to you; d'you mind cooking?'

'I'd rather go out.'

This was a tricky one; if they went out, she was liable to behave in her usual way, touching him up under the table, nuzzling his neck as the evening went on; on the other hand, being in her flat meant he was vulnerable to a sexual proposal. He decided that was less of a risk.

He arrived quite late; as he had feared, she had gone in for the full works. She was wearing a very low-cut black top and some very flared trousers that clung to her flat stomach and, more alarmingly, fitted her so closely round the crotch it was very obvious she was wearing no pants. Her hair swung loosely onto her shoulders: her make-up was light except for her mouth which she had painted a dark plum colour and then piled on the gloss. She smelt very heady; he kissed her, and then drew back.

'Hey,' she said, smiling up at him, 'did I do something wrong?'

'No, of course not.'

'Champagne?'

'Oh – yes, thanks.'

She took his hand, led him into her sitting room; it was, as always, slightly untidy, magazines on the floor, hairbrush on the coffee table next to an empty coffee cup, a half-eaten bar of chocolate. When they had been together it had charmed him, her messiness, even while it annoyed him, it was all part of her sexy, chaotic lifestyle, now it seemed to approach squalor. He thought, without being in the least sure why, of Louise's immaculate, stylish flat, all white and chrome, and how much he liked it.

'Right. I've bought steak, fillet, hope that's OK.'

'Of course.'

'And some other stuff. Oh, and some wine.'

'I've brought some wine.'

'OK, we can drink them both. Mine's a Merlot. I know you'll like it. I told the man in the off-licence it was for a man who didn't like wine and he said there wasn't a man alive who wouldn't like this one. He said it was a very sexy wine, actually, and wished me a good evening.'

'Great!' He was beginning to feel a bit sick. 'But you know—'

'I know,' she said, pulling him down onto the sofa, 'and it's not long now. And we can at least have a bit of an aperitif tonight, don't you think? What you might call a snog?'

Matt did his best; even that, he could tell, was rather unsatisfactory. She pulled away with an irritable sigh.

'Matt! This is so tedious.'

'I'm sorry. I've just – got a lot on my mind.'

'And don't I know it. Oh well – let's go and cook, that's supposed to be an aphrodisiac, isn't it, cooking together?'

'I – hadn't heard it, no.'

'I really don't know what's happened to you, Matt. There isn't anyone else, is there?'

'Of course not,' he said and his voice was so full of genuine horror, he could even hear it himself. She smiled and visibly relaxed.

'That's all right then. OK, one more for the road and then we'll carry on in the kitchen . . . I wish. Do you remember how we used to try doing it on all the floors, see which one was sexiest? And you decided the kitchen?'

'Yes, of course I do,' said Matt.

'So,' said Gina, as they sat down at the table, 'how are things? How's the witness tally? I cannot get over your sister doing that, taking the stand for Eliza. It's just – just gross.'

'I did think that,' he said, in between chews, reflecting that the fillet was tougher than it should have been. He should have done the shopping himself.

'Well – don't you still?'

'Yes. But – it's got a bit better since then.'

'Really? How's that?'

'Well – you know Louise?'

'What, the girl in your office?'

'She was the girl in my office,' said Matt, discovering he felt a certain proprietary pride in Louise's progress, 'she's now Contemporary Hotels.'

'Really? I didn't know that. They're very good. Brilliant facilities, I went to a trade show in the one near Covent Garden last week. She must be clever. Anyway, what's she got to do with the case?'

'She's going to be a witness for me.'

'She's what?'

Gina's eyes had become very sharp, lost their sexy languor.

'She's going to appear as a witness for me.'

'Saying what?'

'What a good dad I am. Would be. All that stuff.'

'But – how? I don't see how she can. She's not a friend, is she? Just a work colleague.'

'Yes, of course, I mean of course she's just a work colleague. But – she offered and I took her up on it.'

'I'm sorry.' Gina had put down her knife and fork. 'I don't see how someone who worked with you, in the office, could possibly carry any weight as a witness to your skills as a father. I can't think why your solicitor's even entertaining the idea.'

'Well, you're wrong about that,' said Matt. In fact Ivor Lewis had been slightly sceptical, but having talked to Louise, and heard what she had to say, had conceded she would be a 'useful backup'. Matt wasn't going to tell Gina that.

'We go back a long way,' he said now, 'she came to work for me when we were just two men and a dog. Me and Jimbo.'

'And Louise was the dog, I suppose?'

Matt felt a rush of anger. 'Don't talk like that, Gina, please. She's a very good friend, she's done a lot for me over the past few months.'

'And I haven't, I suppose?'

'Oh God,' said Matt wearily, 'of course you have. But she's listened to me moaning, tried to cheer me up, taken me out, bought me drinks—'

'How very kind.'

'It was actually,' said Matt quietly.

'Sounds to me as if she's after you, Matt. Trying to get to you the best way she can see at the moment. I'd be careful if I were you.' She smiled at him, twisted a strand of hair round her finger. 'You're very vulnerable and women can sense that.'

'Gina, for Christ's sake, do stop this. Louise is an old friend, we spent most of the time we worked together fighting, she walked out on me when I appointed a new partner and it wasn't her—'

'Good for Louise. Suddenly I like her more. Anyway, I still don't see how she possibly can be a witness to your fitness to look after Emmie. It's going to sound pretty hollow.'

'You don't know what she said,' said Matt, trying to sound calm, 'she was pretty convincing.'

'I bet she was.'

He flung down his napkin.

'This is a ridiculous conversation.'

'Matt, it is not ridiculous. Honestly. And I'd lay a pound to a penny I'm right. Why should a girl do that, pretty scary experience, volunteer to go into the witness box – I presume she did volunteer? Only one explanation, Matt. She fancies you. Thinks maybe she can close in when the divorce is through. Well, if she knew how useless you are in the bed department at the moment, she'd pull out pretty fast, I'd say. Maybe I should warn her—'

'Please stop talking like that,' said Matt, his voice icily polite. 'I know you're not entirely serious but I don't like it. I told you, she's been a good friend to me and . . .'

'Hmm. A friend who takes you out and serves up whisky and sympathy? And then says anything else I can do for you Matt, while I'm about it, oh, speak up for you in court did you say, yes, of course I will, three bags full, Matt. You're more stupid and blinder than I realised, Matt Shaw.'

Matt suddenly had a vivid flashback to the evening in Louise's flat, could hear her voice again working out what she might say. 'I can tell them how much you love her . . . she'll be so proud of you one day, Matt . . .' and he couldn't bear it any longer.

'You'll have to excuse me,' he said, 'I'm not enjoying this very much. I think I'd better go.'

'Oh, don't be so ridiculous,' said Gina, 'I'll start thinking you fancy her back in a minute.'

Matt pushed his chair back and stood up.

'Just shut up, would you?' he said quite pleasantly.

Gina stared at him; she was flushed suddenly, and looked startled.

'You do, don't you?' she said slowly. 'You actually do fancy her.' My God! What a turn-up for the books. A bit of office totty, how terribly, terribly corny – well, I hope it hasn't got out of hand, Matt, that's all I can say. But probably you've been dishing out the same old stuff you've been giving me. Jolly useful cover, I'd say, for not being able to get it up . . .'

Matt left, without another word.

'Eliza, Philip Gordon here.'

'Oh – hello, Philip.' Now what?

'Interesting one here; your psychotherapist has refused to disclose your reports, as she has at this stage a right to do. However, I should warn you that I think the judge will demand to see them. If he does, and she persists in refusing, she could be charged with contempt of court.'

'Oh no! That's awful, she's so lovely and how brave of her. So, what do I do?'

'I think we should warn her of that as a possibility. If she does get called, then you would have to waive patient confidentiality and the reports would be produced. But let's not meet trouble more than half way.'

'No. All right.'

Oh, God. Something else to worry about. Seriously to worry about. Was it ever going to end?

Eliza had taken the week before the case off. Sarah had brought Emmie up from Summercourt on the Monday evening despite the original plan to keep her there; Sarah felt she was too upset altogether to be away from Eliza, she was restless, fractious, clinging one minute, hostile the next. She cried every night in bed, and often woke up in the middle of the night, having wet the bed and complaining of bad dreams. And when on the Thursday night Emmie was sick Eliza decided that a long weekend at Summercourt would do them both good and drove down early the next day. And trying not to think of a time when she might not be able to turn to it for comfort.

They arrived just after nine; it was a perfect morning, and Summercourt looked at its magical best, the front still cool and shadowy, the terrace behind flooded in sunshine and warmth, the meadow grass long and drenched in dew; she felt herself comforted as always, felt her heart almost literally lift, watched, smiling, as Mouse cantered over to greet them, looking for the Polo mints Emmie always brought him; and she sank gratefully onto one of the old weather-bleached wooden seats, savouring the sound of Emmie's giggles as Mouse nuzzled her hand, tickling it with his whiskers; and wishing she could hold this moment still, for evermore, this happy, sunlit, lovely moment, filled with the scent of the roses that climbed up the walls and the songs of the birds surrounding her, free from care, released from dread. And managed to think, perhaps, perhaps it will all be all right. But – how could it be, for whatever happened, whoever won, Emmie would lose. That was the pity of it, the dreadful, sad, unarguable pity; that it was Emmie, who had done nothing, nothing wrong, nothing selfish, nothing wilful, nothing greedy as both her parents had, Emmie who was suffering quite as much as either of them.

Toby Gilmour had tossed and turned much of the night, and then called Philip Gordon that same morning to tell him the bad news: that the judge they had been allotted was to their case what the Miss World contest was to the feminist movement. 'Couldn't be worse, he might have been hand-picked by Ivor Lewis and Bruce Hayward. He's extremely partisan, has come out several times in favour of the husband in divorce cases, feels they get an increasingly raw deal, especially with all this bra-burning stuff that's going on, his phrase not mine, and – wait for this – lost his own two sons to their mother in his divorce ten years ago.'

'His divorce?'

'Yes. Oh, come on, Philip, you must know . . .'

'Oh crikey. Not Clifford Rogers?'

'The very one.'

'Dear oh dear. That is bad luck. Are you sure?'

'Am I sure we've got him? Yes, quite sure, I was at a dinner with him last night, it'll be confirmed this afternoon. Am I sure about his divorce, yes, I met him at the Lincoln's Inn garden party a couple of weeks ago, he was tight as a tick, and he got very maudlin, and held me in a corner like the Ancient Mariner while he told me all about it.'

'Oh, Christ.'

'I know. I've been trying to work out tactics all night; very difficult. He really dislikes women. He's also – and this isn't too good either – a grammar-school boy, one of the first judges to make it, and carries a banner for the new social order, so he won't like our Eliza and he'll think Matt and Ivor Lewis, come to that, both should have whatever he can give them.'

'Jesus.'

'Anyway, I think one of the things that might help is if we can get Eliza's friend Heather into court. Nice working-class girl, friendship spans the class divide – and I'm delighted we've got Matt's sister on our side as well.'

'Surely she's exactly the sort of woman he won't like. Succesful, powerful, self-confident—'

'No, no, I think it'll be all right. She's self-made, you see, clearly no silver spoon because she's Matt's sister—'

'Hmm. Well, I think the case is even further loaded against us. What about Northcott?'

'He'll loathe him. I'm wondering about the wisdom of calling him at all. We've got the editor and he's pretty middle-of-the-road socially – although I'll have to check the cuttings, make sure they haven't had any brushes in the past.'

'What bad luck. Now – thing is, do we warn Eliza or not?'

'I think we have to. She's not stupid, she'll soon pick up on it, surely. And anyway, if we want to get Heather Connell into court, we'll have a better chance if we go through Eliza.'

'What do you think he'll make of the Italian countess or whatever she is?'

'God knows.'

'Now look, I've got back-to-back client meetings all day, clearing the decks for next week. Can you talk to Eliza?'

'I was hoping we could at least draw lots,' said Gilmour gloomily.

'Dream on,' said Philip, 'and you'll have to go alone, I can't spare any clerks, they're all in court. I know it's out of order, but nobody need know.'

'Emmie?'

'Yes?'

'Emmie, I want to talk to you about something.'

'What, the stupid divorce?'

'Well – it's to do with that, yes.'

'I don't want to talk about it.'

'I know, darling. But this is – important.'

This wasn't the best time, but with the case starting on Monday . . .

'I don't care.'

'Sweetheart – please—'

Emmie turned to look at her. They were sitting on the terrace in the sunshine; she was shovelling cornflakes as fast as she could into her small face, the sooner to go and groom Mouse.

'Go on then,' she said resignedly.

Eliza took a deep breath; Matt was totally opposed to what she was about to say, but Emmie hated shocks and surprises – they should, she knew, have broken the news of the divorce slowly and carefully over time to her, rather than hitting her with it all at once. She liked to be in full command of the facts in her small life, so that she could adjust her behaviour accordingly – to control things as best she could, Eliza supposed. And where did she get that from? God, she was like Matt.

'The thing is, Emmie, and I hope this won't happen, but there is a – a chance that the judge – that's the man who's going to decide what will happen afterwards, which house we're – you're going to live in and so on – Emmie, are you listening to me?'

'Sort of,' said Emmie sulkily.

'Good girl. Well, try to listen properly because it's important. The judge might want to talk to you.'

'I don't want to talk to him. I just want you and Daddy to make friends and stop being stupid.'

'Yes, darling, I know, but that isn't going to happen. It just isn't, you've got to understand that.'

A heavy sigh. Emmie started fiddling with the cornflake packet;

636

it fell over and spilled. She started making a pattern on the table with the flakes.

'Darling, don't do that.'

'I want to.'

Eliza fought for patience.

'OK. But – do you understand?'

'Yes.'

'And is that all right?'

She shrugged.

'Emmie—'

'What does he want to talk to me about?'

'Well – what you feel about it all. And – and what you think would be best for us all to – to do.'

There was a long silence. Then,

'I've got to tell the judge man that?'

'Well – hopefully not. But you might have to.'

Another silence.

'I'd like that,' said Emmie.

'You'd like it?' Eliza stared at her.

'Yes. If he's nice.'

'Well – I'm sure he will be nice,' said Eliza. 'That is to say, I'm sure he'll be nice to you. If you do have to speak to him. So – you really don't mind?'

'No. I don't. Can I go and catch Mouse now?'

'Yes, all right,' said Eliza resignedly. She watched Emmie taking the packet of Polo mints out of her jodhpur pocket, climbing over the fence, and holding them out to Mouse, his head collar looped over her arm. She was extraordinarily competent for her age. She was extraordinary altogether.

God knows what a judge would make of her. Or she of him. Of course she didn't understand. What an ordeal for a little girl: to be asked – in essence – which of her parents did she want to live with.

How could Matt do this to her – how?

Chapter 67

'What an exquisite place! Wonderful gardens too.'

'You must tell my mother. She does nearly all the work. Come in – and this is Emmie. Emmie, this is Mr Gilmour.'

'Hello, Emmie. I've heard a lot about you. Is that wild horse Mouse?'

Emmie looked over at the slightly stout Mouse, patently weary after half an hour of being lunged, and another half-hour of pole walking, and giggled.

'Yes. Can you ride?'

'I can. But I don't. Don't have time. Or anywhere to keep a horse. Sad. I love it.'

'You could keep it here,' said Emmie consideringly, 'Mouse gets lonely, in fact Granny's looking out for a Shetland, to keep him company.'

'There you are,' said Eliza, 'you didn't expect to find livery accommodation into the bargain this morning, did you?'

'I didn't. Sounds excellent. Only thing is I haven't got a horse or I'd be down faster than you could say walk-trot-gallop.'

'I like doing walk-trot-gallop,' said Emmie, 'only I can't gallop, so I just walk and trot. I want to have a gymkhana of my own,' she added, 'here at Summercourt.'

'That sounds fun. With just you, or other people?'

'Of course other people,' she said, her voice reproving. 'Otherwise it wouldn't be a gymkhana. Shall I show you how I do walk and trot?'

'Later on. I'd like that very much. Just now I need to talk to your mother.'

'What about?'

'All sorts of things.'

'The divorce?' said Emmie and scowled.

'Well yes, I'm afraid so.'

'It's so stupid,' she said, and her voice was scornful rather than distressed, Toby Gilmour noticed. 'They're so stupid, too.'

'Who, Mummy and Daddy?'

'Yes. I thought they were clever but they're not and we all have to be miserable and a man called a judge will decide what's going to happen to me. How can he, when he doesn't know me or what I want. Stupid.'

'Emmie,' said Eliza, 'you know I told you you may get a chance to talk to the judge.'

'I don't suppose he'll take any notice. You know what I want and you don't.' Her small face looked across at Mouse with an expression of great disdain. 'Horses are much more sensible.'

'I do agree,' said Toby.

'Emmie, Mr Gilmour and I have to go and have a chat. Granny's in the kitchen and she wants you to help her shell some peas.'

'I hate shelling peas.'

'Never mind, they need doing. Now we won't be long—'

'And then can I show you walk, trot and not gallop?' asked Emmie, looking up at Toby.

'Nothing I'd like more. But I might have to take your mother somewhere first.'

'OK.' She shrugged and set off in the direction of the paddock.

'Emmie, I said go and help Granny,' Eliza said; Emmie turned to look at her and gave her a smile of great sweetness.

'And I said I didn't want to,' she said and continued on her way.

Eliza looked at Toby with a slightly shamefaced expression.

'She's a bit – over-indulged at the moment.'

'I'm not surprised. I see a great future for her in the law. Clear-thinking, and very good at marshalling her arguments.'

'Oh, don't. Come into the house, I've put coffee in the drawing room. It's so kind of you to come all this way.'

'Well – it was a bit of a complicated conversation. Best face to face. Besides, we might have to go on a journey together.'

'Heather's not a bit sure he'll agree,' said Eliza, as Toby's BMW pulled into the council estate where Heather lived. 'It's down there, look – yes, just park here. Oh, there's Coral,' she said jumping out of the car. 'Hello, Coral, why aren't you at school?'

'Hello,' said Coral shyly, 'I've got a cold. Where's Emmie?'

'With her granny. I should have brought her. Coral, this is Mr Gilmour, we've come to see Mummy. Is she inside?'

'Yes, she said to look for you. Is Emmie all right, is it true she's got a pony?'

'Only a very little one. You must come and see her one day and ride the pony.'

Heather appeared, a baby on her hip.

'Heather, it's lovely to see you, how are you. This is Toby Gilmour, the barrister, working on the case. Toby, this is Heather Connell.'

'Pleased to meet you,' said Heather.

'And I to meet you,' said Toby. He bowed slightly; don't overdo it, thought Eliza, she's too clever for that.

'Well – come through. I've made some tea, we could have it in the garden.'

The garden was a work of art: the small lawn mown in stripes, every inch of every bed a riot of roses, dahlias, and irises, and every bed edged painstakingly with pansies. At each corner of the lawn was a piece of box hedge, carved into a very neat triangle, and a bird table stood absolutely in the middle of the lawn. A tortoise sat underneath it.

'A tortoise!' exclaimed Toby. 'I used to have one. Coral, I presume it is yours?'

'Yes, he's called Meths.'

'Short for Methuselah,' said Heather by way of explanation.

'What was your tortoise called?'

'Tort,' said Toby, smiling at her, 'which is a sort of law, so it seemed to suit him. My father was a judge.'

'Are you a judge?'

'No, I'm only a barrister. That's a sort of judge in waiting. I hope,' he added.

He was good with children, Eliza thought; she was surprised.

'Now,' said Heather, passing round the biscuits, 'I'm afraid I'm not too hopeful about Alan. He'll be home at five past five, so you can ask him then.'

'If he does say yes, will you do it?' asked Eliza.

'Yes, I will. I won't say I'm not scared, but I will—'

'Well done,' said Toby.

At five past five precisely a Ford Consul pulled up into the small drive.

640

Alan Connell got out. He was dressed in a navy-blue suit with the jacket buttons all fastened in spite of the extremely warm weather, a white shirt and a perfectly knotted navy and grey striped tie. His shoes wore a high shine; his hair was combed very precisely from a side parting, even his moustache looked as if it had been combed. Heather went out to greet him and they had a rather intense conversation; Eliza, watching from the windows, was not encouraged. Alan shook his head twice and when he walked towards the house, his expression was extremely stubborn.

'Good afternoon,' he said, nodding at them. 'So you're Eliza.'

'Yes. How do you do, Mr Connell, we meet at last. I'm sorry we're here, intruding on your weekend.'

'It's not the weekend yet,' said Alan Connell, 'not until midnight.'

'No, I suppose not.'

'I'm going up to change. I like to get into casual clothes as soon as I get home. Helps me relax. Then, Heather, perhaps you could get us some tea.'

This time the tea was served in the breakfast room; Bobby was in his high chair, his face smeared with something unrecognisable, Coral at the table unwrapping Kraft cheese triangles. It didn't look like a meeting which could result in a victory in the High Court.

Alan reappeared, wearing perfectly creased slacks, a short-sleeved shirt, pressed carefully open at the neck, and highly polished brown shoes instead of black. He sat down at the table and took the cup of tea Heather passed him, added two precisely level spoonfuls of sugar, stirred it three times and then sipped it.

'Right,' he said, 'let's get down to business. I don't like this, I said Heather wasn't to appear in court, and I haven't heard anything yet to make me change my mind.'

'Let me explain,' said Toby. 'The point is that the judge we've been – allotted – doesn't like written statements. Indeed, he tends to dismiss them.'

'Why? Not his place, I wouldn't have thought,' said Alan.

'Well, unfortunately the court is his place – while he is presiding over it, at any rate. He can decide what to do, how to run his case.'

'Well,' said Alan, 'I don't hold with pandering to that sort of thing, very arrogant, I call it, but I can see there's not a lot you can do and it is important.'

'Yes, it really is. It could make all the difference to Eliza's case. If Heather could come – if you could agree to her coming – of course, I know it's a long way, but we could arrange to send a car—'

'A car! From here to London?'

'Yes. It would be extremely good of you, and we would want to show how much we appreciated it. There's a lot at stake, you see—'

'Well, no wonder you lawyers charge such high fees,' said Alan. 'I've never heard such rubbish, she can go on the train—'

'Oh, but we'd want you to come too,' said Toby, 'of course. To keep her company. I imagine you wouldn't want her to go through it all on her own, bit of an ordeal. And to make sure you were quite happy with everything.'

'Oh. I see. Well – that might make a difference. That shows consideration, doesn't it, Heather?'

'Yes. It does.'

'And you'd send a car here? To the house?'

'Yes, of course. If you preferred to go on the train, then it would just take you to the station and meet you on your return, we'd pay your fares, but—'

'No, no, a car could be very nice,' said Alan, 'I hadn't realised you'd want me as well. It would certainly make me feel a lot happier. Of course I'd have to ask for the time off work, but I imagine it would be considered a bit like jury service. In that you couldn't refuse?'

'I'm sure. And in the unlikely event of your having to stay, we'd obviously put you both up in a very nice hotel . . .'

'Very generous of you,' said Alan and then, clearly anxious not to be seen as a pushover, 'no more than I'd expect of course.'

'And I would like to help, Alan,' Heather said, 'Eliza was such a good friend to me.'

'Tell me, Heather, in what way was she such a good friend to you?' asked Toby.

'Eliza's just the best friend I could ever imagine,' said Heather simply. 'She was so kind to us, Coral really loved her, she's so good with children and she never complained about giving up that amazing job, although I know she missed it a lot. And later on she was always meeting Coral from school when I was pregnant and not feeling up to it, and doing the shopping, I never had to ask, she just offered, and she used to drive us out to the park for picnics in the holidays. She gave us a TV, she even lent me some money once when – well, when I lost my purse. And she took up our cause with the landlord, argued with the useless plumber and I know

642

it all went wrong in the end, with the article in the paper, but it wasn't her fault. And I was so sorry for her, when the baby died, and she was so brave, and so generous when I fell pregnant again, very soon after, she said she was so pleased for me, not many people could do that. And Coral just loved Emmie, said she was her best friend and she really missed her when we moved away. And I missed Eliza so much as well, it was like a huge hole in my life. She's the sort of person who'd do anything you asked her, I can't think of anything she'd refuse you—'

There was a silence; Eliza rummaged in her bag for a tissue and blew her nose very hard. Toby, who had been sitting looking at Heather as if he was bewitched by her, reached out and patted her hand and even Alan cleared his throat.

'Well,' said Toby finally, 'do you think you could say all that in court? It could make all the difference to Eliza.'

'Of course I could,' said Heather.

'That was brilliant,' said Eliza, as they drove away, having done what Alan called a tour of the garden, and Toby had admired the box triangles, 'you were so clever. So funny, apparently there was a lot of turf on that lawn, the grass seed kept dying and he kept putting down squares of turf in bits and pieces, but he said it didn't count . . .'

'Well, it was a triumph in any case, turf or no turf. Lot of work in the smallest garden, and those beds—'

'Toby!' said Eliza. 'You'll tell me you meant all that guff in a minute.'

'I did,' he said, 'I'd love a garden, I admired yours, didn't I?'

'Yes, you did.'

'Oh Christ, look at that traffic. We're not going to get back for hours at this rate. Are you hungry?'

'Bit. I feel a whole lot more hopeful too. I know one swallow doesn't make a summer and all that—'

'It's a pretty good harbinger of one, even so. Let's find a nice country inn, then, and have a meal.'

'Haven't you got to get back to London?'

'No,' he said shortly, 'I haven't. Nothing on at all, all weekend. OK, we'll drive for an hour, say, and then stop, shall we? Should be somewhere like Buckinghamshire by then. Lovely restaurant at Cookham, I seem to remember, down by the river. How would that be?'

'Lovely,' said Eliza. 'Thank you.'

Chapter 68

Coincidence is a powerful force. It runs in its apparently untrammelled way, linking people across continents, events across time. Everyone has a particularly striking example of it: of the unplanned meeting at a point thousands of miles away of two people from the same street, of a book found in a second-hand bookstall that the purchaser had owned as a child, his name on the flyleaf, of a love letter sent from the battle line and lost in a mailbag for fifty years arriving at its destination and joining writer and addressee in twilight years of happiness.

And it was coincidence, and its close relative chance, at work that lovely summer evening, as everyone concerned with the case of Shaw vs Shaw became increasingly obsessed, as well they might, with its outcome.

'I – um – I wondered if you'd like to have a drink this evening?'

'What, with you?'

'I wasn't suggesting you went with anyone else.'

'Well – why not. Yeah, OK, Matt. Would you like to try one of my hotels? The one near Hyde Park is very good.'

'Yes, nice idea. Thanks, Louise. I've never been to one, and I should. Great.'

'OK. Champagne bar, that's what it is, six thirty?'

'You're on.'

'Gina, doll, this is Freddy.'

'Oh – hi, Freddy.'

Freddy was her business partner; or rather he'd put up most of the money for Dressing Up. He was flashily handsome, gay and extremely rich, the money made by a lucky dip into the oil market and now brilliantly invested; the shop was really a tax dodge.

'I'm in town. Just for tonight. I was wondering if you'd like to have dinner? Maybe go on somewhere – I could do with a bit of nightlife.'

'Well—' She'd been about to refuse then thought it could be a good idea. Freddy was amusing and very good-looking, it would be no disgrace to be seen with him. Even if he did call her 'doll'. And she was buggered if she was going to sit around waiting for Matt to call any longer. She really was beginning to feel she'd had it with him. But – she'd invested a lot of emotion in him, and she was actually extremely fond of him Or had been. And when this bloody divorce case was over, things should steady again.

And she was getting to an age when she would quite fancy a bit of security. You couldn't go on being a good-time girl for ever.

'Yes, that'd be nice,' she said.

'Excellent, I'm staying at that new hotel just below Hyde Park Corner, very nice, quite flashy, you'd like it. They've got a champagne bar, we can start there, and then go on somewhere to eat . . . you choose.'

'What, the Contemporary? Yes, great. See you there.'

Matt was late – of course. God, he was annoying. It had surprised her when they started meeting socially, his pathological lateness. He was never late for a business meeting, she had often been hauled over the coals in the early days for two or three minutes – for social occasions it was always thirty minutes late and often an hour.

She had ordered a glass of champagne, done a quick recce of the reception rooms and the Ladies – always a barometer of a good hotel – and was sitting trying to concentrate on the *Evening Standard* when he finally arrived.

'Good of you to come.'

'Louise, don't start. I've had a hell of a day. But I've got some good news, we've got a judge who's very keen on fathers' rights.'

'Very progressive. I thought judges were all preserved in aspic.'

'I know. Me too. So – could be a good omen. Now I did tell you, didn't I, we may be calling you on Day One, more like Day Two, I'll have a very good idea by lunchtime Monday, so if you could—'

'Stay by the phone? Yeah, yeah. You did tell me. But only about three times.'

'OK, sorry. No need to worry about their barrister, he's a junior, as I said, not much cop probably, and Bruce Hayward will give you a very easy ride obviously. If you can just say – you know – the sort of things you said the other night—'

'Matt, that slightly unattractive solicitor of yours has already gone through it with me. Don't worry. I won't let you down. How's Emmie?'

'She's fine. Well—' He sighed. 'Not really. She was throwing up the other night. But she's down in the country with her mother. For the weekend.'

There was a silence; then he nodded in the direction of her glass.

'Another?'

'Yes. Please. I feel like indulging myself tonight.'

'Why?'

'Oh – not sure. Just feel a bit – a bit like it. But I'll have to be careful, I've got a big day tomorrow, going up to Stratford for a meeting with the builders on site. Not good with a hangover.'

'No. Look – I'll get a bottle, might as well.'

The bottle arrived; they seemed to get through the first glass very quickly. Matt poured them a second.

'Wow, this'll have to be my last,' said Louise, 'I feel a bit dizzy already. I might go to the Ladies now, while I can still walk straight.'

'You look sensational, doll,' said Freddy, 'love the hair.'

'Thanks. Suddenly – one lot of wispy layers too many. Good day?'

'Yup, very.'

'So where's Sam?'

Sam was Freddy's partner, a sober-looking academic, specialising in medieval history, and about as unlike Freddy as a man could be.

'He's at home. He's finishing some paper on the rise of the anti-popes.'

'Christ,' said Gina.

This was not a reaction to the subject of Sam's paper, but the fact that she had just seen Matt across the bar.

'Anything wrong?'

'Could be. Might be best to move on.'

'Gina! I haven't even ordered a drink yet. Have a heart, I'll make it a quick one. You?'

'Oh yes, all right,' said Gina. She had taken comfort from the fact that she and Freddy were in a banquette, fairly well-shielded from view. And the bar was quite dark. She could actually observe Matt without him realising it. She wondered who he was with . . .

✿   ✿   ✿

646

Louise combed her hair, touched up her lipstick and sprayed on some more Miss Dior perfume. She studied herself in the mirror; she looked all right. She didn't look drunk. But then she didn't know what she looked like when she was drunk, it was quite a rare occurrence. On the other hand, it had been a bit hard to walk straight across the bar.

She went back to Matt, who was looking broodingly into his glass.

'Matt! You're not going to survive the weekend if you go on like this. It'll be fine.'

'I – hope so,' he said, but he didn't sound very convinced.

'It will. What are you most scared of? Apart from losing?'

'Oh, reliving it all, in public—'

'What?' she asked, genuinely curious.

'The – the marriage. The marriage going wrong. All the awful things, the fights, the cross-purposes, oh, I don't know, I just feel so confused. Part of me wishes I'd never even started on it—'

'Of course. You'd be weird if you didn't. But—' She struggled for the right thing to say. 'But everything you really care about is worth fighting for – sorry, terrible cliché – and, and surely Emmie comes under that category.'

'Yes, of course. But you know – I was thinking about her the other day, how I was high as a kite after she was born, I could have flown out the window, it was so amazing and we were all so happy. I thought I've really, really got it all now, and – look at us. I did that.'

'Matt, you didn't do it. Well, you did, but you both did. Maybe – maybe the two of you should never have got married. You're so different. I mean, I know you were in love and everything, but there's love, isn't there, and there's marriage and – oh, never mind. I don't know what I'm talking about. Last of the spinsters, that's me. Married to hotels, what a prospect for my old age—'

'I don't know. Could be worse. Someone to look after you. Lots of someones. Not many old people have their own personal chamber-maids—'

She smiled. 'Nice one, Matt. Oh, could you excuse me just a moment, there's the manager, he's spotted me. I'll be back.'

Gina watched Louise as she walked across the bar; she was very stylish. Not exactly fashionable, those shoes were last year's without a doubt and her Little Black Dress was neither mini nor maxi, just knee-length. But that long rope of pearls, possibly the Chanel boutique, was very nice and so were the gold bangles – and her legs were very good indeed. And she had a sleekness about her that meant self-confidence and success – big success. Louise was a tycoon, one of the very first females to be so, not just the part owner of some crummy boutique. Gina suddenly felt rather depressed. No, more than depressed, distressed.

Here was the man she was hoping to – well, actually, marry one day, in the company of a woman who . . .

'Let's go,' she said to Freddy, 'please.'

'OK, doll, but I've left my wallet upstairs, I'll have to go and get it. See you in the lobby.'

'Yes, fine.'

She stood up; as she did so, Louise came sashaying across the room, sat down with a bit of a thump half on Matt's lap and laughed. He wouldn't like that, Gina thought, he hated any kind of public intimacy. But – he smiled back at her and patted her thigh fondly as she slithered off it.

And then – then – no, couldn't be, but yes, yes it was, they stared at each other, clearly quite startled, and there was a pause and then Louise leaned forward and smiled and kissed Matt – OK, very briefly – on the mouth. And then pulled back. And then he did the same. Equally briefly. And then they sat staring at each other again.

Gina couldn't stand it any longer; she walked forward, right up to their table, and squaring up to them said, 'Is this a private love-in? Or can anyone join in?'

'Damn! Shit! Bloody animals. Oh—'

'Fuck?' proffered Eliza helpfully.

'Yes, actually. Fuck, fuck, fuck. Oh, look at it. And it's Friday evening, all the garages will be closed. Oh, bloody hell—'

The cause of this outburst was a couple of sheep that had clearly escaped their field and were ambling peacefully along the country lane; a corner had obscured them from view until the very last minute, whereupon Toby had braked, swerved violently and slithered safely but rather irrevocably half into the ditch.

Eliza got out and looked at the car. A few attempts at reversing had failed, indeed made matters worse; the BMW was now trapped in its own skid trail of wet grass and mud.

Toby got out and joined her. 'We should have stuck to the main roads,' he said.

That 'we' was generous, she thought; it had been her suggestion that they struck off the A road, which was thick with Friday-evening traffic.

'I'm sorry. Bad idea.'

'No, no, it's – well, yes, bad idea.'

'Sorry,' she said again.

'It's – OK.' He scowled at the car. 'Bloody thing. But – point is – what do we do now?'

'God knows. We need a tow—'

As if on cue a very old Ford Anglia pulled up beside them, and a doughty-looking elderly lady peered at them. She was dressed in a barbour and wellington boots in spite of the lovely evening, her grey hair piled up in a straggly bun on the top of her head.

'Looks as if you need help.'

'Indeed,' said Toby, 'and kind of you to stop. But I don't think your car . . .'

She looked at him witheringly.

'Of course not. But there's a breakdown garage in Deep Mallow, that's the village a few miles along. Want a lift there?'

'That would be very kind. But won't they be closed?'

'Oh, without doubt. But Jim – that's the owner – lives on the premises, I know him very well, he'll come and sort you out, come on, hop in.'

Eliza and Toby hopped.

Jim Douglas was clearly in awe of the old lady; he said he was just finishing his tea and then he'd accompany Eliza and Toby back to the car. He revealed as they drove over that she was the widow of one Colonel Rockingham, resident of the manor house and the uncrowned queen of the village.

'Very nice lady, very generous, but you 'ave to do what she says or you're sorry. She says to let 'er know what I make of it all.'

'Oh – OK,' said Toby. 'Very kind of you anyway.'

Jim Douglas managed to tow the car out of the ditch; but there was some damage to the wheel base. 'Can't do nothing with that till tomorrow, if then.'

'Oh, dear. We rather need to get back,' said Toby.

''Fraid you won't. Not in that.'

'Is there anywhere we could hire a car?'

'Not this time of night. In the morning, maybe. If you want to make a few calls, there's a pay phone in the workshop, but I doubt you'll 'ave any joy.'

They didn't. Everywhere was closed.

'Looks like we're stuck. No – no buses, I suppose.'

'What, this time of night? Last one goes at five thirty.'

'No taxi service?'

'What, in Deep Mallow?' He seemed to find this very amusing. 'No, you're here till tomorrow, I'd say. But . . . let's see now – there's a very good pub down the road, you could get a meal there and then my auntie, she's got a B&B, she might be able to put you up, I could ring her. Just the one night, would it be?'

'Yes, but—'

'I'll see what I can do.'

He came back smiling. 'Yes, she's got the one room, nice one, she says, looks over the meadows. Fifty bob with breakfast, OK?'

'Yes, but—'

'I'll tell her then. It's just two houses down from the pub, called White Cottage, nice and convenient for you. You'll be very comfortable, I can vouch for that.'

'Mr Douglas—'

'That sounds perfect,' said Eliza. She smiled sweetly at Toby. 'Very, very kind. Thank you.'

Toby stared at her, his expression a mixture of horror and amusement.

'Well, honestly,' she said, tucking into the very good pie and chips that the pub served, 'we have to stay somewhere, we can't sleep in the ditch, and it was obviously very clean. And so sweet of her, offering to lend us toothbrushes and stuff.'

'Yes, but – I mean – Eliza—'

'Toby, stop it. I'm not trying to seduce you, if that's what you think.'

'No – no, of course not.'

'I've got enough problems. You saw it was quite a big bed, we'll manage. You can put a bolster down between us if you really want to—'

'Oh, God.' He looked quite desperate; she felt half-amused, half-insulted. 'Did – did you speak to your mother?'

'Yes. I just said we'd had to stop for the night in a hotel, she'll obviously assume two rooms and all that. Emmie's fine, exhausted, actually gone to

650

bed, and unless you've got any serious commitments you haven't told me about, I don't see why you're quite so worried.'

'Legal protocol,' he said, 'surely you can see this is appallingly compromising.'

'Toby!'

'No, it's true. Personal relationships between counsel and client are absolutely unethical. It would give your husband and his legal team the perfect opportunity to say I was unable to do the job I am required to do, that of advising the court as well as the client.'

'But we're not in a personal relationship,' said Eliza.

'And who would believe that? Christ. Sharing a room and a double bed. Please, Eliza, use your brain.'

'I don't have much of a one, as you know. And who is going to tell? I'm not, you're not. I doubt if Jim Douglas's auntie will. So do stop fussing and eat your pie, it's awfully good.'

He looked at her and grinned suddenly. 'You seem very cheerful about it.'

'I am. It's a wonderful distraction from Monday. Now do try to stop fussing, Toby. It'll be all right.'

Mrs Rockingham appeared in the pub just as they were finishing their meal. She nodded at them, went over to the bar; Toby jumped up.

'Let me, it's the least I can do. You've been so kind. What are you drinking?'

'Guinness,' she said. 'A pint, please. Very good of you. May I join you for a bit? I won't stay long, never do, just the one and I'm back off home to bed.'

'Us too,' said Eliza with an innocent smile at Toby. She was suddenly hugely enjoying this.

'Toby, please try to relax. You'll have a heart attack in a minute. Now look, I'm going along the corridor to the bathroom, clean my teeth and stuff and you can get undressed. OK?'

'Yes, OK. Well actually – I'll go first. Oh, I don't know.'

He seemed incredibly stressed, stripped of his usual self-confidence. Eliza was surprised. She'd have expected him to take it more in his stride.

'I'll go first,' she said.

When she got back, he was waiting by the door; he bolted out of it. Eliza sighed and undressed down to her bra and pants, then after a

651

moment took the bra off and replaced it with the denim shirt she'd been wearing. It seemed less compromising. She sat down on the bed; it was quite hard and it creaked horribly. But – it was large. They could lie quite easily – on their separate sides.

She decided he would be happier if she turned the light out, but the switch was by the door; he came in and climbed in beside her.

'Goodnight,' he said, very formally.

'Goodnight, Toby. Sleep well. Er – could you turn the light off?'

'Oh – yes, sure.'

She watched him as he half-ran across the room; he was wearing only his underpants. He had a very good body, she noticed – purely out of academic interest of course – he was lean and muscly and his shoulders were much broader than she had realised.

'Night,' he said again, turning his back very carefully on her.

'Night, Toby. Sweet dreams.'

'Gina, please!'

'Please what, Matt? Please go away? Please leave me to what is clearly a very enjoyable evening? Please don't be embarrassing?'

She nodded at Louise. 'Hello. Nice to see you again. You must forgive me for intruding. I've heard how much you've been helping Matt with his case; it seems I was right about your motives. And I might say you're doing a lot better with him than I am. He won't even appear in public with me, never mind snogging. This is a very nice hotel, Louise, I presume you can have a room at very short notice. Most convenient. Well, I'll let you get on. Enjoy your evening.'

And she was gone, her high heels clacking across the hard wooden floor.

'Oh, God,' said Matt, 'I'm sorry, Louise. She's a bit – highly strung.'

'You could say that. Or you could say she was a bit rude. Or a bit mad. Are you still seeing her, then?'

'Not – not really.'

'It sounds as if you are. What was all that about, my motives?'

'Oh – oh nothing . . . Look, you must feel very embarrassed in front of your manager and everything, maybe we'd better go.'

'What, up to a room, as the whole bar will now be expecting? I don't think so. I think we should stay here, nice and calm, and carry on with the champagne. And you can explain, perhaps, exactly what she meant.'

'Louise—'

'No, I want to know.'

'Well – I'll – I'll try.'

He tried.

'That's just totally ridiculous.'

'I know. I'm just telling you what she said.'

'I mean—'

'I know.'

'It's – well, it's crazy.'

'I know.'

'I just wanted to help, that's all.'

'I know.'

'I mean of course I'm very – I'm fond of you.'

'Really?'

'Of course.'

'I thought you hated me.'

'Now Matt, that's just stupid. Of course I don't hate you. As I said, I'm quite – quite fond of you.'

'I know. I mean, I know you don't actually hate me. I didn't realise you were – fond of me.'

'Hang on. Probably I should have said I liked you. Yes, I like you. Quite a lot.'

'Ah.'

'We go back a long way, after all.'

'We do.'

'Years and years.'

'And for most of them, we spent a lot of time fighting.'

'Yes, we did. But you deserved it.'

'Oh, Louise.'

'Oh, Matt. What's the matter, what's gone wrong, you look as if you're going to – to cry.'

'I feel like crying,' he said, 'suddenly.'

'Why?'

'Because I'm a complete and utter bastard. And I've made a complete and utter hash of everything.'

'Not a complete and utter hash. Complete and utter bastard – well, arguable, I'd say.'

'No, don't. Don't start trying to make me feel better about myself. You can't. I'm a bastard, and I didn't deserve Eliza and I've behaved appallingly towards her, for years and years, and I don't deserve Emmie, and I'm behaving appallingly to her, and – oh shit. Shit, shit, shit. Oh, Christ, I think I'd better go home.'

'No. No, don't. Why don't you come back to my place. Just for a bit. Just for some – whisky. Whisky and sympathy.'

Eliza woke up, feeling very hot and longing for a pee. She eased herself cautiously onto her back and lay there for a bit, listening to Toby snoring. His concern about their situation was clearly not severe enough to keep him awake.

She slid as carefully as she could out of bed, cursing the creaking, worked her way towards the door and opened it; switched the landing light on and scuttled along to the loo.

God, it was hot.

Back in the room, it was stifling; she tried to open the window, but it seemed to be jammed. She looked at her watch: only half past two. A long time ahead, to be this uncomfortable. Well – maybe –

She pulled her shirt off, and lay down again. And then her pants. Toby was far too deeply asleep to notice.

She'd never get back to sleep; never. She lay there, trying all the tricks, relaxing all over from her toes up, saying the alphabet backwards, counting backwards, counting sheep – she sighed. At least the snoring had stopped . . .

'You awake?' said Toby.

'Yes. Are you?'

'No.'

She giggled.

'It's awfully hot, isn't it?'

'Yes. I might try and open the window. Let's see – oh damn, stubbed my fucking toe – I'll have to put the light on . . .'

He sank onto the bed, rubbing his toe; and then turned and saw her. Sitting up, stark naked.

'Oh God,' he said, and then again, 'oh, my God,' and then, 'turn the fucking light off, for Christ's sake.'

It all happened very quickly after that.

She came back to the bed, and lay down on it and turned her head to him. And he reached out a hand and touched one of her breasts very gently and slowly. And then he said, 'I – don't think I can stand this any longer. You?'

'I can't stand it either.'

And then he turned on his side, and pulled her into his arms and started to kiss her. Hard. And quite – well, yes, impatiently. As he did most things. And as if he couldn't get enough of her, fast enough.

And then . . . and then . . . and then . . .

She wanted him so much, wanted it so much, it shocked her. Everything, her anxiety, her grief, her remorse was gone, thrown aside in its wake, in a great roaring, raging wave of desire, selfish, greedy, desperate. Her body took his in and could not have enough of it; she yearned, sought, soared into delight, into a clear, bright, brilliant pleasure, that spread through her, swiftly, sweetly, wonderfully, reaching into her most secret self, into her head and into her heart. And when finally she collapsed, trembling, weak with relief and release, she realised he was almost laughing, very quietly, his hand over her mouth, the sheet over their heads.

'God, you're noisy,' he said, and she could hear the smile in his voice.

'I know. I'm sorry.'

'That and the bed combined. It was amazing. You are amazing. I – I loved it,' he said after a pause, and the words surprised and touched her. 'Are you always that noisy?'

'I'm afraid so. Sorry.'

'I should like to think you weren't,' he said, 'I should like to think those extremely unladylike shrieks were simply because of me. Please don't tell me otherwise.'

'I won't. Toby, it was lovely. Really lovely. Thank you.'

'My pleasure. My great, huge pleasure.'

'Do you think—' She stopped.

'What?'

'Do you think it would have happened, if we hadn't been here, if we'd just driven home and—'

'Not yet,' he said, 'most assuredly not yet.'

'That's a bit – insulting. That you only did it because I was here.'

'Fidgeting about, waking me up. Well, yes. But it would only have been a postponement. I've thought about it ever since I first set eyes on you, in Philip Gordon's office.'

'You haven't!' she said, and she was genuinely and most sweetly astonished.

'Yes, I have. I might have seemed to be thinking about witnesses and evidence and rights of access, but actually I was thinking I wonder what she looks like without her clothes on, and I wonder what she's like in bed.'

'I bet you weren't.'

'Maybe not exactly. But I thought how very lovely you were and how you were the very first woman for a long, long time who had – well, moved me, is the only expression.'

'Oh, Toby. That's so – so nice.'

'It's true. And now I know, you look pretty good without your clothes on and you are not half bad in bed. How about you?'

'I just thought you were very scary.'

'Just?'

'Well, I found you a bit – disturbing.'

'Disturbing – such a sexy word. I feel a little bit disturbed again now actually.'

'I—'

There was the sound of a door opening, footsteps in the corridor, the light showed through a crack in the door.

'We're going to get expelled,' she whispered.

'Shush—'

The light went out again, the door was heard to close, the house became silent.

'Phew!'

'Yes, but—'

'Yes, but what—'

'I find I rather want you again. Even more. You?'

'I – might do,' she said, sitting up, pulling the pillows from under them, hurling them across the room.

'What are you doing?'

'Let's do it on the floor. Must be quieter.'

'But – will you be quieter?'

'I'll try. Come on, come on, don't keep me waiting . . .'

She woke up at six, back in bed, to find the sun flooding into the room and Toby gone; she looked round, alarmed. Had he fled, back into the anonymity of London, safe from the disgrace of flouting the rules of the Bar? Had he hitched a ride into Marlow, the nearest town, and picked up a hire car and left her to sort things out without him?

He hadn't. He came back in, one of the very small towels they had been given round his waist, his hair wet.

'Sorry. Went to have a bath. Now listen. We have to have a talk.'

This was it. He was going to tell her it had been great, but it was over, a mere trifle of delight, and they must return to their old selves, of counsel and client, probably never to see one another again, after Friday's verdict when his work was done.

'From now on,' he said, affirming her fears, 'we must forget this. Forget how we feel, how we've behaved, how we discovered one another. I cannot tell you how important that is. The merest hint of what has gone on, and we would both of us be done for in that courtroom. If I am to fight for you and for Emmie, I must do it on my own terms, dispassionately and temperately; as if, indeed, you and I had hardly met. No exchanges of smiles or looks or—'

'Kisses?' she said, her face very serious, and he scowled at her until he realised she was teasing him.

'Kisses, fine. Any time. Just blow them from the witness box, if you feel like it. No, Eliza, nothing. And I have to tell you something else. You may not like me very much as the week goes on. I shall quite possibly give you a hard time; I shall certainly give the other side a hard time. You could see someone quite – brutal. I think you should be prepared for that.'

'Yes,' she said, and she felt quite nervous suddenly, not about the case, but of him. 'Yes, all right. But—'

'No buts. It's too important.'

So it had been just – just a momentary thing. Born of an accident.

'I was going to say afterwards. What will happen afterwards. Will we – can you – should I—' and then because his face had grown quite hard, shockingly so after what they had shared that night, she lapsed into silence, and felt very afraid. That it had been just a one occasion thing. An – accident, born of chance and proximity, a piece of torment from Fate.

There was a long silence. Then he said, 'Afterwards, if you still so wish, and after a very slightly decent interval, we can meet and explore one another and how we feel. We have a long way to go, we've both been hurt, we're both – scared is probably the right word. But – I think, I would like that, if you would. And with time, and possibly even a quieter, softer, less creaky bed.'

'Oh,' she said, and delight flooded her again, delight and relief. 'Oh, God. Is it too late for me to – just kiss you again. I'll lock the door.'

'I really would rather you didn't,' he said, and she felt crushed and foolish, and then she saw that he was smiling, 'because if you did, various sequences might be set in motion and it would be getting late for the seven o'clock breakfast Mr Douglas's auntie has promised us before driving us into Marlow and I would feel bound to repeat all my warnings, and—'

'Oh, do shut up,' she said, 'we can be quick, very, very quick. Please, Toby. Please.'

And Mr Douglas's auntie, downstairs preparing the English breakfast for which she was famous in the area, complete with black pudding, looked up at the ceiling and shook her head at the noise of the bed creaking and thought how she really must replace it and how nice it was to find a married couple who were so clearly in love with one another . . .

And meanwhile in London, in her chic, minimalist flat, Louise was also awake, staring at the bright morning sky, and thinking about Matt and his rather obvious alarm at her invitation back to her flat and the rather feeble excuse he had made about getting home and sorting out a few final details of his case.

Matt was also awake, afraid that he had overstepped the mark and belaboured poor Louise just one too many times with his misery and his remorse and thinking she really was the only person who had ever managed to distract him from it, and what a long way they did indeed go back, and how much he valued her friendship and that he really should not trade on it so heavily. When the case was over, he would make a great effort to leave her alone. And let her get on with her own life. Until then, he seemed to rather need her.

And Georgina Barker, angry beyond anything, was counting down the hours until nine o'clock which she felt was the earliest time she could decently ring Philip Gordon, Eliza's solicitor, who had given her his home number, to tell him that she was prepared after all to appear as a witness.

Chapter 69

'All rise.'

Mr Justice Rogers walked more quickly into the court than most judges. He was, while deeply respectful of its processes and traditions, its power and its frequent glory, impatient of its pomp. His alma mater, Plymouth Grammar rather than the Winchester or Eton of so many of his peers, and his university, Nottingham, not Oxford or Cambridge, had left him perhaps less arrogant than they, but more self-opinionated. He had succeeded, he felt, where most of his ilk would have failed; doors had not automatically opened to him as he left university, the old-boy network had not been available to him, his pupillage had been hard won, and his father, a widowed head teacher from Devon, had had to sell much of his beloved dead wife's jewellery to keep him in it. Cases had been equally elusive for a good while, as the soft burr that still clung to his voice charmed but did not inspire confidence in clients; and even as his reputation gained an increasing momentum, won in the first instance by his brilliant defence of a young woman accused of the murder of her offspring – it was perhaps one of the first recorded cases of what would one day be called 'cot death' – the ultimate prize of a seat on the bench took him a decade longer to win than it did most of his peers.

Along the way, he had lost both his wife and two young sons in a messy divorce; she had grown weary of his long absences as a circuit judge – which had been hard on her, Clifford Rogers would have been the first to accept – and taken up with the dashing young GP who had called so frequently late at night when one or other of the boys was ill.

She had been granted both custody and care and control; the boys were only five and three and she and the doctor could provide a model home. The boys were now fifteen and thirteen and Clifford Rogers had probably spent only a year in their company in total.

He was, not surprisingly, something of a misogynist, deeply suspicious of the feminist movement and almost equally so of the working mother.

His sympathies in the case of Shaw vs Shaw, from his initial very careful reading of the documents, tended towards the father.

From what he had read he was self-made, hard-working, successful and a devoted father; the mother, a fashion editor, and with an undefended adultery to her name, and some history of mental illness, did not present a very satisfactory picture. However, it was a complex case and an interesting one; he had found himself looking forward to it during the course of a rather long and particularly lonely weekend. He found the way many judges came to the court ill-prepared quite shocking and more so if it was necessary to adjourn proceedings for several hours so that they could study the documents more carefully. For Clifford Rogers, the weekend before a big case was the start of his working week.

And it was an impression of impatience, of an eagerness to get on with the matter that he carried with him as he strode into the court.

Ivor Lewis admired Clifford Rogers greatly; he could not believe in their luck in getting him as their judge. He had once heard him speak on the iniquities of privilege in general and public-school education in particular; the likes of Jeremy Northcott therefore, Lewis reckoned, and the upper-class riff-raff from his agency, and even the upmarket tones of Eliza Shaw, must surely struggle to find favour. He watched Rogers now as he settled on the bench, pulling out files, looking round the court with his brooding, restless gaze, and wondered if they could possibly have had anyone more suitable . . . and the other lot hadn't even got a QC. It really was going to be like taking candy from a baby – an appropriate analogy indeed, he said to himself, looking round.

'Yes, Mr Hayward, do please begin.'

Oh, God, thought Eliza, it's started; oh, Christ, thought Matt, this is it; and terror united them, as surely as love once had, terror at what they had done and what was to come, and their eyes met across the court, and both of them would have given all they had to be safely back in the past, with none of it begun.

And then Bruce Hayward rose to his feet and looked around the court; there was a silence, while he appeared to be waiting for absolute attention. He always did that, Philip Gordon knew, for as long as he dared. Which wouldn't be so very long today, Hayward was a wily old gannet and he knew that Clifford Rogers didn't really like theatricals.

Finally then: 'My lord, we are here today to consider the case of Shaw versus Shaw, and the matter of custody of Emmeline Shaw, aged six. This is necessitated by the ending of the marriage due to the admitted adultery of her mother Elizabeth Shaw . . . her father, Matthew Shaw, seeks custody on the grounds that Mrs Shaw is not a fit person to have care of her daughter . . . moreover I intend to show that Mrs Shaw has a history of mental instability and is quite possibly not competent to take care of so young a child . . . that Mrs Shaw took Emmeline on trips abroad without Mr Shaw, where she was not properly supervised . . . and that moreover while Emmeline was still extremely young Mrs Shaw returned to work in the advertising industry, pursuing her career specifically against the expressed wishes of Mr Shaw . . . and quite frequently asked the nanny to bring the child to her office late in the evening, if she was delayed in a meeting . . . it was during this time that Mrs Shaw went on what she describes as a photographic session to Scotland, leaving the child at home with a nanny, specifically against Mr Shaw's expressed wishes, and that the adultery, with the creative director employed by the agency, took place . . .

'. . . It should also be noticed that Mrs Shaw sought to diminish Mr Shaw's public reputation, and that far from being a supportive wife she was a destructive element in his career, even engineering an article in a newspaper critical of his work and methods . . . a career that had of course guaranteed her a very high standard of living and moreover had enabled Mr Shaw to purchase a property which had been in Mrs Shaw's family for many generations but was going to rack and ruin, as there were not the funds to maintain it. And beyond even that, your honour, he had allowed Mrs Shaw's mother, a widow, to remain living in the property, a substantial house in Wiltshire, when she would normally have been forced to move into very inferior accommodation . . .'

Well, Eliza thought, they might as well all go home straight away. There wasn't a hope in hell of getting Emmie, not a judge in Christendom who would have passed her into the hands of so neglectful, so selfish, so manipulative a mother.

'. . . there was also a very unfortunate incident in Milan, Italy—'

'I know where Milan is, Mr Hayward.'

He was irritating the judge, Toby thought; that was a piece of luck, they hadn't considered that as a possibility, that foxy old Hayward with his flashy gestures and smooth voice might prove rather too theatrical for the more basic approach of Clifford Rogers.

'Of course, my lord. Mrs Shaw presented this trip as a distraction from her depression after her baby was born, a depression for which she sought psychiatric help.'

'Yes, yes, and I would like to read those reports. Is there some reason they are not included in the papers?'

'My lord,' said Toby Gilmour, standing up, 'Mrs Miller, the psycho-therapist, has refused to disclose the reports in advance on grounds of patient confidentiality.'

'Has she indeed? Then she must be informed I need to read them. Given the age of the child, and their importance to the case.'

'Yes, my lord. But—'

'No buts, Mr Gilmour. I shall find her in contempt of court if she refuses further.'

'Yes, my lord.'

That was it then, Eliza thought. It would all come out, there was no hope left.

'Do continue, Mr Hayward.'

Mr Hayward continued with a graphic description of Emmie, lost in Milan by one of the Crespis' maids, 'after dark, at the busiest time of the year, in a foreign city, a small child of just five. She was finally found in a department store. Imagine her distress, her panic, indeed.'

'I think I can manage that, Mr Hayward. And possibly of the mother as well.'

'Indeed. Moreover this incident was kept from Mr Shaw and only emerged when Emmeline mentioned it much later. The next night a party of the Crespis' guests was going to the opera. I should have said the Crespis lived on the shores of Lake Como, and Milan was an hour's drive away. Emmeline was left with this same incompetent maid. Although there had been talk of a thick fog coming in, a well-known occurrence in Milan, Mrs Shaw decided to go. And as a result was trapped in Milan that night and again the child was alone in a strange, large house, with a group of servants she hardly knew for company . . .'

It all sounded so terrible, Eliza thought. So, so terrible. Careless, reckless behaviour towards her daughter; and – it had been terrible, how had she been persuaded to do that, how, how?'

'. . . a further incident, deeply distressing for Mr Shaw, indicative I would propose of Mrs Shaw's general irresponsibility, occurred when she organised the appearance of the extremely derogatory article in the *Daily News* which named her husband and some of the properties he owned . . . there was no attempt to allow him to explain the situation, or to warn him. It was a humiliation and a betrayal that Mr Shaw again found indicative of Mrs Shaw's lack of loyalty towards him and responsibility for the family he was working so hard to support.

'We now come to the night which Mr Shaw describes as being the last of his marriage. Mrs Shaw was in Scotland, working, for three days, Emmeline was left in the care of the nanny and her maternal grandmother. Mr Shaw arrived home to find the child unwell; she became dramatically worse, the doctor was called and he advised she be taken to Casualty. She was crying for her mother, crying to speak to her, Mr Shaw phoned the hotel where his wife was staying and was put through to her room; a man answered the phone. The man with whom she was committing adultery. It was at that point, Mr Shaw said, that he lost faith finally in Mrs Shaw not only as a wife, but a mother.

'I would submit therefore, Your Honour, that Mrs Shaw is clearly an unfit person to have charge of her child, and that sole custody be granted to Mr Shaw.'

This was horrible. How could she bear it, how was she going to get through a week of this, of hearing these lies and innuendoes and distortions of the facts? Toby had tried to warn her but nothing could have prepared her for this . . . she looked at him across the court, sitting very still, very calm, studying papers, making notes, listening to Bruce Hayward with great attention, and felt a rush of rage that he could do that, not leap to his feet and her defence, saying that is not so, not how it was, this is not true, most assuredly not true. Well, he had warned her; but he seemed a very different creature from the man who had made love to her only three days before . . .

'. . . Your Honour, I would now like to call Mr Shaw . . .'

He looked very nervous, Eliza thought; she knew that expression, the one of fake bravado, the slightly cocky tapping of his fingers on the witness box, the inability to make eye contact . . . he was really scared. Well – good.

'Mr Shaw, perhaps you would like to tell us, in your own words, why you think you should have care, and indeed custody of your daughter.

You are, after all, a very busy man, you work long hours, why do you think she would be better off with you than her mother? Take your time.'

Matt cleared his throat.

'I have worked very long hours in the past, it's true. But if I was to gain custody of Emmie – of my daughter, I would make sure that didn't happen. I have a large company now, with many employees, and I am very well able to delegate all but the most complex tasks. I am already looking at adjusting my schedules to allow for me to be home very shortly after Emmie is back from school . . .'

'And while you were at work, and she was not at school, if she was ill or something like that?'

'I have already located a very competent nanny, a woman of mature years, Norland trained' – he's learnt this off by heart, Eliza thought – 'who would be available twenty-four hours a day, and would collect Emmie from school, and of course be with her full-time in the holidays. My mother, who has taken care of Emmie regularly from birth, would also be on call during the term time and would spend at least two days a week with Emmie in the holidays . . .'

'Yes, Mr Gilmour?'

Toby rose to his feet. He smiled at Matt.

'Mr Shaw, good morning. A question. Emmie already has a nanny, Miss Margaret Grant, who she knows and loves. Why would you not continue to employ her?'

'I think the woman I have decided upon—'

'You've already decided on her? Has Mrs Shaw met her?'

'No, no, she hasn't. But this person, in my opinion, is of a much higher calibre, more highly qualified, and would work for me – us – full-time. Miss Grant is a shared nanny.'

'Yes, I see. Thank you, Mr Shaw.'

Matt was staring at his hands, seemingly silenced. The interruption had clearly rattled him. Bruce Hayward rose to his feet again.

'Mr Shaw, the court would like to hear more about your plans for Emmie, and the more humdrum aspects of her care. In my experience, this is something we males find rather tedious.'

'Actually, I don't find it that at all,' said Matt and his voice suddenly became stronger, less defensive. 'From the moment she was born, I've enjoyed it, looking after her. And I was there that day – at her birth.'

'You were there?' said Bruce Hayward. 'How very – unusual.'

'Yes, of course I was there. I wanted to be, I felt' – his voice shook slightly – 'I felt it was probably the most important day of my life . . .'

He means it, thought Eliza, you can tell, this is not rehearsed emotion; and she felt, in spite of everything, a lump rising in her throat, and looked at Matt through a blur of tears.

'I see. I have to tell you I am very impressed.'

'Well – I thought it was important for all three of us, my wife, the child and me. And it was an amazing experience. It changed my life. And I think my relationship with Emmie has always been closer as a result. I was the first person to hold her, apart from the midwife who delivered her . . .'

'And would you say this has formed your attitude to the more intimate aspects of her care?'

'Yes, I would, if you mean things like changing nappies, looking after her when she was – well, throwing up, you know. I've never minded it at all.'

'Most admirable.'

'Mr Shaw.' Toby was playing this very skilfully, Philip thought, very calm, almost laid-back, a rather charming contrast to the foxy Hayward.

'I too am impressed. I have not been blessed with fatherhood, but I have always found babies rather messy, smelly objects. I applaud your strong stomach along with your devotion.'

Matt looked at him warily.

'However – you have never done it on a daily basis, have you? Seven days a week, fifty-two weeks a year. It is a kind of recreational duty, wouldn't you say? After a long tough day on the building site or the boardroom, it is probably quite attractive to come back to something completely different.'

'I've never been able to do it seven days a week,' said Matt, 'obviously I've had to earn the money to finance it all, I couldn't just stay at home, everything would fall apart—'

'Of course. I just wanted to make the point that impressive as your record is, it is based on a slightly romantic model.'

'There's nothing romantic about clearing up after a puking kid all night, I can tell you,' said Matt.

'Of course. That's not what I mean. But you have always known that at the end of that night or that weekend, you will be returning to the nice, clean, adult world of your office. You don't have to continue looking after the – er, puking kid.'

'Well – I explained why not.'

'Of course. I merely wanted to make the point.'

Point well made, thought Philip Gordon.

'I also found my wife's attitude towards motherhood difficult to understand,' said Matt, 'she wanted to go back to work, when Emmie was really still very young. I couldn't understand it. A child needs its mother. And looking after a child is surely the most important job there is. Even working part-time, which was what she was talking about – it just seemed wrong to me.'

'But she did not take a job?' inquired Toby Gilmour, his voice honeysweet. 'Why was that?'

'Well – I was very opposed to it. Which she knew.'

'And she acquiesced to that?'

'Yes.'

'That sounds quite accommodating to me.'

Matt became silent again; he had clearly had this planned, but not rehearsed.

Bruce Hayward stood up.

'Mr Shaw, there was another chapter in the story, wasn't there? Which we have only touched upon so far. Tell us about that, Mr Shaw, about the – the other child.'

'Yes. We had a – a tragedy. Another child, a boy, born three months premature. Who – who died. My wife became very depressed . . .'

'Not surprisingly.'

'No, of course not.'

'And what was your role then, did you feel?'

'Well – to try to – to cheer her up, support her. And of course to get things back to normal. But – she was very – very down. She wasn't sleeping, she cried all the time—'

'Would you say this had a bad effect on your relationship, Mr Shaw?' Toby Gilmour had stood up again.

'No. No, of course not.'

'You were able to continue to support her? Even though obviously you went back to work. Of necessity.'

'Yes. But—'

666

'But?'

'She didn't seem to want me to do that. To support her. She – avoided me. Wouldn't spend time with me. She was quite – hostile.'

'And – forgive me, Mr Shaw, had intimate relations between you ceased at this time?'

'Objection, My Lord.'

'No, I think it is relevant. Mr Shaw, answer the question, please.'

Eliza had not thought to feel a shred of sympathy for Matt ever again; she did now, as he looked down, clearly going through the tortures of the damned, remembering her constant rejections, his hurt, forced to this public admission of failure, she felt again a lurch of her heart . . . and looked thoughtfully at Toby, remembering his words and indeed the situation in which he spoke them, 'you may not like me very much as the week goes on . . .'

'Er – yes,' Matt said finally. 'At that time.'

'But – not permanently?'

'No.'

He pulled out a handkerchief, wiped his forehead.

'And then Mrs Shaw saw this psychiatrist, I believe?' Bruce Hayward's tone was thoughtful.

'Yes, yes she did.'

'Who diagnosed depression?'

'Yes. And her behaviour towards Emmie became very – very erratic. She was short-tempered, shouted at her a lot, often took her late to school, I was anxious for Emmie, I felt she wasn't safe.'

'Mr Gilmour?'

'Mr Shaw, I believe the strictly accurate diagnosis was of post-natal depression.'

'Yes, it was.'

'I don't see the relevance of this, My Lord.'

'I simply wanted, my lord, to make it clear that it was not an ongoing problem for Mrs Shaw. She is not a depressive personality, this was a reactive depression, not an endogenous one, there is a difference, as I am sure your lordship would appreciate—'

'Point taken, Mr Gilmour. Proceed, Mr Shaw.'

'There isn't very much more to say. I have come to believe that from that time my wife has simply not been a reliable person, not suited to take care of Emmie. Emmie is my first priority in life, and I – I love her very much, I want to see her happy and safe. I think I can make her and keep her so. That's – that's all.'

'Thank you, Mr Shaw. Time for a break, I think.'

'Want any lunch?'

Eliza shook her head; she was numb with misery. It was so clearly so hopeless, she was being completely pilloried, as Toby had said she would be. Why had he ever encouraged her to go on, why had Philip Gordon encouraged her in the first place? She wanted to run and run, to go Summercourt, stay there hidden where no one could find her . . .

'Let's go to my rooms,' said Toby Gilmour. 'Come along, Eliza, that was the very, very worst part over. As Winston Churchill might have said, the end of the beginning.'

'Why didn't you argue more, why didn't you ask more questions?'

'Because that's not the way it works. I asked what was pertinent for the moment. We have plenty of time and I shall ask plenty of questions . . . try to trust me.'

As they walked into the chambers, Tristram Selbourne swept out, with a rather dismissive nod at Eliza; she gazed after him wretchedly. She had been wrong, she should have had him as her barrister, Toby wasn't up to it, it had been an appalling mistake . . .

Toby, watching her, read her thoughts and felt wretched himself.

'I would like to call my first witness.' Bruce Hayward looked as if he had enjoyed his lunch; almost lit up with adrenaline, his eyes sparkling, his colour high. 'Miss Louise Mullan . . .'

She looked marvellous, Eliza thought, dressed in cream gaberdine, cool, calm, very composed. She must be very fond of Matt to be doing this; and especially after they had had that very ugly professional split . . . very good of her, very good of her indeed.

Bit of a funny choice for a first witness, Philip Gordon thought, someone who knew Matt only professionally; and Toby Gilmour thought the same, that clearly this was the other side's weakest ground, the defence of Matt as prospective sole parent . . .

'Miss Mullan, you've worked with Mr Shaw for – how long?'

'Many years. From when he first founded his company.'

'And Mr Shaw was not then married to Mrs Shaw?'

'No. He wasn't even going out with her. He was – well, he was married to the firm.'

Whoops, Louise. Mistake. That's not going to help at all.

'But it was very early days, it was necessary for him, for all of us, to work round the clock.'

'Of course. But these days?'

'Well – he does work very hard. Of course. But the company is very successful, he employs a lot of people, he can clearly afford to work a much shorter day.'

'And – in your opinion, is Mr Shaw capable of making a good home for his daughter, of acting as both father and mother?'

She hesitated; then she said, 'I do think so, yes. If – well, if devotion has anything to do with it. He is quite exceptionally devoted to Emmie. He has always adored her from the day she was born; I shall always remember him coming in straight from the hospital, high as a kite. He said he felt as if he could have flown out of the window. He said he felt' – 'she hesitated, looked over at Matt – 'immortal.'

'I see. And – did this devotion continue? Many men are extremely excited by the arrival of their children, after all.'

'Yes, it did. He was always coming back from lunch with presents for her, dresses, toys, books to read to her, when he got home; we' – she smiled briefly here – 'we, the others in the office and I, had to listen at great length to her accomplishments, how advanced she was, and if Mr Shaw had to work late, he would always ring her up, say goodnight to her on the phone, sometimes even read to her, sitting there at his desk.'

The tribute went on; about Matt studying horse care, so that he could get involved with the whole pony thing, how he had sometimes come in looking quite exhausted, having been up with Emmie in the small hours. 'I remember when she had measles, it went on for night after night . . .'

'Where was her mother?' asked Bruce Hayward. 'Asleep?'

'I object to the tone, my lord,' said Gilmour.

'I agree. Please continue, Miss Mullan.'

'Eliza was there too, of course, but they did it in shifts, apparently. Except once, when she was very ill, when they both sat up, he told me, one on either side of the bed.'

'Right. That all sounds most exemplary,' said Bruce Hayward. 'No one could fail to be impressed by Mr Shaw's commitment to his daughter.'

'No, they couldn't,' said Louise, 'and I'm very impressed by the way he has everything planned, how he is going to arrange his life around her—'

'Yes, yes, we've heard about that from Mr Shaw. Any more questions, Mr Hayward?'

'No, my lord.'

'Mr Gilmour?'

'Yes, thank you. Miss Mullan, clearly you and Mr Shaw had a very good working relationship. I understand you are no longer business partners.'

'No, that's right.'

'Could you tell us why?'

'Yes, we had a – a disagreement. I resigned.'

'Of a personal nature.'

That was – mean, Eliza thought and then –

'No, of a business nature?'

'I see. So your relationship is purely a businesss one, is that correct?'

'Yes, it is.'

'There is nothing personal between you?'

'Absolutely not.'

'But you are clearly friends? You want to help him.'

'Yes,' said Louise steadily, 'we are friends and I want to help him.'

'I see. Well, you are a good friend, Miss Mullan. I hope he appreciates you.'

Could there be more between them? Could there? Because – no, Eliza, don't fall into that trap, he's just using his legal permission to smear. As she had been smeared so thoroughly that morning. It was a dirty business.

'Did you admire Mr Shaw as a businessman?'

'Yes, very much. He built up the company from absolutely nothing.'

'With your considerable help, as I understand it?'

'Yes, but he was the inspiration behind it.'

'He was one hundred per cent committed to it, I imagine? How do you think he will adjust to a slightly more – detached role?'

'I think it will be hard for him. Very hard. But he's prepared to do it and I think that shows the extent of his love for Emmie.'

'Have you spent much time with Mr and Mrs Shaw and Emmie?'

'No, I haven't.'

'So you're not really very well equipped to comment on his parenting skills? Beyond what you have already told us? I just want to put your – testimonial, passionate as it is, in proportion.'

Louise met his eyes very steadily.

'No. No, I'm not. But I am equipped to comment on his personal ones and he is a very determined person and whatever it is he puts his mind to, he will see it through. And right now, he's put his mind to being the main figure in Emmie's life. He even said to me that he would be prepared to sell the company in order to care for her full-time. If it became apparent that was necessary. And he loves that company, it would be like selling part of himself. One day Emmie will be very proud of her father.'

'I see. Thank you, Miss Mullan.'

She was amazing, thought Matt. Completely amazing. Standing up there, beating the drum for him; putting herself through this, when there was absolutely no need, just because she wanted to help him. Typical lawyer, trying to imply they had something going on between them. They stopped at nothing, these guys, they really did.

He watched her, cool and calm, and so bloody clear-headed and articulate, so impressive, for Christ's sake, refusing to be rattled by any of them, and he felt a sudden thud of – God, he'd thought it was gratitude, but actually it was something a bit – a bit different.

'I would now like to call my next witness, Mrs Sandra Shaw.'

Well, she'd be predictable . . . and she was . . . wonderful son . . . wonderful father . . . wonderful family man . . .

'Mrs Shaw—'

Toby Gilmour had stood up very slowly; he smiled at Sandra Shaw.

'Mrs Shaw. Could you tell us what sort of mother you consider your daughter-in-law to be?'

Good question, Toby, thought Eliza. Very good.

'Oh. Well, I don't really know—'

'Remember you are under oath.'

'I – I think she has been a good mother. In the early days, yes.'

'How would you define good mother?'

'Well – she looked after her very well. She seemed to love her. Emmie was certainly very well cared for. And Eliza used to work very hard at keeping her amused, take her to visit her friends, things like that. She used to bring her over to see me quite often, because she knew I liked that.'

'That must have been – very nice for you both.'

'Yes. Yes, it was. And I used to help her as much as I could, make suggestions, you know. It's hard when it's your first baby, you're nervous. And Emmie was very naughty, she used to play up given half the chance – and with Matt working so hard, I think it was nice for Eliza to have a bit of help.'

'Which she wasn't getting from him? I thought—'

'Well not during the week, no. He had his business to run.' Sandra looked defensive. 'It was a twenty-four-hour job sometimes.'

'Indeed. But hard on Eliza, perhaps?'

'Well, no worse than most wives have to put up with.'

'Really? Did your husband, and the husbands of your friends, work a twenty-four-hour day, as you put it?'

'No. No, they didn't.'

A pause.

'Did you get the impression she was lonely?'

'No, I didn't. She seemed to have plenty of friends. And a car and that, she wasn't tied to the house, she could get out and about.'

'So you were on good terms with her?'

'Yes, yes, we were – then.'

'But not any more?'

'No. We're not.'

'Did you observe any change in your daughter-in-law's behaviour, at any point?'

'Well – when the – the little boy died, she was very low after that, of course. Very low.'

'Did she talk to you about it, how she felt?'

'No. Not really. I used to offer to have Emmie for her then, she didn't often take me up on it. She said Emmie—' She stopped, looked anxiously across at Matt.

'Go on.'

'She said Emmie gave her a reason for living.'

'I see. And – did she continue to appear depressed?'

'For a while, yes. Then she saw this doctor and she got some pills for the depression, and she seemed better.'

'Thank you, Mrs Shaw.'

Margaret was wonderful, Eliza thought; very cool, very calm. She stressed Eliza only worked two days a week, that she and Matt were never out on the same evening, they were both very devoted parents and she dealt quite firmly with the matter of what Bruce Hayward called the habit of taking Emmie to the agency.

'It was not a habit. It was a suggestion of mine that if Mrs Shaw was held up in a meeting, I could save her half an hour or so by taking Emmie to her office occasionally. It was necessary for me to leave on time, as I have an invalid mother to take care of, but the offices are on my way home, and so it seemed to make sense. Mrs Shaw often arrived home in a state of panic, which worried me and this arrangement seemed helpful to both of us.'

'An admirable plan, Miss Grant. I am sure Mrs Shaw was very grateful.'

'She was.'

'But – did this not delay Emmie's bedtime?'

'Only very little. I would give her her tea first, and then drive her to Carlos Place. Mrs Shaw was usually ready when I got there, it was a half-hour journey maximum, twenty minutes if the traffic was light. But it was a very unusual arrangement, as I say, very far from regular.'

'How often? on average?'

'Oh – perhaps once a month at the most.'

'I see. And you would leave Emmie there, with her mother?'

'Well – yes. Usually.'

'And unusually?'

'Well, once or twice, the receptionist would look after her. Just until Mrs Shaw was out of her meeting. She would pop down and make sure Emmie was all right, and then go back to her meeting.'

'I see. So once a month – let us say – a very young child, who should have been in bed, and after her last meal of the day, was dragged across London, into an office environment and left in the care not of a qualified childminder, or her mother, but a receptionist.'

His implication was clear: a receptionist was rather lower on the social scale than a hooker.

'No! No, it wasn't like that.'

'Really. In what way was it not like that? I have repeated exactly what you told me—'

'She wasn't dragged across London for a start. She was in the back of my car, and I am a very good driver. We would sing songs and tell stories on the way. It wasn't late, it was about half past five. Emmie didn't go to bed until at least half past six. And she loved going there, she asked every single day if we could.'

'I see. Thank you. Now we come to the night Emmeline was ill and her mother was away.'

'Yes.'

'Perhaps you could describe the chain of events . . .'

Margaret described them. They were exactly as detailed by Matt.

'But I believe Mrs Shaw's mother was also in the house?' said Hayward.

'Yes, she was.'

'Why would that have been? At whose instigation?'

'Mrs Shaw's. It was the first time she had left Emmie to go away on a business trip and she felt that her mother added a – a safety net.'

'So she didn't entirely trust you, in other words?'

'My lord, I object to the question.'

'I agree, Mr Gilmour. Carry on, Miss Grant, please.'

'Mrs Fullerton-Clark, that is Mrs Shaw's mother, was there as a back-up. She had looked after Emmie a lot and Emmie is very devoted to her. As she is to her other grandmother.'

'Thank you, Miss Grant.'

Toby Gilmour stood up.

'Miss Grant. How would you describe Emmeline? Is she shy, quiet, extrovert – we know little about her. You might provide us with an objective view.'

'Oh – well, she's extremely bright. Very sophisticated in her patterns of thought. Not remotely shy, no. Quite – naughty. A handful, really. Oh, and very popular at school.'

'And – has she been badly affected by the recent train of events?'

'She was very upset, yes, after her parents told her. They kept it from her for a long time. Her father was still living in the house, you see, so it was possible to sustain the fiction that all was well. Since then, she has suffered from nightmares, bedwetting, she has become very much more difficult to handle. I – I feel very sorry for her,' she said simply.

'Thank you, Miss Grant.'

'I think,' said Clifford Rogers, 'we will adjourn for the day. Thank you. We will resume in the morning at nine o'clock.'

✿ ✿ ✿

674

'Eliza – do you want to come back for some tea?'

'No, Philip. No, thank you.' She felt like not just crying but screaming; this was so immeasurably worse than she had ever expected. She felt not only the whole courtroom, but everyone in the Law Courts, in the Strand, in Greater London, must be watching her, the news of her irresponsible behaviour, selfishness, adultery and complete unfitness to be a mother spread by some osmosis throughout the land. 'No, I'll go home. Mummy's there, with Emmie, and Charles is there with them. I think I should go to her.'

'And Matt – will he be there?'

'No, no. He's staying with his old friend and partner, Jimbo Simmonds. We really felt this week it was impossible for us to be under the same roof.'

'Of course. Let us at least get you a cab. I imagine your whistling abilities might be affected.'

She stared at Toby almost as if she had never seen him before, didn't know what he was talking about.

'No, it's fine, there'll be plenty in the Strand. Yes. Who – who will they have on tomorrow?'

'Not sure. Possibly some odious little private eye they've been using. Some of the people from the advertising agency.'

'Oh – yes. Fine. Thanks.'

'Eliza – are you all right?' said Toby.

'Oh yes,' she said, turning to him in a sort of subdued savagery, 'I'm absolutely all right. I mean it's really wonderful, sitting there learning all about what a selfish, amoral slut I am, not allowed to defend myself, seeing any slight chance of keeping my daughter just slipping away. I'm fine. Thank you.'

And she ran away from them, out into the Strand, and hailed a taxi and went home to Emmie. She must enjoy that while she could.

Chapter 70

'Breakfast, Matt?'

'Breakfast? Oh – no, thank you. Couldn't possibly.' He spoke as if she had suggested a five-course dinner, or a pint of bitter.

'You'll need something inside you. Long day again today, I'm sure.'

'Yes, I expect so.'

'Coffee? Go on, do you good.'

God, she was irritating. Attractive in that sort of lush, Jewish way, but – thick. Well, Jimbo had never been too bright. He could see that now. If it hadn't been for Louise, they wouldn't have done nearly so well . . .

Louise. He had tried to see her the night before, to thank her, and to – well, to talk to her. To tell her how great he thought she was. But she'd gone of course, from the Law Courts, and when he rang her office, a girl there said she'd had to go and visit a client.

'Tell her I called, would you?' he said.

'Yes, Mr Shaw.'

'Oh and—' This was difficult, he didn't usually leave messages with secretaries, except to say he was going to be late. But it was important, he felt. Very important. 'And could you say thank you for today and that she was – was really very good.'

'Yes, I will. And – good luck tomorrow, Mr Shaw.'

Suddenly he recognised her voice: that breathy, sweet, South London voice.

'Jenny, I'm sorry, I didn't realise it was you—'

'That's all right, Mr Shaw. You've got a lot on your mind, I'm sure.'

'Just a bit,' he said.

He thought of Jenny, in all her blonde, blue-eyed, cliché-ridden prettiness, of the days when she had greeted him with a smile and an offer of coffee – and biscuits – however unpleasant he had been the day before. He grieved for them, those happy, straightforward days, albeit

676

fraught and frantic, when he had run his life on a wing and a prayer and his worst nightmare had been the collapse of a project and his worst fear had been losing a few hundred thousand pounds . . . not a little girl with huge blue eyes and long dark hair like her mother's, who sat on his knee and made him laugh, and could talk him into anything, anything at all, and who wound her arms round his neck when she went to bed, and told him she loved him. Long after her mother had ceased to do so. And he told Roberta that he wouldn't wait even for the coffee and went out into the world to fight for Emmie some more.

'Eliza, this is Toby Gilmour.'

Toby Gilmour. The barrister. The cold, not-clever-enough barrister, who so far had done almost nothing for her. Not Toby, who had made love to her in a creaky bed only three days ago, and made her think she might be falling in love with him . . .

'Oh, hello.'

'Look – bit of a shock. The judge has called your mother.'

'What! At this stage?'

'Yes. It's extremely unusual, but he's concerned to make sure the child's case is properly understood and he's taking a strong line on it.'

Terror shot through her. This was really the end of it for her.

'I'm sorry. We just have to – to hope for the best. You're doing wonderfully, Eliza. I'm – I'm very proud of you.'

It wasn't very intimate; but it was something, some indication that he was at least human.

'So, just hold tight today and then by tomorrow afternoon we should be in calmer waters. OK?'

'Yes. OK.'

'Oh, and Eliza—'

'Yes?'

'Remember not to pick your nose.'

'Eliza, this is Rob. Look, you know how much I don't want to do this. But – best to, my solicitor says.'

'Rob, it's OK. I understand. And the minute it's over I want to talk about the clothes for the shoot next week.'

'You're amazing. I adore you, babe.'

'Don't tell the judge that.'

Jeremy also called to wish Eliza luck; and then surrendered himself to the agony of contemplating the following night, when he and Mariella would be at Covent Garden at the same time, and it would be almost impossible for them not to come face to face. In the presence of her husband. How was he going to bear it. How?

And Mariella, gazing down on London from the plane as it approached the airport, thought of the love and happiness held within that city that she could never know again and had to fight to contain her tears; and nonetheless managed to smile at Giovanni as he touched her hand and asked her if she was feeling quite well, as she had been so very quiet ever since they had left the villa; and assured him that she was feeling very well, just a little tired. For what was the point in any of this, this savage pain and sense of loss, if Giovanni, the entirely innocent reason for it, was to be deprived of happiness himself?

'Mr Brigstocke, I believe you and Mrs Shaw work together.'

'Yes, yes, we do.'

God, he looked scared, Eliza thought. The cocky little bugger had completely morphed into a rather pale, monosyllabic creature, who gripped the edge of the witness box and clearly would have given a very great deal to be somewhere different.

And he didn't know what the cringing, slimy private eye Jim Dodds had just let him in for.

'She advises you on fashion as it relates to the advertisements you work on. How the models are dressed and so on. Is that right?'

'Yes. Yes, that's right.'

'Is it a close working relationship? We know it extends to the personal, of course.'

'Well – yes. We spend a lot of time together in the office.'

'And do meetings and so on run on into the evening? I ask because, for example, of the need for Emmeline to be brought to the office.'

'Well – yes, sometimes.'

'And why is that?'

'Because you can't stop thinking about a campaign, not if you're really getting going, just because it's six o'clock.'

'Of course you can't stop thinking about it. But – do the two of you continue to discuss it?'

'Sometimes. Not often, because Eliza – Mrs Shaw – always has to rush off home.'

'But if she does – stay – you have meetings in your department?'

'Yes, we do.'

'And do you ever enjoy a drink while you chat?'

'Yes, we do. I don't believe that's illegal.'

Careful, Rob, don't let him rile you. Philip looked at Clifford Rogers, who was regarding Rob Brigstocke with great distaste. Well, he would, he was exactly the sort of person he most disliked, steeped in privilege, doing a job which Rogers would regard as useless, parasitic even, raising two fingers to the law.

'Drink – no. There is talk, according to Mr Dodds, of other – substances. Do you and Mrs Shaw ever partake of those?'

A long silence.

'Mr Brigstocke, you are under oath.'

'We have smoked – er, hash – very occasionally.'

'How would you define very occasionally?'

'Very occasionally,' said Rob, 'oh – once or twice.'

'Once or twice a day?'

'No, of course not.'

Rob . . . careful.

'Then – how often?'

'During our entire association.'

'I see. No more questions.'

'Mr Gilmour?

'No questions, Your Honour.'

'I would now like to call Mrs Sarah Fullerton-Clark.'

This was it. This was when she really finally lost her. Drinking, taking drugs, abandoning Emmie in a foreign city – nothing compared to hitting her.

'Mrs Fullerton-Clark . . .'

Clifford Rogers won't like her either, Philip Gordon thought, looking at Sarah, pale but composed, her dark hair neatly set, dressed in a skirt and twinset, and of course pearls, her grandmother's pearls as Eliza could have told him, she was seldom seen without them – answering the questions in her rather dated, clipped, upper-class voice.

Generations of good breeding stood in that witness box; the kind that Clifford Rogers most resented. Sarah Fullerton-Clark was, as Scarlett Shaw had once observed, deeply posh.

'So you have looked after Emmeline quite a lot over the years?'

'Yes, I have. And enjoyed it, of course.'

'And – did your daughter enjoy looking after her, would you say?'

'Very much, yes. She was an excellent mother. She was very tired of course in the early stages, as we all are, but she coped very well.'

'Did she ever discuss going back to work with you?'

'Well – occasionally. I know she missed it. She always enjoyed being a working gel—'

Philip Gordon could almost feel the judge wince at that pronunciation.

'But she was happy to be at home?'

'Oh – yes. Very happy.'

'Now home for you all is your family seat in Wiltshire—'

'Oh, I'd hardly call it a seat,' said Sarah, 'it's just a small country house.'

'I see. I imagined something more substantial. How many bedrooms does it have?'

'Ten – well, it depends how you count them, whether you include the rooms on the top floor. If you do – then – ten. Yes.'

'Ah, yes. Not too small then. And you have continued to live there since your husband died?'

'Yes. Yes, I have.'

'You son didn't inherit it?'

'Well, in terms of a family trust he did, but his life is very much in London, and—'

'Is it not true that the house required a great deal of restoration, and that no one in the family could afford it?'

'Yes, that's right.'

'And your son-in-law bought the house, that you broke that trust to make it possible and that he has spent a lot of money, doing it up and so on. And he allows you to live there?'

'Yes. That is correct. Matthew has been a very kind, generous son-in-law.'

'Indeed. And how often do the young family come down?'

'Oh – in the summer, most weekends. Emmie loves it there, she has a pony which we keep in the paddock.'

'And which you look after?'

'Oh – well, not exactly, a girl from the village comes every other day to groom and exercise him.'

This gets worse and worse, thought Toby.

'Very good. Now – I want to hear about the time your daughter lost the baby. The little boy.'

'Oh – yes.'

She looked down, fiddled with the pearls.

'It must have been a very sad time for you all.'

'It was, yes.'

'Did your daughter spend much time with you over that period?'

'Yes. Yes, she did. I was very worried about her, she was very low, very low indeed, she couldn't sleep, wasn't eating. Matthew was very upset too, but of course he had to go back to work and – well . . .' Her voice faded.

'Well what, Mrs Fullerton-Clark?'

'It is always worse for the mother.'

'That is your view? That your son-in-law was not as upset by the death of his son as your daughter?'

'No, that is not my view.' Sarah faced him down. 'I said that Matthew was very upset, I simply meant that it is always worse for the mother, she can't escape into the world of work, she has fewer distractions, and I truly believe we feel such loss more, it's in our biology.'

'I see. And – how did Eliza cope with Emmeline at this time? I imagine it must have been difficult for her, a lively – what, three- or four-year-old?'

'Emmie was five at the time. Yes, my daughter did find it difficult, Emmie's a demanding little girl and – yes.' Her voice tailed off.

'Was she – irritable with the child, that sort of thing?'

'A – a little, yes.'

'I see. So – she and the child, did they spend a lot of time with you?'

'Yes they did. I could help entertain Emmie and let Eliza get a bit of rest.'

'What form did this irritability take, Mrs Fullerton-Clark? Did Mrs Shaw snap at Emmie, that sort of thing?'

'Er – yes. That sort of thing.'

'Were you ever worried about her ability to cope with the situation?'

'Not – not seriously. A little, I suppose. Yes.'

'Did you suggest she sought help?'

'Yes, yes, I did, but she didn't want to give in, as she put it. I was very glad when she agreed to go and see a – a doctor.'

'A doctor? Surely it was a psychiatrist she saw?'

'Well – we agreed together she should seek help. We didn't actually define what sort of help. It seemed to me at the very least she needed perhaps some sleeping pills. And to—'

She stopped.

'And to what, Mrs Fullerton-Clark?'

'And to talk to someone. About how she was feeling, how – how wretched she was.'

'And – was there one particular incident which persuaded her this was necessary? Or did she slowly come round to the idea?'

Does he know, Eliza wondered; has he read Mary Miller's notes, and how much had she given away?

'Well – well, she – that is, I—'

'Mrs Fullerton-Clark, please answer the question,' said Clifford Rogers. He sounded irritable.

'Well – she was down one weekend, without Matthew and – and she became very upset—'

'Why was that particularly?'

'Well, Emmie was being very difficult.'

'In what way?'

'She – she wanted to go to the village shop and buy some sweets and Eliza said she couldn't. Emmie was very angry and started having a tantrum. Shouting at Eliza and so on.'

'And—'

'Well – Eliza became very – very distressed.'

'And—'

'And she – she, well, she lost her temper with Emmie.'

'And—'

'Well, and she – she—'

'Mrs Fullerton-Clark, I have to ask you this. Did you ever observe any violence towards Emmie from your daughter?'

Sarah was silent; she looked at Bruce Hayward and then at the judge and then down at her hands, fiddling with her rings. The silence in the courtroom was profound.

Finally she said, 'Yes. Yes, I'm afraid I did. Just – just the once. She – well, she hit her. I wasn't there, in the room, but I heard screaming and

682

shouting and I went in and Emmie – Emmie was holding her head which was bleeding – not from the blow, she'd fallen against the table – we had to go to Casualty, she needed stitches.'

Eliza looked at Matt, who was staring at her, sitting bolt upright, his dark eyes brilliant, blazing in his white face.

She would lose Emmie now; absolutely without doubt. And she would deserve to.

'Oh, darling.' Jeremy held out his arms. They were sitting on the sofa in his drawing room; without being sure why, she had wanted to see him more than anyone. 'How utterly dreadful for you. I wish, I wish I'd been there. Just to – to have been there.'

'It was so bad,' said Eliza, wiping her eyes on the back of her hand, sniffing hard, 'I wanted to just run away. Everyone looked at me, you could see them thinking what an awful, awful creature I must be – and Mummy did try to explain that Emmie had been provoking me beyond endurance, but she hadn't been in the room, I'll get a chance to tell them exactly what she – what she said, and also that she begged me not to tell Matt, but . . . oh, Jeremy, how did all this happen, why did I let it, why am I so awful—'

'You're not awful. You're wonderful. You're brave and very strong. You weren't well, Eliza, you were depressed. Obviously this psychotherapist woman will have made that clear in her report – here, have another glass of wine. You're a superb mother and everyone who knows you knows that.'

'And what about all the people who don't know me?' said Eliza. 'It's in the late editions of the *Standard* tonight, Jeremy, there was a reporter there this morning, "Deb of the Year's downfall" it was called. Oh, God, I wish I was dead.'

'No, you don't. And I certainly don't. This all seems dreadful now, today, but in a few weeks' time, it will all be forgotten. Tomorrow's fish-and-chip wrapping, don't forget, as any old Fleet Street lag will tell you about his scoop.'

'In a few weeks, in a few days, I won't have Emmie,' said Eliza, wiping her eyes again, 'never mind about anything else. So far I've been branded publicly as taking drugs, hitting my child, losing her in a foreign city, and dumping her with your receptionist, while I carried on working, very possibly smoking pot at the same time. Would you grant me custody?'

'Possibly, possibly not,' said Jeremy very seriously, 'but if I was a judge I would be rather too experienced and skilful to be influenced by a lot of sensational evidence. Anyway, it's your turn soon, isn't it? We shall hear the other side of the story. And so will the judge. *Courage, mon brave. Ma brave*, I suppose. All will be very well.'

Which was more than he could claim for his own situation, he reflected; and after she had gone, returned to wrestling with his own demons and the torments that almost certainly awaited him the next day.

'Matt,' said Louise, 'I'm sure, I'm quite, quite sure, it must have been a one-off thing. Otherwise, Emmie would have been frightened of her. Did she ever seem scared?'

'No, but—'

'Listen, we've all done awful things we've regretted. That we're ashamed of, even. Haven't you?'

'What?'

'I said, haven't you ever done anything you were ashamed of?'

'Oh – yes, yes, of course I have.'

'Well, there you are.'

'Yes, but not to a child. Not to my own daughter. And then to lie about it, and obviously to encourage her to lie about it. I just don't know what to do, Louise, I really don't.'

'You don't have to do anything. That's the whole point of all this. The judge will do it for you.'

'And she knew all along, Sarah, that is. I trusted her, you know. And she knew that and she didn't tell me. Left Emmie at – at risk. It's – it's awful. Well, she'll never be alone with Emmie again either.'

'Matt! Emmie was not at risk. Didn't your mother ever wallop you? I know mine did.'

'Yes, of course, but that's quite different.'

'I don't see why. Look, Matt, you decided to do this. You decided to go down this road, to turn Emmie into an object, that you were going to acquire at all costs. Did you really think that it was going to be all over in a few minutes, with everyone being decent to each other and saying they were sorry?'

'Of course not. But—'

'I know this is awful for you. It's awful for everyone. You, Eliza, Emmie, everyone involved actually, your mother, Scarlett, Sarah – it's horrible. Of course it is. It didn't have to be. You chose to do it like this and I've backed you all the way. But I will not listen to you now whining and saying it's not fair. Or words to that effect. Of course it was bad Eliza hit Emmie, and of course it was very – unfortunate she lost her in Milan. But neither of them was as bad as you've made out, there are reasons, explanations, Eliza is not a bad person and nor are you, but the barristers and the solicitors and the judge are turning you into bad people, and you can't blame them either, because that's their job. So just – just grow up, Matt. I'm going home now, I can't stand this any longer. You'd better do the same. Remember me to Jimbo.'

Chapter 71

'I do not propose to retell this story, my lord, even from the different perspective of Mrs Shaw's own experiences. I intend to refute many of the charges against her through the evidence of witnesses. I would merely ask you to consider that there are actually not merely two sides to every story, but frequently three or four. I intend to show the court that Mrs Shaw is a loving, conscientious and intensely caring mother, that her daughter is, as she had said to her mother-in-law, her reason for living; and that while she has been at times thoughtless, reckless even, and might appear irresponsible, her behaviour is always prompted by a genuine desire to do her best for her daughter, and everything that she does is directed ultimately towards her well-being and happiness.

'We need not retrace the story of the adultery; it is in any case undefended and Mrs Shaw deeply regrets her behaviour, which was a rare instance of moral frailty. In the time she and Mr Shaw have been married, there have been no other incidents of infidelity. There was almost an embarrassment of people willing to speak for her devotion as a mother; we have heard of it already from both her own mother and her mother-in-law, and indeed from Miss Grant, Emmeline's nanny.

'And we should not underestimate the career that she gave up in order to care for Emmie; she is regarded as one of the outstanding fashion editors of her generation and we shall hear from just one of the people she worked for that he tried repeatedly to lure her back to work, without success.

'I would not like to depict Mrs Shaw as a perfect example of a stay-at-home mother; she is not. Like so many young women of today she has been highly educated and trained and does not wish to see that education and her own talent wasted. But I believe I can show her as a mother for whom her child, and the security and safety of that child, has always been her first priority, and who struggles at all times to fit her career round that child, rather than the other way round.'

Clifford Rogers spoke. 'Mrs Shaw, please take the stand and try to tell us why you feel Emmeline should remain in your care.'

She is terrified, Philip thought, looking at Eliza's eyes as she stood, gripping the edge of the box, exactly as Matt had, the eyes of a creature facing its doom. She has lost faith in herself and her cause; she does not believe she can win. Which is dangerous – he scribbled a note and passed it to Gilmour.

There was a long silence; finally Gilmour stood up.

'Mrs Shaw,' he said gently, 'tell us about Emmie, and why you think she needs you. What would happen to her if she didn't have you.'

'Oh. Yes. Well—' She took a deep breath, then started to speak, gaining some frail momentum as she went. 'Emmie, like all children, needs security and familiarity. Like all children, she falls apart when faced by change. Her first preoccupation, when my husband and I told her about the divorce, was not which of us she might be going to live with, but whether she would have to have a different house and a different bedroom. She is happy and confident in herself and her life; she has many friends, she is extremely popular. Running her social life alone is quite a full-time job, she's got a busier diary than I have . . .'

Clifford Rogers won't like that, thought Philip; he was already regarding Eliza with a certain disdain, clearly seeing her as a younger version of her mother. She was wearing a very socially neutral outfit, a calf-length Thirties-style dress, in a floral print, and very little make-up. However, there was no disguising the accent, or more importantly the terminology.

'Mrs Shaw,' said Bruce Hayward, standing up, 'are we to infer from this that you feel one of your prime duties as a mother is to organise your child's social diary?'

'I object to the tone of that question, my lord.'

'No, it's perfectly reasonable. Answer it please, Mrs Shaw.'

'No, of course not. Not a – a prime duty. What I meant was that – that – I can't do this,' she said suddenly, 'I think I should leave it to others to speak for me. I'm sorry.'

'Mrs Shaw.' Clifford Rogers looked at her quite sternly. 'You are obliged to answer the questions put to you in court. Otherwise you are in contempt. Answer the question.'

'Yes. Well – well, no, not a prime duty. But one of them.'

'And the other duties?' asked Bruce Hayward.

'Well – to – to see to the child's physical well-being, to give it love and attention, to make it feel secure—'

'And you don't think leaving a child with a nanny and going out to work would make it feel less secure?'

'Um – possibly. It would depend how you – you organised everything.'

'Possibly. I see. So you decided to give it a go. To see how it worked out?'

'No. Not – not at all.'

Another long silence; she was floundering very badly, Gilmour thought. He stood up again.

'Mrs Shaw, tell us how you felt after your baby died. How this affected your performance as a mother.'

'Oh. Yes. Well, I was very, very – unhappy. Of course. And I found Emmie very difficult. She is a very demanding little girl. And she could see – she could see I wasn't—'

'Mrs Shaw, go on.' Toby Gilmour's voice was very gentle.

Another, very long silence. Then – 'I'm sorry. I don't want to go on with this. I can't. There could be no defence of what I did to Emmie that day. However provoked I was. Nothing a child said or did could possibly excuse violence on the part of an adult. I've already tried to explain why I think Emmie would be better with me. I – I can't say any more. I'm sorry.'

This is awful, this is a crucifixion, thought Gordon. We have to get her out of this.

'Mr Hayward,' said Clifford Rogers, looking both impatient and bored, 'do you have any questions for Mrs Shaw?'

'Only one, at this stage, my lord. Mrs Shaw, your psychiatric treatment was clearly very successful, and how fortunate that it was. How long after the – the incident with your daughter were you able to go to Milan? To stay with your friends in their villa?'

He somehow managed to endow the word 'villa' with connotations of debauchery.

'Oh – well – about three months. Maybe two.'

'Where you were obviously able to enjoy yourself quite considerably. Shopping, the opera, dining out – all very therapeutic as well, no doubt.'

Eliza was silent.

'And when you returned, then you began to think about returning to work, as I understand it. That would require considerable self-confidence, surely, after a prolonged absence?'

'Well, yes. Yes, I suppose so. But I knew – well, I thought – oh, I don't know.'

'Mrs Shaw,' said Clifford Rogers, wearily, 'that is not acceptable. I have said before, you are obliged to answer the questions put to you. Proceed, Mr Hayward.'

'I was only seeking to ascertain, my lord, whether Mrs Shaw had found it easy to find the necessary self-confidence to return to work. Mrs Shaw?'

'Not really, no,' said Eliza, 'but I also thought it would help.'

'Help what exactly?'

'My state of mind.'

'Which was?'

'Well – very unhappy. And – and lonely.'

'And – staying at home and caring for your child was not going to help that?'

He was a clever bastard, thought Toby; this was getting worse by the minute.

'Well – no, not really,' said Eliza.

'Thank you, Mrs Shaw. No more questions, my lord.'

Toby was back on his feet. 'I would like to call Miss Scarlett Shaw.'

Shrunk back into her seat, sandwiched between Philip Gordon and his nice, sympathetic assistant, overwhelmed by her failure to perform, Eliza sat and watched Scarlett in awe. She was dressed in a brilliant blue linen trouser suit, her glossy dark hair pulled back from her face; she was not remotely fazed by the situation, indeed she seemed to be enjoying it.

'I have known Eliza Shaw for many years,' she said, smiling briefly across at Eliza, 'and I have seen her with her daughter countless times; I was a frequent visitor to their home. She is a quite marvellous mother. She's endlessly patient, she's fun, plays with her all the time, never stops trying to amuse her, she plans outings, she takes her all over the place, and yet she's very firm with her, she doesn't spoil her. She makes her do her homework, learn her spellings and so on. And she runs her life. It's very, very complicated, Emmie's life, ballet, gym, music, the riding at the weekend, parties – I'd need a secretary if it was mine. And that's one of the reasons I think my brother would find it so hard to cope with caring for Emmie full-time.'

'Is it really so difficult to do?' Toby Gilmour was playing devil's advocate. 'I would have thought a man who ran a considerable business empire could organise a little girl's life for her.'

'Well yes, but not if he was still trying to run the empire. Matt – Mr Shaw – is a very all-or-nothing person, that's how he's achieved what he has. And I know he says he'll give it up, but I don't think he'll be able to, he loves it all too much. He's brilliant, don't get me wrong, I admire him more than I can tell you, but – delivering and fetching to and from parties, taking Emmie to the dentist and the doctor, remembering to buy birthday presents for her friends, getting costumes made for the dancing displays – I've watched Eliza doing all this, at the same time as she's running her own life, and she's brilliant at it. Women are, it's in our genes—'

'What is in your genes, Miss Shaw?' Clifford Rogers was watching Scarlett with a certain fascination.

'Well – you know – doing six things at once. Men – with respect, my lord – usually can't.'

'I – must observe myself more closely,' said Clifford Rogers. There was a polite murmur of laughter round the court.

'Are you telling us, Miss Shaw,' Bruce Hayward had risen to his feet, 'that this and this alone would prevent your brother from being a good parent to Emmeline?'

'No, of course not. And I do think he is completely devoted to Emmie, he's a brilliant father, very patient and interested, he plays with her and reads to her for hours as well, and when she was little he was amazing, he'd actually change her nappies, my dad – our dad – thought it was all a bit, you know, soft, he was embarrassed by it, and actually, I think Matt is quite ahead of his time as a parent, but I don't think he can play both roles. I really don't. They're both brilliant parents, in their different ways, it's such a – a – dreadful shame.'

There was a long silence; then Toby Gilmour said, 'Thank you, Miss Shaw.'

Scarlett stepped down from the witness box; everybody was watching her in various stages of admiration. As she left the court there was a slight disturbance and a clerk came in, gave a note to Sarah Jennings, who read it and reached behind her to give it to Philip. He read it too; then scribbled something on it and gave it back to the clerk. And wrote a note of his own and passed it to Toby.

Eliza, her misery only slightly eased by Scarlett's performance, was too wretched even to notice.

'My lord, I would now like to call Mr Jack Beckham, the editor of the *Daily News*. Mr Beckham, you employed Eliza Shaw as fashion editor on a magazine you edited, I believe? Could you tell us its name?'

Beckham looked round the courtroom and waited several moments before he spoke; he looked relaxed and cheerful and clearly intended to enjoy himself hugely.

'It was called *Charisma*. I edited it from 1963 to 1968. Then I decided it was time I did a proper job and went back to Fleet Street.'

'And Mrs Shaw came to work for you – when?'

'Oh, in 1963, as fashion assistant. I was very impressed with her from the word go. I had my reservations, as I knew she'd been a deb and all that nonsense, I thought she might just be passing the time till she found some chinless creature to marry, but I was wrong. She proved herself in days. She worked round the clock, nothing was too much for her. We gave her husband a big break, matter of fact, included him in a feature on the new young blood around, very good publicity, not sure that he appreciated it enough, but anyway . . . I saw quite a bit of him, when he came to pick Eliza up and so on. They were good together at the time. Damn shame, all this. But it happens, doesn't it?'

'Indeed, Mr Beckham.'

'Try to keep to the point, Mr Beckham,' said Clifford Rogers.

'I'd have thought that was the point. Certainly part of it.'

'And – when did you make her fashion editor?' asked Toby, terrified Clifford Rogers would haul Beckham up for contempt of court. But he actually appeared rather delighted by him, sat looking at him benignly as he certainly had not for the past two days.

'Oh – about nine months later. Everyone said it was too soon, but I knew it wasn't, there wasn't another candidate to touch her, she'd done a fantastic job at the collections in Paris, the fashion editor was ill, and she just took over. Very, very clever girl, always coming up with the goods, wonderful ideas and nothing but nothing was good enough but the best. I'm proud to have been involved in her career. Then she had to throw it all away.'

'Indeed? How did she do that?'

'She got herself in the family way. Pregnant. Said she had to leave, when she'd had the baby. I did everything I could to make her stay, flattered her, promised her the moon, bribed her with more money, but she wouldn't. She said it was out of the question.'

'Did she give a reason?'

'Yes, she did, she said she had to stay at home and look after the child. I tried again a few years later, to get her to come as fashion editor at the *News*, but she said she couldn't. Same reason.'

'Thank you, Mr Beckham.'

'Mr Hayward?'

'Mr Beckham, it was in your paper I believe that the article about Mr Shaw's tenants was published.'

'It was indeed.'

'So – you were still in touch with Mrs Shaw?'

'I don't know quite what you're implying.'

'I'm not implying anything, Mr Beckham. Merely trying to find the background to the article.'

'I had nothing to do with the article, it was done entirely through my property editor, Johnny Barrett. She'd met him, and she got in touch with him herself. I subsequently discovered she tried to get it taken out of the paper, but it was too late.'

'Thank you, Mr Beckham. Could we hear from Mr Barrett next?'

Something was going on; Eliza was puzzled. Both Philip and Toby asked her to excuse them at lunchtime and Sarah escorted her to a local coffee shop for sandwiches. Not that she could eat them, or even swallow more than half her coffee. She felt sick and numb with misery, overwhelmed by her own wretched performance in the witness box.

'I feel I've let you all down,' she said to Sarah, nibbling half-heartedly at a sugar lump; Sarah told her not to be silly.

'We're here to look after you, not the other way round.'

'I know, but I'm making it impossible for you.'

'The reporter, Johnny Barrett, was great, wasn't he?' said Sarah, in a clear attempt to change the subject; and indeed he had been, stressing that Eliza had done her utmost to discourage him from writing the article, even before she had realised the developers were colleagues of Matt's.

Bruce Hayward had suggested it was naïve of Eliza to think that any article about the property business might not be in danger of damaging

Matt; but Johnny Barrett said he had known Eliza for a long time, and he could vouch for the pride she felt in Matt's company – 'First time I met her, she practically bent my ear right off telling me how brilliant he was.'

He had also accepted that what he himself had done, tracking Heather down and coercing her into talking to him, was not entirely honourable; 'But, sorry, Mr Hayward, he that pays the piper calls the tune, and my piper is my editor and he wanted this piece. You know what they say about the British journalist, I'm sure.'

Bruce Hayward said he did not, but he had no wish to either, and Johnny Barrett was free to go.

'What do they say about the British journalist, Eliza?' Sarah asked now.

'Oh – gosh, yes, it's a poem. "There is no way to bribe or twist, thank God, the British journalist; but seeing what the man will do, unbribed, there's no occasion to."'

'Very good. Oh, there's Philip, he wants us to go back. It's your friend this afternoon isn't it?'

'Yes. Yes, it is. Poor Heather, she'll be so frightened.'

If Heather was frightened, she didn't look it, once the first few minutes were over. She appeared calm, sensible and made the same touchingly loyal speech about Eliza and her qualities as a friend and mother as she had a week earlier – omitting by mutual agreement that Eliza had lent her money.

It was immediately apparent it had been a good idea to call her; Clifford Rogers was obviously not only rather taken with her – she did look very pretty, dressed in grey trousers and a blue blouse, her brown hair cut to a swinging bob (at Eliza's expense, but he was not to know that) but he clearly liked the story of their friendship and when Bruce Hayward inquired in honeyed tones if Heather had ever wondered why Eliza wanted to spend so much time with her, he looked across at her most benignly as she said she imagined it was the same reason she had wanted to spend so much time with Eliza, that she liked her and enjoyed her company.

'But – did you really have very much in common?'

'Yes, we did. We had the children, they were the same age and they always got on very well. And we – just liked talking to each other. Doing things together.'

'You didn't feel – that perhaps there was something of Lady Bountiful in Mrs Shaw's relationship with you?'

'My lord, I object strongly to that question.'

'I agree with you, Mr Gilmour.'

'I am quite happy to answer the question,' said Heather firmly, 'and no, there wasn't. We were just good friends. I never felt she was spending time with me because she hadn't got anyone among her own circle, she had lots of – of posh friends, but—' She stopped.

'Do go on, Mrs Connell.'

'She always said they weren't as interesting as me,' said Heather, looking down at her hands.

Clifford Rogers looked as if he would like to embrace her.

'And the article,' said Bruce Hayward, clearly regretting this line of questioning, 'that must have upset you and your husband considerably.'

'Yes, it did, and we weren't on speaking terms for a while, Eliza and me, but that was my fault, not hers. She tried and tried to make it up to me, came to see me and apologised the very next day, and said it wasn't her fault, and she'd tried to stop it, but I was a bit stupid and said I didn't believe her. But I do now.'

'And when was your friendship resumed?'

'A few months ago.'

'She didn't contact you, I suppose?'

'No,' said Heather firmly, 'I didn't know anything about the case, if that's what you mean, I wrote to her because I was missing her . . .'

A few more innocuous questions and then . . .

'Thank you, Mrs Connell. You may go.'

It was the end of the session; Philip and Toby escorted her out of the building, offered her tea in the chambers, said they had something to tell her.

'Eliza – I'm sorry and you must try not to get too upset, but – the old boy has asked to see Emmie.'

'Oh, no, no, please, he can't.'

'He can, I'm afraid. Tomorrow afternoon. She'll need to be brought here, could your mother do that?'

'Yes, yes, of course, but – oh, God, it's awful, so awful, she'll be so upset by it, I know she thinks it'll be fun—'

'Does she?' said Toby sharply.

'Yes. She said she thought it was a good idea when I warned her. I was quite – surprised. But she doesn't know what it means, the sort of things he'll ask her.'

'And what do you think they will be?' said Philip gently.

'Well – I suppose who she loves best, who she wants to live with.'

'Eliza, it will be much more subtle than that, I promise you. He'll be trying to establish how she views it all, how upset she actually is, how much she likes her school, possibly what she thinks about living mainly with Matt, whether any of the other children at her school have parents who don't live together, perhaps how she feels about you going to work, how much she likes the nanny – that sort of thing. It will be quite gentle. Rogers is a bit of an old war horse, but he likes children, he understands them, and he's had two of his own, he'll take it very steady. Try not to worry.'

'Worry? Me? Of course I won't worry . . . Oh, God . . . I'd better go home, tell her, get her used to the idea.'

'Yes, but don't – don't alarm her, make her think it's going to be an ordeal. Will you? That will really be counterproductive. Just tell her he wants to have a little talk with her.'

Eliza looked at them. 'You really do think I'm stupid, don't you?' she said coldly. 'Look, call me a taxi, will you, I've had enough of all this, I really have.'

The opera house was very full: the crush bar packed with perfectly dressed people, smiling, waving, kissing; champagne was poured, drunk, poured again, shreds of conversation were tossed into the heady air; but Mariella, following Giovanni through it all, on the way to their box, felt quite quite alone, isolated in her terror, terror and longing, that at any moment she might find herself confronted by the person she wanted to see most and least in the entire world; and Jeremy, for his part, arriving deliberately as late as he dared, walked slowly up the great red staircase to meet his guests, filled with the same terror and the same absurd longing.

But thus far they had been spared; and the warning bell saw Mariella and Giovanni settled into their box and Jeremy and his guests into their seats in the stalls and it was only as the lights went down and the overture began that Jeremy allowed himself the luxury, the rash, foolish, dangerous luxury of looking round and up at the boxes to the one where he knew she was; and saw her, less rash, less foolish, leaning out just a little, one white-gloved hand resting on the front of the box, the other holding her opera glasses to her eyes, and it was so intensely painful, seeing her, knowing she was there, breathing the same air, listening to the same music, witnessing the same passionate, dreadfully familiar story, that he did wonder how he could possibly survive several hours of it.

The first interval she had been safe; Giovanni had had champagne brought to the box, and had invited a friend he had seen in the foyer to join them. The performance was sublime, but she had seen little of the opera, and heard less; for while aware of the dreadful irony of it, this story of forbidden passion, of the struggle of duty, she could think only of the last time she had seen it, at La Scala the night of the *nebbia*, pulled into her own forbidden love affair.

Perhaps, perhaps they would even now escape. But Giovanni had wanted to stretch his legs, he said and—

'Jeremy! My dear, dear friend, how marvellous to see you. Mariella, *cara*, here is Jeremy—' and Jeremy, bending to kiss her, breathing in her perfume, brushing against her hair, tortured, terrified, said it would be delightful to join them for dinner, but alas he had ten guests with him and they had booked a table at the River Room at the Savoy. 'Then let us have a drink together now,' Giovanni said, 'and we can meet perhaps for lunch tomorrow – after Mariella has made her appearance in court, she is a little nervous I think, a little quiet this evening, but she will be wonderful, Jeremy, will she not, and you must join us at the Ritz at – shall we say, one thirty – no, no refusals, I will not hear of it—'

And then they returned to their seats, away from one another once more, to the doomed love story playing out before them as well as their own.

Chapter 72

Mariella had hardly slept; when she did, after dawn, it was to dream of loss, of parting, of empty houses and silent rooms. She awoke with a start to find Giovanni no longer beside her; anxious without knowing why, she sat up with a start. And saw him standing on the balcony; she stumbled out of bed and joined him, and they looked together over the gardens of the Ritz, a piece of the English countryside come to town, green and filled with birdsong, drenched in dew. Giovanni looked pale, she thought, and said so; he said he had a headache, but it was nothing to worry about, merely too much champagne the night before. He would be better soon, he told her; meanwhile she must get prepared for the day's performance. He said how much he would like to come and watch her, but since it was not allowed, he would wait in their suite for her return.

They had breakfast together on the balcony and then she ran a bath and lay in it for quite a long time, and he sat with her and told her how beautiful she was, and how very much he loved her; and how proud of her he was.

She asked him how his headache was and he said it was perhaps a little better; she offered to stay a little longer, but he told her to go, and that she must do her very best that day for Eliza, who needed her more than he did.

And when they rang to say her car had arrived to take her to the Law Courts, he escorted her to the front of the hotel, kissed her goodbye and said he would see her at lunchtime with Jeremy.

'The perfect English gentleman,' he said, speaking in English, 'how lucky we are to have him as a friend.'

'Good luck, darling, and I'll have Emmie there at three, don't worry.'

'Thank you, Mummy. On second thoughts, I think the Pollyanna sailor dress. It's her favourite and it's very little girly. The judge will like it.'

'She – she says she wants to wear her stripy dungarees. You know, the Osh Kosh ones.'

'Well, she can't. Mummy, you are not to bring her to court in dungarees.'

'No, darling, of course not.'

Toby and Philip were waiting on the steps for Eliza when she arrived; she was feeling different today, she realised, more positive, stronger, after her low of the day before, without knowing quite why. Not beaten. Not yet.

'My lord,' said Toby Gilmour, 'I would like to call Signora Mariella Crespi.'

Judge Rogers nodded rather curtly; he had already formed an opinion of Signora Crespi and it was not benign.

Mariella did not do anything as prosaic as walk; she swept into the courtroom and the witness box. She looked incredible; even Bruce Hayward appeared slightly stunned. She was wearing a white trouser suit, with apparently nothing under the jacket, a thick, thick gold and pearl rope round her neck, and matching gold bracelets on her slender wrists. Her make-up was flawless, her eyes hugely dark, her lips a brilliant red gloss. Her dark hair was piled high on her head and in her ears were large pearl and gilt studs – Chanel, thought Eliza automatically, and that suit was undoubtedly Yves Saint Laurent, the very same design as Bianca had worn for her wedding to Mick.

Toby turned to face her. His face was admirably blank.

'Signora Crespi, you met Eliza Shaw, I believe, while she was fashion editor of *Charisma*.'

'Yes, that is correct. She was very, very important to me, she made me famous. Famous enough to win the best dressed title early this year.'

Clearly no one was to be left in any doubt as to how important she was.

'And then she became one of my dearest, closest friends. She is a most wonderful person, generous, good, so, so kind and loyal, and a most wonderful mother.'

'Yes, indeed. Now – Signora Crespi, perhaps you could tell us about the time Mrs Shaw came to visit you in Milan. In December 1969.'

'Of course. She had been very depressed, after losing the baby, so, so sad, and I invited her to join us for a week or so. It was the beginning of the Milanese season, which starts, as I am sure you know, on the seventh of December, when there is a gala opera performance, usually of Verdi.'

My husband and I always attend, and entertain in our box at La Scala. It was not Eliza's first visit, she had come two or three years earlier, and brought the little Emmie with her. She would never, ever come without her, even though sometimes I thought it would have done her good, made a better holiday for her.'

'I see. And what did you do, the day Emmie went missing?'

'Well, we drove into Milan—'

'You don't live in the city itself?'

'No, no, of course not.' Clearly they were all expected to know this. 'We live in our villa on the shores of Lake Como.'

'I see. Yes.'

'It is perhaps an hour's drive into Milan. There was myself, Eliza, Emmie and one of my maids, Anna-Maria, who cares for Emmie on her visits. Emmie loved her, I cannot tell you how she loved Anna-Maria, and Anna-Maria her.'

'I see,' said Toby again. 'And when you got to Milan?'

'We looked at all the shops and the Christmas displays. Then I had to visit my dressmaker and buy some shoes, and Emmie wanted to go into Rinascente, that is the department store. I suggested she went with Anna-Maria. Eliza was very, very worried about this, but I insisted, I needed her opinion on some buttons—'

'Buttons?'

'Buttons, yes. So it was agreed that we should meet with Maria and Emmie in one half of an hour in the Café Cova, perhaps you know the Café Cova—'

'I do indeed. Delightful!'

Did he? Eliza wondered, jerked out of the fairy story Mariella was telling them all. He was managing her very well.

'But after a little while Anna-Maria arrived, in tears, having hysteria I would say, Emmie had run away from her, she is a very, very naughty little girl, however *dolce*. Anna-Maria had worked very, very hard at finding Emmie, but with no success. But we quickly found her, within a very few minutes, I would say—'

'And where was she?'

'She was in Rinascente still, in the children's shoe department. She had found it by herself, she had said she wanted some new shoes, and when a girl wants shoes, she must have them.'

'And – what was she doing, was she crying, was she distressed?'

'Of course she was not,' said Mariella dismissively, 'she was trying to decide which of two pairs she should buy, she had one on each foot, I often do that myself.'

'And – what did she say when she saw you?'

'She said, and I shall always remember, it was so sweet, so adorable, she said, "Which do you think?" Well of course I said she should have them both.'

'And – how was Mrs Shaw while Emmie was missing?'

'She was very, very upset, quite distraught of course, of course. But it was not for long and there was a happy end. Later that night, over dinner, she said Emmie had run away before, more than once. She is very, very naughty, as I have said.'

'Well, thank you, Signora Crespi.'

Bruce Hayward stood up.

'Signora Crespi, thank you for that very – very vivid account. I wonder – in a crowded, strange city, perhaps it would have been better for your maid to restrain Emmeline in some way. With some reins, for example.'

'Reins? She is not a horse.'

'No, of course not, but there are reins, I believe, for keeping children close to you in such situations.'

'Well, we did not have any reins,' said Mariella with a slightly impatient frown, 'and believe me, Emmie would not have worn them if we had. She knows her own head, that one.'

'Or – perhaps she should have stayed with you?'

'What, in the dressmakers? Of course not. Children have no place in such establishments, and besides I could not have concentrated. No, it was my insisting that Eliza came without her that was to blame.'

'I see. No more questions.'

Clearly even Bruce Hayward could see there was not a great deal of future in cross-examination at this point.

Then a clerk came in with a note for Philip Gordon; he read it, looked at Eliza, looked across at Toby and then whispered, 'Excuse me,' to Eliza and left the courtroom. She felt irritated. How could he leave now, when this was so crucial to her survival? She tried to concentrate on Toby, who had returned to his task – and to Mariella.

'So, Signora Crespi, perhaps you could tell us now about the following evening? When the fog left you stranded in the city?'

'Ah, yes. Our famous *nebbia*. This time it was the fault of Fate, not me, that kept Eliza from her little one. When we left Como, it was clear. When we came out of La Scala, it was impossible to see more than a few metres. No, I would say a few centimetres. It would have been hugely dangerous to try to get back to Como. Emmie would have been left motherless. And – how dreadful that would have been.'

'Indeed.'

'So, Eliza stayed with some friends in their apartment. She did not sleep for one moment, I know. And then she very bravely set out next day, before we would dare to risk it, with some friends, some very, very brave friends, and an exceedingly brave driver, and made a way back to Como through the *nebbia*, to be with Emmie once more.'

'And – who was looking after Emmie at the villa?'

'Oh – so many people. Anna-Maria. The cook. The butler. My husband's valet. All waiting upon her. Eliza spoke to her on the phone many times . . .'

'Signora Crespi—'

'Yes?' Mariella looked at Bruce Hayward disdainfully. She clearly greatly preferred Toby Gilmour.

'Would it not have been better if Mrs Shaw had stayed at the villa with Emmie, rather than gone into Milan in the fog?'

'That would have been extremely rude, do you not think?' said Mariella. 'My husband would have been most offended, having made so many arrangements for her.'

'I think perhaps even so—'

'And besides,' said Mariella, interrupting him, 'we did not know the fog would come. It arrives from nowhere.'

Bruce Hayward gave up. Clifford Rogers would surely see through this ridiculous creature.

But Clifford Rogers was gazing at Mariella in something approaching incredulity; and then called an early break.

'This afternoon I shall see the child. And if there is time we can begin the summing up. Otherwise, that can take place in the morning.'

'All rise.'

Eliza walked out of the courtroom, down into the atrium. It was all beginning to seem rather familiar.

'Eliza—' It was Toby. 'I need to talk to you most urgently. Let's go to my rooms. We have a little time and it's very important—'

She followed him in silence.

'Something has cropped up this morning. Something which could really influence our chances. But – it has to be your call.'

'What are you talking about, Toby? Why now, why not sooner?'

'I didn't know sooner. It's all happened this morning. Philip has been dealing with it.'

'Was that why he rushed out?'

'Yes. Anyway, we have a new witness, but – but I need your permission to call her.'

'What are you talking about? My permission? Who is it?'

'It's Georgina Barker. She rang on Monday, and said she would like to come and see us to discuss the case, but then cancelled; we didn't think it worth worrying you. And then she called again yesterday, but of course I'd left and my clerk couldn't contact me until much later.'

'But – why? I don't understand.'

'She wants to give evidence against Matt. Reading between the lines, I would say he's upset her in some way and she's having her revenge. Pretty ugly actually.'

'But—'

'Apparently he told her he'd hit you once.'

'Oh! Oh, Toby, no—'

'Yes. Well, I always suspected there's been some violence. Was – was that the only instance?'

'Yes. Yes, it was. Oh, my God. How – how weird. I mean that, she should come back.'

'Indeed. But—'

She was silent. Then, 'Toby, I don't think I want that coming out. I don't want her standing up in court and telling everyone.'

He sighed. 'I had a hunch you'd say that.'

'I really don't.'

'It could make all the difference, Eliza. It could win you the case. Win you Emmie. I'm not exaggerating. Please think very, very carefully about it.'

She was silent.

'You OK?'

'Yes. Yes. I'm OK. I think – um – when – when would she be called?'

'This afternoon, possibly. After the judge sees Emmie. Possibly tomorrow morning.'

'So I have a little time to decide?'

'Yes, but only a little. Until Emmie has had her interview with Clifford Rogers at the very latest. We have to get her in, she's at Philip's office, waiting. Eliza, for the love of God, why are you so against it?'

'Two reasons,' she said slowly. 'I'd better tell you what it was about. Not the row itself, it was about the article, in the paper, but what I said to provoke it. To provoke him. I said something appalling to Matt, really appalling, I couldn't even tell you, I'm so ashamed of it – and it would come out, and, well and anyway, I – I don't think I want Emmie knowing her daddy hit me. I really don't. It would get in the papers, God, I can see the headline now, they'd love it, I just can't risk it, Toby.'

'Well – as I say, it could win you the case. It's a gift from God, I'd say.'

'Or the devil.'

She looked at him; he smiled at her.

'Please think about it really carefully. This is probably the most important decision you'll ever make. You have to understand just how important. We are very far from being in a position of strength, you know.'

'I do know. Can we – I mean is it all right not to call her?'

'Yes, of course. No one owns a witness. And besides, we are so far into the proceedings, the judge would be extremely irritated if we produced her now, to put it mildly. I can simply tell Georgina it is too late.'

'But – we could call her? If we wanted to.'

'Oh yes. I'm pretty confident he'd agree. It's pretty compelling evidence. Look – Eliza, please don't rush this, I beg of you. Take your time.'

'Yes,' she said, 'yes, all right.'

Mariella got back to the Ritz just after one. The pain and the suffocating sense of loss had eased with her court appearance; she had enjoyed it, given it her all. It had been a most wonderful distraction: but now she was back, back in the real world, and she had to have lunch with Giovanni and Jeremy.

Panic overwhelmed her; she went and sat in the Ladies and smoked a cigarette to calm her nerves; and then, having sprayed herself with Arpège, smoothed her hair, checked her lipstick, she took a deep breath, lifted her head and walked with great determination into the vast gilded foyer of the Ritz.

✿ ✿ ✿

In his office at the agency, Jeremy was also smoking; and on his second glass of champagne. The ordeal ahead of him was considerable; lunching with the woman he loved more than anything in the world, and with whom he had experienced extreme passion and extraordinary intimacy, while behaving throughout as if she was simply a friend, and all in the company of her husband – combined with the very real danger that they might give themselves away. Giovanni was no foolish old man, he was sharp and sharp-eyed, endowed with much perspicacity; it was not impossible that he would observe a glance, a smile, an awkwardness even, and construe it correctly.

But – there was no help for it. He had considered illness, urgent meetings, pressing family business, and rejected them all. Giovanni would read, correctly, that these were excuses and wonder why they were being proffered.

He walked into the lobby as Mariella did; smiled at her, bowed slightly, and brushed his lips against the cheek she lifted to his.

'Hello.'

'Hello, Jeremy.'

'How did the court appearance go?'

'I think very well. Thank you. Shall we go in?'

'Yes.'

The maître d' bustled to greet them; Jeremy put his hand on her back, very gently, to usher her forward; she turned very briefly – clearly quite unable to help herself – to smile at him; her eyes were huge and very soft; he smiled back into them, unable to help himself either.

Giovanni was already at the table; he saw them approaching, stood up to greet them, clearly delighted that they had arrived together. He was looking particularly wonderful, Mariella noticed distractedly, wearing a soft linen suit, and a shirt of palest blue, his white hair, thick and wavy still, brushed back, perfectly groomed: altogether the epitome of old-world elegance.

He smiled, his enchanting, embracing smile, and his eyes, those piercing blue eyes were, she noticed, particularly brilliant; he held out both his hands in greeting, took a step forward, said 'my' and stopped, then said it again, 'my', and then his face changed, distorted, twisted, his legs buckled and Jeremy only just reached him in time to catch him as he fell, and laid him on the floor where he lay, struggling with dreadful rasping breaths, his eyes wide, his body rigid.

Mariella sank onto the floor beside him, cradling his head; Jeremy knelt beside her, loosening Giovanni's tie, calling for cushions, for help; and just for a moment the world shrank to the three of them, held there, a shocking tableau; and then others moved in, the maître d' said a doctor was coming, a nurse appeared, issuing instructions, and then with extraordinary speed a doctor who took his pulse, listened to his heart, and said he should be taken to the medical room, to await the ambulance he had already called; and Jeremy and Mariella found themselves moved away from the centre of the storm, mere helpless onlookers, and terribly afraid.

But by the time they had reached the medical room, and the stretcher had been placed on the floor, the dreadful rasping breathing had first eased and then stopped; the brilliant eyes had become dim and dull, the face somehow collapsed; and with a final whispery sigh, Giovanni's long and wonderfully blessed life was ended.

The ambulance had arrived, and the medics with it, but Mariella sent them away: 'He is gone now, there is no rush, I want him taken to our room, I want to spend time with him. Please.'

Her tone, initially shaky, became peremptory on that 'please'; the doctor looked at her, looked at Jeremy, paused for a moment and then nodded.

And in a very little while, Mariella and Giovanni were alone together in their room.

She felt strangely calm; they had lain him on the bed, and she sat there beside him, cradling his fine old head, stroking his face, telling him she loved him; the window was open, the table on the balcony still set with the morning coffee he had sent for; and the sweet fresh air filled the room, along with the birdsong, overlaid now with the sounds of London, but it was still very much a safe and private space, and she could still inhabit it with him, and wanted to do so.

And sitting with Giovanni, looking at him as he lay there so sweetly peaceful, she thought that she had anticipated this moment many times over the years, of course she had, but had feared that since the advent of Jeremy into her life there might be something unseemly, unloving, a sense of relief even about it, but she felt only sorrow and loss and a wave of intense gratitude to this man, this brilliant, beautiful, loving man who had done so much to make her into the creature she was and been so proud that he had done so; and she bent and kissed his forehead, and his still, white, oddly empty face, and a tear fell on it, and then another, and she sat there for a long time, holding his hand and remembering all that they had shared and done together and thinking what a truly immense loss to her this was.

Chapter 73

'Oh – oh, Mummy, oh no—'

Sarah looked at Eliza, her eyes large with distress.

'I'm sorry, darling, so sorry.'

Emmie, dressed in blue-and-white striped Osh Kosh dungarees, with a white T-shirt underneath, and sneakers on her feet, smiled at her mother.

'Hello, Mummy.'

'Emmie, darling – I did want you to wear a dress, to look pretty for the judge—'

'I know. But I wanted to wear my dungys. I feel better in them.'

'What sort of better?'

'Just better. More happy.'

'She said—' Sarah spoke in a low voice, 'she said if I made her wear a dress, she'd run away.'

Eliza gave up. She knew actually how Emmie felt. Clothes were great influencers of mood.

'All right, darling. Well – you look very nice. Now come and meet everyone, this gentleman is Mr Gordon, and this is his assistant, Sarah.'

'Hello, Emmie. Very nice to have you here.'

'It's nice to be here,' said Emmie politely. She looked round the atrium with a thoughtful expression. 'It's like a church,' she said.

'I know. But you'll see the judge in a little room.'

'I don't mind big rooms.'

'No, darling, I know—'

'Hello, Emmie.' Toby Gilmour had arrived.

'Hello. I like your wig.'

'Thank you. How's Mouse?'

'He's fine.'

'They're ready, Eliza. Mrs Fullerton-Clark, how nice to see you again.'

'And you. Have you recovered from your enforced sojourn in the Home Counties?'

'Oh – yes. Thank you.'

'How fortunate there was somewhere you could both stay.'

'Indeed.'

'And – how is the car?'

'Oh – fine. Yes. Thank you.'

'Jolly bad luck.'

'Well – in some ways.'

Philip Gordon's default expression was one of courteous interest; this sharpened almost imperceptibly now as he looked at Toby.

There was a sudden whoop of 'Daddy' and Emmie had shaken her hand free of her mother's and shot across the atrium of the Law Courts, almost knocking over a heavily bewigged gentleman, and up into her father's arms.

And Matt stood there, his face buried in her long, shining hair, holding her close; and for a long moment nobody moved, and then, 'Well,' said Philip Gordon. 'Shall we all go up?'

Emmie slithered down and took Matt's hand, then turned to wait for her mother and took hers also and walked up the great staircase between them; and everyone involved in the case, which included Judge Clifford Rogers, on his way to his rooms, became most forcibly aware that what was about to happen to this little family was nothing less than a small, and possibly quite a large, tragedy.

At the top of the stairs, Emmie leaned over the balustrade, studying her surroundings; then, 'Can we explore?' she said.

'Later, darling, later,' said Eliza. She could hear her voice quaver. She mustn't let Emmie think she was nervous: it might affect her.

Standing outside the judge's rooms, she almost panicked; she wanted to grab Emmie, take her away, run down the stairs with her, out into the street, anything rather than subject her to this dreadful ordeal. Her grip on Emmie's hand tightened.

'Now, darling – just answer the judge's questions, all right? And—'

The door opened; a female clerk appeared.

'Is this Emmeline?'

'Yes,' said Emmie before anyone else could speak.

'Come along in, Emmeline. Mr Rogers has tea for you both, and some biscuits . . .'

'Chocolate?' asked Emmie hopefully.

'I believe there are some of those, yes.'

Emmie followed the woman into the room, turning to smile at the small group before she vanished. 'Bye,' she said.

'Give her twenty years,' said Toby, 'and she'll be conducting cases herself.'

They had taken Giovanni away from her now; there had to be a post-mortem, they explained gently; after that, he could lie in a chapel of rest, while she made arrangements to take him home.

'Which of course I want to do, he must be buried in Italy, where he belongs.'

'Of course,' said Jeremy.

They were sitting in the suite, talking; it was where she wanted to be.

'I feel so dreadful, Jeremy, so bad. Supposing that happened because he saw us, coming in together, suppose he guessed—'

'Mariella, he was expecting us together.'

'I know, I know, but you kissed me out there in the foyer, suppose he saw that—'

'Darling one, I kissed your cheek. As I have a hundred times in his presence. You must, must try not to think this way. He had no idea, none at all, he greeted me last night as he always did, you saw, he insisted I joined you for lunch today, he was smiling as he came to greet us—'

'I know. And I – I know you are right. It just feels – oh I don't know. Confused. So frightened.'

'Of course. Of course it is. And there is something very important I have to tell you, Mariella. Very important.'

'What is that?'

'All I feel is sorrow. Dreadful, dreadful sorrow. Nothing else.'

'I too. Just the same. And guilt, of course. I can't help that. That I didn't stay with him this morning. He had a headache, I should not have gone—'

'Did he ask you to stay? Was it very bad?'

'No, no, he said I must go, that Eliza needed me. He came to see me off.'

'Well then. How could you have known?'

'I should. I should have thought, the doctor said it was probably

709

something to do with his brain, perhaps the pain was very bad, and he hid it from me—'

'My darling, he looked the picture of health in the restaurant, you saw it yourself, smiling, strong—'

'I know, I know. Jeremy, the last thing almost he said to me was about you. He said you were the perfect English gentleman and we were lucky to have you as a friend.'

'Well,' said Jeremy, 'that is very lovely. In many ways.'

'It is. I too thought so. We did keep him safe from what we had done, didn't we?'

'We did indeed. And thank God for it.'

'What do we do now?' said Eliza, as Emmie vanished. Matt had gone silently away.

'We wait. Shouldn't be too long. Thirty minutes, maximum. Have you made your decision, Eliza?'

'No. Not yet. Is she – is Georgina here?'

'She's on her way. She knows she may not be able to appear. Why don't you go for a little walk? Have a think.'

'Yes, all right. Thanks, Toby.'

And she walked out of the Law Courts and across the Strand and wandered along towards Fleet Street, her dilemma beating in her head, physically disturbing her. Was it worth it? Would it be worth it? How would she feel, if she stuck to her principles, did the decent thing and then Matt got custody? If she saved him from disapprobation and even disgrace and then he walked away with Emmie? He would get over it, surely, the disapprobation; he was tough, tough as they came, and it wasn't as if he would never see Emmie; indeed, she would probably be a great deal more generous over arrangements than he would. How would she feel, with a life largely emptied of Emmie, with Summercourt possibly gone, with only her career for comfort; did she really want that? All for a touch of righteousness? But – it wasn't a touch. And it wasn't just for Matt, it was for Emmie, it would all come out, not just what Matt had done, but the disgraceful, shocking things she had said to him as well; broadcast, no doubt, all over the court, possibly the papers. The *Evening Standard* had picked this one up and run with it.

But – she would still have Emmie. Probably. Of course nothing was certain . . .

'Eliza! Look where you're going, love. Why aren't you in court?'

It was Jack Beckham, leaving El Vino's slightly the worse for wear, but he'd be sober again by the time he'd walked back to the office, it was the journalist's gift.

'I've got to go back in a bit. Jack, you were so marvellous the other day, I was so grateful to you. I meant to ring, sorry. I promise to buy you lunch very soon.'

'I'd rather you came and worked for me, I can tell you that. No hope, I suppose?'

'Well – there might be,' she said and sighed. 'If I lose . . .'

'I shall say my prayers tonight, then.'

'Jack!'

'Oh, I don't mean it, Eliza. Dreadful lot aren't they, those lawyers. Dirty business.'

'It – it is, yes.'

'Dirtier than ours, if you ask me. We do occasionally give people the benefit of the doubt. That Bruce Hayward, I don't know what he keeps up his arse, but it must be something pretty large and uncomfortable. What are you looking at me like that for, Eliza?'

Eliza giggled. 'Oh, Jack,' she said and reached up to kiss him. 'You've just done me a huge favour. Thank you. I must go. But I will definitely buy you lunch. And come and be your fashion editor, if I lose. If you really want me. That's a promise. Bye, Jack.'

If the editor of a Fleet Street tabloid with scant regard for the feelings of anyone at all thought the law was a dirty business, then who was she to argue?

She turned and ran all the way back to the Law Courts.

As she reached the courts, a taxi was pulling up. Philip Gordon's assistant and Georgina Barker got out of it.

At the same time, Matt Shaw was approaching from the other direction; he saw Georgina and stopped.

Eliza had often wondered what the word 'blench' precisely meant; she felt she knew now. Matt looked as if he had been hit physically, slightly off balance; his face ghastly white and rigid, his eyes wide with shock.

'Hello, Matt,' said Georgina and swept past him into the building.

Eliza decided a little hyper-anxiety would do Matt good, smiled at him sweetly and ran up the stairs to where she had arranged to meet Toby.

711

'Hello,' she said.

'Hello.'

'I've – made my decision.'

'And?'

'And the answer's no. I can't do it, Toby. Sorry.'

'Well,' he said, 'I hope it's the right one.'

'Me too. But you know something? I made another decision in this case, and everyone told me that was wrong.'

'And what was that?'

'To retain you and not Tristram Selbourne.'

'And?'

'That was the right decision. I know that now, without a doubt.'

'I'm glad you think so,' he said. He spoke lightly; but his expression was sombre.

Emmie had re-emerged, smiling and composed.

'He was nice, the judge,' she said. 'We had Penguins.'

It spoke for the strangeness of the day that it would not have surprised Eliza to see a row of black and white birds file out of the judge's rooms. It took her a few moments to realise Emmie spoke of the chocolate version.

'I – don't think we'll be going back into court now,' said Toby, 'as that was so extended a session. I'll check.'

He came back.

'No. Summing up tomorrow. For all of us. And – judgment, of course.'

Eliza and Sarah left to get a taxi. Matt was standing in the atrium as they went through it; looking, still, as if he was shell-shocked.

'Bye, Matt,' said Eliza.

'Where – that is – do you know where Georgina is?'

'Not sure. I think she went off with my team. Yours will know.'

Eliza and Sarah didn't ask Emmie about her hour with the judge; they both felt it would have been an outrageous intrusion and she was not forthcoming. She simply said again that he had been very nice and they had played animal snap.

'You what!' said Eliza.

'We played animal snap. Not for very long, but he didn't know how to play, so I showed him. The lady had to go and get some cards for us.'

712

'I – I see. And – did you have a nice talk with him?'

'Oh yes. I told him what I wanted. He said he'd see what he could do.'

Later, when Emmie was in the bath, she said, 'Do you want me to tell you what I told the judge?'

'Um – only if you want to.'

'I will if you like. But you might be cross. He said I could, but I think I'll let him tell you tomorrow. Specially as you might be cross.'

So – she had told him she wanted to live with Matt. How was she to make sense of that? She sat there, looking at Emmie soaping her small chest, and fought down the tears.

Well, Eliza, that's it then. Dream over. Hopes crushed. You've had it.

Of course, it was to be expected. She supposed she'd always known, really, what Emmie would choose, if she was allowed. Matt did – did spoil her more. And – well, he was a very good father. It wasn't as if she'd have to worry about Emmie. She'd be completely safe, well cared for, happy. But – God, it hurt.

'No, darling, I don't want you to make me cross.'

'But – I love you, Mummy.'

'I love you too, Emmie.'

She put her to bed, read her *The Tiger Who Came to Tea* for what felt like the thousandth time, and then kissed her and said, 'Night darling. Well done today.'

And she went downstairs and told Sarah she really didn't want to talk about it, any of it, and they agreed that they both needed an early night and had a rather modest supper, neither of them feeling remotely like eating, and sat pretending to watch television.

Jeremy rang, with the news of Giovanni's death. 'It was a massive stroke and then a heart attack, apparently. He died in the dining room at the Ritz. I think he would have liked that.'

'I think so too.'

'We saw him collapse. I really don't think he could have known anything about it. I hope to God not, anyway.'

'Oh, Jeremy. I'm so sorry. And Mariella, how is she?'

'Very, very sad. Guilty, of course, that she left him this morning, he had a headache apparently—'

'And she had to come to court for me? Oh, Jeremy, no, I feel so dreadful—'

'Darling, don't you start. He wanted her to do it, he sent her off from the Ritz himself. He told her you needed her more than he did.'

'Oh, God,' said Eliza, a sob in her voice, 'he was such a darling, darling man.'

'He was. But – you should know that Mariella is also relieved on so many counts. Not least that she knew how he dreaded being old and helpless. And he was saved from that, he remained charming and in his own way very young.'

She felt the tears come then; tears of real grief, for she had been truly fond of Giovanni. And then, 'Jeremy, how do you feel?'

'Truthfully, from the bottom of my heart, hugely sad.'

'Of course you do. Darling Jeremy.'

'Darling Eliza.'

She went to bed, to lie awake for many hours; thinking about Giovanni, and Mariella, but mostly about Emmie – and about losing her, and what motherhood really meant.

She thought about her birth and how much it had hurt, and how wonderful it had been; about the early exhausting, confusing days, when sleep had become a strange, distant dream; about the wonder of the first wobbly, uncertain smile, the first joyous, sweet giggle; about the achievements of early childhood, the triumph of standing unsupported, swaying gently back and forwards, the first staggering steps, and tottering run; the first word – enragingly it had been 'Daddy' – and then the tantrums, oh, those tantrums, the arched back, the scarlet face, the screams echoing through shops, buses, playgrounds, screams of 'no, no, NO'; about the childhood illnesses, the fear they brought in their wake; about the sheer tedium of so much of it, the long, rainy days when the hours dragged and they played shops or schools over and over again; the fun of it, pushing her on the swing, running along as she tried to ride her two-wheeler for the first time, before falling off over and over again, and never, ever giving in and then finally 'look, look, look, I can do it'; of the sweet sadness of the first day at school, walking home alone from the gates, looking back with surprise, that those precious first years were actually unbelievably over – and then the sense almost of awe, as she began to read and write, that the tiny helpless creature she had given birth to had become a person: that was what motherhood was, she thought, being there, through it all, seeing it through, enjoying it most of the time, disliking it some of the time, the weariness, the boredom, the anxiety and the love and the sheer, sheer joy of it, and all the time this bond was growing steely strong, unbreakable really, no matter what happened – and it would hold, wouldn't it, through separation, through days, weeks spent apart, surely, surely – or would it begin to fray, to weaken, to fail . . . finally, fitfully, Eliza slept.

And in his large, luxurious bed in Jimbo's house, Matt also lay awake, remembering also, and thinking how much he loved Emmie, how he would quite literally do anything for her, walk on hot coals, give all he had, die for her, and without a moment's hesitation or thought; and how he had felt like that once, and not so long ago, for Eliza, how she had taken his heart that first day on Waterloo station, how he had followed his dream of her, for years and years, how he had won her, finally, taken her, his life's prize, and for how short a while, it seemed now looking back, they had been happy, and then how swiftly and disastrously they had stumbled and fallen at the great differences between them, and how Emmie had held them somehow together, with their shared passion and concern and love for her, and perhaps she could have done so still had he not wrenched her away from both of them, and decreed with his self-absorbed pride that she must belong to him and him alone . . . and in doing so, had possibly lost her . . . finally, fitfully, Matt also slept.

'All rise.'

Judge Clifford Rogers looked more sombre even than usual, and his expression more inscrutable as he walked in; as if he had things on his mind that he could hardly bear to contemplate. And the burdens of his office had become unsupportable.

Toby would sum up first; Eliza sat, her eyes fixed on him as if taking them off would somehow weaken her, scarcely hearing what he said, all the old arguments, the well-worked ground, passing in a blur . . .

'Here we have a little girl born to quite exceptional parents, gifted, successful; both with much to offer to the child they have jointly and successfully raised . . . both excellent parents, both concerned, thoughtful, inspiring, and very loving . . . their marriage has broken down and this joint care is no longer possible . . . Mrs Shaw has worked, and very successfully . . . she believes that Emmie will have benefitted from having a working mother . . . her increased happiness at pursuing her career, and her consequent sense of self-worth has given Emmie a great deal . . .

715

'Emmie is, and this is an inescapable fact, a little girl . . . She needs the kind of input into her life, that only a woman can give. And in the years ahead, as she matures, surely she will need a very female kind of tenderness and understanding . . .'

Just finish, Eliza thought in agony, let's get it over. But then –

'I would like to close with an appreciation of Mrs Shaw. She is a remarkable person, as we have all seen: remarkably loyal, remarkably generous, remarkably talented, and remarkable in her friendships. She has attracted the admiration of many and very disparate people, from all walks of life.

'I would also stress that Mrs Shaw has at no time expressed any wish to end her marriage, or to claim custody of her daughter; it is a situation that has been forced upon her, and to which she has responded with much courage and generosity. I submit that she is the right person to care for Emmeline, and to raise her in her own particular, and care-fully considered, way; I therefore recommend, my lord, that she be granted both custody and care and control, and that generous access be granted to Emmeline's father.'

It had been the right decision, Eliza thought, to choose him; the gentler advocate, the more sympathetic to how she was; the more concerned with Emmie and her welfare. It had been a risk, to go so strong on her working life, but it was a point she had wanted to make most passionately herself and he had done it for her with charm and tact. But . . . then there was Bruce Hayward who, summing up, was gently savage, and his own testimony to Matt as moving as Toby Gilmour's had been to her.

'I am confident that Mr Shaw can provide the kind of emotional support for his daughter that she needs; he is a most unusual father, and we have heard many testimonies to that effect; he is extraordinarily committed to Emmeline, both emotionally and practically. He already has arrangements in place for her, so that he can seamlessly take over her care; and I would recommend that your lordship grant him both full custody and care and control, with access to her mother at his discretion.'

Doesn't look good for me, Eliza thought; just doesn't look good. Her dissolute friendships – how much good really had Mariella done her? – her admitted adultery, her personal ambitions. It just wasn't going to work, any of it; there wasn't enough to be said for her. Literally. And with Emmie throwing her weight in behind her father...

*   *   *

Outside, they waited. Toby was quiet, tense, Philip smiling, over-effusive; the assistants were chattering brightly, Matt's team looking across at them, smiling, patently confident. Eliza felt utterly exhausted, numb, not even frightened; just longing to have it over, the final humiliation, the ultimate pain . . . and regretting – almost – her decision.

'All rise.'

She was going to be sick, she was . . . 'No nose picking,' whispered Toby, trying to smile. She didn't even try to smile back. Clifford Rogers looked at them all with his now-familiar air of weary resignation.

'We have heard a great deal. Some of it revelatory, some of it predictable. Some of it persuasive, some of it frankly incredible. And we are left with – what? Two people, two highly intelligent people, both undoubtedly good parents, both indisputably bad spouses. Two people who love their child so much but are so diametrically opposed to one another that they choose to fight for her, rather than learn not to fight one another for her.

'We have a father, clearly successful and ambitious, who has built up an extremely impressive business, who wants to run his family in the same way, with astonishingly little consideration and generosity for the wishes of the people within it. And a mother who is a most talented editor, admired by her peers and her superiors, but who is not prepared to give up her career in order to do the rather more important job, of caring for her young child.

'Or we could look at it another way, and say we have a child who did not ask to be born, who has every possible right to security and the love of both her father and her mother, and is denied that by both of them.

'I am not over-concerned with the shortcomings of either, as they have been presented to me; it is my considered opinion that the behaviour of both of them is no better and no worse than that of a great many married people, who have had the maturity to find a way to stay together for the sake of the children. Unfortunately neither Mr nor Mrs Shaw are in possession of this maturity. I think Mr Shaw could actually make a very good fist of caring for his daughter as a sole parent, and Mrs Shaw could do pretty well at caring for her in the same situation. The child would clearly be materially well provided for either way. But neither scenario would be ideal for her. Far from it. And it is the interests of the child, the innocent party in all this unhappiness, that have to be paramount.

'So – we need a Solomon. Unfortunately I am not one. I fear I lack both his brutality and his courage. Certainly in so far as a judgment would affect a child.

'But – I have found one. In the child in this case, in the six-year-old Emmeline Shaw, who has, mercifully, more maturity and common sense than either of her parents.

'We spoke at length, she and I; expecting merely to discover in which way and how badly she was affected by the break-up, I found my way forward.

'I think the best thing I can do is tell you what she said. She expressed – of course as all children do in this situation – a passionate wish that things could continue as they were, that she could live at home with both her parents. But she has come to accept that this is not possible. As she put it, rather succinctly, her parents are too stupid.

'She did however propose a scenario which I consider clearly not ideal, but acceptable. Given that her parents are financially succesful, I believe it to be workable.

'She says she would like them to live next door to one another, in houses that were exactly the same, particularly her bedroom. Now, I can see this would be a little difficult to arrange precisely as she desires it, but I see no reason why, in one of the areas of London, with many adjacent streets of extremely similar houses, two identical, or very like, residences could not be found.

'She would like to spend exactly half her life in each house, with each parent. She would like to spend the weekends alternately with each of them, at the house in the country which Mr Shaw so generously bought for the family, and where her pony lives. She would like them all to be together at Christmas and on her birthdays.

'Now it seems to me, that, for a little girl who has already suffered considerably, who yearns to see her parents together, who loves both of them very much, and genuinely enjoys the company of both equally, this is no more than she deserves. Indeed, it is a great deal less than she deserves, as I have already observed.

'I realise it would not be easy emotionally for the parents. I consider, however, that they could and should be able to accomplish it. I am not asking them to live together but for two weekends a year. I would hope they are civilised and mature enough to manage this.

'I am mindful that shared custody in these situations is rarely successful and given the slightly charged potential of this one, particularly so. I therefore grant custody to the father, and care and control to the mother, with access for the father exactly as outlined.'

A long pause ... then ... and was that, several in his audience wondered, a gleam in his heavily lidded eyes, a smile struggling to break out on his lugubrious features?

'I should add that Emmeline's dearest wish, as outlined to me, next to having her parents living together once more, is to hold a gymkhana at the country house in roughly one year's time. I do not, of course, propose to make this a condition of the settlement, but I would say again, that it is no more than she deserves. What I do realise is that it would necessitate that Mr Shaw keep the house, Summercourt, in the county of Wiltshire, and not sell it as I believe he had wished to do. I realise that considerable generosity would be required to do this. But I believe it to be financially possible for him and, given that he is to have custody of his daughter, I would like to think he would show his gratitude by granting her wish. May I say in closing that I am most impressed with Emmeline and what both – and clearly it is both – her parents have accomplished in her upbringing thus far. It is for this reason that I am so unwilling to disrupt her life any further than has already been done.'

'All rise.'

Eliza walked into the house; Emmie appeared, holding Sarah's hand, looking anxious.

'Was it all right? Are you cross with me?'

'It was absolutely all right, Emmie. And no, I'm not cross with you. I can't ever remember feeling less like being cross with you. Come here and give me a big, big hug. And Daddy, he's here too, just to tell you he isn't cross with you either.'

Epilogue

1972

'Mummy! Mummy, get up! It's light and it's late.'

'Emmie—' Eliza forced her eyes open, peering at her watch. 'Emmie, it might be light but it's not late. It's six o'clock.'

'It must be late, there's a man downstairs with a roundabout.'

'A – a roundabout? Oh, you mean – yes. What on earth is he here already for?'

'To put it up, he said. He said the sooner the better. Can I ride on it when he's done it? Please, Mummy, please.'

'No, Emmie, you can't. It's for all the children later—'

'I'm a child.'

'Emmie, for goodness' sake, give it a rest. Go and put some clothes on, your old jodhpurs, NOT the new ones, and I'll go down and let him in. OK? And what about your tack and stuff?'

'I've already done that, and I can't plait his mane and tail without Gail, I can't do the ribbons. I could oil his hooves again . . .'

'Yes, OK, do that.'

Eliza pulled on her jeans and a T-shirt – she could have a bath later – and risked looking out of the window. Rain was her greatest fear for today; rain and what it could do to a gymkhana. She had experienced enough of them, the flying mud, the drenched onlookers, the smell of wet pony, the feel of sodden saddle and slippery reins, the leaking refreshment tent, the rain-cooled tea, the cold fingers holding soggy sandwiches, the icy trickle down the neck . . . and rain had been forecast.

But – 'Oh, my God.' It wasn't raining. It was grey. Very grey. But it was the good grey, the grey of mist, the grey that rolled slowly away into first a hint, then a promise, then a burst of sunshine. A small miracle. No, a large one. Of course it might change . . .

She looked across at the meadow, transformed into a pony paradise, a ring, jumps, all looking very professional, and in the corner nearest the house all the paraphernalia attendant to a gymkhana for later in the day, several bales of hay, dozens of buckets, a stack of chairs, and a large pile of poles, for musical chairs and poles respectively. Beyond that, the rough field had become a car park, already holding two horseboxes – one a very flashy thing, the sort that housed not only horses, but people as well, in an add-on apartment just behind the driver. She looked at it with some foreboding, fearing they had been brought here under false pretences; lured by an article in the *Daily News*, whose editor had insisted on publishing a half-page appreciation of the Summercourt Horse Show and which rather gave the impression that the gymkhana was to be an event only a little humbler than Badminton.

The paper was offering, indeed, a cup for jumping, 14.2 hands and under, to be presented by the editor, Mr Jack Beckham, who would be attending with his own family, the voluptuous Mrs Babs Beckham, one time weathergirl and columnist of the *Daily Sketch*, and their three teenage daughters, who according to their father didn't really know one end of a horse from the other, but liked the boys who rode them.

'They won't find any groovy boys here,' said Eliza briskly; but as it turned out, Gail the girl who looked after Mouse, had suddenly produced her three half-brothers, who lived in Bath with her mother and stepfather, two very presentable and one quite stunning, who bore a distinct resemblance to Marc Bolan, complete with wild head of glossy curls. Eliza, who hadn't seen them for years, and who hadn't believed in the beauty of the Marc Bolan one, although it was much discussed in the village, stared at them open-mouthed when Gail brought them up to the house two evenings before.

'I got them over to help,' she said, 'they all know about horses, course, and Cal, he's the one with the hair, Dad's been after him with the clippers ever since they arrived, he's been at vet college for a year now, so he might be useful with any accidents.'

Eliza said she hoped fervently that there wouldn't be any accidents, and of course they would have a vet in attendance, but it would be very useful to have a second pair of hands just in case; and gazed in fresh awe at Cal, who looked as if he would be more at home on the catwalk or on *Top of the Pops* than in a vet's surgery.

She went downstairs, greeted the roundabout man and told him where he could start to set up – in the furthest corner of the car-park field so as to startle the horses least – and went into the kitchen to make some coffee. Her mother was there already, looking as excited as Emmie.

'It's all so lovely, Eliza, if only Daddy was here to see it, and no rain, you see I told you so.'

'I know, I can't believe it. Now the programmes have arrived I do hope—'

'Not yet, Mrs Horrocks is bringing them over. Mr Horrocks was running them off on the Gestetner until the small hours apparently. But I've got a proof – here – what do you think?'

Eliza looked at it; it was hardly a fine piece of printing. The front cover, which consisted of a drawing of Mouse by Emmie, above all the statutory details, had a considerable list to the left and contained in spite of all her efforts, two typos – one of which was leaving the second 'M' out of Summercourt – but at least the gate charge was now correct, one pound rather than one hundred which had only been spotted, incredibly, at the fourth proofing.

'You should have left it,' Jeremy said when she told him, 'the ordinary punters would have assumed it was a mistake, and you might have got some rich outsiders coughing up, putting you in profit. How much do you think you're going to make, anyway?'

'We'll be extremely lucky to break even,' said Eliza, 'it's a very good thing we've got some sponsors.'

'Sponsors? Darling, how grand. Who would that be?'

'Well, Shaw Construction, funnily enough, and Scarlett's travel company have put in five hundred pounds as well, bless her.'

'Are they coming?'

'Scarlett and Mark? I hope so, but her baby's due on Sunday, so not quite sure—'

'I don't think a little thing like that would deter our Scarlett.'

'Well, she's pretty nervous about it all. What about Mariella, Jeremy, is she coming?'

'Would she miss it? Not for the world. Of course she's coming. Only thing that's worrying me is she's got some mysterious plan.'

'What sort of plan?'

'I don't know, except that it involves arriving at Summercourt long after I do, and she has some appointment quite early in the day just outside Marlborough. We're staying at the Bear overnight, it seemed simpler. Oh, and Pa wants to come too, he's never seen Summercourt, and it's quite famous, of course, being in Pevsner, and he likes houses. And he's quite lonely these days, poor old chap, misses Ma more than he'd ever admit, even misses the bullying—'

'Jeremy, of course it's all right. I love your father, you know I do. I bet he loves Mariella,' she added.

'My God, he does. Whenever we have a row, she threatens to marry him instead.'

'Well, that'd be interesting. Anyway, stay for supper afterwards, why don't you? Loads of people will be there, and Charles is bringing his new girlfriend, she's a teacher, sounds a bit worthy, but perfect for him, and I'd love you to meet her.'

'Try and keep me away.'

The sun was beginning to work through the mist; a pale glow settling on the fields, drifting over the wood. Eliza took her mug of coffee and went to sit on the fence of the paddock. Mouse was tied up, clearly resentful at his curtailed freedom, and Emmie was rather unsuccessfully trying to re-oil his already shiny hooves. Eliza held out her hand to him; he pushed his soft nose into it, seeking Polo mints or carrots, and finding neither pushed his face against her body, jerking his head gently, slobbering onto her T-shirt. Good thing she hadn't cleaned herself up yet.

She looked across at the house, the pale light dusting it, catching the windows, turning the stone lighter, almost luminescent. God, she loved this house. It was such a good friend to her, a gentle, graceful, welcoming friend, always ready for her, to greet her, to contain her.

But a shadow hung over it still. Matt had never – of course, how could he? – loved it as she did. He had bought it for her, because he loved her. He would have bought her anything – then. It had been the hardest part of the negotiations, the house; Matt's initial heady relief at getting custody, thus saving face and his sense of justice, had given way to his usual truculence; why should he, he argued, spend thousands a year on its upkeep for Sarah to enjoy, for Eliza to visit, when another house, cheaper, easier to run, closer to London, would serve as well.

'But what about Emmie and Mouse?' said Eliza tetchily.

'I've seen a couple of houses in Surrey, just outside Guildford, got paddocks, nice little stables. What's wrong with them?'

'They're not Summercourt,' said Eliza.

'No, and not as costly either. I could buy one of them and a cottage for your mother, and still be quids in. Ivor Lewis says I should appeal against that part of the settlement, and I'd be sure to win. Emmie would be fine, what she cares about is Mouse and her weekends with us. She's got a lot of common sense, Emmie has, and she likes her comfort, she won't go mooning about because she's lost Great-great-grandpa's legacy.'

He did appeal and won the right to sell; it would go under the hammer in the autumn.

Eliza told herself that set against losing Emmie, it really wasn't very important. It still hurt though; she could hardly bear even to contemplate its loss from her life.

But, for now, for today, it was theirs; the lovely heart of the family, and at its very best, beautifully on show, preening itself, asking to be admired. Which it would be, of course . . . She slithered off the fence and walked back towards it, determined on only positive thoughts.

'How do you feel?' Mark looked at Scarlett as she lay in the bath, her vast stomach protruding out of the Miss Dior bubbles.

'Wonderful. Like a whale.'

'A wonderful whale. But otherwise?'

'Oh – fine. Yes. No twinges, if that's what you mean. And before you ask, yes, I do want to go to the gymkhana.'

'Dear love, it's a long way. It could shake things up. Get you going.'

'Well – good. I need to be got going.'

'I know, but so far from London, away from the hospital? Is that a good idea?'

'Mark, first babies take at least, at the very least, twelve hours to be born. More like twenty-four. Or even thirty-six. Stop fussing. If it starts, we can just head back. It'll be good, it'll use up some of the time.'

'I know, but dear love, you must remember how important it is you're in hospital. Near all the medical aid.'

'Yes, I know. Double doses of gas and air and pethidine and chloroform if I can get it.. But I still think it would be better to go than sit here waiting for contractions to start. Anyway, the baby's bound to be late, first ones always are.'

'Yes, of course. Well, if you're sure. I'd love to go. But I won't mind if you change your mind.'

Mark was uneasy about Scarlett's insistence on the opposite of natural childbirth. It would have been more than his life was worth to tell her so;

and a great deal more to tell her that his mother had frequently told him how she had given birth to him without any pain relief whatsoever apart from self-hypnosis and infusions of raspberry-leaf tea.

He understood Scarlett's fear of childbirth and sympathised; looking at her vast stomach and thinking of the baby's exit from it, he felt quite fearful himself. He was very grateful moreover that she was as keen for him not to be present at the birth as she was on medical intervention; the thought of seeing this person he loved so much in terrible pain distressed him horribly. Mark was a gentle soul; he planned to spend the time Scarlett was in labour reading, listening to music and getting drunk by the telephone. He hoped for a son; but he would be almost as happy with a daughter, and besides, he very much intended for there to be others. He had a rather unrealistic view of fatherhood; he had been an only child and hated it, and he longed for a large family. The fact that it would bring noise and mess into his life had somehow escaped him; he imagined them all sitting sweetly together in the shade of the garden in Trisos in the summer, or by the big fireplace in the Bloomsbury house in the winter, their heads bent over books, with Mozart or Bach playing in the background.

He was deeply relieved that the rift between Scarlett and Matt was healing; it had upset him horribly. It had taken a while, but Matt loved Scarlett far too much to bear any lasting ill-will towards her, even in a situation as charged as this one: although what would have happened if he had lost Emmie did not, in Mark's view, bear thinking about.

How long ago now it seemed, their own marriage, his and Scarlett's, standing in the little church on Trisos, making their vows before a rather bewildered Greek priest, with only Larissa and Demetrios and the two Aris and of course Persephone to witness it, listening to Persephone's lovely voice reading her epithalamium, and afterwards coming out into the glorious gold and blue day, and looking at Scarlett in all her beauty, in a white flowing dress, with white flowers and ribbons woven into her hair, and thinking what an astonishing and absolutely surprising thing love was.

'Mummy, Gail's here.'

'Oh – good.'

Eliza went to greet Gail, who with Cal was dragging large baskets out of her old truck, filled with potatoes, woolly hats, scarves and gloves, and a lot of extremely muddy wellington boots.

'What are the potatoes for?' asked Emmie

'They're instead of apples,' said the exquisite Cal, who was helping Gail to unload. 'Too early for windfalls and your mum said we weren't to buy them, too expensive, so we hit on the idea of potatoes. Just as good.'

'What, to eat?'

'No, of course not,' said Gail, 'you haven't been listening to me, Emmie, it's for the obstacle race, last heat when you have to get an apple out of a bucket with your teeth and then gallop round the ring. Your mum said she didn't want you in that one, and I think she's right, the big girls always do it and it gets a bit rough.'

'I want to do it,' said Emmie.

'Emmie,' said Eliza, 'if I see you doing that, it'll be last race not just for today, but the rest of the summer. You've got at least two more gymkhanas to go to, and I won't take you if you're naughty today. Is that clear?'

'Yes, it's clear,' said Emmie resignedly. Eliza looked at her sharply; she knew that tone. But Emmie's face was innocently blank, her eyes wide, as she looked back at her mother. God, thought Eliza, what is she going to be like in five years' time . . . Now, maybe she should grab this opportunity to have her bath and change; she didn't want to actually smell when . . .

'Mummy, it's the saints' ambulance.'

'The – oh, St John's. Good. I was hoping they'd be here in lots of time. I'll go and tell them where to set up their tent. Gail, next to the entrance to the ring, do you think?'

'Louise, this is Matt.'

'Oh – hello.'

'Look, I'm – I'm sorry about last night. Really. And – do you want to come today?'

'Well – I'm not sure. Not if you're going to be in a foul mood all the time. And yes, before you say so, of course it's a difficult day for you, but if you could just keep at least looking cheerful, for Emmie's sake, it'll help a lot.'

'I just don't – don't fancy seeing him there. Poncing around. In my house, he's so fucking arrogant, I can't stand him—'

'I know, Matt, and I had gathered that, I think I'd have worked it out even if you'd never actually told me. He seems fine to me. Very nice.'

'I know you do. Bloody smoothie. Smarmy as they come. You don't usually like them like that, Louise, I don't know what you see in him. He's worse than Northcott and that's saying something.'

'If by worse you mean more charming and agreeable, I'm not sure I agree. I've always liked Jeremy. Quite a close-run thing actually, I'd say.'

'Oh for God's sake.'

'What about Mariella, is she coming?'

'I suppose so. They're engaged. She doesn't like me either, but she'll be there, in my house, dressed up in some ridiculous outfit, showing off —'

'Oh, Matt. So – are you getting that place near Dorking?'

'I think so. It's relatively new, about ten years old, very good condition, plenty of room, but not a great barn like Summercourt. Save me a fortune.'

'Has Emmie seen it?'

'Not yet. I'm going to take her next weekend.'

'And – how does she feel about losing Summercourt?'

'I – don't know.'

'What, you haven't told her?'

'Not yet.'

'Matt, that's awful.'

'I don't see why. Long as she's got Mouse, she won't care.'

'I think you might be wrong there,' said Louise. 'See you in an hour.'

She rang off. A year after the custody case, things hadn't changed a great deal between her and Matt. They met regularly for dinner, drinks, occasionally for lunch at the weekends he didn't have Emmie. She still, she supposed – no, she knew – loved him. He didn't seem to love her, or to have any tender feelings for her whatsoever. He'd certainly never indicated that he did; the nearest had been when he told her he enjoyed her company more than that of anyone else he knew. As he seemed to dislike most people it wasn't much of a compliment.

He had adjusted to the custody settlement pretty well; it had, in fact, as Eliza often said, made less difference to his life than it had to hers. His pride had been hurt by Eliza winning care and control, and by Clifford Rogers's very public rebuke, but from a practical point of view, little had changed; he was so often out, so often worked late, that the adjustment required during the week at least was minimal, and he and Eliza had grown used to alternate weekends with Emmie at Summercourt in the run-up to the case anyway. He remained hurt and angry with Eliza; but he would, Louise thought, always love her to an extent in his own difficult way. He had had the occasional fling with women since, more one-night stands than affairs, but there was certainly nothing to be jealous about. She wasn't sure if that made his attitude to her – an impatient, platonic affection was the closest she could come to describing it – feel worse or better.

In every other way, her life was pretty well perfect. Her hotels now numbered ten in construction or already constructed, and she owned three of them; the one just above Covent Garden was still by far her favourite. She described herself as fairly rich; her flat in Paulton Square was extremely luxurious, her twin wardrobes, filled with designer clothes, her latest car – a Porsche – parked outside, and she was in the process of buying a property in the new development of Port Grimaud in the South of France, on the northern tip of the Golfe de St Tropez. She had visited the place the previous autumn and fallen in love with it, with its Provençale-style houses, built in a series of exotic lagoons, each with a landing stage at the bottom of what passed for a garden.

So she had everything she wanted except Matt; and she spent a lot of time persuading herself she didn't really want him, and certainly not as a permanent fixture in her life; love him she might, but the thought of living with him was another thing altogether.

She was told constantly by all her friends (none of whom knew of her feelings for Matt) that she had been unlucky, that Mr Right would eventually come along; she was sure he wouldn't. The only thing that really annoyed her was people asking her if she wasn't unhappy, or lonely or frustrated.

'You wouldn't be saying that to a man,' she would say with varying degrees of irritation, 'why me? I like being single; I have a great life.'

To which they would all nod sagely and say when Mr Right did come along, she would realise what she had been missing; in her darker moments, when she was particularly cross with Matt, she would reflect that even if the unimaginable did happen and he declared some great and undying passion for her, she would have to sacrifice a great deal for it.

Riffling through her wardrobe on that glorious July morning, looking for exactly the right thing to wear to a gymkhana – jeans, a white shirt, cowboy boots and one of Maddy Brown's thick cotton cardigans in scarlet slung over her shoulders seemed pretty exact – she reflected that given last night's altercation with Matt, when he had accused her of being incapable of grasping even half the implications of the developing oil crisis on the property business – she was a great deal better off on her own.

It was just that – he was Matt. God damn him.

'Mummy! Coral's here and her mummy—'

Eliza was halfway up the stairs to have her bath; she sighed and turned round again. She had to greet her best friend in the whole world, as Emmie had christened Heather, probably correctly.

'Heather, hello, it's so lovely to see you. Hello, Coral, hello, Bobby. Goodness, he's grown up. How was the journey?'

'Fine. Alan's just parking down in the village.'

'Look, come on in, let me get you a coffee or something. And Emmie, you take Coral off and look after her, mind.'

'Can I give her a riding lesson?'

'No, Emmie, you cannot, not today, and if I see either of you sitting on that pony even if he is tied up to the fence, the whole thing is cancelled. Come in, Heather. Oh, and hello, Alan, lovely to see you—'

Alan appeared, red in the face, a rather thick tweed jacket buttoned round him, a cap clamped on his clearly perspiring head, his check shirt fastened to the neck and a tie with horses on it clipped to his shirt.

'Nice place you've got here, Eliza. Very nice. Lovely day, too, you're lucky, forecast was terrible, how those people keep their jobs I'll never know.'

'I agree. Look, come inside and have a coffee – or would you rather have a beer, Alan, there's masses?'

'Oh – not beer, not before lunch, thanks. Might have a lager to wash down the picnic, which reminds me, Heather, I noticed you had forgotten the salt, so I don't know if Eliza could lend us some—'

One day, Eliza thought, she must get both herself and Heather drunk enough to ask her why she had married Alan . . .

'Well,' she said, having served them their coffee, 'if you'll excuse me, I must really go and have a bath and change, I've been on the go since six and—'

'Mummy, Mummy, it's Uncle Charles and a lady, Uncle Charles, hello, come and see everything, come and see—'

'Take them round to Granny, darling, I'll be out in a minute—'

She risked a quick peek at Charles's lady from the hall window; she was quite pretty, in a fresh-faced, very young way, holding his hand and looking up at him adoringly. Perfect. Just what he needed.

'Eliza,' called Sarah, running into the house, 'darling, could you go and see the roundabout man, he's having trouble with his generator, it won't start or something . . .'

'Darling, I'm off, as instructed,' said Jeremy, kissing the top of Mariella's head as she lay in the bath. 'I'll see you later. You sure you can find your way from here?'

'Of course. I am not absolutely stupid—'

'Darling, I know that, but you've only been there once before, and you know map-reading isn't your forte—'

'Jeremy, I shall be all right. Now go please, I have a great deal to do.'

Jeremy went. He had learnt not to argue with Mariella unless it was in a very good cause.

She was, he had discovered, in the difficult, heady months after Giovanni's death, the opposite of malleable. However sweet her nature, however genuinely kind and generous her heart, the fact remained she had been extremely spoilt for all the years she had been married to Giovanni: petted, pampered, and over-praised, the subject of hundreds of adulatory articles, painted, photographed, quoted, exclaimed over; no one had crossed her, no one had disobeyed her – except Giovanni. He had kept her in check, had curbed her will, and indeed inflicted his own on her, brooking no argument, deaf to her tantrums, blind to her and her tears. And Giovanni was gone.

In the first rush of her grief, and her remorse, and her loneliness, she was subdued, biddable, grateful for understanding, for kindness; as time passed, as she found herself free, untamed, immensely rich in her own right, she became impossible.

Jeremy, confused and angered by the apparent monster he thought he had loved, struggling to be patient, to understand her, finally cracked one night in October, after a series of rows when she had demanded his presence at the villa, and then demanded he left again when he did not do things entirely to her liking; he told her it was all over between them.

'I'm shocked by you,' he had said, as he waited for the car to be brought round to the front door, to take him to the airport, 'shocked and horrified. I did love you, I quite possibly still do, but your behaviour is intolerable—'

'Don't speak to me like that,' she shouted, her great eyes blazing, her fists clenched at her sides, 'and in front of the servants.'

'You have spoken to me in the most abusive language I have ever heard,' said Jeremy, 'and you won't do it again, Mariella, I assure you. I am very sad to have to end our relationship, but I have to. I won't be humiliated like this. I know you are very unhappy and grieving for Giovanni and I'm sorry—'

'If you were sorry, you would not treat me like this,' cried Mariella, 'you are harsh and cruel, and you have no understanding of me—'

'I have rather too much, I'm afraid,' said Jeremy. 'Now, there is the car. Goodbye, Mariella, I'm sorry it must end like this.'

And he left without a glance at her.

A week later, she turned up in London, pale and remorseful, promising to be 'as you would want'; he forgave her, of course, and the entire scenario was repeated a few weeks later; and then again after Christmas. But that was the last time; they had had rows, to be sure – and Jeremy, whose charmed life had known little conflict, was surprised to find himself more than able to engage in them – but her behaviour and her attitude towards him became reasonable, and, as she put it, respectful.

'Would you like me to make a curtsey to you, when I come into the room?' she said one evening, as they ate dinner at his flat (she had revealed herself an excellent cook) and, 'Very much, yes,' he said, smiling at her, 'not every time, perhaps, just once or twice a day, when my dinner is ready, or I am proposing to exercise my *droit du seigneur*.'

'Oh, no, no, not then, that would be the last time I would do it, at such times I expect you to prostrate yourself before me . . . would you like to do that now, Gentleman Jeremy?'

'Not until I have finished this extremely delicious tiramisu you have made. I expect you remember how you first described tiramisu to me, Mariella?'

'Of course. I said it was like making love. So let us make love, here, at the table, and then we can make love in bed.'

That was the night he asked her to marry him.

Eliza glanced at her watch. It was nearly eleven. The cars and horse trailers – no more full boxes, thank goodness – were streaming in now; Mr Horrocks, who was in charge of parking, was growing more officious by the minute. Ponies were being led round and round the field, by an army of little girls – and a small number of boys; fathers were heaving water carriers and nosebags about, mothers were unpacking picnics. Gail and her brothers were standing by various jumps, Charles was leading Gail's donkey, bearing a seemingly endless queue of little girls up and down the far field, and an even more endless queue was forming for Mrs Horrocks's lemonade. Sarah's business at the tombola was booming.

Everything seemed fine; if she was quick, she could dash up and have her bath and change, before –

'Eliza!' A very flashy Jaguar had driven in; Jack Beckham was waving wildly at her.

'What a day. Blimey, good thing there aren't any of your readers here, fine fashion editor you make.'

'Thanks, Jack. Hello, you must be Babs. I've heard a lot about you. And you three, lovely to meet you. Jack, if you want to park here, in front of the house, do, it's getting very difficult over there. Come and meet my mother, she's serving cold drinks or there's a beer tent over there, next to the orangery—'

'A beer tent!' said Jack Beckham. 'Now you're talking. Well, this is all very nice, Eliza, come on, girls, out.'

The three girls got out, the epitome of Seventies girlhood, all long skirts and long curls and wide over-made-up smudgy eyes.

'I love those skirts,' Eliza said, 'are they—'

But at that moment, Cal appeared, his curls even longer and more luxurious than the girls', carrying two enormous bales of hay; all three of them stood stock still as if they had seen some kind of heavenly vision. Which, as they recounted later to their friends, they felt they had.

''Scuse me, Mrs Shaw,' said Gail, 'but Mum says we should start the jumpin' right away, people are getting restive, so if we can get the judges to come to the table—'

'Yes, of course,' said Eliza. 'Jack, can you sort yourselves out, sorry. Cal will show you everything . . .'

'I bet he will,' said Babs, with the dimpled giggle that had become famous from her days as a weather girl. 'Come on, girls, after Cal.'

Eliza rounded up the judges, grabbed the mike, called the entrants for the first jumping class to come to the collecting ring – the rather grand name for a sectioned-off bit of paddock – and thought longingly of the bathroom.

At last. Upstairs . . . he'd be here soon . . . she must actually smell . . .

✿ ✿ ✿

'Eliza. Hello, my darling. Can I park here, or do I have to go to the field?'

'Oh – Jeremy, no, of course you can park here. Mr Northcott, how lovely to see you, let me take you round to the terrace, you can sit down there and Jeremy can get you a beer or something. Mummy's looking foward to seeing you and we're thrilled you're staying tonight.'

Now . . .

'Eliza – hello. You look wonderful.'

'Mark! I do not, I'm afraid, I keep trying to go up for a bath, but – where's Scarlett?'

'She's run into the house, I hope that's all right, desperate for the loo, poor darling.'

'How is she? It's so brave of you to come.'

'We wouldn't have missed it for the world. She's fine, tired of course, look – I'll go in and find her, don't worry about us. See you later.'

'OK. Thanks. Well, I will then—'

She was hardly inside the house when Scarlett appeared out of the loo, looking magnificent in a white frilled dress, and perilously high-heeled red sandals.

'Eliza, hello.'

'Hello, and you in there.' She patted Scarlett's huge stomach. 'It's lovely of you to come.'

'It's lovely to be here. Wouldn't have missed it. Look – sorry to be a nuisance, but you haven't got any Rennies or anything, have you? I keep getting awful indigestion.'

OK. At least she was on the right floor. Into the bathroom and—

'Mummy, Mummy, Daddy's here. Come and say hello to him.'

Damn. Damn, damn, damn. She would have to go down or it would seem intolerably hostile. This was a difficult day for him, and he'd been very good about it.

'Hello Matt. Doesn't it all look professional? Oh, Louise, how lovely of you to come. You look great. That's one of Maddy's cardigans, isn't it? She's coming later, I hope. Matt, take Louise and get her a drink, the beer tent is over there, turn right after the orangery, you know – I—'

'Yes,' he said, 'I know. Funny place for a beer tent, I'd have thought.'

'Is it, it seemed quite good to me—' She stopped. Matt was looking at her oddly, and suddenly she knew why. She stood very still, staring at him; odd, how things went on affecting you, turning your heart. Even after all that had happened, some things, some memories, good ones, survived. The orangery was one of them, Matt's favourite place here always, special to both of them, the place they had – oh, God – actually consummated his purchase of Summercourt. She should have thought, should have kept it out of today's arrangements.

'Yes,' she said, 'I'm sorry, does it seem a bad place, I just thought—'

'No, no,' he said, 'it's fine. Come on, Louise. Let's go and find Emmie. I presume someone's looking after her?' he added, the old edge to his voice.

'Yes,' she said quietly, 'yes, she's with Gail. In the paddock, which is now the ring, of course, you saw it last week.'

'Yes. Fine. I'll see you later. It all seems very much under control.'

'Yes,' she said, 'yes, it is. I'll just—' She turned to go in for the longed-for bath.

'Mrs Shaw.' It was Mrs Horrocks. 'The local paper's here, they want a picture of the three of you, you and Mr Shaw and Emmie, any hope of that?'

'Not while I'm looking like this,' said Eliza, 'give me five minutes, I'll just go and—'

But – 'Mrs Shaw, Geoff Walters, *Marlborough News*, I see you're both here, where's the little girl?'

'Here!' said Emmie, breathlessly. 'Mrs Horrocks told me to come. Are you from the paper? You can't take a picture and not have Mouse. Come on everyone, this way, this way, and can Coral be in it too, she's my friend, we were born the same day . . .'

The megaphone was crackling into life:

'. . . fourteen hands and under, Number One, Hollyhock, ridden by . . .'

Now, at last, the bath. She could not greet her lover looking and smelling like this –

'Mummy! Uncle Toby's here.'

It had been a slow burn, her relationship with Toby. If they'd been in a film, she thought, they would have run into each other's arms in slow motion in the atrium of the Law Courts and he would have told her he loved her; as it was she felt awkward, diffident with him, even as she thanked him, and when he called a few days later to say he thought they should leave a meeting for at least a couple of weeks – 'give you a chance to recover' – she was both touched and grateful. For she did feel very odd, and rather as if she had had a long and almost fatal illness. She was exhausted, sleeping badly, and when she did, still haunted by bad dreams; demoralised by the character assassination that Matt's team and indeed the whole process had inflicted upon her; and deeply distressed and humiliated by the publicity, which made going into work seem an almost impossible hurdle – until Jeremy called a brainstorming meeting to discuss the re-structure of new client presentations and insisted she was there.

That set a seal on her status at the agency; she got home that night feeling she had at least begun to heal. Just the same, at her mother's suggestion, she had had a few sessions with Mary Miller, and over many boxes of Mrs Miller's extra-strong tissues, began to rediscover some self-respect. But it was painful and slower than she had expected; Mrs Miller chided her for her impatience.

'The psyche has its own timetable, Eliza; follow it, you'll do better that way.'

The house problem had sorted itself out surprisingly easily; she was more than happy to move out, she had always hated the big Fulham house, associating it with unhappiness, and had found a place of her own, only four streets away just off Hurlingham Road, a smaller but very similar house, with a bedroom overlooking the park admirably suited to Emmie's requirements. She fell in love with it at the very first viewing, and nearly lost it while Matt insisted on beating the price down and then down again. This resulted in their first post-divorce row, which turned out to be extraordinarily healing and saw them resolving matters quite cheerfully over a drink in the Hurlingham pub.

Toby had entered her life again tentatively; it seemed rather odd, having shared that astonishing night with him, to be re-cast as lunch companion and a rather bashful one at that. Even dinner, the next step, ended in an almost dutiful snog in his car and she had begun to think they would never get any further, when Fate took over in its usual rather determined way.

She was coming out of the Ritz quite late one night towards the end of September with Rob Brigstocke; Jeremy had thrown a big client cocktail party and then invited a chosen few to stay for dinner. Rob had his arm round her, and as she got into a taxi, she turned to give him a kiss. Next day Toby called her, to say, in his most brusque tones, that he was sorry, he would have to cancel their dinner that evening, as he was probably having to work late.

'And quite possibly tomorrow as well. In fact, best not to schedule anything for a bit. I'll – I'll call you in a week or so.'

Hurt beyond anything, Eliza acquiesced; she had agreed to meet Jack Beckham for a drink that evening, to discuss some possible freelance articles, and was walking along the Strand, jerked into some painful reminiscences, and was trying to tell herself that Toby was indeed very often very busy, and very, very often worked late, when she saw him leaving the Courts of Justice and walking in his swift impatient way away from her – in the company of a very pretty girl. She stared after them, trying neither to care nor to cry, continued to walk after them, and then found herself almost walking straight into him when he stopped dead in his tracks and turned round suddenly as the girl walked on.

'Oh,' he said, 'oh, hello.'

'Hello, Toby.'

And what she should have done, she knew, was walk away coolly, maintaining her dignity: instead of saying, as she seemed compelled to do, 'I thought you were working late.'

'As I am,' he said, his voice very cold, 'I'm taking Verity to a client meeting, she's gone on ahead, I've forgotten something crucial.'

'Oh,' she said, less cool and dignified still, 'is that what you call it, a client meeting?'

'Verity,' he said, 'is my new assistant.'

'Yes, and I'm the Queen of Sheba.' (Oh, really cool, Eliza, really dignified.)

'For Christ's sake,' he said (slightly less cool and dignified himself now), 'you're a fine one to talk. Perhaps you'd like to tell me who you were leaving the Ritz with last night? Some work colleague of your own, I suppose.'

'Toby,' she said (cool beginning to return), 'that was Rob Brigstocke. I'm surprised you didn't recognise him.'

'Ah, yes, of course. The one you smoke dope with. That's a very formal relationship you obviously have.'

And then she said, staring at him, with a sort of incredulity, 'You really mind, don't you?'

'Well, I do, as a matter of fact.'

'And as a matter of fact I really mind that you're walking along with your new assistant.'

'That's absurd. Quite different.'

Eliza began to smile: very tentatively. 'OK, it is quite different. This being the Strand and that being Piccadilly. And Verity being your assistant and Rob being my boss. And if we're both speaking the truth, then we're both being extremely stupid.'

'I'm certainly speaking the truth.'

'And so am I, and nothing but it, so help me God. I'm surprised at you, Toby Gilmour, relying on circumstantial evidence.'

'Oh Christ,' he said after a long silence. 'Oh – this is – awful.'

'Why? It seems rather good to me.'

'Well – actually not, because I really am going to a client meeting. And all I want to do is take you home with me.'

'Well,' she said, her heart and indeed her body lurching most pleasurably, 'that's all I want too, funnily enough, what a coincidence, but I'm going to see Jack Beckham. It'll take about an hour.'

'My meeting likewise.'

'So we could meet after that?'

'Yes, we could. Your place or mine?'

'Yours would be – sort of more appropriate, I think. And I know where it is.'

'Here,' he said, bumbling in his pocket, 'here's a key. In case I'm late.'

'You'd better not be.'

In the event, he was home before her; two glasses by the bed, champagne on ice in the kitchen.

'I sort of think I can't wait to drink that,' said Eliza.'

'OK. We'll have it afterwards. Oh, and I've got some very good news.'

'What's that?'

'The bed doesn't creak.'

And thus had begun a very gentle love affair; Eliza, initially uncertain where it might be leading, but happier than she had been for years, still unsure of herself, aware of the need for tact and care with Emmie, who was still unsettled, still testing both her parents considerably, asked for time for all of them. And Toby, cautious by nature as well as profession, was happy to give it to her.

It was well after Christmas when he announced one night over dinner in his flat that he couldn't stand it any longer; startled, frightened even, she assumed he meant it must be over between them and said, anxious not to appear clinging or feeble, that of course she understood and she would far rather he be honest with her, she really didn't want to hold him against his will, and if he had just been being kind all this time, then she didn't want that either, she'd be absolutely fine, in fact she—

'Oh, for Christ's sake,' he said, his voice at its most impatient, 'you always, always get things wrong—' and, 'Well, I'm sorry you should see it like that,' she said, quite briskly, 'I don't have your advantage of a legal training, I'm not very clear-thinking, never have been,' and she had jumped up from the table, grabbed her bag and rushed out of the flat; and that might have been the end of it, had it not been sleeting, and the steps were slippery and, careless with misery, she had slipped and fallen and when he rushed out after her, he found her crumpled on the pavement, whimpering over a very painful wrist.

Which was broken in two places, it emerged, after a long wait in Casualty, where he insisted on staying in spite of her frequent assertions that she didn't want to waste his time; and finally, when she emerged, white-faced and shaking, her wrist in plaster, he said she must come home with him, she couldn't possibly be on her own. She said she wouldn't dream of imposing on him and if he would just call a cab she'd be fine; whereupon he grabbed her good wrist, pulled her outside and, his face quite dark with anger, told her that she was a silly bitch and he wanted her to impose on him, for as much and as long as he could persuade her to do so.

'Please don't call me a silly bitch,' she said, while feeling her face breaking rather unwillingly into a smile, 'it's not exactly what I need, under the circumstances,' and he said all right, all right and sighed heavily, and then there was a long silence and then he said, 'Would "I love you" be more in order? Under the circumstances?'

And so they went home together, and Toby tucked her up in his bed and said he would sleep in the other room, so as not to disturb her, and brought her a hot toddy and told her he loved her again; and then in the night, rising to go to the loo and seeing his light on under the door, she went in to find him reading 'just some notes for the next day – sorry if it seems heartless', and she said she had never known anyone less heartless, and that middle-of-the-night encounters with him had been rather successful in the past and that she would like to join him, painful wrist or not; adding, quite conversationally, that she had been thinking very hard and she had decided she loved him too. Whereupon, with only a little difficulty, they managed to set a seal on their greatly improved relationship and finally fell asleep so soundly that Toby was almost late in court . . .

It was mid-afternoon, the jumping was finished, Jack Beckham had presented the cup, and what many considered the highlight of the day was about to take place, the 'Mounted Fancy Dress'. Essentially held before the gymkhana proper, while the ponies were still not covered in mud, it attracted a huge entry; ponies and their riders large and small, dressed as fairies, rabbits, foxes, flowers, medieval knights (and ladies) filled the paddock. Emmie had chosen to be a fairy and to wear the tutu she wore for ballet, but at the last minute, in a sudden fit of generosity, she had asked Coral if she would like to enter in her place, and was leading her round the ring. Various jolly tunes were being played over the loudspeaker and judging was about to commence when a very large and glossy horsebox appeared and pulled up beside the others. 'That's too bad,' said Eliza, 'it's far too late, what do they think they're playing at, I'll have to go and—'

But at that point a rather smart-looking grey horse was led out of the box; and out of the passenger seat sprang a figure with very long blond hair, and wearing, apparently, no clothes; she jumped up on the horse with great aplomb, gathered up the reins and rode at a brisk trot, no mean feat, given the horse had no saddle, towards the ring.

'What on earth—' said Eliza.

And, 'Now I've seen everything,' said Jack Beckham.

And, 'Oh, my God,' said Jeremy, 'it's Mariella.'

And indeed it was: in the guise of Lady Godiva, clad in flesh-coloured lycra and a blond wig, smiling radiantly and blowing kisses at the crowd, who were cheering and clapping and laughing.

She was not awarded the prize, of course, for that would not have been fair to the rabbits and medieval ladies and the rest and it went instead to a very sweet ladybird on a Shetland pony; but there was no doubt that for the male spectators it was the highlight of the day, and Jeremy was afraid his father was going to pass out with excitement. He could have done without it himself; but when Mariella joined them, laughing, pulling off her wig, and shaking out her own dark hair, and saying she hoped she had done her little bit for the day, and that it had been a good surprise, he did feel a certain slightly grudging pride and went to fetch her some lemonade in a way that he would not, these days, normally have done.

'Oh, Mariella,' said Eliza, kissing her, 'how Mademoiselle Chanel would have liked to dress you for that.'

The gymkhana was now at full throttle. Countless hooves had thundered round the ring, their riders as hell-bent on winning as if they were at Badminton or the Royal Windsor. There had been enough accidents to keep the St John's Ambulance team on their toes: three major nosebleeds, two sprained ankles, one suspected concussion, one dislocated shoulder (both sufferers shipped off to hospital), and one granny passing out from heatstroke. A number of little girls (and a few boys) were flushed with triumph, walking round with their ponies, their bridles heavily laden with rosettes. Rather more little girls (and a few boys) were tear-stained or sulky or both. Emmeline Shaw, who had excelled herself, given her age, and won her heats in both the pole-bending and the obstacle race and actually come second in the walk, trot and gallop, was now sitting on the terrace with her father, eating her fourth ice cream of the afternoon, and waiting for the sack race, the last gymkhana event of the day.

'How can it be a sack race when it's ponies?' asked Coral. 'Do they put their feet into sacks?'

'No, silly,' said Emmie, 'you—'

'Emmie,' said Matt sharply, 'don't speak like that to Coral, Louise just asked me the same question. Now say you're sorry and tell her sensibly.'

'Sorry,' said Emmie, who was forced to utter the word so often it tripped with thoughtless ease off her tongue, 'and I'm telling you sensibly, what you do is ride round the ring, dismount, get into the sack, and jump back to the start, leading your pony.'

'Oh,' said Louise and Coral in unison.

'What are your duties, Matt?' asked Louise.

'Presenting the best turn-out cup,' said Matt slightly wearily, 'which is after the jumping, and then best-in-show cup, and then please God we can all leave. Or you and I can leave. Look at that wanker,' he said suddenly, 'just look at him. How can she like him, Louise, I just don't get it.'

Louise looked across at Toby. As far as she could see, he was merely drinking some lemonade, and chatting to Sarah and Anna Marchant, who had arrived halfway through the afternoon, without Piers, and looking rather wonderful in what were clearly vintage jodhpurs, a white silk shirt and a pair of tall leather boots.

'I just had to come,' she said, 'I'm so proud of you, Eliza. What a thing to organise.'

'Well – I had lots of help.'

'Of course you did. Is that Archie Northcott over there? Such a charming man, and a surprisingly good dancer, I seem to remember. We had a wonderful flirtation once, during the war, God knows what might have happened if he hadn't had to go back to Egypt, I think it was, but anyway, I think I was quite relieved, Christine would have been a frightful foe. She always found out apparently, about all the mistresses and gave them hell.'

'Were there lots?' said Eliza in awe. 'You never told me that.'

'Of course. He was as good-looking as Jeremy, and rather bored down there in Norfolk. He seems to be chatting up your mother, I feel quite jealous, I shall go and interrupt. Now, how is the lovely Toby?'

'Lovely,' said Eliza, 'yes. Just – lovely.'

She looked at him now, chatting to Emmie, who rather wonderfully continued to like him, and to accept his initially infrequent forays into her life, increasing slowly and helped by his considerable horsiness; in spite of not infrequent bursts of 'you're not my daddy', their relationship seemed set fair.

She had weathered it all very well, but there were inevitable upsets, she still shouted at both Eliza and Matt from time to time, and told them they were stupid, that she didn't like having two houses, that none of her other friends' mummies and daddies lived not together – and, generally, used the situation to the best of her ability. Indeed it had been one of the things that had bound Eliza and Matt together in their new relationship, as important in its own way to Emmie as the old one, that they must acknowledge this and not be either deceived or distressed by her manipulations, her averral that Mummy – or, as it might be, Daddy – had said she could stay up late, eat sweets in bed, have a new pony, and take her whole class to the pantomime at Christmas.

Eliza still quite often hated Matt; she knew she would never forgive him for what he had done to her, while struggling to understand it and to acknowledge her own part in it. She still – occasionally, very occasionally – almost loved him when some fierce memory hit, or he made her laugh, or they were together with Emmie. She resisted it, but it was not to be denied. She was learning to tolerate him, to get along with him; that was new and most difficult but essential for their lives as Emmie's parents, the two people she loved best in the world. As a bond, that remained unbreakable. But it was hard.

'Dearest, are you all right?'

'Yes. Think so. Bit – you know. Uncomfy. Probably just need to pee again. I'll waddle off and see you back here in a little while. I might even – find a bed, lie down for a bit.'

'I'll come and find you. How's the indigestion?'

'Oh – completely gone. Yes.'

Scarlett stood up, stretched her arms, tottered slightly on her high heels; her balance wasn't good. She should really wear flat shoes, but she hated them.

It really was all very uncomfortable; she felt completely invaded by this creature that had made its home in her. Well, not for much longer.

She felt very ambivalent towards it; she viewed its arrival with a certain anxiety, and not just the birth. She so hoped she was going to be a good mother. It was all rather daunting. She might be dreadful at it. The qualities required were very different from those that had served her so well in her life thus far. She would try as hard as she could and she certainly wanted the baby, quite desperately, but supposing she didn't like it? That was Scarlett's secret fear, one that had haunted her through all these long months: one she couldn't admit to anyone. That she would take one look at it and realise she had made a terrible mistake. She didn't really like babies as a race very much: they weren't even very pretty, not at first, scrumpled little things, with their unseeing eyes and flailing limbs. Scarlett liked things to be pretty.

Hopefully, maternal love, whatever it was, would carry her through, and would arrive along with the baby; meanwhile she must just wait.

She did feel a bit odd: as if she was about to burst. Probably be better after she had peed.

'Oh, my God.' She stared at the flood that had formed around her feet in the kitchen as she stood drinking a glass of water. 'My God. Oh – my – God.'

Panic roared through her; she felt completely terrified. What did she do, who could she tell, where could she go? It was awful, she'd spoil everything for everyone, the whole day, and she felt so stupid, so completely stupid –

'Oh – hello.' Scarlett looked round; it was Eliza's friend, Heather.

That was better than some complete stranger – and she'd know about having babies.

'I've come for some water, my little girl's terribly thirsty, do you know where the glasses are—'

'Look,' Scarlett said, stupid in her fear, pointing down at the puddle, 'look what I've done.'

'Oh,' said Heather. And they stood there together contemplating it; and then Heather said, 'Look, you'd better sit down. Your waters have broken. Shall I get someone?'

'Yes, yes, please. Probably – yes, my husband. Only you don't know him. He's quite easy to spot though, he's tall and dark and he's out on the terrace, oh, no, find Eliza, she'll know what to do.'

'Eliza's disappeared, I was looking for her too. Are you having any contractions yet?'

'No, not at all. It doesn't seem to hurt. It will though, I suppose.'

'Just a bit,' said Heather and smiled again, 'but don't worry, it isn't nearly as bad as people say. As long as you relax, that is.'

'I don't feel very relaxed. And I've got to get back to London, to my doctor. Well – maybe you could get Sarah, Eliza's mum. I'll just – just wait here.'

Heather went out of the back door onto the terrace. Sarah was chatting to a man, a neighbour she supposed. She went up to her rather tentatively.

'Mrs Fullerton-Clark. Could you – could you come into the kitchen please. Bit of a, a – problem.'

'What sort of a problem, Heather dear? Not the freezer finally packed up, I hope—'

'No, it isn't the freezer,' said Heather, 'it's a – well it's a baby.'

'A baby!' said Sarah, in tones that would not have disgraced Lady Bracknell. 'What on earth is a baby doing in the kitchen?'

'Well, it's not there yet,' said Heather, feeling increasingly stupid. 'It's – well, it's Matt's sister, Scarlett, I think she's in labour.'

'Oh heavens,' said Sarah, 'I did think it was rather a mistake to come, she looked so huge. Larry, excuse me, I must go. Heather, that's her husband, Mark, just over there, look, tell him to come – and – yes, see if you can find Eliza, dear, as well.'

Scarlett was remarkably composed by now; she was sitting by the open door on a chair, smiling, when Mark came in.

'Darling, we must leave at once. Back to London—'

'Scarlett, we can't drive back to London with you in labour. And don't tell me you're not, I've read the books.'

'Of course we can. We'll have loads of time and I want to be – oh!' She stopped, looked at him, her dark eyes suddenly wide with fear. 'That – might have been something. Oh, it's gone now. Phew. Well, look, go on, find the car, bring it to the front door—'

'Scarlett, my dear, you can't embark on a three-hour journey when your waters have broken,' said Sarah firmly, 'it would be very dangerous. I'm going to call Dr Watkins, he's our GP, and get some advice. He'll probably tell you to go to the nearest hospital, our cottage hospital in the next village is very good—'

'I am not going to a cottage hospital,' said Scarlett, 'I want my own gynaecologist looking after me—'

'Dear love, I agree with Sarah,' said Mark, 'you can't do that drive in labour.'

'Mark,' said Scarlett, 'how many more times do I have to tell you, first babies take at least twelve hours to arrive. I want to get back to Mr Webb, I am going to get back to Mr Webb, and none of you can stop me. It's ridiculous, I – ooh. That was – well, a bit more of something.'

'Scarlett,' said Sarah, and she was very calm now, 'look, we will, of course, do everything we can to get you some expert care.'

'I don't want any expert care, I want Mr Webb's expert care,' said Scarlett, her voice slightly less certain now. 'Please, Mark, go and get the car.'

At that moment, one of the St John's Ambulance men came into the kitchen.

'Sorry, Mrs F-C, but a little boy's passed out, the heat I think, can I get some more water?'

'Yes, you can of course. But first, could we have a bit of advice. This lady's waters have just broken, and her baby is due – when, Scarlett?'

'Tomorrow. So – look,' Scarlett looked at the man imploringly, 'tell them it'll be fine to go back to London, will you?'

'I can't do that, my love. Once your waters have broken you're liable to infection. And that drive, with baby not cushioned by the waters, very dangerous, it could be.'

'Yes, but I'm not in labour,' said Scarlett, 'well, hardly, couple of – of twinges, but . . .'

'My love, you'll have to stay here. You should be resting comfortable.

We can get an ambulance, course, I'll call one right away – where's the phone, Mrs F-C?'

'But – I want—'

'Scarlett,' said Mark, 'no.'

Sarah helped Scarlett up to her room; pulled the eiderdown off the bed, pulled the curtains.

'There you are, my dear, lie down. Do you know, Eliza was born in this room—'

'Yes, well, I don't want to have my baby in this room,' said Scarlett. Her teeth were chattering slightly now with fear. 'I don't mean to be rude, but—'

'Of course not, and you didn't sound rude at all.'

'I'm just so – frightened.'

'Yes, it is frightening at first,' said Sarah, smoothing back Scarlett's hair, 'then you'll find you settle down and it's amazing how you cope. Now the ambulance should be here pretty soon, and Dr Watkins is coming over to see you, just as a precaution. He's a darling man, and very gentle. Don't worry, you'll be absolutely fine. Would you like some tea?'

'Oh – yes, please. That'd be nice. With some sugar. I still think I could go back—'

'Scarlett,' said Sarah firmly, 'you can not go back. Now you try to relax. Easier said than done, I know, and I'll get you the tea. The loo's right next door if you want it—'

Scarlett lay very still, as if any movement might precipitate her baby and its birth into further action. Where was Mark, what was he doing, for God's sake – talking to someone no doubt, bloody man, bloody everything, she wanted to be in London with Mr Webb, she wanted her hospital, her nice expensive private hospital with its nice expensive drugs, suppose the local hospital didn't even know about pethidine, suppose – another pain hit her. She bit her lip, trying to keep calm, fear building faster than the pain . . .

Louise looked at Matt; he was standing on the edge of the ring, holding Emmie's hand. He had slowly relaxed as the afternoon went on, but he was still edgy. It was very difficult for him. He'd actually behaved very well. And once he'd presented the cups, they could leave. She was rather sorry; Eliza had asked them to stay for supper.

'We'd love you to be here, Louise,' said Eliza, 'you and Matt. And Toby, you know, is going. He can't stay anyway. So it won't be too awkward. See what you can do.'

'Thanks, Eliza, but I think probably it would be better if we went. It's – it's not easy for Matt.'

'No, of course not. I think he's been amazing, actually.'

'Have you seen Scarlett? Matt was looking for her.'

'No, but I'm sure she's fine. Mark's looking after her like an old hen – he's so sweet – gosh, I must go, musical ride and then it's over.'

'My dear Mrs Frost, we can't move you now.' Dr Watkins looked at her sternly. 'You're well on your way. Ah, here we go, here comes another one. Deep breaths, that's right. Here, you – what's your name—'

'Mark,' said Mark slightly desperately. He had never been more frightened in his life.

'Go and see what's keeping that ruddy midwife. She should have been here half an hour ago. And then bring some more cold water, sponge your wife down, it's bloody hot. Make yourself useful, man, don't just sit there, like a frightened rabbit . . . well done, Scarlett, well done. You're doing beautifully. Not so bad, is it? Sarah – cup of tea for me, my dear, if you wouldn't mind.'

'She's what! My God. I'll be in in one minute. How – how exciting. A baby, here at Summercourt – first one since – since me. Gosh. Where's Matt? Louise, Louise—'

'Ah, there you are at last. What have you been doing, woman? Come along, here's Mrs Frost, she's doing wonderfully well, but she could do with a bit of gas and air now, and then you can examine her, see how she's getting on. Got all the gear have you, sort her out a bit. Contractions every four minutes, getting nice and strong, I'd say a couple more hours and baby'll be here.'

A couple more hours. Of this? Surely not, surely, surely not. Still – it was going to be less than twenty-four, obviously. And it did hurt, it hurt like hell, but it was – all right. She was just about coping. She hadn't screamed or anything, which she'd been worrying about, right in the middle of the gymkhana – it was actually rather lovely here, in this beautiful room, and fancy Eliza being born here, and her mother coming in and out, and that nice girl Heather, helping with her breathing – she was going to be all right. She was worried about Mark, he looked as if he was going to faint, probably best if he went out, only it was nice to have him there – oh, shit, shit, here came another one . . .

'Matt, Matt, there you are, Scarlett's having her baby.'

'Scarlett's what?'

'She's having her baby.'

'What, here?'

'Yes. It all happened very fast, and she's up in Mummy's room, I was born there, you know, so rather lovely, and no, I don't think you should go and see her, she's quite far on apparently, and the doctor's there and the midwife, and—'

'Toby, you can't go yet. Scarlett 's having her baby. It's really exciting. Please, please stay—'

'Louise, there you are. Look – we can't go yet. Apparently my sister's having her baby. Here, in the house. The doctor's here and a midwife, so she's all right. I hope. What on earth would Mum say . . . Christ, I need a drink.'

'Right, one more push, that's right, good girl, good girl. Well done. Here we are – and it's a – it's a girl, a lovely little girl. Oh, you have done well. There you are, my lovely, there she is – whoops, and there goes the daddy, head between your knees, sir, that's right. Your wife's done so well, now you look at your daughter, isn't she lovely?'

'She's beautiful,' said Mark, looking at his beloved wife, holding her baby, their baby, so safely and sweetly delivered, after all his fears, 'simply beautiful, yes.'

And, 'Yes,' said Scarlett, smiling tenderly down, at the baby's squashed, grimacing, little old man's face, 'yes, she is absolutely beautiful.'

'And – any ideas what you're going to call her?'

'Oh,' said Mark, 'that's easy. She's called Larissa.'

'That's unusual.'

'Yes, it is. It's Greek. It's the name of a very beautiful Grecian lady. Without whom, our Larissa would not be here.'

❀ ❀ ❀

'Matt, come in, come in, come and say hello to your niece. Isn't she lovely?'

'She is beautiful,' said Matt, smiling down at the tiny Larissa. 'Yes. Well done, Scarlett. We're all so proud of you.'

'Oh – it was fine. Not nearly as bad as I feared. I think – I really think being here, in this lovely house of yours, helped. It's so peaceful, such a special place, Matt, and somehow, being with the family, Sarah's so lovely, so calm, she made me feel safe.'

'Yes,' said Matt, 'yes, she is very – nice.'

'I'm going to stay a few days, until I'm strong enough to go home. She's so excited, me having the baby where she had Eliza. And of course Emmie is just over the moon. She says Mouse is Larissa's uncle.'

'Indeed?' said Matt. 'That's a first. Oh – Mark. Congratulations. Well done. I hear you were magnificent.'

'Well, I managed not to faint until it was all right to,' said Mark modestly. 'And Scarlett was so marvellously brave. I feel I should thank you, for hosting the baby's birth . . .'

'Oh – don't mention it,' said Matt. And grinned.

They were all eating Sarah's famous cottage pie round the huge kitchen table.

'Lovely to have the house so full,' she said happily.

'This is splendid pie, my dear,' said Archie Northcott. 'Christine was never much of a cook.'

'Pa! That's so disloyal.'

'Nonsense. She was the first to admit it. How's your cooking, Mariella?'

'It's marvellous,' said Jeremy, 'especially her tiramisu. We always enjoy that.'

'You should come down with the young people one weekend, Sarah,' said Archie. 'Not sure you've ever seen the house. Very fine, Jacobean, you know.'

'Yes, I do. That would be lovely. Thank you, Mr Connell – Alan,' said Sarah, 'another helping of pie?'

'I won't say no. Thank you. Really excellent. Compliments to the chef. And may I say again, it's extemely good of you to put us up. So nice to be part of such a delightful gathering, isn't it, Heather?'

'Yes, Alan, it is.'

'We could hardly send you on such a long journey late at night, after all Heather did to help Scarlett,' said Sarah.

'And I won't say no to another beer,' he said to Matt, 'since you offered.'

'Of course. Then we must go. I'll just go and say goodbye to Scarlett. You coming, Louise?'

'Yes, of course.'

'I'll come with you,' said Eliza, 'make sure she's got everything she needs.'

They went up; Scarlett was drifting in and out of sleep, the baby lying on her breast, Mark sitting rather gingerly on the edge of the bed, gazing at them both. It was a completely charming picture.

'Well – bye, sis. Well done again. Let me give you a kiss. Take care of her, Mark.'

'I will. See you back in London.'

Matt bent over the bed to kiss Scarlett; Eliza suddenly looked at Louise; she was staring at Matt, with a look of naked yearning on her face, her eyes bright with tears. She saw Eliza looking at her and flushed.

'I'll just – just go to the bathroom,' she said.

Eliza followed her out.

'Are you OK?' she said.

'Yes. Yes, I'm fine.'

A tear rolled slowly down one cheek; she brushed it impatiently away.

'Louise—'

'No, don't say it. He doesn't know, he'll never know, he's so – so impossibly emotionally stunted – and so – wrapped up in himself. Oh, sorry, Eliza, I sometimes forget—'

'Louise, you're right. I should know. But he needs someone. And if anyone could put up with him, you could. You know him better than any of us. How you stuck him all those years, I'll never know.'

'Well – you did pretty well.'

'No, I didn't. I was crap. A disastrous wife for him. He's much better off without me.' There was a silence; then she said, 'Louise, you should tell him. Because he'll never see it for himself, never, you're so right. Go on, what have you got to lose?'

'Him,' said Louise. 'At least at the moment I have him as a friend. Not that I'm sure that's exactly a good thing. He's so bloody bad-tempered, always furious about things—'

'Yes, but you're so good for him, you deal with him, without getting cross back. That was my problem. We – oh, hell, that was the phone. Who on earth can that be? I'd better get it. Might be Sandra again. Matt, don't go without saying goodbye. It's been such a lovely day, thank you so, so much for all you've done. I'm – I'm sorry about the orangery. And the beer tent.'

He shrugged. 'It's OK.'

'No, no, it wasn't.'

She came back into the kitchen, having taken the call.

'Matt – that was a man who said he was ready to make an offer to buy – buy Summercourt. He was told you were here by your mum, she was at the – your house apparently. He said he'd like to speak to you. Would you – would you like to take it in the study?'

Matt looked round the room; everyone was pretending not to be remotely interested. Sarah was suddenly very busy with the coffee; Mariella slipped her hand into Jeremy's; Charles and the adoring Pattie started piling up plates; Jeremy poured himself a very large glass of wine and another for his father; Anna pushed her glass forward imperiously. Only Emmie was concentrating on him, her small face dark suddenly, her blue eyes alarmed.

'Daddy?' she said. 'That's not right, is it? You're not selling Summercourt?'

'I – Emmie, let's go and have a talk. Just you and me.'

She slithered off her chair very slowly, walked towards him, as if she was sleepwalking. He held out his hand to her, but she shook her head, as if refusing sweets; he turned and walked out of the room and she followed him into the hall.

'Emmie, sweetheart, listen, I'm sorry, but I have to sell Summercourt.'

'Why? You can't. You can't.' The blue eyes had filled with tears.

'Sweetheart, I have to. Listen—'

'You can't. It's mine and yours and Mummy's, you promised the judge—'

'I know, Emmie, but – listen. It's very, very expensive..

'You've got lots of money. Everyone says so.'

'Everyone isn't always right.'

'Anyway, what would the judge say?'

'I – asked another judge. And he said I could.'

751

'But why? And what about Mouse, where would he go?'

'I've found another house, much nearer London. It's got a stable, Mouse will be fine.'

'He won't, this is his home. And it's my home too, you can't sell it, you can't, I won't come, I'll run away, I'll hate you for ever. You lied to the judge, you must have done. I shall go and find my judge and tell him what you've done. You're horrible, you've spoilt today, you've spoilt every-thing—'

'Emmie—' It was Eliza's voice. 'Darling, listen to me. Daddy has done everything else the judge said, this house is so expensive, and he doesn't get to spend much time here—'

'That's his fault. Not mine.'

'No, darling, it isn't. Daddy has to go to work, listen, I'm sure this other house is very nice, he's told me about it, and Mouse can go there and—'

'No! No, no, NO. You're both doing it now, changing things. I hate you both again, more than ever. I love it here, I want to keep it for ever, I want it to be mine when I grow up . . .'

She was crying now, very hard, her small body shaking, tears streaming down her face. She rubbed her eyes; her hands were filthy and left great streaks of dirt on her cheeks. 'Please!' she said. 'Daddy, please, please, don't sell this house. I'll run away and not come back until you keep it. Please, Daddy, I'll be good, so good.'

Matt stared at her; he had heard that before, many times, in as tear-filled a voice; the pathetic promise that she had made when they told her they were getting a divorce. He went up to her, held out his arms. 'Emmie—'

'No, I won't. I hate you. I'll hate you forever.'

There was a long silence; Matt looked at Emmie, Eliza looked at Matt, Emmie looked from one to the other of them; then with a huge sigh, Matt said, 'All right, Emmie. I won't sell it. You can stay here, you and Mouse.'

'Promise?'

'Promise.'

Eliza expected her to smile then, to jump into his arms, to kiss him; but she just sighed, a heavy, long sigh, an adult's sigh, and looked at him very directly.

'Thank you,' was all she said. And turned and walked slowly towards the kitchen.

'Thank you, Matt,' said Eliza, more shaken by this than the entire scene. 'Thank you so much. I'm – we're very grateful.'

'Oh, it's all right. Of course I can afford it. I just—'

'I know. I understand. It must be so hard for you. I swear I didn't put her up to that.'

'No, I could tell. And thank you for taking my – my side. Fat lot of good it did me,' he added with a lopsided grin.

'And, Matt – I'm so sorry about the orangery again. It was dreadful of me. And, for what it's worth, I often think about it, about how it brought us together and – well, that night, you know.'

'Yes,' he said, 'I know. So do I.'

There was a long silence; then she stepped forward, reached up and kissed his cheek.

'That a thank you?' he said.

'No, no. It's for old times' sake.'

'Well – that's nice.'

They were in the car now, driving back to London. Matt turned to Louise.

'Eliza said you wanted to talk to me about something?'

'Really? I can't think what.'

'Yes, she did. And she said it was important.'

'She had no business to,' said Louise. She felt angry suddenly. How dare Eliza do that to her? Putting her in an impossible position.

'There's nothing important, Matt, I don't know what she's on about.'

'She said it was to do with me.'

'Oh, for God's sake. Oh – shit.' She found she had tears in her eyes.

'Louise. What on earth is it? Come on, you can tell me, surely.'

'No, I can't.' Her voice was rising. 'It doesn't matter. Leave things alone.'

'OK. Calm down, then, it's not exactly restful, driving along with you having a nervous breakdown beside me.'

'I am not having a nervous breakdown. And if I did you wouldn't care. All you want is for me to be good old Louise, hearing about all your problems and difficulties, the endless list of all the people you don't like, I'm just a bloody punchball to you, Matt, nothing more.'

'OK, OK. Give it a rest. I didn't bring you down here to insult me.'

'No, you didn't. So why did you bring me? Just tell me that, Matt, I'd really like to know?'

'Well – I suppose – because I like you. I like being with you. I told you that, Louise, blimey, you're not asking for some kind of romantic declaration, I hope.'

'Absolutely not. As if you'd know how to make one anyway. There's only one person you feel undying love for, Matt Shaw, and that's yourself. Has that ever occurred to you?'

'Don't be so bloody rude,' he said, 'I don't know what's the matter with you, Louise, you've been really – difficult – all day—'

'I have not been difficult,' and she was shouting now, 'it's you who've been difficult, as you always are, bolshie and rude and – I don't know why I bother. Just let's get back to London and then can we please put a stop to this once and for all. I don't see any future in our relationship, and I'd rather not pursue it any longer.'

'Fine,' he said and pushed his foot down onto the accelerator. Outside her flat, he didn't turn the engine off; she got out and and disappeared inside.

Matt arrived home to find the answering machine flashing.

It was Eliza.

'I just wanted to thank you again,' she said when he called her back, 'for keeping Summercourt. It's wonderful of you, and I really, really appreciate it, Matt, we all do.'

'It's not yours,' he said abruptly. 'It's mine. And I intend to set it up as a trust for Emmie. We working-class folk can play these games too.'

'I – can see that,' she said, 'and I think it's a lovely idea. So nice, Matt. Lovely for Emmie, lovely for me. And you, I hope. I know you do like it too.'

'Yes, I do,' he said, surprising her, 'I like it very much. And it was great, Scarlett having the baby there. Quite something. How is she?'

'She's fine. They're all asleep.'

'Good.'

'Now – did you speak to Louise?'

'I tried to,' he said, 'she lost her temper, started shouting at me. She's always doing that these days, I don't know why.'

Eliza took a deep breath. This really couldn't do any harm.

'I'll tell you,' she said. 'It's because she – she cares about you.'

'She what?'

'You heard. She's loved you for years and years, and she thinks you don't care about her, and I think you do and I think you ought to think

754

about it very hard. She doesn't need to know you know, if you want to leave it at that, no humiliation involved. But at least think about it. OK? Now I must go. Emmie and Coral are still awake, high as kites. Night, Matt. Take care. And thank you again.'

Matt put the phone down. He felt weak at the knees suddenly. He could never remember feeling quite so – so shocked. Louise! Louise, loyal, sharp, cool, clever, brave Louise, putting up with him all those years, working with him, fielding his rages, listening to him moaning on and on and on, going into the witness box, speaking up for him – could she? Could she possibly? Surely . . .

He felt as if he was seeing her properly for the first time, as if she had been concealed, behind some strange, distorting glass, unclear, not her true self.

He tried to analyse his feelings for her now and in the past; and wondered if he should have realised how he felt. Which was not how he had thought he had felt. Realised how much she had mattered to him. But – how could he? It had always seemed to him she didn't like him.

Or certainly found it hard to like him. She had so clearly found him wanting, in a great many ways. She tried to put him down. She was desperate to win battles in the office. She usually did win battles in the office. Which annoyed him. Terribly. In fact just thinking about it now made him cross. But – intriguing. She was intriguing. And – viewed without the distorting glass, she was gorgeous. Of course. He'd always thought that. He and Jimbo had often remarked on it. Reluctantly, given how often she got the better of them. So—

He picked up the car keys, and half ran out of the house. Drove to Paulton Square. Parked outside. Looking up at her windows. Got out of the car, rang the bell. Said, 'Can I come in?' into the intercom. She said no. Sounding as if she'd been crying. He rang the bell again. 'Go away,' again.

Then, 'Louise, I've been very, very stupid. Please let me come up. I want to see you.'

'I don't want to see you.'

'Yes, you do. Look – Louise, I'm sorry. I've probably blown it, but – I – I've been talking to Eliza. And she said – well, she said . . .'

'Matt, please go away. Eliza had no right to interfere. She's a bossy cow.'

'Yes, she is. Bit like you. Probably explains a lot.'

'Matt, go away.'

He waited. Then, 'All right, I'll go away now. But will you have dinner with me tomorrow? Please. Please, Louise. I'd like it so much. We have some sorting out to do.'

'You have some sorting out to do.'

'Yes. Yes, all right. But will you? Please?'

A very long silence, then, 'Yes. All right. And you'd better not be late.'

'Toby?'

'Yes. God, Eliza, what time is it?'

'Don't know. Late. I wanted to tell you something.'

'It had better be good.'

'It is. I love you. So much. I just wanted to tell you again.'

It had come to her as she watched them in the kitchen, all of them, thinking this was what happiness must look like, if you could see it – Emmie and Coral, dozing finally on the sofa, Heather and Alan, her head drooping with sleep on his shoulder, his tie rather dangerously loosened, Charles and Pattie smiling at one another, Jeremy and Mariella holding hands, freshly and foolishly delighted with one another, Archie flirting alternately with her mother and Anna – and upstairs the new little family, all contained in Summercourt's lovely walls. It had worked its magic today for them all. And – hopefully in London for Louise and Matt . . .

And it had worked it on her; she had thought, surveying this scene, that she did love Toby so very much. Not wildly, recklessly, desperately as she had loved Matt; that had been a once-in-a-lifetime thing and would not come again: but thoughtfully, carefully, with wiser, less selfish pleasures and gentler, more generous delights. And she needed to tell him, for he might have found today difficult, felt pushed aside; and the fact that she knew he would be pleased to hear from her, even in the middle of the night, proved that she trusted him, to love her and not to fail her.

'I love you too,' he said, 'very much. And thank you for calling. But now I'm bloody tired and I need to get some sleep.'

'Sorry, Toby.'

'Don't say sorry. Just get off the line.'

'Yes, all right. Goodnight.'

'Goodnight, my love. Sleep tight. And don't pick your nose.'

She put the phone down, turned off the light and lay smiling into the darkness. It was all going to be all right.

And Summercourt was not for sale.